WHAT WOULD SCOTLAND YARD DO WITHOUT DEAR MRS. JEFFRIES?

Even Inspector Witherspoon himself doesn't know—because his secret weapon is as ladylike as she is clever. She's Mrs. Jeffries—the charming detective who stars in this unique Victorian mystery series. Enjoy them all . . .

The Inspector and Mrs. Jeffries
A doctor is found dead in his own office—and Mrs. Jeffries must scour the premises to find the prescription for murder . . .

Mrs. Jeffries Dusts for Clues
One case is solved and another is opened when the Inspector finds a missing brooch—pinned to a dead woman's gown. But Mrs. Jeffries never cleans a room without dusting under the bed—and never gives up on a case before every loose end is tightly tied . . .

The Ghost and Mrs. Jeffries
Death is unpredictable . . . but the murder of Mrs. Hodges was foreseen at a spooky séance. The practical-minded housekeeper may not be able to see the future—but she can look into the past and put things in order to solve this haunting crime . . .

Mrs. Jeffries Takes Stock
A businessman has been murdered—and it could be because he cheated his stockholders. The housekeeper's interest is piqued . . . and when it comes to catching killers, the smart money's on Mrs. Jeffries . . .

Mrs. Jeffries on the Ball
A festive Jubilee celebration turns into a fatal affair—and Mrs. Jeffries must find the guilty party . . .

continued . . .

D0008973

Mrs. Jeffries on the Trail

Why was Annie Shields out selling flowers so late on a foggy night? And more importantly, who killed her while she was doing it? It's up to Mrs. Jeffries to sniff out the clues . . .

Mrs. Jeffries Plays the Cook

Mrs. Jeffries finds herself doing double duty: cooking for the Inspector's household and trying to cook a killer's goose . . .

Mrs. Jeffries and the Missing Alibi

When Inspector Witherspoon becomes the main suspect in a murder, Scotland Yard refuses to let him investigate. But no one said anything about Mrs. Jeffries . . .

Mrs. Jeffries Stands Corrected

When a local publican is murdered, and Inspector Witherspoon botches the investigation, trouble starts to brew for Mrs. Jeffries . . .

Mrs. Jeffries Takes the Stage

After a theatre critic is murdered, Mrs. Jeffries uncovers the victim's secret past: a real-life drama more compelling than any stage play . . .

Mrs. Jeffries Questions the Answer

Hannah Cameron was not well-liked. But were her friends or family the sort to stab her in the back? Mrs. Jeffries must really tiptoe around this time—or it could be a matter of life and death . . .

Mrs. Jeffries Reveals Her Art

Mrs. Jeffries has to work double-time to find a missing model *and* a killer. And she'll have to get her whole staff involved—before someone else becomes the next subject . . .

Mrs. Jeffries Takes the Cake

The evidence was all there: a dead body, two dessert plates, and a gun. As if Mr. Ashbury had been sharing cake with his own killer. Now Mrs. Jeffries will have to do some snooping around—to dish up clues . . .

Mrs. Jeffries Rocks the Boat

Mirabelle had traveled by boat all the way from Australia to visit her sister—only to wind up murdered. Now Mrs. Jeffries must solve the case—and it's sink or swim . . .

Mrs. Jeffries Weeds the Plot

Three attempts have been made on Annabeth Gentry's life. Is it due to her recent inheritance, or was it because her bloodhound dug up the body of a murdered thief? Mrs. Jeffries will have to sniff out some clues before the plot thickens . . .

Mrs. Jeffries Pinches the Post

Harrison Nye may have had some dubious business dealings, but no one expected him to be murdered. Now Mrs. Jeffries and her staff must root through the sins of his past to discover which one caught up with him . . .

Mrs. Jeffries Pleads Her Case

Harlan Westover's death was deemed a suicide by the magistrate. But Inspector Witherspoon is willing to risk his career to prove otherwise. Mrs. Jeffries must ensure the good inspector remains afloat . . .

Mrs. Jeffries Sweeps the Chimney

A dead vicar has been found, propped against a church wall. And Inspector Witherspoon's only prayer is to seek the divinations of Mrs. Jeffries . . .

Mrs. Jeffries Stalks the Hunter

Puppy love turns to obsession, which leads to murder. Who better to get to the heart of the matter than Inspector Witherspoon's indomitable companion, Mrs. Jeffries . . .

Mrs. Jeffries and the Silent Knight

The yuletide murder of an elderly man is complicated by several suspects—none of whom were in the Christmas spirit . . .

continued . . .

Mrs. Jeffries Appeals the Verdict

Mrs. Jeffries and her belowstairs cohorts have their work cut out for them if they want to save an innocent man from the gallows . . .

Mrs. Jeffries and the Best Laid Plans

Banker Lawrence Boyd didn't waste his time making friends, which is why hardly anyone mourns his death. With a list of enemies including just about everyone the miser's ever met, it will take Mrs. Jeffries' shrewd eye to find the killer . . .

Mrs. Jeffries and the Feast of St. Stephen

'Tis the season for sleuthing when wealthy Stephen Whitfield is murdered during his holiday dinner party. It's up to Mrs. Jeffries to solve the case in time for Christmas . . .

Mrs. Jeffries Holds the Trump

A very well-liked but very dead magnate is found floating down the river. Now Mrs. Jeffries and company will have to dive into a mystery that only grows more complex . . .

Mrs. Jeffries in the Nick of Time

Mrs. Jeffries lends her downstairs common sense to this upstairs murder mystery—and hopes that she and the Inspector don't get derailed in the case of a rich uncle-cum-model-train-enthusiast . . .

Mrs. Jeffries and the Yuletide Weddings

Wedding bells will make this season all the more jolly. Until one humbug sings a carol of murder . . .

Mrs. Jeffries Speaks Her Mind

Someone is trying to kill the eccentric Olive Kettering, but no one believes her—until she's proven right. Without witnesses and plenty of suspects, Mrs. Jeffries will see justice served . . .

Mrs. Jeffries Forges Ahead

The marriageable daughters of the upper crust are outraged when the rich and handsome Lewis Banfield marries an artist's model. But when someone poisons the new bride's champagne, Mrs. Jeffries must discover if envy led to murder . . .

Mrs. Jeffries and the Mistletoe Mix-Up

When art collector Daniel McCourt is found murdered under the mistletoe, it's up to Mrs. Jeffries to find out who gave him the kiss of death . . .

Mrs. Jeffries Defends Her Own

When the general office manager of Sutcliffe Manufacturing is murdered, Mrs. Jeffries must figure out who hated him enough to put a bullet between his eyes . . .

Mrs. Jeffries and the Merry Gentlemen

Days before Christmas, a successful stockbroker is murdered and suspicion falls on three influential investors known as the Merry Gentlemen. Now Mrs. Jeffries won't rest until justice is served for the holidays . . .

Mrs. Jeffries and the One Who Got Away

The owner of a lodging house is found strangled in a North London cemetery, and it's not the first time Witherspoon has seen her. It's up to Mrs. Jeffries to help him clear up this landlady's mysterious past to find answers . . .

Visit Emily Brightwell's website at emilybrightwell.com

Also available from Prime Crime:
The first five Mrs. Jeffries Omnibus Mysteries
Mrs. Jeffries Learns the Trade
Mrs. Jeffries Takes a Second Look
Mrs. Jeffries Takes Tea at Three
Mrs. Jeffries Sallies Forth
Mrs. Jeffries Pleads the Fifth

Berkley Prime Crime titles by Emily Brightwell

THE INSPECTOR AND MRS. JEFFRIES
MRS. JEFFRIES DUSTS FOR CLUES
THE GHOST AND MRS. JEFFRIES
MRS. JEFFRIES TAKES STOCK
MRS. JEFFRIES ON THE BALL
MRS. JEFFRIES ON THE TRAIL
MRS. JEFFRIES PLAYS THE COOK
MRS. JEFFRIES AND THE MISSING ALIBI
MRS. JEFFRIES STANDS CORRECTED
MRS. JEFFRIES TAKES THE STAGE
MRS. JEFFRIES QUESTIONS THE ANSWER
MRS. JEFFRIES REVEALS HER ART
MRS. JEFFRIES TAKES THE CAKE
MRS. JEFFRIES ROCKS THE BOAT
MRS. JEFFRIES WEEDS THE PLOT
MRS. JEFFRIES PINCHES THE POST
MRS. JEFFRIES PLEADS HER CASE
MRS. JEFFRIES SWEEPS THE CHIMNEY
MRS. JEFFRIES STALKS THE HUNTER
MRS. JEFFRIES AND THE SILENT KNIGHT
MRS. JEFFRIES APPEALS THE VERDICT
MRS. JEFFRIES AND THE BEST LAID PLANS
MRS. JEFFRIES AND THE FEAST OF ST. STEPHEN
MRS. JEFFRIES HOLDS THE TRUMP
MRS. JEFFRIES IN THE NICK OF TIME
MRS. JEFFRIES AND THE YULETIDE WEDDINGS
MRS. JEFFRIES SPEAKS HER MIND
MRS. JEFFRIES FORGES AHEAD
MRS. JEFFRIES AND THE MISTLETOE MIX-UP
MRS. JEFFRIES DEFENDS HER OWN
MRS. JEFFRIES TURNS THE TIDE
MRS. JEFFRIES AND THE MERRY GENTLEMEN
MRS. JEFFRIES AND THE ONE WHO GOT AWAY

Anthologies

MRS. JEFFRIES LEARNS THE TRADE
MRS. JEFFRIES TAKES A SECOND LOOK
MRS. JEFFRIES TAKES TEA AT THREE
MRS. JEFFRIES SALLIES FORTH
MRS. JEFFRIES PLEADS THE FIFTH
MRS. JEFFRIES SERVES AT SIX

MRS. JEFFRIES
SERVES AT SIX

EMILY BRIGHTWELL

BERKLEY PRIME CRIME, NEW YORK

THE BERKLEY PUBLISHING GROUP
Published by the Penguin Group
Penguin Group (USA) LLC
375 Hudson Street, New York, New York 10014

USA • Canada • UK • Ireland • Australia • New Zealand • India • South Africa • China

penguin.com

A Penguin Random House Company

Berkley Prime Crime Books are published by The Berkley Publishing Group.
BERKLEY® PRIME CRIME and the PRIME CRIME logo are a registered
trademark of Penguin Group (USA).

Library of Congress Cataloging-in-Publication Data

Brightwell, Emily.
[Novels. Selections]
Mrs. Jeffries serves at six / Emily Brightwell.—Berkley Prime Crime trade paperback edition.
pages ; cm.—(A Victorian mystery ; 6)
ISBN 978-0-425-27751-5 (softcover)
1. Jeffries, Mrs. (Fictitious character)—Fiction.   2. Witherspoon, Gerald (Fictitious
character)—Fiction.   3. Women household employees—Fiction.   4. Police—Great
Britain—Fiction.   5. Great Britain—History—19th century—Fiction.   I. Brightwell, Emily.
Mrs. Jeffries pinches the post   II. Brightwell, Emily. Mrs. Jeffries pleads her case   III. Brightwell,
Emily. Mrs. Jeffries sweeps the chimney   IV. Title.
PS3552.R46443A6 2015
813'.54—dc23
2014043647

PUBLISHING HISTORY
Berkley Prime Crime trade paperback edition / March 2015

PRINTED IN THE UNITED STATES OF AMERICA

10 9 8 7 6 5 4 3 2 1

Cover illustration by Jeff Walker.

CONTENTS

MRS. JEFFRIES PINCHES THE POST

For Sandra Elaine Diamond—
the "Princess of Quite-a-Lot"
and one of the nicest, kindest people in the world.

Thanks for all the good conversations and great laughs.

The Emily Brightwell website address is
emilybrightwell.com

CHAPTER 1

"I'm afraid there isn't much hope," Dr. Douglas Wiltshire said, as he and his companion walked down the long hall. He glanced at the closed sickroom door. Oscar Daggett, the world's worst hypochondriac, was currently lying in his sickbed suffering from a mild case of indigestion.

"Have you tried everything, sir?" Mrs. Benchley, the housekeeper for Oscar Daggett asked.

"Everything. There's nothing left to be done. Sad as it is, all living things only have so much time allotted to them on this earth. When it's over, death is inevitable."

"It seems such a shame, sir. You've worked so hard to keep the old stick alive, too."

"Even I'm not a miracle worker, and my best efforts simply weren't good enough this time, Mrs. Benchley. It's nature's way, I suppose." He shrugged and smiled as a young maid carrying a stack of linens slipped into the sick man's room. Dr. Wiltshire knew he ought to check on his patient before he left, but he really didn't see the point. He'd already told Daggett he was going to be fine. Besides, he simply wasn't up to listening to the man whine. Except for the indigestion, there wasn't a thing wrong with the fellow. But Daggett would moan and wail as if he had the grim reaper nipping at his heels.

Dr. Wiltshire and Oscar Daggett had played this game many times. Daggett ate too much, drank too much, smoked too much and took absolutely no exercise. Was it any wonder he felt ill most of the time?

"I will see you out, Doctor," Mrs. Benchley said. They'd reached the landing. The housekeeper wasn't surprised the good doctor hadn't poppped in to say good-bye to her employer. If Mr. Daggett caught sight of the man again, he'd bend his ear for hours about his various aches and pains.

"That won't be necessary, Mrs. Benchley." The doctor cast one last glance over his shoulder. "I'm sure you're very busy. But do remind Mr. Daggett of my orders. He's not to have anything to eat today except clear broth and light toast." He smiled to himself as he gave the housekeeper instructions. As Daggett's complaints were actually very mild, there was no reason he couldn't eat a plain, but decent dinner. But Wiltshire wanted the man to suffer a little for dragging him away from his surgery and the genuinely ill patients he'd had to put off.

"Yes, Doctor. And again, I'm terribly sorry your orange tree is dying. I know it was the pride of your conservatory. I do hope Mrs. Wiltshire isn't taking it too hard."

Inside the sickroom, the maid stepped up to the bed. "Here's some fresh linens, sir, and a clean nightshirt. If you'd like me to help you to the chair, sir, I'll change the bed." She'd already changed the linens once today and this was his third fresh nightshirt. She hoped the doctor had given the silly old fool something to make him sleep. She wasn't sure how many more times she could change this ruddy bed. Her back was killing her.

Oscar Daggett, a corpulent fellow with a mottled complexion and thinning blond hair, lifted his head from the six overstuffed pillows. His watery gray eyes were as big as saucers and his expression panic-stricken. "My box, Nelda. Bring me my box. Hurry."

"What box, sir?" She laid the linens on the bedside table.

He threw out his arm, pushing the heavy, red-velvet bedcurtains to one side and pointed at the huge armoire opposite the windows. "My letter box. I must have it. Hurry, I don't have much time."

Daggett was terrified. He'd known his health wasn't good. He was always sure he was on the verge of death. But ye gods, this was the first time his diagnosis had been confirmed by Dr. Wiltshire. He wished the doctor had had the good grace to give him the bad news to his face.

Nelda frowned. "You mean your writing box, sir? The gray paisley one?"

He nodded weakly. He had much to get off his conscience. "Get it quickly, girl." He clutched his stomach as a sharp pain speared his lower abdomen. "I've not much time left."

Nelda hurried over to the huge cherrywood armoire, knelt and pulled open the door of the bottom cupboard. Reaching in, she yanked out a large gray-and-gold paisley box. She took it to the bed and laid it next to Mr. Daggett. "Would you like me to change the bed first?"

"There's no time for that now." Wincing as another pain went through him, he forced his big bulk into a sitting position and placed the writing box across his lap. Opening it, he reached inside and took out a pen and piece of paper. "Come back in an hour. I've a very important letter for you to deliver."

"Yes sir." Nelda was a bit puzzled. It wasn't like the master to miss a chance to loll about in clean sheets. But she did as she was bid and left the bedroom, closing the door softly behind her.

Oscar Daggett stared at the blank paper for a moment. One part of him was desperately frightened of what he was about to do, but another part knew he couldn't meet his Maker without confessing. No, he simply couldn't die without telling the truth. Almighty God would never forgive him for staying silent, and he didn't want to spend eternity frying in hell.

And he was dying. He knew it. He'd heard the doctor's grim prognosis with his own ears. Mind you, he was a tad annoyed with his housekeeper for referring to him as an "old stick." That was quite disrespectful. If he wasn't dying and consequently filled with mercy and forgiveness, he might consider sacking the woman for her impertinence.

He took a deep breath, and another sharp pain shot across his chest. He moaned. He'd best get on with it; perhaps he had even less time than he'd thought.

He straightened his spine, put the paper on the lid of the box and positioned the pen in his right hand. He began to write. "For the good of my immortal soul, I, Oscar Daggett do hereby make this confession of my own free will."

He poured out his confession onto the clean, white pages. By the time he'd finished he was exhausted. He slumped against the pillows and closed his eyes, waiting for the end to come.

Precisely one hour later, Nelda came back to his room, knocked and entered slowly. "Sir," she whispered. "Are you asleep?"

"No. Come closer, girl." He motioned for her to come to stand by his bedside. He reached under his pillow and pulled out the letter. "Take this to number thirteen Dunbarton Street," he told her.

"Where's that, sir?" She was a country girl, recently arrived in London. The address meant nothing to her.

"It's in Fulham, girl. Take the letter to number thirteen and give it to the woman that answers the door. Can you remember that?"

"Yes, sir." She took the envelope and stuffed it in the pocket of her stiff white apron. "Do you want me to take it tonight, sir?"

"Right away. Now. Tell me the address again."

Nelda repeated her instructions. She couldn't read very well, but it wasn't much to remember.

"Good. Go now and hurry. I must know that it's been delivered before I pass."

"But what about Mrs. Benchley, sir? She don't allow us out of the house after dark, sir."

"I'm the master here, not Mrs. Benchley. Send her to see me if she tries to stop you. Now, hurry, go on."

"Yes, sir." Nelda bobbed a quick curtsey and hurried out of the room.

Oscar Daggett sighed peacefully and lay back against the pillows. Now that his conscience was clear, he was quite prepared to meet his Maker.

Upon leaving the master's bedroom, Nelda went down to the kitchen to find the household in a tizzy. Mrs. Benchley had fallen in the wet larder and smacked her forehead against the edge of the shelf. The cook and the other maids were gathered around her trying to stanch the flow of the blood.

"Excuse me, Mrs. Benchley," she said. "The master wants me to take a letter to . . ."

"For God's sake, girl, can't you see Mrs. Benchley is busy," the cook scolded. She glared at the impudent housemaid. Stupid country girls. They couldn't see what was right under their noses.

"I'm sorry," Nelda said miserably. "I can see poor Mrs. Benchley is in a terrible state, but Mr. Daggett ordered me to deliver this letter to . . ."

"For goodness' sakes," the cook cried. "Take the wretched letter and be done with it. Do hold still, Mrs. Benchley, we'll have the bleeding stopped in no time."

Nelda gave up trying to explain. Turning, she grabbed her cloak and hat from the rack and hurried out the back door.

"Mrs. Benchley, don't fret so, we'll have you fixed up in just a moment," the cook assured the housekeeper. But Mrs. Benchley didn't answer. Her eyes rolled up in the back of her head, and she slumped back against the chair. "Oh blast, we'll have to call the doctor," the cook said glumly. "Mr. Daggett won't like that."

"But the bleeding's stopped," Hortense, the tweeny, pointed out. She was standing behind the cook and could only see a portion of the housekeeper's forehead.

"True. But Mrs. Benchley's gone to sleep," the cook replied. "And I don't think that's a good sign. Run along and get Dr. Wiltshire," she ordered the tweeny. "And be sure and tell him it's for Mrs. Benchley and not Mr. Daggett. We want the man to hurry this time."

By the time Dr. Wiltshire arrived, Mrs. Benchley was back in the land of the living. But he was taking no chances. "You have a concussion," he told her. "I don't think it's serious, but with head injuries, one never knows. You must stay in bed for a few days and get plenty of rest."

"Mr. Daggett won't like that, sir," Mrs. Benchley replied. Her head was pounding, and there was a terrible pressure at her temples.

"Not to worry," Dr. Wiltshire assured her, "I'll make it right with Mr. Daggett. He's not a monster, you know; he won't expect you to work when you're ill." He hoped the old boy would see reason, but the fact was, half of his patients were monsters and did expect their servants to do all manner of impossible things, ill or not. Well, dammit, he wasn't going to allow this poor woman to kill herself working. "I'll just pop up and see him." He headed for the back stairs and stopped at the kitchen door. Turning, he addressed the cook. "Have someone help Mrs. Benchley to her room and into bed. Is there someone who can sit with her tonight? She oughtn't to be alone."

The cook hesitated. She wasn't sure what to do. "I suppose Nelda can sit with her." She looked around, wanting to find the girl. "Where is she?"

"Remember, she's gone to deliver a letter," Hortense said helpfully. "She ought to have been back by now. There's a postbox just on the corner."

"Well, go out and have a look for her," the cook ordered. Really, she thought, these country girls were useless. You couldn't depend on them at all. "I'll see that someone sits with Mrs. Benchley," she said to the doctor.

Wiltshire went up to his other patient's room. Daggett was still sitting up in bed, his eyes closed and his hand resting on his protruding stomach. "Egads," he cried, when he caught sight of the doctor, "back so soon. I thought I had another few hours at least."

The doctor was in no mood to put up with Daggett's hysterics. "What are you talking about, man? There's nothing wrong with you but a mild case of indigestion. I told you that this afternoon. Look, your housekeeper's had a bit of an accident . . ."

"I know what you told me," Daggett interrupted. "But I now know the truth. The end is near. The reaper is coming for me. I'm," he paused dramatically, "dying."

Wiltshire wondered if Daggett had ever done a stint on the stage. "Nonsense, Mr. Daggett. You're nowhere near dying. You've got indigestion."

"I'm not dying? Are you sure?" Daggett shot up off the pillows. There was something in the doctor's voice that made him realize he was speaking the truth. "But I heard you talking to my housekeeper. I heard you say there was no hope . . . that the end was near, that it was nature's way and everything had to die."

Wiltshire forced himself to be patient. Daggett wasn't the biggest fool he'd ever dealt with, but he was close. "You overheard me talking to Mrs. Benchley about my orange tree. It's leaves are falling off, and it's dying, not you. Speaking of Mrs. Benchley, I'm afraid she's had an accident. That's why I've come back. She won't be able to work for a few days. I've ordered . . ." He trailed off as he saw Daggett's face go completely white. For once, the fellow actually looked ill. "I say, are you feeling all right?"

Daggett couldn't speak as the enormity of what he'd done hit him full force. He started to get up, but the doctor gently pushed him back. "You don't look at all well. You've gone pale, perhaps I'd better have a look at you . . ."

Daggett shook him off. He had to get that letter back. He had to stop that silly girl from delivering it. "I'm fine," he said. He tossed the bedclothes to one side and swung his legs off the high bed. "Just fine. Not to worry, I'm suddenly feeling fit as a fiddle. I think I'll get dressed and take a bit of air."

Puzzled, the doctor stared at him. "Your color isn't very good, sir. You ought to go back to bed."

"Nonsense." Daggett forced himself to smile. "I'm fine. As you said, it's just a bit of indigestion. Now, what were you saying about Mrs. Benchley?"

He barely listened as the doctor detailed the housekeeper's accident. All he could think of was getting to Fulham, to number thirteen Dunbarton Street, and getting that damned letter back.

"Mrs. Benchley must have as much rest as she needs," he muttered when the doctor finished speaking. He hurried over to his armoire and yanked open the top drawer.

"A day or two should do it," Wiltshire replied, watching him closely. The man's behavior was odd, but medically, he now seemed quite all right. His color had returned to normal. "I'll stop by to see Mrs. Benchley tomorrow."

"Good, good," Daggett said. He yanked a pair of clean socks out of the drawer. "Good night, I'll see you tomorrow then." He wished the doctor would hurry and leave. He had to get moving. Oh God, what on earth was he going to do? Whatever had possessed him to write it all down?

The doctor finally left. Daggett threw on his clothes and raced out the bedroom door, almost running into Hortense on the landing. The girl managed to dodge to one side to avoid being run over. "Out of my way, girl. Where's the other one?"

"Other one, sir?" Hortense had no idea what he was talking about. Alarmed, she stared at him. His shirt was hanging out of his trousers, his hair stood straight up, his tie was crooked and the lapel of his jacket was folded in the wrong way.

"The other girl," Daggett shouted. "Where is she?"

"Nelda's not back yet," Hortense replied. She began to back away from him. "I went and looked for her. I went all the way to the postbox at the corner, but I didn't see her. No one's seen her since she left with that letter you give her."

Daggett's eyes almost popped out of his head, then he turned, bolted down the staircase and out the front door.

Harrison Nye sat across from Oscar Daggett and considered killing the man. He carefully weighed the pros and cons of that solution, and then discarded it. Too many people had seen Daggett arrive. How unfortunate that the fool had come blundering in so hysterical he could barely speak when Eliza was having one of her dinner parties.

No, he decided, he couldn't kill him, and that wouldn't solve the problem anyway.

"I didn't know what else to do." Daggett wiped his forehead with his handkerchief. "I can't think what to do."

"Did it occur to you to go to Dunbarton Street and try to get the letter back?" Nye asked.

"That wasn't possible," Daggett said. "The girl had a good two hours' head start on me. I knew it was hopeless. That's why I came here. We've got to decide what to do."

What Nye wanted to do was to wrap his fingers around Daggett's pudgy throat and squeeze the life out of him. "Don't do anything. I'll take care of the matter. You're sure she still lives there?"

Daggett hesitated. "Yes, of course."

But Nye had seen the hesitation. "Damn it, man. You mean there's a chance she isn't there? Tell me the truth now, it's very important. If she got your damned confession, we might be able to deal with the consequences, but if someone else got it, we could be doomed."

"She was living there last summer. I know because I saw her getting into a hansom on Regent Street. I heard her give the cabbie that Fulham address."

Nye closed his eyes briefly to regain control of himself. He hated losing his temper. It made him do idiotic, impulsive things. But the urge to smack Daggett's fat, stupid face was so strong he had to ball his hand into a fist to keep from hitting him. He'd deal with Daggett later. When he had that letter safely back in his possession. Nye rose to his feet, indicating the meeting was over.

Daggett gaped at him, then lumbered up off the settee as well. "What should I do?"

"Go home," Nye ordered. "Just go home and try to act normal."

"Harrison?" Eliza Nye, a tall, striking redhead in her early thirties, came into the study. "I do hate to interrupt, dear, but we've guests."

"I'm so sorry, sweetheart." Nye smiled at his beautiful wife. She was a good twenty years younger than he. The daughter of minor aristocracy, she'd been the perfect candidate when he'd decided to take a wife. She had breeding, but no money. She was therefore pliable, grateful and willing to overlook his more ruthless character traits. "Let me show Oscar out, then I'll rejoin our guests."

She nodded regally, smiled graciously at Daggett and withdrew.

"You're not going to the house now?" Daggett asked.

"What would be the point?" Nye replied. He started for the door and motioned to Daggett to follow. "She's had time to read it by now. But I doubt she's going to do anything about it until tomorrow. By then, I'll have taken care of the problem once and for all."

They'd reached the hall, and Daggett stopped dead. Behind him, he could hear the sound of the guests through the partially open door of the drawing room. "You're not going to hurt her, are you? I mean . . ." His voice trailed off.

Nye stared at him coldly. "You weren't worried about her welfare fifteen years ago."

"That was different." Daggett swallowed. "What are you going to do?"

"I'm going to take care of our little problem. A problem, I might remind you, that you caused."

"I thought I was dying. I didn't want it on my conscience."

Nye laughed. "We can't have that, can we? Run along home, little man. I'll get that damned letter back, and when I do, I'll be along to see you."

Daggett backed away. Fear curdled in his stomach. "All right, I'll leave it all to you, then." He turned and bolted for the door, almost knocking over a tall, lanky young man who'd just come out of the water closet.

"I say," the young man sputtered apologetically. "Frightfully sorry. I didn't see you . . ." But he was talking to Daggett's back. He turned and looked at his host. "Your friend seems in a deuced hurry. Almost bowled me over."

"Do forgive him, Lionel," Nye said. "He's in a bit of a state. Nervous fellow. You know the sort. Let's go and join the others."

Harrison Nye pulled his heavy overcoat tighter and banged the black-onyx top of his cane against the roof of the hansom. He stuck his head out the side. "Let me off here, if you please."

Obligingly, the cab stopped, and Harrison climbed down onto the wet, cobblestone street. He paid the driver, then waited until the cab turned the corner before he started for his destination. He'd deliberately had the driver drop him here. He was fairly certain she could never be connected with him, but he wasn't taking any chances.

It was past midnight and the October night was cold. A light, misty rain fell. Save for another cab pulling up at a small hotel a little farther up the street, he was completely alone. That's the way he wanted it, no witnesses. Turning, he crossed the road and started for the corner. Dumbarton Street was a long street of small, two-story rowhouses with tiny front gardens. Even in the dark, he could see that most of the houses were unkempt and in need of a good coat of paint.

When he got to the front of number 13, he saw it was in slightly better condition than the others. Nye went up the walkway to the front door. In the distance, he heard the rumble of a train. Reaching in his pocket, he pulled out a small metal object with a thin protruding strip at one end. He stuck it into the lock and turned it gently. But he couldn't hear the small, faint clicks that signaled the opening of the door because that damned train was getting closer. It was so loud now he could barely hear himself think. He tried turning the handle, but the door didn't budge. Damn, he thought, this was supposed to be easy, in and out in a few seconds, just like the old days. No fuss or bother. Why in the hell did she have to live next door to a bloody railway line?

Suddenly, he gasped as a searing pain lanced him from behind. His fingers dropped the lockpick, his arms flailed and he turned to look at his assailant. His eyes widened. "My God, it's you. . . ."

"Where's Betsy?" Smythe, the coachman for Scotland Yard Inspector Gerald Witherspoon, asked as he came into the kitchen. He was a tall, muscular man with dark hair and heavy, rather brutal features. But his true character was reflected in his warm, kind brown eyes and his ready smile.

The housekeeper, Mrs. Jeffries, a short, plump auburn-haired woman in her mid-fifties, pulled out the chair at the head of the table and sat down. "She'll be along directly. I sent her to the station. The inspector forgot his watch, his money clip and his spectacles. He was in a bit of a hurry this morning. But she ought to be back any moment now, she left over two hours ago."

Smythe nodded. "Should I go call Wiggins? He'll need to wash up before he comes to the table. He's covered in filth."

"Yes, thank you; tell him just to wash his hands and face. I'll put a newspaper under his chair to catch the rest of the dirt."

"The lad's worked hard," Mrs. Goodge, the portly, white-haired cook, said as she placed the big brown teapot in front of the housekeeper. "Cleaning them attic rooms is a right old mess. I still think we ought to burn all that old junk instead of having poor Wiggins bring it down to the terrace."

"It is hard work." Mrs. Jeffries picked up the teapot and began to pour. "I told Wiggins he didn't have to do it alone, that we'd get some street lads in to help him, but he was quite adamant he was up to the task."

"Are you going to go through all of it?" the cook asked curiously.

"The inspector wants to see what all is stored up there. He's no idea, you know. From what he learned from his late aunt, most of the stuff in the attic was there when she bought the house. Then, of course, she lived here for a number of years and added to it as well."

"Cor blimey, I've a powerful thirst," Wiggins, an apple-cheeked, brown-haired lad of twenty, announced as he came into the kitchen. He was the household footman. But as the establishment wasn't formal enough to really need a footman, he did any task that needed doing. His face and hands were clean, but his white work shirt and brown trousers were covered in soot.

Mrs. Jeffries got up and grabbed yesterday's *Times* off the pine sideboard. "Don't sit yet," she said, pushing his chair to one side. She put the paper down and motioned for Wiggins to move the chair back onto the newspaper. "There, now you can have your tea in peace without worrying about dirtying the place up."

"Thanks, Mrs. Jeffries," Wiggins replied. Though in truth, he'd not given dirtying the kitchen a moment's thought. He sat down and reached for one of Mrs. Goodge's scones.

"I wish we had a murder," the cook said glumly. "I'm bored." She was also feeling her age. She knew that her contributions in helping to bringing killers to justice was the most important thing she'd done in her life. She wanted to do a bit more of it while she had the chance.

"What's the 'urry, Mrs. Goodge? It's only been three weeks since our last one," Smythe asked cheerfully.

"That's easy enough for you to say," she replied. "You're young and fit. I'm not so young and not so fit. I want to do my part while I've got the chance."

Mrs. Jeffries frowned in concern. "You're not ill, are you?" It wasn't like the cook to be morbid or self-pitying.

"Of course not, I'm just not as young as I used to be and, frankly, helping the inspector with his cases is a lot more important than what I'm going to be fixing for Tuesday's supper." She waved a hand dismissively. "Don't worry about me, I'm not ready to pick my funeral hymns yet; I just wish we had us a nice murder, that's all." She wished she'd kept her mouth shut. Now all of them would be watching her like hawks, making sure she was all right. But then again, that was the other reason her life was so good now. She had a family. They all did. They had each other.

After a lifetime of living in other people's houses and keeping her distance from the staff lest they not respect her, she'd ended up as cook to Inspector Gerald Witherspoon. No one else would have her because she'd gotten old, but Mrs. Jeffries had hired her. Smythe and Wiggins were already there—they'd both worked for the inspector's Aunt Euphemia and even though the inspector hadn't needed a coachman or a footman, he'd kept them on. Then Betsy, half-starved and frightened to death, had been found on their doorstep and the inspector had hired her as a maid. Then all of a sudden they were investigating murders, helping their dear employer bring killers to justice. Not that he knew about their efforts, of course. That made it even sweeter, she thought. Even more important. Here they were secretly helping to do the most noble thing a person could do and only a handful of people knew the truth. It was exciting, and she wanted to do it as many times as possible before she went to meet her Maker. Indeed she did. But she didn't want the rest of the household thinking she'd gone maudlin in her old age.

"Me too," Wiggins agreed. "I'd much rather be out 'untin' for clues rather than luggin' all that junk down the stairs. The inspector's aunt kept everything, rotten old books, boxes of letters, old bits of cloth."

"Perhaps we ought to let the inspector sort out the papers," Mrs. Jeffries murmured. "Family letters can be very personal. As for the rest, we'll have to ask him what he wants done with the stuff. He may want to give the useful objects to charity."

Smythe glanced at the clock on the sideboard. "Betsy should be back by now, shouldn't she?"

Betsy and Smythe were engaged. He tended to worry about the girl when she wasn't right under his nose. She, being the independent sort, generally ignored him when he was acting too much like a nervous Nellie and did what she pleased. They'd agreed to postpone getting married for the near future. Neither of them was ready to give up their investigating just yet.

"I'm sure she'll be here any minute," Mrs. Jeffries replied. She turned her head toward the window. Like many homes in this part of London, the kitchen was lower than the street level, and one could see the street through the kitchen window. A hansom was pulling up in front of the house. "I believe that's Betsy now."

"Why'd she take a cab?" Mrs. Goodge mused.

"I expect she has a good reason," the housekeeper replied. "Betsy isn't one to waste money."

A few moments later, a pretty, slender blonde wearing a straw bonnet and a blue coat hurried into the kitchen. She was shedding her coat and hat as she walked. "I've got news." She put her things on the coat rack and flew toward the table, eager to share what she'd learned with the others. She slipped into her chair, grabbed Smythe's hand under the table and gave it a squeeze. "We've got us a murder."

"Ask and thou shalt receive." Mrs. Goodge rolled her eyes heavenward. "Thank you, Lord."

"Who was killed?" Mrs. Jeffries asked.

"A man named Harrison Nye," Betsy said. She accepted the cup of tea the housekeeper handed her. "He was found stabbed to death in a garden in Fulham."

"Whose garden?" Mrs. Goodge asked. She liked to get as many details as possible. As she did all her investigating right from this kitchen, it was important to get as many names as possible as quickly as possible. Mrs. Goodge had a secret army of informants. Deliverymen, rags-and-bones boys, chimney sweeps, gas men, 'tweenys and street arabs. She plied them with tea and cake and got their tongues wagging. If that didn't work, she used her vast network of former colleagues, which stretched from one end of London to the other, to unearth every morsel of gossip about suspects and victims. She could do a better background investigation on someone than the spies at the foreign office and do it quicker as well.

Betsy took a quick sip of tea. "I don't know. I only got the name of the victim and the address. It was number thirteen Dunbarton Street in Fulham. That's where he was found."

"Harrison Nye," Smythe repeated thoughtfully. "That name sounds familiar. Now where 'ave I 'eard it before?"

"Tell us what happened," Mrs. Jeffries said to Betsy. It was important that they get the full story. She knew that it was easy to leave out something that could be a vital clue when one was telling something piecemeal.

"I got to the station and the sergeant on duty let me go up to the inspector's office. He wasn't there. He was in a meeting of some sort, so I put his things on his desk. Then I left to come home, but just as I was leaving the building, who should pop up but Inspector Nivens."

Everyone groaned. Inspector Nigel Nivens was universally and heartily disliked. The man had made it his mission in life to prove that Inspector Witherspoon had help solving his cases. He was rude, caustic and quite stupid.

"That was my reaction as well," Betsy said with a grin. She'd groaned when he'd waylaid her in the foyer. "But as it turned out, it was just as well. If Nivens hadn't stopped me, I wouldn't have found out about the inspector nor the name of the victim."

"What happened?" Mrs. Goodge asked.

Betsy's grin broadened. "Well, there I was trying to get away from Nivens, who was asking me what I was doing there in the first place, when all of a sudden, who should come racing down the stairs but our inspector and Constable Barnes. He stopped when he saw me, thanked me for bringing his things, then told me to tell you"—she nodded at Mrs. Jeffries—"that he'd be home quite late tonight as he'd just been given a murder. You should have seen Inspector Nivens's face. He got so angry he looked like he was going to have an apoplexy attack. He demanded to know who'd been killed and where it had happened. Of course our inspector told him, and that's how I heard. Then Nivens took off up the stairs muttering something to the effect that this should be his murder and that the chief inspector had no business giving it to our inspector." She broke off and laughed. "Oh, you should have seen him. It was a sight. Even the police constables milling about and the sergeant were staring at Nivens like he'd lost his mind."

"Nye. That name sounds so familiar," Smythe muttered again.

Betsy was glad her beloved was so worried about who the victim was rather than why Nivens had stopped her in the first place. She'd told them he'd been questioning her about why she was at the station and that, to some extent, was the truth. He'd whipped off his hat, done a funny little bow and then grinned at her like she ought to be grateful he was taking any notice of her at all. It had taken a few minutes before she'd realized he was flirting with her. She'd been horrified. He'd actually had the nerve to ask her when was her day out.

She'd told him her day out each week varied according to what the household's needs happened to be. Mercifully, the inspector and Constable Barnes had come rushing down the stairs at that point.

The inspector hadn't noticed anything amiss with her, but she'd seen the constable's eyes narrow suspiciously. Constable Barnes didn't miss much. She'd seen him shoot Nivens a really dirty look too.

She had no intention of seeing Nigel Nivens on her day out, and she'd tell him so the next time she saw him. She couldn't stand the little toad, and she was an engaged woman. She intended to keep it that way.

"Should we send for Luty and Hatchet?" Mrs. Goodge asked.

Luty Belle Crookshank and her butler Hatchet were dear friends. They'd inadvertently gotten involved in one of the inspector's earlier cases and ended up using their considerable resources to help catch a killer. Now they helped all the time.

"I can pop along and get 'em," Wiggins volunteered. "If they're 'ome, I can 'ave 'em back 'ere before noon."

"That'd give me time to nip around to Fulham and see what I can suss out about the murder," Smythe said. "Cor blimey, though, I wish I could remember where I'd heard that name."

"Do be careful, Smythe," Mrs. Jeffries cautioned. "If Nivens is on his high horse, he could well be snooping around number thirteen Dunbarton Street even if it isn't his case."

"I'll keep my eyes open, Mrs. Jeffries," Smythe said. "But we need to get crackin'. It's not often we get a jump on a case like this."

CHAPTER 2

"The doctor is finished, sir," Constable Barnes said to the inspector. "We'd better have a look. The van to take him to the mortuary will be here any moment now."

The doctor, a portly, balding fellow with a huge handlebar mustache, rose from where he'd been kneeling beside the body and started toward the waiting policemen. "I'm Dr. John Boyer," he introduced himself as he drew near.

Witherspoon extended his hand, and the two men shook. "I'm Inspector Gerald Witherspoon and this is Constable Barnes. What can you tell us, Doctor?"

Boyer nodded at the constable. "Not much at this stage," he replied. "Fellow's been stabbed. But I'm not saying that's the cause of death. I won't know that officially until I do the postmortem."

"When will you be finished with the autopsy?" he asked. From the corner of his eye, he could see that quite a crowd of locals had gathered. Several police constables were keeping them well away from the crime scene.

"I'll do it this morning and get the report over to you straight away." Boyer smiled slightly. "Providing, of course, that I don't have any emergencies waiting for me when I get to my office. Now, gentlemen, if you'll excuse me, I must be off. Oh, by the way, you might want to have your lads do a search of the local area. From the size of the wound, my guess, and mind you, it's only a guess at this stage, is that he was killed with a fairly large knife." He nodded one last time and turned on his heel and left.

"That's not good, sir." Constable Barnes pursed his lips. "It's better if we've got the murder weapon."

"I agree," Witherspoon replied. He began walking toward the corpse. "But we don't. As soon as we examine the body, we'd best do as the doctor says and have our lads do a thorough search. Most killers try to rid themselves of the weapon as soon as possible." He turned his head and looked off to where the road ended. Beyond the last house, there was a spindly copse of trees. The Fulham and Putney Railway line was just the other side of the trees. "Have them search amongst the trees."

"How about the railway line? How far should they walk it in each direction?" He started toward the body.

Witherspoon followed. He'd solved many murders, yet sometimes the simplest question caught him off guard. "Uh, well, I'm not sure."

"I'll have them go a mile each way, sir." Barnes reached the victim first. He knelt beside the body. "It's pretty bad, sir," he said. "There's a lot of blood. Looks like the knife went straight in through his back to the heart. Must have hurt like the devil too."

Witherspoon hung back for a few moments, then took a deep breath and stepped to the other side of the dead man. He knew his duty. He hoped he wouldn't disgrace himself by getting sick. Stabbing victims, in particular, always made him queasy. Mindful of the crowd eagerly watching from the sidelines, he forced himself to look down at the corpse sprawled at his feet.

The victim lay on his side, his body half on and half off the stone walkway leading to the front door of the small house. Blood seeped out from underneath the man's back and pooled thinly on the stone. He'd worn a black overcoat, and it was soaked through of course. The inspector noted the position of the fatal wound and looked at Barnes. "Let's roll him over," he instructed. He knelt, took a deep breath and grasped the dead man's shoulder. He and the constable turned him onto his back.

The corpse's eyes were wide-open. "I say, he does look rather surprised," Witherspoon murmured. "But then again, being stabbed in the back is rather unexpected."

"Should we search his pockets, sir?"

"Good idea," Witherspoon replied. He reached into the overcoat and his fingers brushed against its silk lining. He felt around the inside pocket thoroughly. "Nothing in here."

Barnes had plunged his hands into the trouser pockets. "Just what you'd expect, sir," he said. "A money clip loaded with small bills and some coins. Nothing else."

"How was he identified so quickly?" Witherspoon asked.

Barnes jerked his chin toward one of the police constables standing at the edge of the front garden holding the crowd back. "Constable Peters recognized him, sir. He moved him enough to get a good look at his face before he raised the alarm, sir. He said he wanted to make sure the fellow was dead."

Witherspoon nodded. "I'll have a word with him in a moment." He rose to his feet and stared at the silent house in front of them. Then he looked at the crowd being held back by the police constables. "Who lives here?" he called to the nearest constable.

"No one," he replied. "The house has been empty for over two months."

As the small crowd had gone quiet and was now avidly listening, Witherspoon decided it might be best to ask his questions more discreetly. "Thank you, Constable."

"I'll have a quiet word with the local lads, sir," Barnes said. "They'll be able to give us a few more details about this place." He had realized the inspector's dilemma. The police wanted information, but they didn't want the entire neighborhood to watch them getting it.

"Which one of you is Constable Peters?" Witherspoon called out.

"I am, sir." A tall young man with dark brown hair detached himself from the others and came to the inspector. The lad's face was pasty white, and the expression in his hazel eyes haunted.

"Is this your first body?" the inspector asked softly.

Peters nodded. "Yes, sir. And to tell you the truth, I hope it'll be my last. It weren't pleasant, sir. Not pleasant at all." In truth, Constable Peters had almost lost his stomach, but he wasn't about to share that with the legendary Inspector Gerald Witherspoon. Mind you, Peters thought, the inspector didn't look much like a legend. His face was long and kind of bony. Wisps of thin brown hair fluttered from underneath his bowler, and his spectacles had slipped halfway down his nose. No, Peters decided, he didn't look like a legend at all. More like a mustached little mouse of a man. Except for the spectacles, of course. Mice didn't wear spectacles . . .

"Constable Peters, are you all right?" Witherspoon asked sharply.

"Sorry, sir." Peters realized the inspector had asked him a question. "What did you say?"

"Who found the body?" Witherspoon repeated for the second time. Goodness, the poor lad really was rattled.

"A Mrs. Moff. She lives next door."

A police van trundled around the corner, and there was a flurry of activity as the constables holding the crowd back shooed people out of the way so the van could draw up close to the house.

"The wagon's here, sir," Barnes said. "Did you want to have another look at the body before they take it off, sir?"

"No. Let's go have a word with this Mrs. Moff, then," the inspector said.

"Are you finished with me, sir?" Peters asked.

"Not quite, Constable," Witherspoon replied. "There's a café up the road a bit. Go and have a cup of tea, a nice strong one with lots of sugar. As soon as Constable Barnes and I are finished here, we'll be along to get a few more details from you."

Constable Peters hesitated. He was suddenly ashamed of himself for thinking Inspector Witherspoon looked like a mouse. Blooming Ada, the man must be able to read minds, he'd just been thinking he'd give a week's pay for a cuppa. But he didn't want the others to think him a ninny. "I'm all right, sir . . ."

"Go along, lad," Barnes said brusquely. He understood the young man didn't want to appear weak. "Do as the inspector says and have a cup of tea. No one will think any the less of you for it." They moved to one side as two police constables, a stretcher slung between them, hurried up the short walkway to the victim.

Peters, with one last terrified glance over his shoulder at the dead man, muttered a quick thanks to his superiors and took off down the road like a shot. Apparently, watching the victim get hauled away was more than he could stomach.

Barnes watched the police constables in their grim task long enough to ascertain that they knew what they were doing. Then he and the inspector made their way next door.

Witherspoon raised his hand to knock just as the door flew open. A middle-aged woman with a long nose and a flat, disapproving slash of a mouth stuck her head out and glared at them. "It took you long enough. That fellow's been dead for hours."

"I'm sorry, madam." Witherspoon was a bit taken aback. "We got here as quickly as possible."

"Humph," she snorted, and motioned them inside. "Come in, then, and let's get this over with. This whole business has upset my day enough already and I need to get to the shops before they close."

They stepped into a dim, narrow hallway. The walls were painted a pale yellow that hadn't aged particularly well and the air was heavy with the scent of wet wool and stale beer.

The inspector waited until the lady of the house had closed the door. She gave them a disgruntled look as she brushed past them. "Get a move on, then, I've told you, I've not got all day."

"I'm Inspector Witherspoon, and this is Constable Barnes," the inspector said as they trailed behind her. She grunted in response and turned to her left into an open doorway.

They followed her into a neatly furnished small sitting room. White antimacassars were placed on the backs of the sagging gray settee and chairs. The table by the window was covered with a fringed shawl and a spindly-looking fern was doing its best to soak up what little sun it could through the pale muslin curtains.

"I'm Mrs. Moff." She sat down smack in the middle of the couch and looked pointedly at the two chairs.

Witherspoon and Barnes each took a seat. The inspector waited until Barnes whipped out his little brown notebook and his pencil, then he said, "I understand you're the one who found the body."

"Right." Mrs. Moff bobbed her head up and down as she spoke. "I did. Saw him lying there big as you please when I went out this morning."

"What time was that, ma'am?" the constable asked.

"Oh, it was right early. The sun were just comin' up when I stepped outside and saw him lying there. I went dashing over to see what was what, but when I was a few feet away, I saw the blood and I knew he was done for. So I went off and got the copper on the corner."

"Constable Peters," Barnes said to Witherspoon. "This is his patch."

"Right, I see him every morning on my way to the baker's. Mr. Moff and I get us a couple of buns every morning for our breakfast." Mrs. Moff's head began bobbing again. "I got the constable, and we come back here. He took one look at the fellow and gave a mighty blast on that whistle of his and before you could count your linens, there were more coppers about the place than fleas on a dog. Well, I told the constable what little I knew, went on and got my buns and come back inside. Mr. Moff and I had our breakfast, and he went off to work. I've been waiting for you ever since."

Witherspoon stared at her for a moment. She certainly wasn't upset that a murder had taken place right under her nose, so to speak. "Did Mr. Moff see the body?"

Mrs. Moff's thick eyebrows rose in surprise. "No, why should he? He's seen dead uns before."

"Really?" Witherspoon said.

"Course he has," Mrs. Moff said staunchly. "He works over at Fulham Cemetery, has done for nigh onto twenty-two years now. You know, digging graves and that sort of thing. Mind you, they're usually in the box by the time Mr. Moff has anything to do with 'em, but not always. No, no, seein' a dead body wasn't something Mr. Moff wanted to do before he'd even had his buns."

"Er, did you happen to hear anything unusual during the night?" Witherspoon asked.

"Unusual?" She seemed puzzled by the question.

"You know," Constable Barnes interjected, "did you hear footsteps or screaming or anything that might have been just a bit out of the ordinary?" He tried to keep the sarcasm out of his tone but wasn't quite successful.

Mrs. Moff appeared not to notice. "You mean did I hear the killing? No, slept like a log, I did. Now Mr. Moff's a light sleeper. He might have heard something."

"What time will Mr. Moff be home?" the inspector asked quickly.

"Half past six," she replied proudly. "Regular as clockwork, he is. Why? Do you want to speak to him?"

"That's the idea," the inspector replied. He knew there were a number of other questions he ought to ask, but for the life of him, his mind had gone blank.

"Who owns the house next door?" Constable Barnes asked.

"Which one?"

Barnes took a deep breath. He'd met stupider people. He was sure of it, but he couldn't remember when. "The one where the murder happened."

"Oh, that one." She nodded wisely. "Well, as far as I know, Miss Geddy still owns the place. Mind you, I can't say it for a fact, she might have sold it, because she just up and disappeared one day without so much as a by-your-leave. She didn't say a word about where she was goin' or if she'd be back. The house 'as been empty ever since."

The two men looked at each other. Then Witherspoon leaned forward slightly. "What is Miss Geddy's first name? What can you tell me about her?"

"Why do you want to know?" Mrs. Moff frowned. "I just told you, Miss Geddy's been gone for nigh on to two months now. What could she have to do with this killing?"

Barnes opened his mouth to speak, but the inspector beat him to it. "Probably nothing, ma'am. But it's important we know as much as possible. Now, please, just answer the question."

"It's all the same to me," Mrs. Moff said with a shrug. "Her name's Frieda Geddy, and she come here about fifteen years ago. That's all I know about the woman."

Barnes looked up from his notebook. "How long have you lived here?"

"Twenty years." Her eyes narrowed. "Why? What do you care how long I've been here?"

"As you implied you knew very little about your neighbor, I wondered if you'd just moved here," he replied.

"I don't know much about her because she kept to herself," Mrs. Moff shot back. "And I mind my own business, too. There, that satisfy you?"

"Has Miss Geddy any relatives in the area?" Witherspoon asked quickly.

"How would I know?" Mrs. Moff sniffed disapprovingly. "I just told you, she weren't one to get friendly."

"Did she have any visitors?" he persisted. Even if she did mind her own business, she had eyes. She could have seen someone coming and going next door.

Mrs. Moff's expression darkened. "I don't know, Inspector. I didn't spend my time watchin' her, and I don't know why you're goin' on and on about some toff-nosed woman that's been gone for over two months now. What's she got to do with anything? She ain't the one lying out there dead now, is she?"

Smythe hovered on the corner of Dunbarton Street and Hurlingham Road. He didn't dare get any closer to the house, he didn't want to be seen. But by keeping his ears open, he'd learned a lot. For starters, he'd found out the victim wasn't a local man.

"What's goin' on?" he said casually to a young lad who'd come out of one of the houses on the other side of Dunbarton Street.

The sandy-haired lad of about fourteen stopped in his tracks. "Fellow's been murdered. Bloke got stabbed in Miss Geddy's front garden. The body's in that van"—he pointed to the police van—"and they're fixing to take it away."

"Murder." Smythe shook his head. "That's awful. 'Ave they caught who done it?"

"Nah, they'll not catch him." The boy shrugged. "This'll be like that Ripper murder. They'll never catch who did it." His eyes sparkled with excitement as he spoke. "Mind you, my mam thinks it must be the same person who done in Miss Geddy."

"Miss Geddy? You mean someone else 'as been killed?"

"They ain't never found her body," the lad explained, "but she disappeared. Ain't been seen for over two months. And now look what's happened. Some bloke gets himself sliced up in her front garden."

"Harold, what are you doin'? You get on to the chemist's now and quit larking about," a woman's voice screeched at the hapless boy from the window of the house behind them. "I need my Bexley's Pills, I've got a bleedin' headache."

The boy rolled his eyes and sighed, but turned toward the corner.

Smythe hesitated for a split second. He had a feeling he oughn't to let the lad get away from him. This "disappearance" might not be connected to the murder at all, but then again, it might. He fell into step beside Harold. "So this 'ere Miss Geddy disappeared too, you say?"

"One day she was there, the next day she weren't."

They rounded the corner and headed up the road toward the shops. Harold, delighted to have an audience, kept on chatting a mile a minute. "Mind you, me mam says we don't none of us know how long it were before we even noticed Miss Geddy were gone, kept herself to herself, she did. But she's gone, and that's a fact."

They'd reached the shops. "I've got to get me mam's medicine," Harold said.

Smythe racked his brain trying to think of something he needed. "Oh, I need to pop in and get a bottle of liniment for our housekeeper." He pulled the door open, and the two of them went inside.

They made their purchases in just a few minutes and stepped back into the weak autumn sunshine. Smythe had a few more questions to ask the lad. He looked at him speculatively. "I'm goin' over to that café"—he nodded toward a workingman's café a few doors up—"and havin' a cup of tea and a bun. You're welcome to come along."

Harold's eyes narrowed suspiciously.

"Truth is," Smythe continued quickly, "I work for a detective . . ."

"You mean one of them private inquiry agents?" Harold interrupted excitedly.

"In a way," Smythe hedged. He hated to out and out lie to the boy. But he wanted to talk to him. Not only could the lad tell him about this mysterious disappearance, but he'd probably know a number of details about the murder. Young lads like him were natural snoops, and this Harold looked like a bright young chap. "We're workin' on a case. A case that might involve your Miss Geddy and this 'ere dead bloke in 'er front garden."

Harold nodded eagerly and started down the road. "I'll just run Mam's medicine home, then I'll meet ya at the café. Will ya buy me a bun?"

"I'll buy ya more than one if you've a hunger," Smythe promised. Grinning, he watched the boy run around the corner. But his smile abruptly faded as, a moment later, he spotted Constable Barnes and the inspector heading his way. "Cor blimey," he muttered. "What's he doin'?"

Smythe turned on his heel and took off toward the corner. If he was lucky, he could duck into the café without being spotted.

His long legs ate up the short distance in no time. He yanked open the door and stepped inside. His eyes widened as he saw a police constable sitting at a table near the back of the café. Blast a Spaniard, he thought, what's he doing here? Smythe had worked for the inspector long enough to know that police constables didn't sit around drinking tea when a murder had been committed. They were out searching for murder weapons and taking statements and doing house-to-house searches. They blooming weren't sitting around on their backsides drinking tea.

As unobtrusively as possible, Smythe eased out the door, spun on his heel and sauntered off. The inspector and Barnes were less than fifty yards away. But they were so engrossed in their conversation, they didn't notice him.

He hunched his shoulders as he skirted the traffic, waiting for a break between the hansoms, wagons and horses so he could dash across the road. Finally, he loped across and reached the safety of the other side. He winced as he thought of poor Harold. He hoped the lad wouldn't be too disappointed not to get his buns. Smythe dodged around a costermonger pushing a handcart of jellied eels. He'd find the lad tomorrow and do his best to make it up to him.

Constable Barnes squinted at the broad back and the hunched shoulders of the big bloke walking ahead of them. There was something very familiar about the fellow.

"I do think it'll be worth coming back and interviewing Mr. Moff," the inspector said. "He may have heard something."

"Right, sir. Perhaps we can come back this evening."

"That's a good idea, Constable." They'd reached the café. Witherspoon pulled the door open and they stepped inside. A short, red-faced fellow wearing a dirty apron stood behind the counter. There were five small tables scattered around the room and a long counter down one wall. The scent of hot tea and fried eggs filled the air. Except for one table where Constable Peters was sitting, the place was deserted. Constable Peters, seeing them, rose to his feet.

Witherspoon waved him back to his seat. "Would you be so kind as to get us both some tea, Constable Barnes."

"Certainly, sir." Barnes headed for the counter, and the inspector went and sat down opposite Peters. He noticed the man wasn't quite as pale as he'd been. "You look a lot better than you did earlier."

Peters smiled gratefully. "I feel better, sir. I'm sorry, I mean, I didn't mean to get all het up . . . it's just I've never seen someone who's been murdered."

"There's no need to apologize," the inspector said quickly. "I understand. I'd like to say it gets easier over time, but the truth is, it doesn't. Death is bad enough, no one but an undertaker could ever get used to it, but murder is quite different. It's shocking and obscene. I hope to God none of us ever get used to it."

"Here we are, sir." Barnes put two steaming cups of milky tea on the small table and sat down.

"Thank you, Constable," Witherspoon said. "Now, Constable Peters, tell us how you happened to be able to identify the victim so quickly."

"I've seen him before, sir. Lots of times. He lives on Belgravia Square on Upper Belgrave Street. That was my patch when I first joined the force. I used to see Mr. Nye every morning as I was walking my beat."

Witherspoon nodded approvingly. "You'd met him, then?"

"Yes, sir. He was a pleasant enough fellow. Always nodded and spoke when he walked past. I was called to a disturbance at his house right before I was transferred here. Someone had tossed a brick through one of his windows."

"Tossed a brick through his window?" Witherspoon repeated. "How very odd. Was it a robbery?"

"No sir. Someone just chucked a ruddy huge brick through Mr. Nye's front window, then went running off. It was done in the middle of the night, sir. We'd not a hope of catching 'em." Peters gave an embarrassed shrug. "Mr. Nye was rather annoyed. He said we weren't doing our job properly. I think he might have filed a complaint, sir. He was really angry about that window. I was surprised a bit, I mean, like I said, he always seemed a pleasant enough sort."

Witherspoon said nothing. He wasn't sure what to make of this. But then again, perhaps it had nothing to do with Mr. Nye's demise. Random cases of vandalism weren't unheard of, even in the better parts of London.

"How long ago did this happen?" Barnes asked.

Peter's brow creased as he thought back. "Let me see, now. It was a few days before I moved over here, and I've been walking this beat for about two months."

"Two months." The inspector frowned and glanced at Barnes. "Didn't Miss Moff say that Miss Geddy had been missing for about two months?"

"That's what she said, sir. But we don't really know that the woman is missing."

"The neighbors have all talked about Miss Geddy being missing," Peters interjected, "but no one has filed a report, sir. So we've not investigated." He blushed as they looked at him. "Sorry, I didn't mean to interrupt your discussion."

"That's quite all right," Witherspoon said quickly. "We need all the information we can get. So let me see, no one's filed a report so officially, Miss Geddy isn't missing."

"That's right, sir," Peters agreed. "She just hasn't been seen by her neighbors in that time, and now there's been a murder in her front garden."

Witherspoon sighed. He knew this case was going to get complicated. He just knew it. "All right, then, we'll deal with the missing Miss Geddy later. Right now, we've got to get this murder investigation under way.

What is Mr. Nye's address? We really must let his family know what's happened as soon as possible."

"What's taking everyone so long?" Mrs. Goodge asked as she put a plate of scones on the table. "We've got to get cracking on this case."

"I'm sure someone will be back soon," Mrs. Jeffries said calmly. "Luty and Hatchet might not be at home."

"Let's hope Wiggins can track them down, then," Mrs. Goodge muttered. "They hate being left out."

Mrs. Jeffries cocked her head toward the street. "I believe I hear a carriage pulling up as we speak."

"That's them," Betsy said as she came into the kitchen.

"Where's Smythe got to, then?" the cook complained. "He should have been back by now."

"Fulham isn't just around the corner," Betsy said defensively. "It'll take him a bit of time to get there and back. Plus, he's got to be able to nose about a bit. Otherwise, there was no point in him going."

They heard the clatter of footsteps and the babble of voices from the back hallway.

"Howdy everyone." The voice was loud, brash and American. It came from the mouth of an elderly, white-haired woman dressed in a bright blue dress. She had on a huge matching bonnet dripping with lace and ribbon.

Directly behind her came a tall, dignified gentleman with white hair. He wore an old-fashioned black frock coat and a pristine white shirt with a high collar. In one hand he carried his black top hat and in the other, he had an ebony cane.

Wiggins trailed in last. Fred, their mongrel dog, leapt up from his spot by the footman's chair and bounded out to meet them. He gave Luty and Hatchet a perfunctory tail wag and bounded over to the footman. "There's a good boy," Wiggins crooned to the dog.

Everyone greeted the new arrivals. Luty Belle Crookshank and her butler, Hatchet, were not just friends, they were as much a part of the inspector's cases as the others. They took their places at the table.

"Should we wait for Smythe?" Betsy asked. She was as eager as the rest of them to get started, but she didn't want to be disloyal to her intended, either. Mind you, she did think it a tad unfair that he was already out and about.

"We'll give him a few moments," Mrs. Jeffries said. "Why don't you tell them what happened when you took the inspector's things to the station."

Betsy told them how she'd heard the news about the murdered man.

"Harrison Nye?" Hatchet frowned thoughtfully. "That name sounds very familiar."

"That's what Smythe said," Wiggins interjected. He paused as they heard the sound of the back door opening and then footsteps coming down the hall.

"Sorry I'm late." Smythe bounded into the kitchen. He paused by the sideboard long enough to lay down the small, paper-wrapped parcel containing the liniment he'd bought at the chemist's. He hoped Mrs. Goodge could use the stuff. He smiled at Betsy first then the others. "But I've 'ad more than my fair share of aggravation this mornin'." He pulled out his chair and plopped down.

"This ought to help, then." Betsy handed him a cup of tea. "I've just finished telling Luty and Hatchet how I heard we'd a murder. We've been waiting for you, I hope you've plenty to tell us."

Smythe took a quick sip. In truth, he was parched. He felt like he'd run all over blooming London. "You're goin' to be disappointed, then, because I didn't find out much at all. The bloke was murdered, all right. Stabbed in the back. Odd thing is, he wasn't a local. As a matter of fact, the house where he was killed is empty and has been empty for two months."

"Have you remembered where you'd heard his name before?" Mrs. Goodge asked. "Hatchet seemed to feel it sounded familiar to him too."

Smythe shook his head. "No, for the life of me, I just can't remember . . . but I know I've heard it." He glanced at Hatchet. "Where'd you hear it?"

"Unfortunately, I'm in the same quandary as you. I simply can't recall." He shook his head. "It's rather annoying not to be able to bring it to mind . . ."

"The harder you try to remember, the worse it'll get," Luty said. "Just set it aside, both of you. When you're not thinking about who this feller is, that's when it'll come to one of you." She directed her gaze to Smythe. "So this Nye fellow was stabbed in a deserted house?"

"On the walkway," Smythe explained. "I saw the body. It looked to me like the man must have been right at the front door when he got knifed." He glanced at Betsy to make sure she wasn't offended by his rather colorful description, but she was listening as hard as the rest of them.

"What do you mean?" Mrs. Jeffries asked. She didn't doubt the importance of the coachman's observations, she merely wanted more details as to how he'd come by them.

Smythe reached for a bun. "Well, I got there before the mortuary van arrived, and I saw the body before they had a chance to muck it about. It was lying just this side of the front door, on his side, he was. It looked to me like someone had come up behind him and knifed him just as he reached the front door."

"But didn't you just say the house was deserted?" Luty asked.

"That's what don't make sense." Smythe popped a bite of bun in his mouth. "Why would anyone be visiting an empty house in the middle of the night?"

"Why do you think he was killed in the middle of the night?" Luty asked.

"I don't know when he was killed, but I overheard one of the neighbors sayin' as he weren't lyin' there at eleven last night because her husband come home late and he'd have noticed a bloody great corpse in the neighbor's front garden. If she were tellin' the truth, that would mean he had to 'ave been killed later that night."

"Or early this morning," Luty said.

"Whose house is it?" Betsy asked. "Maybe it belongs to this Nye fellow, and that's why he was there so late at night."

"That's another interestin' bit," Smythe said. "It belongs to a woman named Miss Geddy. Seems she up and disappeared herself about two months ago. Some of the locals think she's been murdered."

"You mean we've got two murders?" Wiggins exclaimed.

"I don't know what we've got." Smythe took another fast sip of tea. "I didn't get a chance to find out more. I was going to meet this lad at the corner café and see what he knew about everything, when blow me for a tin soldier, if I don't see the inspector and Constable Barnes coming straight at me."

"They didn't see you, did they?" Mrs. Jeffries asked.

"I don't think so," he replied. "But it were a close call. I thought I'd go back to the neighborhood this afternoon and have another go at sussin' out what's what."

Mrs. Jeffries thought about it for a moment. They didn't know much. But they did have some names and the address where the murder took place. That was enough to start with. "I think that's a very good idea. As a matter of fact, I think we should all get out and see what we can learn."

"I can git over to the city and see what I can find out about this Harrison

Nye fellow," Luty said eagerly. "You always say we ought to start with the victim."

"That's an excellent idea, Luty," Mrs. Jeffries replied. If the murdered man had so much as a farthing invested with anyone in the City of London, Luty would get the details.

"I do wish I could remember where I'd heard that name," Hatchet muttered. "Never mind, then, I've a few resouces of my own to tap. Should I see if anyone has heard of this Miss Geddy?"

"Get all the information you can find," Mrs. Jeffries replied. She glanced at Betsy. "Would you mind going over to Fulham and having a go at the shopkeepers?"

Betsy grinned. "I was planning on it. Too bad this Nye fellow wasn't a local. Maybe I ought to concentrate on finding out about this Miss Geddy . . ."

"You'd best be careful, there's going to be police all over Hurlingham Road. That's where all the shops are. A good many of them know you by sight."

Betsy shrugged. "I'll be careful."

"We'll go together, then," Smythe said. He looked at Mrs. Jeffries. "Will you be here this afternoon?"

Mrs. Jeffries thought about it for a moment. She glanced at Mrs. Goodge. The cook's eyes were sparkling with excitement, and there was a half-formed smile on her lips. Mrs. Jeffries was greatly relieved. This murder really had perked up the cook. "I'm going to do the shopping. I'm sure we're in need of a few things."

"Good. That'll help," Mrs. Goodge said. "I know we're a few days early and we could have made do with what we've got, but if I'm going to feed my sources, I'm going to need provisions right away. I'll give you a list of what I want—oh yes, and could you stop at the greengrocer's and get some apples? Those turnovers Lady Cannonberry gave me the recipe for are very popular. People chat their heads off when I've a plate of those on the table."

That was precisely why Mrs. Jeffries had decided to do the shopping. She knew that Mrs. Goodge had been battling a bit of melancholia lately. This murder had come along at just the right time. She didn't want anything interfering with the cook's enthusiasm for pursuing justice. "Of course. I had a quick look in the dry larder this morning. We seem to be low on a number of things. We can't have that. Your sources expect to be fed."

CHAPTER 3

"Looks as if Mr. Nye was doin' all right for himself," Constable Barnes muttered. He and the Inspector stood on the doorstep of a huge town house on Upper Belgrave Street, right off Belgravia Square. The neighborhood was rich, and so was the victim's house. The door was freshly painted, and the brass post lamps and knocker were polished to a high shine. "On the other hand, as I've learned from you, sir, appearances can be very deceiving."

Witherspoon nodded. "Indeed they can, Constable. I say, this is the very worst part of the job, isn't it?"

Barnes nodded and reached for the knocker. "Telling the family is always hard, sir." He banged it once and stepped back.

After a few moments, the door opened, and a butler appeared. His eyes widened slightly as his gaze took in Constable Barnes's uniform. "Oh dear, you are quick. We only just sent for you."

"Sent for us?" Witherspoon repeated.

"Indeed," the butler said. He opened the door wider and waved them inside. "The footman isn't even back yet."

"Is that the police?" A woman's voice came from above them.

They stepped inside and stared up the curving staircase from where the voice had come.

"Yes, madam, it is." The butler looked very confused. "But I don't quite understand. We've only just sent for them, and Angus isn't even back yet."

"That doesn't matter," she said. "They're here."

Witherspoon glanced at Barnes as a tall, rather lovely auburn-haired young woman flew down the stairway.

"Have you found my husband?" she asked. Her eyes were frantic with worry. "Is he all right? Is he ill?"

Witherspoon sighed inwardly as he realized what had happened. They'd sent for the police this morning when they'd realized that Mr. Nye hadn't come home last night. Drat. "Are you Mrs. Harrison Nye?" he asked gently.

"Yes," she nodded. "I'm Eliza Nye. Where's my husband?"

"Mrs. Nye," the inspector said softly. "Is there anyone here with you?"

"Just the servants." Her brows drew together in confusion. "Oh good Lord, what's wrong? Where's my husband?"

Constable Barnes looked at the butler. "Do you have a housekeeper?" At the man's nod, he continued, "Then get her, quickly. We're going to take Mrs. Nye into the drawing room. Have her join us there and ask the maid to bring some tea."

Uncertain about taking orders from a stranger, the butler hesitated for a brief second, then realized something was terribly wrong and that these two policemen weren't here to give them good news. He gulped audibly and hurried off.

"I think you'd better sit down." The inspector took her arm. "Let's go into the drawing room, madam. I'm afraid I've some very bad news."

The color drained out of her face. But she said nothing. She took a deep breath and led the way across the foyer. They went through a set of double doors and into a beautifully furnished drawing room. Done in creams and gold, there were settees and overstuffed chairs, fringed shawls on the tables, brass sconces on the walls, and a floor polished to a high gloss. But the inspector barely took in the lavish furnishings. His attention was completely on the young woman who stared at him with huge, beseeching eyes. She looked positively terrified.

But to her credit, she didn't give in to the fear so evident on her face. "Something terrible has happened, hasn't it?"

"I'm afraid so," Witherspoon said. He saw the housekeeper come into the room and make her way toward them.

"It's my husband, isn't it? He's hurt."

"It's a bit worse than that. I'm dreadfully sorry, Mrs. Nye, but your husband was found dead this morning in Fulham."

She stared at them for a moment, her expression more puzzled than shocked. "Dead? But that's ridiculous. Why would he be in Fulham?"

"We don't know why he was there, Mrs. Nye. We were hoping you could tell us that."

"Was it an accident?" She seemed very confused, as though she couldn't quite take it in. "Did he fall and hit his head?"

"It wasn't an accident," Witherspoon said gently. "Mr. Nye was murdered."

She gasped. "Murdered. You're not serious. You can't be. We're not the kind of people that get 'murdered'—" She broke off and her eyes filled with tears. "There must be some mistake. No one could murder Harrison." She turned away as sobs racked her body.

The housekeeper looked inquiringly at the inspector. He nodded, and she slipped her arm around her young mistress's shoulder. "There, there, Mrs. Nye."

"Why don't you take Mrs. Nye up to her room," Witherspoon instructed the housekeeper. It was obvious she was in no state to answer questions. "We'll have a word with the staff."

"Come on, my dear," the housekeeper said softly as she led the sobbing woman out of the room.

Barnes walked over to the bellpull and gave it a tug. The butler appeared a moment later. "You rang, sir?"

"I'm afraid we've some very bad news for the household," Witherspoon said. "Mr. Nye was found murdered early this morning."

The butler's mouth gaped open. "Murdered? Mr. Nye? But that's . . . that's . . . awful."

"Of course it is," the inspector agreed. He moved toward a settee. "Mrs. Nye took the news rather badly. She's resting in her room. Your housekeeper is taking care of her. But we'll need to question the staff. Can you arrange it please."

He hesitated again, his expression uncertain. "Well, I suppose it's all right."

The inspector understood the man's quandary. The master of the house was dead, and the mistress was hysterical, so there was no one to give them instructions. Witherspoon sat down on the settee. "Of course it's all right. I'm sure the staff wants to cooperate with the police. Now, why don't you go and arrange things. I'll take full responsibility for whatever happens."

Constable Barnes said. "Why don't I go with him and interview the kitchen staff?"

"Excellent idea." The inspector nodded approvingly, then looked at the butler. "Take the constable to your kitchen and then come back. I'll start with you."

Wiggins cautiously poked his head around the corner of Dunbarton Street and quickly stepped back out of sight. Blast a Spaniard! he thought. The whole street was crawling with police constables. He might have known. The inspector had probably ordered a house-to-house. Them ruddy constables would be there until they'd taken a statement from everyone who lived on the blooming street. That might take hours.

Sighing in disgust, he turned to go. "Ooh . . ." He was slammed from behind.

"Oh, I'm ever so sorry," a young woman carrying a wicker shopping basket said quickly. "I come flying around the corner so fast I wasn't looking where I was going. Are you all right?"

"I'm fine, miss. Really, it wasn't your fault. It was mine. I was dawdling." As she was a rather pretty girl with big brown eyes, dark hair tucked up under a plain white maid's cap and a lovely smile, he wanted to make a good impression on her.

"But I was walking too fast," she said quickly. "I must get to the shops." She gave him a cheeky grin and started to move past him.

But he'd been expecting that move and was ready for her. He fell into step beside her. "It were my fault. I was hangin' about because I'd 'eard there was a man found murdered 'ereabouts."

"He was killed right across the street from us. Mrs. Rather was all up in arms; just because her husband is day superintendent down at the pickle factory, she puts on airs. She didn't like havin' the police come 'round with all their questions, but that made no matter to them." She giggled. "It were ever such a sight watching her tryin' to be so high-and-mighty with that old police constable."

"The police asked you questions?" He made himself sound suitably impressed. He knew exactly how to handle her. Wiggins wasn't being arrogant, he simply knew how hard, boring and tedious it was working as a servant. Especially a lone maid in a small, working-class house like the ones on Dunbarton Street. It meant the girl did everything from scrubbing the floors to pounding the carpets and probably for very little pay as well. Anything that broke the monotony of the day-to-day drudgery, even murder, was to be welcomed. Everyone on Dunbarton Street would be talking about this killing for months. Once they got over the shock of what had happened, they'd talk their heads off to anyone who'd stand still for ten seconds. "You mean you saw it 'appen? 'Ere, let me carry that basket for you. It looks 'eavy."

"Ta." She handed him her basket. "I'm only goin' up to the shops. Usually Mrs. Rather does all the shopping, but this here murder has got her all upset. Took to her bed, she did. My name's Kitty. Kitty Sparer."

"I'm Wiggins. Uh, if you're not in a 'urry, I'd be pleased to buy you a cup of tea and a bun at that café on Hurlingham Road. But you're probably in a rush . . ."

"I've a few minutes," she said. "Mrs. Rather was sound asleep when I left. To be honest, I was only rushin' up to the shops to see if anyone knew anything more about the murder. It's the most excitin' thing that's happened around here since Miss Geddy up and disappeared."

"I'm afraid I don't quite understand the question." The butler's heavy brows drew together in confusion.

Witherspoon didn't think it a particularly difficult question, but he knew the staff had had quite a shock and therefore probably weren't at their best. "What I want to know is if anything unusual happened to Mr. Nye last night?"

Duffy, the Nye butler, shrugged. "Not really, Mr. and Mrs. Nye hosted a dinner party last night, but that wasn't unusual. They had dinner parties every week or so."

"How many people were here?"

"The table was set for twelve, so there were ten guests."

"Can you get me a copy of the guest list?"

Duffy looked doubtful. "I don't think Mr. and Mrs. Nye's guests would appreciate the police pestering them with a lot of questions."

"Would you rather Mr. Nye's killer go free?"

"Or course not," he protested. "But . . . this is very difficult. Mrs. Nye is the great-niece of Lord Cavanaugh. She's very particular about observing the proper social etiquette. With her indisposed, and Mr. Nye dead . . . oh dear, I don't quite know what to do."

"I realize you're in a delicate situation, but murder is murder. You really must cooperate. We need that guest list. I'll take full responsibility." Witherspoon was amazed that someone would be worried about etiquette when there'd been murder done.

"I suppose it'll be all right." Duffy sighed and started to get up.

The inspector waved him back to his seat. "You can get it when we've finished. I've a few more questions. Do you recall what time Mr. Nye left the house last night?"

"Oh dear, I'm not sure I know the exact time. But it was quite late."

"Just give me your best estimate."

"I know it was after eleven." Duffy stroked his chin. "Because I'd overheard Mrs. Ryker ask Mr. Ryker for the time a few minutes before they actually left. They were one of the last to leave, and I'd gotten them a hansom. As I went back into the house to see if Mr. Lionel needed a hansom as well, Mr. Nye was coming out. He didn't say where he was going, he simply instructed me to leave the back door unbolted."

"I see." Witherspoon nodded. "And you say this was about eleven o'clock?"

Duffy thought for a moment. "Maybe fifteen past the hour. I overheard the Rykers sometime before they actually left the house."

"You're sure Mr. Nye gave no indication of where he was going?"

"None whatsoever, and it wasn't, of course, my place to ask."

"Was Mr. Nye in the habit of going out late at night by himself?" Witherspoon thought that a rather good question.

"Well." Duffy frowned thoughtfully. "I wouldn't say he was in the 'habit of doing' such a thing. But he was a man who did as he pleased, if you get my meaning. There were several other occasions I can think of when he went out late at night."

"Mrs. Nye didn't object?" the inspector asked. Being a lifelong bachelor, he was no expert on marriage, but he did think that wives tended to be curious about their husbands disappearing in the middle of the night.

The butler glanced over his shoulder to make sure no one was lurking about the hallway. Then he leaned closer to the inspector. "The first time it happened, she had a right fit. That was just after they married, two years ago."

"But he continued doing it?"

Again, the butler looked over his shoulder. "He kept on doing it, but after that terrible row, he never went out until after Mrs. Nye had retired for the night."

"Wasn't he concerned that she'd wake up and want to know where he was?" This was getting very curious.

"No. Mrs. Nye never gets up once she retires. As a matter of fact, from the day she came to this house as a bride, the staff had strict instructions not to bother her after she'd gone to bed. Seems the mistress is a very light sleeper, and once she gets awakened, she's up for hours. Of course, there are some in the household that think the mistress wasn't to be disturbed because . . . well . . . oh dear, I really oughtn't to say."

"Say what? I assure you anything you say will be held in the strictest confidence unless it directly involves Mr. Nye's murder," Witherspoon promised.

"Well, we think Mr. Nye didn't want us to disturb Mrs. Nye because she's tied to her bed. . . ."

The inspector felt a blush creep up his face.

"None of us have actually seen it," the butler continued quietly. "But it would certainly explain why the master and the mistress were insistent she never be disturbed. Of course it stands to reason, doesn't it?"

"Stands to reason," Witherspoon repeated. He was too embarrassed to even look at Barnes. He'd heard of people doing unusual things in the privacy of their own bedchambers, but it wasn't the sort of thing he was comfortable talking about.

"Of course it does," Duffy replied. "She could hurt herself otherwise. I'm sure it's rather undignified, but it's better than letting her get hurt when she begins her nocturnal rambling."

"Nocturnal rambling?" Barnes repeated. "Are you telling us that Mrs. Nye is tied to her bed because she sleepwalks?"

"That's what we think," Duffy said. "Not that we've discussed it very much, of course. Mr. Nye didn't allow us to gossip. But Mrs. Nye was seen walking about the garden in her nightclothes on at least two occasions. I guess she must have gotten loose on those nights."

Witherspoon sagged in relief. It sounded reasonable. People did walk in their sleep, and being tied to a bedpost could be rather undignified. He wouldn't want his servants seeing him in such a position. "Er, I take it she and her husband had separate bedrooms?"

"Of course. But there is, naturally, an adjoining door."

The inspector thought for a moment. He rather wanted to get off the subject of where people slept. "What did you mean when you said you came back inside to see if Mr. Lionel needed a cab?"

"Mr. Lionel was one of the dinner guests. He's a relation of Mrs. Nye, rather distant, I believe, but family nonetheless. He was actually the last to leave the house last night," Duffy explained. "After I passed Mr. Nye on the stairs I came back inside. Mr. Lionel and Mrs. Nye were in the drawing room. I asked Mr. Lionel if he needed a hansom. He said he didn't need one."

"Mr. Lionel lives close by?" Barnes asked.

"Not really, he has rooms in Bayswater. He generally has us fetch him a hansom, but last night he didn't. He said it was a nice evening, and he wanted to walk home."

"So Mrs. Nye hadn't retired by the time her husband left?" the inspector asked. "I thought you said he usually waited until she'd retired before he went out."

"He did," Duffy replied. "But last night he didn't, and I just assumed he must have told her something or other because she didn't seem upset. As a matter of fact, she smiled at him quite warmly before he left."

"So you think he probably told her where he was going?"

He hesitated. "I would think so. Mr. Nye is quite a strong character, if you know what I mean, but he's very considerate of his wife's feelings. He wouldn't want her to worry. I'm sure he must have mentioned something to Mrs. Nye. He was already a bit in the doghouse, if you know what I mean. What with that silly Mr. Daggett bursting in in the middle of the fish course and disrupting Mrs. Nye's dinner party."

Witherspoon stared hard at the man. "Would you mind explaining that please."

"Mr. Oscar Daggett, he's a business associate of Mr. Nye's. He showed up here last night in the middle of a dinner party and demanded to see the master. I tried to tell him that it was impossible, but he made such a fuss that Mr. Nye came out of the dining room to see what was going on. He took Mr. Daggett off to his study and they were in there for over half an hour. The mistress was most displeased."

"What time was this?"

"Let me see, we'd just served the trout . . ." His round face creased in concentration. "It must have been about half past eight. Yes, it was because the clock had just struck nine when Mrs. Nye left the table to go and get Mr. Nye."

"Where does this Mr. Daggett live?"

"I'm not sure of the exact address, but I believe his house is in South Kensington. His address is in Mr. Nye's study."

"Could you get it for me when you get the guest list?" Witherspoon asked. He tried to think of what would be best to ask next. There really were so very many questions one could ask when someone had been murdered. Sometimes it was difficult to decide which were the right ones. "Did Mr. Nye have any enemies?"

Duffy shook his head. "He was a decent enough master to the household. None of us would want to kill him."

"What about his business acquaintances?"

"I don't know anything about that."

"Has there been anyone lurking about the neighborhood or anything like that?"

"Not that I've noticed." Duffy smiled wearily. "I'm sorry. That's not much help."

"How long have you worked for Mr. Nye?"

"Since right before he and Mrs. Nye married two years ago." Duffy smiled sadly. "Let me explain, Inspector. Mr. Nye bought this house two years ago. Most of us were already here. We worked for Mr. Miselthorpe. When he passed away, Mr. Nye bought the house and hired us at the same time. We've all only worked for him for the past two years and in that time, it's been made quite clear to all of us that we'd best mind our own business."

"I see." The inspector nodded in understanding. "Are you saying that Mr. Nye was secretive?"

"I wouldn't exactly say that. But he did keep his business to himself. Not that it was ever necessary, of course. None of the staff would have ever dreamed of asking the master or mistress questions that didn't concern them." He paused. "This is difficult to explain, but Mr. Nye went out of his way to protect his privacy. The day he moved in he called the staff together and instructed us to mind our own affairs."

"Is that a common practice?" The inspector was rather sure it wasn't. In most large households, he'd noticed the servants didn't speak unless they'd been spoken to first.

"Of course not." Duffy pursed his lips. "We were all rather surprised. As a matter of fact, we weren't really sure what he was talking about. I could tell the rest of the staff was confused, so I asked Mr. Nye to clarify what he meant. He said if we were ever caught gossiping about him or his bride, that it would be grounds for instant dismissal."

The inspector said nothing for a moment as he digested this information. Then he asked, "Has anyone ever been dismissed for gossiping?" He was fairly certain the killer wasn't a disgruntled former servant. Harrison Nye didn't strike him as the type to go all the way to Fulham in the middle of the night to meet with a former maid or footman. But he felt he had to ask the question anyway.

"No one."

"Did you ever hear Mr. Nye mention someone called Miss Geddy?" The inspector held his breath, hoping against hope that there might be a connection between the victim and the place where he'd been found dead.

"No sir, I haven't. Is she a friend of Mr. Nye's?"

"We don't know. But he was found stabbed to death in her garden. Frankly, I was rather hoping you might have heard of her."

Betsy didn't want to be rude to Smythe, but honestly, if he didn't quit dogging her footsteps, she was going to scream. They'd separated when they reached Fulham, but every time she came out of a shop, there he was.

"Will you please go somewhere else," she said. She pointed toward the hansom stand at the end of Hurlingham Road. "There are cabs over there. Go talk to the drivers or something. Having you under my feet is making me nervous."

"I'm not tryin' to get under your feet," he insisted. "I'm trying to find that lad I was talking to this mornin'."

"Why don't you try looking on Dunbarton Street. Isn't that where he lives?" Betsy stepped off the curb, her destination a grocer's shop across the road.

"There's police all over Dunbarton Street." Smythe sighed and fell into step next to her. She shot him a glare. "Now, now, don't look so, lass. I'll not be interferin' on your patch. I'm takin' your advice and goin' up to the cabbie stand. Uh, 'ow much longer do you think you'll be?" The sun was sinking in the west, and he wanted to make sure they headed home together. She was an independent sort, but he didn't want her out on London's streets on her own once it got dark.

"The shops will be closing in another hour," she said. She knew he wouldn't give up, not this late in the day. She decided to give in gracefully.

"I'll meet you at the omnibus stop over there"—she pointed back the way they'd come—"and we'll go home together. All right?"

"The omnibus will be crowded, we can take a hansom."

She opened her mouth to argue with him, then clamped it shut and grabbed his arm. "Oh no, don't look now, but there's Inspector Nivens."

Smythe looked in the direction she was staring. Nigel Nivens stood on the other side of the street, staring at the two of them. "Blast a Spaniard," he muttered. He quickly took Betsy's arm and waved at the inspector. " 'Ello, Inspector. Fancy seein' you 'ere."

Nivens waited till they'd reached the curb before he spoke. "I was just thinking the same about you two," he said. He stared at them suspiciously. "This is an awfully long way from Upper Edmonton Gardens, isn't it?"

"It's only a few miles," Smythe retorted. He racked his brain to think of a good reason for them being here.

"I wanted to see where the murder took place," Betsy said boldly. "It's my afternoon out, so I pestered Smythe into bringing me over here. Smythe and I are engaged, Inspector. Did you know that?"

Nivens's eyes widened a bit, but he managed to nod. "Congratulations."

Betsy could tell by the expression on his face that he got her point. He'd not pester her again; policeman or not, he was no match for Smythe in any way. "The inspector's cases are ever so interesting, don't you think so, Inspector Nivens?"

"I wouldn't exactly call murder 'interesting,' " Nivens said pompously.

"Inspector Witherspoon would." Smythe, who thought he knew what Betsy was up to, decided to join in the fun. "Course, maybe that's why he's so good at catchin' killers. He thinks solvin' murders is real interestin' and real important too. Guess 'e just sees things in a different light as you."

Nivens flushed angrily. "That's not what I meant. Of course it's interesting, but it's hardly a spectator sport. I wouldn't go rushing over to visit the scene of a crime merely because I found it amusing."

"Are you on this case, then?" Betsy asked innocently. She knew he wasn't. "Is that why you're here? Mind you, I didn't realize you and our inspector would be working together again. I'll be sure and tell him we saw you this afternoon. . . ."

"We're not working together." Nivens's face turned even redder.

"Then you're like us, just 'ere to 'ave a bit of a snoop?" Smythe grinned amiably. He loved watching Nivens squirm.

"Certainly not," Nivens snorted. "I'm on my way to interview a robbery suspect over on Hobbs Lane. I do have cases of my own, you know. It's merely a coincidence that I ran into you two. I must be on my way." With a curt nod, he turned on his heel and hurried away.

Betsy sagged against Smythe in relief as they watched him disappear around the corner. "That was a close one."

"But you 'andled it just right. He'll not say a word to our inspector about seein' us 'ere."

Betsy giggled. "When I first spotted him, I started to panic a bit. Then I realized that sometimes you can get rid of a problem by just telling the truth. We are here because of the murder. Even if Nivens said something to our inspector about seeing us, it wouldn't make any difference. Inspector Witherspoon knows how curious we are about his cases."

"But it's not your day out," Smythe reminded her.

"The inspector isn't likely to know that, is he?" Betsy laughed. "He leaves that sort of thing to Mrs. Jeffries."

"That he does. Let's just hope that our inspector doesn't start to figure out that we do more than just have us a look at the murder scene. Speakin' of which, I'd best get to that hansom stand before they're all gone. It's gettin' late."

"And I want to have another go at that girl who works at the green-grocer's," Betsy said.

They each went their separate ways. Betsy was relieved that Smythe hadn't noticed the way she'd announced her engagement to Nivens. It might have led to some pointed questions, and she didn't want to have to lie to him. She retraced her steps and was soon back at the greengrocer's. But the young woman who'd been too busy to talk to her earlier was gone. Standing behind the counter was a tall, thin-faced young man wearing a dirty brown apron.

He glanced up as she entered the small enclosure. "Hello, miss, can I help you with something?" he asked.

Betsy gave him her best smile. "I'm not sure what I want," she said. "Those apples look very nice." She pointed to some pippins at the front of the large fruit bin. "I'll have three of them, please."

"Certainly, miss." He bustled out from behind the counter to get her order.

"Isn't it awful about that man being murdered?" she began. "Honestly, it makes a body frightened to go out the front door."

He shook his head in disbelief. "We were all shocked when we heard the news. Absolutely shocked. Things like that don't happen around here. This is a decent neighborhood. Not like some. Mind you, when I found out where the poor fellow was found, I wasn't surprised."

Betsy decided to play dumb. "Really? Why? What was so special about where he was found? I'll take one of those cauliflowers, too."

He put the apples on the counter. "You're not from around here, are you?"

"No," she admitted. She said nothing else and apparently that satisfied him because he kept on talking.

"He was found in Miss Geddy's front garden. She disappeared a couple of months back." He slapped a cauliflower down next to the apples. "Will there be anything else?"

Betsy wasn't about to lose him now. "Yes, I'll need some carrots. Have you got any pears?"

"We've some right over here." He went toward a bin on the other side of the apples.

"Do go on with what you were saying," she reminded him. "It was ever so interesting."

"I do hope this Mr. Daggett has something useful to tell us," Witherspoon said, as he and Barnes approached the front door of the town house on St. Albans Road in South Kensington. The sun had gone down behind the homes lining the west side of the road, plunging the area into the gray gloom of early evening.

"He must know something, sir," Barnes replied as he reached up and banged the door knocker. "According to what the footman told me, Daggett's visit was the reason Nye decided to go out last night. Otherwise, he'd have sent the footman to order him a hansom to pick him up at a prearranged time. The lad swears Nye always ordered a hansom in advance for his late-night outings. Besides, cabs are hard to find after ten o'clock."

The front door opened and a nervous-looking housemaid stuck her head out. "Oh, you're not Nelda."

"No, we're the police. Who's Nelda?" asked Witherspoon.

"She's the upstairs maid and she's been gone since last night," the maid said quickly. She glanced over her shoulder, took a deep breath and then plunged on. "Mrs. Benchley's all in a state about it and refuses to let us report her missing to the police. Mr. Daggett won't hear of it either, but I'm worried. I think we ought to do something."

"As we're here now, I think you'd better let us in," Barnes said calmly. The girl might chatter like a magpie, but he was fairly certain she'd spotted them coming, seen his uniform and beaten anyone else to the front door. Clever girl. The master of the house hadn't wanted the police called, but the lass had seen her chance and taken it.

"This way, please." She flung the door open wide and stepped back.

"Who is it, girl?" Oscar Daggett stepped out of the drawing room and into the hall just as the policemen stepped inside. "It's blasted inconvenient having Mrs. Benchley laid up like this. These girls don't know the proper way to open the door and announce people at all. . . ." He broke off complaining as he caught sight of the two men standing in his foyer.

"It's the police, sir," the girl said cheerfully. "They want to see you."

Witherspoon stepped forward. He was suddenly quite glad he'd listened to his constable instead of going home. This case was indeed getting strange. Another missing girl? What next? "I'm Inspector Gerald Witherspoon, and this is Constable Barnes," he said. "Are you Oscar Daggett?"

Daggett took a deep breath before he answered. "I am. What are you doing here? What do you want?"

"We'd like to speak to you, sir. We've a number of questions for you."

"If it's about that missing maid, it's all a tempest in a teapot." He glared at the maid. "I told you to leave the police out of this. How dare you go against my orders."

"I didn't go to the police," the girl protested. She edged behind the inspector. "Really I didn't, sir."

Witherspoon decided he didn't much care for Oscar Daggett. "We're here about an entirely different matter," he said firmly. "But if you've a missing girl in this household, we'd like to know about that as well."

"The girl isn't missing," he said, but he'd lost some of his bluster. "She's run off home. These country girls can't be trusted. Now, if you don't mind, I've an engagement for dinner, and I need to get dressed."

"We won't take much of your time," Barnes said. He gestured toward what he thought was probably the drawing room. "Can we sit down, please?" His words were polite enough, but the tone of his voice brooked no argument.

Daggett pursed his lips and turned on his heel. "This way," he muttered. He stalked toward an open doorway.

The maid scurried out from behind the inspector. "Nelda wouldn't have run off like that," she whispered. "She's a good girl, and she's my friend. She'd have told me if she was going home, besides, she wouldn't leave her young man. I don't care what he says. Something's happened to her."

"Don't worry, we'll be down to speak to you about your missing friend," Witherspoon assured the girl, as he and Barnes followed Daggett.

"Thank you, sir." She hurried off down the hall.

They entered a nicely furnished drawing room. It was done in masculine colors of forest green and brown. There were the usual hunting scenes on the wall and heavy, dark-upholstered furniture. Daggett sat on a chair near the marble fireplace. "What's this about?" He didn't invite them to sit down.

Witherspoon didn't mind standing up. As a matter of fact, sometimes he thought being on his feet gave him a distinct advantage. "Do you know a man named Harrison Nye?"

Daggett nodded slowly. "Yes. I've known him for over fifteen years. We were in business together."

"What kind of business, sir?" Barnes asked.

"A variety of things, Inspector. Insurance, shipping, mining, overseas investments." He waved his arm expansively. "As I said, a number of things. Now, what's this all about?"

"When was the last time you spoke with Mr. Nye?" Witherspoon asked.

"Last night. I popped around to have a word with him about a business matter." He shrugged. "Unfortunately, he was in the middle of a dinner party. But we had a quick word together. Why?"

"Harrison Nye was murdered last night." Witherspoon watched Daggett carefully.

Daggett's mouth dropped open. He bolted up from his chair. "Murdered! But that's absurd. No one would murder Harrison."

"But I'm afraid someone did," the inspector said. "Do you happen to know if Mr. Nye had any enemies?"

"He was a businessman. He could be ruthless at times, but I don't know of anyone who'd actually want to murder him."

CHAPTER 4

By the time Inspector Witherspoon climbed the stairs to his front door, his head was pounding and there was a dull ache in his lower back.

Mrs. Jeffries was waiting for him in the front hall. "Good evening, sir," she said cheerfully.

"Good evening, Mrs. Jeffries." He handed her his bowler hat. "I'm sorry to be so late. I do hope Mrs. Goodge isn't put out."

"Not at all, sir. We're all quite used to your odd hours. She's kept your supper warm, sir. I'll just nip down and bring it up."

"Oh, do let's have a sherry first," Witherspoon suggested. "It's been a long day."

"Of course, sir." Mrs. Jeffries hid a smile as she led the way down the hall. This was even better than she'd hoped. He was always so much more willing to talk about his cases over a glass of sherry.

The inspector followed her into the drawing room. He plopped down in his favorite chair as she poured them both a glass of Harvey's. "Here you are, sir." She gave him a sympathetic smile. "You do look a bit tired. Have you had a very difficult time? Betsy mentioned you'd been sent out on a murder."

"Actually"—he took a sip from his glass—"I'm quite pleased with the progress we've made so far. One never likes to think that murder is by any means commonplace"—he sighed—"but there does seem to be a lot of it about these days."

"I suspect there always has been, sir," she replied honestly. "Perhaps in earlier times it was simply easier to hide it than it is now. If you ask me, sir, that's a step in the right direction."

"How right you are, Mrs. Jeffries." He sighed. "Of course, it isn't always easy to distinguish between a natural death and a deliberate murder. I imagine that before the formation of the police, people were popping one another off all the time. There's a number of poisons that simulate heart failure or seizure." He shook his head in dismay.

"Is that how your victim in today's murder died?" she asked innocently.

"Not quite. Poor fellow was stabbed. It was obviously murder."

"How awful, sir." She clucked her tongue. "You've had a lot of stabbings in the last couple of years."

"Only because it's easier for people to get hold of knives than it is guns or poison," he replied with a sad smile. "But nevertheless, I do believe I've already got a suspect for this one."

Mrs. Jeffries didn't like the sound of that. It could only mean one thing, if after less than one day on the case, the inspector already thought he knew who did it, then there probably wasn't much of a mystery to solve. Drat. "So soon? How very clever of you, sir."

"Well, I don't want to get too far ahead of myself, but we do have someone we're keeping our eye on. His story doesn't really ring true, if you know what I mean."

"I'm afraid I don't, sir," she said. "You haven't really told me anything about your case at all."

He took another swig of sherry. "I am getting ahead of myself. Do forgive me, I know how very interested you are in my work. The victim was a man named Harrison Nye. Quite a wealthy fellow, judging by the house he owns. But then again, appearances can be deceiving. For all I know the house may be mortgaged to the hilt and there might have been creditors hounding the fellow every day." He continued talking for the next half hour, filling the housekeeper in on all the details he'd gleaned thus far.

Mrs. Jeffries listened carefully, tucking everything she heard safely into her phenomenal memory.

"So you can understand why I want to keep my eye on Oscar Daggett," he finished. "There was something odd about the man's behavior. Mind you, we've got to pop back in the morning. It's imperative we have a word with Daggett's staff."

"I take it you don't believe he was home when he claimed to be," Mrs. Jeffries asked. Her mind was working furiously. Coupled with the information she already had from the others, she knew this case was more complex than the inspector thought. There were already far too many questions that needed answers.

"It's not that so much as it is what one of the maids told us when we first arrived. It seems a girl has disappeared from the place. A maid called Nelda Smith. I feel a bit bad, actually, I told one of the other young women in the household I'd come down to the kitchen and talk to her about her missing friend before I left. But Daggett was insistent we leave as he had a dinner engagement. Not to worry, though, I've got a constable watching the house. The girl should be all right until tomorrow." He put his glass down and got to his feet. "Not that I think she's in any danger, of course. But short of arresting the fellow, I couldn't do anything else but leave when he made such a fuss."

"I'm sure you did right, sir."

"Thank you, one does worry in these sorts of cases. I would hate for the girl to think I was ignoring her."

"What was the girl's name?" Mrs. Jeffries asked.

"What girl?"

"The one who wanted to talk with you about the missing girl?"

"Hortense Rivers. She seemed quite concerned. But Daggett insisted the missing maid had gone back home to the country." He sighed and put down his glass. "I believe I'll have my tray now if you don't mind, Mrs. Jeffries."

"Of course, sir." She had dozens of questions she intended to ask. "If you'll go into the dining room, I'll pop down and get your supper."

The next morning, Mrs. Jeffries rushed down to the kitchen the moment she closed the door behind Inspector Witherspoon. The others were waiting for her when she entered the kitchen. Even Luty and Hatchet were sitting in their usual spots at the kitchen table.

"The inspector's finally gone, has he?" Mrs. Goodge looked up over the rim of her spectacles. "It took him long enough."

"I thought he was gonna camp out in the dining room all mornin'," Luty declared, "and we've got lots to talk about."

"He's gone." Mrs. Jeffries slipped into her chair at the head of the table. "Should I tell you everything I learned from the inspector last night, or would you all like to have your say first?"

"I'd like to have my say first, please," Betsy said. "I don't know why, it just seems to make more sense when we do our bit first."

"I agree," Mrs. Goodge said stoutly. "Even though I haven't got much to report. As a matter of fact, I've got nothing to report. But I've got a number of sources coming through the kitchen today, so by tomorrow I'll be able to hold up my end of the stick."

The housekeeper nodded at Betsy. "Go ahead, tell us what you've learned."

"Well, it doesn't amount to much, but I did hear a bit about the woman who disappeared. The one who owns the house where the murder took place."

"You mean that Miss Geddy person?" Wiggins clarified.

"Of course she means Miss Geddy." The cook frowned at the lad. "Who else has disappeared and had a murder on their front steps?"

"I like to keep me facts straight." Wiggins sniffed. "It's not good to get muddled, especially at the beginning of an investigation."

"How very prudent of you, Wiggins," Mrs. Jeffries said soothingly. "Do go on, Betsy."

"According to the gossip I got, this Miss Geddy kept very much to herself. But the local shopkeepers liked her all right, she paid her bills on time and didn't ask for credit."

"How'd she pay?" Smythe asked.

Betsy looked surprised by the question. "I don't know, I never thought to ask. Is it important?"

"Probably not." He shrugged. "But it never hurts to know these things. Go on, lass, I didn't mean to interrupt."

"Well, like I was saying, the shopkeepers like her well enough, but she wasn't very popular about the neighborhood."

"How unpopular was the lady?" Hatchet asked.

"She had a tart tongue if she was crossed. She had a run-in at the local post office," Betsy said. "She used to go in there to mail off packages, and the poor man behind the counter made some comment about it. You know, he was trying to be friendly like, make conversation, that sort of thing. But Miss Geddy flew right off the handle. Told the man it was his job to mail the parcel, not make comments for all and sundry to hear her personal business. The post office was full when this happened. There were dozens of people lined up. They all heard it. It caused quite a stir in the neighborhood. More importantly, it happened just a few days before she disappeared."

"How very interesting," Mrs. Jeffries commented. "Anything else?"

"That's about it, I'm afraid." Betsy sighed. "I wish I could have found out where this Miss Geddy was mailing off her parcels to, but no one I spoke to knew that. Do you think it's important?"

Mrs. Jeffries had no idea what was important or what wasn't important. "Find out if you can," she replied. "At this point in the investigation, we don't know what is or isn't important. Who would like to go next?"

"I've not got anything to report," Smythe said. "None of the drivers I talked to had taken any fares to Dunbarton Street. I thought I'd make the rounds of the pubs today and see if I can pick up anythin' there."

"That's an excellent idea." Mrs. Jeffries nodded encouragingly.

"Can I go now?" Wiggins asked. At the housekeeper's nod, he continued. "I met up with a maid that lives across the street from the killin'. Her name's Kitty Sparer. I didn't learn all that much. She was a right talker, but she didn't know much of anything. Nice girl, though."

"Did you find out anything at all?" Mrs. Goodge asked. "Or was your whole afternoon a complete waste of time?"

"I wouldn't call it a complete waste," Wiggins replied cheerfully. "She did tell me that she heard footsteps going up Miss Geddy's walkway last night."

"She heard the killer?" Luty said eagerly.

Wiggins's face fell. "I don't think so. She heard the footsteps fairly early in the evening. She didn't know the time, just that it was early like in the evenin', so it couldn't 'ave been the killer." He shrugged.

"Did she see anyone or just hear footsteps?" Mrs. Jeffries asked.

"She only heard the footsteps," Wiggins replied. "She was busy with the mistress of the house so she couldn't get to the window to 'ave a look."

"How did she know where they were?" Luty snorted. "Seems to me if she only heard footsteps, then how could she tell they was goin' up this Miss Geddy's walkway?"

"She knew it was Miss Geddy's walkway because the steps were shoes on stone, not shoes on dirt. The footpath along Dunbarton Street isn't paved. Miss Geddy's walkway is done in stone. It's the only one along there that is. The road's made of brick, and there's a streetlamp down the far end, but the local council's never paved the footpath. The residents have complained about it, but it's not done any good."

"Wasn't she curious that she heard footsteps on the walkway of an empty house?" Hatchet asked.

"Course she was," he said. "But her mistress was jawin' at 'er something fierce, and by the time she could get away and have a look out the front window, there was nothing there."

"That's very interesting," Mrs. Jeffries muttered. "I do hope she'll have a word with the police and let them know what she heard."

"She will," Wiggins said cheerfully. "She thinks this murder is the most excitin' thing that's ever 'appened. That's all I've got to report."

"Can I go next?" Luty asked. "I found out that Harrison Nye has a list of enemies as long as my right arm, and I'm dying to tell everyone."

"Really, madam." Hatchet sniffed disapprovingly. "You mustn't exaggerate so. You told me yourself it was only his banker and solicitor that disliked him."

"That's a list." Luty sniffed. "Besides, it wasn't just one solicitor, it was two. They were brothers, and they blame Nye for ruining their business."

"Gracious, Luty, that certainly sounds like motive for murder."

"That's what I thought too," Luty said.

"What happened?" Betsy asked eagerly.

"Nye blamed his solicitors for making so many errors on a piece of property he was tryin' to buy that it cost him the deal. They made a bunch of mistakes, and by the time it was sorted out, the man who owned the property had died and his heirs then refused to sell. The whole business cost Nye a lot of money. He'd already raised a packet of cash from a group of private investors, and he ended up givin' it all back."

"And Nye blamed his lawyers?" Smythe raised his eyebrows. "But Nye's the one who's dead, not them."

"Yeah, but he sued the solicitors for damages and actually won. Cost 'em so much they went bankrupt." She grinned at the surprised expression on the faces around the table. "I know, I found it hard to believe too. Usually the legal profession protects its own. But from what I heard, these two were more incompetent than most. Anyway, they had reason to hate Harrison Nye's guts."

"Did you get their names?" Betsy asked.

"It's Windemere," she replied. "John and Peter Windemere."

Mrs. Jeffries tapped her fingers against her heavy, brown mug. This was quite interesting. It was rare that one heard of solicitors actually being sued by their clients, rarer still that the clients actually won. "When did this happen?"

"It's been a couple of years back." Luty hedged.

"A couple of years," Hatchet exclaimed. He snorted derisively. "Really, madam, it happened eleven years ago."

"So what? Sometimes people let their anger fester forever before it boils up and causes them to go dotty. That could have been what happened here. They coulda bided their time until they caught him alone late one night and then did their worst . . ."

"So you're saying they hung around his home waiting for the one time he went out at night unexpectedly, followed him and then murdered him in the front garden of a strange house in Fulham?" Hatchet's voice dripped sarcasm.

"I didn't say it did happen that way, I said it mighta happened that way." She glared at her butler. "Besides, at least I come up with something. You ain't doin' so good, are ya?"

He glared right back at her. "I won't dignify that remark with a response. Investigating a murder doesn't require speed, madam, it requires perseverance."

"Which you both have in abundance," Mrs. Jeffries interjected. She rather agreed with Hatchet; it was highly unlikely the disgraced solicitors had waited eleven years to take their revenge, but it wasn't impossible either. Furthermore, she knew something they didn't. She had a copy of the guest list in her pocket. "Luty, could you find out a bit more about the Windemere brothers? You know, find out their financial circumstances, that sort of thing."

Luty smiled smugly. "I intended to do just that. Plus, I've got my sources workin' on findin' out more about our victim."

"Why'd 'is banker dislike 'im?" Wiggins asked.

Luty waved her hand dismissively. "For the same reason the solicitors did, he tried to ruin the fellow in a dispute over a letter of credit. Only Marcus Koonts was smarter than them solicitors and hired a decent barrister. Nye lost the case but not before he'd caused Koonts a lot of trouble. Besides, Marcus couldn't have killed Nye. He's been in Scotland since last week. He might hate Nye, but he's no killer. I've known him for years."

"I still wish I could remember where I'd 'eard that name," Smythe said. He shook his head. Perhaps he'd make a run down to the docks and have a chat with one of his sources, Blimpey Groggins.

"Does anyone else have anything to report?" Mrs. Jeffries glanced around the table. "Well, then, I'll tell you what I learned from the inspector." She poured herself another cup of tea as she spoke. This might take a while, and she didn't want to leave out anything. They were going to have a lot to do today, and she wanted everyone to be prepared with as much knowledge as possible.

The inspector didn't particularly care for graveyards. He felt they were a tad depressing. But as Mr. Moff had already gone to work by the time he and Constable Barnes had arrived at the Moff home, he had no choice but to go along to the Fulham Cemetery. The entrance was off the Fulham Palace Road. Witherspoon stopped and stared across the open fields of the common. The grass was still green, but the trees had lost most of their leaves, and the air was crisp enough that he was glad he wore his good black greatcoat. In the distance, the mist rose from the river, and the weak autumn sun would make no headway in burning through the thick cloud layer above. All in all it was a depressing gray day, and he was stuck interviewing a witness at a cemetery. Drat.

"Shall we go in, sir?" Barnes inquired. He tried not to smile at the glum expression on the inspector's face. "It won't be too bad, sir."

"Yes, I suppose we must." Witherspoon started through the open iron gates. He stopped just inside and peered through the rows of crowded headstones and gated crypts. "I wonder where the porters' lodge or the caretaker's place might be."

"Are you lookin' for me, then," a voice said from behind them.

Witherspoon jumped and whirled about. Even Barnes was a bit startled. A tall, thin man dressed in a gray shirt and dark gray trousers stood just inside the gate. He held a shovel in his right hand. His eyes were as gray as his clothes and his face was long and weather-beaten. "Are you Mr. Moff?"

"The missus said you'd be wanting to have a word with me," he replied. "You'll have to talk to me while I work, we've one comin' in this morning at ten and that stupid lad's not got the hole dug deep enough." He turned and began weaving his way through a row of headstones.

Witherspoon glanced at Barnes, shrugged and trailed after their witness. They followed him to the north corner of the cemetery, then the fellow seemed to disappear. "I say." Witherspoon came to a halt on the far side of an open pit. "Where'd the man go?"

"I'm right here." This time the voice came from below them. "I expect you're wantin' to ask me if I know anything about that fellow that got himself killed on Miss Geddy's walkway."

Witherspoon looked down and realized Mr. Moff was standing in an open grave. He leapt to one side as a shovelful of dirt came flying out and landed inches away from his good black shoes.

"Did you hear anything unusual?" Barnes asked. He'd moved to the other side of the grave and whipped out his little brown notebook.

"Nah, once I'm in bed, I'm dead to the world." He looked up and grinned. "If you'll pardon the expression."

The inspector didn't think that was particularly funny. Gracious, didn't the fellow have any respect for the dead? "What time did you retire that night?" He thought it was a fairly useless question, but he had to start somewhere.

"Right after nine." Moff went back to his digging. "The missus and I had a bit of a natter and then I went out to the pub for a quick one. I was back by a quarter to, had a wash and then went to bed. The missus was already asleep."

"Did you happen to see anyone hanging about the neighborhood while you were coming back from the pub?" Witherspoon pulled his handkerchief out and whipped a bit of dirt off his sleeve.

Moff stopped and rested on the end of his shovel. "Well, I did see that young girl in Miss Geddy's front garden, but I wouldn't say she was hanging about. She was at the front door."

"You mean she was knocking?" Barnes asked.

"I didn't see her knockin'." He went back to his digging. "I told her that no one lived there, and that seemed to upset her some."

"Upset her how?" Witherspoon leaned closer. This was finally getting interesting.

"She didn't start blubberin' or anything like that," Moff replied. "She said something like 'oh bother,' or 'I'll not bother then,' I'm not sure. I weren't payin' all that much attention to the girl. I was in a hurry to get home."

"You didn't think it strange that she was at the door of an empty house?" Barnes asked. "It's our understanding that Miss Geddy, the owner, disappeared some months ago."

"That's true." Moff looked up at the constable and shrugged. "She up and bolted one night."

"Bolted? That's an unusual choice of words," Witherspoon said.

He shrugged. "What else would you call it when someone sneaks out in the middle of the night?"

"You saw her leave?" Witherspoon asked eagerly. Gracious, this case was getting complicated. He'd no idea how Miss Geddy's disappearance related to Harrison Nye's murder, but he knew it did. He could feel it in his bones.

"I did. Had a bit of indigestion that night, so I got up to get one of the missus's bilious pills. She swears by Cockles, she does, and it did help a bit. When I went back to bed, I happened to glance out the window, and I saw her leavin'. Our bedroom overlooks the street."

"Did she have any baggage?" Barnes asked.

He frowned for a moment, then brightened as the memory returned. "She had a carpetbag with her. I remember because she kept banging it on the side of the hansom when she was climbin' inside."

"Miss Geddy left in a hansom," Witherspoon clarified. He wanted to make sure he understood.

"That's what I said." Moff went back to his task.

"If you don't mind my sayin' so, sir," Barnes said, "the whole neighborhood keeps talking about how this woman disappeared, and you said nothing to anyone, including your own wife, about Miss Geddy leaving of her own free will."

"I know." Moff grinned widely. "It's been a right old laugh watchin' all them tongues waggin'. You should hear some of the things they've been sayin'." He cackled. "I haven't had so much fun in years. Some claim she's been sold to white slavers, some claim that bloke she had a run-in with down at the post office come after her and did her in, and the rest say she were runnin' off to meet her lover. I tell ya, it's been a right old bust-up." He laughed again and went back to shoveling dirt.

Barnes and Witherspoon looked at one another. The constable sighed. "Do you have any idea where Miss Geddy went?" he asked.

"The train station," Moff replied. "I heard her tell the driver to take her to Victoria Station. It was almost midnight and quiet enough to hear a pin drop. I'm surprised I'm the only one who heard her. She weren't botherin' to be quiet about it, and the hansom made enough noise to wake the dead."

"Do you happen to recall exactly what the date was?" Witherspoon asked. He didn't hold out much hope the man would remember. It was, after all, two months ago.

"Course I do," he said proudly. "It was August 12."

The inspector raised his eyebrows. "Gracious, you do have a remarkable memory."

"Not really," Moff admitted. "The only reason I remember is because of my indigestion. I always get it when we go to Winnie's for supper. She's my sister-in-law. It was her husband's fiftieth birthday, and we was havin' a bit of celebration. She's a good enough woman, our Winnie, nice disposition and all that. But she's a terrible cook. Her Yorkshire puddin' was sittin' on my stomach somethin' awful. Kept me awake for hours, it did."

Witherspoon nodded sympathetically. He wished Mr. Moff had gone to Winnie's for supper the night before last; if he had, he might have seen the murder. "Have you ever heard of a man called Harrison Nye?"

"That's the bloke that was murdered," Moff said. "Never heard of him."

"You seem an observant sort of fellow," Barnes said quickly. "I don't suppose you remember someone fitting Nye's description ever coming around to visit Miss Geddy?"

Witherspoon smiled approvingly at the constable. That was a jolly good question.

Moff shook his head. "Nah, she never had any visitors. Mind you, she used to go to the post office quite a bit. She was always mailin' off packages."

"You mentioned she had a 'bit of a run-in with some bloke at the post office'?" Witherspoon didn't think Miss Geddy's disappearance or Harrison Nye's murder had anything to do with an angry postal worker. Civil servants didn't generally come after every member of the public whom they'd had words with, but one never knew.

"You'll need to ask my wife about that set-to," Moff said. He stopped and wiped the sweat off his brow. "She knows all about it. I only heard it secondhand-like. Is there anything else?"

The inspector couldn't think of anything. He looked hopefully at Barnes, but he closed his notebook and slipped it into the pocket of his uniform. "No, sir, there's nothing else. But do contact me if you think of anything else that may be helpful in our inquiries."

Moff grunted agreeably but didn't look up.

Wiggins started to reach for another sticky bun. "So what do we do now?"

Mrs. Goodge pushed the plate out of his reach. "Don't be so greedy. If you eat another, you'll make yourself sick."

"I've only 'ad two," he protested, but he pulled his hand back.

"And you've had upset stomach three times this month," the cook said tartly.

"But you do have a point," the housekeeper interjected smoothly. "What do we do now? We've learned an enormous amount of information, but I'm in a bit of a muddle as to where we ought to focus our attention." They now were in the position of having almost too many avenues of inquiry to pursue.

"I think we ought to do what we always do," Betsy said, "and concentrate on the victim."

"But what about this Daggett fellow?" Smythe argued. "Seems to me it was his visit to Nye that got the fellow killed."

"We don't know that for certain," she replied.

"The bloke barged into a dinner party and insisted on seein' Nye. A few hours later, he was dead."

"But we don't know that Daggett's visit was the reason Nye went to Fulham that night. He may have been planning on going out all along. The inspector told Mrs. Jeffries that Nye had a habit of going out on his own at night."

"But he always waited until his wife had retired for the night," Smythe reminded them. "But this time, he didn't even wait until all his dinner guests had gone before he left. And from what the inspector told Mrs. Jeffries, Constable Barnes found out from the Daggetts' servants that he got up from his sickbed to go to Nye's so whatever sent him there, it must have been important."

"I think you're both right," Mrs. Jeffries said quickly. She meant it too. She had a feeling this case was going to be very, very complex. It was imperative they obtain as much information as possible, especially at this stage of the investigation. "The victim, of course, is important, but so is

Oscar Daggett." She cocked her head to one side and gazed appraisingly around the table. "There are enough of us to do both. We'll have to scatter our resources a bit thinly, but I don't think that's going to be a problem."

Hatchet leaned forward, his expression thoughtful. "Precisely what does that mean? In practical terms, that is."

"It means some of us need to concentrate on learning everything we can about Harrison Nye and the rest of us need to concentrate on Daggett."

"I'll take Nye," Smythe volunteered. "It's nigglin' me that I can't remember where I've heard of him."

"I'll get my sources workin' on both of them," Mrs. Goodge said. "And Mrs. Nye too. Didn't you say she's some relation to Lord Cavanaugh? I only wish we had the names of the guests at the dinner party."

"We do," Mrs. Jeffries said. "The inspector had the dinner guest list in his coat pocket. I slipped down here last night and copied the names out."

"You went through the inspector's pockets!" Wiggins was positively scandalized.

"Of course she went through his pockets," Luty exclaimed. "This is murder we're investigatin'. Sometimes you have to ignore the social niceties. We need all the clues we can git. Don't be such a Goody Two-shoes, boy. It ain't like the man keeps love letters or personal stuff in his pockets."

"Thank you, Luty," Mrs. Jeffries said gratefully. Then she looked at the footman. "I don't want you to think I'm in the habit of violating the inspector's privacy. I only searched the pockets of his overcoat and only then if he's mentioned that he got a list of some sort or another."

"I weren't tryin' to make out like you was doin' something wrong." Wiggins blushed a deep red. He knew the housekeeper wouldn't do anything really wrong. "I was just a bit surprised, that's all."

"Mrs. Jeffries knows that," Smythe said. He could tell that the footman was genuinely embarrassed. "I think you ought to have a gander 'round the Daggett household. You're always right good at gettin' the servants to talk, especially housemaids and such."

"Ya think so?" Wiggins brightened immediately.

"We all think it," Betsy interjected. She gave Smythe a fast, grateful smile. He might be big and hard-looking, but he was the best man in the world. Beneath that rough exterior, he truly had a heart of gold. She loved him more than her own life, and she was pleased to be marrying him; she only hoped he wouldn't pressure her to do it too quickly. But she felt fairly certain he wouldn't push her too hard. He loved their investigations too. "And if you've a mind to head over Daggett's way this afternoon, I'll go along with you. I want to have a word with the local shopkeepers in the area."

"I suppose I'd best keep on seein' what I can suss out about Nye," Luty said. "Iffen that's all right with everyone. I can put out a few feelers about Oscar Daggett as well."

"And let's not forget the missing woman," Hatchet reminded them. "Apparently, it seems this Miss Frieda Geddy's disappearance may have some bearing on the case."

"Would you like to follow up that inquiry?" Mrs. Jeffries asked. It would be easier to keep everything straight if they were somewhat organized in their investigation.

"Certainly, though I do wish we knew precisely when she disappeared. But never fear, I'm sure with my rather extensive network of information sources, I'll soon find out everything we need to know."

"Don't be so modest, Hatchet." Luty laughed.

"Modesty has nothing to do with it, madam. I'm merely stating a fact." He smiled cheerfully. "I have great confidence in all of us."

Luty snorted. "You have more in yourself, though."

"Nonsense, we've all had tremendous successes in our endeavors. What is this, our fifteenth case?" He was toying with the notion of writing a comprehensive history of everything they'd done thus far, but he'd not made up his mind yet. It would involve rather a lot of work.

"Our sixteenth, your fifteenth and Mrs. Jeffries's seventeenth," Wiggins stated matter-of-factly.

Everyone gaped at him.

He shrugged. "I've been keepin' track."

"I can see where Hepzibah"—Luty jerked her chin at the housekeeper—"has one more than me and Hatchet. After all, she started this whole thing by figurin' out them horrible Kensington High Street murders, but I can't see where you all"—she jerked her head in a circle, indicating the rest of them—"have any more cases than us."

"But we do," Wiggins explained. "We helped solve that Dr. Slocum's murder."

"And I think we ought to count the horrible Kensington High Street murders as well," Mrs. Goodge added. "We helped with that one."

"But we didn't know we was helpin'," Wiggins pointed out, "so it don't count."

"It does too," Betsy said flatly. "We helped, and that's that. Besides, we each figured it out on our own before the case actually got solved."

"But Mrs. Jeffries didn't tell us what she was up to until after Dr. Slocum had been poisoned," Wiggins insisted. "So we can't count it as one of ours."

"That's daft," Mrs. Goodge yelped.

"Of course we can count it," Smythe said.

"I think I ought to count the Slocum murder," Luty argued, "I give you plenty of information that helped solve the case, and I figured out what all of you was up to."

"If you get to count that one, then so do I," Hatchet interjected. "I was the one that spotted Miss Betsy and Wiggins asking questions about the neighborhood. You'd have never figured out it was the inspector's household solving the murder if I hadn't told you."

"You only spotted 'em," Luty yelped in outrage. "It was me that figured out what they was up to."

Hatchet's eyebrows rose halfway up to his hairline. "Really, madam, are you having trouble with your memory . . . ?"

"You can all count all of them," Mrs. Jeffries interrupted. She gazed sternly around the table. "Honestly, I don't know why it's so important to you, but the truth is, all of you have helped on all the cases. Except of course, for Luty and Hatchet on the Kensington High Street murders. Now, can we get on with it? We've not got all day, and we do have a killer to catch." But the argument rattled her so much she forgot to mention that both of the Windemere brothers were at the top of the guest list.

CHAPTER 5

Inspector Witherspoon stood in the tiny servants' hall of Oscar Daggett's home. "I say, Constable, for such an apparently wealthy man, he certainly doesn't bother to make his staff comfortable."

The room was pathetically furnished, the long oak table was scratched and stained, the chairs were mismatched and rickety, the floor was plain wood without so much as a scrap of carpet, and the small cabinet that probably held the sugar and tea was padlocked shut.

"He takes good care of himself but can't even spare a tablecloth for his staff," Barnes muttered in disgust.

"Unfortunately, most of the servants' halls in London are at this sort of standard. I don't know why." He shook his head in disbelief. "You'd think people who had so much could spare a few bob a year to make their servants' lives a bit easier. But they never do, do they?"

"You do, sir," Barnes said. "Your servants eat as well as you, sleep in comfortable beds and spend their relaxing hour in that nice big kitchen of yours. So you can't say that everyone treats their staff badly."

"Do you have any positions open?" a timid voice asked from behind them.

They turned and saw Hortense, the maid, standing in the doorway. "I'm sorry, I wasn't tryin' to eavesdrop. But I couldn't help overhearin' and frankly, sir, you sound like a good man to work for." She snorted. "Course just about anywhere'd be better than here."

"Oh dear," Witherspoon replied. "I don't have any positions open right at this moment, but I will keep you in mind if I need anyone. I'm sorry I wasn't able to have a word with you yesterday, but Mr. Daggett insisted we leave."

Barnes covered his mouth with his hand in an effort to turn his laughter into a cough. His inspector was brilliant at solving murders, but the poor man was as innocent as a kitten when it came to dealing with people. Especially female people.

"That's all right, sir." Hortense marched into the room. "I overheard him telling you to go. Scared me a bit, it did. I thought for certain I was in for the sharp side of his tongue after you'd gone, but he never said a word. He just shut himself up in his study until it was time for bed."

"I'm glad you didn't suffer for telling us about the girl that's gone missing," Witherspoon said. He was greatly relieved that nothing untoward had happened to the girl. "Why don't we sit down, Hortense, and we can have a nice chat about your friend."

"I was afraid you weren't goin' to come back," Hortense said as she scurried over to the table and flopped down in one of the chairs. "I kept tellin' Mrs. Benchley that we had to tell someone about Nelda. Her things is still here, ya know. She wouldn't have run home without her trunk. I don't care what Mr. Daggett says. Somethin' has happened to her."

Witherspoon took a seat next to the girl, and Barnes eased his tall frame into the chair at the end. He whipped out his notebook. "Why don't you tell us what happened, lass," he said softly, "and the best way for us to really understand is for you to start at the beginning."

"All right, I guess that's best, I do tend to get muddled when I'm excited." Hortense took a long, deep breath. "It all started day before yesterday. Mr. Daggett took one of his sick spells, and we had to send off for Dr. Wiltshire."

"Dr. Wiltshire?" Witherspoon clarified. "Is his surgery close by?"

"It's just around the corner on Victoria Road. Which is lucky for us," Hortense charged. "Otherwise, we'd run our feet off. Mr. Daggett's always sending us for the doctor."

"I take it his health isn't very good," Witherspoon asked.

"He's as healthy as a ruddy workhorse," Hortense exclaimed. "But he's got more aches and pains than a dog has fleas. Even the doctor gets fed up with him."

Barnes looked up from his notebook. "What happened after you got the doctor around?"

"Doctor couldn't come right away. He told me to tell Mr. Daggett to go to bed and he'd be along as soon as he could get away." Hortense pursed her lips. "Course when I told Mr. Daggett it'd be a while before Dr. Wiltshire come to see him, he got so angry I thought he'd pop. But he didn't. He took to his bed and had all of us, but especially Nelda, fetchin' and carryin' and runnin' up and down those ruddy back stairs for hours. Finally, when the doctor got here, all Mr. Daggett had wrong with him was a bit of indigestion."

Witherspoon frowned thoughtfully. "So Mr. Daggett was ill enough that he stayed in bed, is that what you're saying?"

She nodded eagerly. "Right, took to his bed from the first pain, had poor Nelda runnin' up with fresh nightshirts every hour, he did, and he made her change the bed."

"So when did Nelda leave?" Barnes asked.

"Oh, I'm not sure I know what time it was exactly." Hortense wrinkled her forehead. "Things were in a bit of a mess, you see, what with Mrs. Benchley bleedin' all over the kitchen and us having to send for Dr. Wiltshire again. . . ." She paused. "That's right, it was right after Mrs. Benchley had the accident that Nelda left. She took a letter that Mr. Daggett had given her, and she ain't been seen since."

Barnes and Witherspoon glanced at each other. Daggett hadn't mentioned giving the girl an errand. "What's Nelda's last name?" the inspector asked.

"Smith," she replied promptly. "Nelda Smith. She's from a small village in Lancashire. She's only been in London for a couple of months. She didn't much like it here, but she wouldn't have gone off without so much as a by-your-leave."

"Mr. Daggett is under the impression she went home," Witherspoon said softly.

"She didn't," Hortense insisted. "She wouldn't do something that daft. Besides, she left here with just her coat and hat on. How could she have paid her train fare?"

"We'll have the local police check to see if she's at her old home," Barnes said gently. "It won't take long before we've an answer." But he did find it odd that Daggett was so unconcerned about the girl's disappearance.

"Thank you, sir, I'd be ever so relieved to know that she was home safe. But I don't think that's where she's gone. I think something's happened to her." She shifted her gaze slightly, looking at someone who'd just come into the room. "Oh, Mrs. Benchley, the police are here. I'm telling them about Nelda being missing."

Witherspoon leapt to his feet as a woman with her head bandaged just above the left eye came into the dismal room. She stared at them for a moment, then said, "I'm Edith Benchley. I'm the housekeeper here."

"I'm Inspector Witherspoon and this is Constable Barnes."

"If you're through with Hortense, perhaps the girl can get back to her duties."

"We've no more questions at present." Witherspoon smiled kindly at the girl as she got to her feet. "I promise, we'll let you know as soon as we hear anything."

"Thank you, sir," Hortense replied gratefully. She gave the housekeeper a quick, rebellious glance. "I didn't know Nelda very long, but she was a nice girl. Didn't have much family to speak of, just an old aunt. But I don't think she run off home the way they're all sayin'."

"Did Nelda have a young man?" Constable Barnes asked.

Hortense hesitated for a split second. "There'd been a lad who walked her home from chapel a time or two."

"Chapel?" Witherspoon repeated.

"Nelda was a Methodist," Mrs. Benchley said. "And it was more than just a time or two. He's been walking her home every Sunday and he's escorted her to the park on her day out for the last month. So don't you be trying to fool the police into thinking we're a hard-hearted bunch that doesn't care a whit that a young woman in my charge has disappeared."

"I wasn't tryin' to do that, ma'am," Hortense protested. "But I overheard what Mr. Daggett was sayin' yesterday, and if Nelda ain't run off with Ian, then something's happened to her."

"Nothing's happened to her," Mrs. Benchley said calmly. "And you're not to blame Mr. Daggett for thinking she'd run home; that's what I told him. Now if you'll run along to the kitchen, I'd like to have a word with the police."

The woman's tone brooked no argument, so Hortense bobbed a quick curtsey and hurried away. As soon as she'd closed the door behind her, the housekeeper turned her attention to the two policemen. "I'm terribly sorry I haven't been able to speak with you until now, but I've been somewhat indisposed."

Witherspoon's gaze flicked to her bandage. "Uh, yes, we can see that. Er, uh, I take it you believe the girl's not come to any harm?"

Mrs. Benchley gave them a weary smile. "I don't think anything's happened to Nelda that she didn't want to happen. Oh, Inspector, it's all been a dreadful mess. I understand you're here investigating a murder, is that correct?"

"Right, a man named Harrison Nye was killed the night before last. From what we understand, Mr. Daggett was with him shortly before he died. As a matter of fact, Mr. Daggett had something so urgent to tell Mr. Nye, he interrupted a dinner party. Do you have any idea what that could have been?"

She shook her head. "I've no idea. Mr. Daggett wasn't in the habit of sharing information with his servants."

"We understand he'd been ill that day," Barnes said. "Hortense told us he'd been abed most of the day."

"That's correct. Dr. Wiltshire went up to see Mr. Daggett after he finished bandaging my head. I needed a few days' rest, and he wanted to be sure that Mr. Daggett understood that I wasn't to be on my feet. I don't know what happened, but Mr. Daggett left only moments after the doctor did. Later, we found out that he'd gone to see Mr. Nye and that Mr. Nye had been killed that night."

"Did you actually see Mr. Daggett leave?" Barnes asked.

"No, by that time I was abed myself." She smiled and lightly patted the bandage on her forehead. "But I got a detailed account of everything from our cook."

"I take it, then, you've no idea what time Mr. Daggett returned home that night?"

"I'm afraid not," she admitted. "As I said, I was sound asleep. But you might ask Clark—he generally stays up until Mr. Daggett comes home. He's our footman, and it's his task to make sure all the downstairs doors and windows are bolted."

The inspector nodded and made a mental note to speak to both Clark and the cook. He also decided that their next stop would be Dr. Wiltshire's surgery. He was very keen to know what the doctor had said to Mr. Daggett to send him running out into the night. "Thank you, Mrs. Benchley, we'll do that. Now, could you please provide us with Nelda Smith's home address? I did promise Miss Rivers that we'd see if the girl had indeed gone home."

"Certainly, I'll get it straightaway. But I'm fairly sure you'll find that she isn't there," Mrs. Benchley replied. "I think she's run off with her young man."

"We do need to check," Barnes said. "What's this lad's name and where does he live?" He was fairly sure the housekeeper would have that information. Most households kept a fairly tight rein on the young women who worked for them. Some places even forbade the girls to have outings with young men in case they'd fall in love, marry and leave their posts. But times had changed a bit since he was a young man. These days, there were more and more young women refusing to work in those sorts of households.

"His name is Ian Carr. He seems a respectable enough young man. He works on his family's barge. I believe he lives somewhere near the river, but I'm not sure. Mr. Daggett wasn't overly strict about such things, and I didn't feel it was my place to get every little detail from Nelda. She's generally a sensible young woman."

"So you don't think she's come to any harm?" Witherspoon persisted.

"Hardly, Inspector," she said with a knowing smile. "If I honestly thought Nelda had truly disappeared, I'd have been down to the police station straightaway."

Barnes studied her appraisingly. She stared back without flinching. Finally, he said, "You seem certain she's gone off with this young man, why?"

"Because I think she was fed up with Mr. Daggett." Mrs. Benchley sighed. "The poor girl had run her legs off that day. She'd changed his bed twice and taken him three clean nightshirts."

"But wasn't that her job?" Barnes commented.

"No, Constable. She was hired as a maid, not a nurse."

"But Mr. Daggett was ill . . ." the inspector pointed out.

"Nonsense, there wasn't a thing wrong with him except a little indigestion. Most of Mr. Daggett's ailments are in his head. He has the doctor around here at least twice a month." She pursed her lips and stood up. "Nelda had finally had enough. The last time she went into his room, he gave her some silly errand to run. It was dark, Inspector, and the girl doesn't know the city at all, but that didn't stop Mr. Daggett from sending her out on some silly errand. I think she went out, got a bit frightened, went and found her young man and he took her home. That's what I think and frankly, if I had a young man as good-hearted and handsome as hers dancing attendance on me, I wouldn't stay here one minute more than I had to."

The two policemen exchanged glances. "We'll certainly have a word with Mr. Daggett about that," the inspector said. "He never mentioned sending the girl out on an errand."

"I'm sure he didn't," Mrs. Benchley said coldly. "But that's precisely what he did. Feel free to question the rest of the household. They'll tell you the same thing."

"Thank you, ma'am." Witherspoon rose politely. "We would like a word with the rest of the servants, and do you know if Mr. Daggett is available?"

"Mr. Daggett's gone out. He didn't say where, but I do know he's planning on paying a condolence visit to Mrs. Nye this afternoon."

"I suppose this is as good a place to start as any," Betsy muttered to Wiggins. "But I'm not sure about this. It seems to me we're spreading ourselves very thin."

"It should be all right," Wiggins said easily. "It's like Mrs. Jeffries says, we've not really got much choice. There's a lot of territory to cover. We've got to suss out this Daggett fellow *and* the guests at the dinner party *and* the Nye household."

They were standing on a busy corner in South Kensington. Naturally, before their meeting this morning had broken up, they'd all changed their minds several times on what they were going to do next.

As it happened, they'd finally decided that Wiggins was going to snoop about for a housemaid or a footman from the Daggett household and Betsy was going learn what she could about the victim. Smythe had headed out on a mysterious errand of his own, Mrs. Jeffries had gone to Fulham to learn a bit more about the disappearing Miss Geddy and Luty had gone off with the list of names from the Nyes' dinner party. Hatchet had decided he wanted to find out a bit about Harrison Nye as well—he was very much of the opinion that the more one learned about the victim, the easier it was to find the killer.

Betsy agreed with that assessment too. She wasn't dragging her feet because she was annoyed at her assignment. She was miffed at her intended. He'd been far too vague about where he was going and what he was up to. She hated that. She worried about him as much as he worried about her, and he'd been overly casual when she'd asked him where he was off to this afternoon.

"Oh, 'ere and there," he'd said with a casual shrug of his big shoulders. But she'd not been fooled for a moment. He'd not been able to look her in the eyes, and that meant he was up to something. She knew he went to some dangerous places to do his investigating. Not that he couldn't take

care of himself; he could. He was a strong man. But even the strongest
man couldn't do much if someone shoved a knife in his back or coshed
him over the head to steal his money.

"Are ya all right?" Betsy jumped as Wiggins screamed the question in
her left ear.

"Stop shouting at me." She cuffed him in the arm. "Of course I'm all
right."

"I've been talkin' to ya for five minutes and ya 'aven't answered. I
thought you was fixin' to 'ave one of them fits or something." He gazed
at her accusingly. "I was just tryin' to make sure you was all right."

Contrite, she smiled at him. "Oh, Wiggins, I'm sorry. My mind was
elsewhere. I was woolgathering, and I didn't hear you. I'm fine. Now, I'm
going to take myself off toward Belgrave Square and see if I can get a few
shopkeepers to talk to me. Do you want to meet back here and we'll pop
into that Lyon's up the road and have tea?"

He brightened immediately. "That sounds nice. I do love them hot
cross buns they serve. I'll meet you right here at two o'clock." He gave
her a jaunty wave and stepped off the curb.

"Be careful," she called after him, as he darted between a hansom
and a cooper's van. She held her breath till he was safely on the other side
of the busy road, then she turned and started off in the opposite direction. She hoped one of them found out something useful.

Wiggins spent a good part of the afternoon hanging about near the
front of the Daggett house. He tried to be as inconspicuous as possible, but
when he noticed the butler from the house across the street peering out the
front window for the third time, he knew that his loitering had been noticed.

"Blow me for a game of tin soldiers." he muttered in disgust. But the
game was up, and he knew he'd best take himself off. That nosy butler
would be calling the police in two shakes of a lamb's tail, he knew that.
Irritated with the wasted afternoon, Wiggins trudged off to his meeting
with Betsy. He hoped Betsy and the others were having a better afternoon than he was.

Luty boldly marched up the walkway to the tall, elegant, town house on
Ridley Square and banged the knocker. As the door opened, she plas-
tered a huge smile on her face. A poker-faced butler stuck his head out
and peered down at her. "Yes, madam, may I help you?"

"I'd like to see Mrs. Ryker, please. If she's at home. Here's my card." Luty gave him one of her calling cards.

He pulled the door open wider. "Please come inside, madam, and I'll see if Mrs. Ryker is receiving." He waved toward a tall-backed chair next to a round table with a gigantic fern sprouting out of a Chinese-style pot. "Please make yourself comfortable."

Luty nodded and sat down to wait. She'd just about had a stroke when she got a gander at that guest list from the Nye dinner party. Hilda and Neville Ryker were old friends of hers. She'd known them for years and even better, Hilda loved gossiping more than just about anything. The woman could talk the hair off a cat. She straightened as she heard footsteps coming down the hall. She smiled smugly, glad she hadn't told the others of the connection. They'd be real surprised when she told them about it at their next meeting.

"Mrs. Ryker is at home, madam," the butler said. "Right this way, please."

She followed him into a large, beautifully furnished drawing room. A tall, hawkish-looking woman with salt-and-pepper-colored hair, a long nose and a wide, thin mouth was sitting on a gold damask settee. "Goodness, Luty Belle, do come in. It's been ages since I've seen you. Do sit down, please."

"Howdy, Hilda, it has been a while." Luty sat down on a chair. "Sorry for bargin' in like this, but I was in the neighborhood and realized I'd not seen ya in quite a spell."

"Don't apologize." Hilda Ryker smiled widely, obviously delighted to see her friend. "I'm thrilled you've stopped in to call. It's been ages since we've had us a nice good gossip."

Luty chuckled. "You're a woman after my own heart. It has been too long. So, have ya done anything interestin' lately?"

"'Interesting'? I should hope so!" Hilda's eyes sparkled. "You'll never guess what happened the other evening. I was at a dinner party, and the host was murdered."

"In front of everyone?" Luty pretended ignorance. Hilda wouldn't take kindly to figuring out that she'd only come around to get the goods on Harrison Nye. "Now that's what I'd call an interestin' party."

"No, no, no." Hilda waved her hand. "He was murdered later that night. In Fulham. He was stabbed. I'm surprised you haven't heard of it, it's been in all the papers."

"I've been too busy to read the papers," Luty replied. "Well, go on, tell me the rest. Who was this fellow, and who killed him?"

"He's a business friend of Neville's." Hilda pursed her lips in disapproval. "His name's Harrison Nye. He's a bit of a mystery man, or I should say he was a bit of a mystery. He never spoke much about himself or where he'd come from."

Luty stared at Hilda. For all her wealth and breeding, she generally wasn't a snob. "You don't sound like you liked the fellow very much."

"I know one shouldn't speak ill of the dead," Hilda said, "and I'm sorry he was murdered; but honestly, I wasn't in the least surprised he was killed. He could be quite charming, you know, but only when it suited him. There was something cold about him."

"Ruthless sort, was he?" Luty prodded. She bided her time; she wasn't going to budge out of this chair until she got every last detail about that night out of Hilda.

"Very." Hilda leaned forward eagerly. "He's one of those businessmen who has his fingers in lots of different pies, if you know what I mean."

"And no one knows where he came from?" Luty pressed. "I mean, did he just show up in London with a fistful of cash and start buyin' up everything he wanted?"

"He wasn't quite that blatant. But he certainly managed to find opportunity everywhere he turned. As I said, I'm not surprised he was murdered. I suspect he was the sort that has lots of enemies. What was he doing in Fulham in the middle of the night? That's what I want to know. Mr. Ryker and I didn't leave the dinner party till almost ten-forty-five— that means he must have gone out after everyone had left."

"You were the last to leave?" Luty asked. Now they were getting somewhere. She wanted details about that night. She already knew Nye was shady as all get out.

"Lionel was still there." Hilda waved her hand. "He's Eliza's cousin."

"Eliza?"

"Mrs. Nye. She's a niece by marriage of Lord Cavanaugh." Hilda waved her arms expansively. "Actually, it was the most interesting dinner party I've been to in years. Halfway through the fish course, the butler came in and told Harrison he had a visitor who insisted on seeing him immediately. Naturally, Harrison told the butler not to be absurd, that he was with his guests. All of a sudden, the dining-room door flew open and this wild-eyed fellow burst into the room. We were all quite startled; Neville almost choked on his trout."

"What happened then?" Luty pressed. Hilda was easily distracted, and her favorite subject was her husband.

"That was the oddest part of all, as soon as Harrison laid eyes on the man, he leapt to his feet and the two of them disappeared. He didn't come back until Eliza went and reminded him that they had guests."

"So he came back to the table with his wife?" Luty asked.

"Not quite then. It was a few minutes later. I remember because he came back into the room with Lionel."

"Did he say anything when he came back?"

"Hardly." Hilda looked amused. "Harrison Nye had more arrogance than the Kaiser. He offered no apology. He simply sat down and started eating his charlotte russe."

"Do you know who the man was that come to see him?"

"His name was Daggett." Hilda grinned. "I didn't know who he was, but I overheard Lionel ask Eliza what the dickens that Daggett fellow was doing there. Those were his exact words."

"Did she know why he'd come?"

"Hadn't any idea at all. She just shrugged and kept that silly smile on her face. But you could tell she wasn't happy. Of course, that's understandable, no one likes having an important dinner party interrupted." Hilda laughed. "No one, of course, but the guests. It did liven the party up a bit. This fellow was terribly disheveled looking. His hair was standing on end, his tie was askew and he was panting like he'd run for miles. Neville and I were ever so curious. That's one of the reasons we stayed so late. I had the impression something else was going to happen, and as it was, I was right."

Mrs. Goodge picked up the plate of scones and hurried back to the table. She was in luck today, her source not only talked a blue streak, she also might actually have something useful to say. The cook thanked her lucky stars that she'd had the good sense to ask her old friend Ida Leahcock to come round yesterday afternoon. Ida hadn't known anything about the case, but she'd known who might.

"If you're curious about that Nye murder, you might want to have a chat with Jane Melcher," Ida had said. "Her agency is just around the corner from there, and she's probably heard servant's gossip about the house-hold."

She'd taken Ida's advice and sent Jane Melcher a note yesterday evening inviting her around for morning tea. As she hadn't had any contact with the woman in over twenty-five years, she'd no idea if Jane Melcher would give her the time of day, much less come around for tea. But lo and behold, the woman had turned up right after breakfast.

"Here you are, Jane. You just help yourself now." The cook put the plate within easy reach of her companion and took her own seat.

Jane Melcher, a plump, gray-haired woman dressed in a dark aubergine-colored bombazine dress, helped herself to a scone. "It's been ages since we've seen each other." She picked up her knife and slit the scone in half. "I was ever so surprised to get your note. Nicely surprised, mind you. I said to Harriet, she's my typewriter girl, that I'd pop right along to see you. We shouldn't be too busy today, so Harriet will be all right on her own."

"Well, I do think old colleagues ought to keep in touch. Besides, I didn't know what had happened to you after I left Rolston Hall. I happened to run into Ida Leahcock a while back, and she mentioned you had your own business. I was ever so impressed."

"It's just a small domestic staffing agency," she replied.

"Don't be so modest. You ought to be very proud of yourself. Ida says you're very successful, that you find domestic staff for some of the best families in London." Mrs. Goodge firmly believed it never hurt to butter up your source before you pumped her for information.

Jane smiled modestly and stuck her knife in the butter dish. She slathered the top half of the scone. "I do my best. How is Ida these days?"

"She's doing quite well, not that you could tell by looking at her. She still dresses as plain as a pikestaff."

"She never was one to waste money. Maybe that's why she's got so much of it." Jane chuckled at her own witticism. "So how do you like your position here? You work for a policeman, I believe you said."

"He's an inspector," Mrs. Goodge retorted proudly. "Inspector Gerald Witherspoon. I'm surprised you haven't heard of him. He's quite a famous detective. He's solved ever so many cases. He's working on one right now. That man that was stabbed the other night in Fulham, that's his case." She held her breath, hoping Jane would take the bait. When the two women had worked together at Rolston Hall, Jane Melcher always had to be just that bit better than you. No matter what gossip you'd heard, she'd heard more. No matter where you went, she'd gone to someplace nicer and more expensive. No matter what you got for Christmas, she got something prettier. Mrs. Goodge sincerely hoped that old age hadn't improved Jane's character.

"Of course I've heard about that case." Jane smiled knowingly. "Actually, I heard all about it before it was even in the papers. One of the girls I placed as a kitchen maid in the house next door to the Nyes' came by early that morning and told me everything. My girls all know how I like to know what's what. Mind you, I'm not one to gossip, but one has a responsibility to know about the community when one is placing innocent young women in service."

"You never were one to gossip; but, of course, you've got to do your duty." Mrs. Goodge crossed her fingers under the table and silently prayed the Almighty would forgive her the lie.

"That's exactly how I see it," Jane nodded eagerly. "According to what Ellen told me, the night he was murdered, Mr. Nye scarpered off practically in the middle of a dinner party. His last guest hadn't even gone." She ate a bite of scone.

"You don't say." Mrs. Goodge nodded encouragingly.

"Shocking, it was. Absolutely shocking. But then again, Harrison Nye might have lived in that big house and been married to Lord Cavanaugh's niece, but he wasn't really top-drawer, if you know what I mean."

"Absolutely," the cook agreed. "He's probably one of those people who made their money in trade."

"Humph," Jane snorted, "or worse. He pretends to be a respectable businessman, but I say anyone as secretive as him must have something to hide. It was no surprise to me that he was murdered. Sins of the past catching up with him, that's what I say."

"Secretive? Gracious, that certainly doesn't sound very respectable." Mrs. Goodge had struck gold. All she had to do was keep Jane talking.

"Oh, it's the talk of the neighborhood." Jane waved her knife in emphasis. "He used to insist that his staff never say a word to anyone about his household. Instant dismissal if you were caught gossiping. What's so stupid is when you try that hard to stop talk, it just makes it worse."

"What kind of gossip is there?"

"The usual." Jane helped herself to another scone. "Mrs. Nye is a bit too friendly with that cousin of hers; Mr. Nye sneaks out in the middle of the night—that sort of thing. Mind you, I don't know if it's true."

"I take it her cousin is a man?" Mrs. Goodge asked.

"Lionel Bancroft."

"So, Mrs. Nye is too friendly with her cousin, eh?" Mrs. Goodge repeated. "I wonder if the police know that?"

"Why should they?"

"It was her husband that was murdered. If Mrs. Nye was in love with someone else . . ." She let her voice trail off meaningfully.

"I've already thought of that," Jane said briskly. "But neither of them could have done it. I know for a fact that Mrs. Nye retired for the evening right after the last guest left and Lionel Bancroft, who was the last guest that night, left after Harrison Nye had already gone."

"Maybe she slipped out the back way," Mrs. Goodge argued. She thought that a fairly unlikely scenario. One of the servants would have seen her leave, but she wanted to keep the information coming, and nothing loosened Jane's tongue like someone else appearing to know more than she did.

Jane shook her head stubbornly. "I don't think that's likely. How would Mrs. Nye have gotten to Fulham at that time of night?"

"By hansom."

"Ladies don't take hansom cabs at that time of night. It would be too easy to be noticed, and Eliza Nye would never do anything to be disgraced."

"She mustn't be too worried about disgrace if she's having a romp with her cousin," Mrs. Goodge retorted.

"Oh that's just talk." Jane shrugged dismissively. "She wouldn't pay any attention to that. But she certainly wouldn't have anything to do with murder. Not after what happened to her father. Why, it positively ruined the family."

Mrs. Goodge stared at her. "What did happen?"

"Her father murdered her mother, and then committed suicide. I'm amazed you don't remember it. It happened about twelve years ago. John Durney accused his wife of having an affair with their gardener. He shot her with one of his grandfather's dueling pistols, then turned the other gun on himself. The scandal ruined the girl's chance to make a decent match. That's probably why she married Harrison Nye. I expect her money had run out by the time he proposed."

CHAPTER 6

"Are you saying you haven't interviewed the widow properly?" Chief Inspector Barrows stared at Witherspoon from the other side of his desk.

"It was impossible, sir," Witherspoon explained. "She was quite hysterical. I meant to go back the first thing this morning, but a number of other things cropped up, and I didn't get the chance. Constable Barnes and I were on our way there when I received the message that you wanted to see me."

Barrows leaned back in his chair. "Look, Inspector, I'm not trying to tell you how to run this investigation, but it is customary to interview the victim's spouse as soon as possible after a murder."

"Yes, sir, I quite understand. But as I said, Mrs. Nye was hysterical." Witherspoon cocked his head to one side. "If you don't mind my asking, sir, I've often gone a day or two without questioning a spouse, and you've never objected before. I've always put that fact in my reports, I've never tried to hide it."

"I know. Normally, I wouldn't bother you with such nonsense. But I was walking down the hall with the commissioner's private secretary when all of a sudden Inspector Nivens came rushing in waving an article from the *Policeman's Gazette*." Barrows sighed. "The article said what most policemen already know, that the most likely suspect in a murder is generally the victim's husband or wife. Well, the upshot of the whole business was Nivens managed to work it into the conversation that you were handling the Nye murder and had you interviewed Mrs. Nye yet? By that time Pomeroy, that's the commissioner's private secretary, decided to put his oar in the water and insisted it be done right away."

The inspector knew he wasn't very sophisticated when it came to Scotland Yard and Home Office politics, but he did rather suspect that this Pomeroy fellow and Inspector Nivens were good friends. He'd heard it said that Inspector Nivens was politically and socially very well connected. "As I said, sir, I was on my way to interview Mrs. Nye when I was called here."

Barrows gave a short, bark of a laugh. "Yes, I daresay you were. Now that you're here, you might as well report. How is the investigation going? Is there an arrest on the horizon?"

"It's a very complicated case, sir." Witherspoon frowned. "I don't think we'll be making any arrests just yet. We've a lot of territory to cover first. We think we've a good lead on finding out why Harrison Nye went to Fulham that night. That ought to help clear up the mystery a bit." He glanced at the clock on the wall behind Barrow's. "Er, is there anything else, sir? It's getting late."

"No," the chief inspector interrupted. "I've done my duty and had a word with you. I trust you'll keep me informed as to your progress."

"Yes, sir, certainly." He muttered a hasty good-bye and marched out of the office. Constable Barnes was waiting for him just outside the door. "Everything all right, sir?" Barnes inquired.

"I think so." Witherspoon found the entire episode rather odd. "All he wanted to know was whether or not we'd interviewed Mrs. Nye."

Barnes's bushy eyebrows rose. "He drug us all the way up here to ask you that?"

Witherspoon looked over his shoulder as they headed for the stairs. He didn't want anyone to overhear him. "I don't think he had much choice. I'll tell you all about it as soon as we're outside."

They went down the stairs and crossed the foyer. As soon as they were safely out the door, Witherspoon told Barnes what had transpired in Barrows's office. The constable's eyes narrowed angrily, but he held his tongue.

"I do believe that Mr. Pomeroy and Inspector Nivens are friends," Witherspoon said. "I suspect that Nivens is a bit annoyed that he didn't get this case."

"He's as jealous as an old cat," Barnes said bluntly. He loathed Nivens as did just about every uniformed lad that had ever worked with the man. "You'd best watch yourself, sir. I think Nivens's resentment of you is getting worse."

"Oh dear, that will make things awkward," Witherspoon replied. He waved at a passing hansom. The driver spotted him and pulled over to the curb. "Do you think I ought to have a talk with him?" he asked as he climbed inside. "Take us to Upper Belgrave Street," he ordered the driver.

"I don't think that'd work, sir," Barnes replied as he slid into the seat next to the inspector. He grabbed the hand-rest as the cab started off.

"Really? Oh dear, that is a problem. I don't like to think that Inspector Nivens resents me."

"He does, sir." Barnes wanted to make sure this was understood. It was only a miracle that Nivens's constant undermining of the inspector hadn't already resulted in a transfer or demotion for Witherspoon. "And you can bet your last bob that it wasn't any accident that Nivens 'happened' to run into the chief inspector while he was with the chief."

Witherspoon stared at him over the top of his spectacles. "Are you saying you think the whole event was . . . er . . . orchestrated so that the chief would have reason to call me into his office?"

Barnes nodded. "That's exactly what I'm sayin', sir. It weren't exactly a reprimand, but it wasn't very nice, was it?"

"Not really."

Barnes took a deep breath and plunged ahead. He had to warn the inspector, had to make him understand how damaging Nivens could be. "He's a dangerous man, sir. He sees you as a threat to his climb to the top. He's desperate for power and position. He's not the least interested in justice, sir."

"That's a bit harsh, don't you think?"

"No sir, I don't. I've known the man since he come on the force and he got where he is today by bootlicking, undermining, tattling on his fellow officers and taking the credit for others' hard work. He's out to get you, sir. You'd best watch your back."

Witherspoon gaped at the constable. Barnes was a fair and honest man. He wouldn't make up lies about someone merely because he disliked that person. "But why? I've not done anything to him. Why would he want to harm my career?"

"Like I said, sir, you're a threat to him." Barnes sighed. "Your solving all these murders the last few years has pushed him farther and farther into the background. Before, when you were still working in the records room, most of the inspectors were all much the same. They had about the same number of good arrests and about the same percentage solving their cases. Inspector Nivens, with his political friends and his bootlickin' and backstabbing, tended to pull ahead of the pack a bit. Then you come along and solved them Kensington High Street killings and got started with solving just about every murder that come along. It made him look bad, sir, because it made him look ordinary."

Witherspoon was stunned. "It's not very pleasant thinking that someone dislikes me merely because I'm doing my duty."

Barnes winced as he saw the stricken expression on his superior's face. "You do a great deal more than your duty, sir, and that's what scares Nivens so much. I'm only tellin' you this so you'll keep your guard up, sir."

"I'm not sure I know how to do that," the inspector admitted honestly. "How can one defend oneself against innuendos and er . . . what did you call it, 'backstabbing'?"

"You can't, sir," Barnes said honestly. "But you can fire off a few salvos on your own."

"I'm not sure I understand what you mean." He looked out the side as the hansom pulled up in front of the Nye house.

"For starters," Barnes said as he jumped down, "you can complain to Barrows about Nivens interferin' with your investigation."

Witherspoon handed the driver some coins. "But he hasn't done that."

"Sure he has," Barnes said cheerfully. "Several of the lads who did the house-to-house in Fulham said they spotted Nivens snooping about and what's more, he pulled Constable Peters aside and started questioning him."

"Gracious, really. He did all that?" Witherspoon marched up the walkway toward the house.

"He did, sir, and if you complain to Barrows, that'll get Nivens off your patch for a good while. He's not just a greedy little sod, sir. He's a coward too. It'll scare the daylights out of him to get called on the carpet for stickin' his nose in where it don't belong."

Witherspoon thought about what Barnes told him as they went into the Nye house and waited for the butler to announce them. He was terribly confused. The very idea of running to the chief inspector and complaining about another officer was repugnant to him. Yet he trusted Constable Barnes implicitly, and if he said that Nivens was out to damage him, Witherspoon couldn't ignore the situation. Besides, if he were really truthful with himself, finding out that Nivens was out to do him a disservice was certainly no surprise. He'd never been more than barely civil to Witherspoon. But the inspector had always told himself Nivens's surliness was merely his nature and that it wasn't personal. It seems now that he was wrong. Nivens was out to destroy his career. He took that quite personally indeed.

"If you'll come this way, gentlemen." Duffy's words interrupted his reveries. "Mrs. Nye is receiving in the drawing room."

They followed him down the hallway. Eliza Nye, dressed in widows' black, rose from where she'd been sitting on the settee. A tall, fair-haired man of about thirty-five was in the room with her. "Hello, Inspector, Constable," she said softly. "This is my cousin, Lionel Bancroft."

Both policemen nodded politely, then Witherspoon focused his attention on Mrs. Nye. Her eyes were red and swollen from crying, her face was pale and she had a decidedly haggard air of grief about her. It was difficult to see such a sad, delicate creature as a murderess, but the inspector knew that even the sweetest countenance could mask the heart of a monster. Still, he didn't think she'd be so upset if she'd murdered her husband. "Again, Mrs. Nye, please accept our condolences on the loss of your husband. We'll do everything in our power to bring his killer to justice."

"Thank you, Inspector." She smiled weakly. "I'm sure you will. Let's all sit down. You must have a number of questions to ask me."

"Are you certain you're up to this, my dear?" Lionel Bancroft patted her hand.

"I must," she replied. "Regardless of how distressing it is." She sat back down. Her cousin took the spot next to her.

"We'll do our best to make this as painless as possible," Witherspoon said, as he and Barnes sat down on the opposite love seat. He thought he might as well start with the most obvious questions. "Do you know of anyone who would want to harm Mr. Nye?"

"No, Inspector. I can't think of anyone who would wish him ill."

"He hadn't any enemies? Disgruntled business associates, uh, staff that have been let go . . ."

"He was a businessman, Inspector." She shrugged slightly. "Sometimes quite a ruthless one at that, but as far as I know, no one ever threatened him."

"Would he have told you if he had been in fear of his life?" Barnes asked softly.

She hesitated briefly. "Truthfully, I'm not sure. Harrison was very protective of me."

"Of course he wouldn't have told you such a thing," Bancroft interjected. "He would never have worried you like that." He looked at the policemen, his expression grim. "Mrs. Nye doesn't wish to speak ill of her husband."

"Lionel," she yelped. "What on earth are you doing?"

"I'm telling them the truth, my dear. I don't wish to cause you pain, but if the police are going to find out who killed Harrison, they need to know the truth about him."

"And what would that be, sir?" Witherspoon asked quickly. He didn't want Mrs. Nye stopping her cousin from talking. Sometimes it was unexpected outbursts like these that gave one the very clue one needed to solve the case.

Lionel shot his cousin a quick, beseeching glance, then said, "Unfortunately, Harrison had a lot of enemies. Why, even some of the people who were having dinner here the night of the murder would have wished him dead."

"Lionel, please," Mrs. Nye pleaded. "You mustn't say such things. It's not true. Harrison had made his peace with those two."

"Perhaps it would be easier on Mrs. Nye if we spoke with you alone?" Barnes suggested.

"No," she yelped. Then she appeared to get ahold of herself and took a long, deep breath. She smiled wanly at her cousin. "Lionel, I know you're trying to spare my feelings, but I'd really rather cooperate with the police. The only way I shall ever sleep again is to know the police are doing their best to catch my husband's killer." She looked at Witherspoon. "I'm quite all right, Inspector. Please, do go on with your questions."

"Well, er, now that Mr. Bancroft's brought it up, perhaps he can elaborate on what he meant."

Lionel shot Eliza Nye one quick, anxious glance and then said, "As I said, Inspector, there were two people here who might have had a grudge against Harrison."

"And who would they be, sir?" Barnes asked quickly.

"His former solicitors, John and Peter Windemere."

The inspector looked at Eliza Nye. "Is this true?"

"I'm afraid it is, Inspector." She sighed. "Harrison had a property matter some years ago that they were handling for him. Unfortunately, they mishandled the sale so completely, the deal fell apart. It cost my husband an enormous amount of money. He sued them and was granted damages. It bankrupted the firm."

"Then why'd they come to dinner?"

"My husband asked me to invite them, Inspector. I've no idea why."

Witherspoon frowned slightly. "Didn't you find it strange that Mr. Nye would ask you to invite people who probably had a real reason to dislike him?"

"I didn't think it strange at all," she replied. "I only found out that they had reason to dislike my husband after they arrived that night."

Barnes asked. "Who told you?"

"My husband," she said. "We were just getting ready to come down when Duffy let them in and took them into the drawing room. They were the first guests to arrive. We were standing at the top of the stairs. I started to go down, but Harrison grabbed my arm and told me to wait. He was laughing. He said he wanted them to squirm for a few minutes. I asked him what on earth he was talking about. He told me what had happened years earlier. I was appalled, Inspector."

"Yes, I imagine that would have been a bit of a shock. Er," he hesitated, not quite certain what to ask next but knowing he ought to ask something. "Did your husband offer you an explanation as to why he wanted them at dinner? Forgive me, ma'am, but your description of your husband's behavior doesn't sound like he wanted to make peace with these men."

"No, it doesn't, does it? I suppose that now that Harrison's dead, I'd like to think him a better man than he was." She smiled sadly. "He said he invited them because he had a business proposal that might interest them."

"What kind of proposal?" Barnes asked.

"He didn't say. I was going to ask him about it later that evening, but as I'm sure you realize . . ." Her voice trailed off and her eyes filled with tears. "I never got the chance."

"How did they greet your husband?" Witherspoon thought that a good question. If someone had bankrupted him, he probably wouldn't have been very nice to him. Mind you, he couldn't imagine accepting a dinner invitation from the person responsible for ruining you.

"I don't know, Inspector," she admitted. "As we reached the bottom of the stairs, other guests were arriving, and I went to greet them. Harrison went on into the drawing room."

"I arrived about then with the Rykers," Lionel Bancroft interjected.

"I see." Witherspoon nodded. "Er, how were they all acting when you and your other guests arrived in the drawing room?"

"They weren't there," she said. "Harrison had taken them, and they'd disappeared into his study. They didn't come back until it was almost time for dinner. There didn't seem to be anything wrong. Everyone appeared very cordial. They weren't particularly talkative, but they weren't rude. All the other guests had arrived by then, so Harrison made the introductions."

"It was all very civilized, Inspector," Lionel added. "I'd no idea Harrison had been at odds with any of his guests until Eliza told me the next day. I do think you ought to question these men. If anyone had reason to dislike Harrison, I'm sure it was they."

"We shall have a word with both those gentlemen, I assure you," Witherspoon replied. His head was beginning to hurt a little. This case, which was already complicated, had just been made worse. He hadn't really considered the guests at the dinner party to be suspects. Apparently, he'd been wrong.

"Your husband seems to have spent most of that evening in his study instead of at the dining table," Barnes observed dryly.

Eliza Nye's perfect brow furrowed in confusion. "Oh yes, of course, you're referring to Oscar Daggett's peculiar outburst."

"The man has no manners whatsover," Lionel exclaimed. "He's another one you ought to have a word with."

"We have already spoken to Mr. Daggett," Witherspoon said. "Mrs. Nye, had you ever seen Daggett before that night?"

"Not often," she said. "But he's been here a few times. He and my husband used to be in business together but it was a long time ago."

"They aren't in business now?" the inspector pressed. Oscar Daggett had definitely implied he'd come to the Nye house about a business question.

"No."

"Are you absolutely certain of that?" Witherspoon wanted to be sure.

"Of course I'm sure," she said, her tone just a shade sharp.

"Really, Inspector," Lionel added. "I do believe Mrs. Nye knows who her husband does business with."

"She didn't know about the Windemere brothers' business relationship with her husband," Barnes said calmly.

"That was different," she snapped. "They hadn't had anything to do with Harrison in eleven years. He'd have hardly been likely to mention them, would he?"

Witherspoon decided to try a different tactic. "Your butler gave me the names of everyone who was at your dinner party. I understand Mr. Bancroft was the last to leave that night?"

"I was," Lionel admitted. "I stayed to have a word with Mrs. Nye. I left a few minutes after Harrison did."

"And I retired for the night right after Lionel left," Eliza Nye added.

"Yes, ma'am, we know that. We've already had a word with your staff. Your butler confirmed everyone's movements. Did your husband happen to mention where he was going when he left here?"

"He did not," she replied, "and I was rather annoyed with him about it. Of course I was careful not to show my displeasure in front of our guests."

"I understand he often left the house late at night," Witherspoon persisted.

"Often isn't the word I'd use, Inspector. When we were first married, he went out a time or two. When he saw how much it upset me, he stopped," she said. "Or if he left the house at night, he waited until after I'd retired for the evening."

"But he didn't that night, did he?" Barnes pointed out. "As a matter of fact, he left even before your last guests."

"I was going to speak to him about it later," she snapped. "But I never got the chance."

Mrs. Jeffries stood at the head of the table and double-checked to make sure everything was ready for tea. The others would be back soon, and she had no doubt they had much to discuss.

Mrs. Goodge came out of the dry larder carrying a loaf of plain brown bread. "There's a hot pot in the oven for supper tonight, so I think all we need for tea this afternoon is some bread and butter."

"Are any of the others back yet?" Mrs. Jeffries asked. "I think I hear Luty and Hatchet pulling up outside."

"Betsy's here. She dashed upstairs to change the inspector's linens.

The laundry boy is due by this evening." Mrs. Goodge sincerely hoped the kitchen would be empty by then—that lad was fairly sharp. She wanted to have a moment or two alone to question him and see if he knew anything useful.

"I'm all done." Betsy, her arms loaded with crumpled sheets, hurried over to the wicker laundry basket sitting beside the pine sideboard. She dumped the sheets inside. "Shall I close it?"

"That's the last," Mrs. Jeffries replied. "Can you let Luty and Hatchet in the back door?"

Betsy nodded and dashed off down the hall just as Smythe came down the back stairs. "Where's she going?" he asked the housekeeper.

"To let in Luty and Hatchet," Mrs. Goodge said. "Where's Wiggins?"

"He's right behind me." Smythe slid into his usual chair. "And from the expression on 'is face, I'd say he's not got much to report."

The others came into the kitchen in a pack, with Luty and Betsy in the lead. "Wait'll you hear what I found out," the elderly American exclaimed.

"You're not the only one who learned something useful," Hatchet added. As they'd reached the table, he pulled out Luty's chair and seated her with a flourish. Betsy dropped into the seat next to Smythe and gave him a swift, intimate smile. She was still a bit annoyed that he'd not told her where he went today, but she'd forgiven him.

"I've not found out anything." Wiggins dropped into his seat. He looked hopefully at the plate of bread and butter in the center of the table. Mrs. Goodge shoved it toward him.

"Don't take it so hard, lad," Smythe said. "My day wasn't all that good either." He'd gone to every dirty pub on the eastern docks and he'd not seen hide nor hair of his source, Blimpey Groggins. No one else had seen the man lately either. Smythe was a little concerned. It wasn't like Blimpey to pull a disappearing act like this. Bad for business it was.

"Iffen it's all the same to you, then, can I tell ya what all I learned?" Luty asked.

Mrs. Jeffries glanced around the table, saw no objections, then nodded. "Please, go ahead." She began pouring cups of tea.

Luty smiled delightedly. "Well, since you-all kindly let me have a look at that guest list, I gotta tell ya, I hit pay dirt."

Hatchet raised his eyebrows. "I take it that means you recognized at least one name on the list? Humph," he snorted, "no wonder you changed your mind about what you wanted to do."

"Don't be such a grouch." Luty grinned. "You'd have done the same. Besides, we change our minds all the time about what we're doin' and where we're goin' to be snoopin'."

"So you recognized a name on the list," Mrs. Jeffries prompted. Sometimes these two could waste an inordinate amount of time squabbling like children. "Do go on . . ."

"I decided I'd have a chat with my friend Hilda Ryker. Nice woman, likes to gossip and doesn't give herself airs. She was at the dinner party that night." Luty laughed. "Hilda said she'd only gone because her husband insisted. She didn't particularly care for Harrison Nye, and she didn't like his wife much either."

"Did she tell you why?" Mrs. Jeffries asked.

"I asked her, and she said she wasn't sure." Luty shrugged and reached for her cup of tea. "She couldn't rightly put her finger on why she didn't like 'em, she said she just didn't feel comfortable around either of 'em."

"But she didn't give any specific reason for her feelings?" Hatchet pressed. Sometimes, when madam was vague, it was because she was trying to keep a useful clue all to herself.

"No, like I said, she just didn't like 'em much. But, luckily, she went because Neville wanted her to and she said it ended up bein' one of the most interestin' evenin's she'd had in a long while. Oscar Daggett weren't the only interestin' distraction at that party." She paused dramatically. "The Windemere brothers was at the dinner party."

"Oh dear," Mrs. Jeffries exclaimed. "I meant to tell everyone their names were on the list, but it slipped my mind."

"It slipped your mind?" Betsy repeated incredulously.

"If you'll recall, we ended up in a rather heated argument at our last meeting," Mrs. Jeffries said defensively. "Between trying to determine who had how many cases to their credit and everyone changing their minds about what they were going to do next, I simply didn't think to mention it till everyone had gone. You all did leave rather quickly."

"That's all right, Hepzibah." Luty smiled smugly. "No harm was done. But like I was sayin', they was there that night, big as life. John Windemere sat right next to Hilda. She said you could tell by the way they was actin' that they was upset about something. Every time someone tried to start a conversation, they'd give a one-word answer or mumble something silly: Hilda said it was obvious to anyone who had half a brain that they didn't want to be there. To top it off, when Oscar Daggett come chargin' in lookin' as wild-eyed as a crazy coyote, the two brothers started grinnin' like a couple of fools."

"They knew Oscar Daggett?" Mrs. Jeffries asked.

"Hilda didn't think so," Luty replied. "As a matter of fact, she was sure they didn't. She overheard one of 'em say to the other that Daggett looked like trouble for Nye; he didn't use Daggett's name of course, just said 'the man.' The other one said he hoped so too."

"They were talking like that in front of Mrs. Nye?"

Mrs. Goodge looked at Luty over the top of her spectacles.

"She didn't hear 'em." Luty reached for a slice of bread. "One of the other guests had distracted everyone by gettin' up and leavin' the table. I, uh, think he went to the water closet."

"The water closet? That's an odd thing to do during a dinner party." Mrs. Goodge shook her head. "But then it sounds as if it was a very odd party to begin with."

"You can say that again," Luty said. "Hilda said it was the best one she's been to in years."

Mrs. Jeffries thought about what she'd just heard. It was, indeed, a very strange dinner party. "I wonder why Nye invited them?" she murmured.

"Maybe Mrs. Nye invited 'em," Wiggins suggested. As he didn't have anything useful in the way of information to contribute tonight, he felt duty-bound to ask good questions.

"That's a good question," the housekeeper agreed. "Why don't you see if you can find out the answer?"

Wiggins brightened. "You think it's important?"

She didn't, but as he wasn't doing very well in this investigation, she didn't want to discourage the lad. "Absolutely. See if you can find a servant from the household that might know who put the names on the guest list," she replied. "Now, who would like to go next?"

"I'll go next," Hatchet said. He paused for a brief moment, then plunged right ahead, determined not to let the madam's dramatic revelations bother him in the least. "It wasn't easy finding out anything about Frieda Geddy. But I persisted and did find out a few interesting tidbits." He took a quick sip of tea. "Frieda Geddy spoke Dutch."

"Dutch?" Mrs. Goodge frowned. "You mean she was a foreigner."

"No, I mean she spoke Dutch as a second language," he explained. "Her parents were Dutch."

"They were immigrants from the Netherlands?" Mrs. Jeffries clarified.

"No, no, I'm sorry, I'm not explaining this very well." He took a deep breath. "Her mother was English and her father was from someplace in Southern Africa, some place near Johannesburg. My source wasn't exactly sure, but he did know that Miss Geddy spoke Dutch and that she'd learned it from her father."

"So maybe she was mailin' all them packages off to South Africa," Wiggins suggested. "You know, sendin' mittens and nice things off to her old dad."

"Her father died fifteen years ago," Hatchet said. "He was killed in an accident in the Transvaal."

"Gracious, Hatchet, you have learned a lot." Mrs. Jeffries was rather impressed. "How on earth did you find that out?"

Hatchet gave his mistress a quick, smug grin. He wouldn't admit to anyone, least of all her, that he'd found a former cleaning woman of Frieda Geddy's and bribed her shamelessly. "Oh, I have my ways." He gave an exaggerated sigh. "I only wish I could have learned more."

"What did her family do?" Mrs. Goodge asked.

"My source wasn't certain. She thought perhaps Miss Geddy's family might have been in mining."

Mrs. Jeffries thought about that for a moment. "Did you find out anything else?"

"No." Hatchet's shoulders slumped a bit. "I know we need to find a connection between Miss Geddy and Harrison Nye, but honestly, I'm beginning to think there isn't one."

"But there has to be," Betsy insisted. "He was on his way to visit her; he must have been."

"He was murdered on her front steps," Smythe added. "In the middle of the bloomin' night. There has to be a connection."

"But no one I spoke to had any idea how they could possibly be related," Hatched argued. "Miss Geddy had no friends or acquaintances in common with Nye, she certainly didn't travel in his social circle and as far as I can see, she had no reason whatsover to have anything to do with the man. The fact that she's disappeared and he's died doesn't necessarily mean the two of them have any connection with each other. After all, her disappearance took place two months before he got stabbed on her doorstep. It could very well be a coincidence."

Everyone thought about that for a moment. Then Wiggins said,

"Maybe 'e went there that night because 'e knew that her house was goin' to be empty."

"How would he know that?" Mrs. Goodge frowned at the footman over the rim of her spectacles.

"Maybe 'e owns the 'ouse," Wiggins suggested. "We've 'eard that 'e owns lots of things, 'as his fingers in a lot of pies so to speak. Maybe he owns the freehold where she lives and when she didn't pay 'er rent, 'e knew the place was empty."

Again, there was a silence as everyone thought about Wiggins's observation.

"Cor blimey, the lad might be right," Smythe finally said. "Maybe he was goin' there to meet someone he didn't want to be seen with in public. What better place than a 'ouse he knew was empty."

"That's certainly possible," Mrs. Jeffries murmured. "If he was, indeed, the landlord, he'd have sent his agents around to collect the rent."

"He'd also have a key," Luty said softly. "Let's ask the inspector if they found a key on the body."

"I will," she replied thoughtfully. "Wiggins has raised a very interesting possibility. We need to find out if Harrison Nye had any way of knowing that house would be empty."

"I don't think it's likely," Mrs. Goodge said bluntly. "I think you're leapin' in the dark here. To begin with, we don't know that Nye does own that house, and even if he did, why go all the way to Fulham to meet someone. If he wanted privacy, he could have gone out into the middle of Belgrave Square. That time of night, there'd be no one about to see him. Besides, from everything we've heard, it was Oscar Daggett's visit that night that sent Nye out in the first place. How would he have had time to make any arrangements about meetin' someone in an empty house?"

Mrs. Jeffries smiled sheepishly. "Of course you're right. We are leaping in the dark as you say. But Wiggins does have a point. Nye's going to Fulham may have had nothing to do with Miss Geddy. We'll just have to keep investigating."

"Can I tell what I've found out?" the cook asked. "I think it's pretty interestin'." At the housekeeper's nod, she continued. "I found out a bit about Mrs. Nye today. It seems there's a bit of gossip about the area about her and her cousin, Lionel Bancroft. Some say they're a bit too friendly, even for family."

"You mean they're . . . uh"—a deep blush crept up Wiggins's cheeks—"sweethearts?"

"That's a polite way of sayin' it." Luty chuckled.

"That's one way of puttin' it." The cook tried to keep her expression stern, but it was hard. Sometimes she was amazed at how naive these young people were. "And that's not all I heard. Eliza Nye before she married was Eliza Durney. She's most definitely from one of the best families in England, her mother was Lord Cavanaugh's sister and her father, John Durney, was cousin to minor nobility on his mother's side. But Eliza's chances for a good match were ruined. There was a terrible scandal a few years ago. Her father found out his wife was having an"—she hesitated, trying to pick the least offensive word—"assignation with the gardener."

"Assignation," Wiggins interrupted as he scratched his chin. "What's that?"

"She were playin' about where she hadn't ought to be playin' about," Luty said quickly. "Go on," she urged the cook. "This is getting right interestin'."

Wiggins kept silent. He wasn't exactly sure what an assignation was, but he had a good idea. Nonetheless, he resolved to find out for certain from Smythe when the two of them were alone.

"Right"—the cook bobbed her head—"and in the middle of this . . . uh, assignation, Durney burst into his wife's bedroom and shot both Mrs. Durney and, of course, the gardener."

"Cor blimey." Smythe shook his head in disbelief. "Caught 'em in the act, did 'e?"

"And killed them," Mrs. Goodge said. "Then he turned the gun on himself. Eliza Nye found their bodies. No one else was home that day."

Wiggins was suddenly sure he knew exactly what they were talking about.

CHAPTER 7

Mrs. Jeffries slowly climbed the back stairs. She had much to think about. The evening was quickly drawing in but she was fairly confident the inspector wouldn't be home for a good while yet. Luty and Hatchet had gone home, Wiggins and Smythe were doing a few chores and Betsy was helping the cook finish the preparations for supper.

She stopped at the back-hall closet and took out the big ostrich-feather duster then she made her way to the drawing room. Sometimes she thought more clearly when she was doing a dull, boring task.

She turned on a lamp against the dim light. She walked over to the sideboard and ran the duster along the top. Their meeting had been very productive, and they'd learned a great deal of information. But what did it all mean?

From what they knew thus far, no one appeared to be overly fond of Harrison Nye. His former solicitors had no reason to wish him well that was for certain. He'd ruined their business. But why wait eleven years to take vengeance? Then again, they were solicitors, and waiting such a long time would make the police less likely to view them as suspects than if they'd murdered him when he'd ruined them. She finished dusting the sideboard and made her way to the table near the window. There were still so many unanswered questions. Why had Oscar Daggett interrupted the dinner party? What had happened that had made him leap out of a sickbed and rush over to see an old business partner? She made a mental note to find out if Daggett had received any visitors or messages prior to his going to Nye's house that night.

She finished dusting the furniture, then plopped down on a chair. All their cases tended to be complex, but this one seemed particularly puzzling. She wasn't sure why . . . then she realized it was probably because they had very little information about the victim. Who was Harrison Nye and, more importantly, why would someone hate him enough to kill him? Apparently, he'd quite a reputation as a ruthless businessman—that generally tended to make one unpopular. But there were many such men in London, and most of them didn't get murdered. Maybe they ought to look closer to home—it was certainly not unknown for a wife to want to rid herself of an inconvenient husband. Could it have been Mrs. Nye? According to what the cook had found out, there was ample evidence that Eliza Nye was in love with her cousin and had only married Nye because she needed money. Money was most definitely one of the more usual motives for murdering one's spouse.

But they'd no evidence that Eliza Nye had left the house that night. Beside, how would she have gotten to Fulham? Mrs. Jeffries knew full well that between the inspector's official investigation and Smythe's unofficial one, every hansom cab driver in the area had been questioned thoroughly. So far, none of them had mentioned taking a woman fitting Eliza Nye's description to Fulham.

The case was a puzzle, but Mrs. Jeffries was sure they'd solve it eventually. They generally did.

Even though it was past six o'clock, Dr. Douglas Wiltshire was still at his surgery when the inspector and Barnes arrived. "I'll be with you in a moment," Wiltshire called over his shoulder. He was at a sink on the far side of the examination room scrubbing his hands. "Please seat yourselves. There are chairs in my office."

The two policemen walked past the leather examination table to the small office adjacent to the surgery. They sat down on the two chairs in front of the doctor's simple wooden desk. Witherspoon wrinkled his nose at the harsh smell of disinfectant.

A tall, glass-fronted cupboard filled with bottles, vials and some rather frightening-looking instruments was on one side of the room. The opposite wall was covered with floor-to-ceiling bookcases, most of them medical texts. "I say, he's got rather a lot of books."

"And I use all of them," Dr. Wiltshire said as he came into the room. "There's discoveries being made every day in the medical field, and one has to keep up. The more I know, the better a doctor I can be. Sorry to keep you waiting, gentlemen." He sat down and gave them a friendly, if puzzled smile. "What can I do for you? Neither of you look ill."

"We're here to see you about one of your patients, sir," Witherspoon said. "We've a few questions for you."

"About my patient?" Wiltshire frowned. "I don't know that I'm at liberty to discuss anyone's medical condition without their permission. . . ."

"It's not really his medical condition we're concerned about," Witherspoon interrupted. "It's about Oscar Daggett, sir, and it's in connection with a murder investigation." He'd found that frequently people tended to loosen their tongues a bit when they knew the kind of crime the police were trying to solve.

"Daggett?" Wiltshire snorted. "The only thing wrong with him is he eats too much, exercises too little and takes himself far too seriously. He's got more aches and pains than an entire ward at the infirmary, and all of them are in his head!"

"But you were at his house on October 15," Witherspoon said. "Why did you go if he wasn't ill?"

"I was there twice that day," Wiltshire replied. "Once for him and once for his housekeeper. I go, Inspector, because the fool pays me well. I charge him double my usual fee."

"Double?" Witherspoon was rather shocked. It was rare that someone actually admitted to such a thing.

"Oh yes, patients like Daggett make it possible for me to give my services free of charge to the poor. Once a fortnight I work a clinic in the East End. But you're not here to talk about me. You want to know about Daggett. What can I say? There wasn't a thing wrong with the fellow that day. As usual, Daggett ate far too much at dinner the night before and had a case of indigestion. A simple dose of baking soda would have been adequate treatment for him, but he always sends one of his servants trotting over to fetch me." Wilshire rolled his eyes heavenward. "I've been to attend the fellow three times in the last fortnight, Inspector, and I was heartily sick of it. I had a look at him, ascertained his medical needs were minimal, then had a nice natter with his housekeeper about my dying orange tree. Later that evening, I was called back to attend Mrs. Benchley. She was actually in need of my services. Poor woman had a concussion."

"How was Mr. Daggett when you went back the second time?" Barnes said. "I believe you went up to see him."

"Oh yes, Mrs. Benchley was very worried that Mr. Daggett would be angry with her for needing to stay in bed. I assured her I'd have a word with him about how important it was she stay off her feet." He shook his head. "Actually, that's the only time I was ever seriously worried about Daggett."

"How do you mean, sir?" Barnes asked. He rather liked the doctor.

Wiltshire frowned thoughtfully. "When I got up to Daggett's room, he was still in bed. Before I could even tell him why I was there, he started moaning about how it wasn't fair, that I ought to have told him he was dying because a fellow needed time to get his affairs in order. I asked him what he was talking about and repeated my earlier diagnosis that there was nothing wrong with him but indigestion."

"From what you've told us about Mr. Daggett," Barnes said, "it sounds as if he always thought he was at death's door."

"That's quite true, Constable. But this time was different. He was convinced I'd come back for the deathwatch and that he was dying within the hour. I finally asked him where he got such a notion . . ." Wiltshire broke off with a sheepish smile. "And it turns out that he thought he was dying because he overheard me and Mrs. Benchley talking about my orange tree and how it was dying. He thought we'd been talking about him."

Witherspoon leaned forward in his chair. "Did he believe you?"

"Oh yes," Wiltshire said. "He knew I was speaking the truth. That's why I was so surprised by what happened next."

"What was that?" Barnes prodded.

"He leapt out of bed and began dressing. But what was so stunning is that was the first time since I've been treating the man that he actually looked ill. I got quite worried about him. All the color drained from Daggett's face, his eyes bulged like they were going to pop out of his head and he was in such a hurry to get me out of his room, he practically shoved me out the door." The doctor shook his head in disbelief. "He wouldn't even let me take his pulse or check his temperature."

Witherspoon wasn't sure he understood. "Let me make sure I understand what it is you're telling us. Daggett's demeanor changed dramatically after you told him he wasn't going to die?"

"That's right." Wiltshire smiled faintly. "Believe me, I know it sounds ridiculous. Knowing the fellow as I do, I'd have predicted that upon learning he wasn't going to die, he'd have been dancing for joy. But honestly, Inspector, it was at that moment when the fellow looked the worst I've ever seen him."

Smythe knew that Betsy wasn't going to be pleased with the way he'd crept out of the house this evening, but he simply had to find out what was keeping Blimpey Groggins from his usual haunts. He pulled his coat tight against the chill night air and headed across the darkened communal gardens to the back gate. Smythe unlocked the gate, pulled it open and stepped out onto Edmonton Gardens. Within a few minutes, he was flagging down a hansom on Holland Park Road. "The West India Dock, please," he told the driver as he leapt into the seat. "And there's an extra shilling in it for ya if ya get me there quick."

They made it to the river in record time. "Where do you want to be let off?" the driver called over his shoulder.

"Anywhere along the waterfront will do." Smythe dug some coins out of his coat pocket. A few moments later, he swung out of the cab, paid the driver and headed across the road toward his destination.

Opening the door of the Artichoke Tavern, Smythe stepped inside and paused for a moment so his eyes could adjust to the smoky room. The scent of beer and gin mixed with tobacco smoke and unwashed bodies. Smythe spotted his quarry across the room.

She spotted him at the same time. Lila Clair met his gaze steadily as he made his way through the crowded room. She was a tall, black-haired woman in her fifties, her eyes were deep set, dark blue and had seen more than their fair share of misery. She was sitting at a table with three other girls. As the big man approached, she jerked her head sharply and the girls immediately got up.

"Hello, Smythe." She spoke first. "Funny seein' you here. This isn't your sort of place."

"May I 'ave a seat?" he asked. If he wanted her help, he knew he'd better treat her with respect.

She nodded. "You can buy me a drink if you've a mind to." Without waiting for his answer, she signaled the barmaid. "Bring us another," Lila called to the woman, "and a whiskey for the big fellah here."

Smythe didn't like whiskey, but he wanted her help, so he'd drink what she ordered. "I'm lookin' for Blimpey," he said.

Lila made a great show of gazing about the crowded room. "I don't see him 'ere," she finally said.

The drinks arrived. Smythe paid and picked up his glass. He downed the stuff in one big gulp.

Lila laughed. "You don't like it, do ya?"

"Not really," he admitted. "But as you'd taken the trouble to order it, I thought I'd better have a go. Look, I don't 'ave a lot of time . . ."

"Why'd you come 'ere?" she asked calmly. She took a sip of gin and stared at him steadily over the rim of her glass. "I'm not Blimpey's keeper."

"No, but you're the one that'd know if 'e was in trouble or something," he blurted. "You're about the only person on the face of the earth that Blimpey trusts, and I've got some work for 'im."

She studied him for a moment, then she grinned. "Is it important?"

"Very."

"Ya 'ave money?"

"I wouldn't come to see Blimpey without it."

She tossed back the last of her gin and rose to her feet. "Come on, then. I'll take ya to 'im." She laughed. "He'll not be pleased. He didn't want anyone to see him, but you're a good customer."

"Thanks, Lila." Smythe finished off the whiskey and got up. "I appreciate you takin' the trouble to 'elp me."

"You're a good man, Smythe." Lila smiled wearily. "Some say you and your friends 'ave kept the coppers from arrestin' the wrong people. That's good enough fer me. Besides, Blimpey's gettin' a bit restless. It'll do 'im good to get back to work."

Smythe gaped at her, but as she'd already started for the door, she didn't notice. He took off after her. He wondered what on earth they were going to do now. Blast a Spaniard, he thought, did everyone in bloomin' London know about their investigating?

Betsy was furious. She snatched up the bowl of mashed potatoes and whirled about toward the sink.

"Uh, Smythe's not 'ad supper yet," Wiggins reminded her, "and I know 'e's right fond of Mrs. Goodge's potatoes."

"Then he ought to have been here in time for supper," Betsy said tartly. She put the bowl on the counter and hurried back to the table.

Supper was over and done with. Mrs. Jeffries had already gone upstairs to meet the inspector at the front door and Mrs. Goodge had gone to her room, so it was just her and Wiggins left to clear up.

Wiggins sensed that perhaps he ought to tread lightly. Betsy didn't look very happy. She'd been all right when they first sat down to have their meal; but as it got later and later and the coachman hadn't come home, the maid had gotten quieter and quieter.

"I'm going to clear up," she said, "and if he comes home hungry, that's just too bad." She began snatching up the half-empty bowls and the dirty plates.

Wiggins opened his mouth to protest just as Mrs. Goodge came back into the kitchen. He looked at her for help, but she simply gave her head a barely imperceptible shake. He clamped his mouth shut. Maybe it would be best if he stayed out of this, Smythe wouldn't starve if he missed his supper.

Upstairs, they heard the front door open. Mrs. Goodge, who wanted to distract the maid out of her worry and temper, said, "I expect that's the inspector. You go up and see, then pop back down and I'll fix him a tray."

"But I wanted to finish clearing up," Betsy protested. "He usually has a sherry first."

In the old days, Mrs. Goodge would have flailed the girl with the back side of her tongue for daring to question an instruction, but not now. Betsy was too much like family to be treated like that. But nonetheless, she wanted the girl to have a moment to cool down just in case Smythe came home.

"I know," Mrs. Goodge said firmly. "But sometimes the inspector wants to eat right away, especially if he's planning on going back out."

Betsy put the dirty dishes down on the counter by the sink. "All right, I'll nip up and see what's what."

Wiggins waited till he heard her footsteps on the back stairs, then he said, "I think she's a bit annoyed with Smythe. He didn't tell 'er where 'e was goin' tonight."

"He's done that lots of times," Mrs. Goodge said as she stacked the dirty dishes in a neat pile. "I don't know why she's getting in such a state about it this evening."

"Since they got engaged, they've got an agreement," Wiggins told the cook. "I 'eard 'em talkin' about it. Neither of 'em is to go off without lettin' the other know where they're goin'."

"You heard them discussing this?" Mrs. Goodge fixed the footman with a hard stare. "In front of you?"

Wiggins had the good grace to blush. "Well, uh, they didn't really talk about it in front of me."

"You were eavesdropping?"

"It weren't my fault," he argued. "I was waitin' by the back door for Fred one night, and the two of 'em was in 'ere natterin' away. They didn't bother to keep their voices down. What could I do? I didn't want 'em to know I'd been there all along, so Fred and me waited till they went upstairs before we come in."

Mrs. Goodge sighed. "It's all right, Wiggins. Mind you, the next time you find yourself in that situation, you might call out so they'll know you're there."

He grinned. "But that'd spoil all the fun now, wouldn't it?"

Upstairs, Mrs. Jeffries met the inspector as he came in the front door. "Good evening, sir."

"Good evening." He handed her his bowler. "How is the household?"

"We're all well, Inspector. How was your day?" She helped him off with his coat.

"It was very difficult," he said with a sigh. "Very difficult indeed."

"Would you care to relax with a sherry, sir?"

"Actually"—he gave her a weary smile—"I believe I'll just have my dinner. I shall retire early tonight, Mrs. Jeffries. I'm very tired."

Mrs. Jeffries smiled serenely. "Of course, sir. I'll bring your tray to the dining room."

She met Betsy by the back stairs. "Can you bring up the inspector's tray, please?"

Betsy's eyes widened. "You mean he's not having a sherry?"

"Not tonight; he seems very tired," the housekeeper replied. "I doubt I shall get much out of him tonight."

Betsy turned on her heel. "I'll bring it right up."

Mrs. Jeffries went back to the dining room. If she was lucky, she might get a bit of information out of him before he ate.

The kitchen at Upper Edmonton Gardens was quiet as the grave when Smythe came in at half past ten. "Betsy," he whispered as he poked his head around the door, "did you wait up for me?"

But the room was empty as well as silent. "Blast," he muttered. "She's not 'ere."

"I expect she's a bit annoyed with you."

Smythe jumped and whirled about. "Cor blimey, Mrs. Jeffries, you did startle me some. Uh, you think Betsy's a bit put out?"

Mrs. Jeffries held a covered tray in her hand. "Oh, I think it's a bit more serious than being 'put out,' as you call it." She went toward the table. "But I expect you're hungry. I saved you a bite of supper."

"Thanks, Mrs. Jeffries, I'm right famished." He followed her to the table and slid into his seat.

"Smythe, I'm not one to interfere." She put a plate of cold roast beef, cheese, pickled onions and bread in front of him. "But I do believe your relationship with Betsy might be a bit smoother if you didn't disappear before meals."

He flipped his serviette onto his lap and picked up his fork. "I'm sorry, Mrs. Jeffries, I ought to 'ave told both you and Betsy where I was off to, but I honestly thought I'd be back before supper was over. I only meant to go across town and give someone a message. But things got complicated and instead of giving the message, I got drug off to see the person in the flesh . . . and it was one of them situations where you're not sure what you ought to do and you don't want to make trouble because you really need some 'elp." He paused for a breath. "Am I makin' any sense at all?"

"I think so." She smiled kindly. "I take it you were in a situation where you had no choice but to carry on once you'd arrived at your destination."

He nodded eagerly and stuffed a bite of cheese into his mouth. "That's right. One of my sources 'asn't been around lately, and I needed to get a message to 'im. Only instead of takin' my message, I got took to see 'im in the flesh."

Mrs. Jeffries sat down across from him. "Were you successful in your inquiries?"

"That I was, Mrs. Jeffries." He grinned, thinking of how annoyed Blimpey was when Lila escorted him into the small, rather nice cottage by the river where he was holed up. Blimpey hadn't been at his usual haunts for a very good reason. His gout had flared up badly. "I went to see a feller by the name of Blimpey Groggins."

"And was he able to help you?"

Smythe glanced up as footsteps pounded down the back stairs.

"I thought I 'eard you," Wiggins said cheerfully. He ambled toward the table and plopped down next to the coachman. "Where ya been? I think Betsy's a bit miffed at ya. She kept starin' at your empty place at supper."

Mrs. Jeffries turned her head slightly, as another, lighter pair of feet came down the back stairs. "Smythe was held up by something rather important," she said loudly.

Startled by the housekeeper's tone, Wiggins jerked in his chair. "Cor blimey, Mrs. Jeffries, you give me a fright there."

Betsy came into the kitchen. She'd taken off her apron and had a soft lavender wool shawl around her shoulders. "So you finally came home." She looked disapprovingly at Smythe. "It's about time. I was worried."

Smythe smiled in relief. She looked annoyed, but not angry enough to tear a strip off him. "I'm sorry, I should 'ave told ya where I was off to, but I thought I'd be 'ome in time for supper. Then, once I got there, things sort of got out of 'and."

"Got where?" Betsy crossed her arms over her chest.

"The Artichoke Tavern." He took another quick bite of food. "It's down by the docks. I wanted to get a message to one of my sources . . . but once I got there, I got drug off to see 'im and I didn't want to upset anyone as this source is bloomin' good, if you know what I mean and . . ."

"Did you find out anything?" Betsy interrupted. She slipped into the chair next to him.

Taken aback, he blinked. For a brief moment he was a bit put out that she wasn't more interested in where he'd been. Then he got a hold of himself and thanked his lucky stars that the lass trusted him. "I found out plenty. Now I know why Harrison Nye's name sounded so familiar to me; there was a lot of talk about the bloke when 'e first come to London."

"What kind of talk?" Wiggins asked.

"Let me tell it my own way, lad," Smythe said, "otherwise it'll not make much sense. "No one really knows much about Harrison Nye's background, but what they do know is that 'e showed up one day at the offices of Mayhew and Lundt, Stockbrokers, and bought a fistful of the best stock goin'."

"What's so odd about that?" Mrs. Jeffries asked curiously. "I believe huge numbers of shares change hands each day."

"True, but I'll lay you odds the people doin' the tradin' aren't handin' over gold to buy 'em with. That's what Nye did. He paid for his stock in gold. That's 'ow come I knew 'is name. It were the talk of London."

Mrs. Jeffries was fairly certain that the only people who had heard about Harrison Nye were those who had a genuine interest in the City's financial community. Smythe, even all those years ago, was such a person. Smythe was a rich man. He'd made a fortune in Australia and then come back to England and invested his money. He'd worked for the inspector's Aunt Euphemia. When she'd left this house and a sizable fortune to Gerald Witherspoon, Euphemia had made Smythe promise to 'hang about and keep an eye on the boy' for a few months. But once Betsy had arrived and they'd started their investigating, it had become impossible for him to leave. He enjoyed himself far too much to want to go anywhere else. However, as the coachman went to great pains to keep his true financial worth a secret from the rest of the household (except Betsy), she could hardly blurt this observation out for all and sundry to hear. "I'm sure it was."

Wiggins scratched his chin. "You mean this bloke just slapped a bunch of gold bars or nuggets down onto the counter to buy 'is shares?"

"Just about," Smythe replied. "Supposedly, he did 'is dealin' first, decidin' what 'e wanted to buy and such, then 'e walked over to the bank and exchanged his nuggets for cash. That set a few tongues waggin', I can tell ya."

"Where did he get the gold?" Betsy asked.

"My source wasn't rightly sure."

"Maybe 'e stole it?" Wiggins suggested eagerly.

"Not likely." Smythe shook his head. "My source would 'ave known if there'd been a theft of that much gold in the past twenty years. We're not talkin' about a few nuggets 'ere."

"Nye probably didn't get it in England," Mrs. Jeffries said thoughtfully. "It's hardly a common medium of exchange. So that means Nye probably procured the nuggets somewhere overseas."

"That's what my source thought," Smythe agreed. "I'm goin' to be seein' 'im again tomorrow, 'e ought to know more by then. 'E's workin' on it." He clamped his mouth shut as he realized what he'd just revealed. Blast a Spaniard, no one was supposed to know that his "sources" were anything but ordinary people who just happened to have information about the victim. He glanced quickly around the table and to his amazement, realized that none of them appeared to understand the implied logic behind his statement. Then again, it was late and they were tired. Tomorrow was another day, though, and they all had good memories.

"Uh, 'e's right curious about Nye 'imself," he sputtered quickly, "and when I started askin' questions, he said he knew someone who might know where Nye got the gold. I thought I'd drop around and see if 'e found anything useful out, but then again, I might not."

"I think you ought to find out as much as you can about the gold," Mrs. Jeffries said. "Old sins cast long shadows."

"What's that got to do with anythin'?" Wiggins asked.

"Nothing, probably." She shrugged. "But it popped into my head as Smythe was speaking and I've learned that sometimes it pays to take heed of what comes out of your mouth."

And sometimes it pays to keep your mouth shut, Smythe thought. He hoped the others believed his lame excuse about his source being "curious." It would be right embarrassin' to ever 'ave to admit that his source was a professional and that Smythe had been buying information about their cases for years.

Mrs. Jeffries was waiting in the dining room when the inspector came down for his breakfast. She was determined to find out everything he'd learned the day before, and she was also determined to pass what they'd found out to him. They really must get cracking on this case; otherwise, someone was going to get away with murder.

"Good morning, sir," she said cheerfully as Witherspoon came into the room. "I do hope you slept well. You looked dreadfully tired last night."

"I slept very well, thank you." He pulled out his chair, sat down and gazed happily at the food on the table. "This smells wonderful. I warn you, Mrs. Jeffries, you might have to dash down to the kitchen for seconds. I'm very hungry this morning."

"Eat hardy, sir. I expect you need to keep your strength up, what with this dreadful case." Mrs. Jeffries placed a cup of hot tea she'd just poured by his plate. "I honestly don't see how you do it."

He took a piece of toast from the rack. "Oh, it's not that difficult. Mind you, yesterday did seem a bit long, but then again, we were rather busy." He told her about his visit to Mrs. Nye. She listened carefully, taking in all the details and storing them carefully in her mind. She had dozens of questions she wanted to ask, but she had the feeling this wasn't the time.

"And then I had the most extraordinary interview with Oscar Daggett's physician." He took a quick sip from his cup and a bite of toast.

"His physician?" Mrs. Jeffries prompted. Sometimes the inspector could get a tad distracted by food. "I take it you learned something important."

Witherspoon scooped a forkful of scrambled egg off his plate. "I think so. But I'm not quite sure what to make of it." He popped the food into his mouth and chewed, his expression thoughtful.

Mrs. Jeffries hid her impatience behind a smile. "Really, sir?"

"Oh yes, it's all quite strange." He told her everything he'd learned from Dr. Wiltshire. "So you see, I don't really know if Daggett's thinking he was going to die had anything to do with his visit to Nye or not. It's a bit of a puzzle, but I do tend to think there must be a connection of some sort or another."

"Yes, sir, I think I understand what you mean." She sat down in her usual place. "After all, Dagget had been in his bed, ill and waiting to die until just after the doctor told him there was nothing wrong with him. Then he leaps up and tears out into the night. If the doctor's recollection of the timing of these events is correct, that's the only place Daggett could have gone . . ." She hoped he was getting the drift of her thinking.

"I most certainly do," he interrupted. "After all, Nelda Smith was sent out to post a letter."

Mrs. Jeffries stared at him. She didn't quite see what he was getting at, but she'd learned in the past that it was always important to listen. The inspector could make connections that she sometimes missed. "I don't quite see how . . ."

"I'm not sure myself," he agreed, "but it seems to me that perhaps there was some connection between that letter and the visit to Harrison Nye."

Betsy stuck her head in the dining room. "Excuse me, sir, but Constable Barnes is coming up the front stairs. Should I bring him in?"

"Of course," Witherspoon replied. "Mrs. Jeffries, do bring another cup. I'm sure the constable will want some tea."

A moment later, they heard the front door open and Betsy ushered Constable Barnes into the dining room.

"Good morning, sir, Mrs. Jeffries." Barnes smiled with genuine pleasure at the housekeeper. "Sorry to interrupt your breakfast, sir, but I've had some news, and I thought you'd like it as soon as possible."

"That's quite all right, Constable, do sit down and have a cup of tea." He gestured toward an empty chair. "Then you can give me a full report."

"Would you care for some breakfast, Constable?" Mrs. Jeffries asked as she poured another cup of Darjeeling.

"I've had breakfast, thank you." He nodded his thanks as he took the cup. "We've heard back from the Lancashire Constabulary, and I thought you'd want to know right away."

Now that the constable was here, Mrs. Jeffries could hardly continue questioning the inspector. Reluctantly, she got to her feet and busied herself brushing at the nonexistent crumbs on the tablecloth. She was hoping the constable would get on with it so she could hear what he had to say before good manners actually forced her from the room. Of course, she would nip back and eavesdrop, but it was so easy to miss something that way.

"Do sit down, Mrs. Jeffries," Witherspoon said absently. "You haven't finished your tea."

"Why thank you, sir if you're sure I'm not interrupting." But she quickly took her seat. "I am so very curious about your cases."

Barnes smiled at her over the rim of his cup. His eyes were twinkling, and she had the distinct impression he knew precisely what she was up to. But she put that thought aside; if he did, he would keep it to himself. She hoped.

"All right, Constable, what have we heard from Lancashire?" The inspector took a bite of bacon.

"The news isn't good, Inspector. Nelda Smith didn't run off home. Her family hasn't heard a word from her."

CHAPTER 8

"I thought you'd gone for good," the boy said cheerfully.

"When I turned around and saw you standin' on the corner, I was so surprised you coulda knocked me flat with mam's duster."

Smythe shifted his weight uneasily against the hard surface of the café chair. He felt guilty. He'd told this lad he'd buy him a bun and a cuppa, but that had been three days ago. Mind you, Harold was a nice lad, he hadn't held a grudge when Smythe had "accidentally" run into him again this morning. "I didn't mean to disappear. But somethin' important come up."

"Somethin' with the murder?" Harold asked eagerly.

Smythe winced inwardly, but managed to keep his expression straight. "Yeah. Like I told ya before, I work for a detective."

"I remember." Harold stuffed another bite of bun in his mouth.

"And I'd like to ask a question or two if you don't mind," Smythe finished.

"Go ahead," Harold replied. "Mam says we ought to keep ourselves to ourselves. But I think we ought to tell what we know."

"That's right good of you, lad." Smythe tried to think of what to say. All the questions he would have asked on the day of the murder had already been answered. "Uh, do you 'appen to remember if you saw anyone near Miss Geddy's house on the night of the murder?"

Harold looked down at the table. "Well, Mam says I should keep quiet about it, because it don't mean nuthin' and if I said anything, the police might think I 'ad something to do with the killin'. She's scared of the police, she is. But I don't think that's likely."

"Why would you 'ave 'ad a reason to murder anyone?" Smythe asked casually. He knew the next few seconds would determine whether or not he got anything out of the boy. Harold was a cheerful, eager lad, but Smythe knew he was more interested in the tea and the bun than in answering questions for a stranger. Working people were deeply mistrustful of the police, often for good reason. There were a lot of coppers about that wouldn't look farther than the tip of their noses when a crime was committed, and it was usually those at the bottom of the heap that was looked at first.

"That's what I told Mam," Harold said, "but she said that since the coppers never caught that Ripper feller, they'd grab anyone they could when there was a killin'. But I don't believe that. Besides, that man were murdered hours after I was asleep."

"So you'll tell me what ya saw?"

Harold grinned. "Course I will, not that I think it's got anything to do with the killin', I don't. It were a girl, you see. When I tried to tell Mam, she said it were probably some friend of Miss Geddy's, and I was to think no more about it, but Miss Geddy didn't have friends . . ."

"Slow down, lad." Smythe held up his hand. "You're goin' too fast for me to take it all in. What girl are you talkin' about?"

Harold took a deep breath. "The girl I saw on the night that bloke was killed. I saw her comin' down the street and then she turned into Miss Geddy's place and walked up the front door as big as you please."

"What did she do when she got to the door?"

"She pushed a letter through the mailbox on the front door, then she left. I saw her clear as day, you see. I almost spoke to her, but she seemed to be in a bit of a hurry."

"How could you tell that?" Smythe asked.

"The way she was walkin'," Harold said. "She were movin' really fast, you could tell by the way she watched all the house numbers as she walked past 'em. But that didn't seem to slow her down; once she spotted the one she wanted, she practically ran toward it."

Smythe wasn't sure what to make of this. "Did anyone else 'appen to see the woman?"

Harold's eyes narrowed suspiciously. "Don't ya believe me?"

"Course I do, boy, but it's awful easy to mistake one night for another. Are you sure it was the night of the murder that you saw this girl? You sure it wasn't the night before?"

"I'm sure," Harold said. "I know because it was that night that Mam sent me down to pub for a dram of whiskey for Da's cold. I was on my way back when I saw her. You can ask 'em down at pub, they'll tell ya I was in that night."

Smythe raised his hand. "I believe you, it's just I've got to make sure there wasn't a mix-up. What did this girl look like?"

"Well"—Harold hesitated a moment—"she was wearin' a hat and a dark coat. But she had dark hair, I could see that, she had it tucked up under a hat."

"How old do you think she might be?" Smythe was fairly sure the lad wouldn't have a clue about a woman's age, but he had to ask.

"She looked to be about sixteen or seventeen," Harold said firmly. "About the same age as my cousin Agnes. She didn't have any wrinkles or spots, and I noticed something else, too. She had on a maid's dress. Her coat came open when she started running up the street to her fellow."

"Fellow?" Smythe leaned forward, trying to curb his excitement. "Someone was waitin' for her? Are you sure about that?"

"Sure as I'm sittin' here talkin' to you." Harold gave him a cocky grin. "He was standing on the corner. They went off together. He took her arm and everythin'." He popped the last bite of food into his mouth. "Do you think I ought to tell the police?"

Smythe wasn't sure how to answer that question. It was probably information the police ought to know, but he had to be careful. If he sent Harold along to have a chat with the police, the lad might accidentally mention that someone named Smythe had been along asking questions about the murder. "I'm not sure. That letter or whatever the girl shoved in Miss Geddy's letterbox might be important. It might 'ave somethin' to do with the murder. But then again, it might not."

Harold shrugged. "I'll keep my mouth shut, then. If it's got something to do with the murder, Miss Geddy can take it along to the police herself. She's comin' back in few days."

Inspector Witherspoon stepped down from the hansom and onto the cobblestone road. The neighborhood where the Windemere brothers now lived was grim. On one side of the street was a factory belching soot into the sky, giving the air a faintly copper smell. In the courtyard of the factory, workers loaded barrels onto a rickety-looking wagon.

"Not the nicest area, is it, sir?" Constable Barnes said. He was staring at the row of tiny houses opposite the factory. They were all a dull, uniform gray, had no front gardens and were in various stages of disrepair. The men they wanted to interview lived in one of them. "But then people can't help being poor, can they?"

"No, it's sad that anyone has to live in such places," Witherspoon replied. He sighed inwardly. He'd grown up in a neighborhood not much better than this one, but his home had been well tended and clean. There hadn't been trash in the streets, gutters stuffed with leaves and a noisy factory fouling the air with grime. He reminded himself to count his blessings. He'd also inherited a fortune. Most people weren't so lucky. "But then again, who are we to judge? Home is home." He started off down the street. "Let's hope we can learn something from these gentlemen. I don't mind admitting it, Constable, this case isn't going very well."

"You'll sort it out, sir," Barnes said easily. "You always do."

"Gracious, I do hope so. But it doesn't look good. We've searched the whole area and we still haven't found the murder weapon . . ."

"We probably won't, sir," Barnes interrupted gently. "Dr. Bosworth agrees with Dr. Boyer's opinion. He also thinks that from the size and shape of the entry wound, the killer probably used a common old butcher knife." Barnes had "unofficially" asked their good friend, Dr. Bosworth, to have a look at the body after the police surgeon had finished the postmortem. It wasn't that he didn't think Dr. Boyer was competent; he was. But Bosworth had spent a year practicing medicine in San Francisco. Apparently they had quite a lot of murder there and, consequently, he'd become somewhat of an expert on determining what kind of wound was made with a particular kind of weapon. He'd helped them on a number of their cases, and the doctor had invariably been right in his assessments.

"I know." The inspector sighed. "Which means it's probably sitting in someone's kitchen drawer, and we'll never find it."

"You've solved lots of cases without a murder weapon," Barnes pointed out.

"*We've* solved lots of cases," Witherspoon corrected. "I certainly didn't do it alone. You and everyone else on the force did as much as I did." He held up his hand as Barnes started to protest. "Everyone does their fair share, Constable. I couldn't solve anything without the information you and the other constables come up with. Mind you, this time, we haven't had much useful information at all. Even the house-to-house interviews haven't yielded much. No one saw or heard anything except for a few mysterious footsteps."

"It doesn't seem to make much sense, does it, sir?" Barnes commented. "But we've not spoken to everyone as yet. Something will turn up. It always does." He pointed to the house at the end of the row. "There's the house, sir. Let's hope they're home and that this isn't a wasted trip."

Barnes raised his fist to knock. But before he could strike the blow, the door flew open and a tall, thin-faced man stared out at them. "I've been expecting you," he said. "I'm John Windemere." He pulled the door open and stepped backward. "Come inside, please."

They went into a cramped hallway. A coat rack loaded with jackets, caps, coats and scarves was just inside the door. Next to it stood a tall mottled brass vase with umbrellas sticking out the top. The walls were papered in faded yellow-and-gold stripes, and there was a threadbare brown carpet runner on the floor.

John Windemere closed the door and pushed past the two policemen. "Let's go into the parlor," he said gruffly.

They followed him into a room as dismal as the hall. The furniture was as old and threadbare as the carpet. Limp white-lace curtains, now turned gray, covered two dirty windows and fine layer of dust covered the wood surfaces of the end tables and the one lone bookcase on the far wall.

Windemere flopped down on the settee. "I suppose you want to know where my brother and I were on the night that Harrison Nye was murdered," he said.

Witherspoon and Barnes exchanged looks. It was rare to find someone who got right to the point, so to speak. Then the inspector said, "That would be very helpful information, sir."

"You can't pin this on either of us. We've the best alibi one can have." Windemere smiled thinly. "We were at the Marylebone Police Station."

Barnes whipped out his notebook. "Were you under arrest?"

Windemere gave a short, harsh bark of a laugh. "Why else would one spend the night in such a place. Of course we were under arrest. But it wasn't our fault. We were attacked. Then the police had the sheer, unmitigated gall to arrest my brother and I instead of the real culprits."

Witherspoon frowned. "Could you give us a few more details, sir? Were you attacked by ruffians?" He didn't think that was the case; if it had been, it would have been the ruffians who'd been arrested, not the Windemere brothers.

"Ruffians. I should say so, but because they were dressed nicely and spoke with the proper accent, the police took their version of what happened as the truth."

"Why don't you tell us your version, sir?" Barnes suggested calmly. "And where is your brother, sir? Is he about?"

"My brother is at work, Constable," Windemere replied. "He clerks for a legal firm in Earls Court. He'll not be home till six."

Witherspoon's lower back began to throb. "May we sit down, Mr. Windemere? It appears as if you've quite a bit to tell us."

Wiggins smiled at the housemaid carrying the wicker basket and knew he'd struck gold. "Hortense is a nice name," he said. "It fits you very nicely. Would you like me to carry your basket?"

Hortense, who'd been walking a mile a minute since Wiggins had "accidentally" run into her coming out of the Daggett house, considered his offer. "Well, it is getting heavy, and it's quite a long ways to go yet. Here." She thrust the basket into his waiting hands. "Thanks ever so much."

He was surprised by how heavy it was. The top was covered with a white tea towel. "What's in 'ere?"

She made a face, reached over and flipped the tea towel back. A large, brown bottle was nestled snugly in a cradle of packed towels.

"What's that?" Wiggins asked in surprise. "An empty bottle?"

"That's right," Hortense replied, "I've got to drag this great, heavy thing all the way to Cromwell Road. Can you believe the foolishness of some people? Mr. Daggett, that's who I work for, he's one of those people who think they're on death's door all the time. He thinks this tonic keeps him healthy. It's nothing more than whiskey mixed with a few herbs, but he swears by the stuff. Some old woman makes it up for him, and, wouldn't you know, he ran out of it this morning. I don't usually have to go get it, but what with Nelda and her new husband showing up and havin' words with Mrs. Benchley, things got all mixed up. Instead of the footman goin' to get His Lordship's ruddy potion, I got stuck doin' it. It's not fair. That old woman lives a good mile away, and once this stupid bottle is full, it'll be even heavier comin' back. If I didn't need this position so badly, I'd do just what Nelda did and run off without a word to anyone. Mind you, I don't have a young man to marry now, do I?"

Wiggins wasn't sure how to proceed. On the one hand, he knew this girl was a mine of information, on the other hand, she looked to be a bit annoyed. Females, he'd observed, could be unpredictable when they were angry. He wanted her to talk to him, not box his ears. But there was too much at stake to back off. He had to know what had happened. He decided to proceed with caution.

"I bet you could have someone if you wanted," he said softly. He hoped he was saying the right thing. "I'm not tryin' to be forward, miss, but you're awfully pretty." It isn't exactly a lie, he thought. She's not really ugly. If she smiled a bit and put on some weight, she'd be quite nice-looking.

She stopped dead in her tracks and stared at him. Wiggins's heart sank. This girl had looked in a mirror recently.

"Do you mean that?" she asked.

Wiggins nodded. "Course I do."

A slow smile crept over her face, and she did, indeed, become prettier. "That's awfully kind of you. Where did you say you worked?" She took his arm and they started walking.

"Uh, I didn't. But I work near Holland Park, I'm a footman of sorts."

"That's nice. Is today your day out?" She smiled coyly and batted her eyelashes.

Wiggins had the feeling he might end up regretting this morning's snooping. Hortense might be a very nice girl, but he wasn't really interested in her, only in what she had to tell him about the Daggett household. "Uh, yeah. Actually, I don't get much time away from my work. But sometimes I go out on Saturdays . . ." It was a safe bet that a housemaid wouldn't get a Saturday afternoon off from her duties. They almost always got a day off in the middle of the week and Sunday mornings for church.

"That's too bad," she continued. "My afternoon out is Wednesday. Mind you, now that Nelda's gone for sure, I might be able to get Saturday afternoon off as well. That would be nice, wouldn't it?"

"Uh, yeah, it sure would. Who's Nelda?"

Betsy smiled at the girl sitting next to her on the park bench. "Now don't worry, I'm sure that you'll still have your position. Mrs. Nye isn't going to sell the house right away, is she?"

Arlene Hill, a tiny woman with a narrow face, dark brown eyes and olive complexion, shrugged her thin shoulders. "Who knows what she'll do? Now that he's gone, she's her own mistress, isn't she?"

Betsy, who hadn't had much luck at all on this case, had finally done something right. She'd gone to the Nye house just to have a look at it, get the lay of the land, so to speak, and she'd seen this girl coming out of the side servants' entrance. She'd followed her, of course, and then struck up a conversation with her when she'd been gazing in a shop window. As it turned out this was Arlene Hill's afternoon out and she had no one to spend her few free hours with. Betsy had told her it was her day out as well and suggested they take a walk around Hyde Park. It hadn't taken Betsy long to get the conversation around to the recent murder of Arlene's late master. Arlene was a bit shy at first, but under Betsy's easy approach, she soon had the girl talking freely. As a matter of fact, by the time they had reached the park bench, the girl was talking a blue streak. Arlene was lonely. She didn't have a lot of close friends in the household. Nye's rule about the servants gossiping about the master and mistress apparently had the effect of virtually shutting people up altogether.

"Most women don't like to leave their homes," Betsy said conversationally. "But mind you, you never know what people will do when they're grief-stricken."

Arlene laughed. "Grief-stricken? Her? Not bloomin' likely."

Betsy pretended to be shocked. "Oh dear, the master and mistress didn't get along? That does make it hard sometimes. Especially for those of us who have to work for them."

"They got on all right," she replied, "but now that he's dead, she can do what she likes. She couldn't when she was married to him, could she?"

"Why not? I thought you said the family was rich."

"He had plenty," Arlene replied. "But she hadn't a farthing. Oh, she's from a toff-nosed family, that's for sure, just like her cousin. But they're both poor as church mice. Mr. Nye was the one with the money, wasn't he? Now it's all hers. I know that for a fact because I overheard her tellin' Mr. Bancroft how they'd never have to worry again, how he'd left it all to her."

"Was Mr. Nye a mean husband, then?" Betsy asked.

Arlene looked thoughtful. "He wasn't mean, but you could tell he kept a tight fist on the purse."

Betsy snorted. "That sounds like most men."

"But not all of 'em are like that." Arlene laughed. "The last family I worked for, the missus spent like a drunken sailor and her husband never said a word about it. Mr. Nye would pay the bills, but he always made her squirm a bit, asked her questions about each and every thing she'd bought. You could tell she didn't like it. She was always in a bad mood after she'd been into his study at the end of the month." Arlene laughed again. "But I've got no reason to complain. Come the end of this month, she'll not be answerin' to him anymore, at least that's what I heard her tellin' Mr. Bancroft."

Betsy wanted to steer the conversation along to the night of the murder. "It must be frightening, living in a house where the master's been stabbed to death."

"Oh no, it's exciting. Now that he's dead, we can talk about him all we like," Arlene said. "It's not like before. Like I told you when we were walking over here, we had to be real careful what we said around that house, even to each other. He was a bit of an old preacher about us gossipin'. Mind you, we do have to be careful. It wasn't just Mr. Nye that didn't want us talkin'; she's almost as bad as he was."

Betsy tried to think of what else to ask. She wasn't surprised by the Nyes' rule of silence. It was probably the sort of silly rule most rich houses would have if they thought they had a chance of making it work properly. She was rather amazed at how well it had apparently worked at the Nye house. But now wasn't the time to discuss that. "I guess you're right. As long as you knew the killer isn't in the house with you, it would be exciting."

"I was a bit disappointed that that nice-looking Constable Griffiths didn't want to ask me a few questions." Arlene sighed. "He's got ever such nice ginger-colored hair."

"He didn't speak to you?"

"No."

"So you didn't talk to a policeman at all?" Betsy pressed. She was sure that couldn't be right. Inspector Witherspoon was very conscientious. He would expect everyone in the victim's household to be interviewed, especially the servants.

"Oh I spoke to Constable Griffiths, but only for half a second. He got called away to take care of something, then Mr. Duffy sent me upstairs to air out the top bedrooms. By the time I got back downstairs, the police had gone." Arlene smiled slyly. "Too bad for him, that's what I say. There's plenty I could have told the police about that night."

The afternoon was getting old by the time Witherspoon and Barnes were finished verifying the Windemere brothers' alibi at the Marylebone Police Station. They came out into the busy high street. A cold breeze had swept in from the north and the air was heavy with the feel of rain. The inspector looked up at the gathering clouds. "It's almost teatime, Constable. Let's go back to Upper Edmonton Gardens and have a cuppa. What do you say? It'll be better than anything we can get in a tea shop or a café. We can pick up some umbrellas as well. I think we're going to need them before the day is out."

Barnes's craggy face split into a grin. "You'll not have to ask me twice, sir. Do you think Mrs. Goodge has made scones?"

"I do hope so." Witherspoon waved at a passing hansom. "There's quite a good chance of it, you know. She always seems to bake a lot when I'm on a murder case."

The cab pulled up to the curb and they climbed inside. "Number twenty-two Upper Edmonton Gardens," Witherspoon called to the driver. "It's going to be a very long day for us," he said as he leaned back against the seat. "We've got to review the rest of those house-to-house reports, and I think it might be a good idea to have another interview with Oscar Daggett."

"Yes, sir, I agree. So far, he's about the only suspect we've got. It's too bad both the Windemere brothers were in custody. They'd have made good suspects. They certainly had reason to hate Nye."

By the time the hansom reached Upper Edmonton Gardens, it had started to sprinkle. They paid off the cab and hurried inside. "Hello," the inspector called as he took off his hat and coat.

"Good afternoon, sir," Mrs. Jeffries said from the top of the back stairs. She sounded out of breath. "How lovely to have you home. Constable Barnes, how nice to see you again."

Witherspoon beamed at his housekeeper. "We weren't far away, and I was hoping we might be in time for tea." He sniffed the air. "I say, is that scones I smell?"

Mrs. Jeffries kept her expression calm and mentally crossed her fingers, hoping the inspector wouldn't ask where everyone was this afternoon. She could hardly admit they were all out snooping. As the household was going to have a meeting this afternoon, they were all due back shortly, but they certainly weren't here now. Furthermore, Mrs. Goodge had had her sources coming through her kitchen all day, and the supply of scones was dwindling fast. She had someone in the kitchen right at this very moment. "I believe it is, sir. If you and the constable will have a seat in the drawing room, I'll bring up a tray."

"Oh, that won't be necessary, you mustn't go to any trouble." He started for the back stairs. "We'll have our tea in the kitchen. Much cheerier there than up here. Come along, Constable, let's get some of Mrs. Goodge's delicious scones."

"It's no trouble, sir." Mrs. Jeffries trailed behind the two men.

"No, no, I quite like the kitchen," Witherspoon called over his shoulder. "Is Fred about?"

"He's in the back garden," Mrs. Jeffries replied as she clambered down the stairs behind the men.

But the cook had matters well in hand. In the few minutes between their realization that the inspector had come home and his actual arrival in the kitchen, Mrs. Goodge had managed everything. She'd gotten rid of her source, dumped the dirty dishes in the sink, thrown a clean tea towel over the plate of scones and put the jam and butter back into the larder. "Good afternoon, sir. Constable Barnes." Mrs. Goodge gave them her best smile and brushed her hands off on her apron. "Have you come home for tea, then?"

"Indeed we have." Witherspoon took his place at the head of the table and waved Constable Barnes into the chair next to him. "Your scones are simply too irresistible."

"I'll make the tea," Mrs. Jeffries murmured.

"Not to worry, I've put the kettle on," the cook called cheerfully. She started for the dry larder in the hall. "It should only take a moment."

"Where is everyone?" Witherspoon asked.

Mrs. Jeffries grabbed the teapot off the shelf. "I sent Betsy to the greengrocer's up on Holland Park Road, and Smythe's at Howard's—" She broke off, not wanting to say too much in case someone showed up while the inspector was still here.

"And I sent Wiggins off to get me my rheumatism medicine," Mrs. Goodge said as she came back into the room. She was carrying the jam jar and the butter dish. She put them down on the table and whipped the tea towel off the top of the scones. "Do help yourselves," she offered. "Now, how is your case going, sir?"

Within a few minutes, they were having tea and talking about the murder of Harrison Nye as though they did it every afternoon. By the time the inspector and Barnes were leaving, they'd gotten every detail of the day's activities out of the two men.

Mrs. Jeffries breathed a sigh of relief as she closed the door behind them. She dashed back to the kitchen. "That was a close one," she said to the cook.

Mrs. Goodge nodded. "It certainly was, but it was worth it. We found out an awful lot of information. When the others get here, let's not let them muck about. We've a lot to get through today."

She was true to her word as well. When the others arrived she hustled them to the table, got the tea poured and the buns distributed in mere seconds. "Now," she said, "if no one objects, I'd like to go first."

No one had the nerve to say a word. Sometimes, it was best to let the cook have her way.

"Good, first of all, I found out that my old friend Jane was wrong, someone was dismissed from the Nye house."

"What'd they done?" Luty asked. "Opened their mouth when the boss was in the kitchen? Silliest thing I ever heard of, tellin' your servants they can't gossip."

"It is silly," Mrs. Goodge agreed. To her mind, gossip was one of the things that made life worth living. "But that's not why the girl was sacked and oddly enough it wasn't Harrison Nye that got rid of her, it was Mrs. Nye. The girl was accused of stealing one of Mrs. Nye's nightdresses."

"She pinched a nightgown?" Smythe asked incredulously.

"That's what she was accused of doing," Mrs. Goodge replied. "As to whether or not the girl was a thief, that's open to how you see things. The girl claims she found the nightdress under a cupboard by the back door, tucked up in the corner like. What's odd is that she wasn't sacked because they found the nightdress amongst her things, she was sacked when she took it to the butler and told him what she'd found."

Hatchet's face creased in confusion. "I'm afraid I don't quite understand."

"What I'm sayin' is that my source said the girl wouldn't have been sacked at all if she hadn't tried to do what's right. If she'd just put the nightdress back where she'd found it, she'd still have a position."

"Are you suggesting she might be the killer?" Hatchet asked cautiously. He didn't wish to offend the cook. He had a great respect for her abilities to ferret out information. But stabbing one's employer because one had been sacked seemed a bit extreme.

"I don't think so, this happened over a year ago, but I did think it was worth mentioning." It probably meant nothing, but one never knew what was important and what wasn't until the very end.

"Anything else, Mrs. Goodge?" Mrs. Jeffries asked.

"That's it for me," the cook replied. "I'll let you tell 'em what we heard from the inspector."

"The inspector was 'ere?" Smythe picked up his tea and took a sip.

"He and Constable Barnes stopped in late this afternoon to have tea. We found out a few interesting tidbits," she said. "We can eliminate the Windemere brothers as suspects. I know they were both at the Nye house that night, and they certainly had reason to want Nye dead, but they couldn't have done it. They were locked up in the Marylebone Police Station when Harrison Nye was stabbed."

"They were under arrest? What for?" Betsy exclaimed. She did want to hurry things on a bit, she was eager to tell everyone what she'd learned today from Arlene Hill.

"Fighting," Mrs. Jeffries replied. "Apparently when they were on their way home from the Nye house, they happened upon one of their former clients coming out of a pub. The client, who apparently was most unhappy with the kind of representation he'd once received from John Windemere, started insulting them. Both of the brothers replied in kind. Several of the client's friends then came out of the pub and joined in the shouting. That led to some shoving, which in turn led to fisticuffs. By the time the constable arrived to break it up, half the pub was involved. But it was the Windemere brothers who were carted off to jail. So I'm afraid we'll have to look elsewhere for our murderer."

"Didn't they lose their solicitin' business eleven years ago?" Wiggins asked.

"That's correct." Mrs. Jeffries took a sip from her cup.

Luty looked incredulous. "You mean someone waited eleven years to punch 'em in the nose? Nell's bells, they musta been really bad lawyers."

"Apparently so. Unfortunately, for us it means we must still keep digging on this case." Mrs. Jeffries looked around the table. "Smythe, why don't you go next."

He shot a quick glance at Betsy. He could tell by the expression on her face that she had a lot to report, and he didn't want to steal her thunder. But she gave him a smile so he knew she didn't mind. "All right, then. I went back and finally 'ad that chat with the lad that lives across the way from Frieda Geddy's house." He gave them a quick report on his meeting with Harold.

"So Nelda Smith did run off," Luty said eagerly. "Good fer her."

"But not before she shoved something through Frieda Geddy's post-box," Smythe pointed out.

"It was a letter," Wiggins said quickly. "I know because I had a talk with Hortense today. You know, the maid who works for Daggett, the one who was so worried something 'ad 'appencd to her friend. Well, seems Nelda and her new husband showed up at the Daggett 'ouse today to get Nelda's trunk. Accordin' to Hortense, there was a right old dustup, and words were exchanged. Daggett was screamin' at Nelda that he wanted 'is letter back and she was shoutin' back that if 'e wanted it, 'e could 'auls 'is buns to Fulham and get it 'imself."

Luty cackled. "Did she actually say that?"

"And a bit more." Wiggins grinned. "Hortense said Daggett was so furious 'e looked like 'e was goin' to 'ave an attack of some sort. But there weren't much Daggett could do to the girl. She had her husband with 'er and 'e's a decent-sized bloke who didn't take kindly to the way Daggett talked to his new missus. The 'ousekeeper sent the footman up to get the girl's trunk, and they left, but not before the whole 'ousehold knew that on the day of the murder, Oscar Daggett sent Nelda to Fulham with a letter addressed to Frieda Geddy."

Betsy sank back in her chair. Compared to all this, what she'd learned from Arlene didn't seem to amount to much. But she would tell the others what little she knew, if this lot shut up long enough to give her a chance.

"That means there's a definite connection between Geddy and Daggett," Mrs. Jeffries said, "and it means he lied about it to the police as well. He certainly didn't tell the inspector he'd sent his maid to Dunbarton Street with a letter." Her mind was working furiously trying to sort out all the information into some kind of meaningful pattern.

"Cor blimey, this is startin' to give me a 'eadache." Wiggins laughed. "But it's a good ache, like me 'ead's so full of facts it's goin' to explode."

Smythe leaned forward eagerly. "There's somethin' else I 'aven't told you. Frieda Geddy is comin' home. She sent Mrs. Moff a telegram askin' her to accept delivery of a trunk that'll be arriving tomorrow."

Except for Mrs. Jeffries, everyone at the table started talking at once, trying to figure out just what was going on with this case.

"I know what we've got to do," the housekeeper suddenly announced.

The group fell silent, and everyone looked at her.

"We've got to get that letter. It's the key to everything."

"But it's in Miss Geddy's front hall," Mrs. Goodge pointed out. "I don't see how we can get our hands on it, short of breaking into the house."

Mrs. Jeffries smiled. "I know. But that's precisely what we'll have to do."

CHAPTER 9

"What I'm asking you to do might be difficult," Mrs. Jeffries began, "and I'll understand if you're not willing to put yourself in that kind of jeopardy."

"Don't fret, Mrs. Jeffries," Smythe said cheerfully, "it'll be fine. We can nip in and out in two shakes of a lamb's tail."

"I shall be happy to lend my assistance to the endeavor," Hatchet said as he rubbed his hands together with relish.

"You always get the fun jobs." Luty glared at her butler. She knew that no matter how much she wanted to, no one at the table would hear of her going along on this adventure. Even if she took her gun with her.

"Now, madam," Hatchet said calmly, "This is a job for the men. You know it would be far more efficient if Smythe and I—"

"And me," Wiggins protested. "I'm one of the men 'round 'ere, you know."

"Of course you are," Mrs. Jeffries assured the lad. "But before we do anything, we really must decide if it's possible to even get into the house."

"We'll get in." Smythe smiled confidently. "But I think we ought to wait until later tonight. There's workin' people in that neighborhood, so they'll be to bed early. We ought to plan on bein' at the 'ouse around eleven o'clock."

"That's a good idea," Mrs. Jeffries agreed as she rose to her feet.

"Now hold on a minute." Luty slapped her hand against the table. "Just because you all are chompin' at the bit to bust into Frieda Geddy's house—"

"I would hardly put it like that, madam," Hatchet interrupted huffily.

"We're on a mission of justice to retrieve a piece of evidence that may have a direct bearing on catching a killer."

"Oh, put a sock in it, Hatchet," Luty snapped. "No matter how you try to dress it up, it's still a case of bustin' into someone's house without so much as a by-your-leave. I ain't got no quarrel with that. Hepzibah's right, we do need that letter. But you could at least see if me and Betsy has anything to add to this here meeting."

"I'm dreadfully sorry, Luty. You're absolutely right." Mrs. Jeffries sank back into her chair. "I should have made sure that everyone had their chance to speak. . . ."

Luty waved off the apology. "Not to worry, Hepzibah, I know you're all excited like and we've got a lot to do to get everything ready for tonight, but I've got somethin' to report. I found out where Harrison Nye got that gold."

For once, even Hatchet had the good grace to look embarrassed. "Very good, madam. You're right, of course. We should have waited until everyone had said their piece before we began making plans."

Luty eyed him sternly for a moment and then she grinned. "No harm done. Now, as I was sayin', I found out all about that gold and you're not goin' to believe where it came from. The Transvaal."

"Where's that?" Wiggins asked.

"South Africa," Luty continued excitedly. "But that ain't the good part. I guess what I should have said is you'll never guess *who* it came from."

"But you're going to tell us, aren't you, madam?" Hatchet said patiently. He was quite prepared to let her have her moment in the sun.

"It came from a gold mine that was orginally owned by Oscar Daggett, Harrison Nye and Viktor Geddy, Frieda Geddy's father," Luty announced. "I found the connection. Frieda Geddy's father was in business with the other two. Fifteen years ago, Daggett and Nye bought into Geddy's claim. Geddy was a Dutchman from Holland and the original owner of the claim. But it was a bust. They'd worked it for over six months and hadn't found as much as a nugget. Then Viktor Geddy was killed in a wagon accident. Daggett and Nye, both of whom were English, bought Geddy's share from Frieda Geddy for the price of her ticket back to England. Two weeks later, they hit pay dirt."

"Cor blimey, poor Frieda Geddy," Wiggins said sympathetically. "If her father had just hung on for another fortnight, she'd been rich."

"I'm sure that's precisely what she thought as well," Mrs. Jeffries murmured. To her mind, it had become even more imperative that they get their hands on that letter.

"Anyways, I think findin' all this out is pretty important," Luty said bluntly. "Nye and Daggett worked the mine until it went dry. Nye, probably because he didn't trust banks, kept a good portion of his share of the loot in gold nuggets. Rumor has it that he brought a couple of trunk loads of 'em to England when he came back."

"I wonder if Nye and Daggett knew about the gold before they offered Frieda her passage back to England for her share?" Mrs. Jeffries muttered.

Luty shrugged. "Frieda Geddy accused them of doing just that. Nye threatened to sue her for defamation of character if she pursued the matter. Remember, the next time she saw either of them, they was rich, and she was livin' in that little house in Fulham."

"I'll bet that's how Harrison Nye's fortune started," Wiggins added eagerly. "I'll bet he used the money from the gold to do all his buyin' and sellin' . . ."

"Accordin' to my source, that's exactly how it all started. That's how come he ended up richer than Daggett. Nye put his money to work for him, Daggett just made a few business investments and then spent the rest of his time worryin' about his health." Luty pursed her lips in disgust. "Anyway, that's all I've got."

Mrs. Jeffries turned to Betsy. "Do you have anything you'd like to report?"

Betsy tried not to be depressed, but it was difficult. Everyone but her had found out something really important, something that would help solve the case. She decided to keep her little bit to herself until their next meeting. Maybe it wouldn't sound so pathetic tomorrow. "Not really. Oh, I did learn that it was Mrs. Nye who put the Windemere brothers on the guest list that night, not her husband. I spoke to one of the Nye housemaids. She saw Mrs. Nye add them to the top of the guest list after her husband had given it back to her. That's all."

Smythe gave her a quick, puzzled glance. He was sure she had something more to tell them. But from the look she shot him, he decided to keep his opinion to himself. The lass would say her piece in her own good time.

"That's odd, isn't it. I wonder why she wanted them present that night." Mrs. Jeffries tried to keep her mind on Betsy's information, but frankly, she was too excited to concentrate on anything but getting their hands on that letter. "Oh well, I'm sure we'll sort it out eventually. Now, perhaps we ought to make plans. Luty, can you and Hatchet come back tonight?"

"The madam has a previous engagement," Hatchet said quickly.

"Hogwash," Luty shot back. "I'm not goin' to waste my time at some silly dinner party . . ."

"It'll take us a good two hours to get there and get back here," Smythe pointed out. "If we leave 'ere at ten o'clock, that'd put us back at midnight. You go along in your carriage and I'll pop along to Howard's and get the inspector's for us to use tonight. Will that do ya?" Smythe didn't want an all-out war on his hands. Luty could be very stubborn. For that matter, so could Hatchet.

"I think that's a wonderful idea," Mrs. Jeffries interjected. "The inspector won't need his carriage, not in the middle of a case, and that way, you can have your driver bring you back here after your dinner party."

"Which will give me a ride home," Hatchet added.

"Well, all right," Luty muttered. "But I'll be here before eleven, you can count on that. I only accepted the invitation so I could pump a few of the other guests about our murder."

They broke up a few minutes later. Mrs. Jeffries went upstairs to do some thinking, Wiggins took Fred out for a walk, Mrs. Goodge went to the dry larder to make her grocery list and Betsy hurried up the back stairs. But she wasn't quite fast enough and Smythe caught her on the landing. He grabbed her elbow, swung her around and gave her a fast kiss.

She kissed him back and then pushed him away, but he kept a firm grip on her arms. "Someone will see us," she whispered.

"I don't care," he replied. He searched her face carefully. "Is something botherin' you?"

She wanted to stay irritated, but she couldn't. It was nice to know that he cared so much about her. "Well, not really. Oh, it's just that today everyone else had something interesting to report and all I found out from that silly Arlene was that on the night of the murder she heard footsteps on the back stairs and saw Mrs. Nye change the guest list."

"Why didn't you tell everyone about the footsteps? That could be an important clue."

"You know as well as I do that in a household that size a few footsteps aren't going to mean anything except that someone got hungry and snuck down to the kitchen for a bite of bread."

That was probably precisely what had happened, but Smythe didn't want Betsy to think her contribution wasn't important. "But you don't know that for certain . . ."

"Oh please," she interrupted, "that's exactly what it was. Eliza Nye is stingy with the servants' rations. According to Arlene, that wasn't the first time she'd heard footsteps, and the cook's always complaining that food's been pilfered. Now I know what you're trying to do, but it won't work. I wasted a whole afternoon today listening to that silly girl complain, and what's worse, I've got to waste part of my morning tomorrow taking the goose a pair of my old gloves."

"Why are you givin' 'er your gloves?" Smythe asked curiously.

"Because she doesn't have any and winter's coming." Betsy stepped away from him. "And you've bought me half a dozen pairs, so I thought I'd give the poor girl a pair of my old ones." She gave him a smile. "Now get off with you. I know you've got to go do some mysterious errand and then go to Howard's for the carriage. Don't worry about me, I'm not going to spend the day fretting."

"You promise?" He was dead serious. He hated it when Betsy was upset.

She gave him a dazzling smile. "I promise."

The night was cold and quiet. Smythe pulled the carriage up in a quiet, deserted spot near the railroad tracks just beyond Dunbarton Street. He tied the reins to a post and patted Bow's nose. "Be quiet now, fella. We'll be back soon. You keep Arrow from frettin' if a train goes rattlin' past."

"You talk to them 'orses like they was people," Wiggins said.

"And they understand every word I say," Smythe retorted. "Come on, it's this way. I found a shortcut over the tracks." He led the way past a set of abandoned buildings and over the railway toward Fulham. A few moments later, they emerged at the bottom end of Dunbarton Street.

"How'd you know about this . . ." Wiggins asked excitedly.

"Shh . . . we've got to be quiet." Smythe hissed.

Hatchet pointed to the end of the row of houses. "I'll go along and check the back windows."

"We'll do the front." Smythe and Wiggins hurried along the street to the Geddy house. Wiggins, keeping a sharp lookout over his shoulder, tried the two front windows. He gave his head a negative shake.

Smythe was fairly sure the back ones would be locked tight as well. "Keep a sharp eye out, lad." He dropped to his knees and pulled a flat leather case out of his coat pocket.

Hatchet, his feet making hardly a sound, joined them in the front garden. "No luck at the back," he whispered.

"Any lights come on?" Smythe directed his question to Wiggins, who was acting as the lookout.

"Windows still as black as coal."

Smythe opened the case. A row of gleaming flat metal devices, some with flat edges and some with long thinprongs, were nestled against the felt lining inside of the case.

"Where did you get that?" Hatchet whispered. "No, don't tell me, I don't want to know."

"Cor blimey, what is that?" Wiggins gasped.

"It's a lockpickin' kit," Smythe said softly. "And I've got to return it tomorrow." He mentally thanked Blimpey Groggins for coming through on such short notice. That had been his most important errand this evening. "Now let's see if we can get this lock opened. Keep a sharp lookout, Wiggins, I don't want to get caught with this."

He pulled out an instrument with a long, thin spoke at one end and inserted it into the lock, just as Blimpey had instructed him in today's quick lesson on housebreaking. Turning it softly, he tried to "feel" the tumblers. Nothing happened. Smythe drew a breath, took the prong out, reinserted it and tried again. Blast a Spaniard, it seemed so easy today at Blimpey's. He tried turning the prong in the other direction, felt it hit something and then increased the pressure until he felt the lock click, then click again. "That's it," he murmured. "We're in."

They were back at Upper Edmonton Gardens by a quarter to eleven. The women were sitting at the kitchen table. There was a pot of tea waiting for them.

"We got it." Smythe held up the heavy, cream-colored envelope and handed it to Mrs. Jeffries.

They all took their seats.

"Smythe's got a lockpickin' kit," Wiggins announced. "He's ever so good at it, got that door open in two shakes of a lamb's tail."

"Don't be daft, boy." Smythe glared at Wiggins. "We got lucky, and I told ya, that kit's not mine. I've got to return it tomorrow." He wanted to box the boy's ears. He didn't want Betsy or Mrs. Jeffries to start asking the wrong kind of questions about who'd given him the kit. But then again, both of them would probably approve of Blimpey. He was a scoundrel, but he was a scoundrel with principles.

"I won't ask who you have to return it to," Mrs. Jeffries said with a smile.

"Neither will I," Betsy agreed.

"Is it safe to read the letter?" Hatchet asked. "Has the inspector retired for the night?"

"He came home late and went right up to bed," Mrs. Jeffries replied.

"He didn't even have dinner," Mrs. Goodge added, "and I had Lancashire hot pot."

"Should I open it?" Now that she had it in her possession, she was suddenly uncertain. What they, she, was doing was illegal. What if the letter was something else, something that had nothing to do with the murder?

"Of course you should open it." Luty poked her in the arm. "You read it first, if it don't have nothin' to do with the killin', we'll put it in a new envelope and whip it right back into Frieda Geddy's front hall. But iffen it does have somethin' to do with the killin', then you read it aloud to the rest of us."

Mrs. Jeffries gave the elderly American a grateful smile. "There are moments, Luty, when I think you can read my mind." She picked up the letter opener she'd brought downstairs, slit open the envelope and pulled out one folded sheet of paper. Opening it, she began to read. "It's a confession," she looked up at them. "Shall I read it aloud?"

"Go ahead," Luty urged. "We're all ears."

"*For the good of my immortal soul, I, Oscar Daggett, do hereby make this confession of my own free will. I confess that on September 3rd, 1875, I entered into a conspiracy with Harrison Nye to defraud Frieda Geddy out of her rightful share of the gold mine known as 'Transvaal Mine Number 43.' We perpetrated this fraud by knowingly withholding information as to the value of the mine from Frieda Geddy after the death of her father, Viktor Geddy . . .*"

Mrs. Jeffries read the rest of the statement. In it, Daggett detailed how he and Nye had discovered the rich veins of gold and deliberately kept the information from Viktor Geddy. But before they could buy Geddy out, he'd been killed when his wagon had lost a wheel coming down a steep incline. Daggett hinted that he thought Nye had something to do with Geddy's accident—he had no proof, but he was suspicious of Nye nonetheless. With Viktor Geddy dead and in his grave, it had been an easy task to buy his share of the mine from his grief-stricken daughter for the price of a third-class passage back to England. They'd worked the mine for a couple of years and made a huge amount of money. But Daggett had always felt guilty about what they'd done. *"In closing, I can only ask for your forgiveness. I will be held accountable for my actions soon enough, in that court from which there is no escape and in front of the One who judges us all. I can only offer the feeblest of excuses for keeping silent these long years: fear and greed. Pray forgive me and pray for my immortal soul.*

"I remain your most repentant servant,

"Oscar Elwood Leander Daggett"

"Cor blimey, if anyone had a reason to kill Harrison Nye, it would be Frieda Geddy," Wiggins exclaimed.

"But she's been gone for two months, and she never saw the letter," Betsy pointed out. "So you can count her out as a suspect."

"I think the only person who could have done it is Oscar Daggett," Luty said.

"I agree." Mrs. Jeffries looked at the American, her expression curious. "But I'd be most interested in hearing your reasons."

Luty smiled wanly. "I'm old and a lot closer to death than any of you . . ."

Everyone began to argue that point at the same time.

"You're not old," Wiggins protested.

"You're in your prime," Betsy added.

"You're mature," Mrs. Goodge said.

"Madam, really, you're hardly what I would call old," Hatchet yelped.

Luty laughed and held up her hand for silence. "You're all bein' nice, but facts is facts. I'm old. I don't dwell on it, but I've made my peace with the grim reaper. That's why I think that Daggett must be the killer. He was trying to make his own peace."

"I don't think I understand," Betsy said.

"For fifteen years Daggett felt guilty for what they'd done to Frieda Geddy but he didn't do anything about it because of fear and greed. I can understand the greed, after all the fella's a crook. But Daggett also said he was afraid."

"I should think that was quite understandable as well," Hatchet said calmly. "He did a terrible thing."

"Course he did." Luty bobbed her head in emphasis. "But so what? What did he really have to be afraid of? Even if Frieda Geddy found out they'd defrauded her from her share of the mine, she couldn't prove it. Not after fifteen years and not without Daggett's very own statement."

"I get it," Wiggins cried. "He must not 'ave been worried about bein' a crook because the only way anyone would know he was a crook was if he admitted it himself."

"Right. From what we've learned about Nye, the fellow wasn't stupid. He wouldn't have left any real evidence of the crime lyin' around for Frieda Geddy or anyone else to find."

"So that means he must have been scared of something else?" Mrs. Goodge mused.

"That's what I think," Luty agreed. "Ask yourself. If he felt so danged bad about defraudin' Frieda Geddy, why hadn't he helped the girl out some in all this time? I think it was because he was scared of Nye. I'll lay ya odds that Harrison Nye had ordered him to stay away from Frieda Geddy, and that's exactly what Daggett did for fifteen years. Then he thinks he's dying, so he writes this letter confessing to what they'd done. He finds out he ain't dying, but the girl who he gives the letter to for delivery goes missing so he thinks that Frieda Geddy already has it in her hands. Scared, he hightails it to Nye's place to tell him what he's done."

"But why would he do that if he was so scared of Nye?" Betsy asked.

"Because he knew good and well how Nye would react. He knew he'd go after the letter. I think Daggett lay in wait for him to arrive at Frieda Geddy's house, then he stabbed him in the back. It's a coward's way of killin', and even Daggett admits he's a coward." She crossed her arms over her chest and looked quizzically at the housekeeper. "Well, how'd I do?"

"I couldn't have said it better myself." Mrs. Jeffries laughed. "That's precisely what I thought must have happened."

"So if Daggett killed Nye, and the only evidence we have linking him to the crime is this letter"—Hatchet nodded at the sheet of paper now lying on the table—"how do we get it to the inspector?"

"We don't," Mrs. Jeffries replied. "Smythe has already told us that Frieda Geddy is returning home. I'm sure she'll find out about the murder before she's been home an hour."

"And once she hears about Nye's murder, she'll put two and two together and give the letter to the inspector herself," Wiggins said triumphantly.

"Aren't you forgetting something?" Mrs. Goodge pointed out. "How can she be giving the inspector a ruddy thing if we've got the letter?"

"We'll have to put it back," Mrs. Jeffries said. "But I don't think we need do that tonight." She looked at Smythe. "Did you find out when Miss Geddy is coming home?"

"I'm not rightly sure," he admitted. "But I think I can find out tomorrow mornin'."

She thought for a moment. It was imperative that the letter be back in that house before Frieda Geddy returned home. Yet she didn't want to send the men back tonight. She wasn't certain it was a good idea to send them back at all. They'd been lucky once, and no one had seen them gain entry. They might not be so fortunate the next time. But the letter must go back. It was the only way.

"What are we goin' to do about the envelope?" Wiggins asked. "The top's been sliced open."

"We'll get another envelope," the housekeeper replied. "You can run down to Murray's tomorrow."

"I've got stationery just like this stuff at home," Luty cut in, "I'll bring it by tomorrow mornin' early."

"That's an excellent idea," Mrs. Jeffries said. "Then we can get the letter safely back to Fulham tomorrow night."

Mrs. Jeffries was waiting in the dining room the following morning when the inspector came down for breakfast. "Good morning, sir," she said cheerfully. "I trust you slept well."

He raised his hand to his mouth to hide a wide yawn. "Very well. I am famished, though."

"You had a long day yesterday, sir," she said as she poured him a cup of tea.

He pulled out his chair, sat down and took the silver domed lid off his plate. "Ah, wonderful, eggs and bacon. I can see that Mrs. Goodge has given me extra rashers this morning. Give her my thanks. She has an uncanny way of knowing when I'm going to be especially hungry."

Mrs. Jeffries didn't think there was anything uncanny about the cook's abilities. When the inspector was too tired to eat dinner, it meant that he'd be starving by breakfast. But she could hardly tell him that. "She's an excellent cook, sir. She's always trying to anticipate your every need."

Betsy stuck her head in the dining room. "Constable Barnes is here," she announced.

"I didn't hear the doorbell ring," Witherspoon said as the constable came through the door.

"I came in the kitchen door, sir," Barnes explained. His expression was grave. "I was in a hurry, so I cut through your garden."

"What's wrong, Constable?" Witherspoon half rose from the table.

Barnes waved him back into his seat. "Nothing's really wrong, sir. But I do have some information. Yesterday a hansom driver by the name of Neddy Pifer went to the Hammersmith Police Station and made a statement. He took a man fitting Oscar Daggett's description from the corner of Chapel Street and Grosvenor Place. That's less than half a mile from Nye's house. He dropped him at a small hotel on Hurlingham Road, just around the corner from the Geddy place."

"Did the driver get a good look at the fare?"

"He did, sir. Late at night, the drivers are extra careful. They remember faces. He's sure he can identify him. I've made arrangements to take him along to Daggett's house this morning."

Witherspoon frowned slightly. "Gracious, that is rather important. I suggest we bring a few lads along, Constable."

"Are we going to arrest Daggett?" Barnes asked.

"I'm not sure."

"But we've so much evidence against him, sir," Barnes argued. "He had a motive, sir, and no alibi for the time of the murder. If that driver identifies Daggett, he'll have opportunity as well."

Mrs. Jeffries desperately wanted to ask what motive they thought they had for Daggett being the killer, but she didn't dare.

Betsy had no such inhibitions, though. "Why would he want to kill his friend?" she asked. Then she blushed prettily. "Oh, I'm sorry, I didn't mean to step out of my place, sir. But you know how we all follow your cases so closely."

Witherspoon waved her apology off with his fork. He was now shoveling his breakfast in at an alarming rate. "Not to worry, Betsy," he said around a mouthful of egg. "Naturally, you're all curious . . ."

"His motive was very simple," Barnes interjected. "Nye had called him a fool and threatened to kill Daggett when they were together in the study that night. One of the guests had gone to the water closet which was next to the room they were in; he didn't hear the whole conversation, just the end of it. We figure Daggett thought it was either him or Nye."

"Excuse me, Constable." Mrs. Jeffries now thought it safe to ask a question. "But why did this hansom driver wait so long before coming forward? You generally make it known immediately that you'd like to know if anyone took a fare to the area of the murder."

"He was in hospital," Barnes said. "Food poisoning. He found out from the dispatcher this morning that we were making inquiries about fares to Fulham for that night."

Witherspoon shoved the last bite of bacon in his mouth and stood up. "Let's get going then. Mrs. Jeffries, I may be home quite late tonight."

"I'll wait up for you, sir," she assured him.

As soon as he was gone, she looked at the maid. "Gracious, this is a fortunate turn of events."

Betsy nodded. "It looks that way. Oh drat, I forgot to tell you. Luty's downstairs. She'll want to know the latest development." She began clearing up the table, placing the dirty dishes on the tray she'd brought in earlier.

"We'll have a meeting," Mrs. Jeffries said cheerfully. "If Luty's here, Hatchet is as well. If Smythe and Wiggins are still here, we'll tell everyone an arrest is imminent."

"Do you mind if I don't stay?" Betsy yanked the serviette off the table, wadded it up into a ball and put it on the tray. "I've got to take those gloves over to Arlene at the Nye house."

"I don't mind. I'll tell the others where you've gone."

"Thank you, Mrs. Jeffries, I don't like missing one of our meetings, even when we know an arrest is coming, but I did promise Arlene."

Mrs. Jeffries picked up the heavy tray. "You run along now. If you hurry, you might be back before we finish."

Betsy smiled gratefully. "I'll be back before you know it." She hurried out into the hall, hesitated a split second, then charged up the front steps to her room. She'd left the gloves on her bed.

It took her less than five minutes to gather her coat and hat and be out the door. Betsy was very lucky. The omnibus was just trundling up to the stop when she got to Holland Park Road. Half an hour later, she was ringing the bell on the servants' entrance of the Nye house.

Arlene opened the door. "Oh, you came. I was afraid you wouldn't. Come on in, then." She led Betsy across the narrow hall into the servants' hall. Betsy could hear the muted sounds of people coming from the kitchen.

"I told you I'd be here," Betsy said. "Here, these are for you." She handed Arlene the small, flat parcel she'd wrapped in brown paper the night before. It contained two pairs of gloves.

"Thanks ever so much." Arlene took the parcel and pulled off the string. "Oh, there's two pairs here. This is so nice of you. I don't know what to say."

"Don't say anything," Betsy said. "Just accept them and use them." She looked around the servants' hall. "Is it always so quiet here?"

Arlene made a face. "We're supposed to be a house in mourning. Mrs. Nye's got the butler and the footman up in the attic trying to find the crepe so we can drape the windows with it."

Betsy rolled her eyes. "But no one does that anymore."

"Come on"—Arlene rose to her feet—"I'll show you. She's got the downstairs dining-room windows draped already."

Betsy was curious. She got up. "I don't want to get you in trouble."

"Don't worry, no one will see us." Arlene giggled.

Betsy started for the hall, but Arlene grabbed her arm. "Not that way." She dashed over to the far side of the servants' hall. The wall was paneled halfway up its height in a row of wide oak panels. "See this." She pointed to a small, brass latch on the top of the last panel, pressed it and the panel swung open like a small door.

"It's a door," Betsy exclaimed.

"Most people don't even know it's here," Arlene confided as she ducked inside.

Betsy followed her. They went up a small, narrow set of stairs. "Is this a secret passage?"

"Not really," Arlene whispered over her shoulder. "This used to be a shortcut to the dining room from the kitchen. Made getting the food upstairs while it was hot much easier. It's only one story, it just goes up to the dining room. But they walled it up years ago when the old master stopped receiving."

"Do the Nyes know about it?" Betsy asked. They reached the top of the dark stairwell.

"Mrs. Nye does, I saw her comin' out of it early one mornin'. But I never saw Mr. Nye use it." Arlene reached up, feeling for the brass latch that opened the door. She froze at the sound of voices.

Someone was in the dining room.

"What do you mean she's coming back?" Eliza Nye's voice rang loud and clear. "I thought you said she was in Holland with her relatives."

"She was." The voice that replied was a male's. "But she's coming back tonight."

Arlene began edging backward. "Bother, we've got to get out of here."

Betsy had no choice but to ease backwards down the steps. She strained to hear what was going on behind the wall.

"When did you find that out? You should have told me immediately. We'll have to make plans . . ." Eliza's voice trailed off as footsteps sounded into the dining room.

"Get a move on," Arlene whispered frantically at Betsy. "If she's in the dining room, that means the butler's on his way downstairs. I've got to get back to work or I'll be sacked."

Betsy dearly wanted to hear what was happening on the other side of the wall, but she didn't dare argue with the girl. She edged backwards and down another step.

"Hurry up," Arlene whispered.

"Hold on," she hissed, "it's dark."

But Arlene was in no mood for dallying and before Betsy could hear another word, she was down the shallow staircase and back in the servants' hall. Blast her luck.

CHAPTER 10

"Shouldn't we wait for Betsy?" Smythe asked, glancing hopefully toward the back stairs.

Mrs. Jeffries pulled out her chair and sat down. "She isn't coming. She had an errand to run." Even though the meeting hadn't been formally arranged, everyone else was present.

Smythe frowned but said nothing. Maybe the lass was getting her own back because he'd sneaked off yesterday without telling her where he was off to.

Mrs. Jeffries ducked her head to hide a smile. She knew what it cost the coachman to hold his tongue. He was ridiculously overprotective of Betsy and she, of course, delighted in being as independent as possible. She decided to put him out of his misery. "Betsy's doing a good deed. She's taking a pair of her old gloves to a friend who hasn't any. She ought to be back by lunchtime."

"Oh yeah, she told me she had to do that today." He felt a bit ashamed of himself for thinking that Betsy could be so childish. Of course she'd not try to get back at him. She was too good for that sort of behavior.

"That's right nice of 'er," Wiggins said cheerfully.

"Indeed it is," the cook agreed.

"It's a stroke of luck that Luty and Hatchet dropped by," Mrs. Jeffries said. "We've some news. Constable Barnes came by while the inspector was at breakfast. They're going to arrest Oscar Daggett."

"Arrest him?" Hatchet exclaimed. "On what grounds? They don't have the letter."

"They don't need it," she replied. "They found a hansom driver who remembers taking Daggett to Fulham on the night of the murder." She gave them the rest of the details. "So you see, it probably wasn't as imperative as we thought to get that letter back into Miss Geddy's hallway. Sorry, Wiggins, if we'd known about the arrest, I wouldn't have had to rouse you this morning so early."

"That's all right, Mrs. Jeffries." Wiggins laughed. "Me and Fred 'ad us a nice adventure."

They'd decided to use a ruse to get the letter back into the Geddy house. Early that moring, Wiggins and Fred had made their way to Dunbarton Street and Wiggins had surreptitiously tossed Fred's ball into the front garden, specifically, right at Frieda Geddy's front door. Of course, Fred chased it and that, in turn, gave Wiggins an excuse to go all the way up the walkway of the house in pursuit of his errant dog. Once he was within range of the postbox, it had been easy to slip the letter back inside.

"So I was right." Luty slapped her hand against the table top and laughed. "Nell's bells, I just love bein' right."

"So we see, madam," Hatchet said dryly. "Are we sure that Daggett really is the killer?"

"You can't stand it, can ya?" Luty poked him in the ribs. "You just hate it when I'm right."

Hatchet was unperturbed. "Nonsense, madam. I rejoice in the fact that you've made what is apparently, a lucky guess."

"Lucky guess," Luty yelped. "Guessin' had nothin' to do with it."

"Now, now, Luty," Mrs. Jeffries interrupted. "Hatchet's simply having a bit of fun with you. But in answer to his question, all I can say is that it certainly seems as if Oscar Daggett is the killer. As Luty aptly pointed out last night, he certainly had a reason."

"That's too bad," Wiggins interjected. "Oh, I don't mean it's too bad they know who the killer is, I mean it's too bad they found out so quickly. I 'eard ever so much about Miss Geddy this mornin'. I found out where she'd been mailin' them packages off to."

"What packages?" Mrs. Goodge asked absently.

"The ones she 'ad the dustup with the bloke from the post office about," Wiggins reminded her.

"Oh, yes, of course. Are you goin' to tell us?" Mrs. Goodge asked sharply. She was a tad perturbed as well. Her own contributions didn't amount to much at all. All she'd found out was a bit of silly gossip about the Nye household.

"Rotterdam," Wiggins said proudly. "She's got relatives there. She'll be home tonight, too. Comin' in on the eight-fifteen."

"Cor blimey, boy, who told ya all that?" Smythe asked incredulously.

"Mrs. Moff, her neighbor lady told me." Wiggins laughed again. "She come out when she saw Fred." The dog was lying in a spot of sunshine near the kitchen sink, he raised his head when he heard his name. "Seems Mrs. Moff is right fond of dogs. She and Fred got on nicely, they did. While she was tossin' him his ball, we got to talkin'. She told me ever so much. Too bad it's too late."

"I know what ya mean." Smythe sighed. "When I was over at Howard's this mornin', I found out somethin' interestin' as well."

"What?" Mrs. Jeffries asked. "What did you hear?"

"You know 'ow they rent out gigs and all," Smythe said. "I was givin' Bow a good brush down when I 'eard Bill Cronin, that's the stable master, swearin' a blue streak and poundin' somethin' so 'ard it made the rafters shake. Bill's a nice bloke, not given to losin' his temper, so I went over and seen what was the matter. He was hammerin' the center of the back wheel of a brougham. Said it'd come in wobbly from a couple of nights back, and that he'd not noticed till a man come around that mornin' wantin' to hire the brougham for tonight. Now Bill's not one for rememberin' things very well. Writes everythin' down on bits of paper and old letters he finds in the rubbish." He paused to take a breath. "He'd laid a piece of paper down on the bale of hay that I was standin' next to and I 'appened to glance at it. I saw the name Lionel Bancroft written on it."

"Lionel Bancroft," Hatchet repeated. "Isn't that Eliza Nye's cousin?"

"Some say he's a bit more than that," Mrs. Goodge muttered darkly.

"That's right." Smythe nodded. "So I asked Bill if Bancroft was the man hirin' the brougham for tonight. He said he was. He told me Bancroft 'ad been a customer for years. He was a bit narked at him, said Bancroft had been the last person to have the brougham out and that he ought to have told him it was wobbly when he brought it back in the last time."

"Too bad we didn't know any of this when we was tryin' to solve the murder," Wiggins said. "It might 'ave come in useful."

"I don't see how," the cook grumbled. "All we learned was that Lionel Bancroft rents broughams and Frieda Geddy sends packages to Rotterdam. None of that has anything to do with Oscar Daggett murdering Harrison Nye. More's the pity. I don't think we solved the murder at all. I think the inspector did it all on his own. Mind you, it's not like we had much to work with."

Mrs. Jeffries understood why the cook was upset. In truth, she was a tad irritated as well. It did seem as if the case had come to an abrupt halt. But she wasn't going to share that sentiment with the others. They had done the best they could, and they ought to be proud of their efforts. "Nonsense, we did as much work on this case as we've ever done in the past, and we ought to congratulate ourselves."

They broke up soon after that, and they all went off to take care of the duties they'd neglected during the investigation.

Wiggins went back upstairs to finish cleaning out the attic, Smythe got out a ladder and tackled the gutters along the back of the house, Mrs. Goodge sorted out the dry larder and Mrs. Jeffries went upstairs to organize the linens.

She had just finished putting the towels in the back cupboard when she heard light footsteps on the back stairs. "I'm sorry it took so long, Mrs. Jeffries," Betsy said as she reached the landing and saw the housekeeper, "but I was in a bit of a silly situation."

"That's quite all right, Betsy." Mrs. Jeffries smiled kindly. She didn't want the girl to feel she had to make excuses about her tardiness. "You're a very reliable person, you don't need to apologize for taking a couple of hours off to visit with your friend."

"But . . ."

She held up her hand as the girl started to protest. "Now you run along downstairs and have a cup of tea and something to eat, you must be famished. And pop your head out the back door and let Smythe know you're back. It'll settle his mind."

"But—"

"Now, run along, Betsy." Mrs. Jeffries ushered her toward the back stairs. "You haven't eaten since breakfast."

Betsy gave up trying to explain. Telling Mrs. Jeffries what she'd overheard at the Nyes' would be silly. What, exactly, had she found out? That some woman was coming home from Holland tonight. What did that prove? The little incident had been exciting, but it hadn't meant any-thing. Not now that Daggett was going to be arrested.

There was an air of gloom over the household that afternoon. Mrs. Jef-fries went up to her rooms to do the household accounts but didn't get very far along on them. Odd things kept popping into her mind. She couldn't stop thinking about the murder. She closed the ledger and leaned back in her chair.

On the one hand, it did seem likely that Oscar Daggett was the killer, while on the other hand, it didn't. Annoyed with herself, she frowned, but the truth was, Daggett being the killer simply didn't feel right. Yester-day afternoon it had all seemed so right, so logical. Yet somehow, she knew it wasn't. She couldn't think what was wrong with the situation. It wasn't as if they had anyone else in mind as a suspect.

She glanced out the window and saw that evening was drawing close. She pushed back from the small table she used as a desk and got up. She might as well go downstairs and help Mrs. Goodge fix supper. At least a bit of company would keep her from being maudlin.

Mrs. Jeffries was on the first-floor landing when she heard the front door open. "Gracious, sir, we didn't expect you home so early." She con-tinued down the stairs.

"I know I'm too early for supper," he explained as he took off his hat, "but I was rather hoping I could have a substantial tea. I've got to go back to the station tonight and write up the arrest report."

"That'll be very tiring for you." She started toward the back stairs. "If you'll go into the dining room, I'll bring you up a tray."

"That won't be necessary." He fell into step behind her. "I'd just as soon eat in the kitchen. Taking all my meals on my own is so boring."

Mrs. Goodge must have heard them coming, for she was already put-ting the kettle on the cooker when they came into the kitchen. "Good evening, sir," she said cheerfully. "I'll have something ready for you straightaway."

"Thank you, Mrs. Goodge." He pulled out the chair at the head of the table and plopped down. "I'm very hungry. We didn't have time for lunch. Oh, do sit down, Mrs. Jeffries, and have a cup of tea with me. As I said earlier, I'm heartily sick of taking all my meals alone."

Mrs. Jeffries shot the cook a quick, helpless look, then pulled out the chair next to him and sat down. "Thank you, sir, that would be very nice." She felt very awkward, letting the elderly cook wait on her.

"And bring a cup for yourself, Mrs. Goodge," Witherspoon called, "we might as well be comfortable."

"Thank you, sir," she replied. "My feet could use a nice sit down, and I'm ever so curious about your murder, sir."

In just a few moments, Mrs. Goodge had a hearty tea of bread, cheese, cold roast beef and currant buns laid out in front of the inspector. "Tuck right in, sir," she said.

The inspector speared a huge hunk of cheese with his fork and then took a bite of bread. Mrs. Jeffries poured their tea and handed the cups around.

The cook waited until Witherspoon had swallowed his food before she asked, "Was Daggett surprised when you arrested him?"

"I don't think so." Witherspoon reached for the butter and slathered some across his bread. "He was waiting for us when we arrived at his home; it was almost as if he knew we were coming."

Mrs. Jeffries felt her heart sink. Daggett must be guilty. "Has he confessed, sir?"

"No and I don't think he's going to, either. He admitted taking a hansom cab to Fulham that night, but he claims he didn't go to the Geddy house at all."

"Then why'd he go to Fulham?" Mrs. Goodge asked.

"He refused to say." Witherspoon sighed. "But he insisted he didn't kill anyone."

Mrs. Jeffries realized that the inspector didn't know about the letter. She was amazed that someone from the Daggett household hadn't mentioned it to the police when Daggett was being arrested. But then again, why would they? But surely Mrs. Benchley would have told the inspector that Nelda Smith had shown up unharmed and married.

"Are you going to question Daggett's servants again?" she asked.

"Probably." He finished off the last of the roast beef. "We need to be absolutely certain no one saw him come home at half past nine on the night of the murder." He sighed. "But I've got to tell you, I have grave doubts about Daggett's guilt."

"Doubts?" Mrs. Goodge repeated. "Why?"

He hesitated for a moment. "I'm not altogether sure. There's nothing I can actually put my finger on, it's just that when he protests his innocence, I can hear the ring of truth in his voice."

"You always think the best of everyone, sir," the cook replied.

"I don't think that's it"—he frowned—"and it's not as if Daggett's a particularly likable sort of fellow. Yet I can't help but think he's telling the truth. I suppose it's because there's something about this case that simply doesn't ring true. Something I'm not seeing or understanding . . ." He shook himself slightly. "I expect that sounds silly, doesn't it?"

"Not at all, sir," Mrs. Jeffries said. She had great respect for the inspector's instincts. "I think your 'inner voice' is trying to tell you something." She racked her brain, trying desperately to think of a way to let him know everything they'd learned about the case in the last two days. But short of just blurting it out, she couldn't think of how to do it.

"Do you really think so?" he asked eagerly. "I was rather thinking along those lines myself. Of course, it's not just my feelings that make me think Daggett might be innocent. As I told you, he readily admitted to taking a hansom to Fulham."

Mrs. Jeffries needed to understand something. "Did he say why Nye went to Fulham that night?"

Witherspoon pursed his lips. "No, and that's one of the things that I find most baffling about this case. Daggett still won't tell us why he went to visit Nye that night or why Nye went to Fulham. Frankly, until I know the why of it all, it simply doesn't make sense."

The two women exchanged covert glances. Neither of them were certain they ought to say a word about Frieda Geddy and that letter. Not when Freida Geddy would be home in a few hours and able to take the letter to the inspector herself.

"I'm sure you'll sort it out, sir," Mrs. Jeffries finally said. "You always do. Are you going to be formally charging Daggett?"

"I don't really know." He pushed away from the table. "I'm going back to the station to have another go at talking to the man. If he's innocent, then it's imperative he tell me the truth." He stood up and smiled. "Don't wait up for me. I shall be quite late."

Mrs. Jeffries escorted him to the door, then hurried back to the kitchen. She didn't know what to think. Witherspoon thought Daggett was innocent. She was now almost certain that he was correct. Nothing seemed really right about Daggett's arrest. "What time will the others be here?" she asked the cook.

"Luty and Hatchet won't be here at all," Mrs. Goodge replied. "Remember, we decided this morning that as an arrest had already been made there was no need for a meetin' this afternoon. So it'll just be our lot. Why? Do you think the inspector's right and that Daggett is innocent?"

"I think we'd better have another meeting," Mrs. Jeffries said thoughtfully. She glanced at the clock and saw that it was almost half past five. "And the quicker, the better."

"They'll be coming in for supper soon," Mrs. Goodge said as she got down the drippings bowl from the shelf over the cooker, "and we can talk as we eat."

By the time the rest of them came in for supper, Mrs. Jeffries had given the matter of the murder a great deal of thought. She waited until they'd all filled their plates with Mrs. Goodge's fragrant shepherd's pie. "The inspector doesn't think Daggett's guilty," she said, "and neither do I."

"If Daggett didn't do it, who did?" Smythe asked.

"Oh good," Betsy exclaimed, "Now maybe I can tell some of the things I've found out."

Mrs. Jeffries looked at her, her expression incredulous. "You have information you haven't shared?"

"Just a couple of bits and pieces I found out yesterday and this morning," she admitted.

"Why didn't you tell us yesterday, then?" Mrs. Goodge demanded.

"Because it wasn't much of anything, and yesterday everyone seemed to think that Daggett was the killer. Everyone had so much to say that by the time it got around to me, we'd just about run out of steam."

"It's all right, Betsy," Mrs. Jeffries said quickly. "We understand. Now, why don't you tell us what you know."

Betsy felt just a bit foolish for not speaking up when she had the chance. She glanced at Smythe and he gave her a warm, encouraging smile. "It isn't all that much. Arlene Hill, she's the maid that works for the Nyes, she told me that on the night of the murder she heard footsteps on the back staircase."

"And you didn't think that was something we ought to know," Mrs. Goodge said sharply.

"Not really. Arlene's a bit of a talker, if you know what I mean. I spent two hours with her, and she told me quite a bit about the household. Now everything she told me could be true, but I think she tarted things up a bit to make herself sound a little important. She's a very lonely girl; she doesn't have any family to speak of."

"You think she made up a story about hearing them footsteps?" Smythe asked.

Betsy cocked her head to one side, her expression thoughtful. "I think she heard something on the stairs, but I don't think it was footsteps. She probably just heard the house settling. The next morning, when the police arrived and there was a bit of excitement, she convinced herself she'd heard footsteps. I don't think she out and out lies."

"She just adds a bit onto her tales to make 'em more interestin'," Wiggins suggested.

Betsy nodded eagerly. "That's it. That's what I was trying to say. She adds to things more than makes them up. Not that she'd have to make up any tales about what happened this morning when we were stuck in that closed-up stairwell." She gave them the details of her adventure at the Nye house. "So you see, my information wasn't really all that important . . ." Her voice trailed off as she saw the way the others were looking at her. "What's wrong? You're all staring at me like I've got a wart on my nose."

Mrs. Jeffries leaned toward the girl. "Are you sure about what you overheard? Are you certain that Lionel Bancroft told Eliza Nye that the woman was coming home from Holland tonight?"

"Yes, I know what I heard. Why? What's so special about one of their friends coming home from holiday?"

"Maybe it isn't one of their friends they were talkin' about," Smythe said softly. "Maybe it was Frieda Geddy."

"Frieda Geddy?" Betsy exclaimed. "Why would you think that?"

"Because that's where she was mailin' all those packages," Wiggins replied, "and she's got relatives in Holland. Do you think it could be 'er they was talkin' about? If it was, what do you think it means?" he asked the housekeeper.

"I'm not sure." Mrs. Jeffries's mind was working furiously. She took a long, deep breath, willing herself to be calm. She closed her eyes briefly and let her thoughts go where they would. All of a sudden the pieces began to fall into place and another, entirely different picture of the puzzle started to form in her mind.

"Before we get all het up," Mrs. Goodge warned, "keep in mind that Miss Geddy coming home tonight and their friend comin' home tonight could be a coincidence. Lots of people travel these days."

"But Miss Geddy was always sendin' packages to Rotterdam," Wiggins pointed out, "and this woman Betsy overheard 'em talkin' about 'is comin' in from Holland."

"What does that prove?" the cook asked. She reached for the pitcher of beer on the table and poured more into her now empty glass. "And how would Eliza Nye or Lionel Bancroft know anything about Miss Geddy to begin with? From the gossip we heard, Harrison Nye didn't share his past sins with his wife."

"But it'd be an odd coincidence," Smythe muttered.

"But they do happen," Betsy pointed out.

Mrs. Jeffries remained silent as the argument continued all around her. She was thinking. Everything they'd learned flew in and out of her mind willy-nilly. She didn't try to make sense of it, she simply let the facts come and go as they would.

She looked down at her plate and closed her eyes again, letting the impressions come in their own good time. Oscar Daggett's mad rush to Nye's house after he'd learned he wasn't dying. Harrison Nye's admonitions that his wife wasn't to be disturbed after she'd gone to bed, Lionel Bancroft hiring a brougham, the nightgown hidden in the cupboard by the back door, the gossip about Eliza Nye and Bancroft.

Everything tumbled and swirled about in a seemingly senseless tangle. Facts and ideas pushed and shoved one another for supremacy. Wiggins's question about the origins of the fortune, Frieda Geddy's bitterness, gold from the Transvaal.

"Is there something wrong with the pie?" Mrs. Goodge poked the housekeeper in the arm to get her attention.

Shaken from her reverie, she blinked. "What? What did you say?"

The cook repeated her question.

"I'm sorry." Mrs. Jeffries smiled. "I wasn't paying attention. The pie is excellent." She looked down at her plate.

Mrs. Goodge refrained from asking the housekeeper how she knew as she'd not even had one bite of it. "Well, that's good. We've lemon tarts for afters."

Mrs. Jeffries looked back down at her plate and the room was silent. The others looked at each other, their expressions concerned. They all realized the housekeeper was seriously upset. After a few moments, Smythe cleared his throat, and asked, "Mrs. Jeffries, is somethin' amiss?"

"I'm not sure," she replied. She looked over at the carriage clock on the top of the pine sideboard. "It's just past six," she muttered, "and I'm probably mistaken." But she knew she wasn't. She knew it as surely as she knew her own name.

"Are ya sure?" Wiggins pressed anxiously. "You've not touched a bite of your supper."

She raised her head to find all of them staring at her. "I can't eat," she began, "because I'm worried."

"Worried?" the cook repeated. "What's there to be worried about? Everything's fine. I know we didn't contribute all that much to catching Nye's killer, but sometimes the inspector does get one on his own."

"But that's just it." the housekeeper said urgently. "Even he isn't sure he's caught the right killer."

"Even if Daggett's innocent, there's no need to be concerned. They'll not be hanging the man tomorrow. There's plenty of time to find the real killer," Betsy said.

"But that's just it," Mrs. Jeffries glanced at the clock again. "If I'm right, there isn't. If we don't move quickly, there's going to be another murder tonight."

Wiggins put down his fork and pushed back from the table. "Then we'd best get moving. What do you want me to do?"

Smythe was getting to his feet as well. "Just tell us, Mrs. J, and we'll get right on it."

She was touched by their faith in her. "Before we do anything, I have to admit that I'm not one hundred percent certain I'm right, and if I'm wrong now, it could be very embarrassing for the inspector." And for us, she thought, but she knew they already understood that.

"It's a risk I'm willing to take. You've been right often enough in the past," the coachman said easily. "Now you just give us our instructions and we'll get moving. We must be in a 'urry or you wouldn't keep lookin' at the clock."

Mrs. Jeffries made up her mind. She wouldn't risk a human life because she didn't have the courage to act. If she was wrong, she'd pay whatever price needed to be paid. The others obviously had faith in her. "We are in a hurry. We've got to get the inspector to Frieda Geddy's house by the time she gets home tonight."

"She's not arrivin' before eight-fifteen," Wiggins reported eagerly. "So we've got time."

"Is her train arriving at the station or is that the time she's arriving home?" Mrs. Jeffries pushed her plate away and stood up.

Wiggins hesitated for a split second, "Cor blimey, I don't know for certain, but I thought it was the station."

She turned her attention to Smythe. "Do you know what time Bancroft is picking up the brougham?"

"Not really, but I can nip over to Howard's and find out."

She thought for a moment. "That's a good idea. If he's already picked up the carriage, get over to Dunbarton Street and keep an eye on things. If Bancroft gets to Frieda Geddy before the inspector arrives, he'll try and kill her. So keep a sharp eye out for his brougham. Try and stay out of sight if you can." She looked at Wiggins. "Get over to Knightsbridge and tell Luty and Hatchet what's happened. Tell Luty to come along here and tell Hatchet to get to Dunbarton Street."

"Should I go with 'im?" Wiggins asked eagerly. He reached down and patted Fred on the head. The dog sensed the air of excitement that had begun to build in the kitchen and fairly danced at the lad's heels.

"By all means, but make sure you stay out of sight as well. If our plan works, the inspector should be along shortly after Miss Geddy arrives home. But for this to work, timing is everything, so let's keep our fingers crossed." She looked at the cook. "If Wiggins is successful, Luty ought to be along soon. Tell her what's going on—"

"And exactly what's that?" Mrs. Goodge asked, her expression puzzled.

"Oh dear, haven't I said? I am sorry. I think that Lionel Bancroft and Eliza Nye are going to attempt to kill Frieda Geddy tonight. Probably as soon as she gets home. They know about Daggett's letter, you see, and they can't risk that information becoming public."

"What are you going to tell the inspector?" Smythe asked the housekeeper. "I mean, when he trots along to Frieda Geddy's house and Bancroft's not there yet, what's goin' to happen?"

Mrs. Jeffries bit her lip. She hadn't thought about that yet. She'd put the plan together on the assumption that Bancroft would show up while the inspector was in the Geddy house. "I'm not sure. I think, perhaps, our best hope is Constable Barnes. If he's with the inspector, I've a feeling he'll keep him hanging about the Geddy house until something happens. You'd best hurry, Smythe. We're running out of time."

Smythe nodded and took off toward the back door.

She turned to Betsy. "Come along, let's get our coats and hats. We're going to the station." She hoped her assessment of Barnes was right. She was fairly certain he knew that she and the others helped on the inspector's cases. If he knew that Mrs. Jeffries had been the one to come to the station with an urgent message, he'd make sure the inspector stayed on Dunbarton Street long enough to make an arrest.

"The station!" Betsy leapt to her feet delighted she was going to be part of the adventure and not just sitting around the kitchen waiting for the men to come home. "We're going to see the inspector?"

"Indeed we are and you'd best put on your thinking cap. By the time we get there, we're going to have to come up with a good story to get him to Dunbarton Street in time."

CHAPTER 11

Witherspoon was dreadfully tired, but he knew his duty. "I suppose I'd best go along to Dunbarton Street and see what the problem might be," he said to Barnes as they came out of the station. "It's late, though, and I think your good wife must be waiting for you. There's no reason for both of us to go. I can handle whatever it is Miss Geddy needs."

"Mrs. Jeffries said the street arab claimed it was a matter of life and death. She said the boy had gotten his instructions from someone in the Nye household, sir. I don't like the sound of that." Barnes wasn't going to let the inspector go to Fulham without him. "My wife's used to my odd hours, sir."

"That's very commendable, Constable." Witherspoon peered up the darkened street, hoping to see a hansom. "But do keep in mind that people often exaggerate, and the boy could even have got the message wrong."

"True, sir. But if Mrs. Jeffries came all the way here to tell us, I think we'd best assume it's serious. Your housekeeper's a very sensible woman. She's not easily fooled. As a matter of fact, sir, I took the liberty of asking a couple of the lads to meet us at Dunbarton Street."

The constable was not as innocent as his inspector. He knew perfectly well that when Witherspoon's household began relaying mysterious messages from street arabs about "a matter of life and death," that they'd best be on their toes. Whether the inspector realized it or not, they were probably going to catch the real killer tonight.

"There's a hansom, sir." Barnes put his fingers to his mouth and whistled.

Startled by the sudden sound, Witherspoon jumped. "Uh, well, if you think it's necessary, then I suppose it'll not do any harm."

The hansom pulled up to the curb, and they climbed on board. "Fulham, please," Witherspoon called to the driver. "Number thirteen Dunbarton Street." He sighed and settled back against the upholstery. "I really don't know why people persist in coming to my house," he murmured. "It seems that on every case I've had lately, someone's popped up at my front door with a message or a telegram or a note. You'd think they'd come to the station, wouldn't you? Seems to me that would be far more efficient."

"As Mrs. Jeffries said, sir, there are a number of people in our city who don't like the police or police stations."

"But it's our job to protect our citizens. I just don't understand why so many of them seem to view us as the enemy."

"They don't view you as the enemy," Barnes said. "As Miss Betsy pointed out, you've built a reputation amongst the, how did she put it, the less-than-fortunate, for being fair and honest."

Witherspoon shrugged modestly. "But most police officers are fair and honest. I've done nothing special." Nonetheless, he was pleased.

Barnes turned his head and rolled his eyes heavenward. Inspector Witherspoon amazed him. After all this time, the man was still as naive as a babe in arms. "Believe me, sir, there's plenty of coppers out there that would give the less-than-fortunate short shrift. But I can see your concern, sir. I expect it's not very pleasant for your staff to have strangers bangin' on your front door all the time. But you've got to admit a lot of our cases have been solved with the help of these people. You know what I mean, sir, people who don't want to be seen helpin' the police, so they do it anonymously by sending along a message to your house." Of course, he knew good and well why all these "people" came to the inspector's house. But he wouldn't share that information with his superior. That would take all the fun out of it. If the truth were known, his own career had done nicely since the inspector had become so adept at solving murders. As the inspector's right-hand man, he'd become a bit of a legend himself.

"They don't mind." Witherspoon waved his hand dismissively. "My household is very interested in my work. I'm very lucky in that regard. They do tend to be a bit overly protective of me though. You know, you're not the only one who thinks Inspector Nivens isn't to be trusted. Mrs.

Jeffries has never liked the fellow. Why, by the way, I haven't seen him about much lately. Where's he got to?"

Barnes grinned. "He's kept himself scarce ever since you complained to the chief inspector that he was interferin' on your case."

Witherspoon winced. "I did hate doing that. But I do believe you were right, Constable. Inspector Nivens does seem to resent me very much these days."

"Not to worry, sir. Rumor has it he'll be going up to Yorkshire soon," Barnes replied. "They needed some help on a string of housebreakings that the local fellows can't solve." He didn't tell the inspector that the gossip in the ranks was that Chief Inspector Barrows had gotten fed up with Nivens's playing politics all the time, so he'd sent the fellow off to get him out of Barrow's hair for a few days. "And I must admit, sir, I think you're right about Daggett. I don't think he did it either."

"You and I are the only ones that think he's innocent. I expect it's because he's not a very likable sort." He sighed. "If we want to catch the real killer, we'll have to keep on digging."

"Oh, I don't expect we'll have to dig very far," Barnes murmured softly.

"Cor blimey, I can't see a ruddy thing," Wiggins complained. "We're too far away."

They were flattened against the far side building at the end of the row of homes on Dunbarton Street. They weren't positioned to see Frieda Geddy's home very easily as it was halfway up the block.

"There aren't many hiding places about," Smythe muttered. "And we don't dare be seen. Lower yer 'ead, Wiggins, you're blockin' my view."

"What will we do if things begin to happen, and the inspector's not here?" Hatchet asked softly.

"We'll do what's needed," he said. He turned and gazed at Hatchet's coat pocket. The butler, fully understanding, nodded in the affirmative and patted the pocket. Inside was a small, but deadly derringer. "I brought it. You?"

Smythe looked at Wiggins, who wasn't paying any attention to their conversation, and then back at Hatchet. "I've something with me." He cut a fast glance down to his right boot. Like Hatchet, he'd come prepared. He'd brought his old hunting knife from his days in the Australian outback. It was strapped snugly against his right shin. He hoped for all their sakes he didn't have to use it.

"Cor blimey," Wiggins hissed excitedly, "there's a hansom coming."

Smythe and Hatchet both craned their necks around the corner to get a better view. The hansom pulled up to the front of number 13 and a cloaked figure got down.

"It's got to be Frieda Geddy," Smythe whispered. He was fairly sure the killer was going to arrive by brougham, not by hansom. "Look, she's getting out a carpetbag." They watched her pay the driver and then head toward the front door. She stood on the doorstep for a moment, and then her front door opened and she stepped inside. A few moments later, a light appeared in the front-room window.

"Look, here comes another hansom." Wiggins pointed down the road as a cab pulled around the corner.

Smythe and Hatchet looked at one another in dismay.

"He's got here early," Wiggins groaned. "What are we goin' to do?"

"We'll 'ang on a bit and see what 'appens," Smythe muttered. He looked at Hatchet and saw his own fears mirrored on the butler's face. "Are you thinkin' what I'm thinkin'?"

"I think that's a safe assumption." Hatchet pursed his lips. "It appears as if our killer isn't going to show himself. Apparently, we've been wrong about this."

"We're not wrong," Wiggins insisted. He'd finally started paying attention. "Mrs. Jeffries is dead on about this. It's the only thing that makes sense. Maybe he just ain't got 'ere yet."

"And that's even worse," Smythe insisted. "Because if the inspector leaves after talkin' to Miss Geddy, the killer'll be able to take his sweet time doin' 'er in and Inspector Witherspoon'll never forgive 'imself."

"Then we'll just have to spend the night here," Hatchet said staunchly, "and make certain that doesn't happen. What's happening now?" he hissed at Wiggins, who'd craned his neck back around the side of the house.

"The hansom's pullin' up to the front of the 'ouse," Wiggins replied. "Ow, that smarts."

"Sorry," Smythe replied. Fearing they'd be seen, he'd pushed Wiggins down a bit harder than he'd intended. "Blast a Spaniard, the inspector and Constable Barnes is gettin' out of the hansom."

"This isn't good," Hatchet said. "I think we're going to be here for the rest of the night."

All of a sudden, the quiet night was filled with a blood-curdling scream. It came from inside the Geddy house.

Witherspoon and Barnes jumped and raced toward Miss Geddy's front door.

Another scream came again, followed by a harsh cry.

The two policemen reached the front door. Barnes grabbed the knob and twisted. "It's locked, sir."

"Help, help," a woman cried from inside the house. There was a loud crash, and then the sound of breaking glass.

"Break it open," Witherspoon shouted. He and Barnes both took a step back and then shoved their shoulders hard against the door.

About that time, two police constables, hearing the commotion, came racing around the corner.

"Should we do somethin'?" Wiggins asked worriedly. That scream had just about made him faint, but he'd gotten ahold of himself. "It sounds like someone's bein' murdered in there."

"Let's wait a moment," Hatchet replied. He'd caught sight of the two policemen running toward the Geddy house. "I believe there will be plenty of help."

The two constables raced up to the house just as Barnes and Witherspoon took a step back to try again. One of the constables, a big, burly fellow, said, "Let me try kickin' it, sir." He raised his leg and gave a hard kick against the lock just as another scream came from the house. The door flew open and the police rushed inside.

Wiggins, Hatchet and Smythe came out from their hiding place, hoping to hide in the excitement of the moment and the darkness of the night. "Cor blimey, I wish I knew what was goin' on in 'at house . . . cor blimey, who's that?" Wiggins pointed to a figure who'd just come around the corner. But whoever it was hadn't walked around the corner, they'd crept quietly and kept close to the shadows, as though they didn't want to be seen.

Even at this distance, they could see the figure wore a skirt.

She wasn't watching them; she had her attention fixed firmly on the house midway down the row. Holding her arms stiffly down at her side, she started down the cobblestone street toward the house.

"Who is it?" Wiggins persisted. "And why's she creepin' about like she don't want to be seen?"

"Because she doesn't," Hatchet whispered. "Look, she's heading for the Geddy house." He had a strong feeling they'd better get closer. There was something about the stiff way the woman walked, something about her fixed attention on the house that sent alarm bells ringing in his head.

"What?" Smythe hissed. "You want us to get closer? But what if someone sees us?"

"We've got to risk it," Hatchet persisted. He didn't claim to be psychic or to believe in any of that sort of nonsense, but he knew if they didn't get moving, something awful was going to happen.

Smythe caught something of Hatchet's urgency. "All right, then, let's go." They moved farther out into the street and started walking toward the house. "But you're the one that has to come up with some kind of story when we're caught . . ." He broke off as he saw the woman reach the Geddy house. He also saw why she held her arms so stiffly at her side. She was carrying a revolver in her right hand.

"Blast a Spaniard . . ."

"I know," Hatchet gulped. "I saw it too. Wiggins, go for help. Run and get more police constables; I think we're going to need them."

Inside the house, Witherspoon had plunged ahead of the others. To his right, a curved archway opened into a small sitting room.

"Don't come any closer or I'll slit her throat."

Witherspoon skidded to a halt. The others did as well.

Lionel Bancroft was holding a terrified, middle-aged woman up on her knees by her hair. He held a long, wicked-looking knife at her throat. "I mean it," he snarled. His handsome face was contorted in rage and fear, his hair was askew and a trickle of blood dribbled down his nose.

The room was in a shambles. A chair was knocked over, cushions had been tossed off the settee, and the front of a china hutch had been smashed. The inspector realized that Frieda Geddy had put up a fight. Good for her.

"Let Miss Geddy go," he said calmly. "You don't want to be in any more trouble than you already are."

"Let me go, you great oaf," Frieda Geddy snapped.

"Shut up, you stupid bitch," Bancroft snarled. "It wasn't supposed to happen like this. It was supposed to be easy."

"Now, now, let's not be silly . . ." Witherspoon was terrified the knife was going to slip and sever the woman's neck.

"I said, let me go." Miss Geddy jerked her head to one side and Bancroft lost his grip on her hair. She jammed her elbow back and up as hard as she could. Bancroft screamed in pain, and the knife went flying to one side. Immediately, he was tackled by four policemen.

"Get off of me," Miss Geddy called as she tried to crawl out from the flailing arms and legs of London's finest.

"I've got him," Barnes yelled out. He grabbed Bancroft's collar and heaved the both of them to one side. The two other policemen scrambled to their feet and dived toward Bancroft, grabbing his arms and pinning them behind him.

Witherspoon disengaged his foot from under Freida Geddy's arm. "Are you all right?"

"I'm unharmed," she replied. They were both gasping for air as they staggered to their feet. "Thank God you were here. He tried to kill me . . ." She pointed at Bancroft.

"Take a moment and catch your breath," Witherspoon said. "You've had a dreadful shock."

"He was waiting inside my house," she gasped.

"Are you sure you're unharmed?" Witherspoon persisted as he ran his gaze up and down her person, searching for blood. Barnes, afraid his inspector might be hurt, had dashed over and was carefully, but surreptitiously doing the same to Witherspoon.

"I'm certain," she replied. She glared at Bancroft, who was standing between the constables, his expression defiant. "Why was he trying to kill me? Who is he?"

"He's a fool." The words came from the archway and were spoken by a woman.

Witherspoon and Barnes both whirled about. Eliza Nye stood facing them. She had a revolver in her hand. It was pointed at the inspector's head. "Lionel is a weak fool, but I'm not. I assure you, Inspector, I'll blow your brains out if you don't let us leave. I'm quite a good shot. I shan't miss."

Witherspoon swallowed heavily. There was a hard, crazed look in her eyes. A look that convinced him she was quite capable of doing precisely as she said. "You're already in enough trouble, Mrs. Nye. I suggest you put that weapon down and come along peacefully."

"Trouble?" she laughed. "Don't be a fool, Inspector. I'm going to hang. I stabbed my husband to death. Now do as I say, and no one will get hurt."

"You stabbed him?" the inspector exclaimed in surprise. He cast a quick glance at Bancroft. He wasn't quite sure precisely what was going on here, but he'd sort that out later. The important thing was to get everyone out of the house alive.

"Lionel was hardly up to the task," she sneered. "For God's sake, he can't even do in one lone middle-aged woman." She waved the gun at Miss Geddy. "But enough of this. Now listen carefully, Inspector. Order your men to release Lionel and do it now."

Witherspoon turned and nodded at the constables holding Bancroft. "Step away, lads. We don't want anyone getting hurt."

As soon as he was free, Bancroft raced across the room. "I was going to do it," he told her, "but the stupid bitch put up a struggle. What are we going to do now?" He and Eliza Nye stood with their backs to the door.

"We're going to kill them all and make a run for it," Eliza said bluntly. She took a step forward and aimed the gun at Frieda Geddy. "And she's going to get it first."

"You're a very rude and awful person," Frieda Geddy snapped, "and I certainly hope you'll rot in hell."

Witherspoon, holding out his arms, stepped in front of her. "I'm afraid I can't allow that to happen. Now, please, put the gun down before you hurt someone."

"Good God, you're an even bigger fool than Lionel," Eliza yelped. She leveled the gun at Witherspoon. "All right, then. As you're in such a hurry to die, let's have at it."

Suddenly, Bancroft screamed as he was brought to his knees by a flying tackle. Eliza Nye gasped and whirled around, leaping backwards a bit as the two grappling men crashed into her. Her arms flailed as she struggled to keep her balance. When she righted herself, she was staring down the short, blunt barrel of a derringer.

"Drop your gun, ma'am," Hatchet ordered her. "I assure you, I'm an excellent shot and even if I weren't, at this range, I couldn't miss."

Smythe drug Bancroft to his feet as the room went quiet and everyone's attention turned to the two people with guns. Hatchet's derringer was aimed at Eliza Nye's head, her revolver was down at her side. She hadn't a hope of aiming it before he fired. But still, she didn't drop it.

Eliza Nye and Hatchet stared into one another's eyes. The seconds ticked past and neither of them moved.

"You wouldn't shoot a lady," she said softly. "You're a gentleman."

"I assure you, madam," he replied coldly, "I would. Now drop your weapon."

She smiled slightly and dropped the gun onto the carpet. "I was wrong. You're not a gentleman."

"And you're certainly no lady," he said.

"Cor blimey, I almost fainted when I saw Hatchet take out that gun." Wiggins could talk about it now that they were safely back at Upper Edmonton Gardens. It was very late, closer to morning than midnight. Everyone, except for the inspector, who'd stayed at the station to finish his report, was gathered around the kitchen table.

"We didn't know what else to do," Hatchet said honestly. "We saw her go into the house, and she was holding that gun like she meant to use it. Smythe and I looked at one another and realized that we had to take action. None of the policemen in that house were armed. They couldn't defend themselves."

"It's a good thing we went in when we did," Smythe said. "She 'ad that bloomin' gun aimed right at the inspector's 'eart. All I could think to do was tackle Bancroft and hope that rattled Eliza Nye enough so she'd make a mistake."

"And she did." Hatchet closed his eyes briefly. "She lowered her gun enough for me to shove my derringer in her face."

"You got the drop on her," Luty clarified. Much as she'd have liked to give her butler a good tongue-lashing on his taking such stupid risks, she couldn't. If she'd been there, she'd have done the same. And truth to tell, she was downright proud of him.

"Do you think the inspector and Constable Barnes believed your story?" Betsy asked. She patted Smythe's arm absently as she spoke. She was so proud of him she could burst, but that didn't mean she didn't want to box his ears for putting himself in harm's way. But they'd talk about that privately.

"I don't know," Smythe replied. "By the time we got to the station, he was so busy takin' statements and chargin' 'em, I'm not sure what he thought."

"I think he was quite relieved when we arrived," Hatchet said. "Our explanation certainly sounded plausible. We went there simply to make sure that Miss Geddy wasn't in danger. After all, we knew the inspector and Barnes were on their way, Mrs. Jeffries and Betsy had gone to the station with a life-or-death message." He shrugged. "It certainly sounded reasonable to me."

"Yes and wasn't it a happy coincidence that you just happened to have your derringer because Luty insisted you carry it with you when you went out at night," Mrs. Jeffries added with a smile.

Luty snorted. "That's right, blame me. Come on now, Hepzibah, don't keep us in suspense anymore. How'd you figure out it was them two?"

"And how'd you know they was going to try and kill Frieda Geddy tonight?" Wiggins added.

"That part was easy," she replied. "I knew they had to move tonight. They couldn't afford for Miss Geddy to make the contents of that letter public. Not when they'd gone to all that trouble to kill Harrison Nye. When Betsy told us what she'd overheard, I realized they must have been keeping an eye on Frieda Geddy. Probably since Lionel Bancroft eavesdropped on Daggett and Nye the night of the murder."

"How'd you know it was her they was talkin' about?" Luty asked. "Betsy only heard that someone was comin' back from Holland."

"And you'd told us that Frieda Geddy spoke Dutch, and we knew that she was coming home tonight," Mrs. Jeffries explained. "I knew it couldn't be a coincidence. Once they knew that Oscar Daggett had confessed to what he and Nye had done to Miss Geddy fifteen years ago, they made it their business to find out where the woman was and when she'd be coming home."

"Because of the letter?" Hatchet asked.

"Right."

"Why didn't they do what we did and just break into her place and steal it?" Wiggins reached for another bun.

"They were afraid to go back to Dunbarton Street," Mrs. Jeffries replied. "They were afraid someone would see them. I think their plan was to give it a few weeks, to wait until the excitement about the murder had died down, and then steal the letter. But their plan was foiled when Miss Geddy decided to return home."

"I still don't understand how you knew it was them two," Mrs. Goodge said.

"I didn't until tonight." Mrs. Jeffries closed her eyes briefly, thinking of how close she'd come to getting the whole thing wrong. "It was only when Betsy told us about the footsteps on the back stairs and what she'd overheard at the Nye household that I put it all together. You see, they've planned it for ages."

"Who planned what?" Luty demanded. She didn't want to complain, but honestly, sometimes following what Hepzibah was saying was harder than chasing a pig through a corn patch.

"Eliza Nye and Lionel Bancroft. They've planned on murdering her husband for ages. I think they were actually going to do it the night he was killed—that's why Eliza Nye added the names of the Windemere brothers to the guest list. She wanted to make sure there were plenty of suspects for the police to worry about."

"You think she was going to kill him that night anyway?" Betsy asked incredulously. "Now that is a coincidence."

"Maybe not that night, but I think they were planning on doing it soon. That's why she wanted the Windemere brothers back in Nye's life. They were excellent suspects. When Wiggins told us that it was Eliza Nye, not her husband, who put those names on the list, I didn't understand what it meant. But today I realized she'd done it so the police would be looking at them instead of her. The fact that Oscar Daggett came along with his wild story about his confession only helped their plan along."

"But they didn't know about the confession . . ." Betsy frowned. "Did they? I mean, no one knew but Nye and Daggett."

"Yes they did," the housekeeper interrupted. "Lionel Bancroft got up from the dinner table, supposedly to go to the water closet. I expect he did no such thing; I expect he eavesdropped on Nye and Daggett. Also, remember, he'd hired a brougham for that night as well. I think he waited until Nye left, tipped off Mrs. Nye about the change in plans, then the two of them took off for Dunbarton Street."

"I wonder how she got out of the house?" Mrs. Goodge muttered. "The servants all saw her retire."

"And they were, no doubt, too busy cleaning up the dining room to notice that she'd slipped down the back stairs and out the back door. Remember, none of them dared disturb her once her door was closed for the night. That was quite a clever ruse on her part. I expect she'd done it a number of times. As a matter of fact, I imagine that every time Nye went out late at night, Mrs. Nye was hot on his heels and out the door herself."

"How do ya figure that?" Luty asked.

"I'm not certain, of course," Mrs. Jeffries admitted. "But when I found out about that enclosed staircase it all made sense. She needed time to plot and scheme with her cousin, but she could hardly do that in the house because the servants were around all the time. So what does she do? She gives him some nonsensical story about being a light sleeper and insists that no one disturb her after she's retired. Then she slips out whenever she wants by going through the dining room, down that staircase and right out the side servants' entrance. When I heard about the maid getting sacked over the nightdress, it made sense."

"Huh?" Wiggins frowned and scratched his nose.

"Mrs. Nye nipped out whenever her husband did to see her cousin. She kept a nightdress in a cupboard by the servants' back door, at least she did until one of the maids found it—what better than to toss a nightgown over your clothes and pretend to be sleepwalking. That way, if you were seen coming and going, you had an excuse at the ready so to speak."

"But he was her cousin. Why couldn't they see each other openly?" Betsy asked.

"Because they was always plottin' and tryin' to figure out the best way to kill 'im," Wiggins put in. "Like Mrs. Jeffries said, they daren't do that at 'ome. Someone might overhear 'em."

"But they've been married two years . . ." Smythe muttered.

"I don't think they've met all that many times," Mrs. Jeffries persisted. "But I think they definitely met up on the night of the murder, drove to Fulham in the brougham that Lionel had hired and stabbed him to death before he reached the Geddy house."

"She stabbed him," Hatchet muttered. "She said she didn't trust Lionel to do it right."

"But why?" Betsy persisted. "She didn't have it any worse than lots of other women. Why kill him?"

"Because I think she liked being in control. As long as she was married to Nye, she wasn't. Remember what you told us, Betsy, Nye let her spend his money, but he made her account for each and every penny," Mrs. Jeffries said.

"But why kill Frieda Geddy?" Mrs. Goodge persisted. "With her husband gone, what did it matter that he'd been a thief. She stood to inherit his money, she could have run off with Lionel whenever she liked."

"Maybe not," Mrs. Jeffries replied. "I'm not sure what the law is, but I believe if you build a fortune using money that was obtained fraudulently, which is what Nye did, then the fortune can be divvied up and parceled out to the victims of that fraud."

"In other words, with Oscar Daggett's confession, Frieda Geddy could tie up Nye's estate in court for years," Hatchet said with a satisfied smile.

"Well, we've solved another one." Wiggins leaned back in his chair and yawned. "I think we were right sharp about it too."

"Now we've just got to hope the inspector isn't too annoyed about what all has transpired tonight," Mrs. Jeffries murmured. She cocked her head to one side. "I believe I hear a hansom pulling up now."

They fell silent as they heard his footsteps crossing the hall and come down the stairs. "Yoo hoo," he called. "Is anyone up . . . oh good, you've waited up."

Mrs. Jeffries relaxed a bit. He didn't seem terribly upset. "Yes, sir. Of course we were keen to know what transpired at the station."

He yawned and took a seat next to Mrs. Jeffries. "Well, it was all a bit muddled at first, neither Bancroft nor Mrs. Nye would make a statement. Finally, Bancroft admitted that they'd conspired to kill her husband. It seems the two of them have been . . . ah . . . close for many years. He's completely in her power. Besotted with the woman."

"So he's confessed." Mrs. Goodge asked.

"Yes. But she hasn't. She hasn't said one word. I don't think she's going to either. She's quite a strong-willed woman. I don't believe she's quite sane." He sighed deeply, then looked around the table. "I want you all to know how deeply grateful I am. If you hadn't been concerned about the welfare of a woman you'd never even met and trotted along to Dunbarton Street to keep an eye on her, a number of us would all be dead."

"We were only doing what was right." Smythe blushed a deep red and looked down at the table.

"We were doing our duty," Hatchet added.

"Cor blimey, I was scared to death," Wiggins admitted.

Witherspoon held up his hand for silence. "All of you did far more than your duty and as for being scared"—he smiled at the lad—"so was I. But I do want to make something absolutely clear. I don't want any of you to ever put yourself in harm's way for me again. If something happened to any of you, I'd never forgive myself."

No one said a word. Finally, the inspector rose to his feet. "But then again, I sincerely hope never to be staring down the barrel of a gun again. Again, thank you all. I don't know what I've done to deserve such loyalty and friendship from all of you, but I want you to know, I thank God for you every single day of my life. Without you, I'd be a lonely middle-aged man living a life of terrible solitude."

Smythe had turned even redder, Betsy was dabbing at her eyes, Mrs. Goodge was choking back tears, Hatchet was holding himself so rigidly he looked like he was going to burst and Luty was staring at the tip of her shoe. Only Wiggins was looking at the inspector, and he was grinning from ear to ear.

Mrs. Jeffries rose to her feet and faced her employer. "Without you, sir, we'd be doing the same."

MRS. JEFFRIES PLEADS HER CASE

CHAPTER 1

"They won't get away with it," Harlan Westover muttered to himself as he charged into his flat and slammed his door shut. He winced at the noise and then remembered that Mrs. Lynch, his landlady, was out of town and wouldn't be bothered by his fit of temper.

Harlan tossed his overcoat onto the settee and stalked across the room to the desk in the corner. Yanking out a chair, he sat down, pulled out a piece of paper from the stack in the top cubicle, and grabbed his pen off of the brass inkstand.

He froze for a moment, frowning at the pristine white page and then shrugged. It didn't matter how he wrote the affair up, it only mattered that he got the facts correct.

For ten minutes the only sound in the quiet room was the scratch of his pen across the page. He paused, read what he'd written and then nodded in satisfaction. The prose wasn't elegant, but it told the tale well enough.

A knock sounded on his door, and he started in surprise. The nib of the pen slapped against his fingers, smearing the tips with ink. The knock came again, and without realizing it, he jerked and his stained fingers brushed against his shirt collar. He shoved the paper into the dictionary lying on the edge of his desk, put the pen back in the stand, got to his feet, and crossed the room.

Harlan opened the door. "What on earth are you doing here? Oh, I suppose you'd best come in . . ." he motioned for his visitor to step inside: "If you think to dissuade me from my course, you've wasted your time. There's nothing anyone can say that will stop me from doing what's right."

His visitor said nothing.

Confused by the silence, Harlan frowned. "Perhaps we'd best sit down," he started toward the settee. "Let me move my coat . . ." his voice trailed off, a strangled gasp escaped from his throat, and he toppled onto the plump cushions. A splatter of blood seeped out from the now-bleeding gash on the side of his head and dripped onto the dark paisley fabric of the overstuffed arm of the settee. Then his eyes closed and he lapsed into unconsciousness.

The visitor moved quickly and efficiently. It took only moments to rearrange Harlan's body. As he'd fallen awkwardly, the visitor found it easiest to prop Westover up at the other end of the settee. It was important to set the scene correctly. No one must suspect the truth.

Harlan Westover's visitor pressed a revolver into the unconscious man's hand and then positioned his arm so that the weapon was aimed at the bleeding gash where he'd been struck. The weapon fired once and he slumped to one side, his arm dangling over the end of the settee. The gun was strategically placed on the carpet, just below the man's fingers. It had to look like he'd dropped the revolver himself.

The guest smiled in satisfaction. Harlan Westover was most definitely dead. He wouldn't be telling anyone anything.

The household of Inspector Gerald Witherspoon was gathered around the table in the kitchen for their morning tea.

"I suppose it's just as well that we don't have a case, what with Luty and Hatchet being gone," Mrs. Goodge, the cook, said. She was an older woman with gray hair, wire rimmed spectacles, and a rather portly frame. She'd cooked in some of the finest houses in England but counted herself lucky to have ended up working for Gerald Witherspoon.

"Why'd they want to go off in the dead of winter?" Wiggins, the footman, asked. He was a handsome, brown-haired lad of twenty. He helped himself to a slice of bread and then reached for the butter pot. "Seems to me January is a miserable time to be crossing the Atlantic."

"They didn't have much choice," Mrs. Jeffries, the housekeeper, replied. "Luty's American lawyers insisted on the meeting. Apparently, she's got to make a number of important decisions regarding her properties in that country. She still has a number of investments in her native land."

Mrs. Jeffries was a short, vibrant woman of late middle age. She had auburn hair liberally sprinkled with gray, sharp brown eyes, a ready smile, and a mind like a steel trap.

Betsy, the pretty, blond-haired maid, tossed a quick glance at her fiancé, Smythe. He was a large, rather brutal looking man with dark hair, heavy features, and the kindest brown eyes in the world. He was also Inspector Witherspoon's coachman. Betsy and Smythe had been engaged for several months now and were devoted to one another.

Mrs. Jeffries ducked her head to hide a smile as she saw the quick, rather furtive glance the maid darted at her beloved. No doubt the two of them felt just a bit guilty when the subject of "investments" came up. Betsy, being Smythe's fiancée, knew the truth about him. So did Mrs. Jeffries. She was well aware of the fact that Smythe wasn't just a mere coachman, he was a very rich man with a legion of investments of his own. Every time the subject of money came up, these two squirmed like a couple of guilty puppies. Well, that was to be expected. Keeping secrets was often very uncomfortable, especially for such naturally honest souls as these two.

Smythe, interpreting Betsy's expression correctly, decided to steer the conversation to more comfortable waters. "Did they know 'ow long they'd be gone?"

"Luty hoped they'd be home by the end of the month. They'd like to come home at the end of the month on the *Corinthian*."

"That's a bit quick isn't it?" Smythe reached for a slice of bread. "What's the 'urry. You'd think they'd want to stay a bit. Doesn't Luty ever get homesick?"

"She's scared if they stay too long she'll miss a murder," Mrs. Goodge said bluntly. "Besides, Luty's lived in London for so many years, I don't think that she's got any reason to prolong a visit to America. She doesn't have any family there."

"Funny, isn't it, how so many of us don't 'ave much family," Wiggins said, his expression wistful, but then he looked up and grinned. "It's right that we've got each other, then, isn't it?"

"Indeed it is," Mrs. Jeffries said calmly. But the lad's remark had hit very close to home, she thought. She gazed around the table. Thank goodness they did have each other. They'd come together several years ago when Gerald Witherspoon inherited this house and a sizable fortune from his late Aunt Euphemia.

Smythe and Wiggins were already here, having worked for Euphemia Witherspoon in the capacities of coachman and footman. Even though the inspector had no need for a coachman and was far too informal to use a footman properly, he'd been too kindhearted to turn them out. Gerald

Witherspoon had had no idea how to run a large house, so he'd hired Mrs. Jeffries as his housekeeper. Mrs. Goodge, who'd lost her last position as a cook because she was getting old, had come along and finally, Betsy, half-starved and half-frozen had landed on their doorstep. Though Betsy had no proper training, once she'd regained her strength, the inspector had insisted on hiring her as a maid. They'd been together ever since.

"It's too bad we don't have a case," Betsy muttered. "It seems like a long time since we were out snooping about. It's getting a bit boring." And her beloved was beginning to pressure her to set a wedding date as well. Smythe was a wonderful man, and she loved him with all her heart, but when they weren't actively trying to catch a killer, he tended to forget they'd agreed to wait a bit for marriage. When they were in the midst of a case, he understood how important their investigations were to both of them.

"We just had one," Mrs. Jeffries pointed out. But the truth was, she rather agreed with the maid. Life was boring when they weren't on the hunt, so to speak. However, she did feel it was her duty to remind everyone that murder wasn't really the sort of thing one ought to wish for, regardless of how bored one was.

"That was months ago," Wiggins interjected.

"It was October," the cook said. "And it's wrong to wish someone would die just so we'd have a murder to sort out." Like the housekeeper, she felt morally obligated to defend the sanctity of law and order. But she did love their cases.

"I'm not wishing someone would die," Betsy protested. "I'm just sayin' life is more interesing when we're on a case."

"Of course it is," Mrs. Jeffries agreed. "But according to the inspector there's absolutely nothing on the horizon. He's spent the last week working on an alledged fraud against an insurance company. The only corpses that have turned up have been an elderly man freezing to death on a church porch and a suicide over on Charter Street off Brook Green."

"Someone froze to death outside a church?" Smythe shook his head. "That's disgustin'. Why didn't they do something for the poor old fellow?"

"Perhaps they didn't know he was there until it was too late," Mrs. Jeffries shrugged sympathetically. "The inspector didn't have many details, but there certainly wasn't any suspicion of foul play."

"How about the suicide?" Betsy asked eagerly.

"According to the papers, there was no indication of foul play there either, I'm afraid," Mrs. Jeffries sighed. "More's the pity."

"But you just said it were wrong to wish someone dead just so we'd 'ave us a murder to investigate," Wiggins said, his expression confused.

"I wasn't wishing this unfortunate person dead," she explained, "I was simply hoping it was murder. Suicide is such an ugly circumstance for a death. It's so difficult for the family and friends."

"And he'd be much better off if he'd been murdered," Mrs. Goodge added with a shake of her head, "at least then he'd not be roasting in hell."

Chief Inspector Barrows was a bit embarrassed. He didn't like having to be less than honest with one of his subordinates. But, of course, it wouldn't do to let his discomfort show. "So you see, Witherspoon, we'd best be very circumspect in this matter. Have a bit of a look around on the quiet, if you know what I mean."

"Actually, sir, I'm not sure that I do," Inspector Gerald Witherspoon admitted. "If the coroner's inquest has already ruled the man's death a suicide, I don't understand what it is you want me to do."

"We've some new evidence, Witherspoon. But it's evidence that can be interpreted any number of ways." He could hardly admit that the new evidence consisted solely of the dead man's landlady being utterly convinced that the victim wouldn't ever have committed suicide. But as the landlady was Chief Inspector Barrows's old nanny, he'd promised her he'd have another look at the case.

"What kind of evidence, sir?" Witherspoon asked.

"It's Westover's landlady," Barrows spoke carefully, hoping this most brilliant of detectives would actually understand the delicate political situation they were facing. Magistrates didn't particularly like having their inquest verdicts questioned, especially on this sort of evidence. "She came to see me. She's utterly convinced the fellow wasn't suicidal."

"Westover is the victim's name?" the inspector clarified. He was still a bit confused. If they had new evidence, it was perfectly permissible to ignore the coroner's inquest and open an investigation, mind you, some magistrates got a tad irritated when this happened, but justice had to be served. "I take it he's the fellow who shot himself in the head a couple of weeks ago?"

"Not according to his landlady. She's convinced he was murdered."

"On what evidence, sir?"

Barrows looked down at his desk and then back up at the inspector. "The only evidence she has is her knowledge of the man's character. She claims he wouldn't have killed himself under any circumstances. Harlan Westover was a Roman Catholic. I believe they consider suicide a mortal sin."

As far as the inspector knew, most Christians considered suicide a sin, but he wouldn't debate the point with his superior. "Why didn't his landlady give evidence at the inquest if she knew this?"

"She wasn't home," Barrows replied. "She only returned from the north yesterday evening. She was horrified when she found out her tenant had not only taken his own life, but that the inquest had already taken place and a verdict rendered."

Witherspoon nodded thoughtfully. "So the only new evidence we have is her assertion that he wouldn't have killed himself for religious reasons."

Barrows winced inwardly. As evidence, it was decidedly weak. "That's why I wanted you to have a bit of a look around on the sly, so to speak."

"I think that can be done, sir," Witherspoon nodded. "I'll be very discreet. There's no point in upsetting the apple cart at this stage, sir."

"It's not very good evidence, I'm afraid," Barrows said.

"I wouldn't say that, sir," the inspector replied. "Obviously, the victim's landlady felt strongly enough about it to come and see you. It could well be that she's absolutely correct." But she probably wasn't. Roman Catholic or not, the physical evidence at the scene had indicated suicide to the investigating officers. Still, Witherspoon felt he ought to keep an open mind. "What is the landlady's name?"

"Helen Lynch." Barrows's austere face broke into a smile. "Actually, she's my old nanny. She's expecting you this morning. You're in luck, Witherspoon, she's not touched the flat since she's been home, so the crime scene hasn't really been disturbed. I'll write out her address."

The inspector nodded and pushed his spectacles, which had a tendency to slip down his nose, back into place. "Westover died two weeks ago, right?"

"Correct, the report says it was probably January sixth." Barrows looked up from his writing. "Nanny Lynch returned from Galway on Saturday evening. She came to see me last night."

"So the murder, if indeed murder is what we have here, is a fortnight old," the inspector frowned. "The trail's a bit cold . . ."

"I'm aware of that," Barrows laid down his pen. As all policemen knew, the longer it was between the crime and an investigation, the harder it was to catch the killer. Witnesses forgot pertinent information, important details were overlooked, and physical evidence was destroyed or mislaid. "Look, Inspector, I know we're at a distinct disadvantage here, if, as you noted, a murder has taken place. But as I've already told you, the crime scene's not been touched and as far as I know, Westover's solicitors haven't begun divying up his property."

"Did he have any relations?" Witherspoon asked.

Barrows shrugged. "I don't know. Why don't you go along and have a chat with Nanny Lynch. Westover had been her tenant for the last three years. She can tell you all about him."

"Yes sir," he reached over and picked up the paper with Nanny Lynch's address on it. "I'll take Constable Barnes and pop along to see her straight away. Er . . . uh . . . how discreet do I need to be sir?"

Barrows stroked his chin thoughtfully. "I'll leave that up to you, Inspector."

"Right sir," Witherspoon nodded respectfully and then left. Barrows slumped in his chair. He had a moment of misgiving about this whole business. Witherspoon might be his most brilliant homicide investigator, but the fellow had the social acumen of a tree stump. Sometimes Barrows wondered if the fellow wasn't just a bit backwards, not stupid or anything that harsh, but a bit like one of those terribly sad defective individuals who couldn't tie their shoes but could do multiplication and long division without any trouble at all. Barrows had attended a lecture last year about the subject. He shook himself to dislodge the thought. Witherspoon was the best homicide detective he'd ever seen and a decent chap to boot. But he did hope that the fellow had the good sense to keep a low profile on this investigation, at least until they got some conclusive evidence.

"Do you think there's anything to this, sir?" Constable Barnes asked as they rounded the corner off Shepherds Bush Road and started up Charter Street towards Helen Lynch's house.

The constable was a craggy-faced veteran of London's streets. He'd walked the beat for years before he'd joined up with Inspector Witherspoon. Under his policemen's helmet, his hair was iron gray and his mind as sharp as a razor.

"I don't know," Witherspoon sighed and pulled his heavy topcoat closer against the cold, winter wind. "From the report I read, there doesn't seem to be much in the way of clues."

"If you ask me, the report wasn't very thorough," Barnes complained. "Just a few pages of notes and no witness interviews at all. Here we are, sir." He opened the gate and started up the stone walkway to number 6.

Helen Lynch's house was a neat, two-story red brick affair with a small, enclosed front garden and white lace curtains at the bow front windows.

"The report wasn't very detailed," Witherspoon agreed as they reached the front door. "But then again, the officers were under the impression they were dealing with a suicide. The doors were all locked from the inside, and there was no indication of a struggle." But privately, Witherspoon thought the chief officer assigned to the case had done a very shoddy job.

Barnes reached over and banged the heavy brass knocker. A moment later, the door opened and an elderly, gray-haired woman peered out at them. "So you've finally arrived, have you? It's about time. I told Neddy to get right on this." She stepped back and gestured for them to step inside.

Witherspoon smiled at the idea that 'Neddy' was their austere Chief Inspector Barrows. "Good day, ma'am, I'm Inspector Gerald Witherspoon and this is Constable Barnes." They stepped inside to a small foyer crowded with a wooden coat tree, a huge ceramic umbrella stand, and a trestle table holding a giant potted fern. A staircase with thick, brown carpet was next to the table. "I take it you're Mrs. Lynch?"

"That's correct," she nodded curtly. "Give me your coats and hats, please." They shed their outer garments and handed them to their hostess. Witherspoon noticed there were three large umbrellas in the white and blue stand. He wondered if one of them belonged to Harlan Westover.

"Come along then," Mrs. Lynch ordered, "let's go into the sitting room. Mina will bring us tea. It's so cold outside. But then again, it's the middle of winter so I suppose we can't expect sunshine."

She led the way down a short hall and into a large, nicely furnished sitting room. A fireplace and mantel were on the far wall, and opposite was a rose-colored settee with white antimacassars along the top. On each side of the settee was a straight back chair, with maroon upholstering on the backrest and the seat. The wallpaper was a cheerful rose and green paisley against a white background, and there was a pale gray carpet on the floor. Two huge potted ferns, stood on pedestals at each side of the door.

"Sit down, gentlemen," Helen Lynch gestured toward the settee and the chairs. "I'm sure you've a lot of questions to ask me. I didn't mean to be rude earlier, but I do want this resolved as quickly as possible. Mr. Westover did not commit suicide. I can't imagine why anyone would think he did."

Witherspoon nodded and took one of the chairs. Barnes took the other one, leaving the settee to their hostess. The constable whipped out his little brown notebook. The inspector cleared his throat, but he wasn't quite sure where to begin. Then he remembered something his housekeeper was always saying, "You're so very clever, sir. You always go right to the heart of the matter." Of course, that's where he ought to start.

The door opened and the maid came in, pushing a tea trolley. "Here you are, ma'am," she put the trolley in front of Mrs. Lynch.

"Thank you, Mina." She dismissed the maid with a nod and then looked at the two policemen. "How do you take your tea?"

"Sugar and milk for both of us," Barnes answered quickly. Despite the fire, he was feeling the cold.

She nodded, poured and handed them their cups.

Witherspoon took a quick sip of the warming brew. "Thank you, this is wonderful. Mrs. Lynch, why are you so convinced that Mr. Westover didn't commit suicide?"

She sighed impatiently and put her own cup down on the trolley. "I've already told Neddy . . ."

"Yes, I know that," he replied, "but if you don't mind, I'd like to hear it from you. Learning information secondhand, so to speak, isn't as efficient as hearing it directly from a witness."

She raised an eyebrow. "Is that what I am, then? A witness."

"A very important one, Mrs. Lynch," Constable Barnes interjected. "So far, you're the only one who's come forward with any information at all about this case . . ."

Mrs. Lynch interrupted him with a loud snort. "Seems to me if the police had done their job properly, there'd have been any number of witnesses that could have told you plenty. That's what I told Neddy, too. You've left it a bit late now, and you'll be lucky if anyone can remember seeing or hearing anything about poor Mr. Westover's murder."

Witherspoon rather agreed with her, but he could hardly admit it. "Uh, Mrs. Lynch . . ."

"I know, I know," she waved him off impatiently. "You're still waiting to hear why I'm so convinced it was murder. To begin with, right before I went off, Mr. Westover told me he was going on holiday next month.

People who are planning on killing themselves don't make plans to go on holiday."

"Mr. Westover was going on holiday?" Barnes looked up from his notebook. "At this time of year?"

She nodded eagerly. "He was going to go to Sicily. He said it was warm there and he needed to get away from his work. He'd been working dreadfully hard. Some days he'd leave before dawn and not get home till late in the night. I believe he'd actually booked his tickets."

"Do you know where he booked them?" Barnes asked.

Mrs. Lynch shook her head. "I never thought to ask. Why? Is it important?"

"It could be," the constable looked back down at his notebook.

"What kind of work did Mr. Westover do?" Witherspoon asked. He knew from his quick look at the report that he'd been employed at an engineering firm somewhere nearby.

"He was an engineer," Mrs. Lynch replied. "Quite a clever one too. He worked for a firm off the Kensington High Street. Donovan, Melcher, and Horrocks."

"Did Mr. Westover have any family?" Constable Barnes asked. "There wasn't mention of anyone in the corner's file or the police report."

"He really hadn't anyone," Mrs. Lynch smiled sadly. "He never married, and both his parents were dead. There are a couple of cousins in Bristol, but he hadn't had any contact with them in years."

"No brothers or sisters?" Witherspoon pressed. Like the constable, the inspector wanted to have some idea about who might be likely to benefit from Mr. Westover's death. Generally, the person who benefited the most was someone near and dear to the deceased.

"No, Inspector. As I've said. He was quite alone in the world. It's sad. He was a very nice man. He would have made some woman a good husband. But he was one of those men who are married to their work. Honestly, there were times when he'd be poring over those funny papers of his, and I swear, he'd not hear a word I'd say."

"Funny papers?" Witherspoon wondered what on earth she meant.

"Oh, you know, these funny papers with drawings of all sorts of newfangled nonsense on them," she retorted. "I asked him once what they were, and he told me they were his designs for some sort of engine. Proud of it, he was. He spent a good half hour explaining how the ruddy thing worked, and I had to stand there and pretend to understand what he was going on about." She broke off and looked away. "I wish now I had understood. He was so proud of that silly engine, and all I wanted to do was to get back to my kitchen and have a cup of tea." She sniffed and swiped at her cheeks with her hand.

The inspector cringed inwardly. She was crying. He was hopeless at dealing with weeping women. He'd no idea what to do.

"Mrs. Lynch," Barnes said softly, "don't take it so hard. You weren't to know he was going to die."

She drew a long, deep breath and straightened her spine. "You're right. Of course I didn't know, and he could go on and on about his work."

"Was that the only thing he ever spoke about?" Witherspoon asked. He was grateful that Barnes had gotten her to stop crying.

"Of course not, Inspector. He was devoted to his work, but he read the newspapers. He could talk about what was going on in the world. I miss him very much and not just because he always paid his rent on time and took care to be considerate."

"I take it you and Mr. Westover were quite . . . er . . . friendly," the inspector stumbled over the last few words. He didn't want to imply anything that might offend the lady. She was, after all, his chief inspector's old nanny.

Mrs. Lynch laughed. "Of course we were friends. He was lonely. He spent many an evening in my front parlor chatting with me in front of the fire." She shook her head and smiled wistfully. "I shall miss him. I guess you could say, we were both a bit lonely."

"Was Mr. Westover your only tenant?" Witherspoon asked.

"No, Mr. Baker has the rooms on the top floor. But he's not here very often, he travels for his work. So usually, it was just Mr. Westover and me. He took all of his meals here. Mind you, recently, he'd missed supper a good deal of the time because he'd been working so hard." She stopped and seemed to shake herself. "So tell me, Inspector, what are you going to do about his murder?"

"Ah, Mrs. Lynch, I'm not quite sure . . . uh, so far the only evidence you've given us that the poor fellow was murdered is that he was planning on going on holiday . . ."

"That's not all," she interrupted. "There's a bit more than that. I know Mr. Westover didn't kill himself. He couldn't. He didn't own a gun. So how did he come to blow his brains out then? Answer me that!"

"The inspector's a bit late this evening," Betsy said as she came to stand next to the housekeeper in the front parlor. "I wonder what's keeping him." Neither woman would ever admit it, but they did worry just a little when he was delayed. He was, after all, a policeman, and that wasn't the safest occupation in London.

The housekeeper cocked her head toward the window. "I believe I hear a hansom pulling up outside." She stepped close and yanked the heavy velvet curtain to one side. "Oh good, it's the inspector. He's finally home."

"Should I pop down and get his dinner tray?" Betsy asked as she started toward the door.

Mrs. Jeffries hesitated. "Wait here for a few moments, let's see if he's hungry." Because he was a good hour and a half late, she suspected something might be in the wind. If that was the case, her dear inspector might want a glass of sherry and a nice chat before he had his meal.

The front door opened and Witherspoon stepped inside. His narrow face brightened. "Good evening, Mrs. Jeffries, Betsy."

"Good evening, sir," she held out her hand for his hat. "You're a bit late, sir. Was the traffic terrible?"

He gave her his bowler and started to unbutton his heavy black overcoat. "Traffic was bad," he sighed, as he slipped the garment off his shoulder, "but no worse than usual. I'm afraid I'm late because . . . well, I'm not quite sure how to put this, but I think there might have been a murder."

Behind the inspector's back, the two women exchanged glances. "Shall I go down and get your dinner tray, sir?" Betsy asked.

"I believe I'll have a sherry first," Witherspoon replied. "It has been a very tiring day."

Mrs. Jeffries took his coat and hung it just below his hat. "Come along into the drawing room, sir. A sherry is just what you need. Betsy, why don't you bring up the inspector's tray in about fifteen minutes."

"That'll be perfect," Witherspoon replied. Betsy nodded and hurried off toward the backstairs. Mrs. Jeffries knew that the moment the maid got to the kitchen she'd tell the others to be "at the ready," so to speak.

She led the inspector the short distance down the hall and into the drawing room. He immediately went to his favorite armchair and sat.

She moved to the sideboard, pulled a bottle of *Harvey's* out of the bottom cupboard and poured him a glass.

"Do pour one for yourself as well," he called to the housekeeper. "You've probably had a tiring day too."

"Thank you, sir." She poured another for herself, picked up the glasses, and made her way across the room. Handing him his drink, she said, "Now sir, what's all this about a possible murder?"

Witherspoon sighed and took a sip of his sherry. "It's all the chief inspector's doing. It seems his old nanny came to him this morning all in a dither about stories that one of her tenants had taken his own life."

"The suicide," Mrs. Jeffries murmured aloud as she thought back to the conversation she'd had with the others earlier in the day.

"The suicide," the inspector repeated her words. "How did you hear about it?"

Mrs. Jeffries caught herself. "Oh, I didn't really, sir. It's just that the only thing that's been in the papers the last few weeks is a suicide and an accidental death." She held her breath, praying he wouldn't realize how closely she and the others watched the papers. She couldn't have him suspecting she'd been nosing about, trying to see if he had anything interesting on his plate. "I'm sorry, please do go on."

"You're right. It was the suicide." He took another quick sip. "The chief inspector had me go around and have a quick look-see because he didn't wish to disappoint his old nanny."

"His old nanny?"

"It was her tenant that supposedly took his own life. But honestly, Mrs. Jeffries, I think Mrs. Lynch is right."

"You mean you think her, er . . . lodger was murdered?" She forced her face to stay blank and her tone calm. But inside, her spirits soared.

"Well," he hesitated. "I can't be sure. But she did make a rather interesting point. A few days before Mr. Westover's allegeded suicide, Mrs. Lynch thinks he booked tickets for a long holiday. As Mrs. Lynch pointed out, one doesn't spend all that money for a trip to Italy and then kill oneself."

"Was that her only reason for thinking his death was murder?" She wanted to make sure she got all of the details out of the inspector.

Witherspoon pursed his lips. "No, she claimed that Westover didn't own a gun and therefore, couldn't have killed himself with one. I didn't want to upset the dear lady by pointing out that revolvers are quite easy to acquire."

"But as far as she knew, he didn't have a weapon," Mrs. Jeffries said thoughtfully.

"Correct," the inspector's brows drew together. "She also insisted that Westover wasn't in the least depressed about anything and that he was positively looking forward to the future."

"What, precisely, were the circumstances of the death?" Mrs. Jeffries took another sip of her sherry.

"Actually, I uh, didn't read the file very carefully. I didn't have much time, you see." Witherspoon was so embarrassed he fibbed just a bit. He'd read every word of the file, but he didn't want to admit to anyone, even Mrs. Jeffries, how little information the investigating officer had obtained. "But the long and short of it is, Harlan Westover died of a gunshot wound to his head. The gun was found lying on the carpet right under his fingertips. This happened almost a fortnight ago."

"A fortnight!" She hadn't realized it had been quite that far back. The newspaper account had only appeared last week.

"My sentiments precisely," the inspector shook his head. "The trail, if indeed there has been a murder, is exceedingly cold. But it couldn't be helped. Mrs. Lynch only arrived home herself a couple of days ago. She was quite shocked when she realized that not only had her lodger died, but the coroner had already made a ruling and the case was considered closed."

"Who discovered the body?" Mrs. Jeffries asked. The case had just begun, and it was already a bit muddled.

"A man named James Horrocks, he's the general manager of Westover's firm. When he didn't arrive at work the next day and didn't send a message, they got concerned and went around to his rooms."

"How'd they get in if the landlady was gone?"

Witherspoon's brow furrowed. "You know, I'm not sure. I don't think the report mentioned how Mr. Horrocks got inside. I shall make a note to follow up on that question. However, be that as it may, the fellow got inside, saw what had happened, and then fetched the police. You know what happens after that. The cornoner's inquest ruled the death a suicide, and the case was closed."

"Does Mr. Westover have any family?" Mrs. Jeffries asked.

"Just some distant cousins. From what I gathered from Mrs. Lynch, he didn't stay in contact with them. According to her, he was quite alone in the world. Of course, Mrs. Lynch might not know the extent of his relations."

"Does he have an estate, sir?" Might as well get that aspect out into the open, she thought. People who stood to inherit were frequently those who most had reason to want someone dead. "Even if he's no family to speak of, someone's got to inherit his things."

Again, the inspector frowned. "I don't really know. I suppose I ought to go around to his rooms and see if I can find the name of his solictor." He sighed and tossed back the last of his sherry. "I do hope it isn't a murder, because if it is, the case is already a bit of a mess. Frankly, Mrs. Jeffries, I've not a clue about what's the best way to go about this investigation. The fellow died two weeks ago. Any witnesses there might have been have disappeared. The crime scene has been mucked about, and we don't even know if anyone heard the gunshot that killed the poor man. Where does one begin?"

Mrs. Jeffries understood her employer's dilemma. At the best of times, he wasn't overly burdened with self-confidence. Trying to track down a possible murderer under these circumstances would be a daunting task for anyone.

But she knew what he needed. "You begin where you always do, sir," she said briskly. "With the victim. Learn the victim, and you'll find the killer, that's what you've always said, sir."

"Really?" He sounded genuinely surprised. "I said that?"

He'd said no such thing, of course. But it was sound advice. "Of course you did, sir. You mustn't let a little thing like a delayed investigation make you feel you're not up to the task. Why you know you're absolutely brilliant at catching killers, even killers that think they've gotten away with it." And that would be the case now. If Harlan Westover had been murdered, his killer wouldn't be expecting an investigation at this stage of events. That might just work to their advantage.

She stopped, aware that she was already thinking of the case as a murder. She mustn't do that. Not yet. Not until they knew for certain one way or the other.

"Thank you, Mrs. Jeffries," he brightened immediately and got to his feet. Talking his cases over with his housekeeper always made him feel so much better. She was such a good listener. "I'm flattered by your confidence in me and shall do my best to live up to it."

"But of course you will, sir." She led the way toward the dining room. "Now, sir. Why don't you have your dinner? I'm sure you'll feel much better with something in your stomach."

CHAPTER 2

Mrs. Jeffries questioned the inspector further as he ate his roast beef and mashed potatoes. When he'd finished off his treacle tart and retired to his rooms, she dashed down to the kitchen. Betsy and the others were ready for her. Within minutes, they had the dining room cleared and the dishes done. Then they took their usual places at the kitchen table.

"All right then, have we got us a murder or not?" Mrs. Goodge asked as she lowered herself to her chair. She was eager to begin. She'd helped with the cleanup, even though the others had protested. She might be getting old, but she could still do her fair share.

"It's a bit difficult to say," Mrs. Jeffries hated to dash their hopes, but she had to be truthful. "How much has Betsy told you?"

"Just that the inspector said 'e might 'ave a murder," Wiggins replied.

"So do we or don't we?" the cook persisted.

"I'm not sure," the housekeeper said quickly. "Do you remember that suicide we talked about earlier today? It turns out that perhaps it might have been a murder after all. Chief Inspector Barrows has asked our inspector to have another look at the matter."

"But I thought the papers said that there weren't any signs of foul play," Smythe reminded her.

"Apparently, the papers might have been wrong," Mrs. Jeffries nodded, "and it appears the coroner's inquest may have been a bit hasty in their verdict as well. Therefore, I suggest we assume we've a murder investigation to conduct. The inspector didn't know much at this stage, but I did learn a few facts." She leaned back in her chair, took a deep breath, and gave them a full report.

When she'd finished, the room fell silent as they thought about what they'd just heard. Wiggins shook his head. "Seems to me there ain't no doubt. Fellow was murdered all right."

"Don't say 'ain't'," Betsy told him absently. Like the others, she was thinking of all the questions that needed to be answered.

"I don't know that I like this one," Mrs. Goodge muttered darkly. "Murder or suicide, it's been two weeks . . ."

"The inspector's concerned about that as well," the housekeeper said. "But that certainly shouldn't stop us. We've worked on cases like this before. Providing that is, that everyone wants to give it a good try." She'd bet the next quarter's household money that everyone would want to have a go at it.

"But what if it was a suicide?" Smythe complained. "We don't want to be runnin' about wastin' our time over nothin'."

"As I said, I think we ought to go on the assumption that it's murder. Although he wouldn't come right out and admit it, I think Inspector Witherspoon believes the police investigation wasn't very thorough."

"And his landlady felt so strongly that there'd been a gross miscarriage of justice, that she went to the police," Betsy said firmly. "That's good enough for me."

"Me too," Wiggins added. "This Mrs. Lynch went to the trouble to make a bit of a fuss. The least we can do is snoop about a bit and see what's what. Besides, it's not as if we've got anythin' else on our plates."

Smythe laughed and threw up his hands in mock defeat. "All right, all right, I wasn't sayin' we oughn't to put our oar in, I was just thinkin' we might try and get a few more facts before we make up our minds for sure."

"I agree," Mrs. Jeffries said.

"What do you want us to do first?" he asked her. "This one's goin' to be a bit 'arder. The trail's probably cold as a banker's heart."

Mrs. Jeffries thought for a moment. "This case does have a rather unique set of circumstances, but we mustn't let that assume too much importance in how we proceed. I think we ought to do precisely what we've always done in the past."

"Concentrate on the victim," Mrs. Goodge nodded in agreement.

"Right then," Smythe got to his feet. "I'll get along to the local pubs and see what I can learn about Westover."

"Wouldn't it be better if you started with the hansom drivers?" Betsy asked. "Seems to me that the more time that goes by, the dimmer memories are going to get. Whoever did the killing had to get to the Lynch house that night. Maybe they took a hansom."

He gave her a lazy grin. "I can do both. You just don't want me hangin' about in pubs flirtin' with the pretty barmaids."

"Don't be daft," she gave him a saucy grin of her own. She knew her beloved hadn't even looked at another woman since their engagement. "You do better with hansom drivers than you do with pretty barmaids. They're too busy pulling beer to have time to talk."

"I'll pop along to the Lynch neighborhood and see what I can learn," Wiggins volunteered. "Maybe someone's maid or footman saw something the night he died."

"We don't know that he was killed at night," Mrs. Jeffries pointed out. "His body wasn't found until the next day when he didn't show up at work. Westover might have been killed the previous day."

"This isn't going to be an easy one," the cook frowned ominously. "I can feel it in my bones."

"To be fair, Mrs. Goodge, none of 'em are ever easy," Smythe said dryly.

"True, but on the others we've generally known whether it was murder or not. Or when they were killed or that they had a whole pack of scheming relatives who wanted them six feet under. But this Westover fellow doesn't even have that, just a couple of cousins in Bristol. Where do we start? That's what I want to know."

Mrs. Jeffries could understand Mrs. Goodge's frustration. The cook did her investigating in a far different manner than the rest of them. She needed names. Lots of them. A veritable army of informants trooped through her kitchen. Give the cook the suspects' names and she could pry every last morsel of gossip there was to be had about any of them. Rag and bones men, chimney sweeps, laundrymen, delivery boys, and even street arabs could all be found eating buns, drinking tea, and talking their heads off in Mrs. Goodge's kitchen.

The cook also had a vast network of old colleagues and associates she could call upon when needed. She'd worked in a number of places in her many years of service.

"Why don't you see what you can find out about James Horrocks," Mrs. Jeffries suggested.

"You mean the one that found the body?" The cook's frown deepened. "But he was just Westover's employer. Why would he want him dead? Seems to me if he didn't like the fellow it would be much easier just to sack him."

Everyone laughed.

"You're right, of course," Mrs. Jeffries said. "But according to what Mrs. Lynch told the inspector, Westover spent most of his time at work. Besides, it's as good a place to start as any."

"I'll go along with Wiggins tomorrow and have a word with the local shopkeepers," Betsy said.

"And I'll have a word with Dr. Bosworth," Mrs. Jeffries told them. "Perhaps he'll be able to give us a bit more information about the circumstances of the victim's death."

Wiggins got up. Fred, the black and brown mongrel dog who'd been lying on a rug by the door to the hall, leaped up as well. He trotted over and nuzzled the footman's hand. "All right, fella, we'll go for a walk now." He grinned at the others. "If this does turn out to be murder, Luty and Hatchet'll 'ave a fit that they missed it."

The offices of Donovan, Melcher, and Horrocks were located on the first floor of a three-story white stone building on the Kensington High Street. Inspector Witherspoon and Constable Barnes sat in the reception area of the outer office. They shared the room with three clerks who were sitting at desks behind a low counter. The clerks sat hunched over ledgers and papers, but they couldn't have been getting much work done, they kept sneaking glances at the two policemen.

"I'm sure someone will be right with you," the lad nearest to the inspector muttered. "I told Mr. Horrocks's private secretary that you're here."

On the far side of the room a door opened and a dark-haired man, with a huge handle bar mustache, stuck his head out. He stared coldly at Witherspoon and Barnes. "You may come in now, Mr. Horrocks will see you."

Annoyed at the fellow's tone, Barnes gave him a good frown, but the inspector simply nodded. They followed the secretary down a long hall and past the open doors of the other offices, all of which were empty. They came to the door at the end, and the secretary knocked once, opened the door, and led them inside.

They entered a large office with pale green walls, brown carpet, and three narrow windows looking out on the High Street. At the far end of the room there was a round table with a map of England on the wall. A mahogany desk with two straight-back chairs in front of it was opposite the door. Sitting behind the desk was a bald man with narrow shoulders and a long nose. "I'm James Horrocks," he said.

"I'm Inspector Gerald Witherspoon, and this is Constable Barnes," he said as they went toward the desk.

Horrocks motioned for them to sit down and then looked at his secretary. "This oughtn't to take long, but do see that I'm not disturbed."

"Yes sir," he withdrew, closing the door quietly behind him.

"Why have you come?" Horrocks asked bluntly.

The inspector decided to be just as blunt. "We're here to ask you some questions regarding Mr. Harlan Westover."

"Westover?" Horrocks frowned. "I gave testimony at the coroner's inquest. Dreadful business, but I told them everything I know. Westover's death was a suicide, so I don't understand what questions you could possibly need to ask now."

"Well, uh . . ." Witherspoon knew he had to be careful. There was no need to stir up sentiments against the police if one could avoid doing so. "There are a few areas that weren't covered quite as well as they should have been." Drat, what made him say that? He certainly didn't want to imply that the police had been lax in their initial investigation. Even if it were true.

"What things? The police asked me all sorts of questions when it happened."

"Of course they did, sir," Barnes interjected. "But additional evidence has come to light, and we would be remiss in our duty if we didn't investigate further."

"What additional evidence?" Horrocks leaned halfway across his desk. "What are you talking about? What evidence?"

"We're not really at liberty to say," Witherspoon replied, he shot his constable a grateful look. "But we do hope we can count on your cooperation."

"Cooperation. I never said I wouldn't cooperate," Horrocks blustered. "This is a dreadful business. Dreadful I tell you. Most upsetting for all of us."

"I'm sure it has been, sir." The inspector took a quick, deep breath and tried to remember the questions he needed to ask. "How long has Westover worked for your firm?" Egads, that wasn't what he'd meant to ask.

"Three years," Horrocks replied. He pursed his lips and looked out the window. "He came to us from a small firm in Birmingham. He was our chief engineer."

"What sort of things do you make here?" Barnes asked.

"We don't make anything here," Horrocks said. "This is just our offices. But we've a small factory on Watling Street in Stepney. We make engines. Mainly used in mining operations."

"Did Mr. Westover have any enemies?" Witherspoon asked. That was always a good question.

"No, of course not. He worked hard, got along well with his staff, and minded his own business."

"Can you tell us how you came to go to his rooms the day you discovered the body." That was another good one.

Horrocks shrugged his narrow shoulders. "I got concerned when he didn't show up that morning. Westover was a very punctual man—hard worker. When it went half past ten and we'd heard nothing from him, I knew something was wrong, so I went to his rooms in Brook Green and . . ." his voice trailed off and he looked out the window. "You know what I found."

"How did you get into the house?" Barnes asked softly. "His landlady wasn't home."

"The door was unlocked," Horrocks admitted. "I knocked and when no one answered, I went inside and up the stairs to his rooms."

Witherspoon's brows drew together as he tried to recall what the original report had said. "Was the door to his rooms locked?"

"Oh yes, but the key was right there, so when he didn't respond to my knock, I unlocked the door and went inside."

Barnes looked up from his notebook. "Where, exactly was this key?"

"On the floor," Horrocks replied. "It was just lying there on the carpet. Almost as if someone had dropped it."

"What did you do when you found the body?" Witherspoon wanted to get the sequence of events just right. He wasn't sure why it was important, but he knew it was, and he'd learned to trust his instincts in these matters. As his housekeeper frequently told him, "Let your inner voice guide you sir, it's never wrong."

"What did I do? I went for the police, of course. I'm no expert on these matters, sir, but even I could see that something dreadful had happened and Harlan was dead." Horrocks dropped his gaze to the desk. "It was quite shocking, Inspector."

"When was the last time you'd seen Mr. Westover?" Witherspoon asked.

"Alive?"

"Uh, yes."

"It was the day before he died. He was in his office, working." Horrocks cleared his throat. "Is that all? I do hate to be rude, but I've a very important meeting scheduled . . ." he looked up as the door opened. "Yes, Jackson, what is it?"

"It's Mrs. Arkwright, sir, she's here."

"Then go get Mr. Arkwright," Horrocks ordered.

The secretary winced. "He's gone to Birmingham, sir. Remember, he went to see about the strivets. Mrs. Arkwright is a bit upset, sir. She insists that Mr. Arkwright was supposed to meet her here. I, uh, don't really know what to do with her."

"I suppose she's causing a commotion," Horrocks sighed. "Send her in here, then. I don't want her upsetting the staff. God knows there's been enough turmoil about the place lately."

"Yes, sir," Jackson disappeared and Horrocks smiled apologetically at the two policemen. "I'm sorry, but I shall have to deal with Mrs. Arkwright. She's the wife of one of our general partners. I expect she's gotten a bit muddled about something . . ."

The door opened and a tall, attractive middle-aged woman stepped into the office. She paused just inside the doorway and surveyed the scene out of a pair of dark brown eyes. Beneath an elegant hunter green veiled hat, her hair was the same dark color as her eyes. Her full lips curved into a half-smile. "Oh dear, it appears I'm interrupting something important. I'm sorry."

James Horrocks had risen from behind his desk. "Not at all, dear lady. Not at all, it's always a delight to see you. These gentlemen were just leaving."

Witherspoon shot a quick look at Barnes. The constable shrugged. The inspector realized they probably weren't going to get much more out of Horrocks, so he got to his feet. "Actually, Mr. Horrocks, we do have a few more questions for you, but we'll be happy to speak to you a bit later. Right now I'd like a word with the rest of the staff."

Horrocks, who'd been coming out from behind the desk, stopped in his tracks. "The staff? Why do you want to speak to the staff?"

"It's routine, sir," Barnes assured him. "We've just a few general questions."

"Oh dear," Mrs. Arkwright said. "Are these gentlemen here about that dreadful business with Mr. Westover?"

"I'm afraid so," Horrocks said as he continued toward Mrs. Arkwright. "I'd hoped that was all behind us."

Witherspoon turned to Mrs. Arkwright. "I'm Inspector Gerald Witherspoon, and this is Constable Barnes. You didn't, by any chance, happen to see Mr. Westover on the day he died, did you?"

It was a silly question, and the inspector regretted asking it as soon as the words were out of his mouth.

"Now see here, Inspector," Horrocks blustered. "Mrs. Arkwright barely knew the man . . ."

"It's all right, James," she soothed. She gave the two policemen a dazzling smile. "Actually, I did see Mr. Westover that day. I'd come to have luncheon with my husband. He was going to take me to Wentworths after the board meeting. We saw Mr. Westover as we were getting a hansom downstairs. I must say, he looked quite angry about something."

Witherspoon jerked his head toward Horrocks. "You had a board meeting? Was Mr. Westover in attendance?" He'd no idea what prompted him to ask the question, but ask it he did.

Horrocks scowled. "I don't think we're obligated to make the police privy to our internal company affairs. But yes, we did have a meeting, and yes, Mr. Westover was in attendance. As I told you, he was our chief engineer."

"What was the meeting about?" Barnes queried.

Horrocks gaped at them. "What was it about? I don't really see that it's any business of the police . . ."

"It's our duty to investigate suspicious deaths, sir," the inspector replied. "And everything about Mr. Westover's day might be important." Drat, he thought, that was hardly being subtle. But gracious, it was difficult to be subtle and still get any information out of anyone. Besides, he was getting a feeling about this case. There was something about this "suicide" that simply didn't feel right. As his housekeeper was always telling him, he must have faith in his feelings and instincts. She seemed to think the whole mysterious process was really just his mind gathering information and prodding him along a certain path. He'd no idea what caused him to get these "ideas" when he was on a case, but he'd learned to trust them.

"I'd hardly call Harlan Westover's suicide a suspicious death," Horrocks snapped. "The man blew his brains out in a locked room."

"With a key found just outside the door," Barnes added. "A key that could have been used and then dropped by anyone."

Mrs. Jeffries smiled sweetly at the tall, red-haired man coming out the side door of St. Thomas's Hospital. He caught sight of her and immediately turned in her direction.

"Mrs. Jeffries, how very delightful to see you. I do hope you've come to see me," Dr. Bosworth said.

"Of course I've come to see you," she replied. The good doctor had helped on several of their cases. There was no need to be coy with him. "But if this is an inconvenient time, I can come back later."

"That won't be necessary. My last appointment didn't show up, and I've a bit of free time." He laughed in delight, took her arm, and started off. "There's a tea shop up the road. Let's go have a cuppa, and we can have a nice chat about why you've sought me out."

They crossed the Lambeth Palace Road to a small café tucked around the corner on Crosier Street. Dr. Bosworth pulled open the door to the café, ushered her inside, and seated her at a table by the window. A few moments later, he was back bearing two cups of steaming tea. Placing one in front of her, he sat down and smiled at her. "What's this all about? Another murder?"

Mrs. Jeffries sighed. "I think so, but to be honest, we're not sure."

"Not sure?" Bosworth repeated. "Goodness, this is intriguing."

"You see, the coroner's inquest ruled the death a suicide."

"There's already been an inquest?" Bosworth interrupted.

"I'm afraid so."

"So there isn't a body . . ."

"It's already been buried," she said. She knew why he'd asked the question. In several of their other cases, Dr. Bosworth had been able to examine the victim before the autopsy and before the coroner's inquest. Bosworth had spent several years working in America. He had some rather revolutionary ideas about how close observation of the wounds could give one information about the cause of death. He was of the opinion that one could ascertain from the wound what kind of weapon had been used to do the killing, and sometimes even the precise time of death could be known. Dr. Bosworth had come to his conclusions after working for two years under a doctor in San Francisco. Apparently, there were plenty of gunshot, knife, and bludgeoning victims in that part of the world. "But we're hoping you'll be able to read the autopsy report and give us your opinion."

He raised an eyebrow. "I'm flattered by your faith in my abilities, Mrs. Jeffries. But a report isn't the same as an actual examination. How did the death occur?"

"He used a gun."

Bosworth frowned. "Messy business, guns. What's the victim's name?"

Mrs. Jeffries gave the doctor all the information she'd learned from the inspector. Bosworth listened carefully, occasionally stopping her to ask a question. When she finished, she leaned back in her chair. "Well, what do you think? Is there any chance you might be able to find out anything useful from the police surgeon's report."

"That depends on how thorough the surgeon was," Bosworth shrugged. "Do you know who it was?"

"I'm afraid I don't, but the victim died at home and he lived in Brook Green near Shepherds Bush. Is that of any use?"

"That means the body was probably taken to West London Hospital on King Street for the postmortem. I've a good friend that works there, he can probably get me a copy of the report. I'll tell you what, I'll have a go at it today and see what I can find out." He finished off his tea and rose to his feet.

Mrs. Jeffries did the same. "Shall I call around to see you later in the week?"

"That won't be necessary," he grinned. "I'll contact you straightaway if I've got any useful information."

"Thank you doctor, I don't know what we'd do without you," she replied gratefully.

He laughed. "Oh, I've no doubt you'd do very well, Mrs. Jeffries. Very well indeed."

Wiggins drew his heavy coat closed and then reached down and patted Fred on the head. "You doin' all right, fella? I know it's cold out 'ere, but we've got to 'ang about a bit longer if we're goin' to find us someone to talk to."

Fred wagged his tail and pranced about on the cold footpath. Wiggins sighed and looked up at the row of houses on Charter Street opposite Brook Green. So far, no one had so much as stuck their heads out this morning. Cor blimey, he thought, you'd think someone along the street had to do a bit of shopping or something . . . but no, he'd been here almost an hour, and he'd not seen hide nor hair of anyone. If this kept up, he'd not have anything to report this afternoon at their meeting.

In the house directly opposite him, the curtain in the front window jerked to one side. "Oh blast, Fred," Wiggins muttered. "That bloomin' curtain is twitchin' again. Maybe we ought to get movin'." Nonchalantly, he tried to edge further onto the green. "I don't want anyone rememberin' we was 'ere." Like the others, Wiggins knew the importance of being discreet when he was out investigating one of the inspector's cases.

Keeping his eye on the curtain, he and Fred headed across the footpath. He wished he'd brought Fred's ball along. Playing with the dog would have looked less suspicious than just hanging about.

He breathed a bit easier as he and Fred reached a bench in the center of the green. At least now no one could see him from the street. He decided to have a sit down and think what to do next.

"You're wastin' your time, you know. She's gone home." The cheery voice came from behind him.

Startled, he whirled around and saw a young girl gazing at him. She wore a thin overcoat and a wool hat that had definitely seen better days. The strands of hair escaping from the hat were dark brown, her skin was pale and spotty and her eyes were hazel. "What's the matter," she challenged, "has the cat got your tongue."

"I beg your pardon, miss," he replied. He wondered if she'd mistaken him for someone else. "But I don't know what you're on about."

"Oh who do you think you're foolin'?" she laughed. "Louise said you'd be comin' around. Mind you, it took you long enough. She went home last Thursday on account of her gran takin' ill. We expected you to come 'round the back, though, not hang about in front of the house for the whole world to see. The missus will have a fit if she finds out, but I expect you know that."

Wiggins hadn't a clue what to do. On the one hand, the girl was out here talking to him. On the other hand, it was clear she had mistaken him for Louise's young man. Wiggins decided to go along with the charade for a bit longer. Inquisitive girls like this one were just the right sort to have seen something that might be of interest to him. "Sorry, I guess I should 'ave gone around the back, but, uh, I didn't want to run into the mistress."

"There'd be no chance of that. The missus don't poke her nose into the kitchen before noon. But it's just as well you didn't. That nosy Olga's been hanging about all morning. Anyway, I've got to get a move on, I've got to get to the butcher's."

"Can I walk along with ya?" He asked quickly.

"Why?" She looked at him suspiciously. "There's no more that I can tell you. Louise has gone back to Wales. We don't know if she's even comin' back. The missus knows, but she'll not lower herself to tell us." She started off down the footpath.

"I've got to get back to work myself," he began as he fell into step next to her.

"You've got a position, then?" the girl asked eagerly.

"Uh, yes."

"What kind of a position is it? Oh, it's too bad that Louise isn't here. She'd be ever so thrilled you finally got work."

Blast a Spaniard, Wiggins thought, now he had to keep on lying. Maybe he ought to just wash his hands of this. It was getting a bit messy. "Well, actually . . ."

"Did you get that job down at the rubber factory, then?" she continued. "Louise said you were trying to get on there."

"Uh, no, I got another one." He had an idea. "I got it a couple of weeks back . . ."

She stopped and stared at him. "Louise didn't say anythin' about you having a job before she went home."

"She didn't know," he replied. "I tried to tell her, but she were so full of her own news I never got a word in edgewise."

The girl looked doubtful. "What news? Nothin's happened to Louise acceptin' her granny gettin' sick."

"News don't have to be just what happens to you," he forced himself to laugh. "She told me all about that neighbor of yours that blew his brains out."

"Oh that." The girl pursed her lips. "I don't see why Louise would be excited about tellin' that. Fellow did a suicide."

"That's not what Louise heard," Wiggins fervently hoped Louise stayed in Wales, he was about to use her name shamelessly. "She said she'd 'eard it were murder, not suicide."

"Murder," the girl repeated. "She must have been havin' you on. Even the police said it were a suicide. I know, because Louise told me she heard the gun go off herself and she never said anything about a murder."

"Louise never said anything to me about hearin' a gunshot. If she heard so much, why didn't she go fetch a policeman?" Wiggins countered. He'd no idea how the events surrounding the death had unfolded, but that didn't stop him. He had the girl talking and that was all that mattered.

"Fetch a policeman? Not bloomin' likely. She's not one for stickin' her nose in other people's business," the girl said defensively.

"Cor blimey, she hears a gun go off, and she thinks she'd be a nosy parker if she went for the police," Wiggins shook his head in disbelief.

"She thought it was them lads over on Dunsany Road settin' off some explodin' bon-bons left over from Guy Fawkes. It's happened before, so she claimed she didn't take much notice until the next day when she saw the coppers comin' and goin' about Mrs. Lynch's house."

"About what time did she 'ear this gunshot?" Wiggins pressed.

The girl stopped and gave him another long, suspicious look. "What's your name?" she asked abruptly.

"What do ya mean, what's my name . . ." he sputtered. Cor blimey, what a time for the lass to start asking questions.

"I didn't stutter," she shot back. "Now tell me, what's your bloomin' name? I don't think you're Louise's feller at all. I think you're just some stranger hangin' about the green and havin' me on."

"I wasn't 'avin' you on, I'll admit I was 'angin' about as you put it," he protested, "but well, uh . . . the truth is I've been wantin' to meet you. When you come out and thought I was this 'ere Louise's feller, well, I uh just went along with it." Cor blimey, he was lying through his teeth. He held his breath, hoping she'd believe him. He knew he wasn't a bad looking lad, but he didn't value himself so highly as to think every young woman he met found him attractive. Still, it was all he could come up with on the spur of the moment.

Her expression softened. "You've been wantin' to meet me," she repeated. "Why?"

"Uh, I saw you the other day walking down the street, and I thought you looked ever so nice," he shrugged. "But if you want me to leave you in peace, I'll be off . . ." he picked up his pace and shot ahead of her. "I'll not stay where I'm not wanted."

"Wait," she called. "Wait please. Uh, I don't mind if you walk with me."

Blast a Spaniard, he thought, he'd been half-hoping she'd let him go on about his business. His conscience had apparently jumped out of its matchbox and was now poking at him uncomfortably. He had no right to lead this poor girl on just to get information. But this was about a murder, he argued with himself. Killers didn't have the right to go unpunished. He stopped, turned, and looked at her. She smiled hopefully, and he felt like a worm. "Are ya sure? I don't want to be forward . . ."

Her smile widened. "It's all right, you look like a nice lad, and I'd like the company. What's your name?"

For a split second he considered lying. "Wiggins." He couldn't do it. "What's yours?"

"Marion." They started walking again. "Marion Miller. Uh, do you live 'round here?"

He hesitated. "I work over near Holland Park," he finally admitted. "I'm a footman. 'Ow about you?"

"I'm a maid," she replied. "I work for the Cuthberts. They've got the biggest house on the street. There was four of us worked there, me, Louise, Olga, and cook. Now there's just me and Olga doing all the maid work. Cook's lazy, she won't get off her arse and do anything but prepare meals." She clamped a hand to her mouth. "Oh, that sounded awful, I didn't mean to be coarse . . ."

Wiggins laughed. "Not to worry, I don't think you're coarse. I know what you mean, though. Lots of households work a body to death. Where's the butcher shop?"

"Up on Shepherds Bush Road," she replied. "It's only a few minutes walk."

"I know that area," he said. "There's a café on the corner. Have you got time to stop for tea and a bun?" Wiggins had plenty of coin on him. It was odd, too. He always kept a bit of change in his top drawer, but no matter how often he dipped into it, the pile never seemed to get any smaller. Truth was, it seemed to grow a bit everytime he looked at it. Maybe he ought to mention it to Mrs. Jeffries. But then again, maybe he was just being fanciful.

"I'd like that," Marion's eyes brightened. "I like buns. We don't have them much at the Cuthberts's house. I can't stay too long, though. I've got to get the chops back to cook before luncheon, but they'll not miss me for half an hour or so."

"Sorry, but I can't 'elp ya. I don't remember takin' any fares to Charter Street or Brook Green." The driver untied the horse's reins from the railing of the cabmen's shelter. He shrugged apologetically at Smythe and mounted the cab. "Try talkin' with Danny Leets. He was workin' that night too. He might remember something."

"Where can I find 'im?" Smythe asked.

"Hang about a bit, and he'll be along soon."

"Thanks," he called as the cabbie pulled out into the traffic. Smythe looked around the busy neighborhood. This shelter was just across from Shepherds Bush station, at least a half a mile away from the Lynch House, but it was the closest one. He leaned against the lamppost and peered down the road, hoping to see a cab headed his way. There were omnibuses, carts, water-wagons, broughams, and four-wheelers, but not a hansom in sight. Blast a Spaniard, he didn't want to hang about here much longer, but he'd not had any luck at the pubs around Brook Green either. He was meeting the others in an hour, and he was sure they would have plenty of information. He didn't want to be the only one to show up empty-handed. Just then, a hansom pulled by a huge bay came around the corner. Maybe it was Danny Leets, and maybe, just maybe, he remembered taking a fare to Westover's rooms on the day of the murder.

The cab pulled up at the shelter and a big, burly fellow with a ruddy, pockmarked complexion climbed down.

"Are you Danny Leets?" the coachman asked.

The man's blue eyes narrowed suspiciously. "Who wants to know?"

"Me. I'm not a copper or a crook. I just want to ask ya a couple of questions." He reached into his pocket and pulled out a wad of pound notes. "I'll make it worth yer while."

The cabman's eyes cut to the cash. "I'm Danny Leets. What can I do for ya."

Mrs. Goodge hummed as she set a plate of brown bread in the middle of the table. She couldn't wait for the others to get here. She glanced at the clock and saw that it was almost four. They ought to be coming in soon. She put the butter next to the plate of bread, checked that the roast was cooking properly in the oven, and then put the kettle on the burner.

She'd been so depressed after the others had gone out this morning. She'd been sure she wouldn't find out anything about the murdered man. But goodness, as luck would have it, she'd struck gold on her first try. She glanced at the laundry hamper by the hall door. Thank goodness for delivery boys, especially ones that did deliveries to the same neighborhood where the murder'd been committed. Mrs. Goodge hummed as she flicked a crumb of bread off the tabletop. Oh yes, she simply couldn't wait till the rest of them got here.

CHAPTER 3

The last one to arrive for their meeting was Mrs. Jeffries. She dashed into the kitchen, taking off her hat and coat as she walked. "I'm so sorry to be late, but there was an accident at the upper end of Holland Park, and it tied up traffic for ages." She tossed her outer garments onto the coat tree and took her usual place at the table.

"We've not been waiting long," Mrs. Goodge said as she poured a cup of tea for the housekeeper. "Wiggins has only just got back himself."

Wiggins nodded in agreement. "I was late too, Mrs. Jeffries, and the silly thing about it is I've not found out a thing about our Mr. Harlan Westover. Cor blimey, it were 'ard enough tryin' to find someone to talk to about the bloke, and when I finally did, she didn't know a bloomin' thing about the poor feller." He'd been bitterly disappointed. He'd thought from what she'd told him that he'd learn the time of death. But closer questioning had revealed that the absent Louise hadn't mentioned anything useful to Marion Miller.

"Don't take it to heart, lad," Smythe said. "I've not 'ad much luck either."

"It's still early days yet," Mrs. Jeffries said stoutly. In truth, she'd not learned anything useful either, and from the comments Dr. Bosworth made about police reports, she suspected that even when he'd read the thing, she still wouldn't know much. She cast a quick look around the table as she sipped at her tea. Betsy was frowning at the tabletop, Smythe looked irritable, and Wiggins was slumped in his chair. The only one who looked at all chipper was the cook. "From your faces, I don't think any of us have had much luck except, perhaps, Mrs. Goodge."

"I've learned a thing or two," the cook replied. She pushed the plate of brown bread toward the housekeeper. "I don't know how useful it is, but at least it's a bit of a start."

"That's better than I've done," Betsy muttered. "I talked to every shopkeeper in Shepherds Bush and Brook Green. I didn't hear anything about Westover. No one had heard of the man until he died. Mrs. Lynch does all the shopping for that household. He's not so much as bought a tin of tobacco."

"Don't fret, lass," Smythe smiled at his fiancée. "We'll find out what we need to know. As I said, I didn't find out anythin' either. Westover doesn't seem to 'ave ever set foot in the local pubs."

"Did you have a chance to speak to any hansom drivers?" Mrs. Jeffries asked. Whoever murdered Westover had to have gotten there on some means of conveyance.

"I spoke to a couple of 'em," he admitted, "but no one remembered takin' a fare to Westover's neighborhood on the day 'e died. Maybe our killer walked to the house." His chat with Danny Leets had been useless. The bloke had taken his cash and then not known a ruddy thing.

"That's possible. I take it you're going to keep trying," Mrs. Jeffries reached for a slice of bread.

"There's a couple of drivers I didn't get a chance to talk to. I'll 'ave another go at 'em tomorrow."

Mrs. Jeffries smeared butter on her bread. "Mrs. Goodge, you're the only one who doesn't have a long face. Would you like to share what you've learned?"

"Oh, it's not all that much," Mrs. Goodge said modestly. "But I'll give it a go. Actually, it was almost an accident that I found out anything. I was sitting right here trying to get something out of George Wilkes, you know him, he's the one who delivers the heating fuel. Well, he'd nothing to say at all. He just sat here, stuffing his face with my treacle tarts, when the laundry lad brought back our sheets. The lad overheard me asking George about the 'suicide' over on Brook Green. Luckily, Henry's got no manners . . ."

"Is Henry the laundry boy?" Betsy interrupted.

"That's right, he overheard what I was asking George, and he jumped right into the conversation." The cook laughed. "He said he'd seen Westover on the day it must have happened. He remembered because he was dragging out a huge hamper from the house next door to Mrs. Lynch's when Westover came charging past and almost knocked poor Henry on his backside."

"So all he did was see the man?" Smythe asked.

"Give me a minute," she retorted. "I'm getting to the interesting part." She took a quick sip of tea. "Harlan Westover came charging down the street so hard he barged right into the hamper. Henry didn't see him coming, and he was ever so surprised when all of a sudden a man comes flying over the top of the lid."

"He actually flew over the hamper?" Wiggins asked. He glanced at the household hamper, which was still by the door leading to the back stairs. "Cor blimey, that thing's as big as a trunk. That must 'ave 'urt."

"I expect it did. But when Henry tried to help him up, Westover brushed him off and said for him not to worry, that it was Westover's fault for not paying attention to what he was doing. Then he took off towards his house." The cook looked around the table expectantly, but all she saw was blank stares. "Well, don't you understand? That proves it was murder."

No one said anything. Finally, Mrs. Jeffries said, "I don't quite follow you . . ."

Mrs. Goodge sighed. "Maybe I'm not saying this right, but Henry said he was sure that the man was angry about something . . ."

"He were angry about takin' a tumble over a silly laundry basket," Smythe suggested. "His pride were smartin'."

"No, no," the cook protested. "Hold on, now. Give me a minute so I can get this right. You know how you can get impressions of how people are feeling without actually having them say anything." She paused. "Well, Henry was sure that Westover was boiling mad about something, and it were something that had him so rattled he wasn't watching where he was going. That's why he banged into the hamper in the first place. Because he was so furious, he wasn't payin' attention to his surroundings."

"But why does that make you think he didn't kill 'imself?" Wiggins asked.

"Because he was angry that day, not despairing," she replied. She smiled smugly. "That proves he wouldn't have taken his own life. Angry people don't kill themselves."

Mrs. Jeffries wasn't so sure about that, but she didn't want to quell the cook's enthusiasm. This case could use as much enthusiasm as it could get. "That's a very interesting point of view, Mrs. Goodge. Do you happen to know what time all this took place?"

"Around two o'clock. Henry remembered, because by rights, he shouldn't have been there at all that time of day. Usually he dropped off clean laundry early of a morning. But there'd been a problem and they'd not done their deliveries until the afternoon. That's why he remembered, they was watching the time real close so they could get done by nightfall."

"How did he know it was Westover?" Betsy asked. "Had he met him before?"

"Saw him every week when he delivered the laundry to the Lynch household," Mrs. Goodge replied. "Henry said Mr. Westover was a nice man, always greeted him kindly and had a word or two with the lad."

Mrs. Jeffries thought for a moment. "Why didn't Henry come forward at the inquest and tell them what he knew?"

The cook shrugged. "I didn't think to ask him. But I imagine Henry's the sort who didn't give the incident another thought until he heard me talking about the coroner's verdict in the newspapers. By then it was too late. Besides, he's not the sort to go running to the police unless he had to."

"You're right, that was a silly question. Of course he wouldn't have gone to the inquest." Mrs. Jeffries said. She knew most of London's poor and working class had a real distrust of the police and the courts. Often, they had good reason for their misgivings. "Do you have anything else for us?"

"No, but now that I know Westover was hopping mad, I've got my feelers out."

"For what?" Wiggins asked.

"For whatever had happened at his office," the cook replied. She saw that the others were listening intently.

"How do you know something happened at the office?" Betsy asked. "Maybe something happened to make him angry on his way home."

"I don't know what happened where," the cook retorted. She reached for the teapot. "But I've got to start somewhere, and considerin' the state Westover was in when he went barreling into the laundry hamper, I'm willing to bet that it wasn't something like missing the omnibus that had him in a right old state."

"Do you have any names?" Mrs. Jeffries didn't beat about the bush. "Because if you don't, I should be able to get the names of his work colleagues out of the inspector."

"I've just got the one—you know, Horrocks, the man who found Westover. But it's a place to start."

"I agree," the housekeeper replied. "I expect that's where the rest of us ought to put our efforts as well. Let's have a quick meeting tomorrow morning before we get out and about. By then I'll have spoken with the inspector and we ought to have a few names to track down."

Betsy frowned. "You don't want us to concentrate on Westover's neighborhood?"

"You haven't had much luck with the local shopkeepers," Mrs. Jeffries pointed out.

"I know," the maid admitted. "But he was killed in his rooms, not his office."

All of a sudden, Fred leapt up, barked once, and charged down the hall toward the back door. Wiggins dashed after him. "What's got into you, boy?" he called. "Cor blimey, there's someone at the door." They heard the back door open. "Hello, we've not seen you in awhile. When did you get home?"

They heard the low murmur of voices and the sound of footsteps. A moment later, Wiggins and a blond-haired, middle-aged woman came into the kitchen, Fred trotted at their heels, his tail wagging furiously as he paid his respects to one of his favorite people, Lady Cannonberry.

"Good gracious," Mrs. Jeffries rose to her feet. "Ruth, it's so good to see you. Do come in and have tea with us."

"I hope I'm not interrupting," she replied. "I only got home an hour ago. I simply had to come over and say hello. It's been ages since I've seen you."

Lady Ruth Cannonberry was the widow of a peer of the realm and their neighbor. She was also the daughter of a minister and had a highly developed social conscience as well as a politically radical point of view. Though titled and wealthy, she insisted all the Witherspoon household call her by her Christian name of Ruth. She and Inspector Witherspoon had been developing a very special relationship. Unfortunately, family duty had called her out of town frequently in the past two years, so her and the inspector's friendship hadn't progressed very far.

"Indeed it has," Mrs. Jeffries agreed, "but we're glad you're back. Are you in town for long?"

"I'll get another cup and plate," Betsy smiled and got to her feet.

"Sit right 'ere next to me," Wiggins patted the empty chair to his left. "We've missed you, you know. Are you goin' to stay about for a bit now that you're back?"

Ruth laughed and sat down. "I hope so. Uncle Edgar is on the mend, so I think I'm at home for the foreseeable future. Unless, of course, someone else in the family thinks it's their turn to take ill."

"You've 'ad a spate of bad luck, that's for sure." Smythe said. He liked the lady very much and hoped she'd hang about long enough for her and the inspector to renew their friendship. Now that he and Betsy had their understanding, he was convinced that the rest of the world would be much happier if paired off properly.

"Thank you," Ruth said as she took a cup of tea from Betsy. "I know I should have given you some warning instead of just popping around, but I did so want to see what you've all been up to lately. Have you had any good murders?"

Unfortunately, Ruth, like several others of their acquaintance, had also guessed that the staff had been helping the inspector. When she was in town, she frequently volunteered her services. The others, however, were wary of involving her too closely. It wasn't that they didn't trust her, that wasn't the case at all. They simply didn't want to do anything to harm the budding (albeit slowly) relationship between her and the inspector. Sneaking about behind his back asking questions about his cases could most definitely be considered a hindrance to a harmonious friendship.

Before Mrs. Jeffries could give a nice, noncommittal reply, Wiggins blurted out. "We've got us one now, but we don't know 'ow good it's goin' to be. So far, we've 'ad the piker's worst luck on findin' out anythin'."

"How exciting." Ruth's smile widened. "I got back just in time. I can help you."

"That's very kind of you," Mrs. Jeffries said quickly. "But we don't want to put you to any trouble, especially as you've just got back. You must have much to do in your own household."

"And there's all your social obligations," Mrs. Goodge added.

Ruth waved them off. "I've nothing to do, the butler makes sure everything works properly whether I'm at home or not. As for my social obligations, why, that's the very best sort of places for one to start asking questions. Now, who got killed?"

Mrs. Jeffries was at the front door when the inspector arrived home. Within moments, she had him comfortably seated in his favorite chair in the drawing room. "Dinner will only be a few moments, sir," she said as she handed him a glass of sherry.

He took a sip and closed his eyes. "Oh, this is very nice. Aren't you having one?"

"I believe I will, thank you." She poured one for herself and took the seat opposite him. "So, how did your day go?"

He sighed. "Not very well. So far, we know absolutely nothing except that the fellow is dead."

"Oh dear, I'm sure you must know more than that, sir. It's always this way at the beginning of an investigation."

"I suppose you're right," he took another sip. "But honestly, getting information out of people is very difficult. You'd think they'd want to help the police, not hinder them. Take for instance today, we went along to have an interview with James Horrocks. Frankly, the fellow could barely tear himself away from work long enough to even speak with us. Then, when we did start getting a bit of information out of him, we were interrupted by one of the partners' wives . . ."

"Which one," she interrupted.

"Which one," he repeated. "Oh, it was Mrs. Arkwright. She'd gotten a bit muddled about where she was to meet her husband. But that's beside the point, actually, now that I think of it, it was perhaps a good thing that Mrs. Arkwright interrupted us."

"How's that, sir?" Mrs. Jeffries prompted.

"If she'd not said something, we'd never have known that on the day Westover died he'd been at a board meeting." He sighed. "I don't think Mr. Horrocks would have volunteered that information on his own. Gracious, he didn't even want to tell us where he was on the afternoon of Westover's death. We were halfway out the door before we could get it out of the fellow." He shook his head. "Mind you, as alibis go, his is very weak."

"Really?"

"He says he went to lunch at a local pub and then went to look at some property he's thinking of buying near Shepherds Bush. It's an office building on the Goldhawk Road."

"Then the estate agent can vouch for his whereabouts," she ventured.

"I don't think so. He's already told us he only looked at the outside. Claims he didn't want anyone to know he was interested in purchasing the leasehold on it."

"What about the pub?"

"We'll send a lad to check it tomorrow. But pubs are dreadfully crowded that time of day. Besides, he eats there all the time, they'll not remember if he was there on any particular day."

"Which pub was it?" she asked. She'd make sure she got the name to Smythe at their next meeting.

"The Kings Head," he answered. "It's just around the corner from the office." He sighed. "This is going to be a very difficult case."

"Not at all. So far, you've been very astute, sir," Mrs. Jeffries said. Her mind worked furiously, and she took a quick sip from her glass to gather her thoughts.

Witherspoon stared at her, his expression confused. "I'm not sure I understand what you mean?" If he'd been astute, he wasn't aware of it.

She laughed. "Now don't tease me, sir. I'm on to your methods. You know perfectly good and well that you've learned something of great importance. Why, obviously this board meeting is pertinent to your case, because, as you've just pointed out, Mr. Horrocks quite deliberately didn't tell you about it."

"Er, uh, yes, you're right. He wouldn't have mentioned it at all if Mrs. Arkwright hadn't blurted it out." He nodded sagely. "As a matter of fact, once she did tell me about it, Mr. Horrocks became most unreasonable when I started asking questions about it. Most unreasonable, indeed." He went on to tell Mrs. Jeffries every little detail of his day. In the telling, he became more and more convinced that something was indeed amiss in Harlan Westover's death.

The next morning, she told the others what she'd learned from the inspector.

"Well, it's something, I suppose," Betsy said. "Do we know who all was in that board meeting?"

"Yes, we do," Mrs. Jeffries replied. "The entire board was present. Oliver Arkwright, he's the general secretary, Harry Donovan, he's the chairman, and of course, the general manager, James Horrocks. There's another general partner, Lawrence Melcher. He doesn't have a title but he's on the board. The only other person present was Harlan Westover."

"How long did the meetin' last?" Wiggins asked. He'd no idea why he needed to know, but he felt it was important.

Mrs. Jeffries hesitated. In truth, she'd not thought to ask. "I don't know. I'll see if I can find out from the inspector."

"We ought to be able to find that out ourselves," Betsy said confidently. Now that she had a direction to go in, she felt much better.

"I'm glad you think so," Mrs. Goodge commented.

"It'll be easy. People work in the office, someone's bound to have noticed when the meeting started and stopped."

"That's an excellent place to start," Mrs. Jeffries nodded approvingly.

"Seems to me we'd best be worryin' about what went on in the meetin'," Smythe muttered. He was thinking hard. It would cost a lot to find out what went on behind the closed doors of a board meeting. Luckily, he had plenty to spend. After he'd paid a visit to the Kings Head pub in Kensington, he'd go along to the docks. This might be a job for Blimpey Groggins.

"Oh, I've no doubt we'll find out what went on in the meeting," Mrs. Jeffries replied. "It's been my experience that a closed door doesn't stop secrets from getting out."

"Did the chief inspector agree with you, sir?" Constable Barnes asked softly as he and Witherspoon went down the stairs of the station house.

Witherspoon frowned. "Actually, he seemed a bit annoyed when I told him I thought the case warranted further investigation. I've no idea why. You'd think he'd be pleased that his dear old nanny was right."

Barnes stifled an amused smile. Sometimes the inspector was so naive. Of course the chief inspector wasn't going to be pleased to find out that not only had a coroner's inquest given the wrong verdict, but that they'd apparently done so based on a very slip-shod investigation by the police. The force had barely started to recover from all that Ripper ruckus, it wouldn't look good when and if the press got hold of the fact they'd botched another investigation. Barnes cut a quick look at Witherspoon. He knew something that his inspector didn't, and he wasn't sure if he ought to mention just yet.

"I do hope he's not going to be too hard on the lads that did the initial investigation," Witherspoon said as they stepped out the front door and started across the cobblestone courtyard. "On the face of it, the death did look like a suicide."

The constable decided to keep his secret for a while longer. In the near future, he might need a decent bargaining chip or two. They came to the curb and looked down the busy road for a hansom. Barnes spotted one discharging a fare down the block, and he waved at the driver. "Nonetheless, sir, they did rush to judgment. Even a cursory investigation would have revealed there was something odd about the death. A suicide can't leave a key on the other side of a locked door."

The cab pulled up, and Barnes reached for the handle. "Number 14 Sussex Villas, South Kensington," he called to the driver and then turned back to Witherspoon, "and all they'd have had to do to know that fact was to ask the right questions. Horrocks told us about the key straight away."

"I wonder why he didn't mention it to the constables when he was first questioned?" Witherspoon climbed into the hansom. "Perhaps I ought to ask him. It might be important."

"I agree sir," Barnes swung in next to the inspector. "But more importantly, we've got to find out how that key got on the other side of the door."

"Oh, that's easy," Witherspoon waved his hand. "The murderer dropped it."

They discussed the case the rest of the way to South Kensington. Barnes paid off the cab, and they made their way up a short walkway to a tall, brick house in the middle of a row of town houses. The steps were freshly painted, the brass door lamps polished to a high sheen, and there wasn't so much as a weed in the small patch of garden behind the ornate wrought-iron fence. Witherspoon banged the knocker and a moment later the door opened. A short, plump woman wearing a black housekeeper's dress smiled out at them.

"Good day," the inspector said politely. "We'd like to see Mr. Oliver Arkwright, please. I'm Inspector Gerald Witherspoon, and this is Constable Barnes. I believe Mr. Arkwright might be expecting us."

"Please come in," she opened the door wider and ushered them in. "Wait here please, I'll see if Mr. Arkwright is receiving."

Barnes waited till she'd disappeared into the room at the end of the hall before he asked, "Why would Arkwright be expecting us, sir?"

"Because I'm quite sure that Mrs. Arkwright must have mentioned our visit to his office yesterday. I imagine he knows he'd be next on our list." Witherspoon replied. For some odd reason, he felt strangely confident about this case. Everything was going to fall into place, he simply knew it. He could feel it in his bones.

The housekeeper returned, "Mr. Arkwright will see you, sir. Please follow me."

They walked down the long hall, passing portraits of sour-faced individuals who were probably Arkwright ancestors. The housekeeper lead them through a set of double doors.

A man sat behind a huge desk on the far side of the room. He didn't bother to get up. He had brown hair with a few streaks of gray at the temple and a very disapproving expression on his narrow, thin-lipped face. "I'm Oliver Arkwright." He focused his gaze on the inspector. "I understand you'd like to speak to me."

"That's correct," Witherspoon replied. "This is Constable Barnes, and I'm Inspector Gerald Witherspoon. We'd like to ask you some questions about the death of Harlan Westover." He couldn't help noticing that there were pictures and portraits of Her Majesty, the Queen, on virtually every wall of the study.

Arkwright frowned slightly. "I should imagine the less said about that unfortunate incident, the better. The man's dead and buried, he killed himself."

"We're not entirely sure of that," the inspector said. "That's why we've come. There is some evidence that perhaps Mr. Westover's death wasn't self-inflicted, in which case, it would be murder." He was deliberately blunt. It bothered him that Arkwright hadn't acknowledged the constable's presence by so much as a glance and that he'd not bothered to invite them to sit down. Then he got himself under control. He mustn't let his personal feelings influence his work. This wouldn't be the first time he'd questioned someone while standing up.

Arkwright's frowned deepened. "My wife mentioned that you were around at the firm yesterday asking questions. I supposed it was something to do with his insurance."

"The police do not investigate insurance claims," Barnes said softly. He'd taken out his notebook and pencil.

"I suppose you'd best have a seat," Arkwright motioned toward the two straight-backed chairs to the right of his desk, and the two policemen sat down. "Though I've no idea what you think I can tell you. I never saw Westover after he left the office that day."

"I understand there was a board meeting that day and that Westover was in attendance," Witherspoon said.

Arkwright started in surprise. "Who told you that?"

"Your wife. She mentioned it yesterday when we were talking to Mr. Horrocks. Why? Was there something amiss with Mr. Westover being at the meeting."

Arkwright's mouth thinned even further. "Of course not, I'm just surprised that you'd bother with anything my wife said. For goodness sakes, she's only met Westover a time or two. But that's neither here nor there. In answer to your question, Westover was at the meeting."

"Was that normal business practice?" Witherspoon's gaze was caught by an ornate silver picture frame on the desk. Again, it was a likeness of the queen—taken, he was certain, in celebration of her jubilee. Gracious, the man must be extremely patriotic.

"I'm afraid I don't quite follow you?" Arkwright replied. "What do you mean, 'normal business practice'? Westover worked for the firm, he was there to give the board a report. That's all there was to it."

"What kind of report?" Barnes asked.

Arkwright's brows rose in surprise. "I don't see how our internal business affairs have any connection to his death."

"We've no idea why Mr. Westover was murdered," With erspoon said quickly, "so any help you can give us will be invaluable."

Arkwright sighed. "He was there for the simplest of reasons. We've designed a new engine, you see, and Westover was in charge of the project. We've already sold one, and it's on a ship as we speak. It's being sent to Africa, to be used to run equipment in the gold mines. Westover was giving the board a report on how quickly more engines could be manufactured."

"Did anything unusual happen at the meeting?" Barne asked.

"No." Arkwright shook his head. "He said his piece and then left. I didn't even know he'd left the office until the next day when he didn't come into work."

The study door opened, and Mrs. Arkwright stepped inside. "Oh dear, Oliver, I'm so sorry, I'd no idea you were busy." She smiled warmly at the two policemen. "How very nice to see you again."

"Did you want something, Penelope?" Arkwright asked irritably.

"Only to tell you that the others have arrived. Shall I have Mrs. Grebels show them in?"

Arkwright flushed. "Oh, no, that won't be necessary. Tell them I'll be available in a few minutes."

"I told them you're talking with the police," she retorted "and that you might be tied up for quite some time."

"You oughtn't to have done that." His eyes flashed angrily "What will they think?"

Mrs. Arkwright appeared unperturbed. "They'll think whatever they like. Oh for goodness' sake Oliver, it's just those nosy old fools from the London Architectural Committee."

Arkwright's neck turned bright red as he held himself in check. Finally, he glared at his wife and then turned to the policemen. "I serve on one of His Highness's civil committees."

"That's quite an honor, sir," Witherspoon murmured.

"I'm related to Her Majesty through my mother," Arkwright explained.

"Distantly related," Mrs. Arkwright added. She pulled open the study door and stepped out into the hall.

"I'll be with them in a few moments," he yelled as she moved away. "Have Mrs. Grebels take them into the study."

Witherspoon, who had been both repelled and fascinated by the exchange between husband and wife, knew they weren't going to get much more out of Oliver Arkwright. He glanced at Barnes, and they both rose to their feet.

"Thank you for your time, sir," Witherspoon said.

"Is that it, then?" Arkwright got up, started to extend his hand, but then thought better of it. He'd obviously decided that a police officer wasn't his social equal. "I take it you're finished with me?"

"For the present, sir," Barnes said softly. He'd noticed the aborted handshake and was angry on the inspector's behalf. "But do keep yourself available, sir. We may need to ask you more questions."

"I don't see why," Arkwright sputtered. "I've told you everything I know."

"I'm sure you think you have, sir. But one never knows, does one? Do tend to your guests, sir. We'll show ourselves out," Witherspoon said.

Betsy's feet hurt. She'd spent half the morning watching the front of the offices of Donovan, Melcher, and Horrocks before she realized that once the staff was inside for the day, they weren't likely to come outside again until the office closed at half past five. She frowned at the double-wide front door of the elegant building where the offices were housed. She couldn't face going home this early, and she'd no idea what to do next. Maybe she ought to try some of the shopkeepers on the Kensington High Street, maybe one of them knew something. Just then, the door she'd been watching opened and a young man carrying a large satchel stepped outside. Her spirits brightened. He worked for Westover's company. She'd seen him go inside the offices earlier.

He stopped, put the satchel on the pavement, and adjusted his scarf beneath his heavy coat. A moment later, he'd picked up his burden and was on his way. Betsy followed at a discreet distance until he turned the corner, then she took off at a fast clip. She rounded the corner just as her quarry crossed the road and stopped at an omnibus stand. Unfortunately for Betsy, the omnibus was practically in front of the fellow. Taking a deep breath, she flew across the busy road. Dodging hansoms, carts, four-wheelers, and pedestrians, she raced toward the omnibus. Her hand grabbed the front pole of the platform, and she swung onboard just as the horses pulled away.

She ploughed into the young man. He was still standing in the aisle, his satchel tucked under one arm while he dug in his pocket for coins with his other hand.

"Oops," Betsy exclaimed, "I'm ever so sorry. Are you all right?"

He blushed a deep hue. "Don't fret, miss. It's my fault, I oughtn't to be standing in the aisle . . ."

"Then why don't you sit down," the conductor ordered. He jerked his head toward two empty seats in the front row.

The young man blushed even redder. "I'd best sit down," he sputtered. He eased his lanky frame into the seat. Betsy plopped down in the empty space next to him. She ignored the disapproving look the middle-aged woman in the seat across the aisle gave her. Let the silly cow think Betsy was a forward hussy. She didn't care. There was a killer on the loose.

"Are you sure you're all right, then?" she said chattily. She smiled brightly. "I banged into you pretty hard."

"I'm fine, miss," he smiled shyly in return. "You've no need to apologize. It was my fault." His voice was just a bit on the loud side.

"I'm sure you were just in a bit of a hurry to get home," she soothed, saying anything to keep the fellow talking. She prayed he was going to the end of the line.

He laughed. But the sound seemed to pass through his nose rather than his mouth, and the end result was that he sounded a bit like a braying mule. "If only that were true. I'm on me way to take some papers to our factory over on Watling Street. Then I've got to get back to the office." His voice was even louder than before.

"What office do you work in, then?" she asked. She deliberately pitched her own voice very, very soft. Maybe he'd take the hint and the entire omnibus wouldn't be privy to their conversation.

"Donovan, Melcher, and Horrocks. I'm a clerk. My name's Gilbert Pratting. I'd normally never be settin' foot in the factory exceptin' that our chief engineer has passed away and I've got to get his notes and papers over to our Mr. Barker, he's the factory foreman. Not that he could make sense of them, Mr. Westover, he was our engineer, he was a downright genius. Designed the most remarkable new engine . . . it's so good that a company in Africa bought the first one, sight unseen. It's on a ship right now. I can't see that Mr. Barker will be able to make heads or tails of Mr. Westover's papers. But then again, that's not my problem." He laughed again.

"How sad," Betsy winced. His voice drowned out the loud, London street traffic. The entire omnibus was staring at them. "Was the poor man ill before he passed away?"

"Not as far as I know," he finally lowered his voice a bit. "But he must have had something wrong with him, he committed suicide."

She gasped in shock. "How dreadful."

"Leastways, that's what the coroner's inquest ruled, but now they're all having fits. We've had the police around, you see," he laughed again. "And they're askin' questions like they think it might be something more than suicide. They're acting like someone did poor Mr. Westover in. Murdered him."

Betsy gasped again. "How terrible that must be for you and the rest of the staff."

"It's not terrible for me, I'd no reason to kill him."

"Goodness, you make it sound as if someone else did!" Betsy risked a quick glance around the omnibus. Her heart sank. Everyone, including the conductor, was openly staring at them. She was hardly being discreet. She brushed the problem aside. Right now she had to concentrate on getting as much information as possible out of Gilbert Pratting.

"Not as far as I know," he replied. "Mr. Westover was a harmless sort of fellow. Nice enough and very polite, but like a lot of people, he could really be stubborn. Especially about anything to do with his designs. Had a right old fit when he found out Horrocks had bought cheaper struts than the one's he'd specified. They had a right old blowup about that." He leaned closer to Betsy. She tried hard not to cringe back. She wasn't afraid of Pratting, but she was concerned that if he didn't lower his voice her hearing would be permanently damaged.

"I can't think why Mr. Westover was surprised about them struts," Pratting continued, he shook his head. "Everyone knows how cheap the old man is. Why at our Christmas party last month, all we got was one tiny mince tart and a cup of tea. Can you fathom such a thing? If you're going to be so cheap and nasty about the whole matter, why bother to have a party in the first place?" He paused for a breath, and Betsy tried to think of a question. But she wasn't fast enough, and he continued on. "Mind you, we shouldn't have expected any better than what we got. Mr. Jorgens, he's one of the other clerks, he helps with the books, he claims that if we'd not sold poor Mr. Westover's engine when we did, none of us would even have a job. Oh look, here's my stop coming up. I've got to change to another line." He gave Betsy a smile as he rose to his feet. "You never did tell me your name."

She thought quickly. "It's Henrietta. Henrietta Baker."

CHAPTER 4

A hard, steady rain pelted the inspector and Barnes as they emerged from the hansom in front of the offices of Donovan, Melcher, and Horrocks. They dashed for the door and managed to reach the dim foyer without getting soaked completely through.

Barnes took off his helmet and shook off the water. The damp seemed to soak into him, causing his knees to throb. He frowned at the sliver of late afternoon light coming in through the transom over the doors. He hurt, but he wasn't about to complain. The inspector, kind-hearted fellow that he was, would send him home. Barnes wasn't having any of that. He was a copper, and if he had to stand on his aching knees until the cows came home, so be it. He'd do his duty. But he did hope that whomever they interviewed next would offer them a chair. "Which one do you want to see first?" he asked. "Donovan or Melcher?"

Witherspoon shook the last of the water off his bowler and put it back on his head. "I don't suppose it matters much. Let's see who is here."

"And let's hope we get more information than we got out of Mr. Arkwright." Barnes pulled open the door to the outer office, and they stepped inside.

The clerks looked up from their desks, and the one closest to them got to his feet. "May I help you, sir?"

"I'm Inspector Witherspoon, and this is Constable Barnes."

"Yes, sir, I know. You were here yesterday."

"We'd like to see Mr. Donovan or Mr. Melcher."

"Mr. Donovan isn't in as yet," the young man replied, he smiled faintly. "But Mr. Melcher's in his office. If you'll wait here, I'll announce you."

He hurried across the room and down the hall. A few moments later, a tall middle-aged man with thinning blond hair and dark circles around his eyes appeared at the end of the hallway. He stopped in the doorway and gazed at the two policemen. "I'm Melcher," he said bluntly. "What do you want?"

Witherspoon was taken aback. "We want to talk to you, sir. As I told Mr. Horrocks yesterday, I'm going to be speaking to everyone in the firm."

Melcher stared at them and then waved them across the room. "James did mention you'd been by to see him. Come along then, we'll go into my office." The clerk, who'd been standing behind Melcher, scurried back to his desk.

"Inspector," Barnes said softly. "If you don't mind, I'd like to have a word with the rest of the staff," he jerked his head to indicate the clerks.

Witherspoon frowned slightly. "Hasn't someone already spoken to them?"

"Yes sir," Barnes replied. "A couple of lads took statements yesterday, but if you don't mind, I'd like to have a go."

"Certainly," he replied. He trusted Barnes completely. If the constable wanted to have a word with the clerks, he must have a good reason.

"Come along, Inspector," Melcher called over his shoulder. "I've not got all day."

"Yes, just coming." Witherspoon hurried down the hall and into the first open door. Melcher was already behind his desk. He nodded toward one of the two empty chairs opposite him. "Have a seat, sir."

"Thank you." The inspector sat. He decided to get right to the heart of the matter. "As I'm sure you've heard, Mr. Melcher, we've reason to believe that Harlan Westover didn't commit suicide."

"James told me you think it's murder," Melcher snorted. "A bit late in the day to be poking about looking for a killer, isn't it?"

"Better late than never, sir," Witherspoon replied. "Now, if you'll just answer a few questions, sir. Can you tell me what happened at the board meeting on the day that Westover died?"

Melcher's eyebrows shot up in surprise. "Why on earth do you want to know about that? It was just a board meeting. What's it got to do with Westover's death?"

"He was there, wasn't he?"

"Yes, we'd invited him along to give a progress report on a new engine he'd designed. He gave us his report, and then he left the office."

"Was he upset about anything?" Witherspoon asked.

Melcher shrugged. "He didn't appear to be. Actually, I wasn't paying all that much attention to the man. I'd a lot on my mind."

"Were you here at the office for the remainder of the day?" Witherspoon asked.

Melcher frowned. "I'm not sure I understand the question."

"I'll try to be more precise." Witherspoon wondered how much clearer he could be. "What time did the meeting end?"

"Around a quarter past twelve. Just before luncheon."

"Did you continue working here in the office the rest of the day?"

Melcher shook his head. "No. I went to my club for lunch, and then I went home."

"What time did you arrive at your home, sir?" Witherspoon wasn't sure what good this line of questioning was, they weren't sure what time the murder had been committed, only that it had been done in the afternoon. Still, it never hurt to get as much information as possible.

"I don't know, Inspector. I wasn't looking at my watch." He leaned forward somewhat aggressively, his expression darkening. "What is this, sir? Are you accusing me of having something to do with Westover's death?"

"Of course not," Witherspoon assured him. "These questions are very routine, sir. I had, of course, simply assumed you and the other board members had spent your afternoon working here. Now it appears that you weren't here at all."

"Neither were any of the others," Melcher snapped. "Arkwright and Donovan scarpered as soon as the meeting adjourned, and as I left, I heard Horrocks telling Jackson that he was in charge and to make sure to lock up properly, so he wasn't here either." He paused and took a deep breath. "I think, Inspector, that you'd best ask everyone where they were that day."

"I intend to do just that, sir," Witherspoon said. "So you went directly home from your club after luncheon?"

"That's right."

"Where do you live, sir, and where is your club?"

"I live on Argyll Road in Kensington. Number 19. My club is Jensens, it's just down the street here."

"I know the place," Witherspoon said.

Melcher nodded slightly in acknowledgment. "I was there until half past one. You can check if you like, dozens of people saw me."

"And from there you went home," the inspector pressed. "Did you take a hansom?"

"No, I walked. Traffic was a mess. A coopers van had overturned, and I thought I'd get home faster on foot than if I took a cab. It's not all that far."

"What time did you arrive at your home?"

Melcher shrugged. "I'm not absolutely sure, but I think it was close to two."

"Would your housekeeper recall the time?"

Melcher gave him a thin smile. "She might if she'd been there, but she wasn't. She was out, and before you ask, so was the rest of the staff." He leaned back in his chair and flicked a bit of lint off the sleeve of his brown tweed coat. "I'm a widower, Inspector. My household is small, just a housekeeper and two maids. None of them were home that afternoon. It was their afternoon off. I was home alone until half past six, when Mrs. Brown, my housekeeper, returned from visiting her sister in Colchester."

Witherspoon nodded. He really didn't know what to think. "So you have no one who can vouch for your whereabouts after you left your club?"

"That's correct," Melcher replied. "Frankly, it never occurred to me that I'd have to account for my whereabouts."

"You had no idea that Mr. Westover was upset about something?"

"None at all, Inspector. He seemed perfectly fine at the meeting."

"That's odd, we've already spoken to one witness that claims Mr. Westover appeared to be very angry when he left here."

Melcher snapped out of his languid posture and leaned aggressively across his desk. "There are a number of people around here who have very vivid imaginations, Inspector. I shouldn't take everyone seriously, if I were you."

"We always take witnesses seriously, sir." Witherspoon hoped he wasn't being too indiscreet at this point in the investigation, but his instincts were prodding him to dig just a bit deeper. After all, Mrs. Jeffries was always telling him to trust his "inner voice" and obviously, that voice was prompting him along a certain path. "Why did everyone leave the office after the board meeting? Was that your normal practice?"

"No," Melcher said. "Generally we all went back to work. I can't speak for the others, but I left because I had a headache. Now see here, sir. I don't mind cooperation . . ." he broke off as a clerk stuck his head in the door.

"Sorry to interrupt, Mr. Melcher, but there's a cable just arrived from Cape Town. Do you want me to bring it in?"

Melcher waved impatiently, "Bring it in, boy. Bring it in." He looked at Witherspoon. "I'm afraid we'll have to continue this later. Cables from our customers generally require a good deal of work on my part."

Mrs. Jeffries was reaching for her cloak and bonnet when there was a loud knock on the back door. The cook, who was sitting at the table peeling apples, started to get up. Mrs. Jeffries waved her back to her seat. "I'll get it," she said. "You finish with your apples."

"Thanks, I want to get this pie done and in the oven. I've half a dozen sources coming by this afternoon. They stay longer and talk easier with their bellies full of sweet pie and custard."

The knock came again, and Mrs. Jeffries hurried down the back hall. She flung open the door. "Dr. Bosworth, gracious, this is an unexpected pleasure."

"Sorry to barge in on you, but I've discovered some information that I thought might be useful."

"Do come in," she stepped back and opened the door wider. "You've gone to a lot of trouble, doctor. You should have sent me a message, and I'd have been quite happy to come to you. I didn't mean for you to be inconvenienced on our account."

Bosworth stepped inside. "Please don't fret, Mrs. Jeffries, I had to come over this way today for a meeting at St. Giles Hospital. That's just up the road a piece from here. I thought I'd take a chance on catching you in and kill two birds with one stone."

"That's very kind of you." She led the way down the hall and into the warm kitchen. "Do have a chair, and I'll get us some tea."

Mrs. Goodge had already put the kettle on. She nodded respectfully at their guest. "It's nice to see you, Doctor. We'll have tea ready in just a moment."

Bosworth took off his hat and coat and placed them on the coat tree. "It's good to see you, too, Mrs. Goodge. This kitchen smells wonderful . . ."

he stopped and sniffed the air, smiling in pleasure at the scent of cinnamon and apple. "Reminds me of when I was a boy."

They spoke of trivial things until they were sitting comfortably at the kitchen table with tea in hand and a plate of treacle tarts in front of them. Dr. Bosworth helped himself to a pastry. "This is excellent," he nodded at the cook.

Mrs. Goodge smiled politely, but Mrs. Jeffries could tell by the tight set of her mouth that she was impatient to find out why the good doctor was here. She also wanted her kitchen free.

"We're very curious as to why you're here," the housekeeper said.

Bosworth laughed. "I'm sure you are. Actually, I don't know if my information will be useful or not. But I thought it best to let you make that decision." He took a quick sip from his cup. "I spoke to the doctor who did the postmortem on Harlan Westover. He's quite a competent chap, actually, from what I hear of the fellow, he's a bit more than competent."

"That's always good to know," Mrs. Jeffries replied. There were some doctors that did postmortems that weren't very good at all.

"He was a bit reticent at first, but after we'd chatted for a bit, he told me a very curious thing. He found an abnormality in Westover's brain."

"Abnormality? What does that mean?" Mrs. Jeffries didn't know much about the human brain, but she did know it was a mysterious and complex organ.

Bosworth paused. "An abnormality is a growth in the brain that shouldn't be there. In this case, your Mr. Westover had a small growth on his frontal lobe."

"Did the doctor mention this in his postmortem report?" Mrs. Jeffries asked.

"There was no reason to put it in the report. The postmortem is only concerned with the cause of death. That was quite clear, Westover died from gunshot wounds to his head."

"So once he finds the cause of death, so to speak, the doctor doesn't care what else is in a body," Mrs. Goodge frowned.

"That's right." Bosworth took another bite of his tart.

"Then how did the doctor find this uh . . . uh abnormality if he weren't lookin' for the ruddy thing?" Mrs. Goodge asked.

He laughed. "According to him, it was hard to miss. It was quite close to the bullet entry wound. Just above it, in fact. As far as medical science knows, the growth shouldn't have had much, if any, impact on Westover. But after the doctor and I got to discussing the case, he wondered if maybe there might have been more of them."

"More what?" Mrs. Goodge demanded.

"More growths in Westover's brain," Mrs. Jeffries said softly. "If there were, could these growths cause someone to act out of character?"

"Perhaps," Bosworth shrugged. "It's very possible, but neither I nor any other doctor can say for certain. There is simply too much about the brain that's still a mystery. For all we know the poor fellow's brain might have been peppered with the wretched things, and it wouldn't have had any impact on him at all. Or it might have caused him to behave in ways completely out of character. There's some interesting research being done in Scotland and on the continent, but we simply don't know for sure."

Mrs. Goodge frowned darkly. "Are you tellin' us that if he had these here growths, he might have actually picked up that gun and shot himself?"

He hesitated. "I don't know. But the possibility is there."

"So it might not have been murder after all," Mrs. Jeffries murmured. This was most disappointing news.

"We've a bit of a problem, you see," Bosworth continued. "As I said, Dr. Garner, he's the one who did the postmortem, didn't mention the first growth in his report. He thought it obvious the man had committed suicide. When the coroner agreed, Garner thought no more about the case and went about his business. But when he found out the police were now investigating Westover's death as a possible murder, he realized the information he'd left out of the report might be important."

"What difference could it make?" Mrs. Goodge asked. "You've already told us that doctors don't know if these here growths cause people to act strange."

"But it's still pertinent information. Even though we don't know for certain, many doctors, and I'm one of them, are of the opinion that a growth on the brain could cause someone to act very differently than he normally might."

"Why doesn't Dr. Garner simply tell the police what he knows?" Mrs. Jeffries suggested. "He wasn't negligent. He did ascertain the cause of death."

"Yes, I know, but still, it won't make him look very good, will it?" Bosworth replied. He looked definitely uncomfortable, "Garner's a good doctor, generally takes a great deal of care with his reports. But on that particular day, he was covering two districts. Right after Westover was brought in, he had two other postmortems at St. Bartholomew's to attend to, so he wasn't as detailed as he should have been."

Mrs. Jeffries thought she understood perfectly. "So you want us to make sure the inspector finds out about the growth. That way your friend will be able to keep both his position and his reputation."

"I'm not sure what I want you to do." Bosworth sighed heavily. "Dr. Garner is very worried. He's afraid that Westover's death really was suicide, not murder. He doesn't want to see an innocent person arrested and hung because he left a pertinent detail out of a P.M. report."

"Reassure Dr. Garner that an innocent won't be unfairly tried for this death," Mrs. Jeffries said firmly. "If it was a suicide, we'll find it out. But just because you found a growth in the man's brain doesn't mean it wasn't murder. As you said yourself, the growth may have had no effect on his behavior whatsoever, right?"

"Yes, of course you're correct." Relieved, he smiled. "And you're right to investigate these circumstances as a murder as well. But I did think you ought to know about this."

"Of course," Mrs. Jeffries replied. "It's now quite possible that Westover did take his own life. We must keep that in mind. But we will find out the truth."

"You always do." Bosworth grinned and popped the last of the tart into his mouth.

"Was there anything else, Doctor?" Mrs. Jeffries asked calmly, even though her mind was now racing with this new possibility.

"Not really. The only other thing Dr. Garner mentioned about Westover was that he had inkstains on his fingers and an old bit of chicken pox scaring on his shoulders. I guess one could say that apart from the gunshot wounds and the growth, the fellow seemed to be in quite good health."

Smythe elbowed his way through the crowded public bar of the Dirty Duck. Smoke from the fireplace wafted through the room, helping to mask the stink of unwashed clothes and bodies. Along the walls, narrow benches were filled with men and women drinking beer or gin. Couples and small groups occupied the half a dozen rough-hewn tables scattered in front of the fire, and they were standing two-deep at the bar.

Smythe wedged his bulk between a post and a solitary drinker and caught the barman's eye. "What'll you 'ave, mate?" the publican called over the noise.

"Beer," Smythe yelled. He scanned the crowd, looking for a familiar pork pie hat and checked coat. Nothing. "Blimpey Groggins been around?" he asked, as the publican slapped a mug of beer in front of him. Smythe took care to lay down two shillings, far more than the cost of the beer. He shoved them toward the barman.

"You a friend of 'is?" he asked as he picked up the coins.

"More like a customer," Smythe replied. "And I need to see 'im right away. As a matter of fact, you could say I'm one of 'is best customers." He wanted to make it clear he meant Blimpey no harm. Groggins was a man who had many friends, but the nature of his work insured he had an equal number of enemies.

"Blimpey'll be 'ere in a few minutes, he's just gone to have a word with someone out the back."

Smythe nodded and sipped his beer. While he waited, he relaxed and studied the crowd. It was what you'd expect—dockworkers, day laborers, washerwomen, prostitutes, and probably more than one pickpocket in the lot.

"I thought I might be 'aving a visit from you," the familiar voice came from behind him.

"And how's that?" he asked as Blimpey Groggins stepped up to the spot just vacated by the solitary drinker.

Blimpey Groggins was a short, portly, ginger-haired fellow, wearing a pork pie hat and a dingy brown and white checked coat. A bright red scarf was draped about his neck. He'd once been a petty thief and a burglar. But circumstance had shown him that it was far safer to sell information than stolen goods. He was possessed of an incredible memory, a vast network of contacts, and enough brains to realize he was a lot less likely to hang for selling information than for housebreaking. He'd deliberately set about learning every scrap of information there was to be had about anyone and anything in London. People paid good money to know things, and Blimpey wasn't one to ask questions of his customers. If they wanted to know something, he'd find it out for them.

"I figured you'd be around as soon as I 'eard your inspector was havin' a nose about that Westover suicide." Blimpey grinned at the barman and jerked his head toward Smythe. "He's buyin' so I'll have a double whiskey."

Amazed, Smythe shook his head. He knew the man made his living buying and selling information, but the inspector had only got the case two days ago—and there was even some doubt that there was even a murder at all. "Is there anything in this town that you don't know about?"

"Not much, mate," Blimpey shrugged modestly. "That's my job now, init? I take it you'll be wantin' the usual?"

The publican gave Blimpey his whiskey. "Ta, George."

Startled, Smythe dropped his gaze and fumbled with his pockets. He dug out more coins. Cor blimey, he thought, was he such a regular now Blimpey knew what he'd be needin' as soon as he walked in the door? That took the wind out of his sails. "That's right, we need to know all we can about the victim."

"Harlan Westover," Blimpey shot back. "Worked for an engineering firm by the name of Donovan, Melcher, and Horrocks."

Smythe wasn't the least surprised by Blimpey's knowledge. "Doesn't look like Westover 'ad much of a life outside of his work."

"Don't you believe it, old boy," Blimpey laughed slyly. "Everyone's got a life. It's those quiet, hardworkin' types that are usually full of the most surprises."

"You're right about that, mate," Smythe muttered. "Anyway, find out what you can about 'im, and find out about the people he worked for, too."

"The owners of the firm?" Blimpey asked.

"Right. Their names are James Horrocks, Harry Donovan, Oliver Arkwright, and Lawrence Melcher. I don't know that any of them 'ave anything to do with Westover's death, but we've got to start somewhere." He took another drink of his beer. "How much time do you think you'll need?"

"Give us a couple of days. I'll 'ave something for you by then." Blimpey cleared his throat.

"Right, then, I'll be back here the day after tomorrow."

"Mind you come in about this time."

Smythe drained the rest of his beer and pushed away from the bar.

"What's the rush, then?" Blimpey held up a hand. "I've not seen you in a bit. Stay and 'ave a bit of a natter."

Smythe's eyebrows rose in surprise. He'd known Blimpey for a goodly number of years, but they were more business acquaintances than friends. Still, he liked the fellow. For an ex-thief, Blimpey was a decent sort, and he'd done Smythe more than one favor over the years. For that matter,

Smythe had done Blimpey a good turn every now and again, as well. "All right, I'm in no 'urry." he shrugged. "So what've you been up to lately?"

"Oh, the usual." Blimpey took another quick sip of whiskey and then took a deep breath. "There's somethin' I want to ask you, and I don't want you gettin' all shirty on me."

Curious, Smythe gave him a long, appraising look. Blimpey's face was flushed, and there was a tight, pinched look about his mouth. If Smythe hadn't known better, he'd have sworn that Blimpey looked nervous.

"Well, are ya goin' to hold your temper or not?" Blimpey swallowed hard. "You're generally an easy goin' sort, Smythe. But it wouldn't do to get on the wrong side of you. God knows more than one dockside tough has found that out the hard way. But to be honest, I'd not like to lose you as a customer because I've offended you. This is important though, and . . . well, I need a bit of 'elp 'ere."

"That depends on what you're askin'," Smythe replied warily. "Look, why don't you just spit it out? I'm not that bad-tempered. Leastways I never thought of myself that way."

"You're not," Blimpey sighed. "But a man's got to be careful when he starts askin' personal questions." He raised his arm and signaled to the barman. "Another round over here, George. Put it on my bill."

"Cor blimey, this is a first," Smythe exclaimed. "You must be in a state, if you're goin' to pay."

"It's a measure of how desperate I am," Blimpey replied darkly.

Genuinely alarmed now, Smythe leaned closer to the smaller man. "What's wrong, Blimpey. Are you in some sort of trouble with the police?"

"Oh no, it's much worse than that. My solicitors can handle the coppers." He paused as the barman brought them their drinks.

"Are you sick?" Smythe couldn't think of what else it could be.

"In a way," Blimpey tossed back the second whiskey like it was water. "Truth is, I need to ask your advice about a rather delicate matter. You're the only person I know who was in a bit of the same situation as I find myself in and you came out all right."

"What are you goin' on about?" Smythe couldn't think of anything they had in common. "What turned out for me?"

"The lass," Blimpey sputtered. "You got engaged to your lass."

"Engaged? You mean me and Betsy?"

"Unless you've gone and gotten engaged to another woman since I last saw you." Blimpey took another deep breath. "And that's why I wanted to have a word."

"You're wantin' to get married?" Smythe fought hard to keep from grinning.

"I am. I'm at the age when the idea of settling down and havin' a family begins to 'ave a bit of appeal," Blimpey nodded his head.

As Blimpey was pushing fifty at least, Smythe reckoned he was well past that age, but he kept his opinion to himself. "So if you want to get engaged, why don't you just ask the woman to marry you? I'm assumin' it's someone you've been courtin' regularly."

"That depends on what you mean by 'courtin'," Blimpey replied. "I see her every day, and I think she's got feelin's for me. But how the 'ell is a bloke to know?"

"Ask her," Smythe said flatly.

"But what if she says she don't want me," Blimpey cried. He shook his head. "I want 'er in my life. If I ask and she says 'no', she might not want me about."

"That's a risk you've got to take," Smythe said kindly.

"Easier said than done, my son," Blimpey shot back. "I mean, if I say nothin', then we can go on as we are. But if I ask and she says 'no', then it'd be awkward for us to be together after that. And I'd rather 'ave her as a friend than not at all."

"Then keep 'er as a friend," Smythe suggested. He knew exactly what Blimpey was going through. "But if you want more than friendship, you've got to go that next step."

Blimpey took a deep breath. "So you think I ought to just tell her straight out 'ow I feel?"

"That's right. Beatin' about the bush won't do you any good."

"Is that what you did with your Betsy, ask her straight out?"

That most definitely hadn't been what Smythe had done. He'd danced about Betsy for months before he'd worked up the courage to even hint about his feelings for her. And then he'd only had the courage to pursue her when she'd made it clear she'd had feelings for him. But he wasn't going to share that with Blimpey, the bloke was too close to giving up as it was. "That's exactly what I did. But then again, it were a bit different for me. I was livin' in the same 'ouse as the lass, so I saw 'er all the time."

"Did give ya a bit of an advantage, didn't it?" Blimpey sighed. "Well I guess there's not much else I can do. If I want to be livin' in connubial bliss come this time next year, I'll have to risk tellin' her how I feel."

Smythe nodded wisely. "You can do it, Blimpey. By the way, why'd you ask me for advice? Why not one of your other friends?"

Blimpey shrugged. "Cause you're the only person I know who was in the same sort of situation."

"What do you mean?"

"Just what I said. My lady's a bit younger than me." Blimpey grinned. "You know, just like you and your Betsy."

Smythe winced. He wished he hadn't asked. "There's not that much of an age difference between us."

Blimpey laughed. "There's a good fifteen years, mate. Just about what there is between me and my Nell."

Luckily for Inspector Witherspoon, just as he came into the outer office, Harry Donovan walked through the front door. He was a short, portly man, with dark hair highlighted by thick gray streaks at the temples. He was impeccably dressed in a dark black suit, paisley waistcoat, and white shirt with an old-fashioned collar.

He held out his hand in greeting when Witherspoon introduced himself. "Harry Donovan," he said, his blue eyes flicked toward the hall. "Chairman of the board. James said you'd been by. Come along into my office." He turned his head toward the clerk sitting a few feet away. "Where's Melcher?"

"Mr. Melcher's gone to the factory," the clerk replied. "He had a telegram from Capetown. He said he had to go and see the foreman about making the ship dates."

Donovan nodded. "When he gets back, tell him to come see me. Come along, Inspector, my office is this way."

Donovan's office was twice as large as the others and had a marble fireplace opposite the entry door. Above the fireplace was a huge portrait of an austere-looking gentleman in old-fashioned clothing. "That's my grandfather," Donovan said proudly. "He started the firm."

"That's a very nice portrait," Witherspoon replied. Actually, the fellow didn't look nice at all, but he could hardly say such a thing. Not waiting for an invitation to sit, he went to one of the two green paisley upholstered chairs in front of Donovan's huge mahogany desk.

"Thank you." Donovan sat down behind the desk. "I understand you're investigating our poor Mr. Westover's death as a murder."

"We're investigating the circumstances," Witherspoon replied.

Donovan's right eye twitched rapidly. "The coroner ruled the death a suicide."

"I know, but some additional evidence has turned up and so we must, of course, investigate. Now, I understand that on the day Mr. Westover died, he was present at your board meeting."

Donovan nodded slowly. "Yes, we asked him for a list of equipment requirements. He'd designed a new engine, and we'd shipped the first one off. We've gotten orders for more," he broke into a wide smile. "It's an excellent piece of engineering. Revolutionary, in fact."

Witherspoon no longer cared why Westover had been at the meeting. "Yes, yes, I understand all that. What I'd like to know is if you noticed anything odd or unusual about Mr. Westover that day?"

Donovan sat back in his chair and his right eye started twitching again. "I can't think of anything specifically. But I did notice he wasn't as cheerful as usual."

"Was he generally a cheerful fellow?" the inspector asked. He forced himself not to stare at Donovan's fluttering eyelid.

"He was always pleasant enough," Donovan frowned. "He wasn't of a naturally cheerful nature. I suppose what I ought to have said was that he was a bit more dour that day than usual." He smiled sadly. "I suppose I ought to have been a bit more solicitous of the fellow and asked him if there was anything wrong. I'd no idea he was in such despair that he'd take his own life."

"What did you do after the meeting?"

Donovan looked surprised by the question. "I continued working."

"Here?" the inspector pressed.

"Where else would I work, Inspector," Donovan replied. This time, his left eye twitched.

Witherspoon didn't particularly like calling people liars, but Melcher had already told him that everyone had left after the board meeting. "Are you sure, sir?"

"Sure?" Donovan exclaimed, "Of course I'm sure . . ." his voice trailed off as he realized that the police had already spoken to the others. "Oh dear, of course, of course. I didn't work that afternoon . . . yes, that's right. I've gotten my days mixed up. I left after the meeting." He gave Witherspoon a weak smile. "I'd quite forgotten. It's been several weeks ago that it all happened."

"Where did you go, sir?" Witherspoon prompted softly.

Donovan's bushy eyebrows drew together. "I don't know why I'm having such difficulty remembering. Perhaps it's because it turned into such a dreadful mess, what with poor Westover killing himself. I've quite put the whole day out of my mind."

"Nevertheless, we do need to know your whereabouts."

Both of Donovan's eyes jerked rapidly. The inspector tried not to stare, but it was impossible. The poor fellow's eyes were jerking faster than hummingbird wings.

Finally, after what seemed an age, Donovan sighed. "I took my wife for an early luncheon at Maitlands, and then I went for a walk."

"Did your wife accompany you on the walk?"

"No, she had some shopping to do, so I put her in a hansom for Regent Street."

"Did you happen to see anyone who you knew?" Witherspoon realized that this was quickly becoming a case where movement and timetables might be important. He made a mental note to himself to do up a nice timeline when he got home. Timelines had been most useful to him in the past.

"No, Inspector, I did not." Donovan stood up. "Now, sir, if you'll excuse me, I'm very busy."

It was obviously a dismissal. But the inspector had gotten quite a lot of information. "Of course you're busy, sir, so are the police. Would you mind giving me your address."

Donovan's jaw dropped at the same time both his eyes began to twitch. "Why on earth do you need my address?"

The inspector did his best to ignore Donovan's contorting face. The poor fellow couldn't help his affliction. "We'd like to have a word with your wife, sir. She met you here, correct?" He was guessing, but sometimes he actually guessed right.

"She did," Donovan admitted, "but I don't see why you need to speak to her."

"She might have seen Mr. Westover, might have spoken to him. She might have observed something everyone else missed. I think women sometimes notice things that men don't." His housekeeper was always noticing things that escaped him, but he wasn't going to share that with Mr. Donovan.

"I very much doubt that," Donovan replied. "My wife barely knew Mr. Westover."

"She didn't see him at all?" Witherspoon pressed.

Donovan hesitated. "I . . . uh, well, I can't say for certain. She might have seen him."

"Perhaps even spoken to him . . ."

"All right, Inspector, you've made your point. I live in Mayfair. Number 7 Wywick Place."

"Thank you, sir."

"Please do me the courtesy of being as discreet as possible, Inspector. My grandfather built our house. We have a position to maintain. I shouldn't like my neighbors to notice you going in and out of my home."

CHAPTER 5

"It was terribly disconcerting," Witherspoon said to Barnes. "Everytime he answered a question, one of his eyes twitched. I didn't know whether to look away or simply pretend I didn't notice." The two policemen were in a hansom on their way to the Donovan house. The rain had finally stopped, but the day hadn't improved any. Though it was barely half past three, the afternoon light was fading fast and they still had interviews to do. It would be full dark by the time either of them got home.

"It's hereditary, sir," Barnes said. "Apparently Mr. Donovan's father and grandfather had twitchy eyes as well."

"Gracious, really? How dreadful for them," Witherspoon clucked sympathetically. "At least that proves he wasn't twitching because he was lying. Though, frankly, that had been my impression of the fellow."

"How did the interview go, sir? Was he forthcoming with information?"

"Not particularly. He took umbrage when I asked him to explain his movements the day Westover was killed," he sighed and told the constable everything he'd learned from Harry Donovan.

Barnes whipped out his little brown notebook and took careful notes. When the inspector finished, he looked up, his expression puzzled. "Donovan claimed that the board asked Westover to be there because of equipment requirements? That's odd, sir. One of the clerks told me that it was Westover who insisted on going to the board meeting. That's two of them now that's said the same thing."

"What do you mean?"

"Donovan and Melcher both implied that they'd asked Westover to be at the meeting to give a report," Barnes explained. "But that's not what the clerk said."

"Why, Barnes, how very clever of you to find that out. I hadn't even thought to ask that question. Once I heard Melcher's statement, I simply assumed that Westover was at the meeting at their request." Witherspoon believed in giving credit where credit was due.

"It just happened to come up," Barnes shrugged modestly. Nonetheless, he was pleased.

"Nevertheless, it was clever of you to suss out the truth. Now, which clerk told you, and what, precisely, did he say?"

"He's the senior clerk, sir. He sits in one of the back offices. His name is Miles Wittmer, and he's been with the firm for over forty years. He was hired by Mr. Donovan's grandfather. The old gent started the company in 1848. But that's neither here nor there." Barnes paused for breath. "I'd asked Mr. Wittmer about Westover's last day, and he told me much of what everyone else has said. He'd not noticed anything unusual about Westover, certainly nothing which would indicate the man was thinking of suicide. Wittmer told me a little about Westover's engine and how it was going to change the firm's fortunes for the better. When he was showin' me some of Westover's papers, he dropped a page, and it slipped under my chair. When I bent down to get it, he said not to bother, that it was just the cost sheet and the estimates had been set weeks before the first engine was built. And then he said, and this is the interestin' bit, that it was the cost of parts that had poor Mr. Westover insistin' on being at the board meeting."

"He was certain that it was Westover who wanted to be at the meeting?"

"I didn't press him on the point, sir," Barnes admitted. "I'd no idea it might be important. But he sounded fairly sure of himself as he was talkin'. Wittmer told me that according to office gossip, Westover wanted to go to the meeting so he could complain about James Horrocks buying cheaper struts than his specifications required."

"Cheaper struts?" Witherspoon wasn't sure what a strut was, he made a mental note to try and find out. "That's interesting. Did you find out anything else from Mr. Wittmer or the other clerks? I mean, anything beyond what was in their statements."

Barnes shifted uncomfortably. "Truth is, sir, I don't really know. I've not gone over the statements that carefully." He had, but he couldn't quite remember all the details of what he'd read. He didn't particularly want to share that with the inspector yet. It frightened him. He loved being a copper, and he especially loved working with the now-legendary Gerald Witherspoon. If his memory started to go, he'd have no choice but to resign. He didn't even want to think about that possibility. "Sorry about that, sir. I know I should 'ave been a bit more prepared . . . especially as I was the one who wanted to interview everyone again."

"Nonsense, Constable," Witherspoon interrupted just as the hansom pulled up to the curb. "You're always 'at the ready,' so to speak. I've not gone over the statements all that carefully myself. I simply wondered if there'd been something you read in them that made you want to have another word with the office staff. You're so very good at catching little things people say that might be of significance." The inspector opened the door, got out of the hansom, and waited in the blustery cold while Barnes paid the driver.

"Let's see what we can learn from Mrs. Donovan," he said as the cab pulled away.

The Donovan house was in the middle of a row of Georgian town houses. It stood four stories tall, was made of red brick, and was topped with a dark gray slate roof. The front steps were freshly painted, and the brass side sconces polished to a high sheen. The front door was painted jet black and boasted a bronze cast door knocker, which was a good ten inches in size.

"Yee gods," Barnes muttered, "that thing looks big enough to go clean through the door."

"Let's hope it doesn't," Witherspoon picked up the handle and let it drop against the strike plate. He winced at the loud noise the ruddy thing made and wondered what it must sound like from the inside.

The moments ticked by, and the door remained firmly closed. Witherspoon listened hard for the sound of footsteps on the other side but heard nothing. He was reaching for the knocker again when the door flew open and a tall, grayhaired woman garbed in black stared at them. "Yes?"

"We'd like to speak with Mrs. Donovan," the inspector said. "We're the police."

"I can see that," she flicked a quick look at Barnes's uniform. "Is Mrs. Donovan expecting you?"

As most people weren't expecting the police to drop by, the inspector thought it a silly question. But he understood the rather peculiar habits of the upper class. "I don't think so, but it is important we speak with her."

The housekeeper stepped back and motioned them inside. "I'll see if Mrs. Donovan is at home."

"This isn't a social call," the inspector said, but he was talking to the woman's retreating back. They stood in a large, open foyer with a beautiful persian carpet on the dark wood floor, thin blue and cream striped walls and a huge bushy fern on a round table next to the staircase. Along the wall opposite the staircase were paintings of pastoral scenes, seascapes, and two spectacularly huge bowls of fruit.

The housekeeper appeared at the end of the hall and waved them forward. "Mrs. Donovan will see you now."

They were led into a cozy, but well-appointed room. The two windows opposite the door were draped with blue and silver paisley patterned curtains, and a cheerful fire burned in the hearth. Silver candlesticks and framed daguerrotypes were scattered along the mantle piece.

"If you'd like to have a seat, gentlemen," the voice came from a small door at the far end of the room. They turned and saw a tiny woman watching them. She was very, very small, not more than five feet and quite thin. Witherspoon didn't think she could weigh more than seven stone soaking wet. By the look of her face, she wasn't young. Witherspoon guessed she was closer to fifty than forty. Her hair was more brown than gray, and she wore it up in a topknot with fringe scattered across her forehead. "I'll be quite happy to speak with you." The faint rustle of her maroon-colored day dress sounded loud in the quiet room as she came toward them.

"Good day, madam. I'm Inspector Gerald Witherspoon, and this is Constable Barnes. We're here to ask you some very simple questions. We won't take much of your time."

She smiled and gestured toward the dark blue settee and matching chairs in front of the fireplace. "Take as much of it as you like, Inspector, I've nothing else to do today." Her voice was surprisingly deep.

The two policemen waited politely until she sat down and then they each took one of the blue armchairs flanking the settee. Witherspoon said, "That's most cooperative of you, madam. Now, uh, I'm sure you're curious as to why we're here."

"You're here, Inspector, because you think someone murdered Harlan Westover." She smiled faintly. "My husband and the other partners in the firm are most upset about the whole matter. They'd quite reconciled themselves to a suicide. Murder, of course, is quite a different matter."

"Uh, yes, you're right." Witherspoon's mind went completely blank. He wasn't accustomed to such unbridled cooperation. Generally, women of her class thought speaking to a policeman rather disreputable. Consequently, getting any information out of them was difficult.

"We understand you were at your husband's office on the day that Mr. Westover died?" Barnes asked.

"That's correct. There was a board meeting that day, and my husband promised to take me to Maitland's for luncheon. It's a lovely restaurant, do you know it?"

"I've seen it, ma'am, but I've never eaten there." Witherspoon replied. "Did you happen to see Mr. Westover while you were at the office?"

"Yes, I was a bit early, or the meeting ran a bit late, I don't remember which," she laughed. "But I was sitting in a chair in the outer office waiting, when Mr. Westover came storming out. I said 'good day' to him but he didn't return my greeting. He just stalked past me and left the office."

"Did you think his behavior odd?" Witherspoon pressed. Totally ignoring the chairman of the board's wife seemed fairly odd to the inspector. He'd never ignore Chief Inspector Barrows's wife if she spoke to him, no matter how preoccupied he might happen to be.

"Very. I'd never known Mr. Westover to be rude. But I thought perhaps something had happened at the meeting, something which might have upset him. I couldn't imagine what could be wrong. My husband was thrilled with Mr. Westover's work. The new engine he'd designed and built represented a huge windfall for the firm. They'd already sold the prototype and were in the process of building more. Oh no, they'd not want to lose someone of Mr. Westover's talents."

"Was Mr. Westover thinking of leaving the firm?" Barnes interjected.

"Not as far as I knew," she replied. "But I know how worried my husband was that another firm was going to steal Westover away."

"Had any other firms tried?" the constable pressed.

She hesitated. "Not directly. But I know that the board was concerned about losing him. Of course, since he'd finished the prototype for the engine, they weren't quite as concerned as they had been."

"I take it the firm owns all rights to Westover's design." Witherspoon stated.

"That's correct," she replied.

"Do you know if Mr. Westover had any enemies?" he asked.

"Not that I'm aware of," she replied. "But I hardly knew the man.

You really ought to ask my husband. He's known Mr. Westover for years."

"He knew him before he went to work for your husband's firm?" Barnes asked.

"That's right. Their fathers were at school together. My husband lured Mr. Westover away from Rupert and Lincoln, they're a big company in Birmingham."

"Did his old firm try to get him to stay on?" the constable asked.

"Of course," she laughed. "My husband and the other partners were terrified Westover would change his mind if they left him in Birmingham too long. They got him here as quickly as possible. They even found him a place to live once he'd agreed to come. You know how difficult it is to find decent accommodation these days. Luckily, my husband knew of some rather nice rooms that were available to let." She smiled brightly, "they were in a house he used to own as a matter of fact."

Witherspoon nodded. "Can you tell me if you noticed anything else about Mr. Westover after the board meeting?"

She thought for a moment and then shook her head. "Only what I've already said."

"Did you ask your husband what had happened at the meeting?" Barnes asked. "I mean, did he have any idea why Mr. Westover had been so rude?"

"I asked him, of course. But he said nothing had happened at the meeting and that Mr. Westover probably hadn't even noticed me sitting there," she snorted derisively. "My husband has very little faith in my powers of observation."

"Perhaps, ma'am, he should have listened to you a bit more carefully," Witherspoon said. "What time did you and Mr. Donovan finish lunch?"

"I'm not certain. It was probably about half past one."

"Did you come straight home from the restaurant?" the constable asked.

"I was in no hurry to get home, Constable. I went shopping and then to my dressmakers. I ordered three new gowns," she smiled slyly. "My husband will be furious when he gets the bill."

Smythe stood just outside the back door and watched Betsy step through the gate in the far corner of the communal garden. The gate was so well hidden by shrubs, you had to know just where to look to spot the ruddy thing. But as they all used that shortcut, especially when they were on a case, he knew if he waited out here he could talk to her without the others hearing.

He kept his gaze upon her as she stepped onto the footpath and started across the garden. Cor blimey, but he loved her. But Blimpey, damn the man, had made him think, made him start having doubts. He was older than Betsy. It hadn't bothered him until now, until he'd started thinking of some of the things Blimpey had wittered on about back in the pub.

She smiled in delight as she spotted him. "Are you waiting for me?"

"Always," he went toward her, holding out his bare hands.

"Why aren't you wearing gloves," she chided, as their fingers met. "It's cold."

"Don't fret, lass," he said softly. "I'm fine."

Betsy stepped back and looked at him. She could tell something was on his mind. "What's wrong?"

"Nothing, but I do want to talk to you before we go into the meetin'." He took her arm and led her back out into the garden, toward the huge oak near the center. "I've got something to ask you, and I want you to be honest with me."

"You're starting to worry me, Smythe," Betsy frowned. "What on earth is wrong?"

"Do you think I'm too old for ya?" he blurted. Blast, he'd not meant to say it like that.

"Too old?" she repeated. "Now why would you be thinking that you were too old for me?"

"There's more than fifteen years between us," he continued. "I'm goin' to be thirty-six in April . . ." his voiced trailed off as she stopped and stared at him.

"Smythe," she finally said, "if I'd thought you were too old for me, I wouldn't have said 'yes' when you asked me to marry you. Now who's been putting these silly ideas into your head?"

He could hardly admit that he was getting them from his paid informant, so he just shrugged. "No one. It just occurred to me I might 'ave pressed you a bit. You know, before you 'ad a chance to really think about whether you wanted to marry me. That's all."

She cocked her head to one side and gave him a long, speculative look. "Are you sure you're not the one who's feeling a bit pressed?"

It took a moment for him to understand. "Now don't go thinkin' that, lass," he said defensively. "I'm the one that wants to get married. You're the one that's always puttin' it off."

"Me! You agreed that once we married, things would change and that neither of us was ready to give up our murders." She was incensed by the unfairness of the charge. Mind you, she'd been the one to realize that once they wed, there would most definitely be many changes in their lives. For starters, Smythe would want to give her everything, including her own home. Once that happened, no matter how hard they tried, life would be different. Neither of them was ready to face those kinds of changes. But blast it all, he'd agreed with her.

"You're right," he soothed, not wanting to ruffle her feathers any further. "I did agree. But just because neither of us wants a change just yet, I'll not 'ave you thinkin' I don't want to marry you. I want that more than anything."

"Then what's all this nonsense about?" she complained. "Oh, come on, let's get home. It's cold, and I learned ever so much today. I don't want to miss the meeting. You and I can sort this out later."

"There's nothing to sort out," he fell into step beside her. Betsy knew her own mind, if she didn't think he was too old, then well, he wasn't. But still, that conversation with Blimpey had left him feeling uneasy. "I just wanted to make sure you didn't mind the difference in our ages."

"Don't be daft," she took his arm. "It's not all that much, and it means nothing. I'd never even given it much thought until you brought it up."

Blast, he thought, maybe he should have kept his mouth shut.

The others were already seated around the table by the time they got to the kitchen. Wiggins was bent over, giving Fred a good petting. He straightened up as they entered the room. "I told Mrs. Jeffries you two would be along soon, told 'er I'd spotted you doin' a bit of courtin' in the garden."

"We weren't courtin'," Smythe said. "We were talkin'."

"Why don't you both have a seat and we'll get started," Mrs. Jeffries could tell the coachman was annoyed about something. She hoped he and Betsy weren't quarreling. But then again, it was quite natural for an engaged couple to occasionally have a difference of opinion. "I've quite a bit to report." She and Mrs. Goodge had already agreed that they wouldn't tell the others about Dr. Bosworth's news until the very end of the meeting. She didn't want to dampen their enthusiasm by telling them they might not have a murder at all.

"I wish I could say that," Wiggins gave the dog one last stroke and went to his chair. "Cor blimey, them tarts look good. I'm starved."

"You're not to make a pig of yourself," Mrs. Goodge chided. "Don't ruin your appetite. I've got a nice roast in the oven for supper."

"I think we'd best get right to it." Mrs. Jeffries poured the tea and began handing the cups around.

"Can I go first?" Betsy asked. At the housekeeper's nod, she told them everything she'd found out from the clerk Gilbert Pratting. She always made sure she repeated every little detail that she'd learned, no matter how inconsequential it might seem on the surface. They'd had too many cases solved correctly because of some tiny little fact that had been mentioned right at this very table.

"What's a strut?" Mrs. Goodge asked when Betsy had finished.

"It's a small part that helps fasten other parts," Smythe replied. "You know, it's one of them little bits that don't look important, but if they go missing, the whole contraption can fall apart."

"You mean like the time the pin thing broke off of my sausage maker and the handle fell off? That was a right mess, wasn't it! We had mountains of pork butt all over the kitchen and nothing to grind it with. Just goes to show how important the little bits in life are, doesn't it."

"That's right," Mrs. Jeffries added. She had her own questions to ask the maid. "So Pratting said that the clerk to the chief accountant said they'd not have jobs if Westover's engine hadn't sold?"

"That's what he said," Betsy replied, "and he wasn't unsure of himself when he was talking. He said it like it was the gospel."

"That means the firm is in trouble," Smythe muttered.

"Very probably," the housekeeper agreed. She took a sip of her tea.

"Maybe the firm's in trouble, but some of the partners aren't short of money," Mrs. Goodge added. "Oliver Arkwright has plenty, well, leastways his wife does."

"Did you hear that from one of your sources?" Wiggins asked cheerfully.

"That's where I hear everything," she replied.

"I wish we knew more about the argument that Westover had with James Horrocks," Betsy frowned slightly. "Too bad that lad got off the omnibus when he did. That might have been important."

"If 'e knew about it, I'm sure others in the firm do too," Smythe said kindly. "We'll find out what we need to know, we always do."

"You're right," the maid replied. "I expect I can find out about it tomorrow if I put my mind to it. Anyway, I've said my piece."

"What time is Lady Cannonberry supposed to be 'ere?" Wiggins asked.

Mrs. Jeffries started guiltily. Perhaps they should have waited for Ruth. But she still wasn't sure about the wisdom of discussing everything about the case with her. Ruth and the inspector were getting closer all the time. The housekeeper didn't want to be in the position of having encouraged the woman to keep secrets from Gerald Witherspoon. That wouldn't do their relationship any good at all. Yet telling Ruth she couldn't help out hadn't been a reasonable alternative either. She already knew what they were up to, and she was eager to do her bit. Besides, with Luty and Hatchet away, Lady Cannonberry's social connections might be very useful. They'd given her an easy assignment—to find out what she could about the partners in the firm. "She ought to be here any minute, we'll catch her up when she arrives."

"Don't worry, boy," Mrs. Goodge said. "We'll not leave her out of things. Now, as I was sayin', some of the partners aren't short of money. With or without the firm, the Arkwright's should be fine."

"Does he have money too?" Betsy asked.

The cook shook her head. "He had the aristocratic connections. She had the money. Her family is in trade and property. The gossip I heard is she only married him to get a step up socially."

Fred suddenly leapt up and bounded down the hallway. A second later, there was a knock on the back door. Wiggins was out of his chair like a shot and escorting Ruth into the kitchen a few moments later. She discarded her cloak and hat as she walked. "I'm so terribly sorry to be late, but honestly, it couldn't be helped. I was working on the case, and I simply couldn't leave without getting as much information as possible."

Mrs. Jeffries's heart sank. She hoped Ruth had been discreet. Getting information was important, but keeping their activities a secret was even more important. Not that all of them were always discreet. "Please don't worry about your tardiness, we only just started. Sit down and have some tea. We'll catch you up on what we've learned later. Mrs. Goodge was just telling us about the financial situation of some of the firm's partners."

"Tea sounds heavenly," she sank into the empty chair Wiggins held out for her. Betsy handed her a steaming cup of tea.

Mrs. Jeffries looked at the cook. "What else did you hear?"

"Not much more, only what Betsy's already mentioned, that James Horrocks has a reputation for being tight with money. But I've got my sources on the hunt, so to speak, and I ought to know more in a day or two."

"Excellent," the housekeeper said. She turned to Ruth, "would you like to share what you've learned with us?"

Ruth giggled, then her hand flew to her mouth. "Oh dear, I sound just like a schoolgirl. Honestly, I can't tell you how very excited I am to be a part of all this."

"We're delighted to 'ave you with us," Wiggins said quickly.

"Oh dear, I mustn't ramble." Ruth glanced at the carriage clock on the top of the pine sideboard. "I know we're a bit pressed for time, so I'll get right to it. I had a little chat with one of my husband's old friends, and he gave me some information on the background of Westover's firm." She stopped and looked at Mrs. Jeffries, "Don't worry, I was very discreet."

"I'm sure you were. Do go on."

"The firm was founded by Harry Donovan's grandfather. It was a family firm until ten years ago when Donovan needed to raise capital to expand. He wanted to start doing his own manufacturing and apparently that requires a great deal of money."

"Is that when the other partners bought in?" Smythe asked.

"That's when James Horrocks and Oliver Arkwright bought into the firm, Lawrence Melcher didn't buy in until two years later. It was when Melcher came along that the firm's name changed, it used to be called Donovan and Son. It was actually quite successful when the grandfather and the father were running it."

"I wonder why Arkwright's name isn't part of the company name?" Wiggins mused.

"I asked Jonathan that very question," Ruth said. "Apparently, Arkwright didn't put in enough money to get his name included."

Betsy shook her head. "There's something I don't understand, if the company isn't worth much, then why'd the other partners buy into it?"

"I don't know," Ruth admitted uncertainly. "But if you'd like, I could try to find out."

"That's a very good idea," Mrs. Jeffries said quickly. Company business was all very interesting, but it probably had nothing to do with Westover's murder. In her experience, people were generally killed for personal reasons. "Did you learn anything else?"

"Not really, only that Lawrence Melcher was persuaded to put his money into the company by Donovan. Since the company's fortunes have taken a turn for the worse, there's supposedly quite a bit of rancor between the two men. They had a dreadful argument at the bank a fortnight or so ago. It was so bad the manager asked them to leave."

Betsy shot a quick look at the housekeeper, who nodded almost imperceptibly. The message was clear, the maid was to find out what had happened at the bank. A fortnight ago was roughly the time that Westover would have been murdered.

Mrs. Jeffries smiled warmly at Ruth. "You've done wonderfully. We're very grateful for the information."

"Oh, I want to keep on helping," Ruth said quickly. "It's ever so exciting, and I do believe we're all meant to serve the cause of justice. Unfortunately, tomorrow I'm going to a committee meeting. We're trying to get women the vote, but perhaps I can beg off . . ."

"Oh you mustn't do that," Mrs. Jeffries interrupted. "Your work for the rights of women is important too."

Ruth looked doubtful. "Are you sure? Catching murderers is useful as well. One doesn't like to think killers are dashing about free to do it again."

"Maybe you can do both," Wiggins suggested helpfully. He was totally unaware of the surreptious frowns the others shot him. "You can go along to your meetin' and then come along back 'ere for our meetin'. Besides if you're busy in the afternoon, you can go out lookin' for clues in the mornin', can't she Mrs. Jeffries?"

"Of course she can," the housekeeper replied. She told herself that Wiggins was simply being kind and helpful. However, she decided that she and Wiggins might need to have a little chat tonight after supper. "Now, we really do need to move along. Smythe, have you anything to report."

"Not yet, but I've got some lines of inquiry I'm workin' on. I'll 'ave somethin' by tomorrow."

"Wiggins?"

"Nothin' from me," the lad admitted cheerfully, "but I'll keep at it. I've got a few irons in the fire."

Mrs. Jeffries sighed silently. She couldn't put off the news any longer. "I do have something to report. Dr. Bosworth stopped by today. He had some information for us. Now, before I give you the details, I want you to know that he was very uncertain as to what it actually meant."

Constable Barnes and Inspector Witherspoon waited in the drawing room of the Horrocks house. The fireplace was cold, the lamps unlighted and dark blue curtains wide open to the gloom of approaching evening. The room was getting darker by the moment. Surely, Constable Barnes thought, in a household this large, someone would come along and at least light the ruddy lamps. But so far, they'd seen no one but the maid who'd answered the door. He saw the inspector pull his overcoat tighter and noticed he'd not removed his gloves.

Maybe the interview with Edna Horrocks wouldn't take long, Barnes thought. He was tired, cold, and his feet hurt. But he refused to give in to the discomfort. He might be getting older, but he wasn't going to become lax in his duty or his demeanor. Occasionally, he might forget something, but he was still a good copper. They wouldn't even be here if he hadn't re-interviewed the staff at the office and found out about Edna Horrocks. He was startled by the sudden sound of footsteps in the hall.

"I hope that's Mrs. Horrocks," the inspector said softly. "I'd like to get this over and done with. I'm very tired."

Edna Horrocks swept into the room. She was an attractive woman in her mid-fifties. She wore a black and green striped dress with a dark green overskirt. Her wheat-colored hair was done up in a tight topknot. She didn't look pleased. She stared at them coldly out of a pair of deep set hazel eyes. "What do you want?" she asked.

Witherspoon was so taken aback by her rudeness, he blurted out the truth, "To find out why you were hanging about outside your husband's office on the day Harlan Westover was murdered." He clamped his mouth shut, mortified that he'd not been more polite. He'd never spoken so rudely to a woman in his entire life.

"I was spying on my husband," she shot back. The inspector's uncharacteristic bluntness had surprised her into speaking before she could guard her words. "Oh dear, I oughtn't to have said that." She closed her eyes, sighed, and then sank down on a chair near the door. "I'm sorry, Inspector. I've been terribly rude. Please sit down and let's start over."

"Of course, madam," Witherspoon replied. He nodded at the constable, and the two of them moved to the settee. "I do appreciate your honesty, though. Would you mind telling me why you want to spy on Mr. Horrocks."

"Why do you think, Inspector," she said wearily.

"I've no idea," Witherspoon replied.

She stared at him incredulously. "The usual reason, sir."

"Usual reason?" he repeated.

"I think Mrs. Horrocks is afraid Mr. Horrocks is seeing another woman."

"Thank goodness one of you understands," she said. "I knew there was a board meeting that day, you see, and that meant that James would be leaving the office right afterwards. I decided to follow him."

"You'd actually want to know your spouse was being unfaithful?" he murmured. Gracious, this was becoming a most odd police interview.

"Of course," she replied. "The only way I can get a divorce is if I've evidence of adultery."

It was completely dark by the time the inspector came through his front door. He desperately wanted to discuss this case with his housekeeper. "Good evening, Mrs. Jeffries. It's very cold outside, and I'm dreadfully tired."

She reached for his hat. "Good evening, sir. Not to worry, Mrs. Goodge has a lovely meal in the oven for your dinner. That'll warm you up nicely."

He took off his heavy overcoat. "I'd like a glass of sherry first."

"I thought you might, sir." She hung up his garments and ushered him toward the drawing room. "It's already poured."

"Excellent."

A few moments later, he was settled into his favorite chair and Mrs. Jeffries was sitting across from him. "Inspector, have you thought anymore about what we discussed yesterday?" She did hate to be a nag, but this was one task he'd been avoiding.

Witherspoon winced. "Well, I've been awfully busy, what with the investigation . . ."

"Of course you have, sir. But as I said earlier, you really must take care of your social obligations."

"Can't I just invite the chief inspector and his wife to a restaurant?"

"It's not just the chief, sir. There's also a good number of others who you ought to entertain. There's your neighbor, Mrs. Cross, Lady Cannonberry, and that nice sergeant and his wife. You really must consider it, sir. It would be very good for your career."

An expression of panic crossed the inspector's face. "But I'm no good at that sort of social thingamabobby. I'd be the host, I'd have to make sure that things went along nicely, that people talked to each other . . ."

"You could ask Lady Cannonberry to act as your hostess," Mrs. Jeffries suggested.

Witherspoon immediately brightened. "Do you think she'd do it?"

"I suspect she'd love to, now do think about it, sir. As I said, a nice dinner party would do wonders for your career. Now, sir. Do tell me about your day. Is the investigation going well? Did you find out much today?"

"Quite a bit, actually," Witherspoon said quickly. He was relieved to be off the subject of the dinner party. He could face down a crazed killer waving a pistol and it wouldn't terrify him as much as the thought of playing host at a dinner party. But he knew his housekeeper was right, he did have social obligations to repay. He brushed the dinner party worries aside and began to give her the details of his day. As it had been quite a long day, he went to great pains to remember everything. He'd found talking over his cases did wonders for putting him on the right path, so to speak.

Mrs. Jefries listened carefully, occasionally asking a question or making a comment. By the time he'd finished telling her about his interview with Edna Horrocks, she'd managed to work several of her own ideas into their conversation. By the time he was on his way to the dining room for his dinner, he was utterly convinced that his own brilliant mind had produced a whole new perspective on this case.

CHAPTER 6

———❖———

The morning dawned bright and cold. Smythe caught Betsy on the landing before they went down for breakfast. "Did ya sleep well, love?"

"Wonderfully," she said. She looked around and then stood on tiptoe and kissed him on the mouth. "Now come along, then," she said as she drew back, "let's not be late. I'm fairly sure Mrs. Jeffries got quite a bit of information out of the inspector last night."

"There's no 'urry, love," he murmured, as he reached for her. He wanted a few more moments alone with her, a few more moments where he didn't have to share her with the others or with one of the inspector's cases.

She deftly stepped to one side just as Wiggins came bounding down the staircase. "Mornin' all," he said cheerfully. "Brrr . . . it's cold. Even with the fire in the grate, I didn't think our room would ever get warm. Let's get on down to the kitchen, it's sure to be nice and toasty."

Betsy fell into step with the footman, and Smythe gave up. He trailed after them. He wasn't going to have a chance to talk to her alone again, not this morning. Blast a Spaniard, why had he ever brought up the subject of age? She'd never thought anything about it till he'd rubbed her nose in it. What if she started thinkin' about it, started thinkin' there was too great a difference between them? What then? Bloomin' Ada, but he'd been a fool. He'd tossed and turned all night, worrying about it.

They went into the kitchen and took their places. Over breakfast, Mrs. Jeffries gave them a full report on what she'd learned from the inspector.

"Cor blimey," Wiggins exclaimed, "you mean this Mrs. Horrocks was actually waitin' about, tryin' to spy on her husband?"

"Yes, and it obviously wasn't the first time," Mrs. Jeffries replied.

"Mrs. Horrocks told the inspector she's sure her husband had spotted her. That's why he went to that pub for lunch. It was the sort of place she didn't dare go into unescorted. She waited and waited for him to come out, and when he didn't she realized he must have slipped out the back door. Apparently, it's not a happy marriage."

"Most marriages aren't," the cook interjected, "but most people don't go about wanting to get divorced. I've never heard of such a thing."

"Divorces do 'appen," Smythe said thoughtfully. "But even so, I don't see 'ow Mrs. Horrocks wantin' a divorce can 'ave anythin' to do with Westover's murder."

"Neither do I," Mrs. Jeffries agreed. "Not unless there was a connection between Mrs. Horrocks and Harlan Westover that we don't know about."

"I'll try and find out," Smythe reached for another slice of bread. "Maybe there was somethin' between the two of 'em, and maybe Mr. Horrocks found out about it."

"Does Horrocks have an alibi?" Mrs. Goodge asked. "I mean, other than the lunch at the pub. Oh bother, what's wrong with me! After his lunch, he's supposed to have gone to look at property on the Goldhawk Road."

"He did 'ave lunch at the pub," Smythe said. "I checked. But he was finished by one o'clock and Mrs. Horrocks was right, he did slip out the back door."

"It's a very weak alibi." The housekeeper frowned. "But then, everyone's alibi is fairly weak." She sighed. "I'm not even sure we're investigating the right group of people. For all we know, Westover might have been killed by someone who had nothing to do with his work. Someone from his past. Someone he'd wronged before he started working here in London."

"Not to worry, Mrs. Jeffries, if that turns out to be what 'appened," Wiggins said cheerfully, "then we'll suss it out sooner or later. We always do. Anyways, now that I've found out about Mrs. Horrocks and her wantin' a divorce, I think I'll 'ave a snoop around there. No tellin' what I might find out."

Despite her misgivings, Mrs. Jeffries smiled. It was impossible to be downcast in the face of such optimism. "That's a good idea, Wiggins, but before you do, why don't you have another go at Westover's neighborhood?"

Wiggins's eyebrows shot up in surprise. "All right, if you say so . . . uh . . . but what am I lookin' for?"

She wasn't sure herself. But she knew they were sorely lacking in hard facts. "The killer had to have gotten to the Lynch house by some means. He or she had to have entered the house, through either the front door or the back. Someone might have seen something . . ." her voice trailed off. "Good gracious, we've been quite foolish."

"How do you mean?" Mrs. Goodge asked.

"We really must speak with Mrs. Lynch," she replied. Her mind worked furiously. "We've got to ask her about the front door."

"Front door?" Betsy repeated. "Didn't the inspector say that Mr. Horrocks had said it was unlocked?"

"Yes, but just because he said it, doesn't mean it's true." She turned her gaze to Smythe, "For many people keeping their doors locked is as natural to them as breathing. I'm betting that an elderly woman, living with two lodgers had them both trained to lock the front door the moment they crossed the threshold." She knew she was on to something, but she wasn't certain what it was.

"But we know that Westover was upset," Betsy pointed out, "maybe he forgot to lock up when he came in."

"When something is a habit, we do it without thinking," Mrs. Jeffries replied. "I don't know that Mrs. Lynch insisted the doors be locked, but we must find out."

"You want me to talk to Mrs. Lynch?" Wiggins wasn't sure he was the best person for that task.

"No, I'll take care of it," she replied. "But do go back to the neighborhood this morning. There is still so much we need to find out."

"And as the police didn't even know they had them a murder, they wouldn't have done much in the way of questioning the neighbors," Betsy added. "You might find out all sorts of things."

The housekeeper poured herself more tea. "With Wiggins working that area, we'll at least be sure we haven't missed something obvious. Oh, by the way, Ruth will be here for our afternoon meeting. She might have some information for us as well."

"Is that it then?" Smythe picked up his mug and drained it. At Mrs. Jeffries's nod, he rose to his feet. "I'll be off then, there's a couple more hansom cab drivers I want to talk to today, and if it's all the same to you, I'll have a go at seein' if anyone saw Horrocks on the Goldhawk Road."

Betsy got up too. "Come along Wiggins, let's get cracking. I might as well go with you as far as Holland Park."

"I'm goin' to take the omnibus," he announced, as he stuffed the last bit of toast into his mouth. "It's too cold to walk very far."

Smythe shot Betsy a fast glance, but before he could say a word, she said, "Don't worry, I'll take the omnibus as well." She knew him so well, she was beginning to read his mind.

"The lad is right. It is too cold to be larkin' about the streets." He knew he sounded like a mother hen, but he couldn't help himself.

"Don't worry about me, I'll be fine. Most of my work today will be indoors. I'm going to do my best to find the bank the partners had that row in a few weeks ago," she laughed. "Let's keep our fingers crossed that Melcher and Donovan made a big enough fuss that people still remember all the details."

"I'd try the banks near the office." Mrs. Jeffries suggested.

Betsy headed for the coat tree. "There can't be that many banks in the neighborhood."

Mrs. Jeffries smiled encouragingly as the kitchen emptied out. But one part of her feared they were all wasting their time. She'd spent half the night awake, worrying about what Dr. Bosworth had told them. The truth was, they might be rushing about chasing their tails. Harlan Westover could very well have taken his own life. She'd given the matter a good, hard think and come to the conclusion that unless they got their hands on some very compelling evidence, they simply couldn't be sure if this was murder or suicide. Drat, but sometimes life was so very complicated.

Wiggins pulled up the collar on his thick, heavy coat to fight off the chill. He'd been up and down the street in front of Harlan Westover's house half a dozen times, and no one had so much as poked a nose out. It was too ruddy cold for anyone to be out and about.

He leaned against a lamppost at the end of the block and stared morosely at the quiet street. Nothing stirred. There were no housewives with shopping baskets, no maids armed with brooms or footmen with brass polish. There wasn't even anyone cutting across the green. What was he going to do? He refused to go home with nothing.

Discouraged, he started to turn away when a young lad came racing around the corner and almost crashed into him. The boy leapt to one side. "Sorry, gov, I didn't see you standin' there."

" 'Ow's that then, I'm not invisible," Wiggins replied with a laugh. "What's your rush, boy?"

"It's bloomin' cold," the boy said. But he stopped and stared at Wiggins out of a pair of curious green eyes. His cheeks were flushed a bright pink, and an unruly mop of curly brown hair was visible beneath a knitted green woolen cap. His short gray jacket was clean, but well worn, and the bright blue wool scarf wound twice around his neck was far too long to actually belong to him. "My mam tossed me out this mornin'. She said I was fit to drive her to drink and to go run off some of my fidgetin'."

"How old are ya?" Wiggins asked. He didn't hold out much hope the lad could tell him anything useful, but it was someone to talk to for a few minutes.

"Twelve," the boy grinned. "My name's Derek Wilkins. I live down the street. My mam's the housekeeper."

"Well, Derek," Wiggins said amiably. "I don't suppose you'd like to walk with me a bit. I'm waitin' for my friend, she's applyin' for a post as a maid at a big 'ouse around the corner. It's borin' as bits out 'ere on my own." It was a weak story, but it would do for a young one.

The lad shrugged. "Mam says not to talk to strangers, but you look 'armless enough. I reckon if you try anythin' I could outrun you. I'm a powerful good runner."

"I'll bet you are," Wiggins said. He started off down the street. The boy fell into step beside him. "Anyway, what kind of neighborhood is this? I don't want my fiancée workin' somewhere that isn't nice."

"Fiancée," Derek repeated. "I thought you said it was your friend."

"We ain't officially engaged, not yet. But bein' as you live 'ere, you'd be in a position to know if it's safe or not for Flossie."

"Nothin' much happens around here," Derek said.

"Are you sure?" Wiggins pressed. This wasn't going the way he wanted. "No robberies or missing persons or murders?"

"Well," the boy rubbed his nose. "Mrs. Markham's cat was stolen. That's what she claims, but Mam says the silly old thing probably run off. And Mr. Walters, he lives down at number 17, he lost his topcoat and gloves. Someone took 'em right off the coat peg when he left his door open . . ."

"That's it, then?" Wiggins tried to keep the impatience out of his voice.

"Oh, that poor Mr. Westover who lives across the street from us, he killed himself . . ."

"Killed himself?" Wiggins clucked his tongue. "When did this 'appen?"

" 'Bout a fortnight ago," Derek replied. He pointed toward the opposite side of the road. "He had rooms at Mrs. Lynch's, right up there."

"How'd he do it?"

"Blew his brains out," Derek said eagerly. "And what's more, I heard the gun goin' off. I tried to tell me mam, but she said I were makin' it up."

"Did you tell the police?"

"The police," Derek snorted. "They wasn't interested. When they come around the second time 'cause Mrs. Lynch was raisin' a fuss and callin' 'em fools, Mam said I wasn't to say anythin'. Said not to cause trouble. But I don't see how tellin' what I heard could cause trouble."

Wiggins was elated. If the lad was telling the truth, they would have an exact time of death. "I don't see 'ow it could either. Cor blimey, you must be a clever one to remember about the gun."

Derek tried to shrug as if it didn't matter, but he couldn't quite hide his proud grin. "Weren't nuthin'. I was outside, ya see. Mam wanted me to pick up a loaf down at the baker's. She'd forgot it that mornin'. I'd just started off when all of a sudden there was this 'orrible loud noise, like thunder, only sharper and quicker like."

"What did ya do?" Wiggins pressed.

"Do?" Derek seemed puzzled by the question. "There weren't nuthin' to do. I looked about tryin' to suss out the cause, but I didn't see anything so I went on to the baker's to get Mam's loaf. She'd be right snarky if I didn't get her the loaf, she needed it for the afternoon tea."

"Did anyone else come out because of the noise?"

The boy's brow wrinkled. "Nah, I don't think so. I don't remember seein' anyone. It was a cold day, and there was plenty of traffic on the road. I expect I'm the only one that 'eard anything, but then, I was practically standing outside Mrs. Lynch's when it 'appened."

"I don't suppose you know what time it 'appened?" Wiggins asked casually. From the corner of his eye, he watched the lad's expression.

"Course I know," Derek bragged.

"You 'ave a watch?"

"Don't be daft, course I don't 'ave a watch. I know because when I got to the baker's, it was almost ten past two."

"How long did it take to get to the baker's?" Wiggins asked patiently.

"About five or six minutes," Derek replied. "It's just across from Shepherds Bush Station. Mam don't like the one 'round the corner from us. That means the poor bloke musta done it a few minutes past two o'clock."

Betsy refused to be defeated. She pulled open the heavy door of the London and Leicester Bank and stepped inside. This was the third bank she'd tried this morning, and so far, she'd had no luck whatsoever. She stopped just inside the door and studied the territory for a moment. On the far side of the huge room, clerks dressed in stiff white shirts and narrow ties labored behind a long, high, wooden counter. Each clerk was separated from the one next to him by wooden partitions.

Betsy hesitated. She had a good story at the ready, but it hadn't worked at the last bank. That clerk had been in such a hurry his only concern had been to get rid of her as quickly as possible. She scanned the young men serving behind the counter. The one in the middle was tall, confident, and handsome as sin, the one next to him appeared to be involved in a very intense discussion with a middle-aged matron. Betsy's gaze stopped on the third clerk. He was perfect. Chinless, pale eyes, and already balding even though he was young, she was sure she could get him to talk. She started for her quarry and took her place in his line. It was the longest of the lines.

She waited patiently as the patrons ahead of her did their business. The customer in front of her finished his business and moved off. No one had gotten into line behind her, so if she got the fellow talking, she might learn something useful. Betsy put on her most dazzling smile and stepped up to the counter.

The clerk looked up as he shut the cash drawer. A blush crept up his pale cheeks as he took in her expression. Apparently, he wasn't used to pretty blonds beaming at him. "Uh . . . can I help you, miss?"

"I certainly hope so," she sighed dramatically. "I've got a most unusual problem, you see, and I'm not even sure I'm in the right bank."

"Oh . . . oh . . . do tell me how I can help," he sputtered.

She leaned closer and locked her gaze on his. "You see, about a fortnight ago, my grandmother happened to be in a bank in this area. She only popped in to keep warm. By that, I mean, it wasn't her bank. While she was there, two gentlemen got into such a terrible row. It was such a terrible argument, that the bank manager asked them to leave . . ."

"Oh yes," he said brightly, "I remember it quite well . . . it was Mr.

Melcher and Mr. Donovan. It was quite awful. They started shouting at each other so loudly that Mr. Haggerty asked them to leave . . ." his voice trailed off as the clerk on his left shot him a frown.

But Betsy wasn't going to let some sour-faced bank clerk stop the flow of information. She brightened her smile even further and leaned so far over the counter it's a wonder she didn't bang her head into the fellow's chest. "Yes, yes, that's what my grandmother told me."

The clerk cleared his throat. "Uh, now uh, how can I help?"

"Do you happen to know where either of the gentlemen that were having the row actually live?" she asked boldly.

"You want to know where they live?" he repeated incredulously.

Betsy nodded eagerly, as though it were the most ordinary of requests. "Of course. That's why I'm here. You see one of them dropped his pocket watch. It's quite a nice watch. He dropped it just outside the door. Grandmother left right behind them. She said the man took his watch out, looked at it, and then was so upset that when he went to put it away, he missed his pocket completely, and the watch fell onto the pavement. He was lucky it didn't break."

"Goodness, it must be a jolly good watch," he said thoughtfully.

"Grandmother shouted at him," Betsy continued, "but he was in such a state that he didn't hear her."

He gaped at her. "I'm afraid I still don't understand."

Yee Gods, she thought to herself, the fellow was a bit of a dolt. "Grandmother picked the watch up," she explained patiently. "She tried to catch up with him, but she's an elderly woman and he was walking very fast. He disappeared before she could give the wretched thing back to him. So she took it home and has been fretting over how to get the silly thing back to the proper owner for two weeks now. That's why I've come."

"Why didn't she bring it back here?" the clerk asked. He sounded curious, not suspicious.

"Because she couldn't recall which bank it was," Betsy replied. "She only stepped inside for a moment to get out of the cold." She threw caution to the winds. "Look, can you meet me after you get off work or perhaps at your meal break? I really don't want to take up anymore of your time here, and I don't want to get you into any sort of trouble. But this is very important. Grandmother will have another stroke if I don't give that wretched watch to the proper owner . . ."

"I take my meal at half past eleven," he said quickly. "I could meet you then."

"Excellent, meet me at the tea shop on the corner. I'll be waiting." With that, she tossed him another dazzling smile, turned on her heel, and left. She didn't want to give him time to change his mind.

Smythe knocked softly on the back door of the Dirty Duck pub. It was outside of hours but he didn't want to wait for opening time to see Blimpey. There was too much to do today. He shivered as a blast of cold wind blew off the dark water of the Thames. From inside, he heard the faint sound of steps and then the door opened. A bearded fellow wearing a stained apron stuck his head out. "We're closed, mate. Come back later."

"I've got business with Blimpey. Tell 'im that Smythe is 'ere."

"I'm not his keeper, you know." The publican wiped his hands on his dirty apron.

"Let 'im in," Blimpey's voice came from inside. "He's a right persistent bloke."

The barman stepped to one side, and Smythe stepped through the door. Blimpey was standing at the far end of the corridor, leaning against the doorway of the public bar. "You're out and about early," he said amiably. "Come in and have a sit down. I was just havin' a bite of breakfast."

Smythe followed him into the bar. Blimpey went back to his spot in front of the fireplace. There was a cheerful fire burning in the grate and a plate of cheese and bread was on the table. Blimpey gestured at the food. "Once I'm married, I'll have a proper cooked breakfast. The only hot thing Sam can do is a pot of tea."

"Have you asked her yet?"

Blimpey dropped his gaze and shrugged. "Not yet. I want to do it properly. Wait till just the right moment."

"Haven't worked up the courage, eh?"

"Cor blimey, big fellah. How the hell did you manage?" Blimpey picked up his mug and took a long, slurpy sip of tea. "Scares me to death, it does. I've faced off coppers, thieves, and river pirates, but nothin's got me shakin' in my boots as much as the idea of askin' her to marry me. What if she says 'no'?"

Smythe gazed at him sympathetically. He knew how painful Blimpey's problem could be. He'd been there himself. But right now, he needed information. "That's just a risk you'll have to take. You might ask one of her friends how she feels about you."

Blimpey brightened immediately. "Cor blimey, that's a right good idea. I could ask Cora Werthers to have a word. At least that way I'd know if it was safe to bring up the subject. I don't want to lose her, you know. I'd rather have her as a friend as not."

"I understand." He'd felt the same way about Betsy.

Blimpey sighed and gave himself a shake. "Right then, on to business. You're 'ere a bit early."

"Knowin' you, I was fairly certain you'd 'ave somethin' for me."

"I've got a bit. It seems your Mr. Westover was quite the fellow. His old employers up in Birmingham were more than a little sorry to see him go. They offered him a barrel of money to stay on, but by that time, Donovan had already snared him and lured him to London. Rupert and Lincoln was in a right old snit about it. There was quite a bit of bad blood between the firms. Still is. Old man Lincoln vowed to put Donovan and the others out of business."

"That's a bit harsh."

"Not really," Blimpey said. "Westover wasn't just a bloomin' good designer, he was a brilliant engineer. I can't make 'ead nor tails out of all that mechanical nonsense, but apparently, havin' someone who's got the gift for it in your firm is good. I don't know the ins and outs of it, but when Rupert and Lincoln lost Westover, they started having one problem after another. They make steam engines, you see, for the railways. Westover was their chief engineer, and once he was gone, they couldn't seem to fix anythin' right. It might be worth havin' a look at Lincoln. He was in London a couple of weeks ago."

Smythe thought about it for a moment and then he shook his head. "I'll have a look. But if he was that angry, why kill Westover. Why not kill Donovan?"

"Maybe he considered Westover a traitor," Blimpey suggested.

"But he wouldn't wait three years," Smythe replied. "Or maybe he would. Do you have anything else for me?"

"Not much," Blimpey said from around a mouthful of bread. "I did find out that Harry Donovan's wife was the widow of John Welch."

"Who's he?" Smythe was beginning to get a bit confused.

"A fellow who made a lot of money importing tea. Died a few years back and left every cent to his good wife, who married Harry Donovan just in time to buy the building the firm is housed in, thus eliminating a very ugly eviction process. They've been at that address for a long time. Course now that Mrs. Donovan bought the leasehold, they'll not have to worry about having to move for awhile."

"Cor blimey, you mean the company was in so much trouble they couldn't pay the rent?"

"Couldn't pay the rent, nor the rates, nor their clerks' wages. If Donovan hadn't married the widow Welch when he did, his company would have been doing business from the front parlor of his house."

"How convenient for Mr. Donovan. A rich widow just larkin' about desperate to marry him."

"She wanted to marry him all right, but she's no fool. She bought the building as an investment. Mind you, she did give him a nice lease and put a bit of cash in the business."

Smythe nodded. "If Donovan was so broke, how did he have the money to lure Westover away from Rupert and Lincoln?"

"Different time, Smythe," Blimpey said. "He married the missus about seven years back. She put in enough to keep the concern going for a couple of years and then when that run out, he brought in Arkwright and Horrocks. After that, Melcher come along with his cash and Donovan was set for a bit." Blimpey smiled brightly. "Course, no matter 'ow much you have, it'll never be enough if you keep pissin' it away. From what I've learned, none of the partners in that company knows their arse from their elbows, let alone how to run a business. Sad too, Donovan's father and grandfather are probably spinnin' in their graves. Now those gents knew what they was about, they didn't have to bring in partners to keep the business goin'. "

"Will you be able to find out more by tomorrow?" Smythe asked. He didn't know what to make of any of this. But he was sure that once he told the others, they'd all put it together. They were a clever bunch, even if he did think so himself.

"I've got my sources workin' on it." He sighed. "I just wish that women was as easy as work."

"So do I, mate," Smythe agreed. "So do I."

Inspector Witherspoon wasn't sure what to do next. He'd interviewed the partners and their spouses, and Constable Barnes had spoken to everyone at the office. Twice. "I still don't have any idea where we are with this case," he said to Barnes. They were in a Lyons Tea Room trying to get warm. Witherspoon took another sip of tea. He was taking his time. He wasn't in any hurry to go back out into the cold. Besides, he hadn't a clue where to go next.

"I think we ought to interview Mrs. Arkwright again, sir," Barnes suggested. "She's a bit flighty, but she seems observant, nonetheless."

Witherspoon perked right up. "I say, do you have some questions you'd like to ask her?" This might not be such a dreadful afternoon after all.

"Well, it seems to me she might know a bit more about everyone's movements on the day of the murder."

"Really?"

"Yes, she admitted she was at the firm on the day of the board meeting, the day Westover died."

"She met her husband for luncheon," the inspector added. "She told us that."

"Don't you think it a bit odd, sir," Barnes mused. "She never mentioned that she'd seen Mrs. Donovan there that day. She was waiting for her husband too."

"We don't know that the two women actually saw one another," the inspector pointed out. "Mrs. Donovan waited in the office proper, while I got the impression that Mrs. Arkwright had waited outside." He frowned, "Of course, I don't recall Mrs. Arkwright actually mentioning where she was waiting."

"She said she saw Westover when she and her husband were getting into a hansom," Barnes grinned. "But that doesn't mean she wasn't in the office and didn't see or hear something else that might end up being useful. Besides, I think she's a bit of a chatterbox, sir. If there's something goin' on at Donovan, Melcher, and Horrocks, I warrant we might have a chance of gettin' it out of her."

"I do believe you've got a point," Witherspoon replied. He was suddenly quite eager to get on with it. He reached into his pocket, pulled out some coins, and laid them on the table. "Let's stop at the restaurant Mr. and Mrs. Arkwright had lunch at as well. I want to have another go at the waiters."

"Right, sir. Best that we cover everything." He was biding his time, it wasn't quite the moment to steer the inspector back to the police reports. "For that matter, sir, I think it's odd that all the board members left the office that day. According to what the clerks said, that was very odd. There was generally always one of the partners on the premises. It was sort of an unwritten rule."

"Yes, but that meeting must have been quite upsetting. Someone committed a murder afterwards."

"Acrimony seems to have been the order of the day at that firm," Barnes said.

Mrs. Jeffries was doing a bit of dusting in the front parlor when Betsy arrived back at Upper Edmonton Gardens. The housekeeper stuck her head out into the hall when she heard the maid coming up the back stairs. "Hello, Betsy. I hope you've had a successful day."

"Hello, Mrs. Jeffries. It's been fine, so far," Betsy giggled. "I can't wait till we have our meeting."

"I think Mrs. Goodge has got someone in the kitchen, so I expect we'd best leave her be for a bit longer."

"I'll just finish tidying up the linen closet after I've changed my shoes." She took off her cloak. "You do think she'll be ready for our meeting, don't you?"

Mrs. Jeffries waved her feather duster airily. "Oh, I'm sure she'll be finished by then. Mrs. Goodge is very good at moving people along once she's got what she needs from them. I take it from the happy expression on your face that you had a run of good luck today."

Betsy grinned. "I found out ever so much. I just hope it's useful. How about you?"

"I popped over to Mrs. Lynch's," Mrs. Jeffries replied. "I found out what I needed to know."

"You spoke to Mrs. Lynch?"

"No, but I managed a word with Mr. Baker."

"Who's he?" Betsy asked.

"Her other tenant. He confirmed what I thought . . ." she broke off at the sound of more footsteps coming up the back stairs. "That sounds like Wiggins."

A moment later, the footman appeared at the top of the stairs. He waved in greeting. "Hello, Mrs. Jeffries, Betsy. Cor blimey, it's cold outside. I saw that Mrs. Goodge had someone with her in the kitchen. Do you think she'll be finished by our meetin' time? I think Lady Cannonberry is on her way across the garden."

"I'd best get downstairs then," Mrs. Jeffries tucked her duster under her arm and headed for the back stairs. "You two come on down when you're ready." She trotted down the stairs and was relieved to find the kitchen empty and Mrs. Goodge putting the kettle on.

"Not to worry," the cook assured her, "I kept my eye on the clock." She pulled the big brown china teapot off of the drying rack.

"I wasn't in the least anxious." Mrs. Jeffries headed for a covered plate at the far end of the long table. "Is that for us?"

The cook nodded. "It's lemon tarts, I thought we deserved something really nice today."

The housekeeper knew that meant Mrs. Goodge must have struck gold. She was always generous with treats when she'd learned a lot.

Within a few minutes, everyone had arrived and taken their places. It was obvious all of them had something to report. Ruth Cannonberry was practically bouncing up and down in her chair, Betsy's eyes sparkled, Mrs. Goodge hummed as she poured out the tea, Smythe looked extraordinarily pleased with himself, and Wiggins was grinning from ear to ear. Gracious, this was a fine how do you do. What on earth was she going to do? She almost wished Dr. Bosworth had kept his information to himself. Then she caught herself, what was she thinking? Of course Dr. Bosworth had been right to tell them what he knew.

"Mrs. Jeffries," Mrs. Goodge raised her voice. "Are you all right?"

"Oh dear, silly me," she smile apologetically. "I was thinking about our case. Do forgive me. Now, who would like to go first?"

They all spoke at once. Mrs. Jeffries raised her hand for silence. "Gracious, it seems we're all very eager to speak. Why don't we take it one at a time. Ruth, you're our guest, you go first."

"I don't want to step out of turn," Ruth began, "but if you insist. As you all know, I didn't think I'd have time to do much investigating, not with my women's meeting and everything, but you'll never guess, I heard ever so much at the meeting."

"Just goes to show you never know where you're goin' to find somethin' interestin'," Wiggins said eagerly.

"I don't know if it's useful or not, but I found out that Oliver Arkwright wouldn't have a farthing if it weren't for his wife."

Mrs. Jeffries hid her disappointment. They already knew that.

"I understand she's from a wealthy family," Mrs. Goodge said tactfully.

"Oh yes, I know you already know that, but I'll warrant that what you don't know is that Mrs. Arkwright wants her money back. She had a frightful row with her husband about money she loaned his firm. Mrs.

Merkle heard all about it from her maid who got it directly from Mrs. Arkwright's maid."

"How can she get her money back?" Smythe asked. "He's her husband. What's hers is his and what's his is hers."

Ruth shook her head. "Not anymore. Not since the Married Woman's Property Act. Surely you must have heard of it? It was passed in Parliament several years ago. It gives married women control over any money they bring into their marriage and any money that they inherit while married. Mrs. Arkwright not only brought quite a bit into the marriage, she's about to inherit quite a bit more."

"I thought she already had inherited," Mrs. Goodge said. "Didn't her uncle die recently?"

"He didn't die, he just went into a coma. But he's not expected to live much longer."

"Why'd she loan her husband money if she didn't want him to keep it for awhile?" Wiggins asked.

"She did it so that he could buy in to the firm. He'd convinced her that it was a good investment. Frankly, Mrs. Merkle is of the opinion that Penelope Arkwright loaned her husband the money to buy in as a partner to get him out of the house," Ruth replied. "Apparently, before that, he spent most of his time at home."

"No wonder she loaned him the cash," Mrs. Goodge muttered darkly. "Imagine having to put up with a man under your feet all day."

"They aren't very happily married," Ruth continued. "Mrs. Merkle's maid says that he's always reminding her that her family is in trade while his is related to the Queen."

"That's not very nice," Betsy said.

"She's getting her own back," Ruth grinned. "Mrs. Arkwright has threatened to take her husband to court to get her money back. That'll embarrass him and his family."

"You can do that?" Wiggins asked incredulously.

Ruth nodded. "It was a proper loan. She has a note and made him put up his house as collateral."

"So if she takes him to court and he can't repay the loan, does that mean she gets his house?" Wiggins asked.

"I think so," Ruth replied.

"Cor blimey, that don't say much for the institution of marriage," Smythe muttered.

CHAPTER 7

Betsy got the floor next. "I had a bit of luck finding out about that row between Melcher and Donovan."

"You didn't have any trouble finding the bank, then," Mrs. Goodge commented.

"It was the third one I tried," Betsy replied. "And I was lucky enough to find someone who'd witnessed the whole thing." She paused and shot a quick glance at Smythe. His expression was interested, but not overly so. She felt just the tiniest bit guilty about how she'd flirted with that poor bank clerk to get the information she'd needed, and she was sure that guilt was written all over her face. Her beloved was getting very good at reading her expressions, and even though he wasn't generally a jealous man, she'd just as soon not have him asking her any pointed questions about her sources. "The clerk who witnessed the argument is a real chatterbox. Told me all about it while we were waiting for the omnibus." This time, she didn't look at Smythe. "The row was very noisy. Everyone heard them. Lawrence Melcher got absolutely furious with Harry Donovan and accused him of running the business into the ground."

"That does seem to be the general assessment of the management of that firm," Mrs. Jeffries murmured. An idea popped into the back of her mind and just as quickly popped out again.

"What else did they say?" Mrs. Goodge pressed.

"The clerk hadn't heard the first part of the argument," Betsy explained.

"You said 'e'd 'eard the whole thing," Wiggins reminded her.

"Only from when the shouting started," Betsy said. "But from the exchange he heard, it was obvious the two men had been arguing well before they began screaming at each other. The jist of it was that Donovan wanted Melcher to guarantee another loan at the bank and Melcher didn't want to do it. Melcher, apparently, has plenty of money of his own. He shouted at Donovan that there wasn't any use in getting a loan, Donovan would only fritter it away."

"What did Donovan say?" Smythe asked eagerly.

"Donovan yelled that Melcher was being unfair, that it wasn't his fault that the firm had had a run of bad luck, and that the loan would only be temporary. Once the orders for the new engine began rolling in, they'd have more than enough to pay off all the loans." She paused for a breath. "Melcher shouted back that if Donovan wanted more money, he'd better try getting it from his wife, because Melcher wasn't giving him another penny. Furthermore, there weren't going to be any orders, not if Westover had anything to do with it."

She stopped and waited for the others to understand the implications of that last bit of information.

"Was the clerk absolutely sure about that?" Mrs. Jeffries asked.

"Absolutely," Betsy nodded her head in emphasis. "I knew that bit was important, so I made him repeat the conversation almost word for word. He was sure of what he'd heard."

"What happened then?" Mrs. Goodge asked.

"At that point, they'd gotten so loud, the manager asked them to please leave. From what the clerk said, they were still shouting at each other as they walked down the street." Betsy shrugged apologetically. "But he couldn't hear what they were saying. But it was loud enough that people on the street were staring at them. The clerk saw that clearly enough. That's about it, then. I didn't find out anything else."

"Well done, Betsy," Mrs. Jeffries said. "That is very useful information. But then, I'm sure the rest of you have interesting things to report as well." She didn't want anyone to think what they had to say wouldn't be important. "Though I must say I'd really like to know whether this row was before or after Westover's death."

"It was before," Betsy said quickly. "I'm sorry, I ought to have mentioned that. Donovan and Melcher had the row on the twelfth, which was the day before the board meeting. The clerk remembered because the row happened just a few minutes before the bank had its monthly board of governors meeting, and the manager was so upset he didn't even notice the govs had arrived, let alone greet them properly. Several of them were most put out. My source said the clerks got a good laugh at that. The manager isn't very well liked."

Mrs. Jeffries nodded thoughtfully. "Now that is interesting. It means the partners knew before the meeting that Westover was unhappy about something."

"Probably those cheap struts," Mrs. Goodge suggested.

"Sounds like they knew he meant to do something about it as well," Smythe added. "Anyway, if it's all the same to everyone, I'll have a go next." He told him everything he'd learned from Blimpey, making sure he didn't leave out any details. "So it seems that no matter how much money people invest in the company, within a few years, it's gone."

"Sounds like it would 'ave been gone even sooner if it 'adn't been for Mrs. Donovan," Wiggins commented.

"And Mrs. Arkwright," Mrs. Goodge pointed out. "Arkwright couldn't have bought into the firm without his wife's money."

"Some people just aren't very good at business," Smythe said. "But that doesn't seem to stop 'em."

"Does anyone want to 'ear what I found out?" Wiggins asked. "It's gettin' on."

"Go on lad," Smythe said kindly. "I've said my bit."

Wiggins told them about his meeting with Derek Wilkins and the lad's certainty about hearing the gunshot. "So at least we know what time the murder took place. That's important, isn't it?"

"Very," Mrs. Jeffries said, and she meant it. "The boy was sure of the time?"

"He was. He was sure it was a few minutes past two."

"And after two that afternoon, none of the partners had an alibi," Mrs. Jeffries said thoughtfully.

Mrs. Jeffries sat in her chair by the window, staring out at the faint flickering gaslight across the street. She was thinking, or rather, she was letting her mind drift from one snippet of information to another. This was a technique she'd perfected over the last few years, one she used when a case seemed unduly difficult, or even worse, unduly muddled.

She took a deep breath and let the thoughts come and go as they would. They knew when the murder took place now, but that didn't help all that much. With so many people not having a true alibi, where did one start?

The firm's partners were apparently appallingly bad businessmen, but that probably had nothing to do with Westover's death. Half of the city was filled with inept businessmen. There were always articles in the newspapers about one bankruptcy or another, but there didn't appear to be a corresponding number of murders. And why would any of the partners want to kill Westover? He was the one goose the company had that just might lay a golden egg. Admittedly, they appeared to know that Westover was upset about those cheap struts, but there were many ways to mollify an angry employee. All they would have had to do was to guarantee to replace the things. Surely that would have been easier than one of them murdering the poor fellow.

What if it wasn't murder at all? She frowned as Dr. Bosworth's words came back to haunt her. Could that growth have affected Westover's behavior? Could it have caused him to do something completely out of character like take his own life? If only they knew for certain one way or another. She suddenly realized that there might be a way to find out. Inspector Witherspoon had told her that Mrs. Lynch claimed Westover didn't own a gun. Which meant that he would have had to have gone out and acquired a weapon. One didn't buy a pistol at the corner shop. She decided to put a flea in Constable Barnes's ear. He had much better sources than she did when it came to finding out how one acquired a weapon on short notice. If Westover had purchased a gun, either legally or through some backstreet sources, that would be very strong evidence for the suicide theory.

She shifted in her chair as her eyes focused on the dim flickering gaslight. The one thought that bothered her the most, the one thing they didn't have a clue about was the most important. Why would anyone want to murder Harlan Westover? No one appeared to benefit directly from his death. His estate was too small to kill for, and he had no known enemies. The partners knew he was angry about what they'd done to his engine, but that was hardly a motive for murder. Besides, the engine didn't belong to Westover. It belonged to the company, so even if he was angry, he was no threat to the firm. So who wanted him dead? More importantly, why?

As soon as the inspector had left the house the next morning, they gathered around the kitchen table. With one eye on the clock, Mrs. Jeffries told them everything she'd learned from the inspector after supper the night before. It didn't add much to their store of knowledge, but they were all of the opinion that every little bit helped. "Today the inspector is going to go back to the Ladbrook Grove Police Station. He wants to go over the police reports again. Then he's going to speak to Westover's solicitor."

"He's not done that yet?" Betsy was a bit surprised. "Usually that's one of the first things he does."

"True, but this investigation is a bit unusual," Mrs. Jeffries said defensively. "I think he's having a difficult time. It's really not his fault. After all, the original police reports classified the death as a suicide. Oh, you know what I mean, we all know how seriously he takes his duty. He's not incompetent, he has simply gone about this investigation a little differently. The truth is, he's a bit stuck on this case."

Mrs. Goodge snorted. "He's not the only one. We're movin' at a snail's pace ourselves."

"We're doin' fine, Mrs. Goodge," Wiggins said firmly. "We'll find out who the killer is; we always do. I think we've learned ever so much."

"I agree," Mrs. Jeffries said firmly. She got to her feet. "As a matter of fact, I suggest we all get started. Does everyone have something in mind for themselves to do?"

"I do," Wiggins declared. "I'm goin' to have a snoop about the Horrocks house. I didn't get a chance to get over there yesterday."

"There's a couple of hansom drivers I'm still tryin' to track down," Smythe said.

"I think I'll have a go at the Arkwright neighborhood," Betsy announced. "No one's really taken a good look at them."

"Ruth has a friend she's going to talk to this morning," Mrs. Jeffries told them. She headed toward the coat tree. "And I think I'm going to go out and see if I can catch up with Constable Barnes."

"Constable Barnes?" Wiggins repeated. "Why'd you need to talk to 'im?"

"He might be able to clear up a little matter for me," she replied. "And even better, I want to give him a few hints about some of the things we've learned." This was as close as she'd ever come to telling the others that she suspected Barnes knew and approved of what they did for their inspector. "He's a very astute man."

Everyone stood up. Mrs. Goodge began clearing off the table. When Betsy started to reach for the empty bread plate, the cook shooed her off.

"You go on, now. I'll clear this lot up. Mrs. Jeffries and Wiggins are right. We will find this killer, but we've got to get crackin'."

"Are you sure?" Betsy didn't want the cook overdoing it. She was getting up there in years.

"Get on with you, girl," Mrs. Goodge laughed. "I might be old, but I've been cleaning up since you were a twinkle in God's left eye. You get your hat on and get out there findin' us some clues."

Smythe looked at the darkening sky and frowned. It was well past nine in the morning and there'd not been a hint of the sun. From the way the clouds were rolling in, he didn't think he was likely to see much of anything but buckets of rain. He hoped Betsy had remembered to take her umbrella before she left the house. Cor blimey, he was turning into an old woman. Betsy was no fool, and she could take care of herself. But he loved taking care of her. He shivered as a cold, damp wind cut through him all the way to his bones. Blast a Spaniard, but it was going to be a nasty day, and his beloved was out in the thick of it.

A hansom cab turned the corner and dropped off a fare. Smythe whistled, then held up his hand to catch the driver's attention. He'd already asked about and found out that this particular driver tended to work this neighborhood regularly.

"Can you give us a minute?" he said as he approached the cab. "I'd like to talk to ya. I'll make it worth your time." He reached in his pocket, pulled out a shilling, and held it up."

The driver grinned as he caught sight of the coin. One of his front teeth was missing. "You can have more than a minute if that's what you're payin'." He climbed down from his seat.

"I need some information." Smythe handed him the coin. "I hear you work this neighborhood pretty often."

"That's right. This is my patch. Most of my fares is from hereabouts."

"Do you ever bring fares to that house?" he jerked his thumb toward the Horrocks house on the far side of the road. "Maybe a gentleman?"

"The Horrocks place?" The driver shook his head. "I've taken a few fares there, but I don't remember just takin' a gentleman on his own. Leastways, not recently."

Smythe was very disappointed. He'd been hoping this case would turn out to be something simple like an enraged husband killing his wife's lover. He tried another tactic. Maybe Mrs. Horrocks went to Westover's house. "Do you remember taking Mrs. Horrocks over to a house on Brook Green?"

The driver frowned. "Why are you so interested in the Horrocks? You're not the law, are ya?"

"No, I'm not the law, and I'm not wantin' to do 'em any 'arm. I'm just investigating uh . . . uh . . . an insurance claim, that's all."

"Insurance claim?" The driver looked at him suspiciously. "What kind of claim? Look 'ere, mate, I'm not wantin' any trouble. Not with the likes of the folks that live around 'ere. They'd 'ave my 'ead on a pikestaff if they knew I was goin' on about their business."

Smythe decided to try a different approach. "You took my money," he protested. "What do you think I was payin' for, your company?"

"You paid me a shillin', mate, and that's not enough for the kind of details you're lookin' to buy."

Smythe didn't like being held over a barrel, but he did want more information. He had a feeling there might be a bit more coming his way if he swallowed his pride and opened his pockets. He dug out a handful of coins. "Here's five more shillings if you'll answer my questions."

"Now that's worth talking for, mate," the driver pocketed the money. "Now, what was your question again?"

Smythe held on to his temper. "Have you ever taken Mrs. Horrocks to a house over on Brook Green?" The whole matter no longer seemed important, but blast it, he'd paid the fellow, and he was determined to get what he could for it. They hadn't any evidence that there was anything between Mrs. Horrocks and Westover.

"Nah, never took Mrs. Horrocks to Brook Green."

Smythe felt like he'd just had his leg pulled, but he wasn't going to let the bloke make him any angrier. "You sure?"

"Sorry, guv, nothing like that. Like I said, I've brought lots of fares to the Horrocks," he replied, "and I've taken Mr. and Mrs. Horrocks here and there, but I don't recall ever taking Mrs. Horrocks to Brook Green. I took her to Hammersmith once, but that was over a year ago."

"Alright then," Smythe muttered.

The driver turned back toward the hansom. "Course now I did take Mr. Horrocks to a house on Brook Green."

"Mr. Horrocks? When? How long ago was this?" Smythe asked eagerly.

"A couple of weeks back. I don't recall the exact date, but it was bloomin' cold. I remember it very well. Mr. Horrocks was so upset about somethin', he overpaid me, and frankly, as he's a bit of a tightwad, I took note of it."

"Do you remember exactly where you took him?"

"Course I do, it were only two weeks ago."

"Can you take me there? I'll make it worth your while," Smythe said. He no longer cared if the driver was taking advantage of him or not, as long as the fellow was telling the truth. He'd know when they got to Brook Green.

"Climb in, mate," the driver was already climbing back up to his seat. "And I'll have you there in two shakes of a lamb's tail."

Mrs. Jeffries walked up to the police constable behind the tall counter of the Ladbrook Grove Police Station and said, "Are Constable Barnes and Inspector Witherspoon on the premises?"

The constable, a chubby, older man with salt and pepper hair and bushy eyebrows, stared at her in surprise. "Yes ma'am, they're here. Do you want to speak to them?"

"Only with Constable Barnes," she replied. She held up a pair of spectacles. "I'm Inspector Witherspoon's housekeeper, he's forgotten his spectacles again. I don't wish to interrupt him while he's busy, so if you could just ask the constable to step out here a moment, I'd be most appreciative."

"Yes, ma'am," he stepped away from the counter and disappeared through a doorway.

Mrs. Jeffries didn't feel in the least guilty for having pinched the inspector's eyeglasses out of his coat before he'd left this morning. She had only done what was necessary. The door opened and Constable Barnes stepped into the room. "Why Mrs. Jeffries, how nice to see you."

"And you, Constable." She held up the spectacles. "He forgot these again. Could you give them to him?"

Barnes grinned and came out from behind the counter. "Certainly."

"Uh, Constable, could you step outside with me for a moment?" she asked. "I'd like to have a quick word with you about something else."

His grin broadened. "I was hopin' you'd say something like that."

A few minutes later, Constable Barnes stepped back into the empty office he and the inspector were using. "Mrs. Jeffries brought these by," he handed the spectacles to Witherspoon.

"Gracious, I could have sworn I left them in my coat pocket," he said. "Oh well, I'm very lucky to have such a devoted staff."

"You certainly are, sir," Barnes replied.

Inspector Witherspoon put on his spectacles and looked out the narrow windows of the station. "It looks like rain is coming, and we've still a number of people to see today. I still want to have a word with Mrs. Arkwright again. It's too bad she wasn't at home yesterday afternoon."

Barnes went back to the empty desk he'd been sitting at and picked up the file he'd been reading. Witherspoon was studying the report written by the first officer on the scene—it was less than one page long. Constable Barnes was reading the final report, which included the cornoner's verdict—it was all of seven pages long.

"Mrs. Arkwright's housekeeper said she'd be available this afternoon," Barnes replied. One part of him was thinking about what Mrs. Jeffries had told him. He hoped he'd have time to get on it before the day ended.

Witherspoon frowned. "I don't see anything here that I didn't see the first time we went through this lot. Perhaps this wasn't such a good idea."

"As you've said before, sir, it never hurts to be thorough. Perhaps if there had been a bit more attention paid when Mr. Westover's body was found, we'd already have our killer." Barnes shook his head in disgust. "I can't believe this, sir, they really did a shoddy job. They didn't ask any questions of anyone, including James Horrocks. You should always question the person that finds the body, sir. Any copper knows that."

Witherspoon agreed, but he didn't want to be unduly critical of his own. "I'm sure the officers did the best they could. But you're correct. They didn't follow proper procedure. I wonder why?"

Barnes glanced at the report again. "I did some checking, sir, and the first lad on the spot was PC John Howard. He's only been on the force a few months."

"Inexperienced. That explains it then."

"Inexperienced and upset by a dead body," Barnes snorted. Then he quickly tried to cover it with a cough. Witherspoon was notoriously squeamish around corpses. But the inspector had never let his discomfort keep him from doing his duty.

"We really ought to interview PC Howard," Witherspoon murmured.

"He's on duty at Shepherds Bush today. I checked the roster with the desk sergeant."

The inspector nodded. He'd been avoiding this part of the investigation. It was never pleasant questioning a fellow officer, especially when there was evidence that they'd mucked up a case quite badly. But it couldn't be helped. "After we speak with PC Howard, we'll have to talk to all the officers on the case. That includes the inspector who signed it closed." He reached for his tea and took a sip. "I don't recall the inspector's name."

"That's because the signature is almost illegible," Barnes ducked his head to hide his grin. He knew he ought to feel guilty about this, but he didn't. "But I can make it out now. It's Nigel Nivens, sir. Inspector Nivens had a murder right under his nose, and he signed it off as a suicide."

"Oh dear, this will be awkward. How on earth did this happen? Inspector Nivens doesn't work out of this station."

Barnes shrugged. "You know how it is, sir, he might have been working out of here on a burglary case and uh . . . volunteered to take a look at it when he heard there was a dead body." The constable was deliberately being diplomatic. More likely, Nivens heard there was a body and thought it meant murder. Solving murders is what made a policeman's career, and Nivens wanted that more than anything. The stupid sod probably used his Whitehall political connections to intimidate his way onto the case, and then signed it off without so much as a second thought when it looked like a suicide. Typical Nivens, Barnes thought, barge in, muck it up, and then drop the case when it couldn't further his career.

Witherspoon shook his head in agreement. "I'm sure you're right. Well, awkward as it might be, we will have to question Inspector Nivens. But I'm sure he'll not mind."

He'll pitch a fit and raise a fuss, Barnes thought. "Of course sir. He's at the Yard today. I think he's got a meeting with Chief Inspector Barrows this afternoon."

"Gracious, Constable, you are efficient these days. How on earth do you know Inspector Nivens's schedule?" Witherspoon asked.

Barnes could hardly admit that he'd known all along that Nivens was the original senior officer on this case and that he'd kept his feelers out for Nivens's whereabouts. He felt a bit guilty for keeping that information from the inspector, but he'd had to do it for Witherspoon's own good. Someone had to look out for his inspector. When he'd seen Nivens's signature on that final report, he'd realized that a confrontation was inevitable. Despite Witherspoon's success in solving murders, the fellow was blissfully ignorant of the political realities that affected every government bureaucracy, including the police. Nigel Nivens wasn't in the least ignorant of these realities. He had a huge network of political allies that stretched from the local precinct houses all the way to the home office. "Constable Booker, he's the deskman out front, he mentioned it to me when I arrived this morning. For some reason, he thought it was a meeting involving all of us." Barnes knew that a confrontation with Nivens would go much better in front of Chief Inspector Barrows. The chief inspector had his own political allies and wasn't in the least intimidated by Nivens. Usually.

"I see. Right then, we'd best get moving." He drained his tea and then looked toward the window. "Oh dear, it has started to rain."

It was pouring, but Barnes didn't care. He'd brave a deluge if it meant he got to watch Nivens squirm. "Are we going to the Yard, sir?"

"We do have to talk to Westover's solicitor, and we also need to follow up with Mrs. Arkwright."

"We've time to fit them both in before we go to the Yard," Barnes pointed out. "Nivens isn't meeting the chief until four this afternoon."

"I don't want to interrupt the chief inspector's meeting . . . "

"But sir, he won't mind," Barnes interrupted. "He wants us to keep him informed, and if we pop in this afternoon, we could give him a report at the same time. Kill two birds with one stone, so to speak." He held his breath, desperately hoping his inspector would agree. Nigel Nivens had been trying to ruin Witherspoon for years, and it was time to put the fellow in his place. "By the time we're finished, PC Howard ought to be on duty so we can swing back around this way and have a word with him and PC Smith. They're both on evening duty this week."

"PC Smith?"

"He's the other constable who was on the original case."

Witherspoon hesitated for a long moment. "That does seem to make sense. I don't suppose Nivens will mind speaking to us in front of the chief. He's a reasonable sort of person."

He'd be furious enough to spit nails, Barnes thought. And every copper who'd ever worked under Nivens would give a week's pay to see him squirm.

Lady Ruth Cannonberry smiled kindly at the maid who handed her a cup of tea. "Thank you, dear," she said, taking the delicate Wedgewood cup and placing it on the table next to her.

"It's been such a long time since we've seen you," her hostess, Miss Emmaline Parker said. She was genuinely pleased to see her guest. Lady Cannonberry was compassionate, kind, and more importantly, intelligent. Miss Emmaline Parker was a very rich woman with very few friends. Her outspoken views on politics had seen to that. She was a radical, an atheist, and thought most people in society useless parasites. But she liked Ruth Cannonberry, even if the woman had been married to a lord and was currently having some sort of relationship with a policeman of all things. Emmaline Parker, who didn't care all that much for the male of the species, didn't understand it but thought it brave of Ruth nonetheless. "I understand you've been out of town taking care of your late husband's relatives. Honestly, Ruth, hasn't anyone ever told you that once you're widowed, you're not responsible for his relatives anymore? It's not like they can't hire a nurse. The whole bunch is rich as sin."

Ruth laughed. "Don't be so harsh, Emmaline. I'm all they've got. No one likes to be on their own when they're ill."

"Malingerers, all of them," Emmaline grinned, and for a moment, her long, bony face was pretty. Even seated, one could tell she was a tall woman. Her hair was dark brown and pulled straight back into a bun at the nape of her neck. She was in her late thirties, but made no effort to appear younger. She dressed for comfort rather than fashion. That day she wore a heavy gray wool day dress, plain enough to please a Quaker. "So now that you're back in town, I do hope we can see one another a bit more often."

"Absolutely." Ruth liked Emmaline, she was intelligent, interesting, and funny. "Now, I do have an ulterior motive for coming along this morning. Not that seeing you isn't a worthwhile endeavor in itself, of course."

Emmaline laughed. "This is getting more interesting by the minute. Do go on, you mustn't keep me in suspense."

Ruth took a deep breath. She was mindful that she had to be discreet, but she was also aware that this was one of the people in London who might have the information she needed. "I know you're very well informed on what's going on in the business community, and I needed your advice."

"My advice? Are you certain? Most people think my views are far too radical to be of consequence," Emmaline replied. She was very flattered. "Are you certain you don't want to speak with your late husband's bankers?"

"I'm sure. From what I've observed, you never lose money on your investments . . . "

"Maybe I keep quiet about it when I do," Emmaline interrupted.

"Nonsense, you're not capable of keeping quiet about anything," Ruth shot back. She clamped her hand over her mouth when she realized what she'd said. But Emmaline hadn't taken offense.

She laughed. "Oh, that's good. It's also true. All right, go ahead, ask away. But mind you, my methods are very unorthodox. Did you have any particular company in mind?"

This was the tricky part. Ruth didn't want to give any hint that she was really investigating a murder, and later, once an arrest was made, Emmaline would remember this conversation. So she'd prepared herself by getting the names of several firms to ask about. She'd asked her butler. She hoped he knew what he'd been talking about. "I've been approached to invest in several firms. I'm hoping you'll know which one ought to be the best." She smiled and took a deep breath. "I've heard rumors that Carstairs might be a good firm to invest in, my next door neighbor has it on good authority that they're looking to raise capital."

Emmaline looked thoughtful. "They're quite reputable, but I'd be careful with them. Jonathan Carstairs isn't well, and his brother is supposedly going to take over the day-to-day running of the firm. The brother's a bit dim."

"Oh. Well, what about Riley and Wotmans?"

"They're quite good. Conservative and reliable. You'll not make a fortune but you'll get a steady return on your investment, more importantly, you'll not lose anything."

"And Donovan, Melcher, and Horrocks?"

"Stay away from them. Don't give them a farthing," Emmaline exclaimed. "Now that their engineer is dead, they'll be out of business within the year, you mark my words."

"That does sound strange."

Emmaline leaned closer. "Now I'm not one to gossip, but wait until I tell you about this lot. You mustn't give them any money, Ruth. You must promise me."

"You make them sound postively dangerous."

"They are dangerous," Emmaline insisted. "At least to rich women. That's how they raise their capital, you know. Every time they're in real financial trouble, they bring in another managing partner with a rich wife." She broke off and frowned at Ruth. "Is someone encouraging you to buy into this firm? A man?"

It took a moment before she understood the implication behind her friend's words. She laughed. "Do you mean am I being courted for my money? Absolutely not."

Emmaline smiled in relief. "I thought you'd be too sensible for something like that, but in matters of the heart, people can be awfully foolish, and as I said, this firm has a reputation for running on other people's money, especially women."

"Really?"

"Oh yes, they've been in trouble ever since the second Mr. Donovan died. Harry Donovan, that's the son who took over about fifteen years ago, is a fool. He's virtually run the company into the ground. His own father didn't want him taking it over, he used to berate him publicly about what an idiot he was, but because of circumstances, Harry ended up with the firm."

"How long has this company been in business?" Ruth asked.

"The company was started by Harry's grandfather. He did quite well out of it, bought the family a big house in Mayfair and made sure his children married well. The next Donovan did even better with the firm than the grandfather. He had two sons, Albert and Harry. Albert was the eldest and was going to take over the firm when his father passed on, but Albert died of typhoid fever. Harry wasn't the man his brother was, he drank, gambled, and generally wasn't considered very bright, but when his father died, there was no one else to take the business. As I said, it's been in trouble ever since. Harry Donovan just seems to have a habit of making one bad decision after another."

"That's so very odd. Now, what did you mean about the engineer being dead? That's a very strange reason for a company going out of business."

"Not this company. Let me pour us another cup of tea, and I'll tell you the whole story. You're not in a hurry, are you?"

Westover's solicitor was a middle-aged man named Alastair Greeley. His office was on the second floor of a building on the Marylebone High Street. Greeley was a tall, dark-haired man, with a broad forehead and deep-set hazel eyes. "I've been expecting you, Inspector," he said politely as he gestured for the two policemen to sit down. "I understand the investigation has been reopened."

"That's correct," Witherspoon replied. "We've had new evidence come to light."

"Good," Greeley broke into a wide smile. "I never did agree with the suicide verdict. I tried to tell the other inspector that it was impossible for my client to have taken his own life, but the fellow wouldn't listen to me."

Witherspoon waited until Barnes had gotten out his little brown note-book before he spoke. "That's most unfortunate. But we're here now and anything you could tell us will be most helpful."

Greeley raised his eyebrows. "Let's hope so, Inspector. But it has been over a fortnight since the murder was committed."

"First of all, can you tell us why you think Mr. Westover didn't take his own life."

"Several reasons. To begin with, he was quite a devout Roman Catholic. He went to mass every week. Secondly, he'd bought tickets to go on holiday in Italy, and thirdly, the man simply didn't have the character to take his own life."

"I see," Witherspoon had hoped for something a bit more substantial than that. "We understand that Mr. Westover had no close family."

"That's correct. He's got some cousins in Bristol. I've been in contact with them."

"Are they his heirs?" Barnes asked.

"They'll inherit everything," Greeley replied. "But I shouldn't see them as suspects if I were you. The cousins are two elderly ladies, and I don't think they came to London with murder in their hearts and a gun in their hands. They were quite distraught when they heard the news."

"How big an estate is it?" Witherspoon asked. He was rather annoyed with himself for not getting this information sooner. But gracious, this case was most odd. Most odd, indeed.

Greeley shrugged. "It's a bit more substantial than one would think. There's a house in Birmingham and some stocks. But believe me, sir, Harlan Westover wasn't murdered for his money."

"Would you explain that, sir?" Witherspoon asked.

"I intend to, Inspector," Greeley replied. "Harlan Westover came to see me a few days before he died. He was very concerned about something going on at his firm and wanted to know if he had any legal recourse against them. Unfortunately, he was quite vague as to what the trouble might be. I told him that unless he could give me a few more details, I couldn't give him any advice."

"You have no idea what he thought the company had done?" Barnes asked.

"It had something to do with the factory, I think. He mentioned that he had to pop around there and have a word with the foreman. Then he'd know for sure and he'd get back to me." Greeley closed his eyes and sighed. "He apparently found out what he needed to know, because he made an appointment with my clerk to come see me again. The appointment was for the day after his death. That's another reason I know he didn't take his own life."

"Why didn't you bring this up at the inquest?" Witherspoon asked.

"I was out of town on another case, and the judge wouldn't grant a postponement. I sent a note to the other inspector, hoping the police would do something before the verdict was rendered, but your Inspector Nivens refused. He insisted Westover was a suicide. He was wrong, and furthermore, he's a very stupid man."

"Is there anything else you can tell us?" the inspector asked quickly.

"Only that I hope you catch whoever did this to Harlan. He was a good and decent man. He didn't deserve to lose his life like that."

"No one does, sir," Witherspoon replied.

CHAPTER 8

Wiggins stood on the corner and stared glumly down Argyll Road. Cor blimey, he hated these posh neighborhoods. This morning, he'd been so certain that he was being ever so clever. He'd told the others he was going to go to the Horrocks's neighborhood, but that had been just a ruse to throw them off the scent. After his triumph yesterday in being the one to find out Westover's time of death, he'd gotten greedy for glory, for being the one to bring in the best clue. He'd planned on going along to every neighborhood where a suspect lived, make contact with someone from the household, and then find out which of them actually owned a gun. That would have been really good. He'd even wondered why the police hadn't done it. But blast a Spaniard, he'd been to the Arkwrights and not seen hide nor hair of a servant to natter with, now he was here at the Melcher neighborhood, and it was just as empty. Dead as a bloomin' doornail. What a waste. There wasn't even much traffic around this way today. Wiggins shifted his weight and pulled his coat tighter against his chest. He didn't know what to do next. He decided it was time to head for his original destination, the Horrocks house, when all of a sudden, the side door of the Melcher house opened and a young woman came out. She was carrying a large basket.

Wiggins took off like a shot. He caught up with the girl just as she stepped onto the sidewalk. He scurried around so that he was abreast of her. "Can I carry that for you, miss?"

"Thanks all the same," she replied, staring at him suspiciously. "But I've got it."

"You can trust me," he said, determined not to give up. "I work for a policeman. My name's Wiggins, and I work for Inspector Gerald Wither-spoon. That basket looks awfully heavy."

Just then she stumbled, and he grabbed her arm, steadying her so she wouldn't fall. "You all right, then?"

"Ta." She smiled gratefully. "This bloomin' thing weighs a ruddy ton." She glanced over her shoulder at the Melcher house, hesitated, and then shoved the basket toward Wiggins. "I suppose it's all right. I mean, if you work for a police inspector." She was a plump girl with light brown hair tucked under a housemaid's cap, blue eyes, and a moon-shaped face. Beneath her thin cloak she had on a gray dress covered with a white apron. "God knows I'll not be able to carry it all the way to the laundry."

Wiggins eagerly took the burden from her. "Most houses 'ave their laundry picked up," he said, giving her a friendly smile.

"We generally do too," she replied. "But Mrs. Miller, that's our housekeeper, found these things of Mr. Melcher's under his bloomin' bed, of all places. The stupid cow insisted I had to take them in right away. Can you believe it? The laundry boy is due by tomorrow mornin', and she couldn't even wait a day!"

They had come to the corner. "Which way?" Wiggins asked.

She pointed to her left. "We take it to Mrs. Clifton and she's right behind the butcher's."

"Right then," he started off in the direction she pointed. "What's in 'ere? Bricks?"

She shrugged. "Clothes and shoes. We don't have a proper footman, so we takes Mr. Melcher's shoes to Mrs. Clifton as well. She does the whole lot, and then her boy brings it back the next day. But honestly, I don't know why Mrs. Miller couldn't wait. It's cold out 'ere. I suppose she didn't want Mr. Melcher findin' out she'd not cleaned his room prop-erly. I mean, that's the only thing it could be. She didn't want Mr. Melcher findin' out she hadn't cleaned under his bed for two weeks. Lazy cow! She'd have my head if I waited two weeks to clean under the settees and cupboards in the drawing room."

Wiggins caught his breath as the import of her words hit him full force. He suddenly realized he had to be very, very careful here. "Uh, sounds like you work at a very strange place."

She made a face. "It's not all that strange, our master is just on his own. You know what I mean. No wife to run the household, so he relies on Mrs. Clifton. If you ask me, she's getting too old to be takin' care of such a large place. Mind you, the way she tells it, if it hadn't been for her, these things," she jerked her head at the basket, "would have been lost for good. But I know she's lyin'."

Wiggins shifted the basket slightly and slowed his steps. His mind was working furiously. "Uh how do you know she's lyin'?"

"She said she found these clothes at the back of his wardrobe. But I saw her pulling them out from under the bed. She won't let me or Dulcie up to clean Mr. Melcher's room, so I reckon he tossed these ruddy things under the bed a couple of weeks back and forgot to mention them. She's been too lazy to clean under there properly, so she made up a story about where she found the clothes."

"Uh, how much further is it?" Wiggins asked carefully. He didn't want her to stop talking, but he needed some measure of how much time he had left.

"Just a few more doors up," she replied. "It's awfully nice of you to do this for me."

"It's my pleasure, miss." Wiggins didn't want to get his hopes up. The clothes in the basket probably had nothing to do with Westover's murder. He didn't think he'd be that lucky two days in a row. Still, you never knew, maybe they were a clue. From what she said, they'd been under a bed for the better part of two weeks. He had to find a way to get a look at them.

"It's just here," she turned down a walkway and led him around the back of a two-story brick building. A narrow, rickety staircase went up the rear wall. Wiggins was afraid if he didn't act fast, he'd lose his chance.

"Why don't you stay here," he suggested, "and I'll take 'em up to your laundry. Them stairs look awfully tiring."

She smiled broadly. "That's right nice of you. You are a good fellow, aren't you. I guess that'd be all right. Just tell Mrs. Clifton it's for Mr. Melcher's account and we need it back by tomorrow."

Wiggins nodded and started up the stairs. He glanced over his shoulder at the girl. Cor blimey, she was watching him like a cat tracking a mouse. He wanted to see what was in the bloomin' basket. He stumbled and dumped the basket on the stairs. The sheet covering fell off, and the clothes tumbled out onto the staircase. "Sorry," he called out to her as he bent to pick up the garments. He picked up a heavy, black shoe, gave it a cursory glance, saw nothing interesting and dropped it back into the basket. He picked up the other shoe, two dirty hankies, some undergarments,

several soiled towels, and lastly, a man's dress shirt. He examined each
piece as best he could. But everything looked normal. He popped the shirt
onto the top of the pile and was reaching for the sheet, when a dark red
spot on the sleeve of the shirt caught his eye. As he picked up the sheet, he
took a long, hard look at the shirtsleeve. There were more dark spots
splattered on the white fabric. Cor blimey, he was no expert, but he was
sure them spots must be blood.

"Yo . . . " the girl shouted, "is everythin' all right?"

"Yeah, I just want to make sure everything's back in properly," he
called. He turned his back to her, took a deep breath, and then shoved
the soiled shirt into his coat. Then he hurried up the stairs. The door
opened as he reached the top. The entire time he was giving Mrs. Clifton
the laundry, he silently prayed that parts of the pinched shirt weren't
sticking out anywhere where she could see.

The rain had stopped by the time that Inspector Witherspoon and Constable Barnes got to the Arkwright house. This time, they were shown
into the drawing room. A tiny fire sputtered pathetically in the fireplace,
and a lamp was lighted against the gloomy day. There were heavy blue
damask curtains on the windows and a pale gray carpet on the oak floor.
There were several likenesses of the Queen scattered about the room, the
largest one being set in the place of honor in the center of the mantel.
Witherspoon wondered if Arkwright had ever considered having a pho-
tograph of his wife done.

"Hello, Inspector, Constable," Mrs. Arkwright said as she swept into
the room. She took a seat on the dark blue settee and gestured toward the
matching overstuffed chairs. "How very nice to see you. Do sit down.
Shall I ring for tea?"

"That's most kind of you, Mrs. Arkwright, but please don't bother,"
Witherspoon replied. "We've just had some." He and Barnes sat down.
"Is your husband here as well?"

"He'll be right in," Mrs. Arkwright smiled brightly. "How is the
investigation coming along? I do hope you catch whoever murdered poor
Mr. Westover. I didn't know him well, but he was such a nice man."

"We'll not rest until his killer is caught," Witherspoon assured her.
"Murderers eventually make a mistake and give themselves away."

"It's so terribly upsetting," she continued. "Just when Mr. Donovan was so very certain everything was going to be all right, this has to happen. Of course, the firm has had the worst luck. Some would say it was more than just bad luck . . . I mean, sometimes I think that some people really aren't adept at running a business . . . " She broke off as her husband stepped into the room.

Oliver Arkwright didn't look pleased. "I don't see why you're bothering us again," he snapped. "We've already told you everything we know."

Witherspoon rather wished he could have had a few more minutes alone with Mrs. Arkwright. "I know that you think you have, sir. But I've a few more questions. We've been to see Harlan Westover's solicitor, and he's given us some very interesting information."

Arkwright's eyebrows shot up. "I don't know what he could have possibly told you . . . "

"He said that Mr. Westover was thinking about taking legal action against your firm."

"I don't know what you're talking about," Arkwright sputtered. "Legal action, that's absurd. There's no reason he'd want to take legal action against us. We did nothing wrong."

"He was going to talk with the foreman at your factory and then go to the board with his complaint." The inspector added.

"He only gave us a progress report," Arkwright said defensively. "I don't know what you're talking about, and this solicitor, whoever he is, doesn't know what he's talking about either. Does he have any proof . . . "

"Exactly where again did you go after the board meeting?" Barnes interrupted. He could see that Arkwright was getting rattled and often, a change in the direction of the questions helped that process along.

"I've already told you, I took my wife to luncheon at Wentworths," Arkwright replied, but some of the bluster had left his voice.

"And what time did you finish your luncheon?" Witherspoon pressed. They had checked with the restaurant, and the waiters had confirmed that the Arkwrights were present that day. But no one recalled precisely when they'd left.

"Again, I've already told you. We finished luncheon about two o'clock."

"Oh no dear," Mrs. Arkwright interjected. "It was actually closer to one thirty. I remember precisely. The clock on the bank tower had just struck the half hour as I was getting into the hansom to come home."

Arkwright glared at his wife. "Penelope, I'll thank you to let me answer my own questions."

"Then I suggest you answer them correctly," she replied cooly. "You know perfectly well when we finished luncheon and left the restaurant, you looked at your watch."

"Am I to understand that the two of you went your separate ways after leaving the restaurant?" the inspector pressed. He was annoyed with himself for not finding this out earlier. Gracious, this was very remiss of him. "I was under the impression you'd come home and spent the afternoon here together."

"I've no idea how you got such an idea, I never said that we were together," Arkwright retorted.

"But you certainly implied that the two of you came home that day," Witherspoon insisted. "But as you didn't, I'd appreciate it if you could each tell me exactly where you were that afternoon." He made a mental note to double check anything either of them said. Goodness, how could he have been so negligent in this investigation? A wave of shame swept through him. His actions thus far bordered on incompetence.

"I came right home," Mrs. Arkwright volunteered. "You can check with the maids. They were both here when I arrived. Then I went right up to my room and had a rest."

"Do you remember what time you got in?" Barnes asked. He was angry at himself. As a good copper, he should have verified all this sort of detail right after the first interview. Blast, but he must be getting old.

She frowned as she thought back. "I think I heard the clock chiming two as I came in the front door. But as I said, you can check with the maids. Bessie was cleaning the front stairs, and she saw me." She shot her husband a malicious smile.

Witherspoon watched the interplay between the Arkwrights carefully. He was no expert on married life, but he suspected these two didn't much care for one another. "Thank you, Mrs. Arkwright." He turned to the husband. "And you, sir? Where did you go after you put your wife in the cab?"

"I put myself in the hansom," Mrs. Arkwright said. "My husband had already stomped off in a temper. We'd had words, you see, and he was quite angry at me."

"Penelope, please be a bit more discreet." Arkwright's voice was pleading now. "The police aren't interested in our private business."

"But I think they are," she retorted. "Especially as our argument related very much to your company." She looked at Witherspoon. "My husband was furious with me because I wouldn't give him anymore of my money to pour into the company. As a matter of fact, I told him if the company didn't repay what I'd already loaned them, I'd take them to court."

"Penelope, please be quiet. Our argument has nothing to do with Westover's death," Arkwright said.

The inspector stared at Arkwright. "Why did you need money to put into the firm if this new engine of Mr. Westover's was going to be so successful?"

"That's not really pertinent to your investigation," Arkwright argued.

"It's for us to decide what's pertinent and what's not," Barnes said.

Arkwright's eyes narrowed angrily. "I don't think I have to answer any more questions. As a matter of fact, I believe I'll contact my solicitor."

"He wanted the money to get his name on the company," Mrs. Arkwright said. She glared right back at her husband. "The other partners all have their names on the company. Oliver wanted that as well. But Harry Donovan wouldn't change the name of the firm until he came up with more cash. Now that they had their golden engine, Oliver didn't want to be left out in the cold."

"You know nothing about it," Arkwright hissed at his wife.

"I know something happened at that board meeting that you didn't plan for," she yelled. "I know that because you were beside yourself with anger that afternoon. You could barely eat."

"I was worried, not angry. For God's sake, shut up before you put my head in a noose." Arkwright shook his head in disbelief as he stared at his wife's stony face. "God, I knew you were unhappy, but I didn't think you hated me this much."

She said nothing.

Arkwright's shoulders slumped, and he tore his gaze from his wife and turned to the two policemen. "I think you'd better leave, Inspector."

"Not until you tell us where you went that afternoon," Witherspoon said softly. He felt rather bad for the poor fellow. It was obvious Penelope Arkwright truly loathed her husband and equally obvious that he hadn't had a clue as to her true feelings. Until now.

He sighed and closed his eyes. "If you must know. I went for a long walk."

"That's true, Inspector," Mrs. Arkwright added. "I know because one of my neighbors, Mrs. Gilley, saw my husband over on Brook Green later that afternoon." She smiled sweetly at her spouse and then looked back at the two policemen. "What a coincidence, Oliver. You must have been so close to poor Mr. Westover just as he was dying. What a pity you didn't go around to see him. You might have saved his life."

Wiggins stepped into the back hallway of Upper Edmonton Gardens and carefully closed the door behind him. It wouldn't do to barge in on Mrs. Goodge when she was with one of her sources, made her right testy it did. He cocked his head toward the kitchen but he didn't hear anything. Deciding it was safe, he walked up the hallway and stepped inside the kitchen.

Mrs. Goodge was sitting at the table, staring morosely at the carriage clock on the top of the pine sideboard. Fred spotted him and shot to his feet, wagging his tail and looking just a bit embarrassed that his beloved Wiggins could slip into the house without Fred hearing him!

Alerted by the dog, Mrs. Goodge looked at Wiggins. "You're back early," she said.

"Good boy," he patted the dog. "It looks like it's goin' to rain again, and I decided to come home."

"Sounds like your day has been as miserable as mine," she shook her head. "I've not found out a ruddy thing. This miserable rain has kept everyone away. The grocer's boy just dropped our order and left without so much as a by-your-leave, the chimney sweep from down the road went home early, and I got a note from my old friend Melba that she hurt her ankle and can't come to see me. I was countin' on learning something from Melba. She used to be the cook at a house on Surrmat Road, and that's just around the corner from where the Donovans live."

Wiggins could see that Mrs. Goodge was very upset. She got like that when she felt she wasn't contributing enough to the case. He hated seeing her get all sad and miserable. "I came home early because I need your advice," he said.

"My advice?" she repeated. "What about?"

Wiggins dropped into the chair next to her. Nothing cheered her up more than giving advice. He had been going to wait until they had their meeting before he told the others, but maybe he could cheer the cook up first. "I've found something and I don't know what I ought to do."

"Something to do with the case?" Mrs. Goodge asked earnestly.

He nodded. "Evidence. I've got evidence and the truth of the matter is, I stole it."

Mrs. Goodge gaped at him. "What on earth have you done, lad? You've not broken in to someone's house . . . " she broke off as she realized what she was saying. The truth was, in the course of their investigations, they'd broken into houses before.

"No, it's nothin' like that," he replied, glad to see that she was getting indignant. That was better than her being sad. "I just happened to get my hands on this," he pulled the shirt out of his coat and laid it in front of the cook, "and I think there's blood on the sleeve. I think it's Mr. Westover's blood but I don't know for sure."

Mrs. Goodge didn't bother with silly questions. "Whose shirt is this?"

"It belongs to Mr. Melcher. I stole it from the laundry basket."

"Maybe we should wait until the others get here before you say anymore," Mrs. Goodge said softly.

"I don't think so," Wiggins replied. "Uh, I came home early hopin' you could tell me if I done this wrong or not. I mean, maybe I ought to nip back to the Melcher house and hide this shirt in case we need the inspector to find it. Oh cor blimey, I'm not sayin' this right."

Mrs. Goodge held up her hand and got to her feet. "Wiggins, Mrs. Jeffries and the others are out. We've got plenty of time. I'll make us a cup of tea and you tell me exactly what happened. Then we'll decide what needs doin' and what doesn't."

Inspector Nigel Nivens was already sitting in front of the chief inspector's desk when Witherspoon and Barnes arrived in Barrow's office. Nivens, a plump middle-aged man with dark blond hair and pale blue eyes, wasn't pleased when the other two men stepped inside the office.

Chief Inspector Barrows waved them forward. "I got your message, Witherspoon. Come on in, then, we've a lot of ground to cover." He indicated the inspector was to take the chair next to Nivens.

Barnes stood respectfully by the door. The constable struggled to keep his face expressionless, but it was difficult, he knew that Nivens was probably beside himself by now. Let the man worry, he was the one who'd mucked up the case.

"I thought this was going to be a private meeting," Nivens said.

"Why would you think that?" Barrows looked up from the papers he'd been reading. He turned his attention to Witherspoon. "I under-stand you need to ask Inspector Nivens some questions about his han-dling of the Westover murder."

"It wasn't a murder," Nivens said defensively, "it was a suicide."

"You're wrong." Barrows smiled nastily. "That's one of the reasons you're here in my office. Harlan Westover was murdered and because you didn't investigate properly, the man's death was ruled a suicide. These," he tapped the police reports in front of him, "aren't worth the ink used to write them. I'm appalled that one of my officers would do such a shoddy investigation, and I'm appalled at myself for not realizing it when these reports first crossed my desk."

"I think you're being a bit unfair, sir," Nivens blustered. "My report was based on an assessment of the evidence that I had at the time of the investigation." He tossed a quick glare at Witherspoon. "It's only been since he stuck his oar in, that the case was called a murder."

"I asked him to stick his oar in," Barrows shot back. "And I wouldn't have had to do that if you'd done your job properly."

"I did do my job properly," Nivens insisted. "The evidence pointed to suicide."

"Then can you please tell me how on earth a man could get into a locked room to commit suicide, when the only known key was thirty feet on the other side of the door?"

Nivens opened his mouth to speak and then clamped it shut again. Finally, he said, "All right, I'll admit that I did overlook the significance of that evidence . . . "

"You overlooked everything," Barrows picked up the reports and waved them in the air. "You didn't interview the neighbors, you didn't investigate anything about the victim's life, you simply assumed that because he was lying there with a hole in his head and gun under his hand that he'd killed himself. That's precisely what the killer wanted you to think."

"Now look here, chief inspector," Nivens began, "you've no call to berate me like this. I made an honest mistake . . . "

Witherspoon didn't dare look at Nivens, he felt terrible for the poor man. "He's right, sir," he put in softly. "I think it was just an honest mistake."

"We don't have any room for these kinds of mistakes," Barrows roared. "It hasn't been that long since the Ripper, gentlemen, and in case you have forgotten, we never solved those cases either. The public still doesn't have a lot of faith in our abilities. When the press gets wind of the fact that we mucked up another case, it'll not do us any good at all."

"Perhaps the press won't find out," Witherspoon ventured. This meeting wasn't going at all as he'd hoped.

Barrows and Nivens both stared at the inspector. Even Barnes closed his eyes in disbelief.

"Don't be naive," the chief inspector said. He sank back in his chair and turned to stare out at the darkening sky. "Of course they'll find out and when they do, we'll look like incompetent fools."

Witherspoon cast a surreptious glance at Nivens, who was staring straight ahead, his eyes focused on a spot over Barrows's head. Drat, this had been a most unpleasant encounter, most unpleasant indeed. He wasn't fond of Inspector Nivens, but he hadn't wanted to see him raked over the coals quite so badly.

Barnes was struggling to keep his expression blank. This had been better than he'd hoped. He couldn't wait to tell the lads. Nivens was hated by just about everyone who'd ever worked under him. He was notorious for blaming the uniformed blokes when things went wrong and taking the credit when things went right. He cast a quick look at Nivens. The man was staring into space, his expression thoughtful and his eyes calculating. Barnes was suddenly uneasy. By rights, Nivens ought to be blazing angry, spitting fire, and threatening Barrows with his Whitehall connections. He was too calm. What was he up to now?

Barrows sighed loudly. "It's getting late, and the most useful thing we can do is get this case solved as quickly as possible. Witherspoon, go ahead and ask Nivens your questions."

The inspector relaxed a bit, relieved that they could move onto a discussion of the facts of the case itself. He saw that Barnes had taken out his notebook.

Nivens's mouth curved into a slight smile. "You're quite right, sir. It is time to answer some questions."

Witherspoon cleared his throat. "I don't have all that many, Inspector Nivens. But I would like to know a few more details about the crime scene, so to speak."

Nivens said nothing for a moment. Then he said. "I'm afraid you don't understand, Witherspoon. This was my case, and I'm the one that should be asking the questions."

Smythe hoped the blooming rain had finally stopped for the day, it was damp enough down here by the river without it pouring onto his head as well. He pulled open the door of the Dirty Duck and stepped inside. The pub had only opened fifteen minutes earlier, but it was already crowded. He spotted Blimpey sitting at a table next to the fireplace.

Blimpey waved him over, and Smythe pushed his way through the crowded room. He slid onto a stool across from his informant. "What'll you 'ave?" he asked.

"What'll you have?" Blimpey repeated with a wide smile. "It's on me today."

"Cor blimey, you must be in a tearin' good mood. I'll have a beer." Smythe studied his companion for a moment and then he grinned. "She musta said 'yes'."

"That she did, my boy. That she did." Blimpey caught the barman's eye, held up two fingers and mouthed the word "beer". He turned back to Smythe. "I took your advice before I said my piece and had one of her friends ask a few pertinent questions of the lady. Once I knew she was amenable, well, then Bob's-your-Uncle." He broke off and grinned at the barmaid who brought their drinks. "Put it on my tab, luv," he told her. As soon as she was gone, he picked up his glass and raised it toward Smythe.

Smythe did the same. "All the best, Blimpey, and I mean it."

"Same to you, friend, same to you." He took a quick sip from his glass. "Mind you, we've already set a date, not like you and your lady. We're doin' it in June. Nell's got a sister comin' over from Canada for a visit. We thought we'd wait till then so she could be here for the nuptials."

Smythe shifted uncomfortably at the reminder that he and Betsy hadn't set a date. "That's a nice time for a wedding. Maybe Betsy and I will beat you to it, though. Anyway, what 'ave you got for me."

Blimpey put his glass down and leaned forward. "I decided that as you'd been so helpful to me with my . . . delicate situation, that I'd do a bit of snoopin' about on the 'ouse, so to speak."

"You didn't have to do that, Blimpey," Smythe replied. "All I did was give ya a bit of advice." Nevertheless, he was touched.

"You're a good friend, Smythe. There's lots that would have had a bit of fun at my expense if they'd known what was troublin' me. But you were a real gent about it. Anyways, I put my feelers out over in Stepney. Found out a bit, I did."

"Isn't that where the Donovan factory is?"

"That's right. Struck gold, too." He laughed and took another quick swig. "Seems your Mr. Westover was in a right old state before he died. My sources told me that a day or two before he supposedly blew his brains out, he went along and had a word with the foreman of the factory."

"And what did he find out?" Smythe couldn't believe his luck.

"Seems that your Mr. Westover had designed an engine that was supposedly goin' to put the company firmly in the black, if you know what I mean."

Smythe patiently sipped his beer. He knew all this, but he didn't want to put a damper on Blimpey's day. "That's right, I remember."

"Well, as I mentioned yesterday, the company wasn't doin' all that well financially. They kept havin' to raise capital to keep operating. But this engine was different from their usual goods, it was actually quality. Some would even say it was ahead of it's time. Very powerful."

"I know all that, Blimpey," Smythe said. "What's it got to do with Westover's death."

"It's got everything to do with it," Blimpey smiled smugly. "Seems that the factory foreman told Westover that the struts used on an important part of the engine weren't the ones Westover had specified on his plans. They'd bought cheaper struts to save a bit of the ready. Westover had a fit right there on the factory floor. He was shoutin' so loud the whole place heard him."

Smythe knew about the struts, but he didn't know about the shouting. "What was he sayin'?"

"He started screamin' that the engine wouldn't be safe unless it had the proper struts. That it was too powerful and that it'd blow up and kill someone."

"Why didn't he just make 'em change the struts to the ones he'd specified?" Smythe asked.

"They couldn't. That's why he got so angry. He'd come to see the foreman to insist he change the struts, seems Westover had known about them bein' cheap for a few days. But the engine had already been shipped out. That's the reason he got so het up."

"Bloomin' Ada, no wonder he got so angry."

"And the factory had orders for more engines. Apparently, word about the engine had already got out, and everyone and his brother wanted one. But that's neither here nor there, what is important was that Westover told the foreman that he had to cable the company that was buyin' the thing, that he had to warn them it wasn't safe. The foreman told him he couldn't do somethin' like that, that Westover would have to take it up with the partners. Westover said he would, that he'd go along to their board meeting and make them do what was right. He'd not have it on his conscience that his engine had killed people."

"So that's why he was at the meeting," Smythe murmured.

"And that's probably why he was killed," Blimpey added. "The firm was in trouble, and that engine was goin' to save all their arses. They'd not want any engineer coming in and tellin' them the thing was about to blow up and kill a bunch of people. More importantly, they'd not want their engineer tellin' anyone else the ruddy thing was dangerous. Not when they had orders comin' in left and right."

Mrs. Jeffries decided to postpone their meeting until after the inspector came home. Neither Smythe nor Betsy were home in time for their usual afternoon meeting, so she sent Wiggins over to Lady Cannonberry's with a note telling her to come around about eight o'clock that evening.

As soon as Wiggins left, she turned to the cook. "He was acting a bit strange. He couldn't seem to meet my eyes."

"Young people always act strange," the cook muttered. "I expect he's just a bit preoccupied with this case. We all are. Oh look," she pointed toward the window at the far end of the kitchen, the one that faced the street. "A hansom's pulling up. That's probably the inspector. Should I get a tray ready?"

"Give me half an hour," the housekeeper replied. She hurried toward the back stairs. "I want to find out if he's learned anything useful today."

She made it to the front door just as the inspector stepped inside. "Good evening, sir," she said as she helped him take off his hat and coat. "Did you have a productive day?"

"I've had a very productive day, Mrs. Jeffries. But it was also rather difficult. I didn't get near as much accomplished as I'd hoped. Constable Barnes and I were going to interview the original police constables on the case, but we simply ran out of time. That's the way this entire case seems to have gone, two steps forward and one step back. Then again, one doesn't achieve something without effort."

"Would a glass of sherry help, sir?"

"Most certainly," he headed for the drawing room. She was right on his heels.

She went to the cupboard and poured out the sherry as he settled himself into this favorite chair. "It's been a most upsetting day, Mrs. Jeffries, but I do believe we're making progress. Mind you, things got a bit dodgy today."

"In what way, sir?"

"I almost lost the case to Inspector Nivens."

"Inspector Nivens," she yelped. She almost dropped the sherry but recovered quickly and only spilled a few drops. "What's he got to do with it?"

Witherspoon smiled as he took the drink from her. "At present, nothing. But he was the first inspector on the case originally."

"You never mentioned that," she said softly. She was alarmed that he'd left out such information in their earlier discussions. What else had he left out?

"I didn't know until today," he admitted. "The signature on the original report was illegible, and I didn't give the matter much thought. Today I realized that we had to speak to the original investigators, and, luckily, Constable Barnes had been able to decipher Nivens's handwriting. Oh, by the way, thank you for bringing my spectacles to the station."

"It was nothing, sir. Do go on."

"Apparently, even though Nivens had mucked it up, so to speak, he felt that being the original officer on the case entitled him to get it back. Luckily, the chief inspector didn't share that view. Of course, it might still get a bit messy. I believe Inspector Nivens has some very influential friends in high places."

"But the case is still yours?"

"Oh yes," he replied. "But the chief did warn me to get cracking."

"In other words, he wants it solved right away."

CHAPTER 9

They were all assembled at the kitchen table at precisely eight o'clock. Wiggins had gone across the garden and escorted Ruth so she wouldn't have to make her way over in the dark.

"I think we've quite a bit of information to get through," Mrs. Jeffries said firmly, "so why don't we go around the table. Let's start with you, Ruth. Did you have any success today?"

"Oh yes," Ruth nodded eagerly. "Well, I don't know if the information is useful, but I did hear a bit more about the principals in the case. It's mainly just a verification of what we already know, that the firm is in financial trouble." She paused for breath and then told them everything she'd learned from Emmaline. She was careful to make sure she repeated everything. "And there seems to be an unfortunate tendency of the company to bring in a new partner with a rich wife when the firm is running out of cash," she finished.

"That's the truth," Smythe muttered. "Despite Harry Donovan bein' such a proud one, it sure didn't stop 'im from using other people's money."

"And it's usually ladies' money," Wiggins added. "That don't seem right."

"That might be changing," Ruth continued. "Harry Donovan has spent the last few weeks bragging to anyone who'd stand still for thirty seconds that his firm was going to be doing brilliantly. He's even started hinting that he was thinking of buying his partners out and returning complete ownership to himself."

Smythe frowned. "Why would he do that? It's not like he's got any heirs to inherit from him."

"Perhaps his pride has taken such a beating over the years that he's desperate to prove he's as good as his father and grandfather," Ruth suggested with a shrug.

"Pride goeth before a fall," Mrs. Goodge quoted.

"And it's a silly reason to buy out yer partners," Wiggins added, "especially when it's already been proved that he's not very good at runnin' the business on 'is own."

"Doesn't seem like the bloke was particularly good at runnin' it even with the partners," Smythe put in.

"I wonder if the other partners know of Donovan's plans?" Mrs. Jeffries murmured, her expression thoughtful.

"My source didn't say," Ruth replied, "and I wanted to take care in how much I asked. I don't want to draw undue attention to my curiosity."

"Yes, we quite understand," Mrs. Jeffries replied. But knowing if the other partners knew of those particular plans might be important. She made a mental note to pursue this line of inquiry. It could well be pertinent to motive. If one of the other partners suspected they were being pushed out, they might have been tempted to ruin Donovan by murdering Westover and making sure that goose didn't lay another golden egg. But she'd think about that later, when she was alone. She turned her attention to Betsy. "Any luck today?"

"Not really," Betsy replied. "I tried hanging about the Arkwright house, but that didn't work. No one so much as stuck a nose out of any of the houses around there. Then I happened to spot the inspector and Constable Barnes coming down the street, so I scurried off as fast as I could. So all I've got to show for my trouble is sore feet. But I'm sure I'll do better tomorrow. You can't get lucky every day."

"Of course you will, Betsy," Mrs. Jeffries encouraged. "Perhaps tomorrow you might try and find out some more about the partners' various maritial problems." She had no idea what, if anything, those kinds of difficulties might have to do with Westover's murder, but one never knew where one would find a solution.

"And they've got plenty of 'em," Smythe added. "At last count two of 'em had wives threatenin' legal action, and the other one's wife wants a divorce."

"Puts you right off the whole idea of marriage, don't it?" Wiggins commented.

"Don't be silly," Betsy glared at the footman. "There's lots of people that are happily married."

"And lots that ain't," Wiggins replied. "But not to worry, you and Smythe'll do all right. You're not like most married people. You like each other."

"Thank you, I think," she said.

"I do rather like the lass," Smythe gave her a cheeky grin. "and we'll do better than all right."

"Have you got any idea who killed him yet?" Mrs. Goodge leaned back in her chair and looked at the housekeeper.

"Not yet," Mrs. Jeffries admitted, "but I'm sure we'll come across something that'll point the way very soon." She refused to let the others see how concerned she was about this case. She had no idea who killed Harlan Westover, and there weren't even any nagging little patterns playing about at the back of her mind. Furthermore, after what she'd learned from Inspector Witherspoon today, she'd realized they'd overlooked some obvious sources of information. She was quite annoyed with herself.

"I 'ad a pretty good run of luck today," Smythe said. "I think maybe I stumbled across somethin' important."

"Good," Mrs. Goodge said firmly.

"Mind you," he warned, "it might be nothing." But he knew it was important. He just didn't want to make the others feel bad. He told them everything he'd learned from Blimpey. He didn't mention Blimpey by name, of course. His pride wouldn't let him admit to the others that he got most of his information by paying for it.

No one said anything for a few moments after he'd finished. Finally, Mrs. Jeffries said, "Gracious, Smythe, I think you've found our motive. Thank goodness you had the intelligence to trot along to that factory and ask a few questions. I'd been giving myself a good scolding because we'd neglected to direct any of our inquiries there."

He could feel a flush climbing his cheeks. "Like I said, I just got a bit lucky. I was a bit at loose ends after leavin' Brook Green so I took a chance on findin' somethin' out from the factory workers. That reminds me, I found out somethin' else today." He told them about the hansom driver taking Horrocks to Brook Green. "I'm not saying Horrocks is the murderer. The driver wasn't sure about the exact date," he stressed. " 'E just knew it 'ad been close to a fortnight ago that he took 'em there."

"Cor blimey," Wiggins yelped. "That's no good. I'm sure the killer must be Melcher . . . "

"Not so fast, Wiggins," Mrs. Goodge warned. She was slightly put out that Smythe had stolen their thunder, so to speak.

"What are you talking about?" Mrs. Jeffries watched Wiggins carefully. The lad generally didn't get this excited without good reason. "Why Melcher as the killer?"

"Because I stole his shirt," Wiggins exclaimed, "and it's got blood on the sleeve. Westover's blood. Tell 'em, Mrs. Goodge. Tell 'em what I found out today. Melcher is bound to be our killer."

Everyone started talking at once.

" 'Ow did you get your 'ands on 'is shirt?" Smythe demanded.

"Wiggins, what have you been up to?" Betsy cried.

"Goodness, Wiggins, that was certainly resourceful of you," Ruth said.

"I'm afraid I don't understand this at all," Mrs. Jeffries frowned. "Have I missed something?"

"Everyone, be quiet," Mrs. Goodge shouted.

Startled, everyone immediately fell silent and stared at her.

"Sorry, I didn't mean to shout," she smiled sheepishly. "But it's important you hear the whole of this. I'll explain how Wiggins happened to get his hands on Lawrence Melcher's shirt." She took a deep breath and then told them what had happened. "So you see, Wiggins was in a bit of a state. He had to steal the shirt because it might be evidence, but by stealin' it, he put himself in a bit of a precarious position, you might say."

"You might say that," Mrs. Jeffries agreed.

"Did I do somethin' wrong, Mrs. Jeffries?" Wiggins asked worriedly. "Should I 'ave left it in the laundry basket?"

"Not at all," she said. "Your actions were perfectly correct. Could you go and get the shirt, please?"

He leapt to his feet. "It's in the dry larder." Fred jumped up and dashed after Wiggins. The dog didn't like to let the lad out of his sight.

Mrs. Goodge waited until Wiggins had disappeared. "I didn't know what to tell the lad when he brung it in and told me how he'd got his hands on it," she said softly. "He was in a bit of a state."

"What's wrong?" Ruth asked quietly. "It's evidence, isn't it?"

"Yes, but it can be traced directly to him," Mrs. Goodge answered. "The girl can easily identify him."

"I see," Ruth nodded. "And if we give it to the inspector and he starts asking questions, it'll lead right back to Wiggins."

"I'm afraid so," Mrs. Jeffries replied. "We've found evidence before, but generally, it doesn't point a finger directly at one of us. Or if it did, we would find a way to muddy the waters a bit. But Wiggins didn't really have much choice in the matter. If he hadn't acted, we'd have lost the evidence."

"Down, Fred," Wiggins's footsteps could be heard, and a moment later, he and the dog hurried into the room. " 'Ere it is," he waved the shirt in the air.

"Thank you, Wiggins," Mrs. Jeffries said calmly. "Put it on the table, and we'll all have a good look."

Wiggins did as instructed, laying the garment neatly in the center of the table. He arranged it so the bloodstained sleeve was draped across the front of the shirt. "I know we can't really give this to the inspector," he said cheerfully. "That'd be too risky. The maid could point me out in a quick minute if the police started asking questions. On the other 'and, I didn't want this shirt goin' into the wash, just in case it was important. I thought we ought to see it."

Mrs. Jeffries cocked her head to one side and studied the shirt. "You're absolutely right, Wiggins, it is important that we see. Now, we've got to think how we can get this evidence and all the other things we've learned tonight to the inspector. But before we discuss precisely how we're going to manage that feat, let me tell you what I found out from the inspector this evening. Before we go putting a noose around James Horrocks's neck, you might be interested to know that Oliver Arkwright was seen on Brook Green the day of the murder."

"Arkwright? So both he and Horrocks might have been there that day." Mrs. Goodge pursed her lips. "Things are certainly getting muddled. Oh, sorry, Mrs. Jeffries, go on with what you were sayin'."

"Thank you, I heard a bit more than that." She gave them a complete report. When she got to the point where Nigel Nivens name came up, there was a storm of protest.

"The nerve of the man," Mrs. Goodge snapped.

"First he mucks it up, then he wants it back?" Betsy yelped.

"Stupid git," Smythe muttered. "It's a wonder someone 'asn't put their fist in that man's face before now."

"The inspector isn't goin' to be taken off the case, is 'e?" Wiggins wailed.

"I'm a bit confused." Ruth glanced around the table. "Gerald's never mentioned this person before. Who's Nigel Nivens, and why do you all dislike him so much?"

Smythe and Betsy were the last to leave the kitchen. The moment Betsy put the last teacup away, he grabbed her about the waist, swung her around to face him, and gave her a quick kiss.

She stared at him and didn't like what she saw. Despite the playful kiss, there was a wary look in his eyes and tightness about his jaw. Something was wrong. "Mrs. Goodge will be shocked if she comes in to get a drink."

He shrugged. "She knows we're 'ere, she'll not be back." He knew the others in the household did their best to give him and Betsy a bit of privacy. "I want to talk to you."

"I don't want to hear any nonsense about our age difference," she warned.

"That's not it," he replied. He took a deep breath. He knew he was getting ready to step on thin ice, but he needed an answer. "I think we ought to set a date."

"For the wedding?"

"No, for callin' on the queen. Of course for the wedding."

Betsy had known this was coming. She'd put him off once, and he'd understood. She didn't think she could manage it a second time. "What's the hurry? I thought we'd agreed that neither of us was prepared to give up our investigating."

"We don't know that we'd 'ave to give up anything," he said softly.

"But we agreed to wait a couple of years."

"I know, but what's the 'arm in settin' a date?"

"The harm is once we set a date, we'll have to stick to it."

"What's wrong with that?" he cried. "Don't you want to marry me?"

"Of course I do," she shot back. "But you know as well as I do that once we marry, everything will change. There won't be anymore investigating, there won't be anymore meetings and following suspects and sussing out clues. Once we're gone, it'll be over."

"Luty and Hatchet manage to help out," he pointed out, "and they don't live here."

"And they miss a lot of things, too," she reminded him. "If you're not on the spot, you're going to miss out. We both know that, and neither of us is ready to give this up."

"There's no reason we couldn't stay on here for a bit after we was married."

She stared at him closely. "Do you really mean that? You'd not want to move us into our own home right off?" Though, in truth, she'd been thinking about how wonderful it would be to have a real home of her own. Smythe could give her anything she wanted, and one part of her really did want a place all her own.

"I'm thinkin' we could find a way," he replied. "We're intelligent people, Betsy. I know that once we marry, things will change. But that doesn't mean we'll have to give up our investigatin'. Besides, all I want to do now is think about settin' the date."

She hesitated. There were so many reasons to keep things just as they were. She knew this man, once they married, he'd not be content with her being a maid in some else's home. He'd want to give her the world, and he could. He was a rich man. But much as she loved him, loved the idea of having her own home and her own family, she couldn't give up their cases. Not yet. Helping to catch murderers made her feel special, as if she was doing something so noble it was almost a religious calling. But she also loved him and she could tell this was important to him. "All right, then," she sighed. "I guess we can set the date."

He stepped back, stared at her for a moment, and then folded his arms over his chest. "You don't have to sound so miserable about it. It's a weddin' I'm wanting, not your execution."

"That's not it, and you know it," she retorted. "And no offense intended, but you're not standing there with a big happy grin on your face either. You look right annoyed about something, and you have ever since the others went upstairs." That was a bald-faced lie, but she said it anyway because she felt so guilty.

He nodded. "You know me so well, lass."

"Huh?" She caught herself. "I knew it. What's got your back up?"

"Nothin'. Well, it's somethin', but it sounds downright petty to say it out loud."

"Go on, then. Be petty, it'll make you feel better." She punched him playfully on the arm. "And don't try telling me it's because I didn't want to set a date."

"That's part of it," he smiled sheepishly. "I guess I was a bit put out at Wiggins producing that ruddy bloodstained shirt and stealin' all my glory. I was so sure my information was going to point the way to the killer."

She gaped at him for a moment, then she laughed. "You're jealous of him for getting ahead of you."

"I told you it was petty," he said.

"Your information was important," she said. "We've finally got a motive."

"But do we have the right one?" He took her arm and headed for the back stairs. "That's the question."

"I think so. Westover probably went to that board meeting and threatened them. That's probably why he was killed. He knew who'd bought his engine and where it was being shipped. He was probably murdered to keep him from sending a cable telling the buyers to send it back before it blew up and killed people."

Smythe shook his head. "I don't know, lass. Would someone actually kill a man to keep him from sending a cable? Especially when we know that the only thing wrong with the engine was just some cheap struts. And those could be easily replaced." He took her hand, and they started up the darkened staircase.

"But they already had a terrible reputation as a company," Betsy said. "Maybe whoever killed Westover didn't want any bad news about the engine getting out. Not with all those orders pouring in."

"Let's think about it after we've had a good night's sleep." Smythe stifled a yawn. "We do need to start thinking about a date, though."

"Of course we do," she agreed. "But let's wait till the case is solved. I don't want to have to think about something as beautiful as our wedding while we're trying to catch a ruthless killer."

Mrs. Jeffries was up well before the rest of the household. She left the others a note on the kitchen table instructing them to make sure the inspector ate a good breakfast and that she'd see them all for tea later in the afternoon. She tucked the parcel containing Melcher's bloodstained shirt under her arm and stepped out the back door. It wasn't yet daylight, and it took a moment for her eyes to adjust to the dim light of dawn. She pulled her cloak tight about her and started across the garden to the gate on the far side.

After their meeting, she'd done a good deal of thinking. She still had no idea who their killer might be, but the beginning of a pattern was starting to form in her head. All the partners had a motive and it appeared as both Oliver Arkwright and James Horrocks might have been to see Westover on the afternoon he died.

She reached the gate, pulled it open, and stepped out into the empty street. Turning, she made her way the short distance to Holland Park Road and reached the omnibus stop just as an omnibus pulled up. She got on board, paid her fare, and then settled back in her seat. If she were very lucky, she'd reach her destination just as her quarry emerged from his house.

She took the omnibus to the Hammersmith Bridge, got off, and started across. Traffic into the city was already getting heavy. She stopped and leaned over the stone balustrade, looking at the dark, gray waters of the Thames. Would they ever solve this case? She simply didn't know. She hoped Wiggins was right and that they'd find something soon to point the way to the killer.

She tore her gaze away from the water, crossed the road, and walked the rest of the way to her destination. She rounded the corner just as the front door of the second house down opened and Constable Barnes stepped out.

Mrs. Jeffries stopped. She wanted to make sure that the constable was alone. She didn't want Mrs. Barnes poking her head out with any last-minute words for her husband. But the door stayed closed.

Barnes adjusted the strap of his helmet and started up the street. He stopped in midstride as he saw her. "Mrs. Jeffries? Is everything all right?"

"Good morning, Constable. Everything is fine. I simply wanted to have a chance to speak with you privately."

He cast a quick, nervous glance back at his house. "Let's get around the corner. I don't want Mrs. Barnes asking any awkward questions."

"Oh dear, I am sorry," Mrs. Jeffries said. "I wasn't thinking."

Barnes relaxed a bit when he was no longer in sight of his house. "Don't fret, Mrs. Jeffries. My wife's not a jealous woman. She's just a bit nosy. If she saw you meeting me, she'd pester me silly until I told her everything."

"And what is everything?" Mrs. Jeffries asked softly.

He looked at her, his expression thoughtful. "I believe you already know that, don't you. You and the rest of the inspector's staff help him a bit on his cases, don't you?"

She wasn't going to insult his intelligence by denying it. "Yes, we do. How long have you known?"

"I started suspecting quite a long time ago. But I didn't know for sure until recently."

"Are you going to a . . . "

"Going to what?" Barnes chuckled. "Run telling tales to the inspector about his staff picking up a bit of gossip or passing on some street talk that they hear? Now that wouldn't be right, Mrs. Jeffries, not right at all. Why worry the man with silly talk like that? He's got a lot on his mind."

It took a moment for her to fully understand him. "Of course," she agreed. "One wouldn't want you to go telling tales out of school. Speaking of the . . . uh . . . well, silly gossip that one picks up, I happened to have heard a few things of interest and even stumbled across a bit of what might be evidence." She handed him the parcel, took a deep breath, and then plunged straight in to her tale. She told him everything. By the time they reached the omnibus stop for the trip back to Holland Park Road, she'd passed on every scrap of information they had.

"That's quite a bit of silly gossip," he commented as the omnibus pulled up. He took her arm and helped her board.

Neither of them spoke until they'd made their way to the back and taken their seats. "I'm not sure what this proves," he tapped the paper-wrapped parcel, "and I shall have to think of a way to get this and the rest of your information to our inspector. But never fear, I'll manage it."

"He already knows some of it," she replied. "I dropped a few hints in his ear last night. But I'll leave it to you to direct him as you see fit." Mrs. Jeffries had complete faith in Barnes's intelligence and his discretion. "I'm getting off at Hammersmith Station. So we've not much time. Did you find out anything about Westover getting a gun?"

"So far, there doesn't seem to be any evidence of him buying one through any of the local gunsmiths. But he could have written off and bought one through the post." He grimaced. "And my inquiries on the less legitimate ways of obtaining a weapon haven't turned up anything. But just because I can't find any evidence of a purchase, doesn't mean he couldn't lay hands on a gun."

"But I don't think he did," she mused.

"I don't either," he agreed. "After everything we've learned, I'm sure he was murdered."

"So am I," she replied. "But then I think of Dr. Bosworth's evidence about the growth on the poor man's brain and how that might have had an effect on his behavior . . . "

"But it might not," Barnes argued, "and the evidence of foul play just keeps gettin' stronger."

"How much of a danger to our inspector is Nivens?" she asked.

"Chief Inspector Barrows clipped his wings a bit yesterday," Barnes replied. "But that'll not stop him for long. You and your lot best be careful. Nivens suspects the inspector is gettin' help."

"We'll take extra precautions to make sure he doesn't spot us. I'm sure his pride is wounded."

"That it is," Barnes warned, "and he'll be wantin' to take his fury out on our inspector. But for all his political connections and bluster, he's a bit of a coward. I think we'll be all right. Especially if the inspector hurries up and solves this case."

The omnibus pulled up in front of the busy Hammersmith Station, and the constable swung out of his seat to let her out. "Let me know if you find out anything worthwhile today," he said. "And I'll make sure our inspector learns everything your lot has found out."

"The inspector kept asking me where Mrs. Jeffries had gone," Betsy said as she came into the kitchen. She carried a tray with the inspector's dirty breakfast dishes.

"He was down here askin' me the same thing," Mrs. Goodge replied. "I told him she'd gone to see the fishmonger and the butcher."

"I know." Betsy frowned as she put the tray down on the far end of the kitchen table. "He told me. But then he kept wondering if Mrs. Jeffries had gone because she wanted to order something special from the butcher's and the fishmonger. I hadn't any idea what to say."

"He's worried," Mrs. Goodge snorted. "He's afraid Mrs. Jeffries has already gone ahead and started planning that dinner party she's pressing him to have."

"Men," Betsy laughed and began picking the dirty dishes off the tray. "They're brave enough to face ruffians with pistols, but the idea of social obligation scares them to death."

"Don't bother with that," Mrs. Goodge jerked her head at the mess. "I'll take care of it."

Betsy looked doubtful. "Are you sure? It'll only take a few minutes to get this lot cleaned up. I'm only going over to the Arkwright neighborhood."

"This case isn't goin' to solve itself," the cook retorted. "Now go on with you, and let me get crackin'. I've got some sources dropping by in a bit, and I want this kitchen cleared."

Betsy did as she was told and was out the door a few minutes later. Once the maid was gone, Mrs. Goodge was alone. Smythe had left just after breakfast to do some snooping near the Donovan house and Wiggins had taken it into his head to go back to the Lynch neighborhood. Mrs. Goodge hoped the lad kept a sharp eye out. She suspected the inspector and Constable Barnes might be over in that area today.

It didn't take the cook long to finish the chores. She had just put the last plate on the rack, when there was a knock on the back door. She hurried down the hall, opened up, and blinked in surprise. "Melba? This is a surprise. I didn't expect to see you today." Melba Robinson was a small, thin woman with frizzy gray hair and bright blue eyes. She wore a heavy black coat, buttoned from the tip of her sharp chin down to the tip of her toes.

"I hope you don't think it's a liberty, bein' as I was supposed to come by yesterday."

"Oh no," Mrs. Goodge ushered her inside and down the hall towards the kitchen. "You're very welcome. Let me take your coat."

Melba was already in the process of unbuttoning the garment. "I'm ever so sorry about yesterday. But the most dreadful thing happened. I locked myself outside."

"How awful," Mrs. Goodge replied.

"Not to worry, I got inside," Melba got enough buttons open to slip off the coat and nimbly stepped out of it. She hung it on the coatrack.

"You have a spare key hidden outside?" Mrs. Goodge asked. She ushered the other woman towards the table. "Let's have tea. I've some nice apple tarts baked."

"There's no spare," Melba shrugged. "Tea would be lovely, thank you."

"Do sit down," Mrs. Goodge pointed at a chair and then hurried to put the kettle on. "If there's no spare key, how'd you get inside? Surely you didn't climb through a window." She really didn't care, but she'd found that it didn't matter what her sources started talking about, it only mattered to get them talking. Melba Robinson lived very close to the

Donovan house, and if there were any gossip to be had about them, she'd have it. Melba's house wasn't one of those posh Mayfair mansions, it was a simple modest row house that she'd bought with money both inherited from relations and saved out of her salary over the years.

"Of course not," Melba giggled. "Mind you, I'm still pretty spry for someone my age. I could probably have gotten in that way if I'd had to, but it wasn't necessary. I went to my neighbor, Mr. Courtland, and he let me in."

"He climb in a window?" Mrs. Goodge said absently. She racked her brain for a way to bring up the Donovans. She put a plate of apple tarts in front of her guest. "Tea'll be ready in a minute."

"Don't be daft," Melba snickered. "Mr. Courtland can barely walk. He used to own my house, you see. I bought it off him five years ago this spring. When I told him what I'd done, he mucked about in this old wooden box of his, and lo and behold if he didn't find an old key to my front door. Mind you, it was covered in rust and barely worked, but it got us inside. He'd had it all along and forgotten it was there."

The kettle whistled and Mrs. Goodge finished making their tea. "That's handy," she said. "Him havin' a key and all. Uh, isn't it awful about that neighbor of yours?"

"What neighbor?" Melba demanded. "I've heard nothing about any of my neighbors." She picked up a tart and put it on her plate.

"The Donovans . . . "

"Oh them," Melba interrupted. "Well, it's only to be expected, now isn't it? Mind you, none of us that live 'round there is surprised about it. Well, it was bound to happen, wasn't it?"

For a moment, Mrs. Goodge wasn't sure what to do. Her pride didn't want to let on that she didn't know what Melba was talking about, yet she was greedy for information. In less than a heartbeat, greed won. "I'm not sure I know what you're talking about, Melba."

"What were you talking about, then?" Melba demanded.

"Mr. Donovan's business," Mrs. Goodge replied. "I wondered if you'd heard about the death of his chief engineer. It were ruled a suicide . . . "

"It was murder," Melba interrupted again. "The police have been around to speak to the Donovans and to some of the neighbors."

"Did they talk to you?"

"No, my home is too far away from those posh houses where the likes of the Donovans live. But they spoke to Minnie Carroll, and she told me they're askin' about Mr. Donovan." She paused and took a big bite of apple tart. "Said they wanted to know if she'd seen Mr. Donovan come home on the day the poor engineer fellow died and if she did, what time was it. But Minnie hadn't noticed anything."

"Oh," Mrs. Goodge was very disappointed.

"Mind you, it seems to me they ought to be keepin' an eye on Mr. Donovan. Seems to me if what I heard was right, poor Mrs. Donovan had better take care."

Mrs. Goodge snapped to attention. "What? What's this about Mrs. Donovan?"

Betsy spotted the housemaid as she came out from the side of the Arkwright house. She knew the girl was a servant because she'd come out the servant's entrance and not the front door. But where was the girl going? It was too early in the day for it to be her afternoon out. Even the nicest of households didn't let girls out until after the noon meal, and it had just gone ten. Puzzled, she watched as the girl turned and headed up the street. Perhaps she was on an errand for her mistress? But then why wasn't she wearing her maid's cap?

Betsy decided to follow her. The girl moved quickly, as though she were late for an appointment. Betsy stayed at a reasonable distance, not wanting the girl to see her. But being discreet was very difficult. The girl kept stopping and looking over her shoulder, as though she knew she was being followed. The first time it happened, Betsy pretended to be looking in a shop window, but the second time, she had to dodge behind a post box.

Finally, the girl turned into a tea shop on the Kensington High Street. Betsy held back, wondering if she ought to go in as well. If the girl had spotted her, she'd be done for. But if she hadn't, she might learn something. She took a deep breath and stepped inside the shop.

The place was very crowded. There were people standing at the short counter, and most of the tables were filled as well. It took her a moment to spot her quarry. She was sitting at a table in the center of the room talking earnestly to a middle-aged man.

Betsy hesitated. There was an empty table next to them, but she knew the practice in these sorts of places was to get the tea first and then find a place to sit. Obviously, the man had gotten both their beverages, as there was a steaming cup of tea in front of the girl. But Betsy didn't want to risk someone at the counter grabbing that table. Blast. She made up her mind and hurried toward it. If anyone asked, she'd just pretend she was waiting for someone.

From the corner of her eye, she watched the girl as she pulled out a chair and sat down. The girl didn't appear to notice her. Betsy sat down and unobtrusively twisted herself so that her ear was towards the girl and the man.

"I'm sorry, sir," the girl said to him, "but that's all I was able to hear."

Betsy heard the man sigh. Then he said, "It's all right. Did she say what time he was coming?"

"No, sir, only that she would be seeing him this afternoon." The girl took a quick sip of tea. "I'm sorry, Mr. Arkwright. I wish I had more to tell you. But frankly, sir, she's a bit careful on what she says around us. She doesn't tell me any details."

Betsy held her breath. So, the maid was secretly meeting with her employer, Oliver Arkwright. The secrecy was apparently so that Arkwright's wife wouldn't find out, and it was equally apparent Arkwright wasn't meeting with the girl for the usual reason.

"But you're sure he's coming today?" Arkwright pressed. "It's very important that you be certain."

"Absolutely, sir. I heard her tell cook to have some nice cakes ready for this afternoon. She said Mr. Wellbanks, her solictor, was coming and they'd be wantin' some tea."

CHAPTER 10

Inspector Witherspoon and Constable Barnes turned into the courtyard of the Ladbrooke Grove Police Station. As they crossed the cobblestones, Barnes said, "Perhaps another chat with some of the partners' servants might be in order, sir."

"Really? Do you have any specific sorts of ideas about what we might ask?" Witherspoon pulled open the heavy double oak doors, and they stepped inside.

Barnes nodded at the police constables milling about behind the counter. "I think so, sir. It uh . . . suddenly occurred to me that as Westover was killed with a gun, the killer might have gotten blood on himself."

"But surely, if that were the case, he'd have gotten rid of the damaging evidence." Witherspoon headed toward the counter.

"Not if he didn't know it was there," Barnes replied. "It's quite easy to get a drop or two on a lapel or a shirt sleeve and not even realize it's there." He winced inwardly at how pathetic his argument sounded, but it was the best he could come up with.

"You're right, Constable. I'm no expert on firearms, but surely it's rather difficult to shoot someone at what must have been very close range, without getting a bit of blood on oneself. Blood does tend to splatter." He smiled politely at the officer behind the counter. "Good day, sergeant. We're here to have a word with PC Howard and PC Smith."

"We're all ready for you, sir," the sergeant replied. "We've set you up in the same interview room as before. Go on in, and I'll have someone go get the lads."

They crossed behind the counter, through a door, and into a dim, narrow hallway. The interview room was the last door at the end. In the center of the room was a table with two chairs on each side of it. A tall wooden file drawer with a gaslamp sitting on top of it stood by the window.

"Did you want to interview them together, sir?" Barnes asked.

Witherspoon frowned. "Is there any reason we shouldn't?"

"They did muck up the original investigation, sir," the constable replied. "And they might be worried about being reprimanded. We'd probably get more out of them speaking one on one."

The door opened, and an older PC stuck his head inside. "PC Howard is here, sir. Are you ready for him?"

"Where's PC Smith?" Barnes asked.

"He's at the Marylebone Magistrates Court. He's giving evidence on another case. He ought to be here soon, though."

Barnes and Witherspoon looked at each other. "We're ready for PC Howard," the inspector said. The constable nodded and ducked back out into the hall. They could hear him say, "Come along, lad, they're ready for you."

"Looks like we'll be interviewin' them separately after all," Barnes muttered as he took a seat behind the table. Witherspoon sank down in the other one.

PC Howard was a tall, lanky young man with a bony face, deep-set brown eyes, and russet-colored wavy hair. "Good day, Inspector, Constable." His back was ramrod straight, but his expression was wary.

Witherspoon smiled reassuringly at the young man. "Good day PC Howard. Do have a seat," he gestured at one of the empty chairs.

Howard licked his lips nervously and sat down.

Barnes opened his little brown notebook. "You were the first police officer to arrive on the scene when Mr. Harlan Westover died, is that correct?"

"That's right, sir, I was patrolling over on Brook Green when all of a sudden, this fellow comes running across the grass shouting that he needed help."

"What time was this?" Witherspoon asked.

"It was about half past twelve." He paused. "I think."

"What happened then?" Barnes pressed.

"I went with the gentleman around the corner to Charter Street. He told me that a man was dead and that it looked like he'd been shot. That's when I blew my whistle, sir." He paused again and took a breath. "That's proper procedure, sir. If you know there's been a weapon used, you're supposed to call for help immediately."

"Of course it is," Witherspoon reassured him. "I suppose you got an answering whistle from PC Smith."

"That's right, sir. It come right away so I knew PC Smith was close by. I went on into the house with this gentleman who I later found out was Mr. James Horrocks. By then, there were plenty of people larking about, so I knew someone would show PC Smith where we'd gone."

"Was Mr. Horrocks saying anything?" Barnes asked.

PC Howard shook his head. "Not really. He'd gone quite pale, like he was in shock. We got upstairs, and Mr. Horrocks stayed on the landing. I went inside and saw the victim sprawled on the settee. I felt for a pulse and made sure he was dead. Just then, PC Smith come in, and he checked the fellow as well." He shrugged uncomfortably. "To be honest, sir, I was a bit taken aback. I'd never seen anything like that and neither had PC Smith. PC Smith went out and asked Mr. Horrocks some questions. He come back into the room, and I was goin' to nip back to the station and call out the police surgeon. PC Smith was goin' to search the victim's rooms, but all of a sudden, Inspector Nivens arrived. He took right over."

"Exactly what did he do?" Barnes asked softly.

"He spoke to Mr. Horrocks, found out who the victim was and that he'd worked for Mr. Horrocks's company. Then he stepped inside, had a quick look about, and announced it was a suicide. I said we'd not had a chance to search the premises or ask any questions . . . but he said not to waste our time." PC Howard shifted nervously. "I didn't like it much, but what could I do? He was an inspector. PC Smith tried arguing with him, he told him that we'd not asked nearly enough questions of Mr. Horrocks, but Inspector Nivens told him it wasn't necessary. That Mr. Horrocks was a well-known businessman and he'd take care of speaking to him later. PC Smith even pointed to the fact that there was a drop of blood on the settee. But Inspector Nivens told him not to be impertinent and to do what he was told."

"Where was the blood?" Barnes asked sharply.

"On the arm of the settee," Howard explained. "But it wasn't on the arm of the side where Westover's corpse was lyin', it was on the other side. PC Smith was sure the body had been moved. Which means it was murder, sir. People don't move themselves from one end of the settee to another, not once they're dead."

Mrs. Jeffries stepped through the heavy door of the West London Hospital. She stood in the foyer, surveying the area and planning her strategy. Straight ahead of her was a long narrow corridor with doors and hallways branching off at various intervals. The walls were painted an ugly shade of green that vaguely matched the gray green color of the linoleum.

The place smelled of sickness and antiseptic. Mrs. Jeffries started down the corridor. She passed a door that led into a large ward, but she didn't go in, instead she carried on to the end where a nurse sat behind a desk. The woman looked up at her approach. "May I help you, ma'am?"

"I'm not certain," Mrs. Jeffries gave the woman a timid smile. She had planned her strategy carefully and hoped it would work. "Actually, I've a rather odd problem. I'm not even sure I'm at the right place."

"You don't know where you ought to be?" the nurse said sternly. "I'm afraid I don't understand."

"Let me explain," Mrs. Jeffries replied. "My cousin died recently."

"Did he die here?" the nurse asked.

"No, but he was brought here for a postmortem."

"A postmortem?" the nurse frowned. "Then you'll have to go around to the back. We've nothing to do with postmortems here. We only have sick people on this ward. The operating theaters and the morgue are in the back."

"But I don't need to get him," she said quickly. "I'm looking for his clothes, you see. He's been dead and buried for over a fortnight, but no one seems to know what happened to his things. I've been around to the police, but they've no idea and they told me to come along here. He was fully clothed when his body was brought in. He was wearing a new coat and one of his good work shirts. My nephew Harold is the same size as cousin Harlan and he could use those clothes. Especially the coat." Mrs. Jeffries had decided on the practical approach. Nurses, porters, and orderlies were good solid working people. They knew the value of money, and a relative retrieving a dead man's clothes would not shock them.

The nurse thought for a moment. "You'd best see Mr. Glass, he's the porter. He'd be able to tell you if the clothes are still here."

Mrs. Jeffries didn't have to ask what that meant. In a city teeming with poverty, a perfectly good set of unclaimed clothing would soon end up at a street market or secondhand shop. "Where could I find him?"

The nurse gave her directions, and Mrs. Jeffries made her way to the other end of the building. Mr. Glass, the porter, was sitting behind a desk at the end of a hallway. He was reading a newspaper. Behind him was a closed door. She suspected the door lead to the morgue.

She stepped up to the desk and explained her situation.

Glass, a thin man with a dour expression and greasy brown hair, stared at her for a long moment. "How do I know you're Westover's cousin?" he finally said.

Her heart sank. The clothes were probably long gone. "How do you know I'm not?" she retorted.

"Anyone could walk in here and claim they was anyone, now, couldn't they?" he replied. "How am I to know you're telling the truth? We can't just go giving people's things to anyone who wants 'em."

"I suppose I could get Inspector Witherspoon to vouch for me," she began.

Glass's eyes widened. "Inspector, you mean like a police inspector?"

"Oh yes," she smiled brightly. "He was the one who suggested I come here. He was sure the clothes would still be here. They were, after all, evidence in a police inquiry. By rights, they should have been sent along to the police station as soon as the postmortem was finished."

"There's no need to be bringin' in any police inspectors," Glass got to his feet. "You look like a nice person. I'm sure someone of your sort wouldn't go about pretending to be someone they're not." He edged toward the door behind him. "You just wait here a minute, and I'll nip back and have a look."

"Thank you," she gave him a bright smile.

He disappeared through the door and slammed it behind him. Mrs. Jeffries was fairly certain that Harlan Westover's things were still here. She had no doubt that Glass had planned on selling the things, but had kept them for awhile in case a relative or a solicitor showed up to claim them.

The door opened, and Glass stepped back out. He carried a bundle wrapped in brown paper and tied with heavy string. He handed her the parcel. "Here you are, ma'am, all nice and tidy like."

Mrs. Jeffries gave him a shilling. "This is for your trouble, Mr. Glass. Thank you for taking care of my cousin's things."

Glass blinked in surprise as he took the coin. "That's all right, just doin' my job." But he was pleased nonetheless.

She tucked the bundle under her arm and hurried off. She still had much to do. When she got outside, the day had brightened, but it was still cold and overcast. Traffic on King Street was heavy, but she managed to get a hansom. "Upper Edmonton Gardens in Holland Park," she told the driver. She wanted to examine Westover's clothes before they had their afternoon meeting. She also wanted to have a good long think about the case. She was beginning to see a pattern and hoped that it was the one that would lead to the killer.

Wiggins danced from one foot to the other in an effort to keep his feet warm. He'd not had much luck today, but he wasn't giving up. He'd found a good spot to keep an eye on things, a nice doorway of an empty house that gave him an excellent view of the Donovan house. But so far, he'd seen nothing. Maybe he ought to give up. But then what would he do? He supposed he could go along to the Melcher neighborhood. As far as Wiggins was concerned, Melcher was even more of a suspect than Donovan. He pushed away from the doorframe, and just then, the front door of the Donovan house opened and Mrs. Donovan, followed by her butler, stepped outside. "Shall I get you a hansom, ma'am?" he asked.

She waved him off. "I'll walk." She started down the street. Wiggins let her get half a block ahead of him and then was after her. She walked for a good distance, finally slowing her steps when she reached the commercial area in Knights-bridge. Wiggins didn't worry about being spotted, she never once turned to look behind her.

She stopped at a low, two-story stone building, paused, and went inside. Wiggins dashed across the road and got close enough to read the lettering on the wooden sign above the door. It read, "PG Baines & Son. Solicitors."

He kept walking on past the building until he got to the corner. Turning, he stopped and watched the door, waiting for her to come out. He had quite a long wait, long enough that he realized he was drawing attention to himself by standing on the corner. Keeping his gaze on the office, Wiggins crossed the road to the commercial district. Shops lined both sides of the road at this end of the street so he could stroll back and forth amongst the throngs of shoppers unnoticed. But he kept a sharp eye on that door.

He reached the end of the street closest to the office when the door opened and she stepped outside. A balding, elegantly dressed gentleman wearing spectacles was with her. Wiggins managed to stroll past them just as the man said, "Are you absolutely sure about this? The preparations are all in place. Once he's served, it'll be very difficult for you."

"That doesn't matter. I won't be there. I'm leaving tomorrow morning," Mrs. Donovan replied.

Wiggins unobtrusively slowed his steps.

"We'll take care of it immediately, then," the man said. "My clerk will go before the . . . "

Unfortunately, no matter how slow Wiggins went, he couldn't hear the rest of the sentence. He was out of earshot. He got to the corner, turned it, and then dived back to keep his eye on his quarry. Mrs. Donovan had finished her conversation and had turned and started up the road toward the shops. Wiggins waited until the solicitor went back inside, and then he took off after her. But the crowd of shoppers had thickened, and he lost her. Blast a Spaniard, he thought, she's up and disappeared.

Mrs. Jeffries quietly eased open the back door and stepped inside. Holding her parcel, she tiptoed down the hall. She kept her head cocked toward the kitchen, listening to see if Mrs. Goodge was with one of her sources. But she heard nothing.

"Mrs. Goodge," she said as she came into the room, "are you alone?"

"I'm 'ere as well," Smythe said.

"We've just sat down for a quick cuppa," Mrs. Goodge said. "My source just left and Smythe hasn't had any luck today. What's that you've got?"

"Harlan Westover's clothes," Mrs. Jeffries popped the parcel on the table and began pulling off the string.

"Cor blimey, where'd you get those?" Smythe asked. His voice held a hint of admiration.

"From the West London Hospital where he was taken for the postmortem," she replied. "The police never bothered to pick them up, and neither did any of Westover's relations." She pushed aside the wrapping paper and pulled out a dark gray jacket. She held it up and all of them had a good look.

"Why don't you check the pockets," Mrs. Goodge suggested.

Mrs. Jeffries laid the coat on the table and began rummaging through the pockets. "Smythe, do the trousers."

Smythe pulled them out of the parcel, gave them a cursory examination, and shoved his hand in the front left pocket. "What's this, then?" He held up a key ring; on it were two keys.

"Those must be Westover's house keys," Mrs. Goodge yelped.

"Cor blimey, you'd a thought the first coppers on the scene would 'ave taken these. This is evidence, Mrs. Jeffries."

Mrs. Jeffries dropped the jacket onto the table, she'd not found anything in the pockets except a pencil stub. "It certainly is," she stared at the keys. "It proves that Westover probably let the killer in."

"How does it prove that?"

"We've already established that Mrs. Lynch had her lodgers well trained. They locked the door behind them the moment they stepped over the threshold."

"So if Westover came in and locked the doors behind him and then dropped the keys in his pocket, the killer either had to have a key to the front door or Westover had to have let him in," Mrs. Goodge concluded eagerly.

"What should we do with these?" Smythe held the keys in the air.

"We'd best prove that those are his house keys," she replied. "I don't want to get caught out making faulty assumptions. May I leave that up to you?" she asked the coachman.

"I'll handle it as soon as we're finished 'ere," he replied. "Don't worry, I'll take care not to alarm Mrs. Lynch. She'll not know I'm there."

"Is there anything else worth seein'?" Mrs. Goodge demanded.

"There's some undergarments," Mrs. Jeffries tossed them to one side, "a pair of socks and his shirt." She held the shirt up. "But his shoes are missing."

"They were probably pinched by someone at the hospital," Smythe suggested. "Good shoes are worth a bit on the street."

"That's got a great ruddy stain on it," the cook pointed to the collar.

"Looks like ink," Smythe murmured. "Wonder how long he walked around with that on his shirt."

"Most of the day, I expect." Mrs. Jeffries folded the garment and laid it back on the paper. She picked up the other pieces, began folding them, and stacked them neatly on top of the shirt. "As soon as Smythe confirms the keys, we need to get this parcel to Constable Barnes."

"Does he know about us, then?" Mrs. Goodge asked.

Mrs. Jeffries hesitated.

"Come on, Mrs. J., we all know that Barnes was close to sussin' us out," Smythe said.

"He suspects we help a bit, but I don't think he quite understands how deeply involved we are. Not to worry, though, he's devoted to our inspector. He can keep his own counsel."

"And workin' with our inspector 'asn't hurt 'is career." Smythe dropped the keys in his pocket and got up. "I might be a bit late to our meetin' this afternoon, I'll probably wait till it's gone a bit dark before I try these keys."

Constable Barnes closed the door of the interview office and followed Witherspoon down the hall.

"Are you all finished, sir?" the sergeant asked as they came into the main room of the station.

"For the moment," Witherspoon said politely. "We appreciate the help you've given us."

"I'll bet you're close to an arrest, aren't you, sir," the sergeant said enthusiastically. Like many of the rank and file of the Metropolitan Police, he was a great admirer of the legendary Gerald Witherspoon.

"Well, uh . . . " the inspector tried hard to think of something optimistic yet noncommital. He hadn't a clue whom to arrest.

"We're workin' on it," Barnes said. "You lot will be the first to know when it happens."

The sergeant laughed. "That's right, good coppers always play it close to the chest."

"Where to now, sir?" Barnes asked Witherspoon. He hoped it was someplace that took them a long time to reach, because he had quite a lot of information he wanted to drop in the inspector's ear. Too bad he couldn't come out and just tell him everything he'd learned from Mrs. Jeffries, but that wasn't possible. He'd been feeding the man hints all day about this case. But he wasn't sure if Witherspoon had gotten any of them.

"I was thinking we ought to have another go at talking to the partners. We need to know a bit more about that engine they shipped off to South Africa. It seems to me that engine might be the key to this whole case. Also, I'd like to ask them some questions about the firm's financial situation."

Barnes silently heaved a sigh of relief. "That's a good idea, sir. We've plenty of time to go over there and have a word before they close for the day."

"We'll even have time for a bit of lunch," the inspector said cheerfully. "Come along, there's a nice café just up the road. I could do with a nice chop and a bit of mashed potato."

They had almost reached the front door, when it burst open and Nigel Nivens charged into the room. He skidded to a halt as he spotted them. "I've been looking for you two."

"And it seems you've found us," Witherspoon replied. "Is there news? Has the chief sent you to fetch us?"

"I'm not Barrows's ruddy errand boy," Nivens snapped.

"Then why are you here?" Barnes asked cooly. He looked Nivens squarely in the eye.

"You know good and well why I'm here." Nivens's hands balled into fists. "I made it perfectly clear yesterday that I wanted to be present when you interviewed PC Howard and PC Smith."

"I'm afraid that just wasn't possible," Witherspoon said. "Chief Inspector Barrows was quite resolute on the matter. He wanted us to interview them on our own."

"This is my case," Nivens's face contorted in fury, he raised his fist and stepped toward Witherspoon.

Barnes quickly stepped in front of his inspector. "It *was* your case, sir. It's our case now."

From the corner of his eye, Barnes saw the sergeant start out from behind the counter. The constable knew he wasn't a young man, but he'd been a street copper for thirty years. He was still fairly certain he could handle himself and protect his inspector if tempers got out of hand.

Nivens flicked a quick glance at Barnes, then backed away. "You're going to be sorry you did this," he swore. "I'll not have my career destroyed by the likes of you two."

"Gracious, Inspector Nivens," Witherspoon was deeply shocked. "No one is trying to destroy your career."

I am, thought Barnes. Fellow never should have been a copper in the first place.

"The hell you're not," Nivens snarled. "You've tried to ruin me ever since you stole those Kensington High Street murders out from under my nose. Well you're not getting away with it. You're not going to make me look like a fool again."

"No one's making you a fool," Witherspoon said. "Inspector Nivens, I really have no idea what you're talking about. I'm simply doing my job."

Nivens glanced over Witherspoon's shoulder. A sizeable crowd of constables had gathered around the sergeant. None of them were looking particularly friendly toward him. He began backing toward the door. "You'd best take care how you write your report, Witherspoon. If you make me look incompetent, I'll make you regret the day you joined the force, and don't think I can't do it, I've got plenty of friends in high places."

Witherspoon hated confrontation, especially with fellow officers, but he wasn't going to allow himself to be threatened. "I'll write up my report as I always do, Inspector, with diligence, care, and an allegiance to the truth. Not my career. You may have many friends in high places but that is certainly no concern of mine and most assuredly will not influence one word of my report."

"You really are a fool," Nivens said coldly, "and I'll make you pay if it's the last thing I ever do." He turned and stormed out the door.

The inspector stared after him, his expression utterly stunned. He shook his head in disbelief. "I've no idea why that man hates me so much."

"He was the rising young star on the force until you came along," Barnes said quietly. "Mind you, he was a lousy copper. Bullied suspects into false confessions, bullied the lads every chance he got, and was a real boot licker when it suited his purpose. That's why this case never had a chance with Nivens on it. Harlan Westover was just an engineer, James Horrocks and the partners are rich and powerful men. He'd not want to look at them too closely. Why do you think he was so quick to call the case a suicide right after he questioned Horrocks?"

"I can't believe it." Witherspoon started for the door. "How did he get away with it all this time?"

"He never leaves any proof, sir," Barnes sighed as they stepped outside. "The lads know it's always their word against his. He's got plenty of rich and powerful friends to protect him, and, well, occasionally he does solve a burglary. Anyway, sir, not to worry, he's not the only one with allies. You're a good copper, sir, and after that Ripper fiasco, there's plenty at the home office that'll be watching out for you. They know you're a good copper."

They were all late for their afternoon meeting. It was almost ten past five before Mrs. Goodge got the table laid. She put out the teapot as Mrs. Jeffries came in. "I'm sorry to be so late," she began, but stopped when she saw the empty chairs. "Where is everyone?"

"Late," Mrs. Goodge replied tartly. "But I was late too, so I can't grouse about it. I sat down in my rocker to have a bit of a rest and nodded off."

Mrs. Jeffries laughed. "Not to worry, I did the same thing, only I was sitting at my desk. I do hope the others get here soon."

"Me too," Mrs. Goodge put the teapot down next to a plate of jam sandwiches. "I have a feeling we're going to have a lot to talk about."

Everyone else, except Betsy, arrived within minutes, and they took their usual places around the table. Mrs. Goodge handed around the sandwiches and cakes, while Mrs. Jeffries poured the tea.

"Should we wait for Betsy?" the cook asked. Just then they heard the back door open and the sound of running footsteps. "That's her now."

Betsy came into view. The others gasped when they saw her. Her face was smeared with dirt, her cloak was covered with mud streaks, and there were leaves dangling from her disheveled hair.

Smythe was on his feet and across the room like a shot. "Bloomin' Ada, are you all right?" he grabbed Betsy and pulled her closer into the light. "What happened to you, lass? Are you all right? Are you 'urt? Should we call the doctor?"

"I'm fine, Smythe," Betsy soothed him with a weary smile. "I'm not hurt, just filthy, and it's my own fault."

"Betsy, come have a chair and tell us what happened," Mrs. Jeffries suggested.

"You 'ave a nice hot cuppa now," Smythe lead her to her chair, and still holding her hand, took his own seat. "Cor blimey, you better 'ave learned something good from bein' in this state."

Betsy giggled. "Oh I'm sorry, I didn't mean for anyone to make a fuss, but I know what I look like. There's a very simple explanation. I had to hide in the bushes when I was following Mr. and Mrs. Arkwright. They decided to go for a walk along the river after she'd seen her solictor." She took a sip of tea and then told them about following the maid to the café.

"Well, naturally, once I knew Mrs. Arkwright was seeing her solicitor, I went back and hung about the house. The solicitor went inside and a few minutes later, Mr. Arkwright came home and went in as well. About half an hour after that, the solicitor left and right behind him, the Arkwrights come out together. So I followed them, I wanted to find out what they were talking about, you see. But I didn't manage to get close enough to hear them till they went down to the river. They popped down on a bench, and I had to dive into the bushes to get close enough to hear what they was saying." She sighed. "I'll not bore you with the details, but the jist of it was that Mrs. Arkwright isn't going to sue her husband to get her money back. He was ever so grateful. He told her he loved her and that he would pay her back. He said he was going to sell some property off the family's estate up in Northumberland. I think they've come to some sort of . . . well, I think they realized they still love each other."

"Well blast a Spaniard," Mrs. Goodge snapped. "That's no good. I was sure Arkwright might be our killer. He was seen on Brook Green the day Westover was killed."

"He could still be the killer," Wiggins said.

"I don't think so," Betsy said. "They talked about Westover, and Arkwright swore he hadn't gone into the Westover's rooms. He claimed he went to the door, tried to open it, and then lost his nerve and left. I believe him. Mrs. Arkwright does too." Betsy shrugged apologetically. "That's all I got today."

"Are you sure you're all right?" Mrs. Jeffries pressed. "You must be cold, it's quite damp down by the river. We can wait if you'd like to go up and change into something warm."

"Let's get on with the meeting, I'm fine." Betsy smiled at Smythe. "Really, I am, I'm just a bit dirty."

"Can I go next?" Wiggins asked. At the housekeeper's nod, he told them about Mrs. Donovan and how he'd followed her. "She went to her solicitor's too," he nodded eagerly at Betsy, "but she didn't tell him to stop doin' anything." He repeated what he'd heard the woman say to her lawyer. "And then she disappeared into the crowd and I thought I'd lost her for sure." He crammed a bite of sandwich into his mouth. "But I caught up with her again just as she was goin' into the railway bookin' office. I nipped in 'ot on 'er heels and got right in line behind her. She booked a first class ticket to Paris. She's leavin' from Victoria tomorrow at eleven o'clock."

"Are you sure about this?" Mrs. Jeffries pressed.

"Heard it as clear as I can 'ear you," Wiggins grinned. "What do you think it means?"

"I don't know. Possibly nothing more than a woman wanting to get away from her husband," Mrs. Jeffries replied.

"Apparently there's quite a number of women wanting to be rid of their spouses," Ruth interjected. "I'm sorry. It's not my turn yet."

"It's all right," Wiggins said quickly. "I was finished."

"Yes, do go on, Ruth," Mrs. Jeffries took a sip of tea. "Who is leaving their spouse? One of our suspects?"

"Edna Horrocks. She's moved out of the Horrocks's house and is going to file for divorce," Ruth replied. "She's moved back to her family's estate in Wiltshire."

"She must be really fed up," Mrs. Goodge pursed her lips. "People like that usually don't divorce, they live separately. Are you sure she's actually going to divorce him?"

"I'm positive," Ruth said. "And her family is actively encouraging the divorce. They hate him. He's quite a rich man, but he's such a miser he's made her live like a pauper for years."

"He's rich?" Mrs. Jeffries asked. "I thought all of his money was tied up in the firm?" She was annoyed with herself for not finding this out earlier.

"Oh no, not all of it," Ruth said. "He's far too cautious a person to put all his eggs in one basket. He's got a number of other investments and plenty of real estate that's free and clear."

"So even if the company goes bankrupt, he'd be all right," Smythe muttered.

"As would Arkwright and Melcher," Ruth added.

"So it's just Donovan who would be in dire straits if the company went under," Mrs. Jeffries knew this was important. Suddenly, a number of things began to make sense. But she needed to have a good, long think about this before she was sure.

"Can I go now?" Mrs. Goodge asked. "It's gettin' late, and the inspector'll be home soon."

"If Ruth's finished?"

"I'm done," she replied. "Go on, Mrs. Goodge, what did you find out today?"

Mrs. Goodge told them about Melba's visit. "Mind you, gettin' any sense out of the woman was like pullin' teeth, she kept witterin' on about gettin' locked out of her house and her neighbor, who used to own the house, havin' to let her in. But I finally got a few useful bits out of her." She looked at Wiggins. "Mrs. Donovan went to see her solicitor today because she's havin' him serve her husband tomorrow. The firm's gettin' a notice to quit the premises. Leastways that's what Melba thought it was called."

"But why now?" Smythe asked. "Seems to me the company might just have a chance to be a success."

"That's probably what Mrs. Donovan is afraid of," Mrs. Goodge replied. "According to Melba, she hates her husband and has been looking for a way to hurt him for years. What better way than to wait until he's almost a success and then snatch it away from him."

"Why does she hate him so much?" Betsy asked.

Mrs. Goodge shrugged. "Who knows? But it happens that way sometimes. Anyway, that's all I've got."

Mrs. Jeffries looked at Smythe. "Does the key fit?"

He nodded, pulled them out of his pocket and handed them to her. "They do. I waited until Mrs. Lynch was in the kitchen and then nipped up the front stairs. Both keys fit, so he must have let the killer in."

"Where'd you get keys?" Betsy demanded.

Mrs. Jeffries told her and the others how she'd obtained the parcel from the hospital. They discussed the case for another half hour before they had to stop and take care of the evening chores.

By the time the inspector came home, Mrs. Jeffries's head was buzzing with so many ideas she could barely keep them all straight.

Over their customary glass of sherry, she found out what he'd learned that day. It was enough to add even more fuel to her mental fires.

The inspector retired right after dinner, he claimed he was simply tired, but Mrs. Jeffries thought he seemed a bit upset about something. He didn't eat as much as usual.

She went up to her own room and closed the door behind her. She didn't bother to undress, but instead, went to her chair by the window. She sat down, relaxed her body, and let her mind drift free. Somewhere in all this information was the identity of the killer. She knew it. She could feel it in her bones.

CHAPTER 11

It was still dark outside when Mrs. Jeffries came downstairs. She made herself a pot of tea and sat down at the table, trying to put her thoughts into some semblance of order. She'd spent a good part of the night awake, alternately thinking and letting her mind drift free. By morning, she'd decided what course of action was needed. She only hoped it was the correct one to lead them to the killer.

She heard footsteps on the back stairs, and a moment later, Smythe appeared. He was fully dressed. He grinned at her. "Couldn't sleep?"

"No, I spent most of the night thinking about our case." She got up and fetched another cup.

"So did I," he admitted, taking the seat next to her. "Come to any conclusions?"

"I'm not sure," she poured him tea and handed him the cup.

"But you've got an idea?"

"I think so, but I'm not absolutely certain." She knew she shouldn't be so hesitant, but the conclusion she'd reached in the wee hours of the morning was based on very little hard evidence. On the other hand, it simply made more sense than any other idea she'd come up with. "When you were at the Lynch house yesterday evening, did you happen to notice the locks?"

"It was gettin' dark, Mrs. Jeffries, the only thing I cared about was seein' if the keys fit. To be honest, I didn't pay any attention to the lock proper. Why? Is it important?"

"It might be. I'm sorry to have to ask you this again, but can you nip over to the Lynch house and have a good look?"

"What am I looking for?"

"Age. I want you to see if you can tell if the lock is the original one. I know that might be a bit difficult . . . "

"That shouldn't be too 'ard," Smythe interrupted. "Those houses over on Charter Street are over fifty years old, if it's an original lock it'll be one of them old-fashioned kind with the big strike plate, if it's been changed, it'll 'ave one of them small mortise locks on it."

She stared at him in amazement. "Gracious, how do you know all that?"

"I did a bit of carpentry and 'ousebuildin' when I was in Australia." He shrugged modestly. "Anything else you need done?"

"I need someone to get Westover's clothes to Constable Barnes this morning *before* he comes to pick up the inspector. But I'll have Wiggins take care of that. He can waylay him at the corner."

"Should I get the lad up?" He started to rise, but Mrs. Jeffries waved him back to his chair.

"Not yet, we've got several hours before the constable is due here." She took another sip of the hot tea. "And I need to know about that stain on Westover's shirt."

"The ink stain?"

"That's right, I want to find out if Westover had it on his shirt when he left the office after the board meeting. It's quite a big stain, so if it was there at that time, it would have been plainly visible. Betsy might be able to find that out quickly enough. She can waylay that clerk she spoke to a couple of days ago before he goes into the office."

"I heard my name being bandied about." Betsy came into the kitchen. "Do you want me to do something? What is it?"

Mrs. Jeffries repeated her instructions as she poured the maid a cup of tea. "And I'll need you both back here by half past eight. That's when Constable Barnes is due," she finished.

Betsy nodded eagerly and took a quick sip of tea. "What if my source didn't see Westover that day? Do you want me to find someone else to ask?"

"If you can," Mrs. Jeffries replied. "But I suspect we're going to be up against a very rigid time frame, so you must be back here at half past eight. Let me give you some money, you'll need to take a hansom, it'll save a lot of time."

Betsy stood up. "I'll just get my cloak, then. It's upstairs."

"You've got a few minutes," Smythe protested. "Finish your tea."

She headed for the back stairs. "It's too hot, I'll finish it when I've got my cloak and gloves."

"You can walk her up to Holland Park Road," Mrs. Jeffries pulled some coins out of her pocket. "It'll be light by the time you get there."

"And I can go on to the Lynch house as soon as I see her safely off."

Within a few minutes, the two of them were out the back door and Mrs. Jeffries was left alone once again. She hoped her theory was right, but there was only one way to prove it. And it all depended on the answers these two brought back.

She poured herself another cup of tea and sat back to wait for the others to get up. She'd know in a few hours if she was right or wrong.

Inspector Witherspoon woke with the beginnings of a headache. He hadn't slept well. The altercation with Inspector Nivens had disturbed him greatly. But he wasn't going to let his discomfort stop him from doing his duty. He washed, cleaned his teeth, dressed, and went downstairs. Mrs. Jeffries was waiting at the foot of the stairs. "Good morning, Mrs. Jeffries."

"Good morning, sir. You're up early. It's only half past seven. I don't believe that Mrs. Goodge has your breakfast ready yet."

"That's all right," he shrugged. "I'll pop down to the kitchen for a spot of tea. As a matter of fact, I might as well have breakfast down there this morning. No point in everyone tromping up and down the stairs with my bacon and eggs."

"Are you sure, sir? You might be a bit more comfortable in the dining room." Drat, the others weren't back as yet. They could hardly give her a report with the inspector sitting there as big as life.

Witherspoon went past her, turned down the hall, and started for the back stairs.

"Excellent, sir," she trailed behind him. "While you're there, we can discuss the dinner party."

Witherspoon skidded to a halt. "Dinner party? Oh dear, I'm afraid I've not given that much thought lately. The case, you see. Uh . . . perhaps I will eat in the dining room. Yes, I believe I will. If you could ask Betsy to bring me a pot of tea, I'll read the paper while Mrs. Goodge cooks my breakfast. No point in upsetting the household routine, is there?"

"The tea will be right up, sir. Your paper's on the dining table."

Afraid she'd bring up the subject of that wretched dinner party, he flew down the hall to the dining room and disappeared inside.

Mrs. Jeffries went down to the kitchen. "The inspector is up early."

Mrs. Goodge, who was sitting at the table drinking her tea, rose to her feet and headed for the cooker. "The others aren't back yet. But at least you got Wiggins out to give that parcel to Barnes."

"The inspector wants a pot of tea while he's waiting for breakfast. I'll make it." She fixed the tea and took it upstairs. As she was coming back to the kitchen, she met Betsy coming down the hall.

The girl's cheeks were flushed and she was breathless. "I had the hansom put me out around the other side of the garden," she explained. "I didn't want the inspector seeing me getting out of a cab this time of the morning."

"Were you successful?" Mrs. Jeffries asked as they went into the room. She put the tray on the table.

"Very," Betsy unfastened her cloak. "Westover's shirt was white as snow when he left the office that day."

"You didn't have any trouble gettin' the information?" Mrs. Goodge pressed.

"Not at all." She glanced around the kitchen, saw that Smythe was still out and said. "All it took was a bit of flirting. Honestly, men are such sillies sometimes. I didn't even have to come up with a convincing . . . " she broke off as she heard the back door open.

Smythe came into the room and smiled when he saw she was safely home. "Good, you're back." He unbuttoned his coat. "Cor blimey, it's cold out there. The locks are original, Mrs. Jeffries. Doesn't look like they've been changed since they were put in place."

"Thank you, Smythe. Sit down and have a bite of breakfast now. You too, Betsy." Mrs. Jeffries frowned thoughtfully. She picked up the empty tray off the table and laid it on the counter next to the cooker.

"Well, are you goin' to tell us who the killer is?" Mrs. Goodge demanded. She cracked an egg on the side of the skillet and dropped it into the hot grease.

Mrs. Jeffries barely heard the cook, she was too busy thinking. "Uh . . . yes, yes, that's the way it must have happened. It's the only thing that makes sense." She turned sharply and said to Smythe. "Get up. You need to get to Constable Barnes before he gets here. Bring him to the back door, I've got to talk to him before he sees the inspector."

Smythe, who'd been in the process of pouring himself a cup of tea, leapt up and charged for the back door. "I'll try and 'ead 'im off at the corner."

"Look for Wiggins," Mrs. Jeffries called. "I sent him out with the parcel of clothes, and hurry, please. I've got to speak with Barnes."

"What do you want Barnes to do?" Mrs. Goodge asked as she lifted the fried eggs onto a hot plate.

"Stop our killer from getting away."

Inspector Witherspoon frowned at the contents of the parcel spread on the dining room table. He shook his head in dismay. "Thank goodness you had the presence of mind to retrieve these things, Constable. It's evidence."

"Look at this ink stain, sir," Barnes said. "Seems to me that means that Westover must have written something after he got home from the board meeting."

"Why afterwards?" Witherspoon asked. "Why not before he left the office?"

Barnes was ready for this question. "I think someone would have mentioned it," he said. "He was a very fastidious gentleman, and we did keep asking the staff if there was anything odd about him that day. Someone would have noticed a huge stain like that on his shirt, and they'd have mentioned it to us. You know how people are, sir. They'll tell you all the details if you ask enough." It was weak, but it was the best they'd been able to come up with on short notice. "So I think we'd best get over to the Lynch house and have us a quick search. The man wrote something when he got home that day, and it was probably something to do with the meeting. Something that might point directly to his killer."

Mrs. Jeffries, who was standing in the hall eavesdropping, sincerely hoped they were on the right track, so to speak. It had just gone half past eight, if she was correct, they had a very short window of time to find their evidence and make the arrest.

"Let's get over to the Lynch house, then," Witherspoon said. "I'll just tidy this parcel up."

"Let's leave it, sir," Barnes said quickly. "I'm sure Mrs. Jeffries or someone else on your staff will do it up nicely and send it along to the station."

"Of course we will," Mrs. Jeffries dashed into the room. "Sorry, I couldn't help but overhear your conversation. We'll take care of this, I'm sure you've much to do today." She and the constable exchanged meaningful looks.

"Thank you, Mrs. Jeffries, we are quite busy." He edged toward the door. "Aren't we, sir?"

"Yes, I suppose we are." Witherspoon smiled gratefully at Mrs. Jeffries and trailed out behind the constable.

Barnes kept up a steady stream of conversation about the case as they took a hansom the short distance to Brook Green. He wanted to make sure he planted a number of suggestions in his inspector's ear.

Mrs. Lynch wasn't surprised to see them. "Are you making any progress, then?" she asked as soon as they stepped inside. She led them up the stairs.

"We should be making an arrest shortly," Barnes said quickly. Witherspoon shot his constable a puzzled frown but said nothing.

"Good, whoever murdered poor Mr. Westover deserves to be hanged." She opened Westover's door. "No one's been in here except your lot. But it's a good thing you came along today. His solictor is sending someone in tomorrow to get all of Mr. Westover's belongings." She stood to one side to let them pass. "I'll let you get to it, then. Close the door behind you when you're done."

Witherspoon crossed the room and stood next to the desk. "I suppose if he wrote something, he'd have done it here."

"Stands to reason, sir," Barnes replied as he walked over to the small bookcase by the fireplace. "I'll have a look in these bookcases, sir."

For the next few moments the room was quiet, save for the opening and closing of drawers and the rustling of papers. Witherspoon said, "There's nothing here on the desk." He picked the huge dictionary and flipped open the cover. "Wait a minute . . . what's this?"

"What is it, sir?" Barnes asked.

Witherspoon dropped the book back onto the desk with a loud thud. He held the paper where he could read it. "Good gracious, it appears to be an account of the board meeting." He paused and finished reading the document.

"What does he say, sir?"

Witherspoon handed the paper to Barnes. "Have a look for yourself. Harlan Westover told the board of directors that his engine wasn't safe. That the struts Horrocks had ordered were too cheap and they wouldn't hold. He demanded the board cable the company in South Africa that had bought the engine and tell them to replace the struts."

"That doesn't seem unreasonable," Barnes replied, as he started to scan the pages. He'd been hoping for something a bit more dramatic than that.

"Apparently everyone agreed with him except for one person. Harry Donovan. Donovan claimed the firm's reputation couldn't stand anymore bad news. It would ruin them in the industry. As the major shareholder, Donovan refused to allow them to send the cable."

"It says here that Westover resigned and told Donovan he was going to send the cable himself." Barnes looked up at Witherspoon. "Perhaps we'd better go have a chat with Mr. Donovan."

Witherspoon nodded. "I think that's quite a good idea."

Barnes sighed in relief and surreptiously pulled out his pocketwatch and checked the time. It was a quarter to ten. He'd promised Mrs. Jeffries he'd do his best to get Witherspoon to the Donovan house before Mrs. Donovan left for Victoria Station. If they took a hansom and didn't run into any traffic jams, they ought to make it in time. "There's a cab stand on the other side of the green."

Witherspoon tucked the note in his coat pocket. "Good. I think Mr. Donovan has some explaining to do."

"Will you be making an arrest, sir?" Barnes asked as they stepped out into the hall. He closed the door.

"I'm not sure," Witherspoon replied. They started down the stairs. "It's evidence, but I don't know if it's enough evidence."

Barnes nodded. He knew that the note was enough evidence, but only if taken together with the scenario that Mrs. Jeffries had hinted at during their brief meeting this morning. "Why don't we see what Donovan has to say for himself," he suggested.

They got into a cab and drove toward Mayfair. The traffic wasn't awful, but they weren't making particularly good time. Barnes pulled his watch out for the second time just as they rounded the corner to Wywick Place. Ten fifteen. Good, if they were lucky, she hadn't left yet.

"Are we running late, Constable?" Witherspoon asked as the hansom pulled up in front of number seven. "Do we have an appointment I've forgotten? That's twice you've check the time."

"No sir," Barnes forced a laugh as he swung out of the cab. "I think the watch might be running a bit slow, that's all."

Witherspoon stepped down and reached into his pocket for some coins. All of a sudden the door of the Donovan house burst open and a maid came running out.

"Help, help," she screamed. "He's killing her. He's killing her."

Barnes caught the woman as she careened toward them. "Get a hold of yourself," he demanded. "What's wrong?"

More screams came from inside the house.

Witherspoon leapt towards the front door. Barnes shoved the maid to one side and charged after the inspector. They ran up the short walkway and into the foyer.

"Leave me alone, you bastard!" a woman's voice came from the drawing room.

Several servants were heading for the drawing room, but the inspector waved them back. "Let us handle this," he yelled. "Go to the corner and get the constable on patrol."

"Hold on, sir," Barnes called. "Wait for me."

"I'll kill you, you stupid bitch!" Harry Donovan's enraged voice filled the house. "You'll pay for this."

Witherspoon ran into the drawing room and skidded to a halt. Harry Donovan had his wife on the settee, his hands were wrapped around her throat. "You stupid cow, I'll kill you. You've been trying to ruin me since the day we married . . . "

Witherspoon and Barnes dived for Donovan. The inspector grabbed one of Donovan's arms. Barnes got hold of the other one. "Let go, Mr. Donovan," the inspector ordered. "You're going to kill her."

But the enraged man had enormous strength. "That's the whole idea," he ground out between clenched teeth.

"Uh . . . ooh . . . " Mrs. Donovan's guttural cries filled the air, her feet kicked helplessly as the three men wrestled with all their might. Barnes let go of Donovan's arm, made his hand into a fist and punched the man in the side as hard as he could.

Donovan gasped and lightened his grip on his wife's neck just enough so that Witherspoon could pry his fingers loose. Barnes grabbed his shoulders and pulled him off the thrashing woman, hurling him onto the floor. Panting for breath, he fell into a heap on the carpet.

Another police constable, followed by a wailing serving maid, came running into the room. "Hang on to him!" Barnes shouted, pointing at Donovan, who was struggling to get to his feet.

He turned his attention to the inspector, who was bent over Mrs. Donovan. "Is she all right, sir?"

Mrs. Donovan gasped for air, her breath was coming in small, hard pants. She pointed to her throat. "Tried to kill me . . . you saw . . . tried to kill me."

"Dear lady, don't try to speak," Witherspoon soothed. "We saw everything." He looked up at the servants standing in the doorway. The one who'd been screaming was mercifully quiet. "Can one of you please get Mrs. Donovan some water."

Witherspoon looked at Donovan. He was now standing between Barnes and the constable. "Mr. Donovan, what do you have to say for yourself? This is attempted murder."

"He killed Harlan Westover," Mrs. Donovan gasped the words out as she struggled to a sitting postion. "And he tried to kill me."

Donovan's face darkened in rage, he lunged for his wife. "You stupid cow, you've ruined me."

The constables grabbed him and pulled him back. "We'd better get him down to the station," Barnes said.

Witherspoon looked at the enraged man. "Harry Donovan, you're under arrest for the murder of Harlan Westover and the attempted murder of your wife."

Mrs. Jeffries was pacing back and forth in front of the kitchen table where Ruth, Mrs. Goodge, and Betsy were all drinking tea. Smythe and Wiggins were out. She'd sent them to keep watch on the Donovan house as soon as the inspector had left this morning.

"Why are you so nervous?" Betsy asked her.

"Because I'm not sure I was right about this one," she replied.

"We can't help you there," Mrs. Goodge sniffed. "You haven't told us much of anything."

Mrs. Jeffries looked at the cook and smiled apologetically. "I'm sorry, I'm not being deliberately mysterious. It's just that I'm not sure that there's enough evidence to be sure of myself, let alone for the inspector to make an arrest. And if my theory is incorrect, I don't want to poison the well, so to speak." She sighed. "If the inspector doesn't make an arrest, we may very well have to put on our thinking caps and approach this from a completely different point of view. I don't want to prejudice your thinking if I'm completely wrong in my assumptions."

Mrs. Goodge didn't look convinced.

"We've already had one false start," Mrs. Jeffries explained earnestly. "After Wiggins gave us Melcher's bloodstained shirt, I was thinking he was our killer. As a matter of fact, that was the one thing that didn't fit in with my current theory. But this morning Constable Barnes told me that after speaking to Melcher's clerk yesterday, he'd found out that Melcher had a bad nosebleed the day after the board meeting. The fellow bled all over himself. So you see how easy it is to be wrong."

"We understand," Ruth said cheerfully. "And if nothing happens today, I'm sure there's still plenty of evidence about for us to find. This killer won't get away with it, that's for certain."

Mrs. Jeffries wasn't so sure. She had a vague suspicion that throughout history, many murderers had gone unpunished, at least by human justice. She heard the back door open.

"They're back," Betsy leapt to her feet and ran towards the hallway just as the two men appeared. "What happened? Was there an arrest?"

"It were ever so excitin'," Wiggins said. "We did just what you said, Mrs. Jeffries, we stayed out of sight and kept a close eye on the place. Mind you, we didn't know what we ought to do when all the screamin' started. But just then the inspector and Constable Barnes pulled up in a hansom, and so we didn't 'ave to do anything."

"What on earth happened?" Mrs. Jeffries asked. She motioned for them to sit down and took her own seat at the head of the table.

"There's been an arrest," Smythe said calmly. "Just as you thought, Mrs. Jeffries, Mrs. Donovan's leaving brought things to a 'ead, so to speak."

"Who got arrested?" Mrs. Goodge demanded. "You can fill us in on all the details later, just tell us who?"

"Harry Donovan," Smythe replied. "He was arrested for Westover's murder and the attempted murder of his wife."

"Harry Donovan," Mrs. Jeffries exclaimed. "Are you certain?"

Everyone looked at her in surprise.

"Who did you think was going to be arrested?" Ruth asked curiously.

"Mrs. Donovan," she admitted. "I was sure she was our killer."

"Why would she have wanted to kill Harlan Westover?" Wiggins asked.

"Because she hated her husband and wanted to ruin him." Mrs. Jeffries shook her head. "I was certain she was the one who'd done it. I thought she found the key to the Lynch house amongst her husband's things."

"Why would he have a key?" Ruth interrupted.

"Because he used to own the house," Mrs. Goodge supplied. "And as he used to own the place, he might have accidentally hung on to the key.

It's just like Melba's neighbor lettin' her in to her house when she'd locked herself out."

"That's what gave me the idea," Mrs. Jeffries said.

"So that's why you sent Smythe over there to see if the locks had been changed."

"That's right, people don't realize that they have more than one key to a door when they're selling a house. I thought he'd probably tossed it aside and forgotten about it. We knew that Westover probably locked the door behind him when he came in that day; Mrs. Lynch had her lodgers well trained in that aspect. So I reasoned that whoever had done it, had had a key. That pointed to the Donovans, but I thought it was Mrs. Donovan, not Mr. Donovan."

"What about the stain on his shirt?" Betsy asked. "How would that point to her? She wasn't at the board meeting so anything he might have written wouldn't have pointed to her as the killer."

"True," Mrs. Jeffries said. "But I didn't necessarily think that his note, if indeed he actually wrote a note, would do anything more than give us an idea of what had really happened at the meeting. I never thought it would point to the killer." She shook her head in disgust. "I've been so wrong, so blind."

"I wouldn't say that, Mrs. Jeffries," Smythe said. "You got the inspector and Constable Barnes to the Donovan house in time to save that woman's life. If you hadn't she'd be dead by now. God knows her servants were fairly useless."

"You should of 'eard 'im," Wiggins added. "He were screamin' at the top of 'is lungs that he hated her and she was tryin' to ruin 'im."

"She was going to force him out of the building," Ruth said. "Remember, she'd made him put up the building as collateral for a loan. Obviously, he knew that even with Westover's wonderful engine, the firm wouldn't be able to survive."

"But I still don't see why he'd kill Westover," Mrs. Goodge sounded genuinely puzzled. "He could just as easily have sacked the man if he wanted to be rid of him."

"Probably because Westover was going to do something about that engine being unsafe," Mrs. Jeffries suggested. "We'll have to wait until the inspector gets back to find out all the details. But I must say, I'm very disappointed in myself." With that, she rose from the table and despite protests from the others, she went up to her room to have a good hard think about where she'd gone wrong.

The inspector came in later that afternoon, just as the household had gathered around the table for their tea. He popped his head into the kitchen. "Hello everyone, may I have tea with you?" His eyes widened in surprise as he saw Ruth Cannonberry with them. "Gracious, I didn't know we had company."

"Hello, Gerald," Ruth gave him a big smile and a wave. "Do come in, your staff very kindly invited me to have tea with them."

Blushing with pleasure, he made his way to the table. "We've made an arrest in our case."

"Of course you have, sir. We knew you would." Mrs. Jeffries smiled cheerfully and poured another cup. "Do sit down and tell us all about it."

He pulled out the chair next to Ruth, gave her another quick smile, and sat down. "Thank you, Mrs. Jeffries," he said as he accepted the steaming cup. "It's difficult to know where to begin."

"Who'd you arrest, sir?" Wiggins asked helpfully, even though he already knew the answer.

"Harry Donovan," Witherspoon replied. "It was most extraordinary. We only went over there because I wanted to ask him a few questions, but when we got there, he was in the process of trying to murder Mrs. Donovan. He doesn't much care for her. Apparently she's loaned the firm a great deal of money and he'd used his office building as collateral."

Mrs. Jeffries was desperate to know where she'd gone wrong. She knew precisely what questions she wanted answered. "Why did Harry Donovan want to kill poor Mr. Westover?"

"Westover had resigned from the firm, he was going to send a cable to the company in South Africa and tell them the engine that was being sent to them wasn't safe."

"That's not a very good reason for murderin' someone," Wiggins said.

"It was reason enough for Harry Donovan," Witherspoon's eyebrows drew together. "He's a bit mad, I think. Apparently, the firm has been in financial straits for years. They don't have a very good reputation. He felt that they couldn't stand any bad news about the company so he murdered Westover to keep him from sending off that cable."

"How did he get into the 'ouse?" Smythe asked. "Did Westover let him in?"

"He had a key," Witherspoon replied. "Apparently, he used to own the Lynch house. He set it up to look like suicide but then made a grave mistake when he left. He dropped the key on his way out. I expect he was in a bit in a panic." Witherspoon went on to give them all the rest of the details about the arrest. They listened carefully, occasionally asking a question or making an admiring comment.

Finally, he said, "Thank goodness Constable Barnes suggested we search Westover's rooms again. If we hadn't we'd not have gone to Donovan's house when we did and poor Mrs. Donovan would be as dead as Harlan Westover."

"You're so very clever, Gerald," Ruth patted him on the arm. "You've caught ever so many killers. I think you ought to be promoted."

Witherspoon blushed like a schoolboy. "I'm not so clever. I couldn't solve any cases without a great deal of help. We owe the solving of this one more to Constable Barnes than to me. He had one good suggestion after another."

"Nevertheless," Mrs. Jeffries added. "Lady Cannonberry is right. With your record of solving homicides, you ought to be a chief inspector by now."

His cheeks turned even redder. "Please, no. You give me too much credit. I like being an inspector. I'd be a terrible chief."

"Nonsense, Gerald, you'd be perfect," Ruth insisted. "Of course, you would have to do a bit more socially . . . "

"Like a dinner party," Mrs. Jeffries interrupted. "You see, Inspector, even Lady Cannonberry agrees a dinner party is in order."

Witherspoon knew when he was beaten. "All right, then. But only if Lady Cannonberry will act as my hostess."

"I'd be honored, Gerald." She smiled graciously and started to rise. "This has been lovely, but I do need to get home now."

"Allow me to escort you across the garden," Witherspoon leapt to his feet.

"That would be wonderful, we can talk about the dinner party. I've all sorts of wonderful ideas about it."

As soon as they were out the back door, everyone turned their attention to Mrs. Jeffries. "From what he said, you were right in your thinkin'." Mrs. Goodge said reassuringly. "You just got the wrong spouse is all."

Mrs. Jeffries sighed. "Do you really think so?"

"Course we do," Smythe said firmly. "You sussed out that Donovan was the only one of all the partners who'd be ruined financially if the firm went under."

"Yes, but I thought that meant that Mrs. Donovan killed Westover to make sure the firm went under. Without Westover, the company didn't stand a chance to survive in the long run."

"And you were right about Donovan havin' a key," Wiggins added.

"True, but I was sure Mrs. Donovan was the one who'd used it." Mrs. Jeffries forced herself to smile. "I know you're all trying to make me feel better. But I made a terrible mistake, and that's that."

"Maybe it was a mistake you were meant to make," Betsy said softly. "It saved a woman's life. *You* saved a woman's life."

Mrs. Jeffries stared at her for a moment and then smiled. "You're right. Perhaps I was meant to make it."

After dinner that evening, Betsy sat down at the table and waited for Smythe. He'd gone to the stables to check on Bow and Arrow, the inspector's horses. The kitchen was empty, and the rest of the household had retired for the evening.

She didn't have to wait long before she heard the back door open and Smythe's heavy tread coming up the hallway. She straightened her spine, bracing herself for a confrontation. She didn't think he'd like what she was going to tell him.

He grinned broadly as he came into the kitchen and saw her waiting for him. "You shouldn't have waited up for me. But I'm glad you did. I want to talk to you."

"And I want to speak with you as well."

He dropped into the empty seat next to her. "The case is over, love."

"And I promised we'd set a wedding date when it was finished," she reminded him. She swallowed heavily. "And I always keep my promises."

"I know," he said. He watched her carefully. "How do you feel about bein' a June bride?"

"I was thinking more like October," she held her breath, hoping he wouldn't get upset and think she didn't love him. "I've always fancied getting married in the autumn."

"October," he repeated. "All right. Are you sure, though?"

"Quite sure," she slumped in relief. "That's ten months from now. That'll give us plenty of time to plan a wedding. Much better than June, that's too soon."

Smythe gave her a puzzled look. "Too soon. I wasn't thinkin' of June this year, I was thinkin' next year."

"Next year? But that's almost eighteen months from now!" Betsy couldn't believe it. "Don't you want to marry me?"

"Of course I do, lass," he laughed. "I was tryin' to do what you wanted and give us time. But if you're set on October . . . " he broke off as she poked him in the arm.

"You silly man," she leaned over and gave him a quick kiss on the lips. "You knew exactly what you're about. June it is, then. Next June."

MRS. JEFFRIES SWEEPS THE CHIMNEY

CHAPTER 1

The Reverend Jasper Claypool ran for his life. His legs ached, his lungs were on fire and his breathing was so loud he could no longer hear if there were footsteps pounding behind him. A thick fog had rolled in off the Thames, blanketing the area, and he could barely see three feet in front of him, but perhaps that was all to the good. Perhaps his pursuer couldn't see where he went. It didn't help that he had no idea where he was or in what direction lay help. Generally, though, he'd always thought the London docks fairly teemed with humanity; it had certainly looked that way when he had arrived that morning. But now that he needed someone, anyone, to help him, the place was utterly deserted.

Claypool skidded around the corner, almost lost his footing and then righted himself before his knees hit the cobblestones. In the distance, he could hear the tolling of a church bell for evensong. The Reverend Claypool was a genuinely religious man; he knew the ringing of the bells was a sign from God. "Thank you, Lord," he gasped as he turned in what he hoped was the direction of the church. He hurried across the empty street and paused for a moment to get his bearings. But then he heard the thud of footsteps hot on his heels. The bells kept ringing, so he charged toward them, hoping that he had the strength to make it to safety. But he was seventy-five years old, and he knew he couldn't go much farther. There was a funny rushing sound in his ears, and his vision was starting to blur. "Please, Lord, show me the way," he prayed silently. God must have heard his plea, for just then the fog parted and the church came in sight. "Thank you, Lord." With renewed determination, he raced toward the dimly lighted building. He ran under the wooden eaves and grasped at the handle, but before he could

yank the door open, a hand grabbed his arm and pulled him around. With
ruthless efficiency, his assailant clutched Claypool and half-drug, half-
carried him around to the side of the building.

Jasper flailed his arms at his attacker, but to no avail. He was clasped
around the neck and pulled, against his will, away from the certain safety
of the church. He tried to scream, but he was so short of breath, he
couldn't do more than whimper. When they turned the corner of the
building, he was slammed up against the wall. He gasped in shock and
opened his mouth in surprised horror. But just as the last peal of the bell
sounded, his pursuer fired a small pistol directly into his forehead.
Whether he wanted to or not, the Reverend Jasper Claypool had gone to
meet his maker.

"I don't think I like this," Wiggins muttered. He frowned at the letter in
his hand and then shook his head.

"What's wrong?" Mrs. Jeffries, the housekeeper to Inspector Gerald
Witherspoon, asked. She was a plump woman of late middle age with a
ready smile and a kind disposition. Her hair was dark auburn sprinkled
with gray, her eyes were a deep brown color and her pale skin was dusted
with faint freckles across her nose. She glanced at the footman as she
reached for the teapot. It was rare for the lad to get a letter, rarer still for
him to look so upset by the contents of said letter.

The household of Inspector Gerald Witherspoon was gathered at the
kitchen table for afternoon tea. The last post had arrived, and with it, the
footman's letter.

By this time, the others at the table had realized that something was
wrong. Wiggins, who was naturally a good-natured chatterbox, had gone
very quiet.

"Has the letter upset you, lad?" Smythe, the coachman, asked. Smythe
was a big, brutal-looking man with black hair, harsh features and the
kindest brown eyes in the world. He'd come to work for Inspector Witherspoon's late aunt, Euphemia Witherspoon, years earlier. When she'd died
and left her nephew a house and a fortune, he'd stayed on to keep an eye
out for the inspector. Then he'd stayed on for other, more personal reasons. He took a sip of his tea and watched the boy over the rim of his mug.

"It's not upset me," Wiggins said quickly, as he swiped a lock of
unruly brown hair off his forehead. He was a good-looking young man

in his early twenties, with rounded cheeks, bright blue eyes and a ready smile, but he wasn't smiling now. "It's just a bit of a bother, that's all."

But everyone knew he wasn't being honest. They'd been together too long to be fooled by the lad's attempt at indifference. Mrs. Goodge, the cook, glanced at Mrs. Jeffries. She wasn't sure who should take the lead here. But the housekeeper, aware that the cook and the footman had become quite close over the last year, nodded her head slightly, indicating the cook should do as she thought best.

"Look, Wiggins," Mrs. Goodge said bluntly, "we can all see something's got you in a bit of a state." The cook was an elderly, portly woman with gray hair neatly tucked under a cook's cap, and spectacles that persisted in sliding down her nose. She had worked at some of the finest houses in all of England and had once thought she'd come down in the world by having to accept a position as the cook to a police inspector. But now she wouldn't leave the Witherspoon household even if she were offered the position as head cook at Buckingham Palace. For the first time in her long life, she felt she had a family and, more importantly, a real purpose in her life. "There's no shame in being upset if you've had a bit of bad news."

Wiggins looked down at the table. "It's from my father's people. My grandfather is dyin' and 'e wants to meet me before he goes. He lives in a little village outside Colchester."

No one knew what to say. Though the footman didn't often speak of his early life, everyone knew that the lad's mother had died when he was a boy. Her relatives had taken him in until he was old enough to go into service. None of them had ever heard Wiggins speak of his father or his father's family.

Betsy, the pretty blond maid, finally broke the silence. "Perhaps you ought to go," she suggested. She didn't want to interfere, but she knew how much it would have meant to her to get a letter from a relative. Unfortunately, most of hers were dead. Now the people sitting around the table were her family. She glanced at Smythe, her fiancé, and saw him nod in agreement.

"Why?" Wiggins muttered. "They didn't want to know me or me mam when I was little. They hated her for marryin' my father. I know that because I used to 'ear my Aunt Nancy and Uncle Severn squabblin' about 'avin' to feed me when I 'ad other relations with money. Aunt Nancy was my mother's sister; she took me in when Mam died. They could barely feed themselves, let alone have to feed me too. My father's people didn't want to know me. So why should I go see this old man now?"

"Maybe he's sorry," Betsy said softly. "Sometimes people do things in their life that they regret. Maybe he wants to make it up to you."

"I don't want 'im to make anythin' up to me." Wiggins shoved back from the table and leapt to his feet. The abrupt action spurred Fred, their black-and-brown mongrel dog, to leap up from his spot near the stove. As if sensing the boy's distress, he trotted over and butted his head against the lad's knee. Wiggins absently reached down to pet him. "I just want 'im to leave me be."

"Are you sure?" Mrs. Jeffries asked calmly. "Aren't you in the least bit curious about your grandfather?"

"Why should I be?" He pursed his lips and shook his head. "They've not been curious about me all these years." A sheen of tears welled up in his eyes. "When my father died, he wouldn't even let my mother bury him. I was just little, but I remember it. He come and took the body and wouldn't let her go to the funeral. I hate him for what he did, and I don't need 'im now. I've got me a real family. I've got you lot." He blinked rapidly and looked down at Fred, averting his face while he got his feelings under control.

"Of course you do, lad," Smythe said softly. "And you know we'd do anything for you. But you might want to at least think about meetin' the old man. Not for his sake, but for yours. It's not like you to 'ave so much anger in ya."

Wiggins looked up. "I'm not angry, I just want 'im to leave me alone. I can't be runnin' off to Colchester at the drop of a 'at. I've got me duties 'ere to consider."

Mrs. Jeffries wasn't sure what to say. As Inspector Witherspoon had no more need of a footman than he did a hole in his head, the lad was exaggerating. Though in all fairness, Wiggins did his part in keeping the household running. "I'm sure the inspector will be quite willing to do without your services for a few days. The rest of us can take over your responsibilities."

"I'm not just talkin' about my household chores," Wiggins protested. "I'm talkin' about the other. You know what 'appens every time someone goes off. We get us a murder. Luty and Hatchet still 'aven't got over missin' the last one, and I don't want that to 'appen to me."

"But we might not have one," Betsy interjected. "It's been very quiet lately."

"That's what Luty and Hatchet thought before they went off for America," Wiggins said. Luty Belle Crookshank and her butler, Hatchet, were good friends of the household of Upper Edmonton Gardens. Inspector Gerald Witherspoon was quite a fortunate man. He was not only rich, but he'd made a real name for himself as the best homicide investigator in the country. He'd solved every murder that he'd been given. What he didn't know was that it was his staff, along with their good friends, who supplied him with the clues he needed to crack the case. "The minute they was gone, we had that murder and they missed it all."

"But they were gone for a long time," Betsy argued. "They went all the way to New York. You'd just be going to Colchester."

"You could always come back if we had us one," Smythe pointed out.

"There are telegrams," Mrs. Jeffries assured him. "All you'd have to do is make sure we had your grandfather's address and we'd send for you immediately."

"But I don't want to meet 'im," Wiggins cried. " 'E was horrible to my mother. She went to him when my father died, and the old man tossed her off his farm."

"And maybe he bitterly regrets that action," Mrs. Goodge snapped. She glared at the footman. "Now you listen to me, young man, I'm an old woman. . . ." She broke off and raised her hand for silence as the others began to protest.

"You're all trying to be nice, but the truth is, I am old and there's no getting around that. But what I'm trying to get the lad to understand is this; there are things I did in my life that I regret. Not many, but some. If I could have a chance to make up for some of the unkind things I did or said before I go to my final restin' place, I'd do it."

"You think I ought to go?" Wiggins's shoulders slumped. He didn't look happy.

"I think you ought to give the old man a chance," she replied. "It's only a few hours' train ride to Colchester. It's not the ends of the earth."

"What if he says bad things about my mother?" Wiggins dropped his gaze again and leaned down to pet Fred. "What then, Mrs. Goodge? I'd not like to be rude, but I couldn't stand for anyone to speak ill of me mam."

"If he says one unkind word about her, then you tell the old fool that he's a scoundrel's arse and not worth a decent fellow's bother. Then you nip right back home," the cook replied.

Wiggins lifted his head and broke into a grin. "Cor blimey, Mrs.

Goodge, I didn't think you even knew words like that. All right, then, if the inspector gives me permission, I'll go."

"Thank you, Mrs. Jeffries." Inspector Gerald Witherspoon took the glass of sherry from his housekeeper. He was a slender man in his mid forties. He had thinning dark hair, a rather long, bony face, deep-set gray eyes and a mustache. He was a bit short-sighted, so he generally tried to remember to wear his spectacles. He had them on now. "Do pour one for yourself," he told her.

"I have, sir," she replied. She took the chair opposite his. They were in the drawing room of Upper Edmonton Gardens. "Are you sure you've no objection to Wiggins going off for a few days?" She'd already told him about the lad's grandfather.

"Of course not," he said. "He's right to go and see his father's people."

"We had to talk him into it," she said bluntly. "If left to his own devices, I believe he'd have ignored the letter completely."

"I'm glad he didn't," Witherspoon replied. "Er, do you happen to know why he's had so little contact with his family?"

"From what I gather," she said, eyeing the oriental carpet on the floor, "his father's family wasn't all too happy when Wiggins's parents married. They've a small farm outside Colchester. The village is called Langham. I believe his mother's people were very poor. When his father died, they were quite awful to his mother, and they didn't want anything to do with him." She made a mental note to have the carpet cleaned. It was looking a bit tatty.

"Let's hope it all goes well for the boy."

"He's taking the eight o'clock from Liverpool Street Station," she said. She noticed the curtains were looking a bit dingy too.

"Tell him to stay as long as he likes, we can always manage. Uh, does he need any money for train fare?"

"No, sir, he's fine. He's quite a saver is our Wiggins. He did ask me to ask you to keep a sharp eye on Fred. He'll be a bit lonely without the boy."

"Fred and I are great friends," Witherspoon smiled broadly. He loved the dog almost as much as the footman did. "We'll do just fine."

"Thank you, sir," she said. "Is anything interesting going on at the station, sir?" She and the inspector frequently talked about his work. As the widow of a Yorkshire police officer, she would naturally be interested in crime. More importantly, as the leader of their investigations on the inspector's behalf, she needed to know what was happening at any given moment.

"Not really," he sighed. "Just the usual; a few burglaries, an attempted suicide and some pickpockets. It's been very quiet. I hope it remains that way."

"Yes, sir." Mrs. Jeffries hid her disappointment. "I do believe we'd best get this rug cleaned, sir. Especially now that it's spring." She glanced about the large room. "Those curtains could do with a clean too. As a matter of fact, this floor of the house could use some new paint and wallpaper."

Witherspoon gulped his sherry. The room looked fine to him, but then again, he'd no idea how to care for a large home. He'd been raised in far more modest circumstances. "If you think it's necessary."

"We've nothing else pressing." She got to her feet. "And the house hasn't had a good sprucing up for a long time. Tomorrow I'll see about getting the cleaners in, and we'll give the whole house a nice tidy up. Then I'll call the decorators."

But the next morning Mrs. Jeffries didn't even think about calling in cleaners or painters. A few minutes after they'd put Wiggins in a hansom for Liverpool Street Station, Constable Barnes knocked on their front door.

"Good morning, Mrs. Jeffries." He smiled politely as he stepped into the foyer. "Sorry to pop in so early, but I must see the inspector." The constable was a tall, craggy-faced man with a headful of iron-gray curly hair under his policeman's helmet. He'd worked with the inspector for a long time and knew the household very well.

"Of course, Constable," Mrs. Jeffries replied. She was delighted to see him. When Constable Barnes arrived this early in the morning, it generally meant one thing: they had a murder. "Come into the dining room, Constable. The inspector is having his breakfast." Mrs. Jeffries ushered him down the hall and into the room. "Inspector," she said as they went inside. "Constable Barnes has come to see you."

"Good morning, sir," Barnes bobbed his head politely.

"Good morning, Constable." Witherspoon half rose and gestured toward the empty chair next to him. "Do sit down. Have you eaten?"

"I have, sir," Barnes replied as he took his seat. "But I wouldn't say 'no' to a cup of tea."

"Of course, Constable." Mrs. Jeffries was already on her way to the mahogany sideboard where extra cups and plates were kept. She took her time opening the cupboard door so that she could hear what the constable had to say.

"There's been a murder, sir," Barnes began, "and the chief inspector wants you to take it."

"Oh, dear." Witherspoon shoved another bite of bacon into his mouth. "Do we have an identification? Do we know who the victim is?" He'd always found that was a good place to start.

"Not really," Barnes replied.

Mrs. Jeffries took down a cup and saucer and closed the cupboard. Moving as slowly as she dared, she went to the table and reached for the teapot. She could only dawdle over this task for so long before it would become obvious she was trying to eavesdrop. If she had to, she could always listen out in the hall. She'd done that on more than one occasion.

"It's a bit of a strange one, sir," Barnes continued. He nodded his thanks to the housekeeper as she handed him his tea. "The victim was found propped up against the side of the St. Paul's Church over on Dock Street. It's just up from the London Docks. Luckily, the lads that did the findin' had the good sense not to move the body."

"You mean it's still there?" Witherspoon asked.

"Yes, sir. Chief Inspector Barrows wanted you to have a look at the scene with the body intact." Barnes broke into a grin. "Looks like your methods are starting to have an impact, sir."

"Er, yes. Well, like I always say, one can learn a lot about the murder if one has a chance to see the body before it's moved." Witherspoon wasn't sure when he'd come up with this idea. He thought it might have been right from the very beginning of his career in homicide. He quickly shoveled the remainder of his breakfast into his mouth. "Gracious, we'd better hurry then. Corpses do tend to draw a crowd, and that won't help the investigation any."

"Not to worry, sir, the body is on the side of the chapel, and there's not much foot traffic in that area. The lads should be able to keep everyone back. We've a few minutes. I've arranged for the district police surgeon to meet us there."

As soon as the inspector and Barnes had gone, Mrs. Jeffries flew down to the kitchen. Betsy was at the sink doing the breakfast dishes, and Smythe was sitting at the table with an old newspaper spread out in front of him, oiling the horse's harness. Mrs. Goodge was at the other end of the long table rolling out pie crust.

"We've got us a murder," Mrs. Jeffries blurted out. "And we've no time to lose."

"Oh no," Betsy wailed. "Wiggins will have a right fit. He was afraid this was going to happen. He'll have to turn around and come right back as soon as he gets there." She put the plate on the drying rack and wiped her hands on a dishtowel.

"Who died?" the cook asked. "Anyone important?" Mrs. Goodge did all of her investigating from the kitchen. She had a veritable army of informants that trooped through her domain on a daily basis: delivery boys, rag and bone sellers, fruit vendors, chimney sweeps, laundry maids and even the communal-garden caretakers. She plied them all with tea and pastries while squeezing every morsel of gossip about victims and suspects out of them. Naturally, the higher the victim was on London's social scale, the easier it was for her to get the information. In addition to the people who came through her kitchen, she also had a vast network of people from her former days of cooking in both London and the countryside.

"We don't know yet," Mrs. Jeffries replied. She told them what she'd heard from Constable Barnes. "He and the inspector have just left." She looked at Smythe.

He'd already put the cap on the oil and was now wrapping the harness in the paper. He pushed it to one side and got to his feet. "Should I go get Luty and Hatchet?"

Mrs. Jeffries hesitated. "Not yet. We don't even have a name. But it would be useful for you to nip over to St. Paul's Church and see what you can find out. If we're really lucky, we can get a nice start on this case."

"I'll go along then." He picked up the folded parcel and scooped up the can of oil. "I'll try and get back with some information by teatime."

"We'll have Luty and Hatchet here by then," Mrs. Jeffries replied. "Maybe even Wiggins if we can get a telegram to him and he can get a train right back."

"I don't think we ought to do that," Mrs. Goodge said softly. She looked at the housekeeper. "I don't want to be oversteppin' my bounds here, but I think it will be good for the boy to get to know his father's people. I'd not realized how much bitterness he's got locked up inside him. That's not right. Wiggins is naturally a good lad; he shouldn't walk around with that kind of poison in his system."

"But we promised him," Mrs. Jeffries reminded her.

"I know," the cook replied. "And we'll keep our promise, but as you said, we've not even got a name for our victim. I think we can wait a day or two before we send for him."

"I agree," Smythe said quietly. "Wiggins should have a day or so with his people. They might have mistreated 'is mother, and now they might want to make it up to the lad. Everyone deserves a second chance." He knew all about second chances. He felt he'd been given one in life with Betsy.

Mrs. Jeffries looked doubtful. "All right, if you both think so. But we must send him a telegram by tomorrow. I agree with all you've said, but we did make a promise."

"We'll keep it," Mrs. Goodge said brusquely. "Now, I'd best see what we've got in the dry larder. We're almost out of flour and sugar. I'll do up a list, Mrs. Jeffries, and I'd be obliged if you could get it to the grocers right away. They can deliver by late this morning, and that'll give me time to get some baking done this afternoon. I've got to have things baked to feed my sources."

"I'll take it right away, Mrs. Goodge." She turned to Betsy. "Can you get over to Luty's and tell her and Hatchet to be here this afternoon for tea? If we're very lucky, we may actually know something useful by then."

Betsy was already taking off her apron and heading for the coat tree. "Of course. Thank goodness they're in town. Luty would have a stroke if they missed another case."

"Luty," Smythe exclaimed. He waited by the entrance to the hall for Betsy so they could walk out together. "Hatchet's worse. He was so upset about missin' that last case I 'eard 'im tellin' Luty he wasn't ever goin' to leave London again."

Despite the best efforts of the police, a small crowd had gathered in front of St. Paul's Church. The constables had managed to keep everyone away from the corpse, but they looked extremely relieved when Witherspoon and Barnes arrived. "He's over here, sir." One of the constables pointed to the side of the building.

Witherspoon started in that direction just as a hansom pulled up and a man carrying a doctor's bag got out. "It's the police surgeon, sir," Barnes said. He broke into a grin. "Gracious, sir, it's Dr. Bosworth."

Witherspoon stopped and waited for the doctor to catch up with them. "Dr. Bosworth, I didn't know you were the police surgeon for this district."

Bosworth grinned and extended his hand. "I was just appointed, Inspector." He shook hands with Witherspoon and then shook with Barnes. "Dr. Niels retired and I applied for the post. Have you had a chance to examine the victim, gentlemen?"

"Not yet," Witherspoon replied. They moved to the side of the building, and he cast a quick glance at the dead man. Witherspoon was very squeamish about corpses. But he knew his duty, so he steeled himself and moved closer to get a good look.

The body was propped up against the back wall with the legs sticking straight out like the poor fellow was just having a rest. His arms hung at his sides, and the hands were both balled into fists. He was dressed in a heavy black coat, which was unbuttoned, black wool trousers, a black vest, a white shirt and a clerical collar. His eyes were open and staring straight ahead. There was a neat, blood-encrusted hole in the center of his forehead.

"I don't suppose he's the vicar of this church?" Barnes knelt down next to the victim. He glanced up at the two police constables standing guard.

"No, sir, he's not. We checked that right away," one of the constables replied.

"Who found the body?"

"I did, sir," the second constable offered. He was a young man with pale blue eyes and a thin face. "I spotted it this morning when I was making my rounds."

"What made you look at the side?" Witherspoon asked.

"Sometimes vagrants sleep there, sir," the constable replied.

"Have you searched his pockets?" Barnes asked.

"Yes, sir, they're empty. We think he might have been robbed." He jerked his chin toward the church. "We've sent PC Boyles to get the vicar. We're hoping he may know who the poor man is."

"Good thinking." Witherspoon swallowed heavily and then knelt down on the other side of the body. "If this man is a clergyman, he might have been coming to visit the vicar." That sounded logical. "Dr. Bosworth, could you come have a look, please. I'd like to get some idea of the time of death."

Bosworth knelt down in front of the dead man, put his bag to one side and then touched the man's face. "He's quite cold, I should say he's been dead at least twelve hours. Perhaps even more." He touched the hand and pried at the fingers. "Rigor has set in."

"You think he was killed last night?" Witherspoon asked.

"It's hard to say exactly." Bosworth pried at the fingers of the other hand, and this time a slip of paper fell out and landed on the grass. "I was just trying to see how stiff the poor fellow was!"

Barnes grabbed the paper and handed it to the inspector. Just then, they heard footsteps and low muttered voices coming toward them. It was a police constable, and with him a short, very fat clergyman.

"Good day, sir." The police constable stopped a few feet from them and nodded respectfully. "I've brought Reverend Sanderson, sir. He's the vicar of St. Paul's."

Witherspoon and Barnes got to their feet. Bosworth continued examining the body. "Good day, sir," the inspector said. "We're hoping you can help us."

"I'll do my best, sir," the vicar replied. He spoke to the inspector, but his eyes were on the corpse propped against his church. "But I don't think I'm going to be of any use to you at all. I've no idea who this poor fellow might be." He shook his head sympathetically. "May God rest his soul."

"Are you sure?" Barnes pressed. "Would you like a closer look? Try imagining him without the hole in his forehead."

The vicar leapt backward and shook his head vehemently. "I've never seen him before, sir. I know a number of clergymen, sir, but I've never seen him before in my life."

"So you've no idea why he was near your church?" Witherspoon persisted.

"None whatsoever." Reverend Sanderson took a deep breath and then knelt down by the dead man. "If he was coming to my church, he was coming as a stranger. But even a stranger deserves a prayer." Without interrupting Bosworth, he quietly and fervently said a prayer over the dead man, and then he rose to his feet. "I'll do anything I can to help find this poor man's killer," he said. "But unfortunately, I've no idea why he was killed here."

They questioned the vicar until it became obvious he'd seen nothing, heard nothing and knew nothing. "I'm terribly sorry, Inspector," he finally said. "But I simply have no idea about who this man is or why anyone would want to kill him. Now if you'll excuse me, I must contact the bishop immediately. Perhaps he can be of some use in this situation."

"Bishop?" Witherspoon repeated. "Oh yes, of course. He's wearing a collar." He turned toward Constable Boyles and said, "Go along with the reverend and see if the bishop has any ideas about who this fellow might be."

The reverend didn't look pleased by this request, but he didn't object either. He was muttering to himself as the two of them went back toward the front of the church building.

The police ambulance pulled around the corner and halted in front of the church. It made an enormous racket as it trundled across the cobblestones. Dr. Bosworth stood up and waved the attendants over. "I can't tell any more until I get him back to the morgue and do the postmortem," he told the inspector. "I should have a report for you by tomorrow morning. I'll send it around to the station."

"Thank you, Doctor," Witherspoon said. "We'd appreciate that."

They loaded the body onto the stretcher and into the van. Dr. Bosworth waited till the doors closed and then turned to Witherspoon. "If you don't mind my asking, what's on that slip of paper?"

Witherspoon had almost forgotten about it. He opened it up and read. "It appears to be an address . . . yes, it is. It says Seven Dorland Place, Bermondsey."

On the other side of the road, Smythe dodged behind a tree as the van emerged and pulled out into the traffic. He'd been keeping the large van between himself and the inspector since it had pulled up in front of the church. Now that it was gone, so was his hiding spot. Not that he'd been close enough to hear anything useful, but he'd seen the body. Apparently, someone didn't much like vicars. He stuck his head around the trunk for a quick peek and then just as quickly pulled back. Two police constables were crossing the road and heading his way, but they'd not spotted him. He moved from his hiding place and strolled over to stand in front of a tobacconist's. The policemen got close enough for him to hear.

"I'll start on this side of the road," one of them said to the other. "You take the other side and then we'll do the street across the way."

They must be doing a house-to-house, hoping to find someone who'd heard or seen something. Fat chance of that happening, Smythe thought. In this neighborhood it was see no evil, hear no evil and speak no evil, especially to coppers. He waited till they'd gone past and then ducked back across the narrow road to the front of the church. Witherspoon and Barnes were walking away from the building, toward a hansom stand at the far end of the road. He took off after them.

Smythe made it just in time to see them getting into the one available hansom. He looked around, hoping to spot another cab. But the street, though crowded with traffic, was empty of public conveyances. "Blast a Spaniard," he muttered. He knew he should follow them. But the cab was already moving fast, so Smythe did the only thing he could in the circumstances. He started running.

He managed to keep the cab in sight for a good half a mile, but his legs were aching and his lungs were bursting. Just then, he spotted a cab pulling over to discharge a fare. Smythe leapt across the road and pointed to the inspector's hansom as it disappeared around the corner. "Follow that cab," he yelled at the driver as he jumped into the seat.

The driver cracked his whip and they pulled away. Smythe kept sticking his head out and giving the driver instructions. "Don't get too close," he called.

"Look, guv, I've been driving this cab for ten years, I know what I'm doin'," the driver retorted.

Smythe finally gave up and settled back in his seat. The driver did know what he was about; he kept the inspector's cab in sight without getting too close.

Finally, after what seemed like hours, the cab slowed and pulled over to the side of the road. "Your cab's stopped just up the road in front of that dilapidated old cottage. Do you want out here?" the driver asked.

Smythe cautiously slipped out of the safety of his seat. Inspector Witherspoon and Barnes were both visible and walking up a short path to the front door of the cottage. They weren't even looking in his direction. He reached in his pocket and pulled out a handful of coins. "This is fine," he said as he reached up and handed the driver the fare. "And this is for all your trouble." He gave the fellow an extra ten shillings.

"Cor guv, this is a lot . . ."

"You earned it," Smythe yelled as he dashed down the road. He looked about for a good hiding place in case the inspector or Barnes came back outside. He spotted an oak with a large sized trunk just across the road from the cottage. Its roots were gnarled and it looked as if the ground around the base had sunk a goodly amount, but it would do in a pinch.

Smythe looked about the area and noted that the cottage was the last in a row of tiny wooden houses. But the houses were all detached with scraggly lawns separating them from their neighbors. Across the road was a huge industrial building with a sign that read "Claypool Manufacturing."

He wondered if he ought to try to sneak up to the window to have a good look, but then he decided against it. If he was caught, there was no excuse he could give for being here. No, best he just duck behind the tree.

Inside the cottage, Witherspoon and Barnes stood in the center of the tiny sitting room. The cottage had been locked, but the slightest pressure on the door had popped it open. The room was covered in dust, cobwebs and dirt. It was empty save for a broken footstool and an armchair with all the stuffing pulled out. To the left of the entry was a small kitchen, also filthy, and to the right of the sitting room, a bedroom.

"What exactly are we looking for, sir?" Barnes asked.

Witherspoon hadn't a clue. "I'm not sure. But our murder victim must have had this address in his hand for a reason." He sighed. "I suppose we'd best do a good search of the premises. Perhaps we should have brought some lads with us."

"I think we can deal with it, sir," Barnes replied briskly. "I'll start with the bedroom if it's all the same to you."

"I suppose I'd best begin in the kitchen," the inspector murmured. They worked in silence for a few minutes, opening cupboards, checking floorboards and generally trying to find anything useful in the empty house. After exhausting every conceivable idea he had about where something could or couldn't be hidden, Witherspoon, brushing cobwebs off his bowler, went back to the sitting room. Barnes was on his knees looking at the fireplace. "I take it you found nothing."

"Nothing, sir." Barnes got up. "Just more dirt and spiders. If there is something here of interest, I certainly can't see it."

"Me, either," Witherspoon said. He put his bowler back on his head. "I wonder why these cottages were abandoned? A bit of spit and polish and they could be quite nice."

"They're condemned, sir," Barnes replied, brushing the dust off his sleeves. "There's a small sign at the top of the road. I think the ground must be shifting. Look." He pointed toward the bricks in the fireplace. "See how they're not in straight lines? That means the earth must be shifting underneath."

Witherspoon ambled over to have a closer look. "You're right, none of these lines are at all straight. I wonder how long it's been empty. Look, there's still ashes in the grate."

Barnes laughed. "I expect a few of our less fortunate friends have availed themselves of the place in the past few years. Mind you, though, I don't think the structure is all that secure." He placed his hand against the mantel and pushed. It creaked loudly and something heavy dropped from the chimney.

"Gracious, it really is getting ready to collapse," Witherspoon exclaimed. He looked down at the grate, expecting to see a clump of ash or a bundle of leaves. Instead, he gasped and leapt backward. "Egads, Barnes, is that what I think it is?"

Barnes dropped to his knees and stared at the object. He shook his head. "I'm afraid so, sir." He ducked his head under the front of the fireplace so that he could stare up into the chimney proper.

"What are you doing?" the inspector asked. He got a hold of himself. This was rather surprising, but he'd seen worse.

"Seeing what else is up there, sir." Barnes's voice was muffled. "But it's too dark to see much of anything. There's a police constable on the main road. I'll nip up there and raise the alarm. We need a good lantern to see what's what."

"Yes, I think that's an excellent idea." Witherspoon looked down at the grate again. "I suppose we ought to see if the rest of it is up there."

Barnes crawled out from the fireplace. There were smudges of dirt on his cheeks and forehead. He took off his helmet and wiped his face. "I expect so, sir," he replied as he looked down at the object on the grate. "Generally where there's a foot, there's a body."

Witherspoon swallowed hard. Even though it wasn't particularly disgusting, he couldn't take his eyes off the wretched thing. It was merely bones, darkened, of course, from being in the fireplace. But it was most definitely in the shape of a human foot.

CHAPTER 2

"Blast a Spaniard," Smythe muttered to himself as he saw another police constable enter number seven. "What's goin' on in there?" Something important was happening at the cottage, and he knew he shouldn't leave until he found out what it was. On the other hand, he knew he should get back to Upper Edmonton Gardens by teatime. The others would be waiting for his report, and more importantly, Betsy would be worried if he was late.

He wrinkled his nose as the scent of creosote filled the air. Must be from the factory, he thought idly. The smell was strong but it did bring a bit of relief, considering that he was hiding behind an old privy with a very distinctive odor of its own. The privy was behind cottage number six. He'd changed hiding places when he'd seen Constable Barnes come charging out of number seven and race up the road. He'd known something odd was happening and had decided the risk of getting close enough to see what was going on was worth taking. If any of the policemen came out this way, he thought he could nip over the back fence without too much trouble.

He peeked out around the corner and took another look at the cottage. From here, he could see down the narrow passage between the two houses, and that gave him a view of who was going in or out of number seven. He'd now seen three additional constables go inside. He made up his mind. Betsy would just have to understand. This was too important, he had to find out what was going on in there.

He pulled his coat tighter as another blast of wind whipped the air around him. Hunkering down, he crept out of his hiding place and moved quietly toward the back window of number seven. He pressed his face against the dirty glass and found he could see inside a bit. The door leading to the sitting room was open at such an angle that he had a partial view. There were policemen bunched in a group around the small fireplace. One of the men shifted position, and Smythe could see that a constable was actually hunkered in the tiny opening, looking straight up into the chimney. Inspector Witherspoon was standing to one side, gesturing with his hands.

"Blast a Spaniard," he muttered, "this doesn't make any sense." He stepped back and shook his head. There must be something up in the chimney, he decided. Cor blimey, if it was some sort of evidence, something that had been tossed down the chimney or burned in the grate, he might be here all day before they got it out.

He pulled out his pocket watch and noted the time again. It was gone three o'clock. If he hurried, he could make it back for the meeting. Smythe ducked down and slipped back to his hiding place, took a quick look about to make sure no one had nipped out to have a snoop and then continued along through the small gardens at the backs of the cottages. He reached the last house, turned and headed for the street just in time to see an ambulance coming from around the corner. What's all this about, then? he thought. He crossed the road and slipped behind a postbox. Peeking out, he saw the ambulance pulling up in front of number seven.

No one had been hurt or wounded in the cottage; Smythe was sure of that. So that meant the presence of the ambulance could only mean one thing. There was another body.

He leaned against the postbox and watched. A few minutes later, he saw three constables come outside. Two of them used their hands as footholds and helped the third one up onto the roof. Then one of them handed him what looked like an old broom. The one with the broom made his way to the chimney, peeked inside and then began poking the handle down it. Smythe shook his head in amazement and stopped worrying about being late to the meeting. The others, including Betsy, would kill him if he didn't stay here till the end and see exactly what was going on.

Betsy cast another glance toward the windows over the kitchen sink. Though it was only four-thirty, the afternoon was darkening with a coming rain. She wished Smythe would get here.

"Stop frettin'." Luty Belle Crookshank reached over and patted the girl on the arm. "He'll be here soon."

Luty Belle was a small, elderly American woman with white hair, sharp black eyes and a Colt .45 in the deep pocket of her cloak. She was rich, opinionated and loved helping the staff of Upper Edmonton Gardens solve the inspector's murders. Widowed, she and her late husband had made a fortune in the silver mines of Colorado and then come back to her husband's native land and settled in London. She knew everyone in London and had wonderful connections in the legal and financial communities.

"I do hope he has something useful to report," Hatchet, Luty's butler, said. He was a tall, robust man with a full head of thick, white hair. He'd been in her service for years but didn't let that stop him from arguing with her about anything and everything. "But I suppose I ought to be grateful for small favors. At least this time we weren't out of the country."

"Quit cryin' over spilt milk," Luty replied. She plucked at the white lace on the sleeve of her burgundy day dress. "That last one wasn't anyone's fault. We were gone when it happened."

Hatchet sniffed.

"Speaking of which, we really must send Wiggins a telegram tomorrow," Mrs. Jeffries interjected.

"Too bad no one thought to send us a telegram when the last one happened," Hatchet muttered darkly.

"We were twenty-five-hundred miles away," Luty shot back. "Wiggins is only in Colchester. He can get here by tomorrow evenin'. It would have taken us two weeks!"

"What if it turns out to be nothin'?" Mrs. Goodge said calmly. "Even with a dead body, these things aren't always murder. I don't think we ought to be draggin' the lad back until we know for sure one way or another."

"But we do know for sure," Betsy pointed out. "Constable Barnes told the inspector it was murder. I don't think he'd be mistaken about that." She looked toward the hallway, her attention drawn by the sound of the back door opening.

"That must be Smythe," Mrs. Jeffries said conversationally. "Betsy, pour him some tea."

But Betsy was already filling his mug and heaping slices of rich brown bread on his plate.

"Hello, everyone," Smythe said as he came into the warm kitchen.

"Sorry I'm a bit late, but I've got a lot to tell." He slipped into the chair next to Betsy and gave her a quick smile. Under the table, he grabbed her hand.

"We thought you'd be back earlier than this," Betsy said as she clasped his fingers tightly. "I was starting to worry. It looks like it's going to rain."

"But we assumed you were detained because something important came up," the housekeeper added.

"What happened?" Luty asked bluntly. "Did they find out who the dead man is?"

"Not yet." Smythe took a quick sip of tea. Having had neither food nor drink since breakfast, he was thirsty and hungry. "But he's not the only one we've got to worry about. There's another body."

"What?" Betsy exclaimed.

"You mean there's two murders?" Mrs. Goodge asked.

"Good," Hatchet said. "That'll make up for us missing one."

"Nell's bells, two at once, that's got to take the prize," Luty said eagerly. "Where do we start?"

"We really must send that telegram," Mrs. Jeffries said softly. "Smythe, do tell us everything."

Smythe swallowed the bite of bread and butter he'd just popped into his mouth. "I don't have much to go on," he began, "and I think it would make more sense if I tell it from the start."

"Go ahead," she encouraged.

He gave them all the details starting with his arriving at St. Paul's on Dock Street. "I was sure the inspector would hang about askin' questions and managing the house-to-house, but he didn't. The minute they loaded the vicar's body into the ambulance, he and Barnes were off like a shot. I figured they must have found out somethin' important and that maybe it'd be best if I scarpered along and saw where they were goin'."

"That was good thinking on your part," Mrs. Goodge interjected. "It's always best to find out as much as possible at the beginning of the investigation. It saves a lot of time and grief later."

"And where were they going?" Mrs. Jeffries pressed. She rather agreed with the cook, but she didn't wish to interrupt the coachman's narrative.

"To a house . . . well, it's not really a house, more like a cottage—it's in Bermondsey. Number seven Dorland Place. It's right across the road from a paint factory and down the end of a lane of abandoned houses. It seemed I had to 'ide for ages before anythin' 'appened, and I'd just about decided to come along home when all of a sudden, Barnes comes out of the house and scurries off up the road. I didn't know whether to follow 'im or not, so I stayed put, and a few minutes later, he was back with a couple of police constables. I got right up to the back window and I could see in a little, but I couldn't really tell too much from where I was standin'. I didn't want to be too bold and risk getting caught."

"Did you see anything?" Luty asked impatiently.

"Not much," he admitted with a rueful smile. "But I noticed that everyone seemed to be doin' something with the fireplace."

"Doing what?" Mrs. Jeffries asked. She'd learned long ago that every detail was important, including the ones that might be unusual.

"Mainly, stickin' their head up it."

"It sounds like something may have been hidden up there," Hatchet mused.

"That's what I thought," Smythe replied. "But then the ambulance showed up and I knew it wasn't something hidden up there, but someone."

"You mean there was a body?" Betsy made a face. "Up in the fire-place?"

"Good God, was they smokin' it like it was a Virginia ham?" Luty tried hard to keep a straight face.

"Really, Madam." Hatchet sniffed disapprovingly.

"Well, that's how we smoke hams where I come from—stick 'em up over an open fire and let 'em smoke. Why else would someone stick a body in a fireplace?"

"You said the cottages are abandoned," Mrs. Jeffries said to Smythe. "I'm wondering if the body was placed there to hide it."

"That's more likely," Luty agreed. "No point in smokin' a body. It's not like they's any cannibals around here."

"It's still disgusting," Mrs. Goodge said. "Imagine, putting a body in a fireplace."

"Seems as good a place to hide a body as any," Smythe murmured. "Especially if the place was empty and there weren't any neighbors about to see you do it."

"Wouldn't it smell?" Betsy asked.

"Probably, but if all the other houses around it are abandoned, and the closest neighbor is a factory, who'd be around to complain?" Smythe leaned back in his chair. "I think we're dealin' with a very clever killer."

"Don't you mean two killers?" Mrs. Goodge reached for the plate of buttered bread and helped herself to a slice.

"Two killers?" Mrs. Jeffries repeated. "I'm not sure we can make that assumption. We'd best wait until the inspector gets home tonight and I can find out what's what."

"I didn't tell you the best bit," Smythe said. "The police surgeon on the first body is Dr. Bosworth. I saw him."

"That's a bit of luck." Mrs. Jeffries nodded approvingly. Dr. Bosworth had helped them on several of their previous cases. He'd been very helpful and, more importantly, very discreet.

"What else did you see?" Hatchet inquired. "At the first murder. Any idea who the victim might be? Any clues for us to go on?"

"Only that he's a vicar," the coachman replied. "Leastways he was dressed like one."

"You must have gotten quite close to the body to see that," Betsy smiled at him.

"Not really," he grinned. "I just overhead some talkin' from people who did see the corpse."

"What do you want us to do?" Luty asked the housekeeper.

Mrs. Jeffries wasn't certain. "I suppose you could find out if there's any missing clergymen in the area."

"Maybe he was Roman Catholic?" Mrs. Goodge ventured. "Priests tend to dress alike, don't they?"

No one knew the answer to that.

"They both wear collars," Betsy finally said.

"Not to worry," Hatchet said cheerfully. "Roman Catholic or C of E, we'll find out soon enough if anyone's gone missing." He turned to Luty. "I believe the bishop was a close friend of your late husband's."

Luty snorted. "Close friend, my foot. Every time the man came around he had his hand out for some building fund or missionary trust. Considerin' how much I've funneled that way over the years, the man owes me some information."

"Good," Mrs. Jeffries replied. She looked at the cook. "What about Wiggins? It's definitely a murder. I think we ought to send for him."

"I wanted him to have a chance to meet his grandfather," Mrs. Goodge replied. "But you're right, we did promise him."

Mrs. Jeffries nodded in understanding. "I'll go along to the telegraph office straightaway and send off the message." She turned her attention to Luty and Hatchet. "Can you be back here early tomorrow morning? I'm going to see what I can get out of the inspector when he comes home tonight. We ought to have some decent information for you by then, at least enough details to get us started."

"We'll be here," Luty said. She grinned wickedly. "And tonight, I'll pay that bishop a visit."

"Madam, one doesn't just drop by to see the bishop," Hatchet warned her. "We must make an appointment."

"Fiddlesticks." Luty's bright dress rustled as she rose to her feet. "As long as I'm dangling my chequebook in my hand, he'll see me. You mark my words."

Witherspoon was exhausted by the time he climbed the steps to his home. Mrs. Jeffries waited for him by the door. "Good evening, sir." She reached for his bowler and hung it on the coat tree.

"Good evening, Mrs. Jeffries." He shrugged out of his heavy winter overcoat and handed it to her. "I do hope dinner isn't on the table. I'd so like a sherry before I eat."

Mrs. Jeffries hung the coat next to the hat. "Dinner can wait, sir. Let's go into the drawing room. You look like you could use a rest."

A few minutes later he was settled in his favorite armchair with a glass of Harvey's in his hand. As was their custom, Mrs. Jeffries had poured one for herself and sat down on the settee.

"It's been a rather odd day," he began. "As you know, the day started off with a murder, and then strangely enough, we stumbled onto another body. Mind you, until the doctor does the postmortem on the second one, we don't know if that's murder or death by misadventure."

"And you're certain the first victim was deliberately murdered?" She wanted to make sure she got all the facts in this case absolutely correct. They already had two bodies to deal with; it wouldn't do to get muddled this early in the game.

"Absolutely. Poor fellow had a hole straight through the middle of his forehead." He took a sip of sherry and sighed in pleasure.

"That rules out suicide, then," she murmured. "Most people who shoot themselves put the gun in their mouth or at their temple. Where did you find your second body, sir?" She had to ask; they couldn't let on that they already had any information.

Witherspoon leaned forward as though he was sharing a secret. "In a very unusual place, Mrs. Jeffries. It was in a chimney, of all things. We'd not have found it at all if Barnes hadn't pushed against the mantel. He was trying to show me how dilapidated and unsafe the building was. Well, imagine my surprise when a foot dropped out onto the grate."

"I expect you were quite stunned, sir. It's certainly not what one would expect to happen." She quickly dropped her gaze to hide her amusement. She knew it really wasn't a topic for levity, but the idea was quite funny.

"And, of course, where there's a foot, there's generally the rest of the body." He took another sip. "Sure enough, once we got some more men there, we found the rest of the corpse. It took three police constables to get the poor wretch out as well."

"Exactly how did they get it out?"

Witherspoon visibly winced. "Well, we had no choice, really. It was either remove half the chimney, which didn't seem very safe, or poke at the poor thing with a stick. So that's what we did. We sent a PC up to the roof with a broom handle, and he shoved from the top while we pulled from the bottom. That's the only way we could get the thing down." He shook himself. "I'm being terrible. It wasn't a thing, it was the body of a woman."

"You could tell that much about it?"

"Oh yes, it was quite dreadful, really just a skeleton, but Dr. Bosworth is sure it was a woman's bones we found."

"Dr. Bosworth." Mrs. Jeffries was surprised. Smythe hadn't mentioned Bosworth being present. "He was there?"

"We sent for him after the foot fell out. I'm no expert on corpses, Mrs. Jeffries, but I certainly didn't want to destroy any evidence. So I sent along for the doctor. He arrived with the ambulance lads."

That explained why Smythe hadn't mentioned him, she thought. He'd probably nipped in with the lads and Smythe hadn't noticed him.

"He was very helpful, too, held the lantern and directed the lads on getting the corpse out without too much damage. Mind you, he's got some very advanced ideas on what one can learn from the dead." Witherspoon paused thoughtfully. "He was certain it was a woman almost from the moment he saw the foot."

"How did you come to go to this house, sir?"

"The first victim sent us there," he said. "The address was written on a bit of paper. He was holding onto it. We went there hoping to find someone who could identify him for us, but, well, you know what we found."

"So you have no idea who this poor man might be?" she pressed.

"No, all we know is that he was dressed in clerical attire and had nothing on him except this bit of paper. The local priest didn't know who he was, and as of late this afternoon, the local bishop didn't know of any missing priests either."

"Was he Church of England, sir?"

"We think so, but we're checking with the Roman Catholic archdiocese as well. Honestly, Mrs. Jeffries, how can priests just end up dead practically on a church doorstep and no one has any idea who they might be?"

"I'm sure you'll find out soon enough, sir. You always do." She could tell he was having one of his periodic bouts of self-doubt. "What did the locals have to say about the situation?" She knew his methods well enough to guess that he'd sent police constables on a door-to-door search for information.

He sighed heavily. "Not very much. No one can recall seeing the poor fellow. But Dr. Bosworth thinks he might have been there all night. It's a commercial area, so there wouldn't be many people about once the warehouses and shipping offices closed for the day."

"The doctor has an estimate of the time of death?"

"Not really, it was only a guess on his part. He'll have more for us by tomorrow. He's doing the postmortems tonight."

"On both bodies?" She felt a bit sorry for the poor doctor. He wasn't going to get any rest this night.

"He hoped to complete them both. Mind you, I don't know what he can hope to find out from those bones. But he seemed confident he could learn something."

"Well, he was able to tell you the victim was a woman," she said thoughtfully. Mrs. Jeffries's mind worked furiously. There were a dozen different ways to approach this investigation, and she wanted to have as much information as possible before they all went off half-cocked. "Inspector, I'm sure you've already done this, but have you found out who owned the cottage where the body was found?"

Witherspoon tossed back the last of his sherry. "Indeed I did.

Unfortunately, all the cottages in that row belong to the factory across the street. But no one's lived in them for ten years."

Wiggins was torn between pity and compassion. He wanted to stay really angry at this old man, but it was getting harder and harder to do that as the day wore on. Jonathan Edward Wiggins lay in the center of a huge four-poster bed and stared at him piteously. His eyes were shrunken into his sockets, his face was pale as the sheets and his skin had a waxy sheen to it that didn't look good.

"I'm not sure I know what you're tryin' to tell me," Wiggins finally said. Through the window next to the bed, he could see the open fields of the farm. The sky was darkening with the fall of evening, and Wiggins wished he were anyplace but here.

"I'm tryin' to explain why I was so harsh," Jonathan Wiggins whispered. "It were wrong of me. . . ." He broke off as a wracking series of coughs shook his whole body.

"Grandfather, don't strain yourself." The voice came from the other side of the room, from a lad about Wiggins's age who was his cousin. Albert Wiggins shot Wiggins a malevolent glance. Like his cousin, he had brown hair, round apple cheeks and blue eyes. But there the resemblance to Wiggins ended, for Albert's mouth was a thin, disapproving line, and his chin was almost nonexistent. "You're upsetting him. Why don't you go back where you came from and leave us in peace."

"No," the old man ordered, and even in his disabled state, his voice was authoritative. "He stays. He's family."

"I don't want to cause any trouble," Wiggins replied. Cor blimey, he didn't want to be in the middle of a family quarrel, even if it was his own family.

"Sit down, boy," Jonathan Wiggins instructed his grandson. "Sit down and hear me out."

Wiggins wished he had the meanness or the courage to tell the old man to sod off, but he didn't. He felt sorry for the old fellow. He'd arrived that day and been met at the station by his cousin, the sullen Albert. During the ride from Colchester to the farm, Albert had said very little. When he'd arrived, he'd met his Aunt Alice and Uncle Peter, who were almost as sullen as their son. But they'd shown him his room and then taken him right up to his grandfather's room. The old man had talked to him for a while . . . well, he'd rambled on about how much Wiggins reminded him of his eldest son, Wiggins's father, Douglas. Then he'd fallen asleep and Wiggins had gone to his room.

This was his second meeting today with his grandfather, and he hoped it would be his last. He eased down into the straight-backed chair next to his grandfather's bed. "All right, I'm sittin'. What do you want to say to me?"

Jonathan Wiggins coughed again. "I shouldn't have run your mother off," he muttered. "But I was so angry, I blamed her for your father's death."

"But my father died of pneumonia. How could she have been at fault?" Wiggins replied. He heard his cousin mutter something under his breath, so he turned his head and shot him a fast glare. Albert stepped back and then looked away. Like many others, he'd mistaken Wiggins's good nature for weakness.

"She weren't to blame at all," Jonathan said softly. "But I hadn't wanted him to marry her, and he'd defied me and done it anyway. When she come along looking for help after his death, I wanted someone to blame, and she were the one in front of me. I bitterly regret it." Another series of coughs racked him.

Wiggins got to his feet. "Don't fret, please. You'll harm yourself. I understand. It's all in the past. It's all over."

Tears filled the old man's eyes. "Do you forgive me?"

Wiggins didn't think he could ever really forgive the old man. But right now, he'd say anything to stop the fellow from suffering so much. "Yes, yes, please, stop cryin', you'll upset yourself."

"You're not just sayin' it, are you? You truly forgive me?"

He hesitated, not wanting to lie twice in a row. But he was scared his grandfather was going to die on him if he didn't calm down. "I'm not just sayin' it. Truly, it's over and done with."

"Will you stay for a while?" Jonathan pressed.

Wiggins paused. He didn't want to make a promise he couldn't keep. "I might have to go back to London. . . ."

"Surely your employer will understand," Jonathan pleaded. "I'm an old man, I'm dying. You're my grandson and I need to make my peace with you."

"Well, I'll stay for as long as I can," he finally replied. Truth was, he didn't want to miss a murder.

"Promise," Jonathan asked weakly.

"I promise."

There was a soft knock on the door, and a moment later, a tall, raw-boned middle-aged woman stepped inside the sickroom. It was his Aunt Alice. She handed Wiggins a yellow envelope. "This come for you."

"What is it?" Jonathan demanded. He struggled to sit up.

"It's a telegram," Albert said smugly. "They probably want him to come back."

"But you said you'd stay," Jonathan cried. His eyes filled with tears again. "You promised. Take pity on an old man. Take pity. You promised you'd stay."

"It's all right, it's all right," Wiggins soothed. He knew what was in the telegram. "If I can, I'll stay." He tore open the thin flap and read the words. It was short and to the point.

"We've got one, come quickly."

Wiggins sighed. He wanted to go back to London more than anything. He didn't want to miss this murder, but then he looked at the old man in the bed and knew he couldn't do it.

"Do you have to leave?" Aunt Alice asked eagerly.

"No, I can stay for a bit."

They met as soon as the inspector had retired for the evening. Mrs. Jeffries told them everything she'd learned, and then she sat back in her chair, her expression thoughtful.

"This is an odd kettle of fish." Mrs. Goodge shook her head. "It'll be difficult to investigate anything. We don't even have any names?"

"Cor blimey, this isn't goin' to be easy. Where do we even start?" Smythe added.

Mrs. Jeffries rather agreed with them, but she didn't wish to sound defeated before they'd even begun. Besides, she'd given the matter some thought, and they did have several avenues that might be worth pursuing. "This may indeed be a difficult case, but I think we've got enough to start looking about."

"We do?" Betsy asked.

"Certainly." She held up her hand and spread her fingers. "To begin with, the first victim was found at the docks, and no one appears to know who he was. Now, to my knowledge neither the Church of England nor the Roman Catholic Church actually lose their priests. Yet neither of them reported anyone missing or lost. So, that might mean there is a good possibility our clerically garbed victim only arrived in town yesterday, the day he was probably murdered."

"Which means someone at a shipping company will know who he might be." Betsy nodded eagerly. "I see what you're getting at. One of us should check the shipping lines and see what came in yesterday or the day before."

"That was my thought exactly." Mrs. Jeffries nodded approvingly.

"And one of us should nip around to the neighborhood where the second body was found and see who lived in that cottage years ago," Smythe added.

"I thought those cottages were owned by that factory," Betsy said.

"They are, but someone had to have lived in them at one time or another," Mrs. Jeffries pointed out. "Someone who knew the place and, more importantly, knew they were going to be abandoned for years. I highly doubt that some stranger came along and shoved a woman's corpse down the chimney." She frowned. "Which is odd when you think about it. Why put a body in a chimney in the first place?"

"What do you mean?" Mrs. Goodge asked. She was a bit disappointed that they'd no names as yet. It was difficult for her to do her bits and pieces without names. But she didn't want the others to think she was sulking.

"I mean, why a chimney? Why not just bury the body?" She turned to Smythe. "Were there any places behind the cottage for a burial?"

He thought for a moment. "Actually, there is. All them cottages have back gardens. They're small, but there's room for someone to bury a body. But I don't see what you're gettin' at."

She wasn't sure herself. "It seems to me that putting a body in a chimney involves a great deal of work. Corpses are dead weight. So, whoever put her there had to either stuff her up the chimney, which seems very difficult unless one had enormous strength, or they had to stuff her down the chimney, which means they would have had to have carried the body onto the roof. That couldn't have been easy."

"It probably wasn't easy, but I expect the killer didn't have any choice. There aren't any fences between the cottages. So if you did try to bury her and someone came outside from one of the other houses, you'd have been seen," Smythe said.

"And even if they had a place to put her, maybe they couldn't bury her," Mrs. Goodge suggested.

"Seems to me digging a hole is a lot easier than hauling a body up onto the roof," Betsy said.

"Not if the ground is frozen," the cook replied. "And if you'll recall, we had some rather nasty winters a few years back."

"That's right," Mrs. Jeffries added. "If the murder was done during bad weather, either the ground being frozen . . ."

"Or soaked," Mrs. Goodge put in. "If there'd been days of hard rain, you couldn't bury a body."

"Then that would explain why someone would use a chimney. Especially if they knew the cottages were going to be abandoned."

"Or they already were abandoned," Smythe suggested. "We don't know when the murder was done."

"Aren't we getting ahead of ourselves?" Betsy said. "We don't know for certain the second body was murder."

"Course we do," Mrs. Goodge exclaimed. "People who die from natural causes don't usually end up in the chimney."

"I hadn't thought of that." The maid frowned, annoyed with herself for not seeing the obvious. "Maybe I ought to nip over there tomorrow and learn what I can about that cottage."

"That's an excellent idea," Mrs. Jeffries said quickly. "Any information you can get us will be helpful. Smythe, do you think you can go along to the docks and see if you can learn anything concerning our dead clergyman?"

"What if he came in on a ship that docked at Tilbury?" Smythe mused. "That's where most of the big ships come in at these days."

"But plenty of ships still come in on the London docks," Mrs. Goodge pointed out. "And it was close to there where the fellow was murdered." She was a tad annoyed. In her view, he at least had something to do. The best she could hope for was picking up a few bits and pieces about the murder in general. It was difficult for her to do her investigations without the victim's name. "Besides, most of the shipping lines still have offices at the London docks."

"Right, then," he nodded. "I'll try the offices first, and if I don't 'ave any luck, I'll 'ave a go at the pubs and seamen's haunts. Not everyone who comes in by ship 'as 'is name on a manifest."

"What about Luty and Hatchet?" Betsy asked. "What can they do?"

Mrs. Jeffries frowned. "We did ask Luty to speak to the bishop about whether there are any missing clergy."

"She'll have done that by tomorrow morning," Mrs. Goodge warned. "You'd best have something else at the ready for her and Hatchet."

"Oh, dear, we've so little information to go on," Mrs. Jeffries replied. "I suppose they could do some general nosing about—especially in the area where the clergyman's body was found. With Wiggins being gone, we need at least one of them asking questions around the neighborhood."

"It'd better be Hatchet doin' the askin'," Smythe grinned. "Luty tends to charge in like a bull in a china shop."

"She's direct," Betsy defended her friend. "But she can be as bland as butter when it's necessary."

"You'd better come up with something for her to do," Mrs. Goodge warned, "or she'll be doggin' everyone's heels and gettin' in the way." Translated, this meant that Mrs. Goodge didn't want Luty hanging around her kitchen—not when she was trying to do her own investigating.

"I'll think of something by tomorrow morning," Mrs. Jeffries sighed.

"Are you going to have a word with Dr. Bosworth?" Mrs. Goodge asked.

"Yes, as a matter of fact, I think I'll go along to the hospital tonight."

"All on your own?" Betsy yelped.

"That's not a good idea," Mrs. Goodge said. "The streets aren't safe for a woman alone at night."

"Why do you want to go tonight?" Smythe asked.

"Because he's doing the postmortems on both the victims, and if I'm very lucky, I'll be able to speak with him before he goes home. He may have some valuable information for us. But I wasn't planning on going alone. I was hoping Smythe would be good enough to accompany me."

"Course I will, Mrs. Jeffries." He smiled in relief. "We couldn't let you go off on your own in the middle of the night. What time do you want to leave?"

She thought for a moment. She had no idea how long it would take to do two postmortems, but knowing how thorough Dr. Bosworth was, she suspected he would take his time. "Why don't we leave here about four. There's no traffic at that time, so we'd get to St. Thomas's Hospital by half past. I should think he'd be finished by then."

"Are you sure he'll be doing the postmortems at St. Thomas's?" Betsy asked. "That's a long way from Bermondsey and Dock Street. Wouldn't he use a closer hospital?"

"I don't think so," she replied. "Not all hospitals have the facilities for postmortems."

"We'll not be able to get a hansom at that hour of the morning," Smythe said, "so I'd best nip over to Howards and get the coach."

"Won't Howards be locked?" Mrs. Goodge asked.

Howards was the stable where the inspector's horses and carriage were kept.

"They will, but I've a key." He grinned again. "I told 'em I needed one. What with the inspector bein' a policeman, there's no tellin' when I might have to get the coach and horses in the middle of the night."

"Why, Smythe," Mrs. Jeffries smiled approvingly. "That was most farsighted of you."

CHAPTER 3

Mrs. Jeffries felt a bit silly sitting all alone in the coach. But Smythe had refused to let her sit up with him, and of course, if he sat inside with her he wouldn't be able to drive. She stuck her head out and called, "Are you all right up there?"

"Fine, Mrs. J. We'll be there in a few minutes, so stop frettin' about me. I'm enjoyin' myself. It's been ages since I had the rig out at night."

She popped back down in her seat and then grabbed the handhold as they careened around a corner. "You might slow down a bit," she muttered, but she'd not the heart to shout at him; he was obviously having a wonderful time. She bounced up and down on the stiff leather seats as they galloped through the sleeping city. Finally, they pulled up in front of a long, two-story, gray stone building with lights shining out of the basement windows.

Smythe tied up the horses and helped her down onto the cobblestone street. "There's a light by that door," he nodded at a door to their left. "I expect there's a porter on duty who can let us in."

Moving quickly against the cold night air, they went up the walkway to the door, their footsteps seeming unusually loud in the quiet night. The porter, hearing them coming, opened the door before they knocked.

"Is this an emergency?" he gave them a hard stare. "You both look healthy enough to me."

"Are you a doctor?" Mrs. Jeffries asked quietly. She took Smythe's arm.

"Well, no," he sputtered.

"Then I'll thank you to refrain from attempting to diagnose me. Could you please direct me to the morgue?"

"No offense, madam," the porter replied. "But you're not supposed to go there. It's for dead people."

"We're here to make an identification," Smythe said quickly. "Dr. Bosworth sent for us."

"No one told me." He stepped back and waved them inside. "What are you doing here this time of night? That's always done during the daytime."

"We're leaving for Australia by ship on the morning tide," Smythe said smoothly. "So we're in a hurry. Now be a good fellow and tell us how we find this Bosworth fellow?"

Mrs. Jeffries shot him an admiring smile. He was getting quite good at thinking on his feet.

The porter shrugged. "It's just down these stairs. Go all the way to the bottom and turn left. You'll come right to it, there's a sign on the door so you'll not miss it."

They followed his directions and a few minutes later they were standing at the door to the morgue.

Mrs. Jeffries took a deep breath. She noticed that Smythe did the same. "Now that we're here, I'm not sure I want to see what's on the other side of that door."

"Oh, I don't know. I'm sure it'll be all right. There's probably not *too* many bodies in there," he replied.

"And I'm certain that the dead are decently covered. Right, then." She stepped forward and grasped the handle. "Let's have a look." She shoved open the door, stepped inside and then recoiled as the smell hit her full force. The air reeked; a ghastly mixture of blood, infection, carbolic acid, formaldehyde and the faintest whiff of methane gas. She forced herself to move into the room proper.

"Cor blimey," Smythe muttered from behind her. "This is bad enough to make the dead weep."

The lights were dim but not so low that she couldn't see. Several bodies, decently covered, she was relieved to see, were lying on tables. Along the opposite wall was a row of sinks, and above them, shelves and cupboards filled with medicine bottles, tins of antiseptic, bandages and rolls of toweling.

At the far end of the room, a lone figure was bent over a naked body. "I'm almost done," he called chattily. "Sorry to be so late. I know it's a bother for you, but I'll have a word with the nursing sisters to make sure you're not in trouble. You can't be expected to clean and tidy up when I'm working."

"Uh . . . Dr. Bosworth." Now that they were here, Mrs. Jeffries was a bit embarrassed. The doctor had helped them on several occasions in their investigations, but this was the first time they'd ever hunted him down on the job, so to speak. "I do hope we're not interrupting . . ."

Bosworth whirled around. "Good Lord, it's Mrs. Jeffries. What on earth are you doing here?" He was a tall, red-haired man with pale skin and generally a nice smile. The smile was conspicuously absent at the moment. He looked rather annoyed. In one hand he held a scalpel dripping with blood and in the other a pair of long slender tongs. His collar was undone, his sleeves rolled up, and there were a multitude of hideous stains on the heavy apron he wore to protect his clothes.

"I'm dreadfully sorry to bother you," she apologized. "We were rather hoping you'd have finished by now and we could offer you a lift home. We brought the carriage."

For a long moment, he stared at them and then he grinned. "I might have known you'd show up. It's not often you get two corpses on one case. I'll be finished here in a few minutes. Why don't you wait for me out in the hall? This probably isn't very pleasant for either of you."

"Yes, that'll be splendid," she replied as she turned and hurried to the door. Smythe was right on her heels. They stepped into the hall and took deep breaths.

"Cor blimey, Mrs. Jeffries." Smythe shook his head. "I thought for a minute there I was goin' to lose my supper. How does 'e stand it?"

"I expect you get used to the odor," she murmured. "But it is rather awful. I do hope the doctor will forgive us the liberty of just dropping in on him."

Smythe laughed. "Sure 'e will. The good doctor likes to see justice done just as much as we do."

"Indeed I do, Smythe," Bosworth said as he stepped out and joined them. He rolled down his sleeves. "And sometimes I'm of the mind that if it weren't for you lot, there'd be many a killer walking the streets of London. There's no need for you to take me home, I've still my reports to write, but if you'll come with me, I know a place where we can have a quiet cup of tea."

"At this hour?"

He grinned again. "This is a hospital, Smythe. There's always a kettle on the boil somewhere." He took Mrs. Jeffries's arm and guided her to the staircase. "I know why you're here, so we can spend a few minutes nattering, then I'll tell you what I've learned about your two victims."

By the time they got the coach back to Howards and made their way back to Upper Edmonton Gardens, it was full daylight. Mrs. Goodge and Betsy were both sitting at the kitchen table, waiting for them.

"We've had quite a time," Smythe said. "It's bloomin' cold out there, I don't care if it is spring."

"Have you had any luck in learning anything?" Mrs. Goodge asked.

Mrs. Jeffries slipped into her chair at the head of the table. She noticed that Fred, their mongrel dog, had barely wagged his tail when they'd come inside. "What's wrong with Fred?"

"He misses Wiggins something fierce," Betsy asked. "But he'll be fine soon. I expect Wiggins will take the morning train and be here by this afternoon."

Mrs. Goodge snorted. "He'd better be. We sent the telegram yesterday and he should have gotten it. Should we wait for Luty and Hatchet to get here before you begin? You know how testy Hatchet's been since they missed our last murder."

"That's a very good idea. That way I'll only have to tell it once." She glanced at the carriage clock on the pine sideboard. "It's almost seven. They'll be here right after breakfast."

They arrived moments after the inspector had left for the day. The household had just finished the clearing up, and the cook had brewed a fresh pot of tea for their meeting.

Mrs. Jeffries waved everyone to the table. "Come along, everyone, we've a lot of ground to cover. I want to tell everyone what we learned from Dr. Bosworth."

"Good," Luty declared as she plopped down in the seat next to Mrs. Goodge. "I've got somethin' to report too."

Hatchet gave her a quick glare. "Naturally you do, madam, considering that we barged into the bishop's residence without so much as a by-your-leave last night. I should hope you'd have something to show for your efforts."

Luty grinned. She knew he was annoyed that she'd not only made him wait outside, but she hadn't shared what she'd learned with him. Served him right for trying to stop her from bargin' past the feller's secretary.

"Excellent, Luty," said Mrs. Jeffries. She smiled approvingly and then waited a moment before she spoke. "I won't bore you with the preliminaries of our meeting with Dr. Bosworth," she said. "I'll get right to the heart of the matter. He was able to determine that the first victim . . ."

"That preacher feller," Luty clarified.

"Yes, or as we call him, the vicar, he'd been dead for at least twelve hours by the time his body was found yesterday."

"That would put it at around nine o'clock the previous evening," Hatchet said.

"Possibly." Mrs. Jeffries frowned slightly. "But he emphasized the fact that he could be wrong by several hours either way. That was his best estimate, but he couldn't swear to that time in a court of law."

"So it could have been as early as say, six, or as late as midnight," Hatchet mused.

"But it would have had to have been after dark, wouldn't it?" Betsy said. "If it had been before six and still daylight, someone would have seen the body."

"That's right." Smythe smiled proudly at his beloved and gave her fingers a squeeze. "There's enough foot traffic that someone would have spotted him propped up against that wall, even if he was around the side of the building. I think it's safe to say he was killed after dark, which would mean it had gone six by the time the deed was done."

"But that still leaves a very long time period to cover," Mrs. Goodge complained. "What about the other one?"

"Now that's quite interesting," Mrs. Jeffries replied. "There wasn't much Dr. Bosworth could tell. Essentially, all he had to work with was a skeleton."

"Had she been murdered?" Betsy asked.

"He wasn't able to tell, but he did say there were no obvious signs as to cause of death. No bullet holes or anything useful like that," she replied. "But he was able to determine she'd been in that chimney for a good number of years. He's having a friend of his take a look at her."

"You mean another doctor?" Hatchet asked. "Good gracious, why?" He didn't much like the idea of even more people snooping about in the inspector's cases. It meant there'd be less for he and the rest of them to do.

"I think it's a doctor." Mrs. Jeffries shrugged. "Apparently, this person is an expert on bones, and he might be able to tell Dr. Bosworth something more about the victim. I didn't really understand the details of why he thought it necessary to bring another person in to have a look, but I've faith that Dr. Bosworth knows what he's doing. He's going to stop by on his way home this evening if there's any more information."

"Is that it?" Mrs. Goodge asked. She really needed this kitchen empty if she was to get anything done at all on her bits and pieces.

"That's all we know," Mrs. Jeffries replied. She looked at Luty. "Were you successful at learning anything about our unknown vicar?"

Luty smiled smugly. "I learned that no one, including the bishop, knows anything about the fellow. As far as he knew, there aren't any missin' priests from any of the London parishes. He's pretty sure the man must be from one of their overseas missions."

"That doesn't mean there aren't any missing priests from other parishes," Hatchet point out tartly. "Just because Bishop Andrews hadn't heard anything doesn't mean there isn't one missing from somewhere. In case you don't know, there are over a hundred bishops in England, and unless you're going to toddle over to the House of Lords and speak to each and every one of them personally, you can't possibly know that this priest isn't from Cheshire or Yorkshire or Nottingham."

"I don't have to go to the House of Lords," Luty said. "I've got a meetin' this morning with the archbishop."

"Of Canterbury?" Hatchet looked positively horrified. "You're barging in on the Archbishop of Canterbury?"

"I'm not bargin' in," Luty retorted. "Bishop Andrews made the appointment for me. Mind you, I did write out a big check for the Bishop's Building Fund, but I like to think he'd have done it even if I hadn't given him any money. Don't get your nose out of joint, Hatchet, I'll be discreet. I've got a good story all cooked up."

"You're going to lie to the Archbishop of Canterbury?" If possible, Hatchet was even more horrified. It wasn't that he considered it a grievous sin to lie to the archbishop; he was simply afraid she'd muck it up and they'd be caught snooping in the inspector's case. "But madam, you can't do that."

Luty smiled smugly but said nothing.

"Hatchet, I'm sure Luty will be most discreet in her efforts," Mrs. Jeffries said soothingly. Luty was rich enough and wily enough that the housekeeper was fairly certain the worst that could happen was that she'd be considered an eccentric American. In England, there was a long history of tolerance for such people. "And I'm equally sure she'll do her best to get us more information. Now, unless anyone has anything else to add, I suggest we do our chores as quickly as possible and then get cracking."

Betsy stared at the row of abandoned cottages and then straightened her spine. There was no point in hanging about staring at the empty houses. They weren't likely to speak to her. The workers at the factory had already gone inside for their shift, so there was no information from that quarter, so she'd best get on up to the commercial areas and start talking to shop-keepers. Surely someone would know something.

She turned on her heel and retraced her steps. It took less than five minutes before she was standing on the busiest street corner in Bermond-sey. Betsy leaned against a lamppost and surveyed the area. There was a greengrocer's, a fishmonger, a butcher shop, a dry goods store and a draper's shop. She decided to try the greengrocer's first. She crossed the cobblestone street and went inside. A middle-aged woman was serving a short line of customers. Betsy waited her turn. Luckily, no one had come in behind her, so she was alone with the proprietress.

"What can I get for you, miss?" the woman asked politely as she wiped her hands on her apron.

Betsy smiled shyly. "I was hoping you could help me."

The woman frowned slightly and dashed a lock of frizzy, light brown hair off her cheek. "What do you need, girl?" As Betsy wasn't actually a customer, she'd gone down a peg or two in the woman's estimation.

"I was wondering if you know anything about those abandoned cot-tages down by the factory."

"They're empty," she retorted. She turned away and began straighten-ing a bin of onions.

"I mean, do you know who owns them?" The moment the words were out, she wanted to bite her tongue. Inspector Witherspoon had already found out who owned them.

"The factory people own the whole lot of 'em," the proprietress said. She looked over her shoulder and stared at Betsy suspiciously. "Why are you so interested in 'em?"

"I'm trying to find someone who used to live in one of them." Betsy already had a story at the ready. "My aunt and my cousin used to live in num-ber seven. My family emigrated to Canada and we lost contact with them. Me mam died, and I've come back. I've come a long way to find them."

The woman snorted in disbelief. "Didn't your people ever hear of writing letters? Sorry, girl, no one's lived in those places for years. The council forced everyone out when the ground began to shift. They're none of 'em safe."

"So you've no idea where the people who lived there went?" Betsy wisely decided to ignore the comment about letter-writing.

"No." The woman turned to help a customer who'd entered the shop so quietly Betsy hadn't heard her come in. "What can I get you, Mrs. Pangley?"

Betsy mumbled her thanks to the woman and hurried out. She wasn't certain what to do next. But she wasn't going to give up. Someone around here had to know something about those cottages. She started for the butcher shop. But she had no better luck there. Nor did she find out anything at the fishmonger's, the dry goods shop or the draper's.

She stared at the busy street. She supposed she could try the shops on the next road, but that was even farther away from where the houses were located. She'd learned nothing except that the houses had been abandoned for years.

"Excuse me, miss," came a woman's voice from behind her.

Betsy whirled around. It was the lady from the greengrocer's, the one who'd come in so quietly.

"I'm Ada Pangley," she continued. "I couldn't help but overhear your conversation at the greengrocer's." She was a tall woman with graying brown hair, blue eyes and thin lips. She was dressed in a sensible brown coat, plain brown bonnet and sturdy shoes.

"You know something that might help me?" Betsy couldn't believe her luck.

Ada Pangley shrugged. "I'm not sure. But I did know someone who used to live in those cottages. I used to do some sewing for the people who lived in number five. Where did your people live?"

Betsy was ready for this question. "I'm not sure. You see, I was just a little girl. It might have been number seven or number six. It was one of the ones at the end."

"It must have been number six, then," Ada nodded wisely. "The woman in number seven didn't have any children."

Betsy wasn't going to let this lady get away. Not if she knew something about the woman who'd lived in number seven. "Is there a tea shop nearby? I'd love to buy you a cup of tea and ask you a few more questions."

"There's nothing like that around here," Ada replied. "But I live just around the corner. Come along, I could do with a cuppa myself."

"Oh, I don't want to put you to any trouble."

"It's no trouble at all." Ada smiled again and started for the corner. "Since my Stan died, I'm a bit lonely. Come along, it'll be nice to have some company."

Betsy trailed after her. "If you're sure it's no trouble." She knew that if Smythe found out she was going off with some stranger, he'd have a fit. But this lady looked harmless enough, and it was worth the risk if she was going to find out anything useful.

Hatchet was determined to find out something important today. He stared at the spot where the dead vicar had been found and saw absolutely nothing but an empty wall. Well, what had he expected? A clue the police had overlooked. Not likely. His mind worked furiously. There was no point in questioning anyone at the church proper because the police would have taken care of that task. He turned and headed for the end of the street, coming out on a busy road with a host of shops, offices and businesses lining each side. He wasn't sure where to start, so he walked into the first one, which was a secondhand furniture shop.

The shop was poorly lighted and crowded with all manner of old furniture, most of it in fairly bad condition. Tallboys with missing handles, uneven tables, and oversized chairs with half their stuffing missing were piled haphazardly around the room. Broken footstools, chairs and even some small tables were suspended on hooks along the walls.

A long narrow counter ran the width of the room, behind which stood a tall, thin woman wearing a beige dress and a stained brown apron. She stared at him. "May I help you?"

Hatchet gave her his most charming smile. It appeared to have no effect whatsoever. "Thank you, madam. I'm just having a good look around, if you don't mind."

"Looking for anything in particular?" she pressed.

"Actually, I came into your charming establishment because of the plethora of quality goods I saw from the window," Hatchet replied. She'd been a handsome woman in her youth, he thought. Her eyes were a nice color of blue, and she had a lovely bone structure.

She smiled faintly. "That's funny, them windows is so dirty you can barely see inside."

Hatchet wanted to tell her that her manner wasn't the best approach to insure a sale, but he thought better of it. But before he could say a word, she spoke.

"Look, let's not shilly-shally about. You're no more interested in my goods than the man in the moon. People like you don't buy this kind of old furniture." She gestured around the shop. "So let's talk about what you are interested in."

"And what would that be, madam?" he asked curiously. He should have worn one of his old suits and his scuffed shoes before venturing out to this neighborhood. The polished top hat and his gold-handled walking stick didn't help his cause either. In the future, he'd leave them at home.

"You're one of them reporters from the newspaper, aren't you? And you're interested in that there dead vicar they found propped up by the church wall."

Hatchet stared at her in surprise.

"If you want any of my information," she said bluntly, "you'll have to pay for it. It's not like we're made of money around here, you know."

"How much?"

"A couple of quid."

Hatchet hesitated. He wasn't sure whether reporters actually paid for information or not, but then again, he wasn't a reporter. But a real journalist would negotiate. "How do I know what you've got to tell me is worth that much?"

"That's just a risk you'll have to take," she shot back. "If I didn't say nuthin' to the police, I'm not likely to say much to you unless you cross my palm with silver."

He reached in his pocket and drew out his purse. Opening it, he took out two half-sovereigns and held them up. "Let's start with these," he said to her, "and if what you've got to say is worth it, I'll give you two more."

Her eyes narrowed but she grabbed the coins. "It'll be worth it, just you wait. Come along to the back. We might as well give my feet a rest while we're talking."

Hatchet followed her through a dingy gray curtain that separated the shop from a back room that was even darker than the shop. She struck a match and lighted a tiny gas lamp that stood on a table. She motioned for him to take a chair, and then sat down herself.

Hatchet lowered himself into the flimsy seat very carefully, and they sat facing one another. The woman said, "My name's Jane Bilkington." She stared at him, her expression expectant. It suddenly occurred to him that she was waiting for him to introduce himself.

He was suddenly a bit ashamed. This woman was poor and quite willing to sell information, but she was still deserving of common courtesy. "My name is Hector Clemente," he said, using the name of a deceased friend of his who didn't need it anymore.

"What paper you work for?" she asked conversationally.

Again, he hesitated. Did real reporters reveal who they wrote for? He didn't know. "I'd prefer to keep that confidential." He gave her a sly smile. "If you don't mind."

She shrugged. "As long as you're payin', I don't care who you work for. I was just bein' sociable-like. Anyways, let's get on with this, I've got work to do."

"Thank you, Miss Bilkington," he replied.

"Mrs. Bilkington," she corrected. "I'm a widow."

"Sorry, Mrs. Bilkingon. If you'd tell me what you know about the dead vicar, I'd be most appreciative."

"I can tell you he weren't alone, that's for certain," she sniffed delicately. "He was runnin' helter-skelter when he come past here last night. Mind you, it was hard to see anything, what with the heavy fog and all, but he weren't alone. I know that much."

"Why don't you tell me exactly what you saw?" he suggested. "Start at the beginning."

"I'd gone out front to bring in a new entry table we'd just bought, nice thing it was too, just had a few scratches and nicks on the top. We'd sold it already, you see. Course I knew it would sell fast, that's why I bought it. Entry tables do well for us. A lot of our customers live in small places, and a decent-sized entry table can be used to eat on . . ."

"Yes, I'm sure that's true," he interrupted. "But what did you see?"

"Just give me a minute," she scolded. "As you're payin' for this, I want to make sure I get it right. Anyways, like I was sayin', I was bringing in that table when all of a sudden, I hears footsteps comin' down the road. They was comin' fast and hard, too, so I stopped what I was doing and stepped out a bit into the street. It was dark, and with the fog and all, you couldn't see more than a foot or so in front of your own face."

"Do you know what time it was, exactly?" Hatchet asked.

"It was almost six, I know that. We close at six and I was due at my sister's at half past. She lives up on Rayners Lane, which is a good twenty-minute walk. So I timed it to bring in the table, lock the shop and then go. Well, as I said, I heard footsteps coming hard down the road. They kept comin' closer and closer, but with the fog I couldn't see anything even if it were right in front of my eyes. All of a sudden, when the vicar couldn't have been more than ten feet from me, there was one of them partings that you get. You know, one of them spots where the fog shifts and you can see. Lo and behold, I saw the man runnin' like the hounds of hell was on his heels."

"Did he see you?" Hatchet had no idea why that was important, but for some reason, it was.

"No, he were too busy lookin' over his shoulder, but he was lookin' the opposite direction. Then, before I could do so much as a by-your-leave-sir, the fog closed in again and I couldn't see anything. Just heard his footsteps. A few seconds later, I heard a second set. They was runnin' hard too."

Hatchet drew a sharp breath. "Did you see this second person?"

She shook her head. "The fog was too thick. Mind you, I thought it odd, but then again, it never pays to stick your nose into things that don't concern you."

"You mean you didn't summon a policeman."

"How was I to know the vicar was in danger? I thought the man was runnin' to get to church on time. It was almost time for the service."

He stared at her in disbelief. "Let me make sure I understand. You saw a gentleman wearing a clerical collar come running past your establishment and a few seconds later you heard another set of footstep, apparently chasing the poor man, but you didn't think it wise to summon a policeman?"

"And tell him what? That I saw a vicar runnin' toward St. Paul's?" She glared at him, shoved back from the table and got to her feet. "You've got no call to be passing judgment on me. Like I said, the evensong bells was ringing. I thought they was late for church. It was only later that I realized what I'd really heard. Now get out of here."

"I'm sorry, Mrs. Bilkington. You're right, I've no right to pass judgment on you." He got up as well. "Please accept my apologies." He reached in his pocket for his purse, but she held up her hand.

"I don't want any more of your money, just get out of my shop."

Hatchet realized he'd deeply offended the woman and that there was no going back. She might have wanted money for the information she had, but she'd genuinely not known the vicar was in danger. He walked out of the room and into the shop. She followed him. At the door, he stopped and turned. "Again, I'm sorry to have offended you."

She said nothing.

Hatchet stepped out into the sunny spring day.

Witherspoon buttoned his coat as he and Barnes stepped out of the offices of the Far East and India Shipping Company. The traffic on the Commercial Road was heavy, but Barnes spotted a hansom and gave a toot on his police whistle. A few moments later, they were climbing into a cab. Barnes gave the driver an address in St. John's Wood.

"It was very clever of you to think of this." Witherspoon gestured at the offices they'd just left as the cab pulled back into the traffic.

"It wasn't me that thought of it, sir. It was Mrs. Barnes. I was telling her over breakfast how frustrating it was not to be able to identify the victim, when she suggested the vicar might be from overseas." Once Barnes had suggested the idea to the inspector, it had then been decided that as they had no other clues to follow, it wouldn't hurt to check with the shipping companies to see if any priests had come in recently on one of their vessels. Armed with copies of the *Times* detailing arrivals from foreign ports, they'd started making the rounds of the shipping companies. The Far East and India line had been the fourth one they'd tried. Their vessel, the *Eastern Sun*, had arrived on Monday morning, the day before the priest's body had been discovered.

"Then thanks to your good wife for being so clever. At least now we might have a name."

"The Reverend Jasper Claypool." Barnes repeated the name they'd gotten off the passenger manifest at the shipping offices. "Now why does that sound so familiar? Let's keep our fingers crossed it's him. We've had a bit of luck on this one, sir, and that's a fact."

They'd not only found out a priest had come in on the ship, but they'd gotten his local address from the manifest and learned that the man had relatives here in the city.

"Hopefully one of his relatives ought to be able to identify the poor fellow," Witherspoon said. "That'll give us a place to start. It's very difficult to investigate a murder properly when one doesn't even know the name of the victim."

Barnes grabbed the handhold above his head as the hansom hit a particularly deep pothole. "We ought to know fairly soon, sir."

The traffic didn't get any better, and it was almost two o'clock by the time the hansom pulled up in front of number four Heather Street in St. John's Wood. The house was a three-story red-brick Georgian with a white painted door on the left-hand side of the building. There was a huge fanlight over the top of the door and freshly painted white trim around the windows.

Witherspoon and Barnes went up the short walkway, and the constable reached for the knocker. But before his fingers touched the brass, the door was flung open and a butler stuck his head out and inquired, "May I help you?"

"We'd like to see . . ." Witherspoon hesitated. He didn't actually have a name of a person.

"The master of the house," Barnes put in smoothly.

The butler raised his eyebrows. "Do you mean Mr. Christopher?"

"Is Mr. Christopher a relation of the Reverend Jasper Claypool?" the inspector asked.

The butler's eyebrows climbed even higher. "No, but Mrs. Christopher has an uncle by that name."

"May we speak to Mrs. Christopher, then?" Barnes asked. He was getting impatient.

The butler looked uncertain. "If you'll come in, I'll see if she's at home." He held open the door, and they stepped into a wide foyer with a beautiful Persian rug on the floor. Through an archway just ahead of them was a wide staircase carpeted in deep red. A huge fern in an ornate brass urn stood next to the staircase. Its twin stood on the second-floor landing which they could clearly see from where they stood.

"This isn't a social call," Barnes said to the butler. "It's a police matter. Kindly tell your mistress it's urgent that we speak with her."

The butler look faintly alarmed, but he nodded and hurried off past the staircase to a room farther down the hall. They could hear the low murmuring of voices, and a moment later, the butler reappeared. "Please follow me."

He led them into an opulently furnished drawing room. The walls were painted a pale green, green velvet drapes with gold fringe framed the tall windows, there was a parquet floor with another beautiful Persian carpet and several glorious paintings of the English countryside were on the walls. Twin cream-colored chairs were on each side of the marble fireplace, and there were also several cabinets, two occasional tables covered with Dresden figurines and a three-seater cream-colored sofa, as well as a padded satin emerald-colored settee.

A beautiful woman with red hair was sitting on the settee. She stared at them curiously out of eyes the same color as the walls. "Good day, gentlemen. My name is Hilda Christopher."

"Good day, madam," Witherspoon replied. "We're sorry to barge in on you so unexpectedly, but I'm afraid I might have some very distressing news for you."

"Distressing news? For me?" She rose to her feet, her expression confused. "I'm afraid I don't understand."

Suddenly they heard footsteps pounding down the hall, and a second later, a tall, dark-haired man burst into the room. "Hilda, what's going on? Blevins said the police were here."

"They are." She gestured toward the two men.

"I'm Carl Christopher. Why are you here? Has something happened?" He crossed the room and stood next to his wife.

"I'm Inspector Witherspoon and this is Constable Barnes. I'm afraid we might have some rather unpleasant news for your wife." He directed his attention to Mrs. Christopher. "Do you have an uncle named Jasper Claypool, and is that person a clergyman?"

Hilda Christopher looked even more confused. "Yes, but my uncle's in India."

"I'm afraid not, madam," the inspector replied. "Your uncle arrived in England two days ago. We'd like you to come with us."

"Come with you?" Carl Christopher protested. "What's this all about? Why should we come with you?"

Witherspoon hated this part of his job. "We'd like you to come with us to the morgue at St. Thomas's Hospital. We need someone to identify a gentleman who was found dead yesterday. He was wearing clerical garb and we have reason to believe he might be Jasper Claypool."

"Dead? Do you mean he's had a stroke or a seizure of some kind?" Hilda Christopher said.

Witherspoon winced inwardly. But knew he must do his duty. It was better she be told the truth in advance than see it at the morgue. "No ma'am, I'm afraid he's been murdered."

CHAPTER 4

Mrs. Goodge held the telegram in her hand and read it for the third time.

"Grandfather very ill. Can't come home yet."

Considering that she'd been the one to insist the lad go visit his grandfather in the first place, she wasn't sure if she should be pleased or annoyed. But it wasn't like the boy to miss a murder. On the other hand, he was a kindhearted sort, so if he'd arrived and the old man had whined at him to stay, he'd do just that.

She sighed and looked over at Fred, who was staring at her with a forlorn expression, as though he understood what was written on the slip of paper in her hand. "Sorry, boy, he's not comin' home just yet."

"Who's not coming home?" Mrs. Jeffries asked briskly as she stepped into the kitchen. She noticed the telegram. "Ah, I see. It's our Wiggins. So they've prevailed upon him to stay?"

"Afraid so." She pursed her lips. "Maybe I oughtn't have encouraged him to go. He didn't want to and now he's going to miss the murder."

"Of course you should have encouraged him." Mrs. Jeffries stepped over to the table and began setting out the plates that were stacked on the end. "He needs to make peace with his family, not for their sakes, but for his. Now don't you fret over it, Mrs. Goodge. You did the right thing."

The cook put the telegram in her apron pocket. "I like to think so. There may come a day when the lad will be glad he's got a family to give him aid and comfort. We'll not be here forever. I'd best get that kettle on the boil; the others will be here soon."

"I'm going to set an extra plate," Mrs. Jeffries announced as she went to the pine sideboard and opened the cupboard, "just in case Dr. Bosworth arrives in time for tea."

In the next ten minutes, the others drifted into the warm kitchen and took their usual spots at the table. Mrs. Jeffries waited till everyone had a cup of steaming tea and a thick slice of freshly baked bread before she made her announcement. "Before we begin, I want to tell you that we've heard from Wiggins. Apparently his grandfather is quite ill and he won't be coming back just yet."

"Poor Wiggins," Betsy said. "He's going to miss the murder."

"More like poor Fred." Smythe reached down and patted the animal on the head. "He's so lonely he's even doggin' *my* 'eels."

"Fred will be fine as soon as the inspector gets home," the housekeeper replied. "He'll take him right upstairs with him and then they'll go for an extra long walk."

"And probably let him sleep on his rug too," Mrs. Goodge said. "But enough of this. If no one minds, I'd like to go first. Frankly, without names, I'm workin' in the dark, so to speak. But I did find out a bit about those abandoned cottages. Oh, bother, I didn't really find out anything about the wretched things except that the gossip is they're used for nefarious purposes."

"Nefarious purposes," Hatchet repeated. "You mean by criminals?"

"No, no," Mrs. Goodge wave her hand impatiently. "The other sort of nefarious dealings. Unmarried men and women doing things they wouldn't confess to the vicar."

"I think we all understand," Mrs. Jeffries said quickly. "Did you learn anything specific?"

Mrs. Goodge shook her head in disgust. "Not yet. But as soon as I have some names, I'll track down all sorts of good gossip."

"I found out something interesting," Betsy said slowly. She wasn't sure if her information was useful or not. "One of the people in the shops told me that some of those cottages weren't let at all. The one on the end, the one they found the body in, never had any real tenants. But everyone who lived along the row knew that someone occasionally stayed there. But they never knew who it was. Only that it was a woman, because no matter how careful she was, someone would spot her going in or out."

"What did she look like?" Mrs. Goodge asked eagerly. "Did your source know?"

"No, she always wore a heavy veil when she arrived."

"How often was she there?" Mrs. Jeffries asked.

"My source wasn't sure," Betsy replied. "She said the neighbors some-times spoke of her like she was a tenant, which would imply she was there quite often, and sometimes they talked about her like she just occasionally came for a visit. She always came in at night and locked the shutters tight so no one could see inside."

"You mean someone was just using the place without permission?" Mrs. Goodge looked confused.

"That's the funny part," she replied. "This Mrs. Pangley that I was talking to said the neighbors had gone to the factory supervisor and reported what they'd seen. They were told it was none of their affair and to leave it alone."

"Did you get the name of the foreman?" Mrs. Jeffries asked. This was very intriguing.

"No, Mrs. Pangley didn't have that many details. She didn't actually live there, she was just repeating the talk she'd heard."

"How long ago was this?" Smythe asked. "I mean, how long ago was it that there was gossip about someone usin' number seven?"

"Well, she did know that everyone had to leave the cottages about ten years ago, but I didn't think to ask her how long before that the neighbors had been talking." Betsy sighed. "That was silly of me. That might be important."

"Don't fret, love," he said softly. "I wouldn't have thought to ask it either, and if it's important, we'll find it out another way."

"That's excellent, Betsy." Mrs. Jeffries nodded approvingly. Considering how little information they'd started with, they were doing quite well. "Who would like to go next?"

"If it's all the same to everyone," Hatchet said, "I do believe I've found out something interesting." He told them about his visit to the used furniture shop and his talk with Jane Bilkington. "So it sounds as if our victim knew he was being pursued," he finished. "According to Mrs. Bilkington, he was running like the devil was on his heels."

"That doesn't sound like he was just worried about bein' late to church, either," Luty added. "Poor feller. Must have been awful, an old man like him bein' chased down like that and killed."

"So he was killed around six o'clock," Mrs. Jeffries murmured. She was trying to think of how she could get this information to the inspector. "Too bad this Mrs. Bilkington didn't share this with the police."

"We'll find a way of seein' that he gets it," Luty replied. "Anyways, if that's all Hatchet's got, can I go next?"

"All that I've got?" Hatchet glared at her. "I'll have you know, madam, that learning the time of death is no small accomplishment."

"Course it ain't," Luty grinned. "But if that's all you got, I'd like the floor now. You ain't the only one who found out something useful."

Mrs. Jeffries decided to intervene. "Go ahead, Luty. Tell us what you found out."

"The archbishop says our dead vicar is from overseas. So we was right to send Smythe off down to the docks to have a snoop around the shipping offices. The murder is causin' quite a stir, what with the victim bein' a clergyman and all. So I guess the archbishop already had his minions lookin' into how they could help identify the feller. Anyways, when I got into his office, he had a list of clergymen that were supposedly comin' to England from their overseas churches."

"I don't suppose he shared the names with you?" Mrs. Jeffries asked.

"Course he didn't, but I didn't let that stop me. The list was sittin' right there on his desk—we got lucky, his secretary had just brung it to him a few minutes before I arrived. Anyways, when we was alone, I pretended to faint so that when he went to get me a glass of water, I memorized the three names on the list."

Hatchet laughed, Betsy giggled, Mrs. Jeffries smiled, Smythe chuckled and even Mrs. Goodge snickered.

"Sometimes my bein' an old woman works to our advantage." Luty grinned broadly. "Anyways, when he jumped up to get me that water, I got a good look at them names. First one was John Smithson, the second was Edgar Woodley and the third was Jasper Claypool."

"Very good, Luty. You are a clever one." Mrs. Jeffries was very pleased. "Now we've really got something to go on."

"It's too bad them names didn't have any dates with 'em." Luty shrugged.

"I don't expect that matters much," Mrs. Goodge put in. "Seems to me the archbishop probably only asked for the names of people who'd only just arrived in the country. Anyone who'd been here awhile would have been reported missing if they didn't turn up at their home or their hotel. According to the inspector, no one's reported any priests missing."

Mrs. Jeffries nodded in agreement. "That sounds logical." She turned to Smythe. "I don't suppose you came across any of those names during your inquiries today?"

"Only one of them: Jasper Claypool. He came in on the *Eastern Sun* early Monday morning. She came in from Calcutta. No one mentioned any of the other priests."

"They might have come into Southampton or Liverpool," Mrs. Goodge suggested.

"Was Claypool's luggage picked up?" Mrs. Jeffries asked.

Smythe winced. "I forgot to check. Cor blimey, I must be losin' my mind. That's important! If we've time after our meetin', I'll nip back and see if I can find out."

"Why is it so important?" Betsy frowned thoughtfully. "I don't see what difference it makes . . . oh, of course. Now I see what you're getting at. He didn't have any luggage with him when he was running through the streets, otherwise that Mrs. Bilkington would have seen it."

"Right, which means that he either had it sent somewhere else, in which case why hasn't the hotel or the boarding house where it went made inquiries as to his whereabouts. Or, he didn't take it with him when he left the ship."

"Why wouldn't he take it with him?" Mrs. Goodge asked.

"Sometimes you leave it at the shipping company," Smythe replied. "When I made my trips to Australia, I used to leave my bags down at the dock until I could find a nice lodging house. He probably wasn't sure where he was goin' to stay and didn't fancy carryin' his bags with 'im. Whatever it was, I'll make it my business to find out tomorrow."

Fred suddenly leapt up, paused for a split second and then charged toward the back door, barking as he ran.

"What's got into him?" Smythe charged after the animal.

They heard the excited sound of the dog's paws bouncing against the floor, the door opening and then a familiar voice saying, "This is a fine greeting. Hello, old fellow, I haven't seen you in ages. Looks like you're being fed very well."

"I hope that's Fred that Doctor Bosworth is talking to," Betsy giggled. "Otherwise, Smythe's nose will be out of joint."

When the two men and the animal came back into the kitchen, it was obviously the dog who'd been the focus of the good doctor's attentions. Fred was bouncing at the doctor's heels and his tail was wagging furiously.

"Good evening, Doctor," Mrs. Jeffries got to her feet. "We're so glad you decided to drop in. Do have a seat." She pointed to the empty spot they'd saved for him. Betsy was already pouring him tea, and the cook was loading his plate with bread, butter and buns.

Bosworth gave Fred one final pat on the head and sat down. "I can't stay long. I've been up for hours and I've got to get some rest. But I did want to give you a quick report on my findings. Ah, this looks wonderful." He nodded his thanks to Betsy as she handed him the tea and took a quick sip. "I won't bore you with too much detail, but it appears that our victim that was found in the chimney was a young woman."

"Any idea how old she might have been?" Mrs. Jeffries asked.

"She could be anywhere from fifteen to thirty," he replied. "At least that's what I thought when I examined her, but Dr. McCallister—he's that friend of mine I mentioned to you," he said, nodding at Mrs. Jeffries. "His opinion is that she was probably in her early twenties when death occurred."

"Does he know what he's about?" Betsy asked softly. She couldn't think how someone could become a "bone expert," but she didn't want to insult Dr. Bosworth or his colleagues. Besides, she knew she was ignorant of such matters.

Bosworth grinned. "He knows what he's about. He's been studying bones for years now and knows more about them than anyone."

"Did he have any idea of how long the bones had been up there?" Smythe asked.

"His best guess was ten years. The bones were beginning to weather from the elements. That means they've been up there a fair bit of time. Considering that the cottages were inhabited up until ten years ago, I think it's fair to assume that if someone had been living in the house, they'd have noticed a corpse in the chimney."

"But that's just it, no one was living in that particular cottage," Mrs. Jeffries said. She gave him the information Betsy had gotten from Mrs. Pangley.

His expression grew thoughtful as he listened and then shrugged. "Even if the cottage was uninhabited, if this woman was occasionally coming in and using the place, she'd have noticed the smell. I know there's a paint factory across the road and it smells awful, but you couldn't miss the scent of decomposing flesh if you were inside the cottage proper. And if you tried to light the fireplace, well," he shrugged and made a face. "Let's just say it wouldn't be very nice."

"Could the body have been up there less than ten years?" Mrs.

Jeffries wanted to clarify this point as much as possible. The entire investigation could go badly if they operated under a false assumption as to when the body had been placed in the chimney.

"That's doubtful." Bosworth gulped more tea. "As I said, the bones had begun to weather, and that does take time." He yawned widely. "Forgive me but I'm dreadfully tired. I've been on duty for over twenty-four hours straight." He rose to his feet and Fred jumped up as well. "I really must be going. Oh, there is one other thing I noticed about the corpse. She'd broken her right arm in childhood and it hadn't been set very well. It was a very old break and done well before the murder."

"Do you have any idea what killed her?" Mrs. Jeffries asked. Gracious, that was one of the most important points, and she'd almost forgotten to ask.

"There were no obvious signs of trauma on the bones." He yawned again. "But she could easily have been asphyxiated or even stabbed to death. There are a number of ways to commit murder without disturbing the bones. Poison, stabbing through soft tissue, a garrot." He stifled another yawn. "I must admit, I'm very curious as to how these two murders can possibly be connected. Do keep me informed."

Mrs. Jeffries knew she had to let the poor man go home. He was dead on his feet. "We'll do that, Doctor." She got up and followed him out of the kitchen. "Let me walk you to the door."

Inspector Witherspoon was always uncomfortable around bodies, but even more so when he was escorting some poor unfortunate to identify a loved one. He glanced over at Mr. and Mrs. Christoper and was relieved to see that they were quite calm.

Barnes pushed through the door that lead to St. Thomas's mortuary and held it open for the others.

Inside, a porter stood respectfully at attention, waiting for them. "Inspector Witherspoon? We got your message, sir. Everything is all set up in the viewing room." He turned to his left and beckoned for them to follow, leading them to a small room off a short corridor.

Witherspoon blinked as he entered. The room was unnaturally bright. Even though it was daylight, all the gas lamps had been lighted and there was a good half-dozen lit lanterns hanging from hooks along the wall. He looked at the oblong table in the center of the room. A sheet-draped body lay on top of it. "I'm afraid this isn't going to be pleasant," he said to the Christophers. They'd come just inside the door and then stopped. The inspector didn't much blame them. He didn't fancy looking at that dead body either.

"Must my wife do this?" Carl Christopher put his arm around her protectively. "Can't I identify him?"

"Did you know your wife's uncle very well?" Witherspoon asked.

"Well enough to know if it's him," Christopher replied.

"It's all right, Carl." Mrs. Christopher smiled bravely. "Let me do it. It's been years since you've seen Uncle Jasper."

"And it's been the same amount of time since you've seen him," her husband replied softly.

"Yes, I know, but he virtually raised me. So no matter how long it's been, I'll recognize him." She looked at Witherspoon and Barnes. "Is he horribly disfigured? I mean . . ."

"He was shot in the head," Barnes put in quickly. "There's a hole, but it's a small one. He's been cleaned up as much as possible. But it'll not be very nice."

"I understand." She moved away from her husband's protective embrace and stepped to the table.

Barnes went over, picked up the sheet and held it back so that she could get a good look at the deceased. "Is this your uncle?"

She gasped, bit hard on her lip and closed her eyes. Then she nodded her head affirmatively. "That's him. That's my Uncle Jasper. But who on earth would want to kill him? Who would want to harm him?"

"Are you certain, ma'am?" Barnes pressed. "It's been a long time since you've seen your uncle."

"It's him." She drew a long, jagged breath and covered her face with her hands. "Oh God, why would anyone hurt Uncle Jasper? He was such a good man."

Carl Christopher rushed over to his wife and drew her away from the table. "Oh darling, this must be dreadful for you."

"Let's go outside," Witherspoon said quickly. "Now that we know he's your uncle, unfortunately, we've a number of questions we must ask you."

Mrs. Christopher kept her hands over her face as her husband lead her out of the room. Once outside, Carl Christopher said, "My wife's had a terrible shock. Must you pester her with questions just now? Can't you ask them later?"

The inspector hesitated. The woman didn't look very well, but on the other hand, they really couldn't waste any more time. "I'm sure your wife is most dreadfully upset," he replied. "But we really must have some answers to move forward on this investigation. Perhaps we could go back to your house and you could answer some of our questions. If Mrs. Christopher isn't feeling up to it, we could come back tomorrow to speak with her."

"I'm fine, Carl," she said. "It's been a shock, but I'm capable of coherent thought." She looked at the two policemen. "I don't know what you think we can tell you. We didn't even know Uncle Jasper was in England."

"Nevertheless, we must speak with you," Witherspoon insisted.

Barnes secured two hansoms and they went back to St. John's Wood. The Christophers arrived first, so that by the time the two policemen entered the drawing room, a maid was pouring tea.

"Please sit down," Carl Christopher said, nodding toward one of the settees, "and let's get this over with."

They each took a seat and accepted a cup of tea from the maid. The cups were delicate bone china that looked like it would crack if you so much as breathed hard. Taking great care, Barnes set his tea down on an end table covered with a fringed shawl, then he whipped out his little brown notebook.

Witherspoon balanced his cup and saucer on his knee and hoped he wouldn't disgrace himself by dropping the wretched thing. "When was the last time you communicated with your uncle?"

"We had a letter from him three months ago," Mrs. Christopher replied. "He said nothing about returning to England. It was one of his usual missives, he told us all about his church doings and his congregation. That was all."

"Do you have any idea why he would have come home?" Barnes asked.

She shook her head. "None at all. He was quite happy living in India."

Witherspoon took a quick sip. "Had he been there long?"

She smiled sadly. "Almost ten years. He retired from St. Matthew's in Finsbury Park and was at loose ends. For some odd reason, he took it into his head to go out to India and take up a church there. I gather it's quite difficult for the church to find priests who are willing to work overseas."

"How old was your uncle?" Barnes asked.

She thought for a moment. "He's seventy-five."

"Perhaps he came home because he wanted to retire here."

"No. He loved India. He planned on staying there for the rest of his life. He owns property and has a wide circle of friends. Oh, dear, I expect I'll have to write to them now, let them know he's not coming back."

"And you've no idea why he came home unexpectedly," Barnes pressed.

"She's already said she hasn't," Carl Christopher snapped. "Now look, we've told you all we know. Uncle Jasper was probably killed by a robber or something."

"We doubt that, sir," the constable replied. "Most robbers don't murder their victim. Especially a victim of your uncle's advanced years. It would have been much easier simply to knock him down and take his purse instead of putting a bullet through his forehead."

Witherspoon asked, "Do either of you know anything about a cottage at number seven Dorland Place in Bermondsey?"

For a moment, neither of them spoke. Then Carl Christopher said, "That's a very odd question, Inspector. I presume you have reason for asking."

"When your uncle's body was discovered, he was holding a slip of paper in his hand that had that address on it. Do you have any idea why?"

It was Mrs. Christopher who replied. "Actually, we do know that address. Oh dear lord, what am I thinking? He doesn't know about Jasper. He and Eugenia will be so upset. Nothing like this has ever happened to our family before." She covered her face with her hands and began to weep softly.

Witherspoon winced, but Barnes looked unperturbed.

"There, there, dear." Carl Christopher put his arm around his wife and drew her close. "It's all right. I'll tell Horace and Eugenia straightaway." He looked at the policemen. "Horace Riley is my wife's cousin. He's also Jasper's nephew. His father was Uncle Jasper's half-brother. He's one of the owners of the factory across the road from those cottages you mentioned. We all are. As a matter of fact, the cottages belong to the factory as well."

"That's why the name sounded so familiar," Barnes murmured. "Claypool Manufacturing. It was written on the sign in front."

Christopher nodded. "We all own part of that factory. Including Uncle Jasper. Actually, he owns the lion's share."

Witherspoon didn't wish to upset Mrs. Christopher any further, so he wasn't sure it was wise to mention the body in the chimney.

"Could you give us Mr. Horace Riley's address, sir?" Barnes asked.

"We've found a body in the chimney of one of those cottages, and we're hoping that he, or perhaps even one of you, could shed a bit of light on it."

Smythe glanced at the clock on the sideboard. "It's not gone five yet. If I 'urry, I can make it to that shippin' office before it closes and see if Claypool's luggage is still there."

Mrs. Jeffries got up as well. "While you're there, see if you can find out from one of the clerks if there is a London address for the man. That would at least give us a start tomorrow morning."

He nodded and turned to Betsy. "Walk me to the door, love."

"All right," she replied cheerfully. "Then I've got to finish dusting upstairs. I want to have plenty of time tomorrow to get out and about."

"Smythe's errand will give the rest of us time to get things caught up around here," Mrs. Jeffries said. They were a very efficient lot, but when they had a murder, they were always a bit pressed to get their household chores done properly.

Smythe and Betsy walked down the dim back hall, and as they reached the door, Smythe drew her close for a quick kiss.

"They know what we're doing," she whispered. "But I don't care."

"Neither do they," he said as he touched her cheek. "I won't be too late, so save me some supper."

"We'll not eat until you get back," she promised.

Mrs. Jeffries met the inspector at the front door that evening. "Good evening, sir," she said brightly.

"Good evening, Mrs. Jeffries," he said, handing her his bowler. "Is there any word from our Wiggins?"

"His grandfather isn't doing very well, sir." She took his coat from him and placed it on the coat tree just under his hat. "Would you like a glass of sherry before dinner, sir?"

"That would be lovely," he sighed. "It's been a very full day." They went down the hall to the drawing room, and within moments, he was sitting in his favorite chair. Mrs. Jeffries poured him a Harvey's and then, as was their custom, poured one for herself. "How is your investigation proceeding, sir?"

"Actually, it's going quite well," he replied. He smiled proudly. "We know the name of our first victim. He's the Reverend Jasper Claypool, and apparently he's just arrived from India. We were able to track down his relations, and they identified the body."

"I must say, that was good work on your part, sir. Do tell me how you did it?"

"Thank you, Mrs. Jeffries. We were rather proud of ourselves." He told her every little detail of how he and Barnes had solved their identity problem. Then he went on to tell her of his meeting with the Christophers. She listened carefully, occasionally asking a question or making a comment.

"I must say, Mrs. Christopher was quite calm until Barnes mentioned the body in the chimney. Then she got most upset."

"Did she know who it was?"

"Oh, no no," he replied. "Nothing like that. As I said, we'd just come from identifying her uncle's body and I think that when Constable Barnes mentioned the cottages and the body, it all became a bit overwhelming for the poor woman. She'd held up rather well until that moment. But it was a rather gruesome conversation, and I'm afraid Constable Barnes did rather blurt it out in a, well, rather frightening sort of manner." He took a quick sip from his glass. "Anyway, as I was saying, it turns out that by mentioning the cottages, we did find out who owns them." He gave her the remainder of the details of his visit with the Christophers. "By the time we'd finished with the Christophers, I'd found out that Dr. Bosworth's reports on both the . . . uh . . . victims had been sent to the station. I wanted to have a look at them before I proceeded any further."

"Was there anything interesting in the reports?"

He told her essentially the same thing they'd already learned from the doctor. As usual, she listened carefully and discreetly asked question after question. By the time he was ready for his meal, she had more than enough information for them to tackle the next day.

Witherspoon ate his dinner and then took Fred for an especially long walk. Both man and dog were tired when they returned. Fred stayed close to the inspector's heels and trotted up the stairs with him. Before the inspector retired for the night he gave them instructions to wake him a bit earlier then usual. He had a very full day planned.

So did the household of Upper Edmonton Gardens, but they didn't
share that information with their dear employer.

Wiggins wasn't in the least bit hungry, but he knew if he didn't eat every
bite of the shepherds pie his Aunt Alice had given him, she'd be offended.
She was easily offended. So was the rest of the family, except for his
grandfather. No matter what he did, no matter what he said, the whole
lot of 'em wouldn't give him so much as a smile. They were a silent, sullen
bunch of people, and he bitterly regretted that he'd agreed to stay.

"What's the matter, the stew not good enough for you?" Albert asked
nastily.

"The stew's fine," he replied quickly. He picked up his spoon and
shoveled it into the bowl.

"You'll not get your fancy London food here, boy," his uncle warned.
"You'll get plain, good country cooking. Won't he, Alice?"

"Yes, sir." Wiggins wouldn't have minded plain, good country cooking, but his Aunt Alice's food was either half-raw or burnt beyond recog-
nition. Tonight's offering was a combination of both. The carrots in the
stew were almost raw while the meat had the consistency of an old shoe.
"It seems that Grandfather's feelin' a bit better today."

"You a doctor now?" Albert sneered.

"No, but his color seemed a bit better, and he was able to sit up without coughin' his lungs out."

"Eat your supper," Alice snapped. "I'm wanting to get this kitchen
cleared."

"Yes, ma'am." Wiggins looked down at his bowl and doggedly took
another bite. When he looked up, his cousin smiled at him maliciously.
Wiggins wished he were anywhere but here.

The next morning, Luty and Hatchet arrived less than ten minutes after
the inspector had gone. Mrs. Goodge and Betsy had already cleared
off the table, so everyone took their usual place.

"We've got a lot to go over this morning," Mrs. Jeffries said briskly.
"We have confirmation that the first victim was Jasper Claypool. He's
been in India for the past ten years, and according to his relatives, he'd no
plans for coming home."

"That's an interestin' bit," Luty muttered.

"Agreed," the housekeeper nodded. "But what's more interesting was the connection between Jasper Claypool and the cottage where the second corpse was found." She told them everything she'd gotten from the inspector, taking care not to leave out any detail, no matter how insignificant it might seem. More than one of their cases had been solved on seemingly insignificant details.

When she'd finished, no one said anything. But by the expressions on their faces, it was obvious they were all considering their next step.

Finally, Luty said, "It seems to me I ought to find out everything I can about the finances of the Christophers and the Rileys. If they're his relations, they might be the ones who'd benefit from his death."

"Don't you think you ought to find out if he had any money to leave them?" Hatchet said softly. "I believe most churchmen take a vow of poverty. . . ."

"That's Roman Catholics," Luty interrupted. "You can be rich as sin and be a priest in the Church of England."

"Are you sure about that, madam?" he asked skeptically.

"Archbishop of Canterbury didn't look like he was hurtin' none," she shot back. "Fellow lives in a palace. Besides, it seems to me if this here Claypool's got the cash to buy a ticket all the way from India, he probably ain't hurtin' none either. Matter of fact, I think I'll make it my business to see what I can find out about how much money he had and, more importantly, who he left it to."

"That's a wonderful idea," Mrs. Jeffries said quickly. "Finding out who directly benefits from someone's death is always a good idea."

"But if no one knew he was coming home," Betsy mused, "how could any of them have had him killed?"

"Because I, for one, am not sure that the family is as much in the dark as they profess to be." Mrs. Jeffries tapped her fingers on the tabletop. "The trip from India to England is quite a long one. Most vessels make several stops on the way. Surely, unless the gentleman was estranged from his family, he'd have let someone know he was coming home. And if he didn't, why not? I certainly think we ought to find out."

"What about the servants?" Betsy asked. "I mean, if Jasper Claypool did let someone know he was coming home, wouldn't a servant know?"

"That's an idea worth pursuing," she replied. "He'd have had to have sent a cable, and someone in one of the houses must have seen it arrive, if, indeed, he contacted anyone."

"I'll work on the Christophers," Hatchet said. "Miss Betsy, why don't you see what you can find out about the Rileys?"

Betsy nodded.

"And I'll track down where that luggage was taken," Smythe put in.

"You mean Claypool's luggage?" Mrs. Goodge looked confused.

"Oh, dear," Mrs. Jeffries smiled apologetically. "I forgot, Smythe found out quite a bit at the shipping office last evening."

He'd told Mrs. Jeffries and Betsy, of course, but not the others. "I 'ad a bit of luck when I got there," he grinned. "One of the clerks had gone home sick, so there was only one person in the office when I went inside. I've found that people talk more easily when there's no one else about, especially if it's late in the day like that and they're wantin' to go home." What he didn't tell them was that when he'd seen the clerk on his own, he'd whipped a couple of sovereigns out of his pocket and dangled them under the fellow's nose as he'd asked his questions. He'd found it was much easier that way. But he didn't want the others to know how often he paid for information. "It seems Claypool's luggage was picked up. But it was picked up by a freight company on Monday afternoon."

"Freight company?" Luty frowned. "That's odd. Why would Claypool have done that? Why not send a hansom for the luggage, or a street arab? That's what most folks would do."

"I don't know, but I'm goin' to find out," he replied. "It's just one more piece of the puzzle. We'll suss it out eventually."

Betsy frowned. "This isn't goin' to be easy, especially as we don't have Wiggins. We're spread a bit thin on this one. Who's going to keep on about the woman in the chimney? We can't forget her. We don't even know who she is."

"Don't worry, Betsy," Smythe soothed. "We'll not be forgettin' her."

He knew she was very sensitive to people who were overlooked or neglected. She'd seen members of her own family die because no one cared enough to provide even the kindness of a crust of bread or a bowl of soup. That was one of the reasons he loved her so much. She genuinely cared about those less fortunate than herself. "We'll find out who killed her and make sure she gets a decent burial."

Even if he had to pay for it himself.

CHAPTER 5

———◆◆◆———

"This is the house, sir," Constable Barnes said to Witherspoon as their hansom pulled up in front of a four-story red-brick detached house. "Number sixty-eight Canfield Lane, Hampstead. Looks fairly posh but not quite as fancy as the Christopher home." He paid off the driver and stepped down. "Let's hope Horace Riley's not gone off to work already, sir."

"It's still quite early," the inspector replied, "and if he's not here, we'll go to his office at the paint factory. At the very least, we'll be able to have a word with his wife."

They went up a short, paved walkway to the white painted front door. Barnes lifted the heavy, brass doorknocker and let it fall. A moment later, the door opened and a middle-aged woman wearing the dark dress of a housekeeper stared out at them. She raised her eyebrows at the sight of Constable Barnes. "Yes?"

"May we please speak with Mr. Horace Riley?" Witherspoon asked politely.

The housekeeper hesitated for a moment and then held the door wider. "Please come inside. I'll tell Mr. Riley you're here."

They stepped into a large foyer that was wallpapered in deep red brocade. The floor was covered with a crimson and gray patterned rug, and directly ahead of them was a mahogany staircase that wound around to the upper floors. On the wall across from the staircase there was a lamp table with a marble top, and above that, a painting of a huge bowl of colorful fruit in a gold-painted baroque frame. Two brass urns, each of them with ostrich feathers sticking out the top, flanked the sides of the table.

"This place is bright enough to make you blink," Barnes whispered.

"The house looked nice enough from the outside, but I wasn't expecting this."

"Obviously, Mr. Horace Riley is doing quite well," the inspector replied. A hallway running the length of the house ran off the far side of the staircase, and Witherspoon watched the housekeeper as she disappeared. "At least we know he's home."

"Yes, let's just hope he's able to shed some light on this case, sir," Barnes replied. "If you don't mind my saying so, sir. It's a real baffler. It's not often that we get two bodies on the same case."

"If it *is* the same case," Witherspoon murmured.

"It must be sir," Barnes said. "It would be too much of a coincidence that a dead man would be holding an address in his hand for a house with a body stuck in the chimney. Coincidences do happen, sir, but not like that."

"I rather agree." The inspector sighed silently. He wasn't at all sure he was going to solve this one. If that second body hadn't been stuck in that ruddy chimney, the first murder could have been classified as a simple robbery gone wrong. It happened that way sometimes, the victim shouted or tried to run off or even fought back, which would cause the robber to panic and fire his weapon. It happened that way sometimes—not often, but sometimes. Then Witherspoon caught himself. He mustn't think like this. These victims deserved justice. It didn't matter how hard the cases were going to be, he must do his best to bring their killers to trial. "Coincidences like that simply don't happen."

The housekeeper returned and motioned for them to follow her. "This way, please. Mr. Riley will see you in his study."

She led them down the hall and into a room with heavy rust-colored drapes on the windows, dark paneling along the walls and an amazing number of tables, tallboys, bookcases and cabinets, all of which seemed to have an equally amazing number of figurines, knickknacks, vases, candleholders and china bowls on top or inside of them.

A man of younger middle age with stringy brown hair sat behind a huge desk next to the fireplace. He stared at them over the top of his spectacles. He didn't get up. "I'm Horace Riley. My housekeeper says you want to speak to me. Why?"

"I'm Inspector Gerald Witherspoon and this is Constable Barnes. We'd like to ask you a few questions about your uncle, Jasper Claypool." From the corner of his eye, he saw Barnes take out his little brown notebook.

Riley drew back in surprise. "My uncle. What on earth has my uncle to do with the police?"

"Mr. Riley, I take it you haven't been in communication with your cousin, Mrs. Christopher." Witherspoon found it odd that Carl Christopher hadn't sent him a message. He'd said he would inform the family. But then again, perhaps he hadn't really wanted to take care of such a grim business.

"I haven't seen Hilda since Christmas. Now what's all this about?" He gestured toward two straight-backed chairs in front of his desk. "Please sit."

They did as he requested. Witherspoon decided to be as tactful as possible, but he had the impression that Horace Riley wasn't going to become unduly emotional about the death of his relation. "I'm afraid your uncle is dead. He was murdered two days ago. Your cousin and her husband identified the body."

Horace's jaw dropped. "Uncle Jasper dead? But he's in India. How could someone kill him if he's in India? I don't understand this. I don't understand this at all."

"Do you know if your uncle had any enemies?" Barnes asked quickly. He watched Riley carefully.

"Enemies? Why would he have enemies? He was a priest. He never harmed anyone. Good Lord, he spent his life in service to his church. Where did it happen?"

Witherspoon gave him the barest facts about the case. He didn't want to give too much away. One never knew with family—they could act dreadfully upset about the departed while at the very same time hiding the fact that they'd helped dispatch the poor victim into the next world! "Did you know your uncle was coming to England?"

Riley shook his head. "No. I had a letter from Uncle Jasper last month. He never mentioned coming home."

"May we see the letter?" Witherspoon asked. He'd no idea why he thought this important, but he did.

"Why?" Riley looked perplexed. "It was simply his monthly duty letter. He said nothing of importance in it."

"He wrote you every month?" Barnes asked. He made a note to remind the inspector that the Christophers apparently didn't hear from their uncle as regularly as Horace Riley. They hadn't heard from Claypool in three months, or so they claimed.

"Like clockwork," he replied. "I receive them the first week of every month."

"You say you got one last month," Witherspoon said. "It's now the fifth of April. Did you get this month's letter?"

Riley's mouth opened in surprise. "Gracious, that's right. I haven't received one to date. I should have noticed . . ." He opened the drawer on the side of his desk, reached inside and pulled out an envelope. "Here's his letter from March. You can read it if you like. But it won't help you. He simply natters on and on about his congregation and the weather and some very dull old family matters."

The door to the study opened and a woman wearing a beautifully fitted sapphire-blue jacket, and matching veiled hat and gloves stepped inside. Though not a great beauty, she was nonetheless quite pretty and a good fifteen years younger than Horace Riley.

She stared at the two policemen and then at Riley. "Horace? What on earth is going on? I was just on my way out to go shopping when Mrs. Staggers told me the police were here."

Horace got to his feet. "My dear. I'm afraid we've some bad news. Uncle Jasper's dead." He turned to the policemen. "This is my wife, Mrs. Riley."

Witherspoon and Barnes had both risen when she'd entered the room. They nodded politely at the introduction.

"I'm sorry for your loss, madam," the inspector said.

"Thank you," she murmured. She looked at her husband, her expression confused. "I still don't understand why the police are here. Uncle Jasper's in India. He's in some little village outside of Calcutta. Is that why they've come, because something happened to Uncle Jasper in India? Did the bishop send them?"

"No ma'am, the bishop has nothing to do with our being here," Barnes said quickly. "Your uncle was murdered, and it didn't happen in India. It happened at St. Paul's Church over on Dock Street."

Smythe wasn't having any luck at all. He'd tried every freight company within two miles of the West India docks and hadn't come up with anything. He sighed as he stepped outside the offices of Winklers Freight Forwarding and stared glumly at the heavy traffic. What was he to do next? It was past noon, and he had the feeling that whoever had picked up that luggage hadn't been a local company. Which meant there were dozens of firms from all over the greater London area that could have done it. He wasn't sure why Claypool's baggage was important, but he knew it was. A vendor pushing a fruit cart trundled past and almost collided with a boardman advertising a pantomine. "Watch it, mate," the vendor shouted.

"You watch it," the boardman shouted back. "You don't own the ruddy streets."

Smythe deftly moved around the skirmish and headed across the road. He wasn't going to waste more time. He was going to see an expert on information. He hailed a hansom. "The Dirty Duck. It's a pub down by the river—"

"I know where it is, mate," the driver called back.

It took less than ten minutes before the cab pulled up in front of The Dirty Duck Pub. Smythe paid off the driver and then pulled out his pocket watch. He was in luck; there was still a good half hour before closing.

He stepped inside and paused for a moment to let his eyes adjust to the dim light. The air was a pungent combination of beer, gin, unwashed bodies and smoke from the fire. The pub catered to dock workers, day laborers, food vendors and all manner of working people from the great commercial area of the docks. It was also the unofficial office of one Blimpey Groggins, ex-thief and purveyor of information to most anyone who'd cross his palm with silver.

"Over here, Smythe." Blimpey's voice rose above the din of the crowded pub.

Smythe spotted him at a table by the fireplace. Blimpey's companion, an elderly man dressed in an old-fashioned top hat, got up and went to the bar as Smythe made his way to Blimpey's table.

"Nice to see ya, Smythe." Blimpey was a short, round, middle-aged man with ginger-colored hair and a ruddy complexion. He was dressed in his usual brown-and-white checked coat, a white shirt that had seen better days and a brown porkpie hat. Around his neck he wore a long, red scarf. He nodded at the seat across from him. "Have a sit down and rest your feet."

"Thanks." Smythe sat. " 'Ow are ya?"

"In good order, my fine fellow, in good order. The plans for the nuptials are proceeding nicely." Blimpey grinned broadly. Smythe had given

Blimpey some advice that had helped him work up the courage to ask his Nell, a woman who was a few years younger than himself, for her hand in marriage. She'd agreed, and they had a June wedding planned. "How are the plans for your own wedding coming along?"

Smythe shrugged. "We're in no 'urry. But we're thinkin' of a June wedding as well." He wasn't going to admit to Blimpey that it was going to be June of the following year. "Anyways, I need some information from you."

He laughed. "You always do, mate. What is it this time?" Blimpey had started his career as a small-time housebreaker and thief. But when he'd realized that his phenomenal memory, coupled with a vast network of information sources, could provide him with a rather large income without the attendant risks one ran as a thief, he'd changed his course and not looked back. As a purveyor of information to all sorts of people, including, it was whispered, the Foreign Secretary, Blimpey was honorable, honest and very reliable. He was also careful in who he worked for, and wouldn't pass on information to anyone planning grievous bodily harm to another human being—unless, of course, he was of the opinion that said human being deserved grievous bodily harm.

Smythe thought for a moment. Now that he was here, he might as well get Blimpey to find out as much as possible. He could well afford the man's services. "There's a couple of things I'd like you to look into. Let me get us some drinks." He waved at the barmaid and held up two fingers. "Two pints, please," he called. Then he turned his attention back to his companion. "You might 'ave a bit of a problem trackin' this down, but I want to know the name of the freight company that picked up some luggage from the Far East and India line. It came in on the *Eastern Sun* this past Monday. More importantly, I want to know where they took the luggage."

Blimpey raised his eyebrows but said nothing as the barmaid brought their drinks. He waited till she'd moved out of earshot before he said, "That's goin' to cost you a bob or two, *and* I'll need a few more details."

Smythe told him as much as he felt Blimpey needed to know, mentioning only the victim's name and not the fact that he'd been murdered.

"Jasper Claypool?" Blimpey repeated the dead man's name. "He's that one who were murdered the other day and propped up outside St. Paul's over on Dock Street."

"How'd you find out about it?" Smythe asked. "His body was only identified yesterday afternoon."

"It's my business to know about things like that," Blimpey replied modestly. "I've got sources all over town, includin' the hospital morgues and the police stations. It pays to know who's died or been nicked."

"Cor blimey, no wonder you know everything that's goin' on in this town."

"And I'll tell you somethin' for free, 'cause I owe you a favor," Blimpey said earnestly. "Claypool wasn't killed so he could be robbed. It weren't none of our local villains that did him."

"You know that for a fact?" Smythe took a sip of beer.

"Wouldn't say it if I didn't know it," he replied. "I put my people on it as soon as I heard a priest had been killed. Don't hold with murderin' children, women or parsons."

Smythe was grateful. "Thanks, I appreciate you tellin' me."

"So what else do you want me to find out about the Reverend Claypool?" Blimpey asked.

"Anything you can," Smythe replied. "He arrived in England from India at six A.M. on the morning he was murdered. But he wasn't killed till six that night. So what did he do for that twelve hours?"

"Something that got him killed, apparently."

"And I want you to get me some names of the other passengers who were on the vessel with him. Preferably, people who he spent some time with."

Blimpey nodded and finished off his beer. "This is goin' to cost you an awful lot."

Smythe shrugged. "I can afford your rates providin' you give me something worth havin'."

"Don't be daft. I always give you your money's worth," Blimpey grinned. "Anything else you want?"

Smythe considered it for a minute. He was tempted to tell Blimpey about the body in the chimney, but the truth was, the fellow probably already knew. Besides, if he came up with too much information about both cases, the others would really get their collective noses out of joint. "This'll be all for now. But there might be something later." He got to his feet, pulled a half-sovereign out of his pocket and tossed it to Blimpey. "Make sure the barmaid gets some of this."

"Right, mate," Blimpey caught it easily. "One thing I like about you,

Smythe. You're always generous with your coin. Give us a day or two and then nip back here in the afternoon. I ought to have something for you by then."

Betsy stood in front of the tobacconist's window and pretended to read a sign advertising a lecture on the fascinating subject of mesmerism, but she was really keeping an eye on the middle-aged woman who'd just gone into the shop. She was hoping her quarry was the Riley housekeeper.

She'd spent half the morning keeping an eye on the Riley house in Canfield Lane, hoping a servant or even a tradesman would come out so she'd have some chance at finding something out. But the only activity she'd seen was Inspector Witherspoon and Constable Barnes going inside. Then, just when she was about to give up, this woman had come out carrying a shopping basket.

She'd been following her now for a good hour. They'd traversed the length of the High Street, and Betsy had watched her go to the grocer's, the fishmonger's and the baker's. But she was of two minds about approaching the housekeeper. Betsy had noticed the woman didn't smile very often, not at the shopkeepers and certainly not at any other pedestrians on the busy street.

Betsy wished she'd been able to find a footman or a maid. She'd found that the lower the servant was in the household pecking order, the looser their tongues. But the hours were passing quickly, her feet were hurting and she'd not found out a blooming thing. The door of the tobacconist's opened and her prey stepped outside. The woman moved directly ahead, crossing the road and nimbly dodging hansoms, wagons and omnibuses before making it safely to the other side.

Betsy was right after her. The housekeeper turned onto a side street and was now moving very fast. Betsy quickened her pace, keeping sight of the woman as she weaved in and out amongst the heavy foot traffic. Finally, after a good five minutes, Betsy saw her quarry stop and then enter a building. When Betsy came abreast of the place, she saw it was a pub.

She went in after her. The light was dim, the air reeked of stale beer and the place was crowded with people.

Betsy stood on tiptoe and looked around. She spotted the woman standing at the far end of the bar, a glass of gin in her hand. As it was nearly closing time, Betsy knew that if she wanted to make contact, she'd best be quick about it. She pushed her way through the crowded room and squeezed in next to the woman. "Crowded in 'ere, isn't it?" she said conversationally.

"It's a pub and the drink's cheap. Of course it's crowded," the woman replied. She didn't look at Betsy.

"Can I buy you another one?" Betsy asked. She signaled to the barman, who promptly ignored her.

The woman slowly turned and stared at Betsy, her expression suspicious. "Why would you want to buy me a drink?"

Betsy's mind worked furiously. She'd come up with and discarded several different stories since walking into the pub, but all of them sounded silly. "I want some information," she said bluntly, "and I'm willing to pay for it by buying you as much gin as you can drink."

Because of Smythe, she had more than enough coins in her pocket to buy a few drinks. He was adamant that she not to leave the house without plenty of money for a hansom home or any other kind of trouble that might come her way.

"Information about what?" The woman's eyes were still suspicious, but she also looked curious.

"Your employer," Betsy replied. She waved at the barman again, and this time, he ambled toward her. "So will you talk to me, or do I have to go elsewhere?"

"I'll have another gin," she smiled slyly.

"Two gins, please," Betsy told the barman. She wasn't much of a drinker herself—the truth was, she couldn't stand the stuff. It brought back too many bad memories from when she was a child and living in the East End. But she'd choke a few sips down if it would get this woman talking. "I'm Betsy," she said to her companion.

"I'm Lilly Staggers. So what do you want to know about my employer?"

"You do work for Horace Riley?" Betsy nodded her thanks to the barman as he put their drinks down on the counter.

"And Mrs. Riley." Lilly grinned and took a long, slow sip of her gin.

"Aren't you curious as to why I'm asking?"

"Not in the least," Lilly shrugged. "I don't care. If talking about them will do them harm in any way, that's fine by me. She's probably going to sack me as soon as she finds another housekeeper. Goes through staff at a fairly good clip, she does. Anyway, what do you want to know?"

Betsy wasn't shocked. Many domestic servants loathed their employers.

But generally, they didn't share their opinions with strangers. Obviously, Lilly Staggers didn't care, though. Yet now that she was here, she wasn't quite sure what to ask. "Uh, were both the Rileys at home around six in the evening this past Monday night?"

"Monday night?" She frowned thoughtfully. "As a matter of fact, they weren't. Mr. Riley didn't come in until seven forty-five, and Mrs. Riley came home a few minutes later."

"Was that the time they both generally arrive home?" Betsy asked.

"Oh, no. Mr. Riley is usually home for his dinner by six every evening, and Mrs. Riley is almost always there, if you get my meaning. The only time we ever have a moment's peace from the woman is when she's out shopping. But ever since her husband's put his foot down about her spending, she's always at home, always hanging over your shoulder, always looking to catch us out doing something wrong . . . honestly, she's a terror, she is." She paused long enough to take another quick drink of her gin. "That's why I remember them being out so late that night. It was nice and peaceful for a few hours that day."

"Do you know where they were?"

"She'd not tell the likes of us her business," Lilly replied.

"So you've no idea where she went?" Betsy pressed.

"No."

"What time did she leave the house that afternoon?"

"Around one o'clock. I remember that because she stuck her head in the drawing room as I was measuring for the new curtains and told me she was going out." Lilly laughed. "At the time, I thought perhaps she'd sweet-talked that old fool she's married to into reopening some of her accounts."

Betsy took a sip of her gin and tried not to make a face. "Had anything unusual happened that day?"

"Unusual? Nah . . . don't think so . . . wait a minute." Her words slurred slightly as she spoke. "I tell a lie, something did happen. We got a telegram. That's right. It came at eleven o'clock and I remember Mrs. Riley was in the study with the door closed so I couldn't give it to her right away. We're not allowed to disturb her when she's got the door closed. So she didn't see it till she came out for lunch."

"Did she read it right away?"

"She read it all right," Lilly snickered. "Turned dead white, she did. Didn't even bother to eat the lunch that cook had made. Just went upstairs, changed her clothes and then went off. Didn't come home till that evening."

Betsy wasn't sure what to make of this. "Do you know what she did with the telegram?"

Lilly finished her drink and shrugged. "Don't know. Probably tossed it away." She was staring at Betsy's unfinished drink. "You don't really like that, do you?"

Betsy pushed the glass toward her. "Help yourself. But, uh, don't you have to go back to work?"

"Should be back there now." Lilly snatched up Betsy's glass and drained the contents in a single gulp. "But I'll come up with some story to keep the old bitch at bay. Truth is, she can't afford to sack me until she's got someone else. Mr. Riley said he wasn't paying the agency's rates anymore, so she's got to find someone on her own, and that'll take her ages."

Betsy suddenly thought of something. "Was Mr. Riley surprised when he got home Monday evening and she was still out?"

"Time, people. Drink up," the barman announced.

She thought about it for a moment. "Not really. Come to think of it, when he came in that evening, he didn't ask about her at all." She burped softly and stepped back. "Well, dear, it's been lovely, but I've got to run. The silly cow isn't the smartest pig at the trough, but even she can read a clock." She headed for the door, moving easily through the thinning crowd.

Betsy dashed after her. "Won't she notice the . . . gin . . . I mean . . . the smell?" She couldn't think of a polite way to ask the question. But she didn't want the woman to lose her position. Now that she'd asked her questions, she felt a bit guilty about plying the woman with alcohol.

Lilly reached the door and pulled it open. "Don't worry about me, love. She's got no nose. She could be standing in a privy and if she had a blindfold on, she wouldn't know where she was." She stepped out into the street. "Oh, there's one other thing about that day. When she did get home, she and Mr. Riley went into the study and had a right old dustup. They was tryin' hard to keep their voices down, but I could hear them going at it like two cats tossed in a barley sack." She started up the road.

Betsy hurried after her. "Do you have any idea what they were fighting over?"

"Like I said, they was keepin' their voices down. But I did hear Mrs. Riley say that if he had botched it up, she'd take care of it herself." She increased her pace.

"Thanks for talking to me," Betsy said. "Getting information hasn't ever been this easy for me."

"Glad to be of help." She gave Betsy a sly, sideways glance. "Truth to tell, girl, I figured you for one of Eric's girls. Blighter's been trying to get control of the factory for two years now, and I reckoned he sent you along to find out the lay of the land. Mind you, I don't care. He's always been decent to me, better than that one I work for."

"Eric who?" Betsy dodged around a couple of ladies walking arm and arm. Keeping up with Lilly was proving harder than expected.

"Eric Riley, Horace Riley's half-brother." She started moving even faster. Betsy was almost running to keep up.

Lilly halted briefly at the corner and then started across the road, neatly dodging the traffic. Betsy charged after her. She cleared the wheels of a hansom by inches but managed to stay on Lilly's heels. "How could Eric get control of the factory?"

"His uncle's back from India," Lilly called over her shoulder. "Eric's been trying to get the old fellow to turn control of his share of the firm over to him. Oh bother, I really can't talk anymore. I've got to get back. I don't want to make her too angry. If she has one of her tantrums, she just might sack me on the spot." With that, she took off at a run down the street.

"Well, blast a Spaniard," Betsy muttered as she watched the woman disappear. "Trust me to spend my time asking all the wrong questions."

Mrs. Goodge set a plate of treacle tarts on the table and then picked up the teapot. "Don't be shy now, Letty. You help yourself," she told her guest as she poured out the tea.

Letty Sommerville was a woman well into her middle years. She had a round face, brown eyes and a generous mouth. She was dressed in a brown bombazine dress that was only fitting as she was a housekeeper and she wore her graying brown hair tucked neatly up in a tidy bun. "Thank you, Mrs. Goodge," she replied as she reached for a tart. "These look wonderful. But then again, you always were a good baker."

Mrs. Goodge laughed and took the chair across from her. "I've always enjoyed baking much more than cooking." She stared at her old colleague. The two women had once worked together in the same house. Only then Letty Sommerville had been a downstairs maid. "I was a bit surprised to see you when I opened the door this morning."

"I hope you didn't mind my coming by," Letty replied. "But I happened to run into Maisie Daniels, and she mentioned you were working for a policeman. Of course after I'd chatted with her, I had to come along and talk to you myself. Especially as I happen to work just around the corner from Heather Street. That's where the Christophers live, and they've had them a murder in their very household! Can you imagine it?" She snorted delicately. "Back in our day it wouldn't have done at all. People didn't work for houses where murder was done, did they?"

"Well, I expect it happened a bit more often than we'd like to think," Mrs. Goodge replied. She was racking her brain, frantically trying to remember the conversations she'd had with Maisie. She remembered inviting Maisie for tea on one of their earlier cases, but for the life of her she couldn't recall what case it was or what she had actually said to her old friend. How much had she given away about their activities? Gracious, did the whole town know they helped their inspector on his cases?

Letty grinned. "Of course it did. I always wondered about old Mrs. Claxton's fall down those back stairs when we worked at Claxton Hall. But back in our younger days, no one had the nerve to suggest that the young master's gambling debts gave him a good reason for helping his grandmother to go meet her maker."

"Do you really think he pushed her?" Mrs. Goodge had already left Claxton Hall when the "accident" had occurred, but she'd heard the gossip.

"Everett Claxton was no good." She shrugged. "He was quite capable of pushing that poor old woman down them awful stairs. But if he did, he was careful and he didn't do it in front of anyone. But I didn't come here to talk about old news, I come to tell you what I know about Carl and Hilda Christopher. Mind you, I don't think they had anything to do with Jasper Claypool's death. Jasper Claypool helped raise Hilda and her sister. I don't think she or her sister will inherit very much. Not that it'll make any difference to Hilda Christopher—the only thing she's ever spoken about wanting was his collection of rare books."

"Are they valuable?"

"Probably. But not valuable enough for her to have wanted her uncle dead."

"Maybe the other sister wanted him dead?" Mrs. Goodge said the first thing that popped into her head.

"Edith's not even in London. She's off on the continent doing who knows what and having a high old time, she is. She was the scandal of that family before she left. I think she's one of the reasons the Reverend Claypool went off to India, probably hoped to set an example for the girl. Not that it did much good—Edith left town within a day or two of her uncle's sailing. I daresay the rest of the family was relieved. No, it seems to me your inspector shouldn't be wasting his time looking at the Christophers. I can't imagine that they had anything to do with Reverend Claypool's murder."

"How do you know all this?" Mrs. Goodge interrupted. She couldn't believe her ears. They were in deep, deep trouble. The entire town apparently knew what they were up to.

Letty blinked in surprise. "How do I know?" she repeated. "Oh, that's easy. I've told you, I work just around the corner from the Christophers. I have tea every week with their housekeeper, Mrs. Nimitz. She doesn't care all that much for her employers, but she's well paid and they keep enough staff that her work isn't too difficult. Mind you, she's always complaining that they work her to death, but if you ask me, she's a bit of a whiner. Anyway, as I was sayin', you ought to have your inspector take a look at Horace Riley or his half-brother, Eric. They are the ones that'll get a good bit of what the Reverend Claypool had in this old world, and from what I hear, they both need it."

"And I take it the good reverend had quite a lot?" Mrs. Goodge interjected. Oh Lord, what on earth were they going to do? She simply couldn't think of a way out of this mess. She could hardly tell Letty to shut up, that she wasn't interested. But the more she spoke, the more obvious it was that she was fishing for information.

"He had plenty." Letty took a quick sip of her tea. "Mind you, I think he was going to leave it all to Edith and Hilda. He was very close to them both. They're so identical he was one of the few people who could tell them apart. But then there was pressure put on him by others in the family not to leave his nephews out of his will. Horace is the general manager of the factory, and it's common knowledge he wants his uncle's share of it for himself. Eric works for Horace, but the two of them don't get on, even though they're half-brothers. Why, Horace Riley only hired Eric because the reverend forced him to do it before he went off to India."

"Really." Mrs. Goodge could barely take in what the woman was saying, she was still so upset by the realization that all her efforts to be subtle about her investigations over the years had been for naught. Everyone could see right through her.

"Of course." Letty reached for another tart. "Both the Rileys have very big plans, at least that's what I've heard. They want to sell off all the adjacent property to the factory and put the capital back into the business."

Mrs. Goodge got a hold of herself. Worrying that everyone knew about their activities wasn't going to stop her from doing her duty, but there were a few things she did want to make clear. "Uh, Letty, I'm not sure what Maisie said to you, but I don't really have that much interest in the inspector's investigations."

Letty stared at her blankly. "The inspector's investigations? What on earth are you on about? I only mentioned your inspector to be polite."

"But . . ."

"The only thing Maisie said about you was that you loved a good gossip."

Mrs. Goodge's jaw dropped. "She said I was a gossip!"

"Oh yes," Letty grinned widely. "And that was just fine with me. I like a good natter myself. Now, where was I?"

"It's most unfortunate that Mrs. Riley got so upset," Inspector Witherspoon said. "I'd have liked to have asked her a few more questions."

"We can always go back, sir," Barnes assured him. "I'd like to have a word with their staff . . . you know, confirm that both of them were home on Monday evening."

"Do you think they're lying?" Witherspoon kept a lookout for a passing hansom.

"I'm not sure, sir," Barnes replied. "But their answers sounded almost as if they'd rehearsed them in advance. I think there's a cab stand around the corner."

"Good." The inspector started for the intersection. "I can never tell if someone's lying. But if they are, we'll find out. We really should get over to the factory and try to have a word with Mr. Eric Riley before it gets too late today."

"We can have another look at those cottages while we're there,"

Barnes agreed. As they rounded the corner a hansom was discharging a fare, and the constable waved it over.

Witherspoon frowned as he climbed aboard. "I do wish we had more information on the chimney corpse. What if those two deaths don't have anything to do with one another?"

"The Claypool factory on Dorland Place in Bermondsey," Barnes told the driver as he swung in next to the inspector. "Not to worry, sir. We'll get it solved one way or another. I'm sure they are connected. As you pointed out, corpses don't stuff themselves in a chimney. Someone went to a lot of trouble to hide that body up there, and I'm sure it's the same someone that put a bullet through that poor vicar's head."

"Yes, er . . . well, that's the assumption we're working under, so to speak." He couldn't recall pointing anything out, but that happened to him quite frequently. He no longer worried about all the intelligent things he said that he couldn't remember. "What did you think of Horace Riley?"

"I think he's worried," Barnes said bluntly. "As I said, sir, I want to have a word with his staff. I think he's hiding something about his movements on the day his uncle was killed. When we asked him what time he'd come home from the factory on the day Claypool died, he was a bit too ready with the answer."

"I agree. If he really was home by half past four, as he claims, someone in the household other than his wife should be able to vouch for it."

"Maybe Mr. Eric Riley will be able to give us some additional information." Barnes grinned. "Matter of fact, I have a feeling we'll get an earful from him."

"Why is that?" Witherspoon asked curiously.

"Because, sir. I was watching Horace Riley very carefully when he mentioned his brother, and if I'm not mistaken, I don't think he likes him very much. Every time he said Eric's name, his hand clenched into a fist."

CHAPTER 6

Luty glared at the three men sitting on the other side of the long mahogany table. "All I'm asking for is an itty, bitty favor," she said. "It's not like I'm wantin' you to bust into Westminster Cathedral and steal the gold plate." She thumped her parasol on the carpeted floor for emphasis.

None of them so much as blinked. They were used to her tantrums. Herndon Rutherford, Thomas Finch and Josiah Williams had been her solicitors for over thirty years. Rutherford, a tall man with a long face, gray hair and a perpetually disapproving expression, spoke first. "Madam, it's not that we don't wish to accommodate you, it's that what you're asking us to do is quite difficult."

"I don't see why. This feller's already dead," Luty exclaimed. "Before too long, his will is gonna be a matter of public record. Nellie's whiskers, they publish that kind of information in the *Times*." Blasted lawyers. Why wouldn't they just do what she told them to do and stop giving her so much trouble? Generally, she got her information through other, less rigid, sources. But she'd been in a hurry to find out who was going to benefit the most from Jasper Claypool's death.

"That's correct, madam," Thomas Finch agreed, "but only after the estate's been through probate and all the other necessary legal steps." He was a short, rotund, balding man with brown eyes and a perpetually worried expression.

"Oh, forget I asked," she snorted. "I'll find out what I need to know myself." She started to get up.

"Now, now, madam," Josiah Williams, the youngest of the three, waved her back into her chair. "Let's not be hasty, here. I'm quite sure we can get this information for you, it's simply going to take us a day or two."

"A day or two," Herndon snapped. He glared at his associate. "I don't think we'll be able to get it at all. We have no business snooping about in this deceased person's business."

"But I already told ya, Claypool's dead. He ain't goin' to give a tinker's damn about whether or not we find out who his heirs might be."

"Reverend Claypool's attitude isn't relevant." Herndon's frown deepened. "Our firm has a reputation for discretion, and I intend to see that we keep it."

"Can you tell us, madam, why you want this information?" Josiah asked softly. Despite the fact that she was an American, he'd always liked her more than their other clients.

Luty shrugged. "I need it for a friend." She was sure that she'd made a mistake. She should have known better than to come here for her snooping. "I don't have any more time to waste with you all. Since ya can't help me, I'll be on my way." She got up, shot them one last frown and started for the door. "I ought to fire the bunch of you," she muttered.

"But then you'd just end up hiring us back," Herndon replied. "We're the best, and whether you'll admit it or not, you're actually quite fond of us."

Luty snorted and thumped her parasol on the floor again. What he said was true. She did like them, even if they were a bunch of nervous nellies.

"Let me walk you to the door, madam." Josiah Williams hurried after her.

As she went into the outer office, she waved at the grinning clerks. They waved back. Luty was a favorite amongst the staff.

"Let me get that for you, madam," Josiah reached past her for the handle to the front door. "If you'll give me a day or so," he said softly, "I'll get that information for you."

Luty stared at him. "You think you can?"

"I'm fairly certain I can find out something," he replied. He shot a quick look over his shoulder to make sure neither of his partners had followed him out. "As you pointed out, the man is dead, so it's just a matter of time until the contents of the will are a matter of public record. I'll stop around to see you as soon as I know one way or the other."

She grinned broadly. "Thanks, Josiah, you're the only one of the bunch with a sense of adventure."

"I'm not sure that's a good attribute for a solicitor," he replied, but he was smiling as he said it.

Witherspoon wrinkled his nose as the clerk led him and Barnes down a long corridor toward the offices. The air had an acrid, chemical smell that wasn't very pleasant. As a matter of fact, it made his eyes water. He wondered how the people who worked here could stand it, and then assumed they must be used to it.

"It's just in here, sir." The clerk opened a door and ushered them into a large office with two young men sitting opposite one another at desks. Both of them had open ledgers in front of them. At the far end of the room was a door leading to an office, and opposite that, on the other wall, was another office. The clerk turned to his left and popped his head into the nearest office. "The police are here to see you, Mr. Riley." He turned to the two policemen. "Go on inside."

A tall, thin man who looked to be in his mid thirties rose to his feet. He had dark brown hair, deep-set brown eyes and a fine-featured face. "Hello, I'm Eric Riley. I've been expecting you. Please make yourselves comfortable." He gestured at the empty chairs in front of the desk.

"Thank you. I'm Inspector Gerald Witherspoon and this is Constable Barnes." They each took a chair, and Riley sat back down behind his cluttered desk.

"We've come to ask you a few questions about your uncle, Jasper Claypool," Witherspoon said.

Eric sighed sadly. "Horace told me what happened. I can't fathom it. No one even knew Uncle Jasper was coming home. Who would want to kill him?"

"That's what we're going to find out," Witherspoon replied. "When was the last time you had any communication with your uncle?"

"Let me see," he stroked his chin. "I'm not really certain. We didn't correspond regularly. But I did send him the occasional letter, and he always replied. I received a letter from him at Christmas."

"Did he mention that he was thinking of coming back to England?" Barnes asked.

"No, he wrote about his congregation and how he wished they'd more money as the church roof needed repair and the hymnals needed replacing.

That sort of thing." Eric leaned back in his seat. "He mentioned a few mundane family matters."

"What kind of family matters?" the constable pressed.

Eric's dark eyebrows shot up. "I don't really think it's of any consequence. It was just the musings of an elderly man. He wished my brother and I were closer, he wished we'd all spent more time together when we had the chance; he wished that my cousins, Hilda and Edith, were closer. He was getting on in years, Constable, and frankly, I think he was getting a bit maudlin. But he never said a word about coming to England."

"Where were you on Monday evening?" Witherspoon asked.

Eric looked surprised. "Where was I? I was here, Inspector. I worked late that evening. I was going over some invoices."

"Can anyone verify your whereabouts?"

He shook his head. "I'm afraid not. My clerks leave at half past five, and the night watchman doesn't come on duty until eight. I saw no one, Inspector. But I assure you, I often work late here on my own."

"Was your uncle one of the owners of this concern?" Witherspoon waved his hand about, indicating the factory. He already knew the answer, but he wanted to hear what Riley had to say and, more importantly, how he said it.

"He owns half an interest," Eric replied. "But he controls more than that, and of course, it isn't just the factory. There's a good bit of adjacent property."

"What do you mean, he controls more than his share?" Witherspoon asked.

"He owns half an interest. The other half is divided up into four shares. Horace and I each inherited a share when our father died, and each of the twins inherited their shares when their mother died."

Barnes looked up from his notebook. "What's the other sister's name?"

"Edith Durant. Their mother was Uncle Jasper's sister, Elizabeth Claypool Durant. For what it's worth, Horace and I have control of our shares, but Uncle Jasper controls the twins' share. So even though he only owns half, for all intents and purposes, he's a majority shareholder in the concern. But he wasn't interested in running a business. He was a clergyman, a servant of his church."

"So he had no interest in the factory at all?" Barnes pressed.

"None whatsoever," Eric replied. "He never interfered. He left the day-to-day running of the business to Horace and myself."

"Then can you explain, sir, why in his letter to Mr. Horace Riley, he asked for a full report on the company's profits and losses?"

Eric frowned and shook his head. "A full report? But he's not due for a report until the end of the year."

"Nevertheless, he asked Horace Riley for a report in his last letter. Mr. Riley showed us the letter," Witherspoon replied.

"I've no idea why he'd want to know such a thing, Inspector," Eric replied slowly. "It certainly isn't like him. He's shown no interest in the factory whatsoever for the past ten years. We only send him an annual report out of courtesy. I'm sure he never reads it."

"Well, he apparently was developing an interest," the inspector said softly.

"Did you ever visit the cottages across the road?" Barnes asked.

"Of course, they're part of the property. Horace and I both have had occasion to examine them. But I've no idea who that corpse you found up the chimney could possibly be. Those houses haven't been inhabited for years."

"Do you have the names of the last tenants?" Barnes asked. "We'd like to interview them."

Witherspoon had no idea what he ought to ask next. He was profoundly grateful the constable was taking such an active part in the inquiry. It gave him a chance to think. But no matter how hard he thought about the matter, between the dead vicar and the corpse in the chimney, he was completely confused. What he needed was a nice long chat with Mrs. Jeffries. She was so very helpful in helping him to sort all the bits and pieces out correctly.

"I've already had my clerk make up a list," Eric replied. "Good luck finding these people. It's been ten years. Most of them have probably moved on."

The inspector suddenly thought of a good question. "Why weren't the cottages torn down when they were deemed unsafe?"

"We wanted to do just that," Eric replied, "but my uncle wouldn't let us . . ." His voice faltered as he spoke. "Oh my God, I've only just realized. It was Uncle Jasper who wouldn't let us tear the wretched things down. He wouldn't hear of it. He kept putting it off, saying that we couldn't stand the expense."

Barnes looked at the inspector. He could tell by his expression that both of them were thinking along the same lines. "So it was your Uncle Jasper who refused to let them be torn down? Are you certain of that?" the constable asked.

"Absolutely," Eric replied. "I remember it very well. We met with Jasper only hours before he boarded the ship because he kept putting off making a decision. But he was in a foul mood that day, which was very unusual for him. He'd just had a terrific row with Edith, and that had upset him. She was always his favorite. Horace told Uncle Jasper he was going to get an estimate for a tear-down price from a local firm, and Jasper had a fit. He told us to board the cottages up and leave them alone. He was adamant about it. We were both rather stunned."

"For a man who didn't take any interest in the running of the business, Reverend Claypool certainly seemed to have strong opinions about the cottages," Witherspoon pointed out softly.

"He was occasionally a bit eccentric," Eric replied. His voice had a defensive edge to it. "After all, he took it into his head to go out to India at the age of sixty-five."

"From the way the ground has shifted, it doesn't look like those cottages will ever be safe," Barnes said. "Do you have any idea why your uncle wanted them left alone?"

"He didn't say."

"Did anyone ever ask him?" Witherspoon asked. It seemed to him a perfectly reasonable question.

"Horace wrote him a number of times about the issue," he replied. "But Horace never saw fit to confide our uncle's reasons to me. At that time, I'd just started here and was a lowly office clerk." He smiled bitterly. "Unlike my dear brother, I actually had to work my way up in the family business."

Witherspoon was as confused as ever, but that didn't stop him from forging ahead. "But you owned equal shares in the company."

"Yes, but Uncle Jasper had appointed Horace the general manager. You've got to understand my position, Inspector. I was very much the odd man out. My mother didn't come from money. Her people were in trade. She was our father's second wife and not overly popular with the rest of the Claypool-Riley clan. Horace was very put out when I was born." He gave a short bark of a laugh. "Our family isn't in land, sir. No primogeniture. When my parents died, our father's fortune was split between Horace and I. But there wasn't a lot of cash, just his share of the factory and some shares of stock."

"I don't suppose you know who's going to inherit your Uncle Jasper's estate?" Witherspoon asked.

Eric laughed. "All of us, I expect. Uncle Jasper was always very fair in his dealings with the nieces and nephews. Not that cousin Hilda needs anything from this place. Their father was very rich. When he died, she inherited his estate outright."

"What about the other girl?" Witherspoon asked.

"Edith was the second born of the twins." Eric shrugged. "She inherited some of the money, but the bulk of it went to Hilda as the eldest. Their father was very old-fashioned, he didn't believe in splitting up the family money. Besides, Edith had already shown herself to be a good deal more independent than their father thought proper. I expect he thought that Hilda, who was always the sensible one, would take care of her sister."

"And has she?" the constable queried.

Again, Eric laughed. "Edith is the last person to need taking care of, Constable. She's . . . how can I say this without being indelicate? . . . I suppose the kindest thing one can say is that she is an adventuress, or perhaps a better word would be courtesan. She never lacks for male companionship. The family never speaks of it, but I do believe that she's been seen cavorting about Brighton with the heir apparent."

It took a moment before Witherspoon understood. "Oh, dear," he murmured. "Then I expect she doesn't know her uncle has been murdered."

"I don't expect she'd much care," Eric replied with a sad smile. "As I told you, the last time she and Uncle Jasper had any contact was just before he left for India. They had a fierce row over how she was living her life. She was involved with a married man at the time. Horace later told me that Uncle Jasper told Edith he never wanted to see her again. It must have broken his heart, too." He sighed and looked away briefly. "Poor Uncle Jasper. I hope he was happy in India. Frankly, we were all amazed at how long he lasted out there. We fully expected the place to kill him."

"Apparently it was coming home that killed him, sir," Barnes said.

"I've got you a sherry already poured, sir," Mrs. Jeffries said as she took the inspector's bowler from him. "Dinner will be a bit tardy, sir. The butcher's delivery didn't get here until quite late this afternoon." The truth was, she wanted to hear what he'd learned that day. She'd already decided that a case this complex was going to require all of her mental agility and listening skills.

Witherspoon slipped off his coat. "That's quite all right, Mrs. Jeffries. I could do with a drink. It has been a very difficult day."

They went into the sitting room and took their usual places. Mrs. Jeffries picked up her sherry from the table. "I take it the investigation isn't going very well?"

He sighed and took a sip. "That's just it. I don't really know. I feel we've learned an awful lot, but I'm not terribly certain that everything I've learned has anything to do with the case. For instance, we went along and had a chat with Horace Riley—he's Jasper Claypool's nephew." He told her everything about his visit to the Riley household. "And of course, I felt a bit odd reading his private letter from his uncle, but then again, he did offer to let me see it, and this is a murder investigation."

"What did the letter say?" she asked.

"Not much, really. Just the usual sort of thing one would expect an elderly vicar to be concerned about. His church in India needed new hymnals and pews, and there was never enough money to do anything properly. He was distressed by the lack of converts but he found the local people wonderfully kind. You know, that sort of thing, grousing about the lack of support from the church here in England."

She nodded. "I see. So the letter was all about his life in India?"

"Not completely," Witherspoon frowned. "At the very end he did mention that he wished the family was closer to one another."

"Did he mean closer physically or emotionally?"

"It wasn't really clear." The inspector pushed his glasses up his nose. "It could have been either."

"So perhaps he was hinting that he might be thinking about coming home," Mrs. Jeffries suggested. "Which would mean that perhaps Horace Riley wasn't completely surprised by the news that his uncle had come to England." She had no idea what the letter might or might not have meant. She was merely throwing suggestions out to see if any of them might be useful. It never hurt to stir the waters a bit and then have look after the silt had settled.

"I hadn't thought of it like that," he replied. "But I suppose it's possible." He took another sip from his glass and then told her about the rest of his day. "I must say the smell around that factory is rather appalling. I can't think how the workers stand it."

"I expect they're used to it," she replied. "And of course, a smelly factory would be quite handy if one wanted to stuff a body down a chimney. It would hide the scent of decompostion."

"Is that how you think they did it?"

"I should think it would be much easier to put the body in the chimney from the top rather than trying to stuff it up from the inside of the fireplace. That would have taken enormous strength."

"But putting a body down a chimney would require you going outside and carrying the corpse up to the roof. That's very risky for the murderer. He might have been seen."

"True, but perhaps he did it late at night."

"Yes, I suppose that's possible. It certainly sounds like a logical way of going about such an activity."

"I don't suppose you're any closer to identifying who the victim was?" she asked softly.

"Not really. Only that it was a young woman." He sighed. "We've got a list of former tenants, and we'll be interviewing anyone who lived there that we can find. Perhaps that'll shed some light on this mystery. I've also got some lads going over old missing-persons reports for young women. But frankly, that's not going to be worthwhile. There are a lot of young women that go missing, and we've no real idea how long that body was up in the fireplace. Dr. Bosworth's expert could only give us a guess. Mind you, he was fairly sure she'd been up there close to ten years. Something about the bones being weathered . . ."

"You spoke to Dr. Bosworth today?" she interrupted.

"We stopped by to see him after we'd seen Eric Riley," Witherspoon replied.

Her mind worked furiously. She had dozens of ideas and questions racing around her head, yet she knew she needed more facts before any of them could coalesce into a useful pattern.

They discussed the case for another fifteen minutes, and then Betsy popped her head into the drawing room and announced that dinner was served. Mrs. Jeffries accompanied him to the dining room, got him settled and then went down to the kitchen for her own dinner.

The kitchen was empty except for Fred. Dutifully, he wagged his tail, but Mrs. Jeffries could see his heart wasn't in it. "I'm sorry, boy, but he's still not back." She leaned down and patted his head. "I'm sure Wiggins misses you as much as you miss him. I'll tell you what, let's give it a few minutes, give the inspector time to eat his meal and then I'll take you upstairs. He'll take you for a nice, long walk."

"You chatting with Fred now?" Mrs. Goodge inquired as she came into the kitchen. She was carrying a sack of flour.

"Just trying to cheer the poor thing up a bit," she replied with a laugh. "Where is everyone?"

"Smythe's gone to Howards to give the horses a bit of a run, and Betsy's upstairs putting the linens away so she won't have to bother with it tomorrow. It's going to be a busy day for all of us."

"That's true. Do you think we ought to send Wiggins another telegram?" She still felt very guilty about the lad not being there.

"He knows we've a murder," the cook replied. "So his not being here is more or less his own doing. He's not bein' held against his will."

"That's true." She smiled suddenly. "I guess he needs to take care of his relations with his family. They've obviously become important to him."

"Get out of my way." Albert shoved Wiggins to one side and hurried over to the kitchen table. He gave him one last glare and then sat down and picked up his fork. "Well, what are you waitin' for?"

"Hurry up, Wiggins, it's time for supper," Aunt Alice snapped. "I don't want to spend all evening cleanin' up this kitchen because you can't get to the table when it's ready."

"I was reading the newspaper to Grandfather," Wiggins replied. He sat down at the table. But he had no appetite. His relatives were a sorry lot. They obviously hated him. He wished he'd not given the old man his promise to stay. But what was done was done, and now he was stuck here with this miserable bunch. Cor blimey, but having a conscience could sometimes cost a body a lot. He'd give anything to be back in London with the others.

"Don't know why he needs to have the paper read to him," Uncle Peter muttered. "Seems to me he ought to be resting, not getting all upset over the troubles of the world."

"He asked me to read it to 'im," Wiggins said defensively. "And I didn't want to leave 'im till he'd fallen asleep. I was only tryin' to be nice."

"We know what you're trying to do," Albert sneered.

"What does that mean?" Wiggins was more mystified than angry.

"You two stop it now, and eat your dinner," Aunt Alice warned. "These walls are thin, and sound carries right up them stairs. You don't want to be waking Grandfather now that he's finally asleep."

But Albert apparently wasn't in the least concerned with waking his grandfather. "You show up here and all of a sudden the rest of us is no more to the old man than a tick in a feather bed," he snapped at Wiggins. "Let me tell you something, no matter how much you lick his boots, you'll not be getting your hands on this farm. It'll belong to us when he goes. You understand. Us. Not you."

"I don't want the ruddy farm," Wiggins cried.

"Hush, Albert," his father warned. He shot Wiggins a quick glance. "He didn't mean that. He's just a bit jealous is all."

"I'm not jealous of him," Albert snapped as he glared at Wiggins. He shoved his chair back and got to his feet. "I don't know why everyone's fallin' all over themselves to be nice to him. He's nothing more than the blow-by of a whore who wasn't even properly married to his father."

Wiggins jumped to his feet with such force his chair went flying. "You take that back," he shouted, his hand balled into a fist. "My mother was no . . ." He couldn't bring himself to repeat the word.

"Whore," Albert laughed maliciously. "That's the word you're looking for, boy. She was a whore. A common, street-walking whore who got her hooks into poor Uncle Douglas. . . ."

Wiggins swung at his cousin, wincing as his fist connected solidly with Albert's jaw.

Luty and Hatchet arrived only moments after the inspector had left for the day. "I've got a lot to do today," Luty announced as she plopped down at the table, "so let's get this meetin' started."

"Really, madam." Hatchet took the seat next to his employer. "I do believe we can take the time to be properly civil to one another."

"I wasn't sayin' we ought to be rude." Luty put her muff on the table and pulled off her green kid gloves. "I was sayin' we ought to be fast. We're a man short on this investigation, and in case you've forgotten, we've got us two murders."

"We're well aware of that, madam," Hatchet replied. He smiled at the others. "But I, for one, am of the opinion that the two killings are connected."

"So am I," Mrs. Jeffries added. "We just have to keep moving right along. Luty is correct, though. We do have a lot to cover this morning. If you don't mind, I'll start." She told them everything she'd learned from the inspector, taking care not to leave out even the smallest detail.

"I heard about Eric Riley," Betsy said as soon as the housekeeper had finished. She told them about her meeting with Horace Riley's housekeeper. She left out the bit about the pub. "She was ever so chatty. I think she hates Mrs. Riley."

"And she was sure about the time that Mrs. Riley left the house?" Mrs. Jeffries pressed. This might be very important information.

"She was, and equally sure of the fact that both the Rileys were late getting home that night," Betsy said. "I only wish I could get my hands on that telegram."

"Maybe we can," Smythe said softly. "If she tossed it in the dustbin, it might still be on the property." He looked at Mrs. Jeffries. "How important do you think that telegram is?"

"Very," she replied. "The contents of it sent Mrs. Riley out of the house without her lunch. It might have been from Jasper Claypool."

"Should I try my hand at getting hold of it?" Smythe grinned. "I've a feelin' I can lay my hands on it."

"It might not still be there," Betsy warned. "She could have tossed it in the cooking fire."

"But she might not 'ave," he countered. "At least let me give it a try."

"Mind you don't take any risks, Smythe," Betsy said lightly. "It'd be ever so awkward if you got arrested for trespassing." She tried to keep her tone casual, but he could tell she was concerned.

"Don't worry, I'll be careful." He patted her arm under the table. "I'll nip over and suss out the lay of the land this afternoon."

Betsy opened her mouth to speak, to tell them the best part about her meeting with Lilly Staggers, but before she could get the words out, Mrs. Jeffries started asking questions.

"Were you able to find out where Claypool's luggage had been taken?" she asked the coachman.

He shook his head. "I'm still working on that one. But I did find out that Claypool's murder wasn't a robbery. At least that's the word down at the docks. I got that from a good source, too, so we can rule out a common by-your-leave bit of pilferin' gone bad."

"That's useful to know," Mrs. Jeffries said thoughtfully.

"And I'm workin' on getting names of the other passengers from the ship," Smythe added. "But that might take some doin'."

"Perhaps I might be of some assistance there," Hatchet offered. "I could stop by the Far East and India offices and see what I can learn.

Frankly, it would be a relief. I'm not having a lot of luck finding out any information about the Christophers."

Smythe could hardly admit he'd already hired Blimpey to find out that information. "Thanks, that would be good. Save me a bit of trouble."

"It'll be my pleasure," Hatchet replied.

"I take it that means you've not had much success," Mrs. Jeffries queried. She knew how easy it was to get downhearted when one hadn't found out anything useful.

Hatchet sighed. "Not really. The best I managed was a bit of old gossip about Mrs. Christopher's sister. Apparently, Edith Durant was a complete hoyden, and the only person who had any influence on her whatsoever was her Uncle Jasper."

"So you weren't able to find out if either of the Christophers had an alibi for the time of the murder?" Mrs. Jeffries pressed. They already knew about Edith. What they needed now was to know where everyone was at the time of the killing.

He shook his head in disgust. "The only person from the household that I managed to speak to was the tweeny, and she didn't know much of anything." He didn't reveal that he'd paid the girl for the pathetic scraps of information he'd brought to their table. "Unfortunately, the day of the murder there were painters at the Christopher house, so most of the staff had gone out. She knew nothing."

"But she knew gossip about Mrs. Christopher's sister," Betsy said. "Someone she hadn't even met."

"Oh, but she had," Hatchet replied quickly. "Apparently, Edith Durant visits her sister every once in a while. She never stays more than a few hours, but the girl had glimpsed her going in and out."

"We do need more information about the Christophers," Mrs. Jeffries said. She looked at Betsy. "Do you think you could have a chat with the local shopkeepers tomorrow?"

"Of course, but before I nip along there, you might want me to go back over to the Riley neighborhood. I wasn't finished with my telling. I found out something else today, something that I think is important. Apparently, Eric Riley knew his Uncle Jasper was back in London."

"How'd you find that out?" Luty exclaimed.

"From Lilly Staggers, she sort of yelled that at me as she was leaving today and I didn't have a chance to ask her any more questions. I've got to talk to her again."

"Of course you must," Mrs. Jeffries replied. She was annoyed with herself for not realizing that they'd all interrupted the girl. "And from now on, if you're not finished with your report, do let us know."

"That's right, we don't want to be interruptin' you," Mrs. Goodge added.

"It's all right," she smiled sheepishly. "I should have said something."

"How are you going to speak to her again?" Mrs. Goodge asked. "Won't she get suspicious?"

Betsy shrugged. She'd planned on watching the pub tomorrow about the same time she'd been there today. To her way of thinking, the Riley housekeeper probably visited that pub quite often. "Not really. She's got quite a loose tongue on her."

"It seems to me that if the housekeeper to the Horace Rileys told Betsy that Eric Riley knew Claypool was coming home, then it stands to reason that there's a good chance the Horace Rileys knew he was comin' home too," Luty said.

She was a bit put out. Suddenly, learning the contents of Jasper Claypool's will didn't seem so very important. But then again, you never knew what was going to be useful or not till you got to the very end.

"I don't see the connection, madam," Hatchet said.

"I do," Mrs. Goodge put in. "Unless she had reason to be talking to Eric Riley directly, Lilly Staggers probably overheard Horace Riley telling Mrs. Riley he'd heard from Eric that Claypool was coming home."

"I think she did have reason to talk to him herself," Betsy said quickly. "She seemed to know quite a bit about Eric Riley and his doings. Did I mention that she said he'd been trying to get control of the factory for the past two years?"

"You didn't mention that time period," Mrs. Jeffries said softly.

"I'm sorry, I'm getting sloppy." Annoyed with herself, she shook her head. "Now that I think of it, her whole manner was odd."

"Odd how?" Smythe pressed.

"Odd in the sense that she seemed almost like she was used to reporting on her employer." Betsy smiled sheepishly. "I'm sorry. I'm being silly, it's just now when I look back on the whole thing, that's the impression I get."

"Your impressions are usually very reliable," Mrs. Jeffries said. "Do you think it's possible that Lilly Staggers is working for Eric Riley? Reporting to him about the Horace Rileys?"

"I think it's worth finding out," Betsy replied. She wondered how much gin it was going to take to get Lilly to tell her the whole truth. "And I think I know how I can do it."

"You be careful now, lass," Smythe warned. "This woman may not take kindly to bein' accused of spyin' on her employers."

"I'll be very subtle." Betsy gave him a reassuring smile. "I'll be talking to her in broad daylight in front of dozens of people. I don't think she'll try and box my ears if I offend her."

"Can I have my turn now?" Mrs. Goodge asked. At the housekeeper's nod, she told them about her visit from her old colleague, Letty Sommerville. "So you see, according to Letty, both the Riley men have big plans for that factory and all the property."

"And apparently, Hilda Christopher gets nothing but a set of old books." Luty shook her head in disgust.

"Not necessarily," Mrs. Goodge replied. "Letty only gets gossip thirdhand, it might not be worth much. Besides, from what Mrs. Jeffries told us, it looks like Hilda's the only one who doesn't need an inheritance from her uncle."

"It would be interesting to find out about Edith Durant's financial situation," Hatchet mused.

"It would be nice if we just knew her address," Mrs. Jeffries added. "But apparently, not even the police have been able to find out where the woman lives."

"I expect once the word that he's dead gets spread, she'll come out into the open," Luty said. "Especially if she's one of his heirs. Money always brings relatives sniffing around, even ones that don't need it."

"But he'd told her he never wanted to see her again," Betsy reminded her. "So maybe she doesn't care if he's dead."

"He told her that ten years ago," Smythe said. "They might 'ave made it up by now." He looked at Mrs. Jeffries. "Do you want me to try and find out where she lives?"

"Do you think you can?"

"I'll give it a try," he replied. He'd get Blimpey on it right away. If anyone could find the woman, he could.

"From everything we've learned about Jasper Claypool," Mrs. Goodge muttered, "it seems he liked his nieces a good deal more than his nephews. Who knows what he actually left them in his will?"

Luty stifled a grin. By this time tomorrow, she certainly hoped she'd know who got what from the good reverend.

CHAPTER 7

Mrs. Jeffries yawned as she went down the stairs the next morning. She hadn't slept well. There were far too many bits and pieces swirling about in her head for a restful night's sleep. She hurried into the kitchen and came to an abrupt halt.

Wiggins and Mrs. Goodge were sitting at the table. There was a plate of buttered bread, a dish of orange marmalade and a pot of tea in front of them. Fred was sitting next to the footman's chair with his head resting against the lad.

"Gracious, Wiggins, this is a bit of a surprise. Welcome back."

"I took the early train back this mornin'. I'm glad to be 'ome, Mrs. Jeffries," he replied. "It feels like I've been gone for ages instead of a few days."

"How is your grandfather?" She got a cup down from the sideboard.

"Well, uh, he's about the same," Wiggins said softly. He reached down and patted Fred. "I come 'ome because I 'ad a bit of a dustup with my cousin."

"He punched him in the nose," Mrs. Goodge added. "But from what Wiggins told me, the boy had it coming. He kept insulting Wiggins's mother."

"I see," Mrs. Jeffries poured herself a cup of tea. "If that's the case, then it's just as well you came back."

Wiggins looked up and met her eyes. "I tried to get along with my relations, Mrs. Jeffries, I really did. But the only one who wanted me there was my grandfather. My aunt and uncle weren't very nice either, and my cousin hated me from the second he picked me up at the station.

But I didn't mind all that, I tried to keep out of everyone's way. But when Albert started callin' my mam them horrible names . . ."

"You don't have to explain to us." She held up her hand. "We know you, Wiggins. You're a good and gentle soul. If you resorted to fisticuffs, I'm sure it was for a good reason." She couldn't believe she'd just said those words. She'd always believed violence never really solved anything, but then again, perhaps she'd been wrong. Perhaps there were moments when a good smack in the nose was just what the situation needed. "So, now that you're back with us, let's get you out there working on our case. We've been stretched a bit thin on this one."

"Course you 'ave," he nodded eagerly, relieved not to have to keep talking about his dreadful relatives. "What with there being two corpses and all."

"I've told him everything we've learned so far," Mrs. Goodge said as she got up and walked over to the counter. She lifted the cloth off her bread bowl and frowned at the dough. "I don't think I've left anything out. Oh blast, this is takin' its sweet time to raise. Perhaps it's just as well I've got those hot cross buns in the larder. I've got my sources coming along this morning."

Wiggins looked at Mrs. Jeffries. "What do you want me to be doin'?"

She thought for a moment. "I think we need someone working on the Bermondsey murder. We haven't really covered that neighborhood very well. Betsy had a bit of luck a couple of days ago, but since then, we've found out very little. I think it would be a good idea if you went around there and had a go at it."

He took a quick sip from his cup. "Exactly what should I be askin'? From what Mrs. Goodge told me, no one has any idea who that poor woman was."

"Just find out what you can about either the woman or the cottage," she replied, "and follow your nose. You've always been quite good at that sort of thing."

The housekeeper was referring to their last case, when Wiggins had taken the initiative and ended up stealing a piece of evidence.

"Just see that you don't get in trouble," Mrs. Goodge warned. "And be back here by teatime for our meeting."

"I'll be 'ere," he said. "Where's the others? Out and about already?"

"Everyone had an early start," the cook replied. She sat back down. "But they'll all be here this afternoon."

"What about you, Mrs. Jeffries? Are you goin' out lookin' for clues today?"

"Certainly, just as soon as I get the inspector fed his breakfast and out the front door." She pushed back from the table and got up. "I thought I'd see what I could learn about Jasper Claypool before he went to India. Claypool was at St. Matthew's Church in Finsbury Park. The family is from that area. Perhaps I'll find out something useful about either our suspects or our victim."

"I'd best get crackin', then." Wiggins finished off the last of his food and got up. "Come on, Fred, let's go see what's what."

They waited till they heard the back door slam before either of them spoke. Then Mrs. Goodge said, "He was in a terrible state when he arrived this morning. His knuckles are red from where he hit his cousin, but it's his conscience that's really hurting him. He told me he'd broken his promise to his grandfather by leaving. Apparently, the old man had got him to give his word that he'd stay until the grandfather either died or got well."

"But the old man didn't see to it that his family kept a civil tongue in their heads," Mrs. Jeffries mused. "And from the sound of it, they made our Wiggins miserable."

"They're afraid the grandfather is dying and that he's going to leave part of the family farm to Wiggins. Albert, the cousin that Wiggins smacked, accused Wiggins of licking the old man's boots to get a share of the estate."

"I don't think I like Wiggins's family much," Mrs. Jeffries said. "Perhaps it's just as well he came home."

"I hate seein' him so upset," the cook muttered.

"You think he wants to go back?"

"He wants to be right here," she replied. "But he doesn't like breaking his promise."

"Then let's hope he can find a way to make peace with his decision," Mrs. Jeffries said softly.

Constable Barnes waved a passing cab over to the side of Holland Park Road. "Where to first, sir? The Mayberrys are in Islington, and that's the closest."

"Let's give them a try," Witherspoon said as he climbed into the hansom. They had the list of the former tenants of Dorland Place they'd gotten from Eric Riley. "Let's keep our fingers crossed that someone will give us a clue to who that poor woman was."

Barnes gave the driver the address and then settled back next to the inspector. He whipped out his notebook. "If we don't learn anything useful from the Mayberrys, we got the address of a Mrs. Colfax who used to live at number three on that road. She lives in Chingford now and is quite elderly."

"Were those the only two names we were able to track down?" Witherspoon asked. As the days passed, this case was becoming more and more difficult. They had no real suspects, no motive, and one of the corpses hadn't even been identified. He was beginning to think he wasn't ever going to solve this one.

"I'm afraid so, sir," Barnes admitted morosely. "Ten years is a long time. We only got these two addresses because they'd kept in touch with the local vicar."

"I suppose it's a start. Has there been any sign of Claypool's luggage?" Witherspoon asked.

"None, sir," Barnes replied. "No one can remember what freight company picked it up, only that they had the proper documents and took it away."

"But they did confirm that it was picked up on the Monday?"

"Right, sir." Barnes scratched his chin. "Which is odd, when you think of it. If he was killed Monday evening and the luggage was picked up Monday afternoon, was he the one that sent for it, and if so, where did he have it taken?"

"I take it the bishop was no help on this problem?" Witherspoon had no idea what this missing luggage meant, but he knew it meant something.

"No, sir, he checked with Claypool's old parish and with some of his former associates and the bags weren't taken anywhere he could find."

"And they weren't taken to either of the Rileys or the Christopher home or the factory." Witherspoon shrugged. "Then where on earth did they go?"

"Maybe they were picked up by Miss Durant, sir," Barnes suggested. "She's the only one in this case we haven't spoken with."

"Do we have an address yet?"

"Not yet, sir. I was only mentioning her as a possibility. Also, sir, I've got the final reports from the lads that did the door-to-door. We've got a report from a woman who actually saw the poor man running down the street."

"Egads! You mean she saw him being chased by his killer?"

"She didn't exactly see his killer, but she did see Claypool running towards the church," Barnes said. "It was a real pea-souper that night, and all she caught was glimpses of him running through the fog. She didn't think anything of it because she thought the man was simply late to church. But she was able to pinpoint the time for us, sir. It was six o'clock."

"And she didn't see the murderer?" Witherspoon asked, his expression hopeful.

"No, sir, but she did hear another set of footsteps. But again, she took no notice. She thought it was someone late for church. That's about it, sir. No one else saw or heard anything."

For the duration of the journey, they discussed the few facts they had about the case. Barnes, who'd had a brief word with Mrs. Jeffries when he'd gotten to Upper Edmonton Gardens that morning, dropped some pertinent bits of information and a goodly number of helpful hints in the inspector's path. But he didn't think they were having the desired effect on his superior, for by the time the hansom pulled up in front of a tiny house in Islington, Barnes could tell by the his inspector's glum expression that he was still having grave doubts about the case.

"Constable, I fear this case is going to be one of those that get away from us." Witherspoon closed his eyes briefly. "We're dealing with a very clever killer."

"Not to worry, sir. We'll get the blighter." He pulled some coins out of his pocket and paid the driver. "Like you always say, sir. They always make a mistake."

"I certainly hope so," Witherspoon said fervently. "But honestly, I do admit this one has me baffled. Frankly, Constable, I'm not even certain whether we're looking for one or two murderers." He peered at the small row houses. "What's the address?"

"It's number eight." Barnes pointed to the middle of the row. The two-story brick house had dilapidated drainpipes and needed a decent paint job about the window sills. "Let's hope there's someone home."

The door opened almost as soon as the constable had finished knocking. An elderly woman wearing spectacles and a clean white apron over her brown housedress peered out at them. "Yes? What is it?"

"Are you Mrs. Mayberry?" Witherspoon asked politely.

"I am, and who might you be?"

He introduced himself and Barnes. "We'd like to come in and speak to you, if we might."

She opened the door. "Come into the parlor, then." She gestured to a room that opened off the tiny entranceway.

They entered a small sitting room containing an aged three-piece suite of an indeterminate dark color and two side tables with brown matching lamps. Antimacassars were laid neatly on the backs of the settee and chairs.

"Please sit down." Mrs. Mayberry indicated the settee. She took a seat in the chair. "Now what's this all about?"

"We'd like to talk to you about when you lived in Bermondsey," Witherspoon began.

"You mean on Dorland Place? That was ten years ago." She looked at him, her expression mystified.

"Actually, we'd like to know if you ever saw any activity at number seven. That's the one at the very end of the row."

"I know which one it is," she said. She smiled slyly. "No one lived in that one, you know."

"We understand that," Barnes said. "But just because no one lives in a place doesn't mean it doesn't get any use."

She laughed. "You can say that again. Mind you, they always tried to be crafty about it when they was using the place. But all of us knew what was goin' on."

"Uh, exactly what was going on?" Witherspoon wanted to make sure he understood her correctly.

Mrs. Mayberry shrugged. "What do you think? They was usin' it for immoral purposes, that's what."

"Immoral purposes," he repeated. "You mean for illicit assignations?"

She nodded eagerly. "Supposedly the people that owned the factory across the road, they were our landlords, you understand, they was supposed to be keeping number seven empty for their own use, but the only time it ever got used was when he was meetin' her."

"When who was meeting who?" the inspector pressed. It would be most helpful if she knew their names.

Mrs. Mayberry shrugged again. "I don't know their names. Actually, they were pretty crafty about stayin' away from pryin' eyes. But I know they used the place because sometimes you could see smoke comin' out of the chimney, and even though they'd pull the blinds, you could see light comin' from out the bottom crack."

"Did these people break into the cottage?" Barnes asked.

"They had a key," she replied. "There was never any windows broken, and the one time one of the neighbors went over to the factory to speak to them about it, they were told to mind their own business."

"So you never saw the people who were using the place?" Barnes pressed.

"Only once, I saw a woman come out late in the afternoon. She stood at the door and tried to wait until she thought it was safe before she showed her face, but I was back behind the tree across the road and she didn't see me. I saw her all right. She was a tallish woman, well dressed and posh looking if you know what I mean."

"What did she look like?" the constable asked. "Could you describe her?"

"No, she had on a veil. But she was dressed fancy and carried herself like a queen, I remember that much. I never got a look at the man, but I know there was one because my Billy was creeping around the back of the cottage when they was in there and he heard them talking."

"How often did they uh . . . use the cottage?" Witherspoon asked. Gracious, this was a very peculiar conversation.

She pushed her spectacles up her nose. "Let me see, they only really started usin' the place the last year we lived there. I don't remember how often they was actually there, but it was more than a few times. Too bad you can't speak to Mrs. Hornby, she was right next door to the place. But she died last year, had the scarlet fever, she did, and it took her in less than three days."

"Are you sure it was the same people all the time?" Barnes asked. "Or did different people use the premises?"

"It was the same ones all the time," she said.

"But how can you know for certain?" he pressed.

"Because they come in the same way each time," she insisted. "They come by hansom cab and the woman always wore a heavy veil over her face and the man had his collar pulled up high. He looked pretty silly when it was summertime. But it was always the same—they went to a great deal of trouble not to be recognized. Seems to me that casual people using the place wouldn't have taken such care, would they."

"Yes, I see your point." The inspector nodded. He wasn't sure what any of this meant, but it had to mean something. "Do you recall the last time you saw anyone at the cottage?"

"Not really," she smiled. "It was ten years ago, Inspector. I only remember about the man and woman because it was so interesting."

They asked her more questions, but it was soon obvious that she'd told them everything she could remember.

"Is there anyone else here who was in your household when you lived at Dorland Place?" Barnes asked.

She smiled sadly. "My Billy is gone for two years now, and we never had any children."

Witherspoon felt very sorry for the poor lady. She sounded very lonely. He got to his feet. "Thank you for your time, Mrs. Mayberry. You've been most helpful."

She started to get up but he waved her back to her chair. "It's all right, ma'am, we'll see ourselves out. Good day."

Mrs. Jeffries stepped out of the train station at Finsbury Park and stopped to survey her surroundings. She needed someone local to point her toward St. Matthew's Church. Across the road, she spotted a newsagent's. She slipped around a hansom cab and darted through the heavy traffic to the other side. She waited till the shop was empty before stepping inside. "Hello," she smiled at the woman behind the counter. "I'm hoping you can help me. I'm trying to find St. Matthew's Church."

"It's up the road a piece." She gestured toward the window and to her left. "It's a good fifteen minutes' walk from here."

A few moments later Mrs. Jeffries, armed with precise directions, started up the busy road. As she walked, she thought about the case. They had two bodies, two victims, but the murders might be as much as ten years apart. Then again, what if the two killings weren't even related to one another? No, she shook her head as she turned the corner, she simply didn't believe that. It would be far too much of a coincidence for the first victim to be holding an address that had a second victim up its chimney.

But then again, coincidences did happen.

She slowed her steps as the idea took root in her mind. Life was full of coincidence. What if this was one too? Then what? They'd have wasted a huge amount of time and effort trying to tie the two killings together instead of investigating them separately.

She pulled her jacket closer against the sudden cold from a gust of wind. The neighborhood had changed as she walked, going from small row houses with tiny gardens to larger homes the farther one walked from the station. A row of tall oaks lined each side of the road, and the homes were set well back from the street. Most of them had gardens with deep green lawns and beautifully tended flowerbeds.

She came to the intersection and stopped. St. Matthew's was on the corner. It was made of gray stone and set back in a churchyard that was surrounded by a low stone fence with a wrought iron gate leading to the church door. She walked up to the gate and stared at the building. It was only half past ten, so there might not be anyone in the church. Well, then, she'd wait about until someone showed up. She pushed through the gate and stepped into the yard. She was almost to the door when a voice said, "You'll not be able to get inside. They don't unlock the doors till noon."

She whirled about and saw an elderly man standing on the path. He was holding a wheelbarrow. "Are you wantin' to see the vicar?"

"Actually, I'm not certain." She smiled hesitantly. "I'm trying to locate a Reverend Jasper Claypool." Though Claypool's murder had been in the papers, she was pretending ignorance, hoping the mention of his name might get someone to talk to her. In her experience, people were always willing to pass along a bit of bad news.

He sat the wheelbarrow down and gazed at her sympathetically. "You're not a relative are you?"

"No, we were on the same ship coming back from India. I got off in Cherbourg. I arrived back in England late yesterday. Unfortunately, I've lost the address where I was supposed to meet him, but I do recall him saying he was coming up here to visit his family. I've got some contributions for his church building fund in India, and I wanted to give them to him personally."

"You must have misunderstood him, ma'am," the gardener shifted uneasily. "Reverend Claypool's got no family around here. They all left the area years ago. But that's not the worst of it, ma'am. I'm sorry to have to tell you this, but the Reverend Claypool is dead. He was murdered a few days ago near the London docks. It was in yesterday's papers."

She gasped in pretend surprise and clasped her hands together. "Oh no, who would want to kill such a nice man?"

"They don't know, ma'am. The police haven't caught anyone." He reached into his pocket and pulled out a key. "You look a bit pale, ma'am. I've a key here, so if you'd like to go inside and have a sit down, I'll unlock the doors for you."

"Thank you, I would be very grateful." She felt just a bit guilty. But she shoved the feeling aside and carried on with her plan. She wanted this man talking. He'd apparently been here for quite a while and was a good source of information. "I do feel a bit faint." She stumbled ever so slightly.

Alarmed, the gardener leapt to her side and took her arm. "Let me help you, ma'am. This 'as been a real shock to you, I can tell."

She let him lead her through the narthex and into the sanctuary. He helped her into a pew on the last row.

"Thank you," she said softly. "I simply can't believe he's gone. He was so looking forward to coming here. He was so looking forward to seeing his family. He'd missed them all so much, especially his nieces and nephews."

"I'm sure he did miss 'em, ma'am. He helped raise the twins after their parents died," the gardener said. "And it weren't no easy task, either."

"It's never easy for a single man to raise children," she murmured. She hoped she was saying the right thing to keep him talking.

"Oh, even if he'd had a wife, raising the girls all those years would have turned him gray. I'm Arthur Benning," he said. "I've been the groundsman here for twenty years."

"I'm Penelope Mortiboys," Mrs. Jeffries said. She hoped that God would forgive her for lying in his house. After all, she was trying to catch a killer, and surely that took precedence over a petty white-lie sin. "I hadn't realized that poor Reverend Claypool had spent so many years rearing his nieces."

"Oh, yes," Benning smiled broadly. "He was ever so kind to those girls. Mind you, Miss Hilda was always as good as gold and Miss Edith wasn't a bad girl, just a bit high-spirited. He was a good man, the reverend. He didn't have to be their guardian. His half-brother and his wife was quite willing to take the girls in and give 'em a proper home."

"You mean their aunt and uncle?" She wanted to make certain she got the details correct.

"Right," he frowned slightly. "Mr. and Mrs. Riley would've been quite chuffed to give the girls a home, but Reverend Claypool said it were his responsibility. He was the one named guardian in their father's will. Course, the gossip was that the only reason the Rileys offered was to get their hands on Miss Hilda's money. But I don't put much credence in that sort of talk. John Riley was a decent sort, and both of his wives was real nice women. The girls spent a lot of time at their house as they were growing up. And the Rileys didn't even make too much of a fuss when Miss Edith played that awful prank." He laughed. "I expect they was used to it. Miss Edith was always doin' something naughty, she was."

"All children play pranks," she said conversationally.

"Not like this," he said. "She leapt out the bushes waving a cloth when young Mr. Horace had all the children in the pony cart. It spooked the horse so badly he reared up like a stallion and the cart overturned. The children were tossed out onto the embankment and poor Mr. Horace ended up with a broken ankle and missed a whole school term because of it. Mr. Eric was just a toddler, and he landed on a clump of grass with just a few bruises, and Miss Hilda broke a bone or two, and, of course, Miss Edith walked away without so much as a scratch." He laughed again. "But that was generally the way of it. Miss Edith always seemed to get out of most things with no mishaps."

Mrs. Jeffries sighed sadly. "I know the reverend was hoping to reconcile with his niece. He mentioned they were estranged."

"Miss Edith's been estranged from the whole family," Arthur Benning said bluntly. "They'd left here by the time it happened, but everyone around here knew about it. Well, you couldn't expect the reverend to forgive something like that, could you?"

Mrs. Jeffries knew she had to be careful. She couldn't let on that she had no idea what he was talking about. "No, of course he couldn't. But all the same, it's a shame the way it all turned out."

"Oh, I don't know, last I heard, Miss Hilda was happily married to her Mr. Christopher and Miss Edith is off running about the continent, doin' what she wants and answerin' to no one. Mind you, I expect the way she's livin' her life probably upset the good reverend, him bein' a vicar and all."

At that moment, a man dressed in clerical garb stepped into the front of the church and peered at them from behind the baptismal font. "Arthur, is something wrong?" He advanced down the aisle toward them.

"This lady felt a bit faint, sir," he replied, gesturing at Mrs. Jeffries. "I brought her inside to have a sit down. She was lookin' for Reverend Claypool and didn't know that he'd died."

"Oh my dear lady, how very unfortunate," the vicar said kindly.

"It was a bit of a shock." She smiled and got to her feet. "But your Mr. Benning has explained everything and been most considerate. Obviously, I misunderstood Reverend Claypool. From what Mr. Benning has told me, both he and his family left this area some time ago."

"That's correct. I never met the man, but he was quite well-loved in the parish." He pulled out a pocket watch and checked the time. "Arthur, you'd best get that trimming done on the Harcourt graves. They'll be here fairly soon to pay their respects."

"Yes, sir." Arthur smiled a good-bye and nodded his head at Mrs. Jeffries.

"Thank you for your kindness," she said. Then she turned to the vicar. "It's such a shame about the poor man. Do they have any idea who killed him?"

"I'm afraid I don't know," he said. He took her elbow and began edging them down the aisle toward the door. "It's most unfortunate, but the police are quite good at catching murderers. I'm sure they'll find out who did it." He hustled her down the aisle and out the front door before she could gather her wits about her to ask more questions. "Do have a good day," he said as he hurried back inside. She stared at the closed door for a moment and then glanced around the churchyard. Arthur was nowhere in sight, and besides, she didn't want to get him in trouble by taking him away from his work any more.

She went up the path to the pavement, turned and stared at the church. On the property next to the church, there was a house made of the same kind of stone as the church. She guessed that was the vicarage. She decided there was no harm in spending a bit more time in the neighborhood. No telling what she might be able to find out.

"I'd like to have a word with the staff," Barnes said to the inspector. "Now that we know when Claypool was killed, it'll be interesting to know if Mr. and Mrs. Christopher was at home." They were seated in the Christophers' drawing room waiting for either the master or the mistress.

Witherspoon frowned slightly. "Do you suspect something?"

Barnes shrugged. "We're not learning much, sir. I keep thinking that

Claypool arrived back in London early that morning, yet he didn't die till six o'clock in the evening. Where was he all that time?"

Mrs. Christopher swept into the room. She was dressed in a fur-trimmed fawn jacket and carried a pair of gloves in her hands. "My housekeeper said you wanted to speak to me," she said softly.

"Actually, either you or your husband would do." Witherspoon rose to his feet. The constable got up as well.

"My husband is out," she replied. "So you'll have to speak with me."

"I was wondering, ma'am, if you've any idea where your uncle might have gone on the day he arrived here?"

Her eyes widened in surprise. "I'm not sure what you mean."

"I mean, he arrived in London early that morning and he didn't die until that evening. He must have been somewhere for all those hours. Mr. Horace Riley insists he wasn't at the factory or at his home, and Mr. Eric Riley says the same thing. You and your husband both say he wasn't here, so we're hoping you can give us some idea of where he might have gone."

She said nothing for a moment. "I've no idea. Perhaps he went to visit old friends."

"I doubt that, ma'am," Barnes said dryly. "There's been plenty of newspaper coverage about his death. We've asked for anyone who'd seen him to come forward and make a statement. No one has. Also, ma'am, would you mind if we had a word with your staff?"

"My staff? If you mean the servants, there'd be no point. Most of them never even met my uncle. They could tell you nothing." She pulled on one of the gloves.

"So you've no objection to our speaking to them," Barnes persisted.

"None whatsoever." She pulled on the second glove. "Now, if there's nothing else, I must be off. I've several appointments this morning."

"Actually, ma'am, there is something else. I believe you have a sister. Does she live here in London?" He knew she didn't, and from everything he'd been told, Edith Durant was a fairly delicate subject. He wanted to be as discreet as possible, but he had to ask. They couldn't find hide nor hair of the woman anywhere.

"My sister lives abroad," Hilda Christopher said coolly. "In Paris. The Metropole Hotel."

"Does she ever come to visit you?" Barnes asked.

"Not often. But she does come occasionally. We saw her last year as a matter of fact, on Boxing Day." She sighed. "Look, Inspector, Constable, my husband doesn't really welcome Edith into our home, so I generally meet her somewhere else."

"Is it possible your uncle was meeting her on the day she died?" Barnes asked softly.

Her shapely brows drew together. "I suppose it's possible. But if that's the case, then why hasn't Edith contacted you about it?"

The two policemen looked at one another.

Mrs. Christopher followed their glance, and then a puzzled expression crossed her lovely face, quickly followed by one of outrage. "Now see here, Inspector. What are you implying?"

"Absolutely nothing, Mrs. Christopher. We're merely asking very routine questions," Witherspoon said quickly.

"My sister may be a bit unconventional, sir, but I assure you, she isn't a murderess." Hilda straightened her spine. "The very idea is unthinkable."

"Does your sister own a gun?" Barnes asked softly.

"A gun." Hilda Christopher repeated the word as if she'd never heard it before. "Why on earth are you asking me that?"

"Do you own a gun, ma'am?" the inspector interjected. "As I said, our questions are merely routine. We're asking everybody." He was annoyed with himself. He'd not thought to ask Horace or Eric Riley if they owned a weapon. He made a mental note to rectify that error as soon as possible.

"I don't understand this. My uncle, who I didn't even know was in England, gets murdered, and all of a sudden, my family and I are subjected to these humiliating questions." Her voice had risen perceptibly, and her beautiful eyes filled with tears. "You have no right to come in here and make these disgusting implications."

"As I said before, ma'am," the inspector said, wishing she'd calm down, "our intention was never to imply anything untoward, we're merely trying to find your uncle's killer. You want us to find out who did it, don't you?"

"Of course I do," she cried. She clasped hands together in distress. "Of course I want you to find his killer. I loved Uncle Jasper, he was like a father to me."

The drawing room door opened and Carl Christopher charged inside. "Hilda, what on earth is wrong?" He crossed to her and drew her close, his expression concerned. "I could hear you from outside."

"I'm sorry, darling." She gestured at the two policemen. "I'm afraid I've let myself get upset. They were asking some questions about Edith. About whether or not Uncle Jasper might have met with her on the day he died. About whether or not Edith has a gun. It was most distressing, and I'm afraid I allowed myself to get terribly overwrought."

"We didn't mean to upset Mrs. Christopher," Witherspoon said quickly. "As I pointed out to her, our questions are merely routine."

"They asked me if I had a gun," Mrs. Christopher added. "And if I had any idea where Uncle Jasper might have been those hours before he died."

"We know your uncle arrived quite early that morning," Barnes said. "And we asked Mrs. Christopher if she had any idea where he might have gone."

"They also want to speak to the servants," she said.

"Of course they can speak with the staff," he said smoothly. He turned to Witherspoon. "We're not trying to be uncooperative, Inspector. We'll answer any questions you like."

"Do you own a weapon, sir?" Witherspoon asked.

"No, neither I nor my wife own a weapon of any sort."

"Does your sister-in-law own a gun?" Barnes asked.

He hesitated for a fraction of a second and then looked at his wife. "We have to tell the truth, dear."

She made a sound of distress.

"Hush, darling." He put his fingers over her lips. "We'll not do Edith any good by lying for her." Turning back to the inspector, he said, "Edith owns a small revolver. She carries it for protection, as she travels so much."

CHAPTER 8

"So what do you think of this turn of events, sir?" Barnes whispered to the inspector. They were downstairs in a small, dimly lighted sitting room, waiting for the housekeeper.

"I'm not sure," Witherspoon replied. He glanced at the partly closed door, not wanting to be overheard. "It's a bit difficult to question someone who doesn't appear to have an address. Miss Edith Durant sounds very much like an adventuress. We've no idea if she's even in England."

"But at least we know she had a gun," Barnes pointed out. He turned toward the door as they heard the sound of footsteps coming down the hall. A moment later, the door opened and a tall, austere middle-aged woman wearing a gray dress stepped into the room.

She nodded respectfully at the policemen. "Good day, I'm Irma Nimitz. Mrs. Christopher said you'd like to speak with me."

Witherspoon smiled warmly. "I'm Inspector Witherspoon and this is Constable Barnes."

"Do you mind if I sit down?" She moved toward an old, overstuffed chair on the far side of the settee. "I like to rest my feet whenever I've a chance."

"We wouldn't mind in the least," he assured her. "I believe I'll have a sit down too." He took a seat at the end of the settee closest to her. "We won't take up much of your time."

She smiled wanly. "Take as long as you like, I could use the rest. This is a big house, and frankly, there simply isn't enough staff to run it properly. But that's neither here nor there. You're not interested in our domestic arrangements."

"Er . . . uh could you tell us if anything unusual happened on this past Monday?"

"The day the old vicar was murdered," she said. "I can't think of anything."

"You didn't have any unexpected visitors or unusual messages," Barnes asked.

"Not that I know about," Mrs. Nimitz replied with a shrug. "But then again, I was out for most of the day. The painters were here doing the downstairs, and the smell was awful. We couldn't do our work so Mr. Christopher let most of us have the day out."

"The whole day?" Witherspoon asked. "That was very generous of him."

"Not really," she shrugged again. "We took the day in lieu of our normal time off for the week. It was a bit annoying, if you know what I mean. We knew the painters were scheduled to come that day, but the master hadn't told us we'd have to take our day out then. It was a trifle inconvenient. My usual day out is Wednesday, and I'd already made plans to go to see my niece in Hackney on Wednesday afternoon."

"So getting the day off was a surprise to the staff?" Witherspoon asked. He wanted to make sure he understood her correctly. That was the sort of fact that ended up being most important. Sometimes.

"Yes."

"What time did you leave the house?" Barnes leaned against the table.

"Are you going to repeat what we say back to them?" she jerked her chin upward, toward the drawing room.

"We do not tell employers what their staff say about them in the course of an investigation," Witherspoon said firmly. "Your statements are completely private unless used as evidence in a court of law."

Her expression was still skeptical.

"We don't run tellin' tales," Barnes added softly. "If we did, no one would tell us a blooming thing."

She still didn't look completely convinced, but her expression relaxed a little. "Right, then. It was a bit of an odd day. We all left fairly early. Blevins, he's the butler, had come downstairs at seven to tell me to get everyone out of the house as soon as breakfast was over. The painters arrived just after eight. As soon as the breakfast things were washed and put away, I let the kitchen girls go on. Then I went upstairs and checked that the beds were made. By the time I came downstairs, Mrs. Christopher had shooed everyone out and was pushing me to go as well."

"Mrs. Christopher was still here?" Barnes looked up from his notebook.

"Yes, both she and Mr. Christopher were still in the house. They planned to stay the day, too, despite the smell."

"They told you that?" the inspector asked.

"No, they gave the impression they were going to be going out as well. Supposedly, that was the reason she was rushing us out the door. She kept muttering they had a train to catch. That they were going to spend the day in Brighton. But I know that was a lie. I had to run back upstairs to get my coat, you see." She smiled impishly. "They thought I'd already gone. I'd left, but before I got to the corner, I'd realized it was too cold for just my shawl so I came back to get my coat. The front door was unlocked, so I slipped inside. That's when I overheard them talking. Mrs. Christopher was telling Mr. Christopher that no matter what, they were to stay here until it was finished. I just assumed she was talking about the painters."

"Why would they insist the staff leave because of the smell and then inflict it upon themselves?"

"Rich people do plenty of things that don't make sense," Mrs. Nimitz replied. "I've been in service all my life and I've seen things in other houses that would drive a saint to drink. Frankly, I was so glad for a chance to have a few hours off my feet, all I could think of was getting out of here before they changed their minds and decided they needed someone to stay here and fetch and carry for them. Knowing Mrs. Christopher as I do, she probably insisted they stay to make sure the painters did the job right. She's real particular and," she tossed a quick glance at the door, "not very trusting, if you know what I mean."

"I'm not sure I do," Witherspoon said. "Do you mean she keeps a close eye on her staff?"

The housekeeper grinned. "Not just her staff, Inspector. She keeps a pretty good eye on her husband too, especially if that sister of hers comes to town."

"Does she come very often?" Barnes asked.

"Not anymore. She used to come around a lot right after the old vicar went off to India. I know because every time she'd been here, Mr. and Mrs. Christopher would have a blazing row."

"What about?" Witherspoon asked.

"About Miss Edith bein' in the house," Mrs. Nimitz replied. "Mr. Christopher kept insisting that her reputation was so awful he didn't want the neighbors seeing her come here to visit Mrs. Christopher. Finally, Mrs. Christopher must have had enough of his carping because the last few years she's always met her sister at a hotel."

"Which hotel?" Barnes looked up from his notebook.

"The St. John's on Teesdale Lane," she replied. "It's a small but very posh place. Miss Durant stays there when she's in town."

Witherspoon was confused. "I don't understand. You said Mrs. Christopher kept a close eye on her husband when her sister was in town, yet you also said he doesn't want Miss Durant in the house? Could you explain that remark?"

Mrs. Nimitz glanced at the door. "Like a lot of men, he's a hypocrite. He's terrified the neighbors will get wind of Miss Edith and her wild ways, but at the same time, he's a yen for her himself if you know what I mean." She leaned closer and lowered her voice. "I heard that before he married Miss Hilda, Mr. Christopher was madly in love with Miss Edith. It's not just gossip, either, because I've seen Mr. Christopher at the St. John's with Edith Durant twice in the last year. Plus, a couple of times when Mrs. Christopher was out of town visiting her mother's people, he'd bring Miss Durant here late at night."

"How do you know he was with Miss Durant?" the inspector asked. "I understand the women are identical in appearance."

"They may be identical twins," Mrs. Nimitz replied. "But you can tell them apart by the way they act and the way they dress. Believe me, I can tell Miss Durant from the mistress, that's for sure."

"Quick, come inside." Luty grabbed Josiah Williams's arm and fairly drug him through her front door. "I don't want him to see us together." She pushed him toward the drawing room and through the double oak doors. She shoved him quite hard. "He's way too nosy and he'll want to know what you're doin' here."

Josiah stumbled on an exquisite Persian carpet, righted himself and then staggered toward a cream-colored overstuffed chair. For a tiny elderly lady, she was very strong. "Who don't you want to see us?"

"Hatchet," Luty said grimly. She glanced up and down the hall and then drew the doors shut. "I've got Jon on guard duty, but Hatchet's crafty, he could easily get past the boy."

Faintly alarmed, Josiah leapt to his feet. "Excuse me, madam, but are you frightened of your butler? Has he been threatening you?"

"Threatening me?" Luty repeated incredulously. She threw back her head and laughed. "Of course not, he just asks a lot of questions. Now sit down and tell me what you found out. I hope you didn't go to much trouble."

"It was actually quite easy. Uh, excuse me for asking ma'am, but you never mentioned why you needed this information." He looked at her expectantly.

Luty had a story ready. "Oh, let's just say that a long time ago, I knew the feller. He's a good man and he always dreamed of giving a big chunk of his fortune to those less fortunate than himself. Unfortunately, he's got a whole pack of relatives bending his ear about what's right and proper. I guess you could say that I want to know if he was able to leave any of his money to a particular charity that I know he supported. If he couldn't, then in his honor, I'll make the contribution for him." She watched his face as she spoke, hoping to tell by his expression if he believed her. She knew he wouldn't actually challenge her on the matter. After all, she was an important client and paid a good part of his salary. But it would be nice to know that she could be convincing.

But Josiah Williams was too good a legal man to give anything away by so much as a twitch of his nose. "I see. That's most generous of you, madam. But the fact is, Jasper Claypool's will hasn't changed in ten years. The only bequest he makes to charity is to a benevolence fund for retired clergymen. Was that by any chance the charity you thought he supported?"

"Nah," she shook her head, "I was thinkin' he'd leave a few pounds to the foundling home in Watford. But I guess he didn't. Well, Nellie's whiskers, the old fellow swore to me that he'd leave some money to them poor children." She narrowed her eyes at Josiah. "Are you sure about this?"

"Of course I'm sure," he replied stiffly. "The division of his estate hasn't changed in ten years, not since he left for India."

"But that's about the time he swore he'd leave them younguns some money," Luty insisted. "Right before he left, he told me he'd leave the bulk to his nieces and nephews but that he'd give a good ten percent to the Watford Foundling Home."

"Apparently he wasn't entirely truthful to you," Josiah retorted, "because he left his estate to his nephews, not his nieces. One of them was specifically disinherited and the other was only left his collection of rare books."

"And you're sure the will hasn't changed?" Luty pressed.

"Very sure," Josiah said. "I spoke to the clerk myself. No one at Claypool's law firm has seen or heard from him for ages. So if he was coming back to England to change his will, he didn't let his solicitors know and he'd not made any appointments to see them."

The door opened and Hatchet stuck his head inside. He pretended to look surprised. "Excuse me, madam, I didn't realize you were with your solicitor. May I remind you, madam, we are expected in Holland Park in half an hour. We really mustn't be late. I've taken the liberty of having the carriage brought around. I trust you'll be through with Mr. Williams shortly."

"Keep your collar on, Hatchet. I'll be ready to go by the time the carriage is here."

"Thank you, madam." Hatchet smiled politely and withdrew.

Luty snorted faintly and then turned back to her companion. Hatchet was already picking at her. That meant he might not have had much luck today either. "I'm real grateful to you for getting me this information."

"It was my pleasure, madam." He rose to his feet. "Would you like me to contact the Watford Foundling Home on your behalf?"

As Luty wasn't even sure such a place existed, she shook her head. "That's all right, I'll take care of it myself."

"It wouldn't be any trouble," he persisted. "I'd be happy to do it for you."

"That's kind of you, but I'd prefer to handle it myself," Luty couldn't swear to it, but it seemed his face twitched a bit, like he was trying not to laugh. "But I'm much obliged for the offer." She'd been going to ask him which niece had been disinherited, but she thought better of it. Besides, she was fairly sure she knew which one it was.

"Do let me know if I can be of further service." He smiled broadly. "Your inquiries are always so much more interesting than my usual work at the firm."

Luty stared at him suspiciously. All her lawyers knew about her close association with the Witherspoon household. Her "inquiries" had nothing to do with charity and everything to do with snooping for clues in the inspector's murder cases. She made a mental note never to ask her law-yers for help again. The old stodgy ones wouldn't give it and this one was too clever by half. "Uh, thank you, I think. Uh, you won't get in trouble with the others for helping me, will you?"

"Not at all, ma'am. You're our best client and the truth is, they're all very fond of you. Now, if you'll excuse me, I'll be on my way." He turned toward the door, and she started to get up. "Don't bother to show me out," he called over his shoulder. "I know the way. Do have a nice time at the illustrious Inspector Witherspoon's household."

Mrs. Jeffries was the last one to arrive for their afternoon meeting. She dashed into the kitchen, taking off her hat as she walked. "I'm terribly sorry to be late, but the train was held up just outside the station."

"We only just got here ourselves," Luty said.

"Wiggins has been tellin' us all about his visit to his relations," Betsy added.

"And we're glad to 'ave 'im back," Smythe interjected smoothly.

Mrs. Jeffries gave them a grateful smile, approving of the way they were making Wiggins's return to the fold less awkward. "Indeed, we told the lad we've been stretched thin on this case." She took her seat at the head of the table and reached for the teapot.

"If no one has any objection," Mrs. Goodge said. "I'd like to go first." She paused a moment and then plunged ahead. "I don't have much to report, but I did hear a bit of gossip this morning. I'm not even sure it has anything to do with our case, but it might. It seems that Horace Riley isn't overly fond of his half-brother, Eric. Supposedly, before Claypool went to India, Horace was trying to talk him into making sure that he had complete control of the factory. Seems he went out of his way to imply that young Eric was incompetent. Apparently, the lad was quite wild in his youth and had a bit of a gambling problem."

"You mean Horace Riley wanted his brother's share?" Wiggins asked. He looked disgusted.

"No, he couldn't get Eric's actual share of the property, it was left to him by their father. But as Claypool controlled both of the twins' share and owned half of the factory himself, he could easily have kept Eric Riley from having a position at the factory. That's really what Horace Riley wanted," Mrs. Goodge explained. "The reverend didn't go along with it. He had very strict views on what was fair and what wasn't. He insisted that Eric be given a position in the family firm and allowed to work his way up. Another thing I heard was that Eric has proved to be far better at business than his half-brother."

Mrs. Jeffries thought for a moment. "So Horace Riley approached his uncle before he went to India?"

"That's right," the cook nodded eagerly. "My source said they had words over it. Mind you, supposedly Horace was already upset with his uncle over the old man's refusal to let them sell off the cottages."

"But wouldn't those houses be worthless?" Betsy asked. "The ground is shifting. They're not safe to live in."

"You can fix that," Smythe said. "There's no great caverns or anything like that under London, so it probably wouldn't be that big an engineering effort to find out what's causing the cottages to shift. Believe me, that's a big piece of property sitting there doin' nothin'. Considerin' the cost of land in London, there's plenty of developers that would go to the trouble and expense of making that patch of ground safe for something or other."

"Why was Claypool so determined to hang on to them old houses?" Luty muttered.

"Maybe when we know the answer to that, we'll know who killed the poor old fella," Wiggins replied sadly.

Mrs. Jeffries glanced at the footman. He was staring morosely at the floor. Poor lad, she thought. He wasn't very happy. Well, he'd have to make peace with his decision one way or another. That wasn't a battle she or any of the others could help him with. "Would you like to go next, Wiggins? That is, if Mrs. Goodge is finished."

"I'm done," the cook assured them.

Wiggins took a deep breath. "Well, uh, actually, I didn't find out much of anything. None of the shopkeepers could remember anything about any of the former tenants of Dorland Place, and the only other person I talked to was an elderly woman who couldn't remember what day it was, let alone anything that happened years ago." He sighed. "I'm sorry. I'm not bein' very helpful, am I."

"Don't fret, lad," Smythe said quickly. "You've just got back. There's lots of times when we go out and find nothing."

"You'll do better tomorrow," Betsy insisted brightly. "You just wait. Besides, you're not the only one who didn't have any luck today. I spent hours trying to make contact with Lilly Staggers, and she didn't so much as stick her nose out the door. But I'm not letting that stop me. I'm going right back out there tomorrow and trying again." She turned her attention to the housekeeper. "I also thought it would be a good idea if I went over to Eric Riley's neighborhood and see what I can learn about him. He's the one we know the least about, and he might have had a reason for wanting his uncle dead."

"That's a good idea," Mrs. Jeffries replied. "Smythe, did you have any luck today?"

"A bit," he grinned. "My source wasn't able to tell me where Jasper Claypool's luggage went; it seems to have disappeared into thin air. But I did have a bit of luck in another area. I got the names of a couple of people who were on the ship with Jasper Claypool." He dug a piece of paper out of his pocket. "There's a Mr. Adam Spindler of number twelve Hobbs Lane in Chelmsford and a Miss Eudora Planter of Barslee Cottage in Richmond. We need to try to speak to either of these two right away. That's the only way we're goin' to find out why the vicar was returning to England unannounced."

"But he wasn't unannounced," Hatchet pointed out. "According to what Lilly Staggers told Betsy, Eric Riley knew his uncle was in town. If he knew, maybe the others did as well."

"I wasn't able to find out what was in that telegram the Rileys received on the day Claypool was killed," Smythe said quickly. "There were too many people hanging about the street when I nipped over there this morning. But I'll try again. Maybe *they* knew their uncle was coming to town too."

"Let me have a go at finding out about that telegram," Betsy insisted. "Like I said, I'm going to talk to Lilly Staggers again, and if she doesn't know anything, I'll try someone else at the Riley house. Surely someone snoops through the dustbin. And I'll try and find out if Lilly's been reporting to Eric Riley about her employers."

"I'll see what I can learn about Eric's comings and goings on the day Claypool was killed," Smythe volunteered.

"Excellent." Then Mrs. Jeffries said, "Does anyone else have anything to report?"

"I've got a bit," Luty tossed Hatchet a smug smile. He might have had a good idea, but she had some real information.

"I found out about Jasper Claypool's will. Feller hasn't changed it in ten years." She gave them the rest of the details from her meeting with

Josiah Williams. "I know it's not much, but at least we know that he wasn't at his lawyer's changin' his will before he died."

"That is useful to know," Mrs. Jeffries agreed. "Do you think you can find out if he had contacted his solicitors? Perhaps he was killed to stop him going to see them."

"My source had spoken to the clerk, and he claimed the firm hadn't heard from Claypool in ages. So that means if he was going to change his will, he hadn't mentioned it to his lawyers." She shrugged. "Anyways, that's it for me. Oh, wait a minute, I'm forgettin' something. I did find out something else. Seems that Horace Riley is in some fairly dire financial straits."

"You mean the factory isn't doing well?" Betsy asked.

"The factory is doin' just fine. They've got more orders than they can fill, and as the general manager, Horace Riley makes a good salary," Luty explained. "But according to what I heard, his missus spends it faster than he can bring it in. They've got creditors hounding them all the time. One or two of 'em are threatening him with legal action."

"So if his Uncle Jasper died and he inherited half of Claypool's estate," Smythe murmured, "that might help him out a bit."

"More than a bit," Luty replied. "I'm still workin' on finding out how the Christophers are doin' financially. But I should have a report on them by tomorrow."

"You've done very well, Luty," Mrs. Jeffries said. "If everyone else is finished, I'll go next." She paused for a moment and waited to see if anyone had additional information to contribute. But they were all looking at her expectantly. She told them about her visit to Finsbury Park and her meeting with the gardener at St. Matthew's Church. "I got the impression that Claypool wasn't just annoyed with his niece over how she lived, but over something specific in her life," she concluded. "It was really bad luck that the vicar choose that moment to interrupt us. We were having a very useful conversation. Of course, I've no idea if it has anything to do with our case."

"So far we've no idea what has to do with our case," Mrs. Goodge muttered. "But that's all by-the-by. From now on, I'm going to concentrate on learning what I can about the Christophers and the Rileys. At least they've got names and addresses."

"And I'll have a go at finding out anything I can about the Christophers," Wiggins added. "Surely in a big house like theirs, someone will know something."

"Perhaps I ought to try to learn what I can from the other passengers," Hatchet said. "Perhaps one of them will know if Claypool cabled anyone from the ship. Perhaps that's how Eric Riley learned his uncle was coming home?"

"Can you go to Chelmsford and Richmond in the same day?" The housekeeper looked doubtful.

"I think I can do it," he replied. "There's an early train from Liverpool Street station. It should get me to Chelmsford by half past eight. If I can't get to Richmond by the afternoon, I can do it the following day. That'll be all right, won't it?"

"It should work very well. But do let us know if you need someone else to go see the lady in Richmond." Mrs. Jeffries smiled happily. This case was very confusing, but they weren't, as she'd feared, losing heart. "And I'll have another go at Finsbury Park. I was going to speak to the people who live next door to the vicarage today, but I wasn't able to make contact with anyone. You'd think on a fine day someone would be outside, wouldn't you? Perhaps my luck will be better tomorrow. There's bound to be someone out and about. From what I heard from the St. Matthew's gardener, family scandals for the Claypools and the Durants were common knowledge."

Witherspoon was tired as a pup when he got home that evening. He was truly grateful that his housekeeper had a glass of sherry at the ready. "This is heavenly." He took a sip and sank back into the overstuffed chair. "It's been quite a day, and I'm exhausted."

"You look tired, sir." Mrs. Jeffries took her own chair. "How is the case progressing, sir? Any new leads?"

The inspector sighed heavily. "We did find out some new information. The trouble is, I'm not sure what it all means."

"How so, sir?"

"We went to see Mr. and Mrs. Christopher again, and, well, I'm not certain, but it appears as if Mrs. Christopher's twin sister, Edith Durant, might end up being our chief suspect." He gave her all the details about their visit.

Mrs. Jeffries listened carefully, occasionally nodding her head or asking a question. When he was finished, she said. "So this Miss Durant is the only suspect you have so far that you know owns a weapon."

"Correct, but that doesn't necessarily mean much. Just because the Christophers say they don't have a weapon doesn't make it true."

"Did you speak to the staff, sir?"

"We did, but unfortunately," he hesitated, "I neglected to ask that question. Silly of me."

"Not to worry, sir, you can always nip back in and have a word with the housekeeper tomorrow," she smiled reassuringly. She knew how easily he lost confidence in his own abilities.

"I suppose I got a bit distracted by what the housekeeper told me," he mused.

"And what was that, sir?"

He told her about the staff being given a surprise day out because of the painters, and then he told her about how the housekeeper was sure the Christophers were both lying. "You see, they'd said they'd be leaving themselves, but then when she nipped back to get her coat, she overheard Mrs. Christopher telling her husband they weren't going to leave. That they were going to stay no matter how long it took. That was rather peculiar, don't you think?"

"Indeed I do, sir." Mrs. Jeffries took a sip of her sherry.

"And then, of course, the woman went on to imply there was a bit of impropriety between Mr. Carl Christopher and his sister-in-law." He repeated to Mrs. Jeffries exactly what the housekeeper had said. "And of course, I was a bit confused, because according to Mrs. Christopher, her sister wasn't even allowed in the house. You can see how very confusing it all is."

"Indeed I can, sir." Mrs. Jeffries wasn't in the least confused, but then again, she had a much less innocent view of human nature than the inspector. She made a mental note to ask Betsy to find out what she could about a relationship between Carl Christopher and Edith Durant. "But I'm sure you'll sort it out in the end. You always do. Is that it, sir or did you find out anything else?"

He drained the last of his sherry. "We were able to track down one of the tenants from Dorland Place." He told her about his visit to Mrs. Mayberry and then rose to his feet. "Now, of course, we've only her suspicion that the cottage was used for illicit purposes, but what I do find most odd is her assertion that the management of the factory knew about the situation and approved of it." He started for the door.

She trailed after him. "That should be an easy thing for you to confirm." She and the others had already heard this gossip, she was glad that it had finally reached the inspector's ears.

He stopped and turned to her. "Really? Do you think so?"

She realized he wasn't quite getting what she was saying. "Of course, sir. All you have to do is find a few of the factory workers or office staff who were around ten years ago and ask them."

"Do you think they'd know?" he asked curiously.

"I think there's a good possibility," she replied. "If the neighbors knew what was going on and that the company was looking the other way while it went on, then I think there's a good chance the staff knew about it as well." She made a mental note to have Wiggins find out exactly who it was in the management who'd "looked the other way," so to speak. It could only have been Horace, or perhaps Eric Riley.

He thought about it for a moment and then continued walking toward the dining room. "I'll add that to my list of inquiries we need to make tomorrow."

They spotted Betsy coming down the hall carrying the inspector's dinner tray. "Good evening, sir. I hope you're hungry. Mrs. Goodge has outdone herself tonight." She smiled brightly and went into the dining room.

"It smells wonderful." Witherspoon hurried after her. "What have we got?"

Betsy put the tray down and lifted the cover off the dinner plate. "Roast chicken, roast potatoes and carrots with butter sauce."

"Excellent." He took his seat and picked up his serviette. "I must admit I'm very hungry."

"Good, sir. There's a lovely rice pudding for dessert." Betsy picked up the tray and started to leave.

"Oh, I forgot, sir. Wiggins is back," Mrs. Jeffries said quickly. From the corner of her eye, she saw the girl pause for an instant and then carry on.

"Did his grandfather get better?" Witherspoon speared a bite of chicken.

"Not really, sir," Mrs. Jeffries said. She wondered just how much about Wiggins's trip she ought to reveal. "But he felt it best to come home. The old gentleman wasn't getting any worse, and he felt his presence was a bit disruptive for the household."

Witherspoon nodded in understanding. "Do tell the lad that if he needs to go back, it'll be quite all right. I suppose Fred will move back in with Wiggins for a while now."

The dog was supposed to sleep on his rug in the kitchen. But everyone knew he slipped up to Wiggins's room as soon as the lights were out.

"Has he been sleeping in your room, sir?"

"Only since the lad's been gone," Witherspoon said quickly. "He came up that first night and scratched on my door. I didn't have the heart to send him back downstairs."

"Yes, sir, well, we'll make sure your rug gets a good brushing, then." She gave him a polite smile.

"Yes, and perhaps the bedspread as well." He smiled sheepishly. "He got up on the bed a time or two."

Mrs. Jeffries was fairly certain the hound had slept on the inspector's bed every night. "I'll see to it, sir. Now, do you need anything from the kitchen?"

"No, I've got my dinner and my evening paper. I'll be fine."

"I'll be up with your dessert in a few minutes, sir," she said as she withdrew. She hurried down the back stairs and into the warm kitchen. The others were all there. Betsy and Mrs. Goodge were tidying up, Wiggins, with Fred dodging his heels, was pushing the huge wicker laundry basket out into the back hall, and Smythe was at the far end of the table oiling a door hinge.

"Everyone, come quick, I want to give you a report on what I've learned from the inspector."

As soon as they were seated, she told them what the inspector had found out that day. "So you see," she finished, "I think we'll have to do a bit more tomorrow than we'd planned. Smythe, do you think you can find the painters that were at the Christopher house?"

"The Christophers probably used one of the local commercial firms," he said. "I'm sure I can track it down. You want me to find out if Claypool was there that day."

"Yes, and anything else that might be important." She turned to Wiggins. "You can get over to the factory and try to find out who in management told the neighbors to mind their own business."

"You mean who was coverin' up for the dalliance?" A faint blush climbed his round cheeks. "I'll see what I can suss out."

"I can try and track down the gossip about Mr. Christopher and his sister-in-law," Betsy said. "I should have plenty of time. Even if I can meet Lilly Staggers, what she has to say shouldn't take too long."

"And she might be a good source of information about Carl Christopher and Edith," Smythe added. "You never know how far the gossip had spread."

"I don't believe I'll be going to Finsbury Park after all," Mrs. Jeffries said. "I think it would be best if I had a word with someone at the St. John's Hotel. I want find out just how often Edith Durant stays there and, more importantly, was she there on the day her uncle was murdered." She looked at Wiggins. "Before you go to Bermondsey, can you stop by Luty's? I think she'll need to use her international resources to find out if Edith Durant really has rooms at the Metropole Hotel in Paris."

"Why is that important?" Betsy asked.

Mrs. Jeffries couldn't say, but something about the twins was nagging at the back of her mind. "I'm not sure. But I think as Edith Durant is the only suspect who supposedly owns a weapon, we ought to find out everything we can about her."

Betsy nodded. "Should I find out if anyone at the Riley household owns a gun?"

"Yes, please," the housekeeper replied.

"And what should I do?" Mrs. Goodge demanded. Though they knew she wasn't going to leave the kitchen, she still didn't want to be left out.

Mrs. Jeffries had a task for her at the ready. "I want you to find out exactly when Hilda and Carl Christopher were married."

CHAPTER 9

Constable Barnes got down from the hansom carefully. His knee was giving him trouble today, but he was in far too good a mood to be bothered by something as petty as pain. On Mrs. Jeffries's advice the day before, he'd sent some lads to question the local hansom cab drivers, and this morning, he'd gotten their reports. He was annoyed with himself, and if the truth be told, with the inspector as well, because neither of them had thought to do it earlier. It was shoddy police work, and he'd not make that mistake in the future. But at least now this case might start moving in the right direction. "Do you want me to ask permission from either of the Mr. Rileys before I start questioning the staff, sir?"

Witherspoon drew his coat tighter against the chill. "No. Go on to the factory floor and speak to the foreman. Tell him we're making routine inquiries. If he is uncooperative, come back to the office and I'll ask one of the Mr. Rileys to intervene."

They started across the cobblestones toward the main entrance. "Do you think either of them will tell us who was using the cottage, sir?" Barnes pulled the wrought iron gate open and they stepped inside.

"I don't know." Witherspoon shrugged. "But we must ask. We've got to find out. If the management knew what it was being used for and looked the other way, it means one of them must know who was using it."

"They were protecting someone," Barnes said softly, "and knowing human nature as I do, I suspect someone around here must have a good idea who it was."

When they stepped inside the front entrance, they went their separate ways. Witherspoon went down the hall to the executive offices, and Barnes went to see the factory foreman.

Witherspoon stuck his head inside the office and smiled at the two clerks. "Excuse me, but is Mr. Eric Riley available?" he asked the man closest to the door.

The clerk blinked in surprise. "Mr. Riley's out on the factory floor making his morning rounds, but he ought to be back soon."

"Do you know if Mr. Horace Riley is in yet?" Witherspoon asked.

"Yes, sir, he got in a few minutes ago." The clerk rose to his feet. "If you'll come this way, sir."

Witherspoon followed the man to the office at the far end of the room and waited while the lad announced him. "I'm sorry to barge in like this," he said as he entered Horace Riley's office, "but I've a few more questions for you."

Horace had partially risen from his desk. "Yes, uh, what is it?" He waved at an empty chair.

"This won't take long, sir," the inspector said as he sat down. "But I'd like to know if you own a weapon."

"A weapon?" Horace repeated the word like he'd never heard it before. "You mean like a sword or a gun?"

"We're actually more interested in whether or not you own a gun, and if so, what kind?"

His mouth opened in surprise. "Of course I don't own a gun. Why would I? London is hardly the wild west."

"You do realize, sir, that I'll be asking your servants this question."

"Now see here, exactly what are you implying? I don't make it a habit to lie, Inspector."

"I wasn't suggesting you did, sir," Witherspoon replied. Though, of course, that was exactly what he'd done. "However, it's sometimes possible that one forgets exactly what one does own. You have a very big house, sir. Are you sure that there isn't an old revolver or derringer tucked away somewhere?"

"Of course there isn't." Horace's face flushed red. "Well, at least, I don't think we've a gun. I don't recall ever buying one. But as you said, Inspector, it's a big house. It belonged to my wife's family. But I assure you, neither of us killed my uncle."

"Where were you on the afternoon your uncle was killed?" Witherspoon asked.

"As I told you before, I was right here," he shot back. "You can ask my clerks."

As he'd probably threatened the clerks with immediate dismissal if they said differently, the inspector didn't think they were a particularly good source for an alibi. "Mr. Riley, this morning we found out you left the office early on the afternoon the Reverend Claypool was murdered. Why did you think it necessary to lie to us? Why not tell us you'd left?"

Horace hesitated and then glanced toward the door. "The truth is, I didn't want Eric to know I'd been gone," he replied. "I went home because I had a dreadful headache and I didn't want Eric to find out. He'll do anything to get control of this factory, and I didn't want him writing to Uncle Jasper with tales of my being ill all the time."

Witherspoon looked over his shoulder at the open office door. You could see straight through to Eric Riley's office. "Wouldn't he notice you weren't here?"

"Not if my door was closed," Horace smiled slyly. "I often close it when I don't want to be disturbed. All right, Inspector, I'll admit I should have told you the truth. But I had nothing to do with my uncle's death, and it was only a small lie . . ."

"Small lie," Witherspoon interrupted. "Excuse me, sir. But we're investigating a murder. There's no such thing as a small lie under those circumstances. Now, tell me the truth. I want to know exactly what time you left and exactly where you went. Please don't lie to me anymore. We know you took a cab that day to a street off the Lambeth Palace Road."

Outside in the factory, Constable Barnes wasn't having much luck. "I just need a list of people who worked here ten years ago," he explained to the foreman. "I'll not take up much of their time or keep them from their work."

They were inside the foreman's office. The place was tiny with only a small table and a couple of rickety chairs. The walls were made of bare wood, most of which was streaked in small lines with paint of different colors. The floor was coated with what smelled like creosote, and the one tiny window was grimy with dirt. Empty paint tins were stacked waist-high in one corner, and in the opposite corner there was a peculiar-looking machine with nasty-looking hooks dangling from the edges.

Barnes and the foreman, a portly man with a florid complexion, black hair and truly awesome, bushy eyebrows, were standing opposite each other across the table.

The foreman's eyebrows drew together. "Well, I suppose old Markle might be worth talking to. He's been here since the place opened."

"Is he the only one?" Barnes asked incredulously.

"Oh no, we've a lot who've been here ten years or more," the foreman replied. "But they work the line and I can't pull 'em off. We'd have to stop the line, and I can't have that."

Barnes sighed deeply. He could threaten the fellow or he could try to find a way around this problem. He decided to find a way around it. You generally got more information out of people when you didn't push them around as if they were nothing. "How long have you been here, sir?"

The foreman's eyebrows shot straight up in surprise. "Me? Oh, let's see now, it's been a good fifteen years since I came on."

"Then can I ask you a few questions?" Barnes asked patiently.

"Me?" The foreman grinned. "I suppose it'd be all right." He nodded toward the rickety chair as he pulled out his own chair and sat down. "Have a seat then, guv, and ask me anything you like."

Hatchet opened the door of the first-class compartment and stepped on to the platform. Immediately, he turned and helped Luty out. "I don't know why you felt it necessary to come along," he said petulantly. "I'm quite certain I can get Mr. Spindler to speak to me."

Luty snorted. "If Spindler was ridin' first class from India to here, he's probably as toff-nosed as you are. He'd come closer to talkin' to me than you." In truth, she'd tagged along because she couldn't think of anything else to do to help the case. Wiggins had come along early that morning and asked her to find out about Edith Durant's hotel room in Paris, but that hadn't taken long to do, just a couple of minutes to write out a telegram to a friend of hers at the Bank of Paris.

Hatchet shrugged. "Much as I am loathe to admit it, you do have a point. Besides, the story you've come up with is far better than the one I was going to use. Come along, then, madam. I believe there's a hansom stand just outside the station. If we're in luck, we'll soon have our answers."

A few minutes later, they were in a cab and heading toward number twelve Hobbs Lane. Hatchet glanced at the fur muff in her lap. "You didn't bring your gun, did you?"

Luty was very fond of her Colt .45. "With a nervous nellie like you ridin' with me, of course not."

"I am not a nervous nellie," he protested. He often carried a small revolver of his own, especially when they were coming toward the end of a case. "It's simply that you've no need of a weapon here. This isn't Colorado or San Francisco, where, I believe, one can have a gun pointed at one for no reason whatsoever excepting that someone doesn't like one's expression."

"Fiddle-faddle." Luty waved her arm dismissively. "You're exaggeratin'. Anyways, I don't have my peacemaker so you can quite worryin'." But she made a mental note to tuck it in her muff in the event things began to happen.

They argued amiably until the hansom pulled up in front of number twelve. Hatchet instructed the driver to wait and then helped Luty out onto the grass verge.

They stood in front of a huge, orange-red brick house with black trim around the roof and windows. The grounds were well-tended with an expansive lawn extending from the front to both the sides. Around the edges, a few tiny daffodils and shoots from bulbs burst out of the neatly dug flower beds.

"This ain't a poor man's house, that's for sure," Luty muttered. "Come on, let's get this show on the road." She grabbed Hatchet's arm and practically drug him up the stone walkway to the front stairs.

"Really, madam, do be careful, this is a new suit," he protested when she gave his sleeve another yank.

"Sorry," she said. They'd reached the front door. Hatchet reached for the ring-shaped brass knocker, lifted it and let it fall. A few moments later, a woman dressed in housekeepers' black opened the front door and stared out at them. "Yes, may I help you?"

"Is this the residence of Mr. Adam Spindler?" Hatchet asked.

"It is," she replied.

"May we see him, please," Luty asked meekly. She reached up and adjusted the veil of her sapphire-blue hat, holding her hand in such a way so that the housekeeper couldn't fail to notice the diamond rings on her fingers. Luty didn't often flaunt her wealth, but she'd observed that people were far more likely to confide in you if they thought you were from the same class as themselves. She'd made it a habit to dress plainly when she was snooping amongst working people and to dress fancy when it was the upper crust. "It's very important. I'm hoping he can help me find my long-lost brother."

The housekeeper looked them up and down, assessing their wealth, background and probable class by the cut of their clothes and the size of their jewels. "If you could give me your names, I'll see if Mr. Spindler is receiving. He only arrived home late last night. Please step inside."

"I'm Edward Hadleigh-Jones," Hatchet whipped off his top hat as he entered the foyer. "And this is my American cousin, Anna Hadleigh."

The woman acknowledged the names by the slight inclination of her head, then she turned and went past the staircase down the hall.

The housekeeper returned a few moments later and led them into a sitting room. An elderly gentleman with wispy white hair rose from the settee. He smiled as they entered the room. "Good day, madam, sir, I understand from my housekeeper that you're seeking my assistance?" His expression was curious.

Luty charged toward him with her hand extended. "I'm Anna Hadleigh," she introduced herself, "and this is my cousin," she gestured at Hatchet.

"Edward Hadleigh-Jones," Hatchet said quickly as he extended his own hand.

"Adam Spindler." The gentlemen shook with both of them and then turned his attention back to Luty. "Do sit down, please." He gestured toward the coral-colored settee. "How may I be of assistance? My housekeeper mentioned a long-lost brother."

They settled themselves into seats and Luty folded her hands demurely in her lap. "Well, I know this is going to sound strange, but years ago, my younger brother ran off to India to do missionary work." She sighed theatrically. "Now understand, when he left England . . ."

"Excuse me, ma'am," Spindler interrupted, "but your accent doesn't sound very English."

"I moved to America as a small child," she replied quickly, "and the longer you stay there, the more you sound like them. I only came back a few days ago. I'd gotten word from my cousin, here," she jerked her head toward Hatchet, "that Oliver might be coming back to England from India."

"I see," he nodded in understanding. "Please go on with your narrative."

"Like I was sayin', when my brother left here, he was a good Presbyterian. But for some reason, once he got out to India, he converted to the Anglican faith and joined that church. Well, my father was furious, and a number of letters were exchanged between the two of them. By then, we'd moved to Colorado, and Papa was first deacon at the Pueblo Presbyterian Church. Anyways, Papa finally got so angry he disowned Oliver and refused to allow Momma or any of us to get in contact with him."

"How very sad. Exactly when did this happen?" Spindler asked.

"Oh, it was years ago, back when I was a girl." Luty lifted her white lace handkerchief and dabbed at her eyes. "You know what happens then, the years pass and we get on with our lives." She sighed. "But finally, I realized that I had to find my baby brother. That's where you come in. I understand you recently came back to England from India and that onboard that ship was a clergyman?"

"That's true." Spindler cocked his head to one side and smiled slightly. "But his name wasn't Oliver."

"My brother's full name was Jasper Oliver," she said quickly. "And we think he might have been using my mother's maiden name because he got so angry at our Papa."

Spindler nodded. "Let me see if I understand you correctly. Your father disowned your brother because he became a member of the Church of England?"

"That's right," Luty replied.

"And you think I might be able to help track this person down, is that correct?"

Luty had a sinking feeling in her stomach. By now, Spindler should have been so moved by her tale that he was spilling his guts about being on the same ship as Jasper Claypool. "Uh, yes, that's right. We have it on reliable authority that a clergyman came in on ship from India this past Monday. But as the poor fellow's disappeared, we were hoping you could help us."

"We think this man might know where my cousin's brother lives in India," Hatchet added. He didn't dare look at Luty. He'd suddenly realized there were a number of inconsistencies in their story and was doing the best he could to recover. "You see, her dear brother retired in India and doesn't seem to have given anyone his address. We're hoping this other English clergyman might know where he lives." He laughed confidentially. "I imagine the English religious community is actually quite small, don't you?" He could feel Luty's eyes on him and knew she wasn't pleased.

"Yes," Spindler said slowly. "I imagine it is."

"Well, do you think you could help us?" Luty asked. "Did you talk to this here English preacher while you were on the ship together? Do you have any idea where I could find him?"

"The only place you'll find this poor man is at the cemetery," Spindler replied sadly. "He was murdered soon after he arrived in London. It was in the newspapers. Frankly, madam, I don't wish to be rude, but your tale is a complete fabrication that only a moron or an innocent would believe."

Luty tried to look outraged, failed miserably and finally said, "It was pretty bad, wasn't it?"

"It was absurd," Spindler replied. "To begin with, if he were your younger brother, then by the timeline you gave me and you'd moved to America when you were a small child, your brother must have gone to India as no more than a newborn. As mighty as our Lord is, he rarely sends babies out to make converts of all nations. Furthermore, for a Presbyterian to disown someone for becoming a member of the Church of England is ridiculous."

"I told you to be an Anabaptist," Hatchet hissed at her.

"You never said any such thing," Luty shot back. "You admitted my story was better than yours."

"Only because mine was pathetic."

"Excuse me," Spindler interrupted, "but would you mind telling me why you're here?" He no longer looked angry, merely curious and a bit sad.

Luty looked at Hatchet. He shrugged. "We might as well tell him the truth. We're here to find out if you spoke to Jasper Claypool on the voyage out from India."

"I spoke to him many times. As a matter of fact, he and I were very good friends in India. I was the one who encouraged him to come home." Spindler's eyes filled with tears. "I wish I hadn't, now. If he'd stayed in India, he wouldn't be dead."

"I'm dreadfully sorry," Hatchet said sincerely. "You were obviously very good friends."

"We were indeed." Spindler turned away and looked out the window at the gray day.

"We're sorry he's dead too," Luty said, "and we aim to help find his killer."

He jerked his head back and stared at Luty. "Isn't that a task for the police?"

"Absolutely," she replied. "But sometimes they need a little help. Look, I'm goin' to tell you the truth now. I'm Luty Belle Crookshank and this here's Hatchet. He works for me."

"I take it you weren't born in England?" Spindler queried with a smile.

"No, but my late husband was. Now I ain't goin' to waste your time with any more foolishness. But we're tryin' to help find out who killed the poor

Reverend Claypool. Whatever information we get will make its way to Inspector Witherspoon, the policeman in charge of the case. You've got my word on that. I keep my word; you can check my references." She rattled off an impressive list of London's best-known politicians, churchmen and financiers. She would have given him even more names, but he held up his hand.

"I believe you, Mrs. Crookshank." He got up and went to the bell-pull by the door. "As a matter of fact, I was going to go to the police today and have a word with them. I'm fairly certain my information will be quite useful."

Luty and Hatchet exchanged glances.

"If you don't mind my asking, sir," Hatchet asked, "What's taken you so long? Reverend Claypool has been dead for a good few days."

"I didn't know he'd been murdered until late last night. My housekeeper told me when I arrived home. I was out of the country on an errand for Jasper." Spindler sighed heavily. "Let me ring for tea and we can discuss this matter like civilized people."

"Thank you, sir," Hatchet said softly. "I do apologize for entering your home under false pretenses. But I assure you, we had the best of motives for our actions."

"I'm sorry too," Luty added. "We shouldn't have lied to you." She ignored the fact that they frequently lied to people when they were obtaining information.

"Oh, that's quite all right, ma'am. Sometimes the truth can be frightfully inconvenient."

Betsy walked slowly past the Horace Riley house and tried to appear inconspicuous. But this was her third time down Canfield Lane, and if someone didn't come out soon, she'd have to move along. She got to the corner and crossed the street. Glancing over her shoulder, she saw a young woman coming out of the house from the side servant's entry. The girl stopped and fiddled with the neck of her brown jacket. She wasn't wearing a maid's cap, so Betsy thought it might be the girl's day out. The girl turned and headed off in the opposite direction from where Betsy stood.

Betsy was after her like a shot. She followed her for a long ways, dodging in and out of traffic and trying to keep her in sight without being spotted. The girl turned into the railway station at Finchley, and Betsy ran to catch up with her.

She was lucky, the girl hadn't bought her ticket yet. She got in line right behind her and when she went up to the ticket agent, Betsy cocked her head and listened hard.

"Amersham, please, second-class return." She handed over her money.

Betsy dug coins out of her pocket and saw that she had plenty enough for a ticket. When she reached the ticket clerk, she bought the same as her quarry. She raced on to the platform just in time to see the girl slip into a compartment at the far end of the train. Betsy managed to slip inside just as the conductor blew his whistle, and the train began to move.

"Thank goodness." She smiled broadly as she sat down, "I thought I was going to miss the train."

The girl was in a seat by the window. She smiled timidly as Betsy flopped down next to her. "You don't mind, do you?" she said brightly. "I hate traveling on my own."

"I don't mind," the girl replied. "But I'm not going far, just to Amersham." She was a small young woman, very thin, with a long bony face, dark brown hair and deep-set hazel eyes.

"That's where I'm going." Betsy grinned. "Do you live there?"

"Wish I did." She shook her head. "I'm going to see my auntie, she works there. It's my day out. My name's Carrie Parker, what's yours?"

"Oh, I'm Betsy. Betsy Smith," she lied. "It's my day out as well. I'm going to visit a friend. Do you work for a nice household?" The use of the term, "day out" identified both of them as servants.

"Not really," she frowned. "Mrs. Riley generally only gives us an afternoon out once a week, but she told me I could go early today."

"That was very kind of her," Betsy said brightly.

The girl turned her head and stared out the window. Betsy noticed her hands were clenched so tightly together her knuckles were turning white.

"Are you all right?" she asked softly.

The girl jerked her head around and stared at Betsy. "I'm fine."

"I'm sorry, I didn't mean to be a nosy parker." She smiled kindly and looked pointedly at Carrie's clenched hands. "You just looked a bit nervous, that's all."

Carrie looked down at her hands and slowly pulled her fingers apart. "You're trying to be kind and I'm being nasty. I'm sorry. It's just that I am nervous and I've no idea what I ought to do."

"About what?"

Carrie took a deep breath. "Mrs. Staggers, that's the housekeeper, says she thinks Mrs. Riley wants me gone all day in case the police come around."

"Police?" Betsy repeated. "Why would the police be coming around?"

Carrie shrugged. "Some old uncle of Mr. Riley's got himself killed Monday last."

"How dreadful." Betsy pretended shock. "And your mistress doesn't want you talking to the police about it, is that it?"

"That's what Mrs. Staggers says." Carrie bit her lip. "But honestly, I don't know what I could tell them."

Betsy wasn't sure what to ask next, so she decided to plunge straight ahead. "If you think you were given the morning off to get you out of the way, then you must know something."

"Not really," Carrie countered. "Leastways I don't think I do. I didn't do nothin', you know. But Mrs. Staggers and Mrs. Riley, they saw me readin' that telegram before I burnt it, and Mrs. Staggers says it's important and that Mrs. Riley don't want me sayin' anything about it to the police." She bit her lip and looked out the window again. "I'm confused. That's why I'm going to see my auntie. Maybe she can tell me what to do. I don't want to lose my position. I'm not really very well-trained, you know. Finding something else would be hard. But if the police ask me, I've got to tell them what I read. I don't want to go to jail, and that's where you go if you lie to police."

"You're not going to go to jail." Betsy could tell the girl was genuinely frightened. She reached over and touched her hand.

"How do you know?"

"Because I work for a policeman," Betsy replied. "He's ever so nice. He'll not let anyone put you in jail or hurt you."

"I'm not scared of Mrs. Riley hurtin' me," Carrie cried, "I'm scared of bein' on the streets. I've been there before, you see. It's horrible not to have a roof over your head."

"I know exactly what it's like," Betsy said firmly. She took both Carrie's hands in hers. "I've been in that situation myself. But if murder's been done, you must tell what you know."

The train was pulling into Edgeware Station. There wasn't much time left. Betsy had to get the girl's confidence before they got to Willesden Junction. They could change trains there for a train to Uxbridge Road. From there, they could walk to Upper Edmonton Gardens and the Ladbroke Grove Police Station. One thing was for certain—she didn't want to end up all the way out in Amersham with important information that might help solve the case.

"But that's just it," Carrie cried, "the telegram wasn't important."

"Wasn't it from the murdered uncle?" Betsy charged. She forced herself to lower her voice. Shouting at the girl wasn't going to inspire much confidence.

"No, it was from Mr. Riley, and all it said was that Mrs. Riley was to hurry and meet him at the Bishops Head Restaurant by half past one. That's all. It didn't say a word about his soddin' old uncle."

Mrs. Jeffries smiled at the man behind the desk. "I'm sorry, would you mind checking again? I'm sure my niece told me she was staying here. She always stays here."

He sighed heavily and gave the open ledger page a cursory glance. "I assure you madam, we all know Miss Durant quite well. She isn't here."

"Did she go back to Paris?" Mrs. Jeffries pressed. She wasn't certain what she hoped to find out, but she was finding out a few bits and pieces.

The desk clerk, a morose-looking man with an overly large mustache, shook his bald head. "I'm afraid Miss Durant didn't disclose her plans when she was last here. Now if you'll excuse me . . ."

"That's nonsense. Surely she left an address so her mail could be forwarded."

He glared at her. "I assure you, ma'am, any mail that comes for Miss Durant is sent to a local address. . . ."

"A local address," Mrs. Jeffries pretended outrage. "Why haven't you given it to me? I must find my niece."

"Madam, we're not in the habit of disclosing our clients' personal information."

"But I'm a relation and I've something very important to tell her."

"It's out of the question, madam." He turned his attention to a man who'd just come up to the desk. "Yes, sir, may I help you?"

Mrs. Jeffries couldn't press any further. She couldn't risk any more of a scene than she'd already created. But she wanted that address. Where was Edith Durant's mail being sent? Find that address and she was one step closer to finding something useful about this case.

She walked out of the small but elegant lobby and turned the corner onto Ordnance Road. The traffic was heavy, and there were plenty of hansoms going past. But she decided to take the train. It was too late to get to Finsbury Park and back by teatime, so she might as well take a train home instead of a hansom or an omnibus. She had plenty of time.

She went past the St. John's Wood Barracks to Queens Road, thinking about the case as she walked.

On the one hand, things were beginning to move quickly, while on the other, she'd no idea if they were moving in the right direction. Eric Riley was the only one who supposedly knew his uncle was back in London, but she wasn't sure that was really true. There was some evidence that the others might have been aware of that fact as well. The Christophers had certainly behaved strangely that day, as had both Mr. and Mrs. Riley. But she needed proof that they knew, not just gossip that both households had been acting oddly.

She dodged around a vendor pushing a water cart. There were still so many other questions to be answered. Why had Jasper Claypool decided to come back to England at this particular time, especially as they knew he'd planned on retiring in India? Yet something had made him come back. What could it be? And where was his luggage?

By the time she reached the Marlborough Road Station, the only conclusion she'd come to was that she'd used the wrong approach at the hotel. Pretending to be Edith Durant's relative hadn't gotten her anywhere at all. She should have found a maid or a clerk and bribed them for information about the woman. Money always worked.

For once, everyone arrived for their afternoon meeting on time. "I hope the rest of you have had better luck than I have," Mrs. Jeffries announced as she sat down. "The only thing I learned is that Edith Durant's mail is sent to a local address when she's not at the St. John's Hotel."

"Which local address?" Mrs. Goodge asked.

"There's the rub," Mrs. Jeffries sighed. "I wasn't able to find out. As I said, it hasn't been a very useful day for me. Now, who would like to go first?"

"Mine shouldn't take long," the cook said casually. But no one was fooled by her tone. "I found out when Hilda and Carl Christopher were married: it was about a year before Jasper Claypool went to India. They were married in Claypool's old parish up at Finsbury Park. I found out something else, too," she grinned. "According to the gossip, Carl was going to marry Edith until her sister Hilda inherited all their father's money."

"He didn't have any money of his own?" Betsy asked.

Mrs. Goodge shook her head. "Not a cent. He's got good looks and aristocratic ancestors and that's about it. I don't think he expected that Edith would be virtually disinherited and that Hilda, the boring sister, would get it all."

"Why would Hilda want to marry him?" Wiggins asked. "If she and Edith Durant were identical, why didn't she get her own feller?"

"Apparently the sisters had a long history of coveting what one another had," Mrs. Goodge replied. "Unlike most twins, these girls weren't best friends. If Edith had something, Hilda wanted it, and if Hilda had it, then Edith couldn't rest till it was hers. Supposedly, Edith was the worst of the two. She was supposedly as bold as brass and always had been. Never afraid to try anything and always one step ahead of trouble, that's the gossip about Edith. Hilda was the quieter of the two. But despite their differences, they do try to see one another. Edith used to come visit Hilda quite a bit up until the last few years. Now she spends most of her time out of the country. Leastways, that's what the gossip says. That's all I found out."

"You found out a lot more than me," Wiggins announced glumly. "I spent two hours tryin' to find someone from Eric Riley's house to talk to and I didn't 'ave any luck at all. His landlady was makin' the staff 'ave a spring clean. They went in and out, fetchin' and carryin' and bangin' on carpets, but every time I tried to get close enough to speak to one of the housemaids, the landlady would pop her head out and ruin it. You'd have thought with all them open windows and doors I'd'a found out somethin'."

"It happens that way sometimes," Smythe told him. "Don't take it so 'ard. You'll 'ave better luck tomorrow. I found out a bit today. I tracked down one of the painters who were at the Christophers' house on the day Claypool died. The other painter is doin' a job near Epping and I'm going to talk to him tomorrow. But the one I spoke to today told me that Mr. and Mrs. Christopher were both at the house all day."

"What time did he leave that day?" Mrs. Jeffries asked.

"They had the job done by four-thirty," Smythe replied. "But with cleanup and all, they didn't leave until a quarter to five that evening."

"Then why did the Christophers let on to Mrs. Nimitz that they were going to Brighton for the day?" Luty demanded. "That don't make sense."

"Nothing about this case makes much sense," Wiggins complained. "I can't make hide nor hair of anything."

"Perhaps they pretended they planned on leaving and then changed their minds?" Betsy suggested. "People do change their minds."

"Perhaps," Mrs. Jeffries grew thoughtful. "Or maybe they received a telegram or a message that morning, something that made them change their minds?"

"I'll have a go at finding that out tomorrow," Wiggins offered. "I can check at the local telegraph exchange."

"The painter didn't say anything about them receiving anything," Smythe said. "But he was down in the kitchen. I think the other one was doin' the back hall and the stairs. Tomorrow I'll ask his mate if he saw any messengers. That's it for me."

"I found something out," Betsy said. She told them about her meeting with Carrie Parker.

"And all the telegram said was for Mrs. Riley to meet him at a restaurant?" Mrs. Jeffries clarified.

Betsy nodded. "That's right, and she'd no idea why it was important, but Lilly Staggers was sure it had something to do with Claypool's murder."

"And supposedly, that's why Mrs. Riley gave the girl the day out, to make sure she wasn't there if the police came back?" Hatchet asked.

"Yes, but Mrs. Riley is in for a disappointment. I talked Carrie into coming back here and popping into the Ladbroke Grove Police Station. She's going to tell Inspector Witherspoon what she knows."

"She know anything about whether or not Lilly Staggers is working for Eric Riley?" the cook asked as she poured herself more tea.

"Carrie doesn't know anything about that," Betsy admitted. "But she did tell me that tomorrow morning, Lilly Staggers is to do the household shopping. I'm going to try and talk to her then."

"Does the girl know if anyone in the house has a gun?" Mrs. Jeffries asked. "Or did you think to ask?"

"I asked," Betsy said proudly. "But she didn't know. She's not been at the house very long. That's all I found out."

"You learned quite a lot, Betsy," Mrs. Jeffries replied. She was a firm believer in telling people when they'd done a good job. She smiled at them. "All of you have."

"We've got something to say," Luty said. "We found out where Jasper Claypool's luggage went."

"Where?" Smythe asked eagerly.

"Adam Spindler's," Hatchet said solemnly. "Not only did Claypool's luggage go there, but apparently that's where Claypool was going to stay while he was in England."

CHAPTER 10

"Gracious, you did find out quite a bit," Mrs. Jeffries exclaimed.

"Wait till you hear," Luty said excitedly. "Claypool was goin' to stay with Adam Spindler and not one of his relatives."

"Spindler was one of the people on the ship with Claypool, right?" Mrs. Goodge asked. Sometimes she had a bit of trouble keeping everyone straight in her head.

"That's right." Luty nodded. "But that ain't the half of it. He and Claypool knew each other in India, he's the reason that Claypool came back when he did. Course he feels real bad about it, seeing as poor old Jasper ended up with a bullet in his head."

"Really, madam," Hatchet chided. "Let's have a bit of respect here. Poor Mr. Spindler is utterly devastated. . . ."

"I didn't say he wasn't," Luty defended herself. "Oh, let's not pick at each other, let's just tell 'em what we found out. Go on, you take it from here. I don't want you claimin' I hogged the whole story for myself."

"If you insist, madam," he replied. He put down his teacup. "As Madam has told you, we went to see Mr. Spindler. The gentleman had only learned of Claypool's death last night."

"But it's been in all the papers," Wiggins pointed out.

"True, the English papers," Hatchet replied. "But Mr. Spindler had been in France and only returned last night. He'd been on an errand for Jasper Claypool."

"Let me guess, he was checking the Metropole Hotel for Edith Durant," Mrs. Jeffries said.

"That's right," Luty interrupted. "So now it don't matter whether my friend Mr. Saunière has any luck finding out about the woman. Adam Spindler's already done it."

"Exactly what did he find out?" Smythe asked.

"Edith Durant rarely uses her rooms at the hotel. As a matter of fact, in the last few years, she's only been there a couple of times."

"Does that mean she's here in England?" Betsy asked.

"We're not sure," Hatchet responded before Luty could hog the floor again. "But we think she might have a flat in Brighton. That's what the clerk at the Metropole told Mr. Spindler."

"Where do they send her mail?" Mrs. Jeffries asked.

"That's another funny thing," Hatchet said. "When Spindler asked, he was told that they didn't forward it anywhere. On her instructions, Edith Durant's mail was picked up by a private messenger service every month."

"It's almost like she doesn't want anyone to know where she is," Betsy murmured.

Mrs. Jeffries was beginning to have an idea of where she was, but she would keep her opinion to herself until she had more proof. "At least now we know a bit more about Claypool. But I still don't understand, why exactly did Spindler say Jasper Claypool had come home? He'd told his family he was going to retire in India."

"And he'd even bought property," Mrs. Goodge reminded them.

"Supposedly, Jasper got a letter from one of his relations that upset him very much." Hatchet took a quick sip of tea. "The letter was from Eric Riley. He virtually accused his half-brother of embezzling money from the company. Eric claimed that Horace Riley is in desperate straits financially and that if Jasper wanted there to be anything left for the rest of them, he'd best come home and take care of Horace."

"That's true," Mrs. Goodge agreed. "We've already heard that his missus spends like a drunken sailor and that he's got creditors on his heels day and night."

"Spindler was planning on returning home to England," Hatchet continued, "and he could see how upset his friend was over the letter, so he encouraged Claypool to come home with him."

"Tell 'em the good part," Luty insisted.

"In due time, madam." Hatchet sighed in exasperation. "As I was saying, Claypool decided to come to London, but he didn't want to give any of them advance notice of his plans. He didn't tell Mr. Spindler why, but he was adamant it was to be a surprise visit. On the morning they arrived, he prevailed upon Mr. Spindler to go on to Paris and ascertain the whereabouts of his niece, Edith. He told him he wanted to reconcile with her. That same day, Spindler accompanied him to the telegraph office, and he sent messages to both Eric and Horace Riley, asking them to meet him. He was to meet Horace for luncheon at a restaurant near Lambeth Palace at half past one, and he was to meet Eric for tea at half past three. Spindler was quite sure of the times."

"What about Hilda Christopher?" Mrs. Jeffries said. "Didn't he send her a message too?"

Hatchet shook his head. "No, he didn't. He told Spindler he wanted to drop by their house unannounced. Apparently, there's been a bit of estrangement between him and Hilda Christopher for the past couple of years."

"Did Spindler know why?" Mrs. Jeffries asked.

"Supposedly, Horace and Eric had been pressing Claypool to sell those empty houses, but he'd promised Hilda he wouldn't. However, he'd decided that the houses should be sold, and he was going to prevail upon her to change her mind. He told Adam Spindler quite a few details."

"But I thought it was Claypool who wanted those cottages left alone?" Mrs. Goodge looked confused.

"It was, but only because Hilda wanted it that way. She'd asked her uncle to pretend he wanted them left alone. That way, her cousins wouldn't harass her over the issue." Hatchet shrugged. "After all, Claypool was thousands of miles away, so her cousins could only annoy him by mail. She was afraid if they knew it was her that wanted the property left undeveloped, they'd bother her constantly."

"This is very confusing." Betsy said what the rest of them were thinking.

"I know," Hatchet smiled wearily. "Even poor Mr. Spindler was confused. But he was quite adamant about everything he told us. Claypool and he had a long voyage together, and apparently the vicar confided in him completely."

Wiggins reached for another bun. "Why did Hilda Christopher want them left alone if the property's so valuable? Is she so rich she don't want any more money?"

"She told her uncle that she wanted them left alone as an investment, that she wanted to insure there was something left for any children she might have one day. Her argument was actually quite sound. London property never goes down in value."

Mrs. Jeffries was trying hard to assimilate all the facts and assemble them into some semblance of order. But she wasn't being very successful in her attempt. She was as confused as the rest of them. "Are you sure you can trust this Mr. Spindler? He seems to know an awful lot."

"We can trust him," Luty answered. "Leastways, I think so. He didn't act like he knew what all this information meant; it was more like Jasper Claypool had bent his ear about it all the way from India."

"So it was Hilda Christopher who wanted the property left alone so her future children would have something?" Smythe's expression was clearly skeptical.

"That's what Claypool told Spindler," Hatchet replied.

"But Hilda Christopher doesn't have any children," Betsy pointed out.

"Right, and that's one of the reasons that Jasper came back. He wanted to get the issue settled once and for all. He didn't think it was fair to his nephews to let the property sit there empty, especially as Mrs. Christopher wasn't producing any offspring."

"So he came back to see if Horace was robbin' him and to settle this property issue." Mrs. Goodge reached for the teapot. "Is that right?"

"And to reconcile with Edith," Luty added. "That's why he sent Spindler to Paris. He was takin' her a letter."

"Is Spindler going to go to the inspector?" Mrs. Jeffries asked.

"He's going to see him tomorrow morning," Hatchet replied. He shrugged. "I don't know what it all means, but at least now we know why he came home and, more importantly, that he saw his nephews and possibly his niece on the day he died."

"I knew it," Mrs. Goodge said. "The whole bunch is lying."

"Yes," Mrs. Jeffries murmured. "But which one of them killed him?"

They spent another half hour discussing the case, but no one came to any conclusions about what it all meant. "I think we ought to meet again tomorrow morning," Mrs. Jeffries told them as the meeting began to break up.

"Why?" Mrs. Goodge stared at her suspiciously. "You have an idea about who the killer is?" The only time they met twice a day was generally when a case was coming to a head.

"I'm not sure," she admitted honestly, "but I've got a nagging feeling in the back of my mind."

"A nagging feeling about what?" Betsy pressed. She had great respect for Mrs. Jeffries's "feelings." She wished she could grow some of her own.

The housekeeper shook her head in frustration. "That's just it, I don't know. But something is bothering me, and I think we need to be 'at the ready,' so to speak."

"That's good enough for me," Luty announced. "We'll be here at eight."

As soon as Luty and Hatchet left, they went about their household chores. They wanted nothing left undone if they had to leap into action, so to speak.

Mrs. Jeffries went upstairs and began to dust the staircase. Boring, mundane tasks tended to free her mind to think. But an hour later, when every speck of dust on three floors had been banished, she was still no closer to any conclusions. But she had realized one important thing: there was only one person with a real motive to want Jasper Claypool dead. Horace Riley. He was the only one with something to lose by his uncle's return. If Claypool received proof that Horace was embezzling cash from the firm to keep his creditors at bay, Claypool would probably fire him and put Eric in charge. He might also disinherit the man. He'd already disinherited a niece for immoral behaviour. Surely, to a clergyman, thievery was equally as wrong as adultery.

But something was still nagging her. She took the feather duster to the cupboard under the front stairs, opened the door and tossed it inside. The inspector would be home soon. Maybe he'd have more information, something tangible that would help her to see the pattern in these murders, the connection. There was always a pattern or a connection of some kind.

A few moments later, he was home and she had him cozily ensconced in the drawing room with a glass of sherry.

"This is wonderful." He took a sip and sighed in pleasure.

"Have you had a good day, sir?" She watched him carefully as she took a sip from her own glass. He seemed in good spirits, and that generally meant he'd made progress on the case. She made a mental note to talk to Constable Barnes the next morning when he arrived to fetch the inspector. It was important that he hear what they'd learned, and she could take the opportunity to find out if he'd picked up any tidbits the inspector neglected to share with her.

On one of their previous cases, Barnes had admitted to her he'd figured out she and the others helped the inspector. But as his own career had benefited from their efforts, and as he had genuine respect and affection for Gerald Witherspoon, he'd kept their secret.

"We've made quite a bit of progress today," Witherspoon said. "Barnes sent some lads around the factory area to speak to the local cabbies, to see if either of the Rileys had left the premises on the afternoon Claypool was killed." He paused and took another sip. "Both of them had left."

"So they were both lying about their whereabouts? Where had they gone?"

"Horace Riley would have lied about that as well," Witherspoon said, "but I told him the cabman remembered precisely where he'd taken him. So he finally told me the truth. He went to meet his Uncle Jasper at a restaurant on Paradise Street."

"Gracious, so he did know his uncle was in London."

"Right, as did Mr. Eric Riley. He had tea with his Uncle Jasper later that very afternoon." The inspector was still amazed at how often people lied to the police.

"But why did they lie about seeing Claypool in the first place?" Mrs. Jeffries asked. "Surely they must have realized you'd eventually catch them out. They were seen in public places with a clergyman who was later found murdered."

"Ah, but both of those public places were frequented by lots of clergymen," the inspector said easily. "And they both hoped no one would notice them. They would have gotten away with it, as well, if they hadn't both been foolish enough to use a local hansom cab."

"I don't understand, sir," Mrs. Jeffries admitted.

"Lambeth Palace, Mrs. Jeffries," Witherspoon explained. "Home of the Archbishop of Canterbury and the seat of administration for the Church of England. Clergymen were the main customers for both the restaurant where Claypool met Horace and Eugenia Riley, and at the hotel lobby where he had tea with Eric Riley."

"I see," she said slowly. "That's why no one came forward when his death was announced in the papers. No one at either place noticed him at all, why would they? He was just another old priest amongst dozens of them."

"It's sad, but understandable," Witherspoon said.

"Do either of the Rileys own a gun?" she asked. She decided to go right to the heart of the matter.

"Neither of them admitted to owning one," he said. "But we're going to talk to Horace Riley's servants again and see if one of them has ever seen a weapon at the house."

"What about Eric Riley?" she asked.

"Constable Barnes and I are going to have a word with the woman who does his cleaning, and with his landlady. He rooms at a rather nice house in Bermondsey. If he has a gun, we're hoping one of them will have seen it."

"You've had quite an interesting day, sir." She gave him an encouraging smile. "But then, you always find the killer in the end."

"Thank you, Mrs. Jeffries, but I'm afraid we've still a long way to go on this one. Constable Barnes tried to find out a bit more about our poor lady in the chimney but didn't get very far." He finished his sherry. "We know good and well that the management of the factory looked the other way while that cottage was being used by someone, but no one appears to have known about it but the neighbors."

"You mean none of the factory staff knew what was going on?" She found that hard to believe.

"If they did, they'll not admit to it," Witherspoon replied. "Barnes spoke to the foreman today, and the fellow insists he'd no idea anyone but legitimate tenants used number seven. He claimed the workers had nothing to do with the cottages and for us to ask the Rileys."

"Did you, sir?"

"They're sticking to their story, that the cottage simply hadn't been let and they'd no idea anyone ever used the place." He put his glass down on the table and got up.

"Not to worry, sir." She rose to her feet, picked up his empty glass and gave him a broad smile. "You'll sort it out, sir. You always do. Was that all that happened today?" she asked as he started for the door.

"Oh, we had a young woman come in with some information. One of the maids from Horace Riley's household. She confirmed what we'd already found out." He took a deep sniff of the air. "Something smells wonderful. I tell you, I could eat a horse tonight."

Mrs. Jeffries spent another night tossing and turning. In the wee hours she got up and made her way to her chair by the window. A strong wind had blown in from the west, leaving the night clear and clean, with no hint of smoke or fog. She stared at the gaslight across the road, focusing on the pale yellow flame and letting her mind go free. What was the motive for this murder? She had a feeling that was the key. But she'd no idea what that motive might be. Could it be plain old-fashioned greed? Could Horace Riley be so desperate to pay his creditors and hang onto his position that he'd murder his uncle? People had certainly been murdered for less. Perhaps it wasn't even Horace who'd done it. Perhaps Mrs. Riley had decided she didn't wish to give up what was decidedly a lavish lifestyle. She came home that night after her husband. After lunching with Jasper Claypool, she could easily have followed him, frightened him into running and then chased him down and put a bullet in his brain. Mrs. Jeffries knew better than anyone that the fairer sex could be deadlier than the male.

She sat up as another thought occurred to her. Why was Claypool killed where he was killed? St. Paul's Church on Dock Street wasn't near any of the suspects, nor was it near the Claypool factory. What was Claypool doing in the area? Did it have anything to do with his murder? Then she realized something. Dock Street was in the East End, near the railroad stations that went to Chelmsford and Adam Spindler's house. That was probably why he'd been killed at that particular spot. He'd been on his way to his friend's house when his assailant caught up with him.

She sighed and shifted in the hard chair. What about Eric Riley? He was the one with the most to gain. But he could only benefit if Jasper Claypool remained alive. He needed Claypool to sack his half-brother and appoint Eric as general manager of Claypool Manufacturing. With Claypool dead, Eric would inherit half of Claypool's estate, but Horace would inherit the other half. They'd still be equals.

So who would be able to say how the company was going to be run? Obviously, whoever controlled both of the twins' shares. But who would that be? She thought back to what Luty had told them about Claypool's will. But she couldn't recall if that point had been discussed. All she remembered about the twins was that Edith Durant had been disinherited from Claypool's estate and that Hilda Christopher was going to get a set of books. Which meant that neither of them had a motive to murder their uncle.

By the time dawn was breaking and Mrs. Jeffries went downstairs to the kitchen, her sleepless night hadn't brought her any closer to an answer.

"You're up early this morning." Mrs. Goodge gave her a cheerful smile.

"I didn't sleep well." Mrs. Jeffries poured herself a cup of tea. "This case simply doesn't make any sense." She told the cook some of the thoughts and ideas that had occurred to her in the wee hours of the morning.

Mrs. Goodge listened carefully. Finally, when she was certain the housekeeper was finished, she said, "Perhaps we're making this too hard. Maybe it's a lot simpler than we think."

"But how could it be?" Mrs. Jeffries wished that were true. "Two murders, ten years apart, and the only thing that links them is an address in Jasper Claypool's dead hand."

"Why'd he need to write the address down, anyway?" Mrs. Goodge asked. "Surely he knew where the place was."

"Maybe not." The housekeeper took a drink of tea. "Except for his insistence on leaving the cottages alone, he seems to have had little to do with the factory or the cottages."

"Do you think he might have been the one who killed the chimney lady?" Mrs. Goodge grabbed a sack of flour from the counter and put it on the table. "After all, we've only his word to Spindler that it was Hilda Christopher who insisted on keeping the cottages empty. Maybe it was him all along, and maybe he didn't want any builders in them because he knew Our Lady of the Broken Arm was stuck up in number seven."

"Our Lady of the Broken Arm," she repeated. She said nothing for a long moment, merely stared at the cook with a stunned look on her face.

Mrs. Goodge blushed. "Oh, sorry. I shouldn't have said it like that, it's just that's the way I've thought of her ever since Dr. Bosworth told us she'd had a broken arm. I'm sorry, I didn't mean any disrespect. . . ."

But Mrs. Jeffries wasn't listening. She'd pushed back from the table, leapt to her feet and charged to the coat tree. "Mrs. Goodge, you're a genius." She snatched her cloak down, swung it around her shoulders and reached for her hat.

"I am? Where are you goin? The others will be here soon . . ."

"I'm going to Finsbury Park." Mrs. Jeffries felt in her cloak pocket and made sure her change purse was still inside. "Tell Smythe to find that other painter today and find out for certain if anyone, a messenger or anyone else, came to the Christopher house that day. And send Wiggins along to the neighborhood as well. Have him find out if anyone saw a visitor go in or out of the Christopher house late that afternoon."

"But . . . but . . . what about our meeting?" Mrs. Goodge protested.

"You'll have to do it without me," Mrs. Jeffries cried. "Oh, I'm dreadfully sorry to dash off like this, but it's urgent. You've just made me see what's been right under my nose all the time. Have Betsy get over to the St. John's Hotel and find out how often Edith Durant has been here in the past few years and, more importantly, was she here when Claypool died. Have her bribe someone if she must." With that, she dashed for the back door, leaving the cook staring after her.

When the others arrived, she told them what happened and gave them their instructions. "But I've no idea what she found out from the inspector last night, because she was out of here too quick to tell me."

"What's she up to?" Luty demanded. She was a bit put out, as Mrs. Jeffries hadn't left any instructions for her to do something.

"I imagine she's got a reason for going to Finsbury Park," Hatchet said. "But I can't think what on earth it could be. None of the principals in our case have lived there in over ten years."

"All I know is what she told me," Mrs. Goodge replied. "But I've a feelin' you three," she gestured at Wiggins, Smythe and Betsy, "had best get crackin'. It'll not take her all day to get there and back."

They all got up and started for the coat tree. Smythe grabbed Betsy's cloak and wrapped it around her shoulders. "Stay warm," he said. He handed Wiggins his jacket and then reached for his own coat. "Right, then, we're off. Everyone, let's try to be back as quick as we can. I'm wantin' to find out what Mrs. Jeffries has got up her sleeve."

When they left, the other three looked at one another. "What'll we do? I don't want to sit here twiddlin' my thumbs," Luty complained.

Mrs. Goodge had given the matter a bit of thought. "I think you ought to snoop over at the Christopher house. I overheard the inspector tell Constable Barnes that they were going to see Eric Riley's landlady. So you'd best not go there. Then the constable happened to mention that he had some police constables talking to the servants at the Horace Riley household, so that's not a safe place to snoop either."

Barnes had made sure Mrs. Goodge had overheard these plans when she'd nipped upstairs during the inspector's breakfast and told the constable about Mrs. Jeffries's trip to Finsbury Park. The household had found a useful ally in the constable, and she wanted to make sure he was fully informed.

"Humph," Luty snorted. "I suppose it's better than nothing."

"Now don't be downcast, madam," Hatchet soothed. "We could

always go to Richmond and see the other passenger from the ship. Perhaps Jasper Claypool confided something in her."

"Don't be a jackass, Hatchet." Luty glared at her butler. "Spindler already told us that Claypool barely spoke to the woman. Oh, fiddlesticks, I know what you're doin'."

"I'm doing nothing, madam, except making a reasonable suggestion."

"You're tryin' to rile me up so I won't feel bad about bein' left out." Luty snorted again. "But there's no need. I know that Hepzibah was in a hurry when she left this morning." Hepzibah was Mrs. Jeffries's Christian name.

"She didn't leave you out," Mrs. Goodge exclaimed. "She knows you better than that. She knows you'll get out and keep snoopin', you don't need instructions from her to do your duty."

"Precisely," Luty grinned. She felt much better. "We'll be back by teatime. Come on, Hatchet. Let's go snoop."

Inspector Witherspoon and Constable Barnes stood outside the door to Eric Riley's room. His landlady, Mrs. Davies, stood on the landing with them. She reached past them and knocked on the door. "Mr. Eric, there's some policemen here to see you."

"Just a moment," Eric Riley called. When the door opened, he was in his shirtsleeves with a towel wrapped around his neck and a bit of shaving soap on his chin. He didn't look pleased to see the policemen. "What are you doing here?"

"May we come inside, sir?" Witherspoon asked. He knew he had no legal right to force his way in without permission. They didn't have a warrant. But when they'd arrived that morning and spoken with the landlady, she'd mentioned that Mr. Riley was still there. Witherspoon had decided to take the opportunity to ask him a few more questions.

Eric stepped back and motioned them inside. "All right, but do make it quick. I've got to get to the factory. Uncle Jasper's lawyers are going to meet me there."

"What about your half-brother, sir?" Barnes asked. "Is he invited to the meeting?" The moment he'd stepped inside, he'd begun having a good look around the premises. He studied the line of the furniture along the floor, trying to see if any of the pieces had been moved recently.

"No, he isn't. Thank you, Mrs. Davies," he said as he closed his door.

The two policemen edged farther into the small, cluttered sitting room. But before they could ask any questions, Eric said, "If you must know, I'm going to contest Uncle Jasper's will. I don't think he'd have liked his share going to an embezzler, and that's what Horace is."

"That's a very serious charge, sir," Witherspoon said softly. "You told us this yesterday, but you never mentioned what evidence you had against your brother."

"I'll show that to the solicitor," he replied.

"Embezzling is a police matter," Barnes reminded him. He noticed that the skirt of the fabric on the settee was jutting out slightly at the corner. Curious, he moved toward it.

"We're not a public company," Eric replied. He frowned at the constable. "Embezzling is only a crime if I or my cousins press charges, and we're not prepared to do that as yet. What are you doing, Constable?"

"Uh, yes Constable, what are you doing?" Witherspoon asked curiously.

Barnes had bent down next to the settee and was sticking his hand underneath it. "I was just wondering why this bit of fabric was jutting out, sir. Oh goodness, what's this, then?" he pulled his hand back out and held up a small, dark object with a handle. It was a gun.

Eric Riley's jaw dropped. "I've never seen that before in my life."

Barnes sniffed the barrel of the weapon. "It's been fired recently," he said to Witherspoon. "And according to Dr. Bosworth, it's one of the type of guns that would leave a small hole in the victim."

"I tell you, I've never seen that before in my life," Eric wailed. He looked very frightened now. "You can't think I killed my uncle. You can't."

"Mr. Riley, no one is accusing you of anything," Witherspoon said. "However, we will need for you to come with us to the station. If you like, you can send a message to your solicitors. As a matter of fact, I think contacting your solicitor is probably a very good idea."

The others arrived back at Upper Edmonton Gardens by four o'clock. Mrs. Goodge had tea laid on the table, but as the minutes went by, the head chair remained empty. By half past four, they were all anxious but trying hard not to let it show.

It was always in the back of their minds that they chased killers, people who had already proved themselves capable of taking a human life.

When one of them didn't show up on time, the others tried their best not to think of the worst.

"Where is she?" Luty demanded. "I'm startin' to get worried."

"Now, now, madam," Hatchet soothed. "Let's not allow our imaginations to run away with us. I'm sure Mrs. Jeffries will be here momentarily."

"She better be," Wiggins exclaimed. "It's raining out there now. Did she take her umbrella?"

"I don't think so," Mrs. Goodge said.

"I wonder what's keeping her?" Betsy looked at Smythe, who smiled reassuringly.

"Don't fret," he said softly, leaning toward her. "Mrs. J knows how to take care of herself."

"She was only going to Finsbury Park, right?" Hatchet directed the question to the cook. "She wasn't going to confront any of our suspects?" He broke off as they heard the back door open. "Wait a second, there she is."

"I'm terribly sorry to be late," Mrs. Jeffries apologized as she raced into the room, taking off her cloak and shaking off the water. She tossed the garment onto the coat tree and hurried over to her place at the table.

"We were starting to worry," Mrs. Goodge said accusingly.

"How long does it take to get to Finsbury Park and back?" Luty complained. "We thought you'd fallen into a well and were about to come lookin' for you."

She gave them an understanding smile. "I'm so sorry, I didn't mean to worry anyone. But when I found out what I needed at Finsbury Park, I realized I had to stop by and see Dr. Bosworth. It took me a good hour to track the man down. St. Thomas's is quite a large hospital. Now, before I tell you anything, I have to know if you were successful?" She looked at Smythe.

"I had a word with the other painter," Smythe said. "And he 'ad seen somethin' more than 'is mate. He was workin' on the walls at the back stairs, so he was goin' up and down usin' the front door to bring in his equipment. His mate had the kitchen door blocked with a great ruddy ladder, so even though it was a bother, he had to use the front of the house." He broke off and grinned. "Lucky for us he did, too. Because he did see someone come to call and it weren't no messenger. It was Jasper Claypool himself."

"Claypool was at the Christopher house?" Mrs. Goodge was determined to keep everything straight in her mind.

"That's right. He showed up just before the painters was gettin' ready
to leave," Smythe replied. "That's how come the fellow knew he was
there, he'd come up the back stairs and was takin' the last of his paint
tins outside. Just as he was walkin' down the hall, he sees this clergyman
standing inside the drawing room starin' at Mrs. Christopher. He kept
on walkin' toward the front door, but he overheard what was bein' said.
This clergyman was sayin' something like 'My God! What 'ave you done?
Hilda! Hilda!'"

Mrs. Jeffries interrupted. "Had Mr. or Mrs. Christopher seen the
painter as he went down the hall?"

"No, he was moving real quiet. He said he always moved quiet when
he wasn't usin' a servants door. Besides, he said the parson was making
such a racket any one could have heard him. He thought the whole thing
odd, but he's seen lots of odd things in houses where he's worked, so he
went on about his business. Outside, he and his mate start loadin' their
wagon with their equipment, and just then, the clergyman comes runnin'
out like the devil himself was on his heels."

"Then what happened?" Betsy asked.

"The painters pulled out into the traffic just as the old man made the
corner and climbed into a hansom. But as they pulled their own wagon
around the corner, John Collier, that's the name of the painter, happened
to look behind him." He paused and took a breath. "He saw Carl Christopher flagging down a hansom, and, a second later, that hansom taking
off in the direction Claypool's had gone."

"Now that's very interesting," Mrs. Jeffries said. "Anything else?"

"Not really. John said he and his mate talked about it for a bit but
decided it weren't none of their affair," Smythe replied. "This is important, isn't it?"

"Oh yes," she said. "Very important. Wiggins, did you have any luck?"

"Sorry," Wiggins said glumly. "None of the servants in the neighborhood saw anything goin' on at the Christopher house. Absolutely
nothing."

"That's fine, Wiggins, I'm sure you did your best." She glanced at
Betsy.

"Edith Durant hasn't stayed at the St. John's much at all in the past five years." Betsy replied. "But she was there on Monday night. But she just stayed for the one night."

"Of course she was, and I imagine she arrived unexpectedly and quite late that night, didn't she?" Mrs. Jeffries replied.

"That's right," Betsy said. "That's exactly what the maid told me."

Mrs. Jeffries sighed heavily. "I don't quite know how we're going to do this, but I'm fairly sure I know who the killer is and more importantly, why the killing was done. But proving it is going to be difficult."

"But not impossible," Mrs. Goodge said. "Right?"

"Let's hope so," she replied.

"Hey, don't anyone want to know what we found out?" Luty demanded.

"Of course we do," Mrs. Jeffries said quickly.

"Well, as you know, Hatchet and I didn't have much to do, so we went along to the Christopher neighborhood too." She shot Wiggins a quick grin. "You're gettin' good, boy, we didn't spot you anywhere."

"That's nice to 'ear." He smiled proudly.

"But we did see something else," Hatchet interjected. "A messenger from Thomas Cook's came to the house."

"From Thomas Cook's? The travel people?" Mrs. Goodge asked.

"That's right," Hatchet replied with a nod. "He brought Mr. and Mrs. Christopher train tickets. They're leaving for Paris tomorrow morning at ten o'clock."

CHAPTER 11

Mrs. Jeffries was silent for a long moment, then she said, "Are you certain about this?"

"Course we are. I paid good money for that information. I bribed the messenger lad a half a guinea to tell me what he was bringing to the Christopher house." Luty gave a half-embarrassed shrug. "I oughtn't to be admittin' it, but sometimes it's easier just to put out a few coins, especially when you're in a hurry."

"We've all done it," Smythe agreed quickly. He was pleased to know he wasn't the only one who put out coin when the situation called for it. "And it sounds like it was money well spent." He looked at the housekeeper. "Is them leavin' goin' to be a problem?"

"Oh, yes," she replied. "So we'll have to work fast. As a matter of fact, we'd best try and move things along tonight." She fell silent, her expression thoughtful.

The room was so quiet the only sound was the faint ticking of the carriage clock. Finally, Mrs. Jeffries said, "It's a risk, but I think it'll work."

"Who's the killer, Mrs. Jeffries?" Wiggins asked eagerly. "Can you tell us?"

She hesitated. "Oh dear, I really don't want to say. You see, we're going to take an awful risk tonight, and if I'm wrong, I don't want the rest of you to have had anything to do with the whole process, if you get my meaning."

They all stared at her suspiciously.

"Generally, Mrs. Jeffries, you keep the name of the killer to yourself when you're not certain you've got the right person," Hatchet said.

"I'm not certain," she admitted. "And if we act too quickly and I'm wrong, the inspector could look like a fool."

"But you're usually right," Betsy told her. "You're good at figuring out these complicated cases."

"But that's just it," Mrs. Jeffries interrupted. "The case isn't complicated. It's very simple, and that's what frightens me. What if I'm wrong? What if we take action tonight and get the inspector involved and I'm absolutely one hundred percent wrong? It could ruin his career."

"Seems to me 'e wouldn't 'ave a career if it 'adn't been for you," Wiggins said softly.

"But he has one now," Mrs. Jeffries said, "and I don't want to ruin it for him. But honestly, it's the only solution that makes sense. It really is."

"But if you do nothing and the Christophers leave, you'll be letting a killer escape? Is that it?" Mrs. Goodge pressed.

"That's right."

"Then I say let's do it," Betsy declared. "Seems to me justice is more important than anything else. Especially for that poor woman that's been stuffed up a chimney for ten years."

There was a general consensus of agreement around the table.

"Betsy's right," Mrs. Goodge said stoutly. "We might be devoted to our inspector, but we do have a higher calling as well."

"I agree," Smythe murmured. He took Betsy's hand. "We can't start bein' afraid at this point. We've got to do as we think best and not worry about the consequences."

"Even if we're wrong about this case," Luty said, "the inspector could survive one blot on his record. Mind you, I don't think you're wrong at all."

"You rarely are, Mrs. Jeffries," Hatchet added.

"But I haven't even told you my theory."

"Doesn't matter," Luty shrugged. "We know you and we all know good and well that any idea you've come up with is based on fact."

Touched by their faith, Mrs. Jeffries blinked back tears. "Right, then. We'll do it. We've got to work fast, though, and after everyone's done what's needed and come back here, I'll tell you my theory." She began issuing orders like a general. "Wiggins, get over to Ladbroke Grove Police Station and see if the inspector and Constable Barnes have returned for the day."

Wiggins got up, and Fred immediately trotted over to him. "Sorry, boy, you'll have to stay here. I can't risk you spotting the inspector. Should I get Constable Barnes to come back with me?"

"No, I don't want to risk compromising the constable. I just need to know where he is so we can put the plan into action." She turned to Hatchet and Luty. "I need one of you to find me someone who can act the part of an informant, and they'll need to do it tonight. Someone who will either walk into the police station or be willing to waylay Constable Barnes on his way home. Do you have anyone who might be willing to do that? I also need that person to then disappear. It would be awkward if he were summoned to give evidence in court."

Luty looked doubtful. "I know lots of people, but this is kind of short notice."

Hatchet grinned broadly. "I know just the right person," he said.

"Who?" Luty demanded.

"Never you mind, madam. But take my word for it, it's someone who'll do anything for the right price."

"I don't want you spending your money," Mrs. Jeffries exclaimed.

"He can spend mine," Luty put in. "I've got plenty of it and I ain't goin' to hear any arguments about it, neither. Better to spend money on something good like catchin' a killer than just lettin' it sit pilin' up in a vault and makin' my bankers rich. Now what do you want this here informant to say?"

Inspector Witherspoon had just settled into his chair with a glass of sherry. "I'm sorry to be so late tonight," he told Mrs. Jeffries, "but it was a very busy day. Then Constable Barnes got called away, and well, I hung around the station for a while waiting for him to return, but he never came back. I do hope everything is all right."

"I'm sure he's fine, sir." Mrs. Jeffries took a sip from her own glass. She tried hard not to watch the clock, but if everything moved according to plan, Barnes should be on his way here at this very moment. "Perhaps someone had some information for him, sir. I believe that happens sometimes. He's been on the force a long time and I imagine he has a number of informants that feed him bits and pieces from time to time."

"Yes, I expect you're right." He yawned. "I suppose I ought to eat my supper, but . . ." He broke off at the sound of knocking on the front door.

"Gracious, I wonder who that can be?" Mrs. Jeffries got to her feet and hurried out to the hall. Opening the door, she feigned surprise. "Constable Barnes. What are you doing here at this time of night?"

He charged right past her. "I've got to see the inspector, Mrs. Jeffries. It's very important."

"Of course. He's in the drawing room." But he wasn't, he'd come out into the hall when he heard Barnes's voice.

"Constable." Witherspoon stared at him in concern. "Is everything all right?"

"No sir, it's not. We need to get to the Christopher house right away."

"The Christopher house?" Witherspoon repeated. "Now? Tonight?"

"Yes, sir. I've just heard from an informant. He's told me the strangest story." Barnes gave a half-embarrassed shrug. "At first I didn't believe the man, but he knew one or two details about the victim from the chimney, details that weren't in the news accounts. I had to take him seriously. We've got to get to St. John's Wood tonight. The Christophers are leaving town tomorrow."

Witherspoon was heading for the coat tree. He grabbed his bowler and his heavy black coat. "Right, then, you can give me the details on the way."

"Shouldn't you send someone to the station for a few more police constables?" Mrs. Jeffries asked. "I mean, if you're making an arrest?"

"I really don't think we can take the time," Barnes said. "My informant was pretty adamant we get there as soon as possible. I had the impression that he was afraid they'd run for it tonight instead of tomorrow."

"Should I send Wiggins to the station?" she pressed. She knew just how dangerous this killer could be. There were already two dead bodies. "Perhaps he can ask them to send some lads around."

"That's a good idea," Witherspoon called over his shoulder. "Have them send a couple of constables to number four Heather Street, St. John's Wood. But tell Wiggins to have the sergeant have them wait outside the house. We'll use the whistle if we need them."

As soon as they were gone, Mrs. Jeffries raced down to the kitchen. "Wiggins, get to the station. The inspector needs a couple of constables sent to the Christopher house." She gave him the rest of the inspector's message.

"Right." He was off like a shot.

Mrs. Jeffries looked at Smythe. "I think you'd best get over to the Christopher house as well. Stay out of sight but keep your eyes open."

Smythe nodded. He knew she was asking him to watch out for their inspector. "Right. I'll be back as soon as it's over."

Betsy walked him to the back door. She put her arms around him and pulled him close in a fierce hug. "Mind you take care, Smythe. I'll box your ears if you let anything bad happen to you."

He chuckled and gave her a quick kiss. "Now that we're together, lass, I'll not be taking any foolish chances. I'll just be keeping an eye out. Now that you've agreed to walk down the aisle with me, I'll not let any power on earth keep it from happening."

"Are you sure your informant is reliable?" Witherspoon asked as the hansom pulled up in front of the Christopher home. Barnes's informant had given them the strangest sort of story.

Barnes sighed inwardly. He wasn't in the least sure about the man's reliability. As a matter of fact, the only thing he was positive about was that his informant probably was acting on instructions from the inspector's own household. But he appreciated the fact that they'd tried to protect him by sending him this information via an anonymous stranger rather than confronting him directly. At least now if they were wrong, the worst that could happen was a bit of embarrassment for the inspector and himself. On the other hand, if they were right, they'd be solving a double homicide. "Actually, sir, I can't know for sure. But he certainly knew a lot of facts about this case."

Witherspoon swung down from the hansom. "Oh well, it can't hurt to have a look in and ask a few questions. Oh good, the lights are still on. At least we're not waking them."

"It may be an odd story, sir." Barnes handed the driver some coins. "But it does make sense. It fits with all the facts."

"Let's have at it, then." Witherspoon hurried to the door and banged the knocker. "I expect the worst that can happen is they'll show us the door."

Blevins, the butler, opened the door and peered out at them. "Inspector Witherspoon? Is that you, sir? What on earth are you doing here?"

"We'd like to see Mr. and Mrs. Christopher," Witherspoon said. "It's rather urgent."

Blevins hesitated. "I'm afraid it's not convenient, sir. The master and mistress are preparing to go away. The household is in a bit of disarray."

"Yes, we know," Barnes said calmly. "That's why we've got to speak to them tonight."

"Blevins," Carl Christopher appeared behind the butler. "Who is it? Good Lord, it's you lot. What do you want?"

Barnes elbowed the door lightly, forcing both of them to step back. "We need to speak to you, sir. Please let us in."

"Open the door," Christoper instructed the butler. "Come on, then. But it's most inconvenient."

They followed their reluctant host into the drawing room, walking past trunks, carpet bags and cases stacked neatly in the hallway. Barnes noticed a small strongbox sitting on top of a stack of hatboxes.

Mrs. Christopher was sitting at a small writing table next to the fireplace. Mrs. Nimitz, the housekeeper, was standing next to her mistress with a ring of keys in her hand. Annoyed by the interruption, Hilda Christopher glared at the two policemen. "What is the meaning of this? How dare you barge in here."

"We'd like a few moments of your time," the inspector began. "We've had a very serious allegation made against you and your husband, and we thought it prudent to give you an opportunity to defend yourself."

Mrs. Christopher reached for the key ring. "You may go, Mrs. Nimitz. We'll continue this later."

The housekeeper bobbed a quick curtsey. "Yes ma'am."

"Just a moment." Witherspoon stopped the woman when she would have left. "I've a question for you."

"This is outrageous," Carl Christopher snapped.

The inspector ignored him. "Mrs. Nimitz, please answer this question truthfully."

"I always tell the truth, sir," she replied as she cast a nervous glance at her mistress. "Always."

"In the last ten years, have you ever seen Mrs. Christopher with her sister, Miss Durant?"

Hilda Christopher gasped. She got to her feet. "How dare you! I'm sending Blevins for our solicitor! Nimitz, you don't have to answer these absurd questions."

But Mrs. Nimitz ignored her mistress. "I've seen Miss Durant in the house, sir, and I've heard them together in the drawing room when Miss Durant used to visit."

"But did you actually see them together in the drawing room?" he pressed. "Or did you only hear them?"

She thought for a moment. "I only heard them, sir. And that was several years ago, Inspector. Miss Durant hasn't been here in ages."

"Now see here, Inspector," Carl Christopher stepped toward his wife. He went to put his arm around her waist, but she brushed him aside.

"How old were you when you broke your arm?" Witherspoon addressed the question to Mrs. Christopher.

"I don't have to answer to you," she snarled. Her beautiful eyes blazed with fury. She whirled around, turning her back on the policemen.

"Hilda, darling," Carl soothed. "Don't lose your temper, dear. I'm sure this can all be sorted out."

Hilda ignored him and started for the drawing-room door. "You can talk to these fools if you want. But I don't have to answer these ridiculous questions."

"I'm afraid you do, ma'am." Barnes hoped those constables would get there soon. He knew something was going to happen, and better yet, he knew they were on the right track. These two weren't in the least mystified by the questions, only angry. "Unless, of course, you'd rather accompany us to the station."

But Hilda wasn't listening; she'd stormed out of the room and slammed the double oak doors shut with a resounding bang. A moment later, they heard a faint click.

"Good Lord," Carl Christoper muttered. He looked completely stunned. "She's locked the door." He ran to the door. "Hilda? Hilda, come back. Don't leave me here. Hilda!"

Then they heard the front door slam.

Barnes raced to the window and tossed back the curtains. "She's running, sir," he called to Witherspoon. He saw her racing down the street with a small, square box in her hands. Barnes guessed it was the strongbox.

The inspector was already on the move. He pushed Carl aside and banged his fist against the heavy wood. "Hello, hello, Mrs. Nimitz. We're locked in here. Mrs. Nimitz, can you hear us." He kept banging as he spoke.

Barnes was struggling with the window, but he couldn't get it to budge. "It's painted shut, sir."

Carl Christopher stumbled backward, his gaze still fixed on the door.

He had a dazed, uncomprehending expression on his handsome face. "She left me here. She's gone. I don't believe this. She left me here."

Witherspoon was still banging. "Mrs. Nimitz, anyone. Can you hear me?"

"Just a moment, sir," the housekeeper's voice came through the wood. "I'm trying to get the ruddy thing open, but it's locked. Blevins, get out of the way."

Barnes dashed to the other window and tried opening that one. "It won't budge either," he muttered in disgust. He turned to look at Christoper and saw that the man had sat down on the settee and was staring blankly ahead. "Do you know where your wife has gone, sir?"

Christopher gave a faint shrug. "My wife? She's gone. She's left me here. Somehow I always knew it would end like this. I knew it."

Barnes didn't like the man's color. His skin had gone from white to ashen. "Are you all right, sir? Do you need anything?"

"All right?" he repeated dazedly. "Why would I be? She's gone and she's left me to face it on my own. She knows I can't do without her. She knows how much I need her. But she's gone. She always goes when she gets bored, but this time, she won't be back."

The inspector banged on the door again. "Mrs. Nimitz, are you still there?"

"Yes sir, I'm trying to get it open, but it won't move."

"Have you got a spare key?" Witherspoon shouted.

"I've sent Blevins downstairs to have a look in the butler's pantry. It'll be just a minute, sir."

But in fact, it took them twenty minutes to free the three men, and of course, by that time, Mrs. Christopher had disappeared without a trace.

"Sit down, Betsy," Mrs. Jeffries told the maid. "It might be hours before they're back."

Hatchet poured himself another cup of tea. "I'm glad to hear that my friend was able to convince Constable Barnes of the truth of our tale."

"Are you goin' to tell me who this feller was?" Luty demanded.

Hatchet thought about teasing her a bit, but he could see that the others were equally curious. "His name is Michael Pargenter and he's an actor friend of mine. This was just another job for him, only instead of pretending to be King Lear, he played the role of a disreputable informant with a grudge against Carl Christopher."

"That's quite a good touch," Mrs. Jeffries said. "I'm glad you thought of it."

Hatchet shrugged modestly. "I had to give our mysterious informant a reason for going to the police. I thought an old grudge against Christopher would be just the thing. But he did say he had a rather hard time convincing the constable the story was true."

"Let's hope it is true," Betsy murmured. "Otherwise there's going to be lots of red faces around here."

"And mine will be the redddest." Mrs. Jeffries sincerely hoped the sequence of events for both murders was correct. Otherwise they'd have gone to a great deal of trouble over nothing. But the others had agreed with her that as far-fetched as it appeared, it made sense.

They heard the back door open, and Betsy leapt up from the table. But before she could get down the hall, Smythe came charging into the room. "She's done a run for it," he announced. "And they've lost her completely."

"What?" Mrs. Jeffries rose as well. "Who's run for it?" She hoped it was the right person.

"Hilda Christopher." Smythe plopped down in the chair next to Betsy. "I was standing across the street, keepin' an eye on the place, when all of a sudden, she comes racing out the front door. At first I thought something 'ad gone 'orribly wrong and she was lookin' for help of some sort. But then she took off running like the devil 'imself was chasin' her. I didn't know what to do. I was afraid if I took off after her that the inspector might be in trouble, but then I heard all this shoutin' comin' from the house. Blow me if a minute later I didn't see Constable Barnes at the window. He was tryin' to get the ruddy thing open and I could hear shoutin' from inside. It was the inspector. I realized he was all right, so I hot-footed it after Hilda Christoper. But she had too much of a lead on me and I couldn't catch up with her."

"What happened then?" Luty asked eagerly.

"Then I got as close to the house as I dared and I heard more shoutin' comin' from the drawing room. I think they were locked in."

"Locked in the drawing room?" Mrs. Goodge asked, her expression incredulous.

"That's right. I think Hilda Christopher had locked all of them, including her husband, in the room, and run for it."

"He's not her husband," Mrs. Jeffries said slowly. "And she isn't Hilda Christopher. She's Edith Durant."

It was almost dawn by the time the inspector arrived home. He went straight down to the kitchen. "Ah," he smiled as he saw his entire staff gathered around the table. "I suspected you'd all still be awake. It's not necessary, you know. I don't expect you to wait up for me when I get called out on a case."

"We know it's not necessary, sir," Mrs. Jeffries replied. She'd relinquished the chair at the head of the table. "But none of us could sleep until we knew you were safely home. What happened, sir? Did you make an arrest?"

Witherspoon slipped into her chair at the head of the table, and she handed him a cup of tea. "Well, yes, we arrested Carl Christopher. But I'm afraid his . . . er . . . well, she's not really his wife, she got away. We're watching all the train depots and docks, but so far, she's not to be found."

"Carl Christoper, sir? Is he your killer?" Mrs. Jeffries prodded. They were all well aware of most of the facts of the case.

"He killed Jasper Claypool." Witherspoon took a quick sip. "But he claims that Edith Durant did the other killing. That's right, Edith Durant." He closed his eyes briefly. "It's quite an ugly story. But at least now it makes some sort of sense."

"Did you find out who the woman in the chimney was?" Wiggins asked. Mrs. Jeffries had told them they had to ask questions, that they had to let him tell them what had happened.

"Yes." Witherspoon sighed heavily. "And that's part of what makes it such a sordid tale. The woman was Hilda Christopher. She was murdered ten years ago by her own sister."

"Gracious, that's shocking," Mrs. Goodge pursed her lips.

"Oh, that's terrible," Betsy cried.

"How dreadful," Mrs. Jeffries said softly. She was pleased to see that none of them were overacting too much.

"It is a dreadful tale," Witherspoon said, "and unfortunately, very true."

"How did you figure it out, sir?" Betsy asked.

"I didn't really. An informant flat-out told Constable Barnes that the woman living as Hilda Christopher was really Edith Durant. He said they'd killed Jasper Claypool because he'd come back to England unexpectedly and he could expose their charade." The inspector shrugged. "As the informant also said the Christophers were getting ready to flee the country, we had to go round there straightaway. When we got there, I started asking the servants if they'd ever seen the two sisters together. You see, we had no proof of any of this, so I was trying to get some circumstantial evidence, so to speak. When all of a sudden, Mrs. Christopher runs out and locks all of us, including Carl Christopher, in the drawing room. I suppose I ought to be glad she made such a precipitous move, because if she hadn't we'd not have had a hope of a successful prosecution. But luckily, when Carl Christopher realized she'd abandoned him, he started talking."

"He confessed?" Smythe asked. "That's a bit of luck."

"Yes, wasn't it," Witherspoon said. "He insisted on telling us everything."

"But how on earth did they get away with it?" Mrs. Goodge asked. "You can't pretend to be someone else for ten years."

"But you can," the inspector said. "The girls were identical twins and the only one who could ever tell them apart was Jasper Claypool."

"If Carl Christopher was in love with Edith Durant, why did he marry Hilda?" Betsy asked.

"Hilda inherited all her father's money." Witherspoon took another swig of tea. "He and Edith continued seeing one another after he married Hilda. Then, when Jasper announced he was going to India, they saw their chance. Jasper was literally the only person who could tell the girls apart. Once he was gone, Edith could take Hilda's place, live with her lover and do whatever she pleased. They lured poor Hilda to the cottage they'd been using for their assignations, and then Edith strangled her with a scarf."

"But why put her body in a chimney, sir?" Mrs. Jeffries poured herself more tea.

"The ground was too wet for them to bury her," Witherspoon replied. "And of course, once they'd murdered her, Edith had to come up with a tale to keep everyone, including builders, out of the cottages, so they convinced Jasper to leave them alone as a sort of future investment for

Hilda's future children." Disgusted, he shook his head. "Carl claimed they always meant to come back and get her, but they never did it."

"So they murdered that poor man just because he could tell them apart?" Wiggins pretended great shock.

"Awful, isn't it." Witherspoon sighed. He talked about the case for another few minutes, answering their questions, making comments and generally telling them every little detail about the encounter. Then he yawned and got up. "Since you waited up for me, I insist that you take the day off tomorrow. We can get our meals from a restaurant and everyone can have a nice, long rest tomorrow morning."

They protested, but their inspector insisted. Then, after giving Fred a final pat on the head, he went upstairs to his bed.

As soon as he was gone, Betsy said, "But I don't understand how they could have been so sure they'd get away with it."

"They were sure because they knew that very few people knew Jasper was coming home," Mrs. Jeffries replied. "They got very lucky when both the Rileys lied to the police as well."

"But why did they lie?" Wiggins asked. "Why not tell the inspector they knew he was in town and 'ad seen 'im?"

"Horace Riley lied because if he'd said anything, the whole issue of why Jasper came back to England would have come out." Mrs. Jeffries shrugged faintly. "He wasn't going to admit his uncle had come home to fire him for embezzlement."

"But what about Eric?" Mrs. Goodge asked. "Why didn't he say anything? He'd not stolen or murdered anyone."

"No," Mrs. Jeffries agreed, "he hadn't. But I expect it was Eric who knew that Edith and Carl were using the cottage. Once that body was discovered in the chimney, I suspect Eric had a very good idea who it was. He wanted control of the factory. To get it, he needed his own share of the company and control of both the twins' shares. Once Jasper was dead, I think he decided he was going to blackmail Edith and Carl. They had plenty of money. They didn't need the factory income."

"How'd you suss it out?" Smythe grinned at her. "Come on, tell us."

"I wouldn't have if Mrs. Goodge hadn't mentioned the chimney victim's broken arm. Then I remembered something Arthur Benning had told me. When the cousins were all children, Edith had pulled a prank that resulted in broken bones for Horace and Hilda. She'd rushed out in front of a pony cart and they'd all been thrown." Mrs. Jeffries smiled faintly. "That's why I went back to Finsbury Park. I needed confirmation that it was Hilda's arm that had been broken. Benning said it was her right arm that had been broken all those years ago. He remembered because there had been so much gossip about the incident. Then I stopped by to see Dr. Bosworth, and he confirmed that our chimney victim's broken arm was the right one."

"Then it was just a matter of puttin' two and two together," Wiggins supplied. "I mean, the clues was all there, right under our noses so to speak."

"Absolutely," she agreed. "Edith Durant had no known address but was seen occasionally in Brighton. I suspect that everytime 'Hilda' got a bit bored with Carl, she took off and pretended she was Edith. She went to Paris or to Brighton or someplace else and made sure people saw her. And, of course, the fact that she'd been doing it less and less in recent years proved that they thought they'd gotten away with it. It must have been an awful shock when they opened the front door and saw Jasper Claypool."

"Why were they acting so strange with their staff on the day Claypool showed up? Why pretend they were going to Brighton?" Mrs. Goodge picked at a few crumbs that had fallen on the table.

"Because I think that when the staff was to return that evening, 'Edith Durant,' would show up unexpectedly and demand to see her sister. As the staff thought the Christophers were gone, they'd never suspect the subterfuge. I suspect that the Christophers used those kinds of opportunities to keep up their charade."

"Why do you think she left him? Carl, I mean. Why do you think she ran off and left him to face it on his own?" Betsy asked softly. She glanced at Smythe. Nothing would ever make her leave him.

"Because as soon as the inspector started asking questions, she knew the game was over. I don't think she planned to run, it was simply convenient. Providence had placed the key to the drawing room in her hand, the strongbox was sitting in the hall, and she knew her only hope was to get away. Once the police started looking, the charade was sure to be exposed."

"And she knew Carl was weak," Smythe said. "From what the inspector said, it was Edith that was the stronger of the two."

"And the smarter." Betsy grinned.

"I don't understand why Jasper Claypool had the address of the cottage in his pocket," Wiggins said.

"I thought about that as well and I must admit I'm a bit perplexed. As we all know, Claypool knew where the cottage was so he wouldn't have needed the address," Mrs. Jeffries replied. "Perhaps it's one of those things which will remain a mystery."

"I know why," Mrs. Goodge said. "I've done it myself a time or two. Claypool wrote it down because he was an old man. He was probably planning on taking a hansom cab to that address and he didn't want to forget it when he had to tell the driver where he wanted to go." She smiled sheepishly. "Sometimes when you're older, you forget the silliest things. It can be very embarrassing."

"That's probably exactly what happened," Mrs. Jeffries said quickly. "It certainly sounds logical."

"Do you think they'll ever catch her?" Mrs. Goodge asked. She was irritated that the woman had gotten away.

"I'm sure they will," Mrs. Jeffries replied. But she wasn't, not really. She suspected that Edith Durant had planned some sort of escape route long before. The woman probably had money stashed all over Europe and the Americas in a whole variety of names. Apparently, she was quite good at pretending to be someone she wasn't. "Let's keep our fingers crossed that they get her." She yawned and got up.

The others started to clean off the tea things, but she stopped them. "Go on up to bed. We can take care of this later."

The others left for their rest, except for Wiggins.

He'd picked up the big brown teapot and was taking it to the sink. "It's no trouble, Mrs. Jeffries," he said. He looked past her, making sure the rest of them were gone.

"What's wrong, Wiggins?" she asked.

"Uh, if it's all same to you, I think I'd like to go back and check on my grandfather." He gave an embarrassed shrug. "I'd like to make up with my cousin, too. I don't want them thinkin' the worst of me, and leavin' like I did, well, it's bothered my conscience something fierce."

"I think that's a very good idea," she replied.

"You don't think the inspector will mind, do you?"

"He'll not mind in the least, Wiggins. Not in the least."